I0822480

MARINA SIMCOE

COMPLETE TRILOGY

DARK ANOMALY TRILOGY

Marina Simcoe
Marina.Simcoe@Yahoo.com
Facebook/Marina Simcoe Author

Cover Design by Naomi Lucas and Marina Simcoe
First Edition
Spelling: English (American)
Editing and Proofreading by Cissell Ink

Dark Anomaly is a Science-Fiction romance. It contains graphic descriptions of intimacy, violence, and discussion on topics that may be triggering for some. Intended for mature readers.

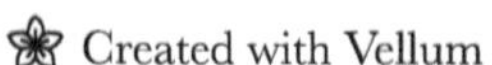
Created with Vellum

DARK ANOMALY

Complete Trilogy

MARINA SIMCOE

GRAVITY

Book 1

Chapter One

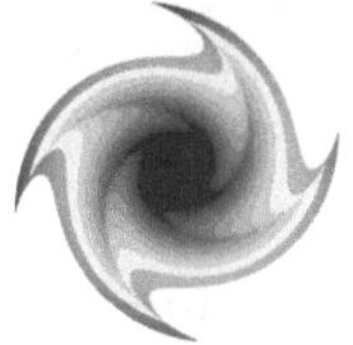

Svetlana

Was I dead?

I felt bruised whenever I moved.

Do dead people feel pain?

I was still inside my spacesuit, which meant unless I'd taken it with me into the afterlife, I must still be alive.

What had happened, though?

The damage from the impact with an asteroid wasn't that big, I had fixed it in minutes. Then, I made it back inside my one-person spacecraft. But before I had a chance to get out of the bulky suit, all hell had broken loose.

The instruments went haywire. The last memory I had was that of the screens of instruments on the control panel blurring into a wide colorful ribbon of light around me. My spacecraft plunged off course, spinning out of control, as I was suspended inside.

Now, all motion had stopped. But I didn't remember when and how.

I must have passed out at some point.

Carefully, I took a deep breath and lifted my head inside the helmet, then moved my arms and legs to assess my body for injuries. My muscles hurt, but my limbs appeared to be functioning. The suit must have saved me from the worst.

Had there been a crash?

I had no idea where I was.

Lying on my side, I didn't get up while wearing the suit. Bulky and strong, it had been built to withstand the enormous pressure of the planet Omphi's bottomless ocean. However, it was not exceptionally comfortable to move in when it wasn't powered on.

Instead, I rolled onto my back and lifted my arm, bringing the screen built into the sleeve up to the glass of the helmet.

The light of the communication device was on, but I couldn't send a message out. Despite the light, the device was not functioning.

The readings of the environment outside of the suit were off, but not by much. The pressure and the oxygen level remained stable. There appeared to be no breach in the ship's hull.

Carefully, I opened the hatch on the chest of the suit, then crawled out of it.

My head swam with dizziness when I attempted to stand. My stomach roiled, and I dropped to my knees, vomiting onto the floor.

Not the *floor*, I realized, staring at the warped and cracked wall panel under my knees. The ship lay on its side. Save for the few emergency lights on the control panel above me, the power was off. However, gravity was keeping me, my suit, and thankfully the mess I had just made down.

The gravity was real. If it were the artificial kind created by the ship, I would have been on the floor, not on the wall.

I had most definitely crashed.

But *where*?

The Anomaly was the nearest space object to my ship when the asteroid hit it. However, I was well aware of the Anomaly's enormous gravitational field, and I had stayed far away from its reach.

I had studied the mysterious space abnormality for years. At first, it was thought to be just another black hole. However, it had exhibited behaviours vastly different from that.

Shortly after my graduation from the Academy, I applied for the mission to explore the Anomaly.

It'd been well into my first year of working on the station orbiting Omphi, the closest planet to the Anomaly, before we had enough data collected by unmanned probes to send a person even closer. I'd volunteered.

It was supposed to be a day trip. I had stayed the calculated safe distance away from the Anomaly. The blow from the asteroid might have nudged me a little closer, but still nowhere near close enough that I would have to worry about the Anomaly's pull.

Something had happened, and I needed to figure out what.

First things first. Where was I?

Had the computer on my ship somehow activated the return route after the incident with the asteroid, sending me back to Omphi?

Then I might now be in that planet's ocean.

Why the spaceship had crashed, instead of safely docking with the station, remained unknown, but its system would have sent a distress signal upon impact. The search and rescue team should have already been deployed, as per the protocol.

I needed to see if the ship's communication system was still functioning, even if the suit's wasn't.

A faint screeching noise caught my attention.

Hands on the wall, I listened carefully. It seemed to come from the outside.

Omphi was a water world with no land. If I'd crashed into its ocean, shouldn't I feel the rocking of the waves? The vibration of them splashing against the hull, maybe?

Yet the spaceship remained stationary, albeit on its side.

The screeching noise grew louder, then bright sparks shot out in a spray from the opposite wall.

Someone was trying to get on board my ship by cutting a hole in its hull.

Why would the rescue team damage the ship like this? Unless the crash had been bad enough to disable all entrance points at once?

I moved over to the control panel. The stream of sparks had completed a full circle. The cut-out fell with a loud thud. A stream of smoke or steam blew in, filling the interior. Its chemical scent was unfamiliar, and I held my breath, trying not to inhale too much of it.

The smoke cleared quickly, revealing an inky silhouette in the glaring light streaming through the hole in the wall.

From the first glance at the person, it was clear—they were not from my station.

Tall and broad, the being had a humanoid form with male proportions. Dressed only in a pair of worn dark pants and heavy boots, he was holding the tool he'd used to cut the hull.

Tossing the tool aside, he stepped inside my spacecraft, remaining but a large shadow in the faint light.

"It stinks in here." He rubbed his nose with his forearm, then added a long curse that got simply translated as "fuck" through my device.

I touched my fingers to the universal translator implanted in the back of my head.

My entire team had gotten the implants before leaving Earth. It had been only a few decades since the extra-terrestrial Federation had made the first contact with Earth. Humans had finally discovered another intelligent life form in our galaxy. However, it came not as a single race, but dozens of them. The Federation included representatives of seven populated planets from five different solar systems. All of them were much closer to the Anomaly my team had been studying than to Earth.

The male who had just barged into my spaceship must have been one of the species that belonged to the Federation. He obviously spoke a language recognized by my translator, though I couldn't immediately place him.

If I understood what he had said, chances were he'd understand me. The translation implants had been mandatory for thousands of years among the members of the Federation. Many nations had them implanted within the first year of a person's life. His would now be automatically updated with a number of languages from Earth, even if this was his first contact with a human.

Hope sparked inside me. As a member of the Federation, he would be obligated by law to assist me.

While I was gathering my thoughts to come up with an appropriate greeting, he clicked on the light strapped to his upper arm, illuminating my empty spacesuit on the ground.

At its sight, the newcomer leaped back. Raising both fists in defense should my suit attack him, he seemed fully prepared to fight back.

"Wyck," he said over his shoulder.

Another one of his kind climbed in through the hole. Just as intimidating in size, with wide shoulders and massive arms, this one wore dark pants similar to the first one. In addition, he also had on a short leather vest.

A chain was wound around Wyck's thick wrist. He yanked at it, and I nearly yelped in shock as a large, terrifying animal leaped into the ship. Black, with red markings, the monster had three heads, each maw open, displaying several sets of sharp, translucent teeth.

"See if this one is alive." The first newcomer ordered Wyck, tipping his chin at my spacesuit.

Wyck led his animal to it. The three-headed hound from hell took a sniff at the suit, then pivoted my way instead. All three of its heads lowered to the ground, the middle one gave out a loud hiss. My insides leaped from fear, but I straightened my spine.

"Greetings…" I cleared my throat, addressing the one with the flashlight on his arm, since he seemed to be the one giving orders here. "Under the interplanetary law of the Federation, I request your assistance. My ship—"

The one with the flashlight twisted my way, illuminating me. I blinked at the beam of light directed at my face and quickly covered my eyes with my arm.

"Well, *this* one looks very much alive," the male sneered. Something thick and heavy in his voice sent icy shivers of dread down my spine.

This didn't seem right.

These individuals and their behaviour were unnerving and intimidating. Their rugged appearance raised concern. The clothes they wore were not recognizable uniforms. Several rips and slashes in them seemed to have been made by teeth, claws or blades.

My throat went too dry to speak.

The monstrous animal moved my way. "Back, Lesh." Wyck yanked on the chain.

"I've got to get out of this stench." With an enormous hand, the first one grabbed me roughly by my arm, dragging me to the hole in the wall.

"Wait…" I tried to protest, but it was like attempting to stop a tugboat. I could either hurry and catch up or fall and be dragged behind.

"Vrateus will want to see this, Crux," Wyck pointed out.

"We didn't break any of his precious rules…yet," Crux scoffed, shoving me through the opening into the bright light outside. "He'll see it soon enough. But *we* got here first."

The "outside" turned out to be a long corridor, lit by strings of light suspended from the ceiling. The panels on the walls and the ceiling here were cracked and bent out of shape, just like the interior of my ship.

Did our spacecraft collide in space, somehow? Was that the reason for their unjustified rude behaviour toward me? Were they angry with me for crashing into them?

"Let me see what was sent to us this time." Painfully squeezing my arm, Crux yanked me closer.

His skin was the color of clay with a reddish tint to it. It darkened to charcoal gray on the three bumpy ridges that ran along his bald skull. Similar ridges stretched the entire length of his massive shoulders and down his thick arms.

A wide rugged scar crossed one side of his face, narrowly missing his eye. It must have been a nasty wound when it was fresh.

"Excuse me, but…" I started, hoping to reach some understanding here. Could it be that this male lacked the implant for some odd reason? He didn't appear to understand me at all.

He touched his nose to my temple, making a loud sniffing noise.

"A female," he growled low. "What a boon."

A shiver of revulsion ran through me. I fought to free my arm from him, but he wouldn't budge.

"I'm Svetlana Kostyk," I said as loud and clear as I could manage, hoping that if he didn't understand my words, he would at least catch from my tone of voice that I disapproved of his behaviour. "I'm on a peaceful research mission from Earth. Our station is orbiting the planet Omphi. I need your help in contacting my team, please."

It remained unclear if Crux understood any of that. He stared at me with his yellow eyes, focusing on my mouth for a moment then sliding his gaze further down my body. His wide nostrils continued to flare as he sniffed the air around me.

Surely, this brute couldn't be the leader of any spacecraft.

"I need to speak to whoever is in charge here." I desperately looked around, hoping to find someone with a better grasp of the situation.

The wide corridor was quickly filling with all kinds of creatures. Some had humanoid body shapes. Most were bipedal. However, I didn't recognize any of the species here. They all gaped at me, their mouths open, drool dripping off their fangs, and their tongues rolled out. It was impossible to tell if any of them were at all intelligent.

"If you just could..." I made another attempt to free my arm from Crux's grip, wishing to put some distance between us, but he only held tighter. Fear pulsed inside me. Crime had been all but eliminated back on Earth and on most of the civilized planets of the Federation. I'd never been threatened in my life, never felt as vulnerable as this man was making me feel. "By intergalactic laws, I am guaranteed personal freedom and respect," I desperately reminded him.

A memory from a history class rushed to mind. Centuries ago, space pirates had travelled these parts of the Galaxy. Could some of that remained here?

Was this a pirate ship?

I regarded this motley crew of individuals of all shapes, textures, and colors. None of them were dressed in anything that resembled a uniform of any known government.

Fear vibrated through me, but I inhaled deeply, forcing myself to act as calmly as possible. Pirates could still be negotiated with. Hopefully, even the one who kept holding me…

My hope for any intelligent communication with him had quickly evaporated the moment he licked my ear then bit on my neck.

“Hey! That hurt!” I yelled, trying to twist out of his grip once again.

He finally let go of my arm, but only to grab me around my waist next.

Stricken by panic, I forgot all about diplomacy.

“Let me go!” I jammed an elbow into his gut.

“Yesss,” he hissed into my ear, his hot humid breath slinking down my neck. “Fight me. I like it.”

Was he insane?

“Crux. Drop her,” suddenly came from the crowd. It was said not exceptionally loud but in a firm voice that carried authority.

I exhaled with relief. Finally, someone in charge here.

A tall man stepped out of the thickening crowd. Subdued whispers from others reached me.

“Vrateus…”

“Captain is here.”

Nearly as tall as Crux or Wyck, the newcomer appeared to be leaner. His silver-white hair looked more like long fur, streaked with black. It had been shaved off above his pointy ears, the skin there decorated with intricate tattoos. The same fur covered his forearms and the back of his hands. He flexed his fingers, and a set of black, curved claws slid out.

This one definitely could be a pirate. He even dressed the part, complete with a wide-sleeved white shirt and tall boots. Two long swords were strapped to his back by embossed leather belts. Huge gems glistened on his fingers, and a row of golden hoops decorated each of his ears.

His outfit appeared to come straight from some theater play. To my knowledge, no one in the Galaxy dressed like that anymore. No one.

The noise of shuffling feet and rumbling voices lowered to a hum with his appearance.

"Sir," I said with renewed hope. "I am Svetlana Kostyk, on a research mission from Earth. My spaceship suffered an accident…"

The newcomer paid absolutely no attention to me. His focus was fully on Crux.

"I said, drop her," he growled, baring a pair of long, white fangs.

He slowly raised his arm. With a hard click, a metal gun appeared in his hand, seemingly coming out of nowhere.

I stared at it in shock. Was it an actual weapon? I had never seen one before.

He pointed the gun at Crux.

Chapter Two

Vrateus

His eyes on Crux, he mentally dared his second in command to disobey. That would finally give him a legitimate reason to shoot the *errock*.

Vrateus had given him an order, twice. There was no third time.

Crux knew it. With a hard swallow, he finally released his grip, letting his prize drop to the ground.

Vrateus suppressed a sigh of relief. With Crux, open disobedience was just a matter of time.

"I saw her first." The *errock* took a wide stance, not moving away from the girl.

Vrateus didn't spare her a glance. She didn't matter. If Crux got his way, she'd be dead before morning anyway.

And if the *errock* didn't get his way, Vrateus risked a mutiny.

There was no place for a woman on the Dark Anomaly. The last few females brought to the Anomaly by its gravitational field had died within hours, brutally raped to death, their bodies eaten by the *ognats* and *kreers*.

That was ten years ago.

Vrateus had been the captain for seven years, now. He'd fought hard to gain control over the feral shipwreck population. And he had been working even harder to maintain the fragile order ever since.

Now, the sudden appearance of this female threatened to undo the results of his labor in seconds.

"She is mine," Crux gritted through his teeth.

The *errock's* jaw muscles twitched, his massive hands fisted at his sides. He was obviously waiting for a better moment to start a fight, to claim what he had already believed was his—the girl.

Vrateus's hackles rose in response. His tail lashed against his boots.

"Yours?" he forced himself to lower his arm but didn't send the gun to its holster. "For how long?"

"For as long as I want her." Crux glowered at him.

"Which would be an hour. Maybe?" Most likely less than that. At least a decade older than Vrateus, Crux had taken an active part in that last brutality. The lives of at least a few females killed that night were on Crux's hands. Rough and vicious, he would give the woman zero chances of survival. "Then what?"

Crux rubbed the back of his neck. "Who cares?"

"I'm sure the rest of them would." Vrateus tipped his head over his shoulder, gesturing at his crew.

"Let all of us have her then!" one of the *ognats* yelled, Naizu, the most bloodthirsty of them all. His eight pairs of skinny limbs were undulating impatiently.

Vrateus's law forbidding cannibalism was especially detested by *ognats*. However, they were not the only race on the Dark Anomaly that would eat sentient beings if given a chance. Most of Vrateus's crew would want to fuck the girl first, but some might also eat her afterwards.

"And how is that going to work?" he asked, sarcastically.

"We'll take turns!" someone excitedly shouted from the crowd.

Several growls supported the idea.

That would create a fuck frenzy that Vrateus wished to avoid—for the female's sake, he realized with annoyance. Part of him wished the girl would have died in the crash. Saving her life seemed to be a nearly impossible task now.

Maintaining power over his people meant carefully balancing the often-opposing interests of different groups and species. As long as Vrateus kept them divided, he held control over all of them. The presence of the female now gave them a reason to unite against him.

The simplest thing to do would be to give her to them. Let them do whatever they wanted with her—fuck her or eat her.

There were over seven hundred of them, though. Most wouldn't get anywhere near her before every trace of her ravaged body would be annihilated. Then there would be fights, murders, and more cannibalism.

Restoring order would take everything he had with no guarantee of success.

He rubbed his face. Running this place was exhausting.

A huge issue was that he had already stopped Crux. Letting the *errock* have his way now would make it look like Vrateus was giving in. He did *not* give in to anyone. For seven years, Vrateus had ruled with undisputed authority. He could not afford to have his decisions questioned publicly—even the decisions he hadn't made yet.

He had no idea what to do with the girl.

"Yeah, so, who's going first?" Naizu hissed, inching closer on his skinny legs. Saliva dripped from both corners of his lipless mouth. His long, body—black, glossy back and beige, mottled belly—slithered her way.

"Me!" Crux stood over the girl, his fists raised to defend his prey. "I saw her first."

"But you didn't fight for her," Krakhil, a huge *dimo*, roared, placing all four of his hands on his hips.

"We need to pull numbers! Lottery!" The shouts came out of the crowd.

"That's fair," others agreed.

The air in the corridor was charged with lust and aggression—an explosive mix waiting for the slightest spark to detonate into violence.

"Fuck the lottery. I want her now." Naizu dove for the girl, grabbing her ankles. His long black tongue slicked out, running over his sharp teeth.

She jerked back with a grimace of utter horror, letting out a panicked scream.

That scream…

It pierced Vrateus's brain with memory, painful and toxic.

"Back, I said!"

He shot. The bullet hit Naizu in the back of his head.

Thick, greenish blood splashed over the pristine white of the girl's bodysuit. The scream caught in her throat, turning into a gurgle of shock as the *ognut* dropped to the ground, dead, his head landing between her legs.

"Anyone else want to try?" Vrateus released the second gun from its holster inside his sleeve and wrapped his fingers around the smooth metal handle.

He had a laser gun strapped to his thigh, a knife hidden inside each of his boots, two swords attached criss-cross to his back, and a dagger concealed in its sheath at his chest. That was his light, everyday armament. Had he known there'd be a female on the new shipwreck, he'd have at least doubled it.

His crew stilled, those in the front shuffling back. No one but him was allowed to wear weapons of any kind on the Dark Anomaly. Vrateus was the only one armed. He had made sure of it.

"All right." He took a pause, sweeping the crowd with a heavy stare to make sure all attention was on him. "There are seven hundred and forty-four—" he glanced at the dead body of the *ognut*. The girl had shrunk away from it, hugging her legs. "…forty-*three* of you. And only one female."

"We'll take turns," Brel, a *kreer*, suggested again, only in a slightly less sure voice now.

"*Seven hundred and forty-three*, Brel. She'd be dead within the first hour if you all get on her at once. Most of you would get nothing at all."

"We'll space it out." Krakhil elbowed a *yourlu*, shoving his hard-plated elbow into the *yourlu's* soft shoulder. "Qen here wouldn't mind waiting for his turn. Would you, Qen?"

Qen rubbed his shoulder with one of the three tentacles he had instead of a left arm.

"How long would I have to wait?" he squeaked.

"Good question." Vrateus shifted his weight to his other foot. "If each of you got her for a day, how long do you think those at the back would have to wait?" He paused for effect, not expecting an answer—math skills were not one of the strengths of his crew. "Almost two years."

Groans of frustration filled the corridor.

"She can be fucked more than once a day," someone grumped, disheartened. "Twice? At least?"

"That would still be nearly a year wait for those at the back," Vrateus retorted. "And that is if the guy before you has been gentle enough for you to get her alive." He leveled a pointed stare at Crux. "You know there's an excellent chance she will not survive that long. Not all species have the endurance for that lifestyle. And she is…" He finally took a good look at the girl, trying to identify what species she was.

She glared at him with her big, dark eyes, the color of aged bronze. The long filaments on her head looked more like hair than fur—a deep shade of brown. Her skin was of a similar color to his, maybe a shade or two lighter. He saw no wings, horns or claws on her. The only tail she had was on the back of her head, but it didn't seem to be functional, hanging limply down her back. She might have injured it during the crash.

What was she?

"Who are you?" he asked.

She straightened her back. Her composure was admirable, though it wouldn't help her situation.

"I told you, my name is Svetlana Kostyk. I am the mission specialist with the research team from Earth. My planet is the newest member of the Federation—"

"Species?" he cut her off.

Her dark eyebrows moved closer together as she levelled him a disapproving glare.

"Human," she gave him a clipped reply.

He searched his memory for the species with that name and found nothing. He was certain he'd never seen anyone like her before.

Staring at her, he'd lost his train of thought and had to gather his focus before addressing his crew again.

"As I said, the wait for those at the back would be nearly a year." He still had no definite plan, working on it as he went. "Do you want to spend that much time, not getting a thing from our bounty here?" He glanced down at the girl again, and she gave him another glare, filled with shock and resentment.

"What other choices do we have?" came a question from the crowd.

Over the years, he had trained them to expect solutions to problems from him.

"I'd say, fuck the waiting. Let's have fun now!" Krakhil roared, his deep, rumbling voice rising over the noise.

"It would be a very short-lived fun, I'm afraid." Vrateus kept his own voice calm and even. Showing any emotions would only fuel the excitement of the males already charged with lust in the female's presence.

"You want to keep her to yourself!" Crux growled accusingly.

Vrateus considered that option briefly and quickly dismissed it. Taking the girl for himself would ignite a riot. Crux would be the one to start it. The *errock* had laid his hands on her—in his mind, the girl was already his property. If denied any access to her now, Crux would snap, all *errocks* would follow, quickly joined by the others.

All seven hundred united against Vrateus.

The exact situation he had been masterfully avoiding for years.

"Give her to us," several voices demanded. "Even if for just one night of fun."

The strangled gasp of the girl reached him. Without looking at her, he sensed her tension. Her fear.

"It might be fun. But only for some." He let his words sink into their minds. An idea formed in his head, but he knew he needed to lead them to it carefully. "What do you do for fun now?"

"Fight!" many yelled.

That was true. Most of them participated in the nightly fights he organized to let them work out some aggression.

"What else?"

"Eat!" someone shouted.

After the years of hard work Vrateus had put his crew through, the Dark Anomaly finally was producing enough food to sustain them all. There was enough to eat for fun, not just for survival.

"Gardening," came a quiet voice.

Malahki.

The *damirian* spent a lot of time in the in-door gardens, taking care of plants. Vrateus didn't expect to see Malahki here. The *damirian* had no gender. It was neither male nor female. Lust didn't affect its species at this stage of their development.

Curiosity was not a gendered quality, though. Anything out of the ordinary passed for entertainment on the Dark Anomaly.

"What else?" he prompted. "What else do many of you do for fun before falling asleep?"

"Fuck!" Trox, one of the *errocks*, smirked.

"You can't call it *fucking* if you're on your own." Nocc, another *errock*, guffawed, shoving an elbow in Trox's side. "You jerk off."

"Right." Vrateus tilted his head, carefully keeping the mood of his crew in focus. "How about if you had a female sitting next to you while you did that?"

"While I'm jerking off, you mean?" Nocc huffed another laugh. "She wouldn't be sitting *next* to me! She'd be right on top of me!"

"Or under!" Someone yelled, cheerfully.

"With both of my cocks deep inside her!" Nocc guffawed.

The crowd grew loud with approval, threatening to get out of control at any moment.

"We've already established *that* can't happen!" Vrateus raised his voice, speaking over the increasing noise. "You can't *all* have sex with her and make the fun last. But you *can* have her next to you—"

A series of confused exclamations interrupted him.

"What for?"

"Naked?"

"Is she gonna touch me, Captain?"

He lifted his arm in a wordless call to silence.

"No touching. But you can *see* her." He gazed over their faces, gauging their reaction. "And yes, she'll be naked."

"Watching her while I'm jerking off?" Crux stared at him with less hatred and more confusion.

"You can see her naked flesh as you stroke yourselves," Vrateus explained, evenly. "You can hear her moans as she touches herself—for all of you to watch."

Crux's green-spotted yellow eyes flashed with lust. Vrateus forced down the uncomfortable feeling. Sexually exciting his second in command was not his intention tonight, or any night for that matter.

The words worked, though. He put an image in the heads of the males. Now he needed to firmly nail that idea to their brains.

"You will be able to watch her every week, for as long as she shall live. And *this* way, she shall live much longer than just for a night. We'll start tomorrow."

It was time to leave.

He needed to remove the girl while the males mulled over his idea. Having her sitting here as an invitation for immediate action was dangerous.

Vrateus also needed to keep Crux from touching her again. He had to put the scent of another male on her, to eliminate any trace of Crux's claim.

"Wyck, get her up," he ordered to the youngest *errock*.

As soon as Wyck complied, Vrateus motioned for him to take the woman down the corridor, keeping the rest of the crew in his view.

The crowd's excitement ran too high to settle right away.

"Why tomorrow? Why not right now?" they shouted at his back as he headed after Wyck and the female.

"She's hurt and filthy," he threw over his shoulder, not slowing down the pace. "Once she has eaten and rested, she'll moan louder."

Chapter Three

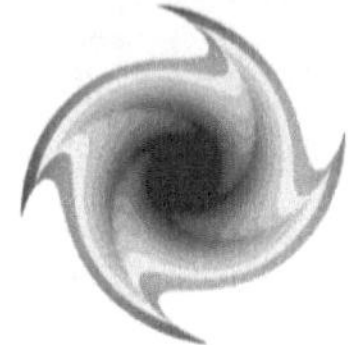

Svetlana

What on earth had just happened?

Could any of this be real? Or was I hallucinating, still lying unconscious after the crash?

With Wyck's meaty hand around my arm and Vrateus walking on my other side, I was hurried down the corridor to keep up with their pace. It was especially challenging over the uneven floors, bulging up in some places and dipping in others. It required concentration not to trip.

More creatures stared at us from side corridors and doors as we passed. Some moved my way, but Vrateus and Wyck shoved them aside.

My stomach was tied in knots, my head swam with dizziness, and my legs barely obeyed my brain.

There must be something wrong with my translator. Otherwise, I would have to believe that the leader of this bizarre group had just promised his people some sexual favors on my behalf.

It was absurd. Illegal. And unethical. Immoral, too. Yet he seemed to find it absolutely acceptable.

I hesitated to clarify anything with him while we remained in the presence of others. Though I wasn't looking forward to being one on one with him, either.

"Here." Vrateus stopped in front of a round, pewter double door. "She'll stay in this room." He hit the side panel with his palm, making the doors slide open, then walked in.

Wyck let go of my arm but didn't follow his boss. Instead, he silently nudged me toward the open doors.

"Are you coming?" Vrateus snapped at me, with an annoyed glance over his shoulder.

The clear resentment in his eyes baffled me. What have I done to deserve any of this?

Anger flared inside me. I dug my heels in defiantly, folding my arms across my chest.

"I believe you owe me an explanation," I said in a much less diplomatic tone of voice than before.

Crux and some of the others came into view at that moment. They rushed our way down the corridor. Wyck's chained monster hissed.

Even annoyed at me, Vrateus still seemed like the lesser of two evils, and I promptly entered the room. He immediately hit the door's side panel, shutting the doors with a soft swishing sound.

"You'll stay here." He stepped aside.

My breath suddenly caught in my throat with a gasp.

The room was made entirely out of glass. Like a soap bubble with a flattened bottom for the floor, it protruded from the wall of the ship into the vast space beyond.

Outside looked like nothing I had ever seen, even after nearly a year of working in space. Shimmering waves of multi-colored lights ebbed and curved through the absolute darkness surrounding me. Beyond the lights, the distant stars twinkled.

Standing on the clear glass, surrounded by undulating lights from all sides, made me feel like I was falling.

"Ahh!" I exhaled in shock, spreading my arms in an attempt to hold on to something.

Then the sensation of floating in space came.

"You're not afraid of open spaces, are you?" Vrateus asked calmly.

"No. Not afraid. It's just…" I swayed, struggling to find a reference point for at least a modicum of balance as everything around me appeared to move along with the lights. "Unsettling. Like a free fall. Or flying. Weird, but not scary."

"Good." He moved back to the entrance, leaving me in the middle of the floor, my arms spread wide like wings. "*Errocks* are terrified of open spaces. They'll never come in here."

His comment hardly registered.

"What's generating the light?" I asked, mesmerized. "I've never seen anything like it."

His chest expanded with a deep breath as he folded his arms across it.

"That is the Dark Anomaly. You must have known you were near it when you crashed."

"Do you mean space anomaly GR-A8502?"

"We call it 'the Dark Anomaly.' But sure, why not assign it a number?" He shrugged on his way to the door. "I have to go. There is always a lot of work with each new ship's arrival. Don't stare at the lights for too long. They can drive you mad."

The space abnormality my team had been studying had looked *dark* on the images. Upon its discovery, it had been initially mistaken for a black hole. Professor Zhang Wei Liu was the first one to calculate a number of dissimilarities in its behaviour. A significant one being that unlike black holes, the Anomaly did not grow. Neither did it suck in any celestial bodies nearby. It didn't absorb planets or stars.

We'd been unable to peer inside it, but the gravitational force of it was strong enough to rival that of a large star or a giant planet. Unlike them, however, its gravity behaved differently, too.

"How did you get this close to it?" I couldn't tear my gaze away from the hypnotic lights. "How come the gravity doesn't pull us in right now?"

"Because we're already inside it, human," he said before exiting the room. "You're looking *out* of the Dark Anomaly, into the open space beyond."

I KEPT STARING AT THE LIGHTS LONG AFTER HE HAD LEFT. AFTER A while, the awareness of this room and the glass around me had completely disappeared. All that remained was the feeling of floating in space, surrounded by the undulating colors and light.

"Don't stare at the lights for too long. They can drive you mad."

I understood what he meant. The sense of reality was no longer there, but I didn't miss it. The brutal aliens, their captain, this insane grotesque world—all seemed to be just remnants of a bad dream. A nightmare I hoped to wake up from soon.

The sound of the doors opening yanked me back into reality again.

"Dinner," the captain's voice sounded behind me, and I slowly turned around.

Carrying a tray in one hand, he rolled a small table in with the other. A group of his thugs lingered outside the door, peeking in over his shoulders. Their smirking faces proved even more sobering.

This was real. I still didn't understand why or how, but this world truly existed.

The wall between the room and the corridor was of the same solid pewter-colored metal as the doors. Both provided a stable point of reference that helped me finally ground myself. Facing the wall, I felt the floor under my feet once again.

The captain deposited the tray on the table. When he turned around to get more things from his crew, his tail came into view.

He had a tail! How could I have not spotted it before? Covered in long, silver-white fur, it swayed delicately, the black tip reaching the tops of his tall boots.

I'd never seen an alien this close before. Despite the dreadful situation, my undying curiosity won over fear for the time being. I openly ogled him as he brought in a roll of blankets and a metal box.

His skin color was that of deep tan, as if he indeed was the captain of an ancient pirate ship, with his skin bronzed by the sun and weathered by the ocean winds. The hard features of his face seemed to be chiselled out of a mountain cliff. He wasn't beautiful, but he could still be considered handsome, in some harsh, rugged way.

His black eyebrows furrowed the moment he caught me staring.

"Sleeping pallet." He tossed the bed roll at my feet. "May I suggest you place it in the part of the room farthest from the door. We'll search for a real bed for you later."

"Listen…" I scrambled to collect my thoughts.

He pressed an open metal box into my hands, obviously uninterested in anything I had to say. "Here are some toiletries. Everyone is allowed a five-minute shower a day. And no, the minutes do not roll over into the next day. Use them or lose them."

I mechanically clutched the box to my chest.

"What is this place?" I asked one of the gazillion questions that crowded my brain.

"Dark Anomaly." He lifted an eyebrow. "I thought we've already covered that."

"Can you…fly your ship in and out of it?"

The Anomaly did not absorb celestial bodies. However, it had sucked in any probe or unmanned research vessel we had ever sent near it. Past a certain point, which was slightly different for each object, all transmissions stopped. And we had been unable to retrieve any of the probes or vessels.

"Dark Anomaly sucks things *in*. No one gets *out*." He said it slowly, as if depositing every word into my brain then waiting for me to absorb it.

"Have you tried to steer the ship—"

He tilted his head, not letting me finish. "Which one of the millions of wrecked ships would you suggest I *steer*?"

Despite the thick sarcasm in his tone, I replied as calmly as I could manage, "Whichever is in the best shape. My spacesuit actually could—"

"No, it couldn't," he cut me off. "The solid part in the center of the Dark Anomaly, where we are, is made entirely of crushed spaceships. For ages, this thing has been sucking them in, smashing them into each other, then squishing them together, into a disk. We are on the very edge of it here, where the newly arrived vessels still have room between the walls. Using the energy we get from the lights of the Anomaly, we have made this sector of the disk habitable. This is home. Yours too, now. The only one you'll ever have. The sooner you accept it, the higher your chances of survival will be."

"This place is not my 'home!'" It could never be.

He barely dignified me with a look in response.

My dire situation was turning into a nightmare, and I feverishly searched for a way to end it.

"How about contacting the ships passing by, outside of its gravitational field? My station is—"

"The Dark Anomaly absorbs any kind of communication waves," he explained with a tired expression. "Reaching the outside world is impossible."

I blinked at him, lost for words for a moment.

Vrateus might fully believe what he was saying, but I couldn't blindly accept any of this as facts without testing them first. There had to be a way out of here. He just hadn't found it yet. Or he simply wasn't interested in helping me.

He obviously mistook my silence for acceptance.

"Well, let's see…" He slid an assessing gaze down my body. It wasn't immediately clear what exactly he was *assessing*. "I'll organize a search for clothes for you tomorrow. There are not enough hours left for that today."

Only now had I noticed the slight slump in his wide shoulders and signs of exhaustion on his face.

"I don't need clothes," I protested. My bodysuit was self-cleaning and required minimal maintenance. Besides, I wasn't planning to stay here for long. "My team will be searching for me."

"The only way anyone can find you is if they crash here, too. We'll deal with that when or if it happens," he dismissed.

Our protocol required for a search party to be sent to look for a missing person. However, I doubted my team leader would send anyone inside the Anomaly. Even if they discovered exactly how I had disappeared, the risk of losing another person without knowing what to expect inside this abnormality would be too great.

With or without the rescue party, however, I was determined to find my way out of here.

"Vrateus, I'll be leaving here, one way or another—"

"No, you won't." He wouldn't listen.

He brushed his hand over his face in a gesture that betrayed how tired he was.

Maybe right now wasn't the best time to argue or even try to reason? Would he be more agreeable if he rested?

He raked his fingers, tipped with black claws, through the fur on his head. It seemed thick and soft, bringing the fur of an arctic fox to mind. It ran in a wide stripe up his nape and along the middle of his head, ending in a thick wave hanging over his forehead. The visual softness of it clashed with his chiseled jaw and sharp cheekbones. And with his hard attitude, too…

"Eat." He pointed at the bowl on the tray, piled high with things not all of which I would consider food. "Then rest. You'll need your strength for tomorrow night."

Alarm shot through me at that reminder.

"You weren't serious about that, were you? You don't really want me to…um, do what you told them I'd do?"

No one would expect a person to do anything of that sort. Would they?

He glanced at me, confused.

"I promised my crew some entertainment. That's the reason you're still alive," he said it as if he had done me a huge favor by bargaining with my body without my permission.

"You must know it's illegal to force me." I shook my head in disbelief. "You didn't discuss anything with me. All I wanted was some assistance—"

"What *you* want is irrelevant." He jerked his head to the side, impatiently. "There are over seven hundred males in here. They all want a piece of you, some literally. The trick was to convince them to want *less* of you. And I have accomplished that."

Lifting an eyebrow, he leveled me a stare. Was he expecting me to be grateful for what he'd done "for me?"

"You've promised them what wasn't yours to give!" I snapped. "How are you planning to deliver it? Surely, you don't think I will act out your perverted fantasies?"

His jaw flexed. He folded his arms across his chest, his tail lashing against his boots.

"What choice do you have?"

"The choice *not* to do it." I widened my stance.

"And who would protect you from the wrath of their disappointment? Do you know what hundreds of sex-starved males can do to one female?" He flinched.

I grimaced, too, trying not to imagine what he had implied.

Was he trying to scare me? Why?

Several interplanetary laws guaranteed my freedom and well-being anywhere in the Federation's territory. I could recite them all by heart. All intelligent races of the Galaxy abided by the law of the Federation—the crime had been practically non-existent for decades.

"Why are you threatening me?" I asked.

"It's not a threat. Just the simple truth."

My mind flashed back to the scene in the corridor. Vrateus had shot one of his people in front of everyone, with no repercussions.

True, the male who'd attacked me had crossed the line, but I didn't think he deserved to be killed without getting a chance to defend himself. He had been a talking, thinking individual—a life that shouldn't have been disposed of so easily.

Obviously, the captain didn't respect any interplanetary laws.

My mentality struggled to adjust to this new reality. I felt disoriented, outside of my normal frame of reference.

Did Vrateus want me to beg for his personal protection?

"I suspect next you'll say you'll save me from the big, bad guys out there, but there's a price? Is that it?"

He frowned.

"I've already done all I can to save you. The rest is up to you."

With another irritated flip of his tail, he left.

Chapter Four

Vrateus

There was still so much to do before he could call it a night. Each newly arrived ship had to be stripped for every piece of equipment that could be reasonably used as a weapon. It had to be done tonight, no matter how tired he was.

As he worked on cataloguing the items and sorting them into boxes, his thoughts kept coming back to the woman who had arrived on this ship.

What an infuriating, ungrateful female she'd turned out to be.

He had left her alone, in the relative safety of the observation capsule of the ship that had crashed on the Dark Anomaly about a decade ago. The decade as calculated here, according to the arbitrary clock he had established and maintained.

He had long suspected that time on the Anomaly did not flow quite the same as it did outside of it. It appeared to run much slower here.

Whenever a new ship crashed, Vrateus would analyze the data, weapons, and equipment it had. He would estimate the amount of time that had passed in the world outside against the age of the data and technology that he'd recovered from the previously crashed ship.

For every year on the Dark Anomaly, about three hundred years passed on a regular, inhabitable planet like Nofoi, the home of his family. Which meant he had been missing from that world for over six thousand years, now.

Not that it mattered, anyway. No one was there to actually *miss* him. Everyone who'd ever known his family must be long dead by now. And no one outside of the Dark Anomaly would ever see him again. As far as the rest of the world was concerned, none of the people inside the Anomaly existed.

This was a world on its own.

Suppressing a yawn, he pinched the inside of his wrist, forcing himself to stay awake and alert as he inspected the rest of the human's ship.

Crux and Nocc stood nearby.

"To keep watch," Vrateus had told Crux.

In truth, he wanted to have the *errock* close by to keep an eye on *him*. By having Crux close, Vrateus ensured he wasn't out there stirring trouble among the rest of the crew.

Crux was ambitious, unpredictable, cruel, and dangerous. He was also the leader of the *errocks* on the Dark Anomaly, the largest and physically strongest species.

Vrateus had relied on their brawn to keep his crew members in order, especially during the first years of his rise to power. Strong, huge, and ruthless, *errocks* proved useful at enforcing his rules and establishing his authority over the rest.

Leading this community of shipwrecks wasn't easy. Being the only one of his species left on the Anomaly, Vrateus needed the assistance of others. Not that he ever could trust anyone here completely.

He blinked, trying to chase away the sleep that had been clouding his brain with increasing persistence.

With a glance at the watch on his belt, he realized he had been awake for over twenty hours now. Dealing with the aftermath of the crash of the human's little spaceship had taken all his evening and most of his night.

"We're done here for today," he called over to Crux, entering the last piece of equipment into the catalogue on his tablet.

The human wasn't lying when she said her mission was peaceful. Judging by its equipment, the ship had a scientific purpose, not a military one. Although unfamiliar with most of it, he realized that the things he had catalogued must be tools, not weapons. However, if they could effectively kill, he qualified them as weapons.

The rest could wait until tomorrow, he decided, sweeping his gaze over the warped walls of the damaged spaceship. In a few centuries, Anomaly time, all of this would move closer to its center. As the disk rotated, the ships crushed and compressed until there was no more space left between the walls. The pressure grew even stronger in the very middle of the disk, fusing all materials in a homogenous matter that bulged up into a sphere at the center.

In a few centuries time, he would be gone one way or another, and none of this would matter.

Until then…

"Come," he ordered Crux and Nocc.

Each of them lifted a box with the catalogued equipment, taking it down the hall to his room. It was identical to the one he had assigned to the female, located just a short distance down the corridor from hers.

Passing by her door, he realized he wasn't done for the night.

At the entrance to his room, he let Crux and Nocc go, then hauled the boxes with tools inside on his own.

He had chosen to live in this room for the same reason he had put the female in hers. The *errocks* had an extreme fear of large open spaces. They would never enter a room made entirely out of clear material, and it was therefore the only place in the Dark Anomaly where he could get some sleep.

The sleep would have to wait tonight, though. After quickly shoving the boxes into the secret storage room he had opened from his bathroom into the wreck of the spaceship one layer below, Vrateus left for the library.

He had promised his crew that the human woman would moan in pleasure. Judging by her words and the glares she had given him, she was not inclined to cooperate in delivering on that promise. Her resistance would end up costing her her life. And the death would not be one he'd wish on his worst enemy.

To keep her alive, he needed her to prove her value to his crew. She had to convince them all that they would get more entertainment from her being alive than from killing her.

He was not against helping her with that, but he needed to educate himself first.

The library was a large room he had expanded into the mass of compressed wreckage, off the main corridor. Here, shelves with opal tablet inserts lined the walls, organized by subject then by the *themul* alphabet of his species.

Heaving a sigh, he contemplated what exactly he needed. Although, he had never heard of humans before, there might be some information on them in the data he had added to his collection in recent years.

The female spoke of the Federation. If humans now were a part of it, there could be mentions of them in the information he'd retrieved from the recently crashed, unmanned ships.

Pulling out the few inserts off the shelves, he grabbed some on mating rituals of *themul* and other humanoid species that might be biologically similar to the woman in his care.

Back in his room, he kicked off his boots, got out of his clothes then unclipped, unholstered, and unstrapped the weapons from his body. Running his hands through the thick fur on his head he arched his back, stretching the muscles and letting the tension of the day finally drain a little.

His gaze drifted to the small figure of the human in the capsule beside his. He had dimmed the glass of his room from the outside. However, he had kept *her* glass completely transparent to keep an eye on her.

As a result, he remained invisible to her, but he could see her clearly.

With her arms wrapped around her, she was sitting on her knees on the floor at the farthest end of her capsule. Her forehead pressed to the glass, she stared straight into the raging storm of light.

He had spent many nights doing the same, wishing he could reach out beyond the lights and into the world.

No one escaped the Dark Anomaly, though. The human was trapped here for life—just like the rest of them were. All she could do was try to survive.

He turned away. Grabbing his tablet frame, he slid the first opal insert in. The surface of the insert came to life, turning into a glowing screen in his hands. Stretching in his narrow, metal bed, he started reading.

As he had feared, there wasn't much information on humans. When the ship before hers had crashed, they had just been discovered, but hadn't been contacted by the interplanetary Federation yet.

The notes on her species were scarce and dry—the expected lifespan, the natural habitat, the general characteristics. Only a few facts on reproduction.

Apparently, some humans mated for life, but some didn't. Breeding was spontaneous, largely unregulated by their governments. Thankfully, like most species he knew, humans appeared to enjoy having sex as recreation, not solely for reproduction.

He found a diagram of male and female bodies and examined it, then compared it to the similar diagrams of other species.

His main goal was to figure out what to do to make the female moan tomorrow night and every night thereafter, but he got sidetracked, watching the mating videos of *themul* and other species.

Vrateus viewed his own arousal as just another function of his body that needed to be addressed from time to time.

When he was hungry, he ate. When his bladder got full, he used the bathroom. When his cock got hard and achy, he stroked it until the climax brought him release.

Never before had he used an outside stimulation to cause an erection. Being in a state of arousal was distracting.

For the same reason, he stayed away from the *irsen* flowers that

Malahki grew in a hidden corner of the gardens. The sweet juice from the flowers would make him temporarily forget about the struggle for survival on the Dark Anomaly, about the brutal murders he had witnessed most of his life, about the screams of men being ripped apart alive, and women being brutally raped when his family ship crashed here over two decades ago… One of the women was his mother.

As much as he would welcome the oblivion, losing control over his mind around here could mean losing his life. For Vrateus, survival came with staying alert and aware at all times. All he allowed himself was a glass of berry wine on some exceptionally hard nights.

Like the juice of the *irsen* flowers, the arousal blunted his awareness, which made it just another weakness to him. He never searched for extra stimulation, dealing with physical desire as it came—once or twice a week.

Watching the videos of the different species having sex was an unfamiliar experience for him, causing a wide range of emotions.

He knew that *ognats*, for example, chewed the heads of their females off during copulation. The larvae resulting from the insemination consumed the female's body while growing inside her. The video of that was just as revolting as it sounded, and he promptly skipped it.

Several other species he had chosen, although they looked like the human at first glance, had very different insemination processes and reproductive organs.

Akuks didn't copulate at all, for example. The females of the species detested being touched by males. They laid eggs in a room of their house and left for the day while the males inseminated the eggs in their absence.

Finally, he turned on the videos of *themul*, his own species, which he had tried to avoid, unsure of the emotions they might bring out in him.

Vrateus was the only one left of his kind in this place. As an eight-year-old boy, he'd escaped the bloody carnage and a brutal death by hiding on the day of the crash. He then spent years surviving out of sight of the crude and violent inhabitants of the Anomaly.

He had stolen and begged for food, eating garbage when he had to.

When a ship crashed that had *vasai* centipedes on board, they escaped, populating the deep bowels of the Dark Anomaly. He learned to hunt the giant centipedes, eating some of the meat and trading the rest for things he needed.

During all that time, he had been gathering information on the variety of species occupying the Anomaly. Reading and learning, watching and listening, he had been biding his time until he had become strong and smart enough to take over and name himself their captain.

He had never seen a *themul* female he wasn't related to. Or if he had seen one, he didn't remember.

He had certainly never seen one bare or touched one.

The bodies of the *themul* females in the video were of a similar shape and proportion to the human female. Like her, they were narrower in the middle, with wider hips. Unlike hers, their chests were much flatter. *Themuls* had between two to six young per pregnancy, and had three rows of small, dark-nippled breasts on their chest and upper belly.

In the diagram on his tablet, the human female had two, larger breasts. And he distinctly remembered two lumps pushing against the material of the woman's bodysuit.

The males of one of the tribes on Nofoi apparently had their females collared during the wedding ceremony, the way Wyck had chained Lesh, his pet. The end of the leash was attached to the male's belt.

Something about that tradition appealed to Vrateus. He liked the idea of having his female nearby and of what the collar represented: possession and connection.

Although, he had to admit that it would not work on the Dark Anomaly. It reduced the female's chance of survival if he were killed. She would be trapped, chained to him, with a limited range of movement to fight for her life, and with no way to run and hide.

When the couple in the video were left alone, they came closer to each other, bringing their mouths together. The male then licked down the row of nipples on the front of his female, making her moan and squirm. Flipping her on her stomach, the male fisted his hand in the thick white-with-black fur of her scruff, ramming his cock into her from behind.

She threw her head back, baring her canines and growling in obvious pleasure as he pounded into her, their tails intertwined between their legs.

The primal passion of the couple, combined with the display of their mutual pleasure, shot straight to his groin. He shifted in his bed, making room for his growing erection. This was unexpected—definitely outside of his usual schedule of about once or twice a week.

Setting the tablet aside, he rose on his elbow and fisted his straining cock. It throbbed and ached, growing harder as he slid his hand up and down its length. The images from the video, now stored in his mind, spurred his arousal, sending him to his back with a groan. He arched his spine, pumping faster, the impending orgasm building up.

Rolling his head on the pillow, he faced the human's room. She was no longer in sight, Instead, he saw the outline of her form under the covers of her sleeping pallet by the wall.

The climax hit him, stronger than ever before, shuddering his entire body. He growled, baring his teeth and lashing his tail as the release pumped out of him in thick, ivory spurts.

After that he lay spent, wondering how much more of his measured, carefully organized life of survival was about to unravel because of one little female who couldn't steer her spacecraft away from the clutches of the Dark Anomaly.

Chapter Five

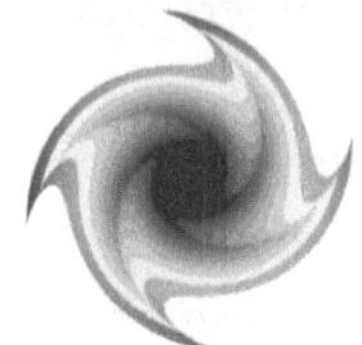

Svetlana

Surprisingly, I had gotten some sleep, though it was hard to tell how long I slept. When I woke up, the lights of the Anomaly continued their dance—ever-changing, yet perpetually the same.

I had eaten some of the food that Vrateus had brought last night—a mouldy smelling stew garnished with some leaves and a few pieces of sour fruit that looked like spotted tennis balls.

Thankfully, my stomach felt much better this morning. The food, as unpleasant as it was, must have agreed with it.

Next, I picked up the box with the toiletries Vrateus had given me and headed to the wall with the door in search of the bathroom.

Our conversation last night didn't go well. Maybe, he was too tired to think logically? Now, that he'd hopefully had some rest, the chances to find some understanding between us might be better.

How long had he been here, in this place, away from the real world? That could explain why his perception of things was so different from mine.

The Anomaly turned out to be nothing like what humans had

expected. Not once during our mission had the theory of life existing inside it been brought up.

I'd read reports of ships disappearing in this area during the early days of space travel. The last disappearances of live beings had happened centuries before humans made contact with the other species populating our Galaxy.

How long had this crew and their captain been surviving here? What generation of survivors could they be?

The word *errock* finally triggered my memory. It was the name of one species I had learned about in the academy. *Errocks* were a civilized nation, living on Hexol, one of the planets of the Federation.

No wonder I didn't recognize them when Wyck and Crux barged into my ship. The pictures I had seen of the *errocks* were those of well-groomed politicians and scientists, dressed in sleek, tailored suits or lab coats. None of them looked rugged and wild like Crux, Wyck, and the rest of this feral bunch. I was certain their out-of-control behavior would not be tolerated on their home planet, either.

Whatever this place was, my priority remained finding a way out of here.

My mission commander must have sent a search party when I had failed to return to the station yesterday. However, I couldn't realistically expect anyone to rescue me. At the very least, I needed to find a way off the Anomaly on my own to meet the search party outside of its gravitational field.

I found the bathroom behind the door next to the entrance of my room. The door slid open the moment I touched it. The water in the shower turned out to be barely lukewarm, not inviting me to linger. I barely managed to wash and rinse my hair before it stopped running. My five minutes had run out.

Finding a towel, I dried myself then slipped back into my bodysuit.

I was combing my hair with the ornate comb I'd found in the box with the toiletries when the door to my room opened and Vrateus entered, carrying another tray with food.

"Good morning." He stopped by the door, closing it quickly, then gaped at me with a curious expression on his face.

"What time is it?" I asked, since there was no time-keeping device in this room.

He kept staring at me, following the movement of my comb with his eyes.

"It looked just like a real tail," he muttered under his breath, setting the tray on the table.

"Tail?" I touched my hair, confused.

"Never mind." He shook his head on his way out.

"Wait." I rushed after him, stopping him by the door. "Can we talk for a minute, please?"

"About what?" He gave me a suspicious glance.

"I'm afraid we didn't start off well." I clutched my hands together in front of me, determined to give diplomacy another chance. "I'd like to apologize for our misunderstanding last night."

I took a pause, waiting for an apology from him in return, but it never came.

Well, he had obviously been brought up away from civilization. A lack of manners could be expected.

"Anyway," I continued as he just stood there in his usual position, his hands folded across his wide chest. "I offer to organize a rescue mission for everyone on the Anomaly, in exchange for your help in my departure from here."

"Departure?" he scoffed. "There is no leaving this place."

Was he intentionally keeping me prisoner here? The thought was disturbing.

"I believe," I started carefully, "I may have the means to leave—"

"You *believe*?" he smirked, taking a step closer and leaning my way. "You still don't understand. Do you? The Dark Anomaly sucks things *in*. It releases nothing or anyone. Ever."

The job of a scientist was to question generally accepted opinions that were not backed by facts. Fighting the urge to shrink away from him, I stood my ground.

"Well, has anyone ever *really* tried to leave?"

"Plenty of times." He huffed a sad laugh. "All have crashed right back here—smeared on the wreckage along the edge of the disk."

That gruesome description gave me pause.

"How long has it been since the last attempt?"

"A few years now," he said, then specified, "Anomaly years."

"Are those different from the universal year definition of the Federation?"

He nodded. "According to my calculation a year here equals about three hundred universal years."

"What?" Shock suddenly made it difficult for me to draw a breath.

"I should probably get you a watch," he muttered, running his hand through the thick fur on his head.

My insides chilled as I made a quick calculation in my head. "If one year here is about three hundred universal years. Then during the day I've spent here, almost a year would have passed there?"

"About ten months." He rolled back a shoulder. "Give or take a few days."

A universal year was an equivalent of an annual rotation of an average habitable planet of the Federation. It equalled a year and eight days on Earth.

If ten months had passed since my disappearance, any rescue efforts would have been over by now.

I most likely had been declared dead…

"Are you sure?" I struggled to stay upright as my knees shook.

I prayed for this just to be another misunderstanding. It wouldn't be hard to assume that Vrateus had made a mistake in his calculations.

Deep in my gut, though, I feared he was right.

The clothes Vrateus and his crew wore, his weapons and other objects around me weren't costumes or theater props. They were old. Really, really old.

From what I knew about the cultures and history of the nations of the Federation, the comb I used to brush my hair must be from at least a millennium ago. Vrateus's handguns were probably at least a few centuries old.

Even the interior of the ships I'd seen so far, all seemed severely dated in décor and finishes. Though most were in much better shape than they should be, considering their age.

"Are you sure, Vrateus?" I repeated meekly, grasping at straws.

"Nothing can be for sure as far as the Dark Anomaly is concerned," he said firmly. "One thing is certain. You cannot leave it."

I HARDLY ATE ANYTHING THAT MORNING.

Over and over, I sifted in my mind through everything that humanity had discovered about the Anomaly, including the knowledge shared with us by alien races.

Somehow things didn't add up. I knew its gravitational field was extremely strong. Yet here I was, not crushed. In fact, the gravity here felt no different from the artificial gravity we had at my research station or that of Earth.

Did the pull of the Anomaly mostly apply to metal objects? Was that why the asteroids moved by freely when our probes ended up being sucked in from much further distances?

We had explored that possibility before. The nature of the gravity had proven not to be magnetic. The probes made entirely of the newest strongest plastics ended up sucked in just as well.

"Nothing can be for sure as far as the Dark Anomaly is concerned."

Was that why humans still had so few results, even after decades of researching this mysterious abnormality in space? There had been so many inconsistencies observed, nothing was definite.

Around lunch time, Vrateus came in again. In addition to bringing food, he also rolled in a rack of clothes. The bright colors of the fabrics rivaled those of the lights outside the glass of my room.

"Choose something else to wear tonight," he said. "I'll come for you after dinner."

He sounded dreadfully serious.

"Hold on." I shook my head. "I said I'm not doing this. I'm not changing, either."

He stopped, sliding his gaze down my body once again.

"Would you rather wear this? Do you want them to associate their sexual pleasure with your regular clothes? You know they will only salivate more over you every time they see you dressed like this. Is that what you want?"

His words sent a shudder of disgust down my back.

"I don't want their *sexual pleasure* to be associated with me, in any way." I frowned.

"That is, unfortunately, not an option I can give you."

His morose composure scared me. I felt more alone than ever before—even more than while spinning through the vastness of space all on my own, my ship out of control.

"Why not? What would happen if I just stayed in here tonight?"

"If you don't show up, they will come for you. *Errocks* wouldn't dare enter this room, but everyone else won't hesitate to break in." He heaved a sigh. "Once they get out of control, they won't stop with raping you. Every trace of your body will be gone before morning."

I fought the horror descending on me.

It couldn't be true. He'd said it to intimidate me.

He was using my fear to get me under his control.

People of the Federation didn't rape and eat each other. The very notion was beyond my comprehension. Sentient beings didn't act like wild animals.

Did they?

The image of Vrateus shooting one of his men came to mind again. I remembered the grip of the alien's chitin covered hands on my ankles, the sinister glint in his black beady eyes. What would he have done had Vrateus not stopped him?

This place could never be my home. I didn't care for whatever mind games Vrateus was playing. Even if the search for me had been called off, I needed to get out of here. And I might have an idea how I could do that.

My ship had been damaged possibly beyond repair, but my

spacesuit should still be functioning. The way it was constructed, the suit was basically a little spaceship of its own. I could use the spare fuel cell from the ship to power the suit and leave the Dark Anomaly. A carefully calculated trajectory would send me back toward Omphi and several trade routes that passed by the water world. Once beyond the energy field of the Anomaly, I would send out a distress signal. Someone would intercept it and come to pick me up.

It could work. In any case, it was worth to try.

Then, I would organize a rescue mission to save these poor wretches here. Brutal and uncivilized, many of them might still be sentient beings, therefore falling under the law of the Federation. Their lives were precious, even if they didn't realize it.

Surely, their captain would welcome the opportunity to rescue his people.

"You see," I started, carefully. "This situation here could be resolved easily if you just let me go."

"Go where?" He stared at me with confusion.

"Back to where I came from. Just let me get to my ship—"

"Oh, for fuck's sake!" He threw his hands into the air. "Not this again? As much as I'd love to get rid of you, you're stuck here now. Forever. And I'm stuck with you. Do not make me regret my decision. Do what you're told. Get dressed and be ready to get naked out there."

I fought the rising anger that was fueled by indignity.

"As a figure of authority," I squeezed through my teeth, struggling to keep any kind of composure. "It is your responsibility to ensure my safety from the people under your command." My self-control finally snapped under frustration and desperation, and I yelled at him, "You're giving me to them with no effort to protect me!"

He stared back at me, in shock.

"How can you *not* see it?" His voice rose, too. "I *am* protecting you. This is the only way to keep you alive."

"By…exposing my body? Don't you try to pose as my saviour!" I shouted, my hands shaking. "You're not better than the rest of them. You're breaking the interplanetary law. Which makes you a filthy criminal."

Rage flashed fire-bright in his eyes.

"I invite the Federation Forces to come and hold me responsible, then." He swiveled to leave. "Around here, there is no law but mine!"

Everything inside me bubbled with resentment. No, it was no longer just that. Fear and indignation grew into panic and bred hot, searing anger.

Vrateus wouldn't listen to me. He had no intention of letting me go, refusing even to let me try. Obviously, he wasn't interested in being rescued, either. Why would he want to leave this place?

"Around here, there is no law but mine."

He could do anything he wanted on the Anomaly. There was no fear of retribution for him. He could write his own laws and alter them at will.

I didn't change out of my suit. I couldn't even look at the clothes on the rack. They had been collected from the shipwrecks. The women who'd worn them long gone, and I couldn't even bring myself to speculate on how they might have perished.

When Vrateus came for me later, he gave me an exasperated look, seeing me still in my bodysuit.

"I said I'm not doing it," I muttered gruffly.

"Then, I must take you in as you are." He moved my way, and I quickly retreated.

Instead of chasing me around the room, he stopped in the middle. "You know that except for *errocks*, none of the other species would hesitate before entering this room. They will come here if I don't present you to them in a few minutes as promised."

I just glared at him, my head low.

"If they get in here once," he continued, "they will no longer view this room as off-limits. Even if you survive tonight by some miracle, you'll lose your one safe place in the Anomaly. They will come back."

Misery flooded through me, smothering all my senses. I felt helpless as the situation seemed inescapable.

"Can't you see? This is the only solution for them to leave you alone." He took a small step toward me, his voice soothing as if he were talking to a skittish animal. He obviously thought of me as nothing more than an animal if he believed he could put me on display in front of a crowd like that. "You will let them look at you tonight, let me touch you in front of them. Just me, no one else. Only then can I guarantee your life and safety."

"I—I can't…" I hated the way my lip shook, and my voice trembled. I hated the feeling of being all alone, already exposed and vulnerable, even if still fully clothed.

Heaving a sigh, he said in a somber voice, "You have to."

I shook my head, wrapping my arms tightly around myself.

"Svetlana." The sound of my name from him shook me. I snapped my gaze to his face as he stared at me imploringly. "I want you to live."

I hated him so much at that moment. He even somehow schooled his features into a kind expression, using a soft voice with emotion, even saying my name to get his way.

One thing he had been right about: it really didn't matter what I wanted.

He had the means to make me do what *he* wished. Whatever sick game he was playing here, I could only play along. At least for tonight.

Then, I would start working on my escape plan from this hell. On my own. I was now glad that Vrateus hadn't let me share the details of my idea with him. I'd have to do it without his assistance, and against his "rules."

Stepping closer, he suddenly placed his hand on my throat, causing a spike of panic. His expression remained calm, if severe. This gesture, however, could mean anything, from anger, to aggression, to threat. His grip remained gentle enough, though. He wasn't compressing my throat, just touching it.

His face came close enough for me to see the true color of his eyes for the first time. They were of an intense shade somewhere between brown and yellow—burnt orange—with black pupils shaped as vertical slits, like those of a cat.

I stilled under his intense stare, the fur on the back of his hand tickling my chin, the warmth of his hand seeping through my skin.

"Will it be just *you* tonight? Touching me?" I croaked, not believing myself. Was I actually about to go along with this depravity?

"Yes," he said softly.

"No one else?"

I'd glimpsed enough slimy tentacles, hard scales, and sharp talons on some of the males to make my stomach drop with terror at the mere thought of those coming anywhere near my naked body.

"No," he promised.

"And you won't hurt me? I mean there'll be no physical pain?"

The focus in his eyes sharpened with a sudden flash of heat. "Unless you want it to be—"

"No!" I shook my head vehemently. In no way did I trust anyone here, Vrateus included, to deliver any kind of erotic pain. "Please, don't hurt me."

"I won't, then." He held my stare, keeping his hand on my neck.

"I have to change," I half-whispered, unable to stand the contact any longer.

He had made an excellent point when he said I shouldn't wear my own clothes for this.

"Right." He let go of my neck, and I drew in a breath.

Even though his grip on my throat hadn't been tight, his mere proximity seemed to have deprived me of oxygen.

"Can you leave?" I asked. "So I can change?"

"No."

Fine. Over seven hundred men were about to see me naked. It might as well start now.

Something inside me went numb the moment I had agreed to this. Little mattered, now.

I tugged down the front closure of my suit. Vrateus, at least, had the decency to turn around when the suit opened.

Walking over to the rack, I yanked the first garment off the hanger, something in canary yellow. I got out of my suit and threw the dress on over my bra and underwear. It had a long puffy skirt and a wide belt that I tied around my waist.

The entire process took me only a few seconds.

"I'm ready."

He turned around, giving me an assessing look.

"Do you want to change out of your boots, too?"

"Really?" I huffed a sharp laugh.

Did he need me in a well-coordinated outfit for this?

Arguing, however, would only prolong the whole thing.

"Fine." I kicked off my boots and rummaged in the long chest on the bottom of the clothing rack.

Finding shoes that would fit me wasn't as easy as the dress. Many had been worn by alien women with feet shaped differently than mine. Some were long and flared at the toes, some had been obviously made to fit over hooves. Finally, I fished out a pair of golden sandals with adjustable straps.

"Done." I straightened after fastening the straps over my feet and around my ankles.

The sooner this nightmare started, the sooner it would be over.

Chapter Six

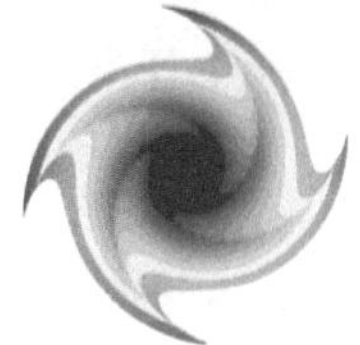

Vrateus

His hand around Svetlana's arm, he steered her down the corridor and toward the mess hall. Crux and Nocc led the way. Trox, Wyck, and Lesh were at the back.

The dress she was wearing had no sleeves. The acute awareness of her bare skin under his palm was unnervingly distracting. He needed to keep his focus on the *errocks*, watching them as they watched everyone else. Yet his attention kept drifting back to that one warm spot of contact with her body.

The mess hall was the largest room they had on the Dark Anomaly. The layout of the living area had been changing over the years, with new ships crashing to the outer edge and the old ones compressing closer to the center. However, the changes were slow, and he had used this room for major gatherings for the entire seven years of his being the captain.

His crew already filled the space. Males sat on the chairs and tables that had been haphazardly arranged around the room. Some of the climbing species clung to the walls higher up. At least a dozen or two swung on the glowing ropes of light suspended from the ceiling.

Svetlana skipped a step, coming to a sudden stop at the entrance, her mouth agape, her dark eyes wide open.

He tried to see the scene through her eyes. The sweaty, mostly naked male bodies of all shapes, colors, and sizes. The musky scent of their combined anticipation hanging heavily in the air. Leering eyes. Smirking mouths. Bared teeth, dripping with saliva. All of this must be disconcerting to her—terrifying, judging by her expression.

"They won't touch you." He forced more reassurance into his voice than he felt.

The space was charged with lust and aggression, making him worry about his ability to keep his promise. Over the years, he had successfully dealt with his crew's rage, frustration, and aggression. However, he could not predict with any certainty what their combined arousal would do.

A rumble of growls, groans, and grunts rolled through the room when Svetlana finally took a tiny step in. It was followed by a shower of leers and screamed obscenities that he had no desire to focus on—as long as they weren't threats.

"This way." He walked Svetlana to the wall to the right.

Keeping his attention on the crowd, he made sure not to put anyone but his personal guard of *errocks* at his back. When he reached the spot he'd chosen for her performance, he edged the *errocks* out of the way, too, by stepping back to the wall until his tail touched it.

He moved Svetlana in front of him, turning her to face the room, her back to his chest. Her body trembled in his arms. He wrapped his hand around her neck, to check her vitals again. Through the sensors in his palm, he took a note of her pulse, body temperature, blood pressure, and rate of breathing—all significantly higher than what they had been in her room.

"Ready?"

"I never will be," she gritted through her teeth.

That was worrisome.

"I promised them some moans."

"Well, *you* can go ahead and moan then," she bit off.

He might not know much about women, but he assumed that to make Svetlana orgasm he'd need her co-operation.

"They're expecting to see and hear *you*." If she continued to stand there like that, tense and glaring at everyone, he suspected his crew would complain bitterly. Unfortunately, most of them complained aggressively. He'd need to kill many. They would want to kill him. And her. "You don't have a choice."

"And I hate you for that," she hissed.

Him?

The shock of surprise rushed through his brain, echoing deep in his chest.

Why would she hate *him* when every single thing he'd done from the moment she'd crashed here was to save her life? Her lack of gratitude for that had been puzzling.

Was she not glad to be alive?

It occurred to him that he had never asked her if she wanted to be saved. He'd assumed her species had similar self-preservation instincts to his. However, he'd read about some instances of individuals preferring death to pain or dishonor.

The situation didn't leave Svetlana much of a choice—either entertain his crew by disrobing and pleasuring herself for their entertainment, or risk being raped and eventually killed by them instead.

He could, however, offer her something else. Something he hadn't considered before.

"Would you rather die?" he asked earnestly.

Sliding his hand between them, he bared one of the blades he carried hidden on his body. He pressed the tip of the dagger below her left shoulder blade.

He could give her a clean, fast death—a luxury compared to the fate of any other female who had ever had the misfortune of landing on the Dark Anomaly.

"I'll make it quick," he promised. "And as painless as possible."

Deprived of their entertainment, his crew would most likely end up ripping him to pieces right after. That fact somehow wasn't at the front of his mind at the moment.

She stilled under his blade. The males in the room quieted down too, expectant. Some unfastened their pants, leaning back. Ready.

Her pulse beat faster under his palm. Her breathing turned to shallow, irregular gasps.

"No," she said softly, and he exhaled in relief.

For some unexplained reason, he wanted her to stay alive more than he had ever wanted anything else in his life.

"I'll do it." She yanked at the belt around her waist, untying it.

A roar of approval rolled through the mess hall.

He discreetly slid the dagger back into its sheath at his chest. His shoulders still ached from the strain and tension he'd felt while waiting for her answer.

Her hands trembling, Svetlana opened the front of her dress, revealing a pink harness underneath that holstered her breasts. Moving her hands behind her, she unhooked the closure at the back. The harness slacked around her chest.

Groans, wet sounds of approval, and clicking noises of unfastened clothes filled the room. Crux leaned back against the nearest table, whipping out both of his cocks. The *kreers* under the ceiling produced their genital clusters from the pouches on their segmented bellies. Crawling over each other, *yourlu* spread their tentacles open in a circle. Their undulating reproductive organs snaked out from the middle.

Svetlana staggered back, coming flush with his chest. "You do it…" Her throat bobbed with a swallow under his palm. "Please."

With a deep breath, he slid his other hand to her front, praying he'd get it right.

The sight of naked males groping themselves couldn't be helpful in getting her to relax, he assumed.

"Close your eyes." He tried to sound confident, hiding his inexperience.

She obeyed with a brief shuddered sigh.

Thinking back to everything he had read and watched during

his recent research into female pleasure, he lifted his hand to her chest, cupping one full breast through her pink harness.

Her breasts were much larger than those of the *themul* female in the video. Heavy. He understood why Svetlana would need to strap them for support.

Her breathing hitched, and he moved his hand higher, sliding the dress and the straps of the harness from her shoulders. The dress slipped off, the voluminous skirt pooling at her feet. The harness followed.

He touched her bare breast, carefully. The images of the thrashing and growling female in the video came to mind again. Was that the way it had to be done? Was that how women liked it? Rough and furious?

"Don't hurt me," Svetlana had pleaded.

It didn't feel right to grab her by her hair.

Pushing the memories of the video aside, he followed his instincts instead. In addition, he kept one of his hands around her throat at all times, consulting the pattern of her erratic vitals.

Palming her naked breast, he found it surprisingly soft, her skin exceptionally smooth and silky. It wrinkled around the tip as the nipple hardened under his thumb. He marvelled at the change, rolling the tight bud between his fingers.

She exhaled sharply. A tiny sound vibrated in her throat.

An echo of a moan?

A sudden urge to taste her skin rose in him, like the male in the video had. Except that he couldn't do that here. His attention was already spread thin. He had to concentrate on his next move with her, continuously watching her reaction while also being mindful of everything happening around them—keeping track of the positions of everyone on his crew while gauging everyone's mood.

So far, they seemed to be enthralled, whether with lust or curiosity. The sight of a half-naked female was a novelty to many of them. However, not all would find her body alone appealing enough. The physical differences between humans and some of the species here were just too great.

They needed to see her thrash in the throngs of passion, to hear her moan, just as he had promised. Then, he hoped, their imagination would fill in the blanks to complete whatever image or fantasy each of them needed to achieve satisfaction.

He moved to fondle her other breast, while stroking the side of her neck with the thumb of his other hand. Not wanting to remove his hand from her throat, he reached with his tail. Wrapping it around her leg, he stroked the inside of her thigh with the tip.

She released a slight gasp at the caress of the fur of his tail.

He slid his hand lower, down her stomach and under the waistband of the short underpants she was wearing.

Several disgruntled growls came from the room, reminding him she had to be completely naked. He tugged her shorts down, past her hips and she wiggled her legs to make the underwear slide down to her ankles.

He discovered with surprise that she had fur between her legs. Short and springy, it differed from the long, silky hair on her head. He parted it with his fingers, finding by touch the small nub he had read would bring an orgasm to a *themul* female if stimulated. He hoped it would cause a pleasurable sensation in Svetlana, too.

He circled it with his finger, applying a little pressure while stroking her inner thigh with his tail.

Her breathing deepened, and she bent forward slightly, prompting him to finally remove his hand from her neck. Instead, he wrapped his arm around her chest, cupping one of her breasts as he continued to rub between her legs with his other hand.

She grabbed his hand on her breast, lacing her fingers with his. Her body relaxed into his arms, a small shiver running through her in response to his touch.

He blinked, amazed and thrilled by the reactions he was causing in her. It felt like a dance where he led, and she followed. The harmony that the two of them hadn't been able to achieve through conversation was suddenly happening wordlessly.

Tossing her head back on his shoulder, she whimpered softly.

He caught a glimpse of a new expression on her face. It conveyed both pleasure and ache. The same sweet torture he was experiencing that very moment as her backside pressed against his straining erection.

Then, he sensed her body tense. She circled his wrist with her fingers and yanked at his arm, shifting his hand away from the spot between her legs.

Whatever he had just ignited inside her, she forced it down, unwilling to let go.

"Pretend, if you must," he whispered.

She drew in some air then released a moan. Strong and loud, it was immediately echoed with grunts and groans from the males who rubbed, stroked, and fondled themselves.

She continued to thrash in his arms, making sounds that he now knew were fake.

A moment later, she stilled. Her eyes still closed, she appeared to be listening to the room, hugging his arms to her.

He glanced around the mess hall quickly, noting the slumped positions of the males. Most appeared satisfied. The rest were catching up. Crux reclined in a chair by the table, a limp cock draped over each of his thighs. A greenish puddle glistened on the floor between his feet.

"Are we done?" Svetlana asked in a hoarse whisper, letting go of his arms.

"Yes." Vrateus bent over quickly, picking up her dress. She grabbed it from him, wrapping it around herself, then snatched her underpants and her breast harness off the floor.

He spotted Wyck at the entrance. Lesh was nowhere around. The *errock* must have chained the animal somewhere to leave both his hands free for the event. Wyck's pants were on, however, with no green puddles around. The bulge in his pants seemed bigger than ever.

Vrateus couldn't concern himself with *everyone's* satisfaction. They all had their chance. If Wyck preferred to pleasure himself in the privacy of his own bed later, it was his choice.

He caught Wyck's eye, tipping his chin toward the exit. It was time to get out of here, and he needed at least someone from his guard for protection on the way back to Svetlana's room.

Wyck nodded, joining them. Vrateus wrapped his arm around Svetlana's shoulders, leading her out of the mess hall.

Chapter Seven

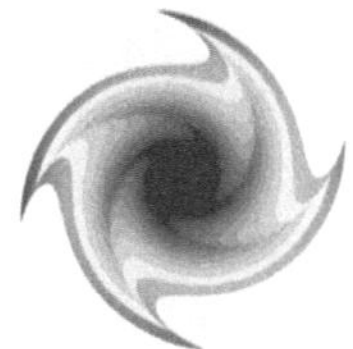

Svetlana

My knees shook and my hands trembled as I walked down the corridor back to my glass room. Then the whole-body shudders started, and I was grateful for the firm grip of Vrateus's arm around me.

I should not have opened my eyes until he had led me out of that hall. The sight of the sweaty males of various species now had been burnt into my brain. Glistening chests. Arm muscles straining as they stroked and jerked themselves off. Shoulders moving as hands pumped... Their mouths agape, fangs bared, hungry stares devouring me.

Even with my eyes closed, I had not escaped their grunts and groans, the sounds of flesh hitting flesh, the wet noises...

The smell of sweat...

The heavy, musky odor of semen rising into the air...

A shudder jerked my shoulders when Vrateus finally dragged me through the open doors and into my glass room.

"You did good."

The praise felt worse than a slap on the face would have. His words set off the explosion of rage, humiliation, and disgust inside me.

"Fuck you!" I snapped, shrugging his arm off me.

What was he praising? My performance during that grotesque show of mass masturbation?

Was I supposed to be proud of *that?* Did I need to strive to do *good?*

Centuries of civilization had just been stripped from me. All progress that humanity had made. The respect and equality I had earned because of my own work and the work of the women who had come before me. All of that meant absolutely nothing as tonight, I had been reduced to just a naked body to gawk at and be used for someone else's slobbering pleasure.

It was easy to hate them all, but it gave no satisfaction of revenge, since the rest of the males couldn't hear me curse at them.

It was Vrateus who'd had his hands on me. And at him, I directed my anger.

I hated him for ever coming up with this perverted idea. For somehow convincing me to agree to it.

Back in the hall, he had actually given me a choice worth considering. He had offered me a clean, quick death. By choosing to live, I had turned myself from a victim into a willing participant in what had happened.

I despised myself for that, too.

But most of all, I was angry that he'd made me *like* some parts of that horrible experience. Nothing about his actual touch had been revolting.

And I hated him for that the most.

Sitting on my sleeping pallet, hugging my knees, I couldn't stop the bouts of shakes that kept running through my body.

I didn't hear the doors open and close and had no idea when Vrateus had left my room.

When a small cluster of waxy yellow flowers slid into my view, I realized he had come back. Now, he was kneeling beside me, holding the translucent branch covered with tiny blossoms in his hand.

"What's this?" I gave him a sideway glare.

"*Irsen* flowers. Chew on them slowly, without swallowing. Their juice will help you fall asleep tonight." He put the branch into my hand and watched me as I mechanically shoved the entire thing into my mouth.

The bitter-sweet juice thickly coated my tongue when I started chewing. Then a fuzzy haze descended on my mind, warming my chest. My limbs grew heavy, and I sank back into the bedding of my pallet.

"Just this once," Vrateus murmured, tugging the covers over me.

He tucked me in as the feeling of soaring beyond the lights of the Anomaly swept me into a blissful delusion.

I did not hear when he left again.

I WOKE UP AT THIRTEEN MINUTES PAST NINE THE FOLLOWING morning. I knew the exact time because of the large, metal analogue clock left near my sleeping pallet.

Right away, I dashed to the bathroom to get rid of the nasty, sticky mess of chewed up flowers in my mouth. Spitting it out, I vigorously brushed my teeth, then took a quick cool shower, which brought me back to life.

Last night had drifted away, like nightmares always did in the morning. I had an amazing clarity of mind, and my body buzzed with energy. I didn't want to dwell on what had happened, I was ready to focus on the future.

Ripping a piece of cloth from one of the dresses on the rack that remained in my room, I wetted it and wiped down my bodysuit and undergarments. The self-cleaning material took care of the rest by absorbing the moisture and dissolving impurities into the air.

Fully dressed, with my hair brushed and put up in a ponytail, I sat down to eat my breakfast. It was a bowl of some grainy matter with the meaty taste of stew. Vrateus must have brought it earlier this morning, as it was still lukewarm.

Escaping this place appeared to be very executable today. Pieces of the plan turned in my head, like a puzzle about to be solved.

I could reasonably assume that my spacesuit had sustained only minimal damage during the crash. I knew the ship's fuel cells had been designed to fit on the suit, in case of an emergency. Their power would be enough to combat the gravity of a planet many times larger than the solid mass of the Dark Anomaly.

I had to make more accurate calculations, of course. For that I needed to know the exact combined mass of the metal wreckage of the Anomaly. I'd also have to get to my ship and the spacesuit somehow with enough time to assess it for any damages, fix them if necessary, then connect the fuel cells and program the trajectory.

Then, I would need to find my way out to the surface of the Anomaly disk.

To figure all of this out, I needed information that Vrateus must have. He was the captain of this place, after all. Which meant that as little as I wished to speak to him again, I would have to.

The door swished open as soon as I finished my breakfast, making me wonder if I had been watched.

"How are you?" Vrateus entered.

His appearance in my room jolted me with a shock of awareness through my system.

He must have just had a shower. The fur on his head, hands, and tail appeared damp. The faint scent of the same soap I used drifted my way. On him, it had the added flavor of male spice—his very own unique scent.

I had been apprehensive about seeing him this morning, but the effect was even stronger and somewhat different from what I had expected.

Was it because he had touched me? The phantom sensation of his hands on me glided over my body.

Hoping to escape his scent, I took a step back. My eyes however kept taking in the sight of his tall, well-build body, dressed in another one of his ridiculous, wide-sleeved, crispy-white shirts that he somehow made look appealing.

This must be some lingering side effect of the flowers.

Why else would I find anything about this man *appealing*?

His arms folded across his chest, he drummed the fingers of his right hand against his left bicep, waiting for my answer.

I made an enormous effort not to think about *where* those fingers had been last night when he held me so close to him.

"I'm fine." My voice came out husky, and I cleared my throat, schooling my expression into something hopefully neutral and casual. "I'm very good, actually. Feel free to show up here with a whole bouquet of those flowers next time."

"You can't have them often." He shook his head with a grim expression on his face. "If you give in to the craving, the juice of the *irsen* flowers would eventually rot your brain."

"Isn't that true about many kinds of cravings?" I muttered, blankly staring at his hand.

When was the last time I had a man make love to me? Definitely not while on the mission. Relationships didn't last long in the cramped environment of the research station. My parents had me during the one and only assignment they had ever worked on together in space. Neither of them had planned for me to happen, and neither wished to have anything to do with me or with each other when the project ended.

The last thing I wanted was to repeat their mistakes when they had treated me as the biggest mistake of their lives for as long as I remembered.

I no longer did relationships. The couple that I'd had, I'd made sure to end myself, leaving them before they left me. I knew way too well how much it hurt when people I loved left, and I refused to give the power to cause that kind of pain to me to anyone anymore.

Now, nearly a year of no physical contact whatsoever had made me suddenly ogle with appreciation the man who had publicly molested me just a few hours earlier.

Disgusting.

"Possibly." He reached for the empty bowl in my hands.

I blinked, snapping back to the task I had identified for myself.

Information.

I needed him to tell me more about the Anomaly, to hopefully show me as much as possible of it, too.

"I'd like to go for a walk, please." I clasped my hands in front of me, giving him a friendly smile.

"A walk?" He stared at me as if I had just asked for something unreasonable, like going on a spacewalk in the nude.

"Yes. I've been here for two days now, but still haven't seen much of this place. You told me this is going to be my home now. I'd love to learn more about it. How do you operate things to ensure your survival? Where does the food come from? The layout of the entire habitable area. How large is it?"

"You want to leave the room?" he said slowly, as if struggling to grasp the concept of my simple request.

"Yes, please," I kept my voice light and friendly, almost imploring. "You can set a time limit if you wish, and I promise to return before it's up."

"It's not safe out there on your own."

As if I didn't know that. The amount of rude behaviour I'd encountered in the past two days by far exceeded anything I'd ever faced during my entire life prior.

"I'm well aware of that, and I'll be careful. I can go out at night when everyone is asleep. Or any other time of the day you'd suggest. I'll stay out of everyone's way. I won't talk to anyone…"

He shook his head, his sharp features hardening into a frown.

"It'd be too dangerous any time of the day. You *know* we have the worst kind of predators here."

"Predators?"

He arched a long, thick eyebrow. "Yes. I'm their captain."

Exactly. As their captain, shouldn't he have some control over them? Or he simply didn't want to exercise it on my behalf?

"Didn't your crew already get what they wanted?" I rolled my shoulders back, trying to hide my embracement at bringing up the last night. Unsuccessfully, it appeared, as I could already feel the blush creep up my neck. "You used me for their entertainment in exchange for my life and safety. That was the deal, wasn't it?"

"Yes. But only in exchange for your life. *Safety* is never guaranteed around here."

"That seems hardly fair." I bit my lip to prevent it from trembling. "I went along with..." I swallowed hard, unable to come up with an adequate name for the last night's depravity. "And none of that bought me even one safe passage through the corridors, deep at night, when everyone sleeps?"

He kept shaking his head, unyielding.

"You cannot leave this room. Definitely not on your own."

"Well...Can you come with me, then?" I'd rather have him for a company than not leave here at all.

"I'm busy," he bit off. "And I have no escort to give you, either. I don't trust anyone around here enough to leave you in their care."

I drew in some air, fighting dread and frustration. An argument would not be in my best interest right now. I needed his cooperation.

"You're not even trying to search for a better solution with me," I managed, calmly enough.

"I've already found the best solution there could be in this situation."

"Keeping me locked up? Around the clock?" My composure crumbled, and my voice leaped higher. "Why?"

"Because this is the safest place for you!" he snapped back. His own patience was obviously even shorter than mine. "Out there, someone will always want more from you than what is allowed."

"But that's not what has been negotiated. You said 'once a week' only, and I believed you..." My voice rang high and brittle to my ear. Frustration burned my eyelids with tears.

I'd gone through the most degrading experience in my life, and it bought me nothing. No safety, no freedom.

If I wasn't allowed to leave this room, my only chance for escape disappeared.

I could not stay here forever.

"You're their captain, aren't you?" I pleaded, already knowing he wouldn't listen. "Order them to leave me alone. That was the deal."

"I can't guarantee my orders will be followed, unless I personally supervise their execution."

"Sounds like something a micromanaging control freak would say," I couldn't hold back the snappy remark at his excuses.

He stretched his neck, his jaw tightened.

"You chose to live," he growled at me. "Your survival is now *my* responsibility. *I* decide how it can best be accomplished."

"And locking me in this room is the *only* solution?"

"Yes."

I groaned exasperated. "Forever?"

"Until the next week's session."

Session? Sounded so proper and legit, it made me want to puke.

"The jerk-off fest, you mean?" I called it what it was. "Is that all my life is now? You'll keep me locked up in here, like an animal in a cage? Letting me out only for that pathetic *entertainment* you've invented?"

He flinched at my words but recovered quickly.

"It's not my fault you crashed here." He kept his voice even, but a flush of color on his bronzed cheeks and the wild lashing of his tail against his legs betrayed his agitation. "Do you understand how much disruption your arrival has caused? I've spent years establishing the current order, and I have to work daily on maintaining it."

"Well, excuse me, for *choosing* to crash on your neat little freak fest and to wreak havoc with my arrival!" I no longer cared about preserving any kind of diplomacy, spurred by the frustration, shame, and desperation. And fear. The cold, brutal fear that I might be forced to remain here forever. That *this* would be the only life I'd ever know. "Do you think I wanted to come here? This shithole is the last place I want to be!"

He huffed, leaning toward my face and fully invading my personal space. The burnt orange of his irises lit up with barely contained rage. His hot scent wrapped all around me, making my breath hitch.

"I promised you a fast, clean death," he gritted through his teeth. "The offer still stands if you change your mind. Otherwise, you are to do what I say. Just like everyone else in this *shithole*."

This was an outright threat. The heat of it made my blood boil.

"If you think that I—" I started, not even sure yet how I was intending to finish the sentence but determined not to let him have the last word.

"You're staying here!" he bit off, his voice hard and cold like steel. "Locked in and safe."

Pivoting on his heel, he stormed out of the room, with an angry whip of his tail against the door frame.

Asshole!

I yelled in my head as the door closed, taking him out of the earshot.

Pervert.

And a brute. Despite all his fine shirts, embossed leather, and jewellery, he was no better than the last of his crew dressed in rags—a barbarian like the rest of them.

I paced the glass floor, raging inside.

I despised them all. However, the rest of the crew were mostly just one homogenous mass of sweaty bodies and leering eyes to me. Hellfire could come and burn them all en masse for all I cared.

Their captain, however, I yearned to strangle with my own hands. I wished to have *his* life in *my* control for a change, to see something else than that calm focus in his bright orange eyes.

Spotting the fiery glow of rage in them a minute earlier stirred something in me.

I was glad he'd left. Yet somewhere deep inside, I wondered what would have happened if he'd stayed.

He didn't matter.

I shook it off.

Even without his help, I would get to my ship. Sooner or later, I'd be out of here. And he could stay and rot in this place, along with his crew of degenerates.

Chapter Eight

Svetlana

The day dragged on. The hours between meals felt like weeks. Vrateus would bring my food and take back the empty dishes—all without saying a word, hardly throwing a glance my way.

Fine, be that way.

Sitting on the sleeping pallet, I watched the endless light show outside the glass during the brief few minutes he spent in my room each time.

The silence grew heavier with each of his visits and harder to bear. With no one to talk to, the loneliness grew. I had to speak with him to get some information, but more than that, I just wanted to *talk*—with anyone.

The next morning, I showered and dressed, unsure of why I even bothered. As far as anyone in this place was probably concerned, I could have stayed in bed for the next several days. As long as I showed up to excite them during their weekly public masturbation sessions, no one cared what I did the rest of the time.

"Good morning," I offered the greeting first when Vrateus brought my breakfast.

He froze, holding the tray with a huge metal bowl and an ornate metal cup on it. Narrowing his eyes, he gave me an assessing stare.

"Morning," he replied tentatively, still obviously sulking.

If he were expecting an apology from me, he would have to wait for a long time. I would not apologize for demanding to be treated as a free person with dignity, even as he had deprived me of both dignity and freedom.

I was not going to apologize this time. However, I couldn't bear to sit in silence, day after day, as years passed by in the outside world —the world where I belonged.

"I don't like this…" I waved my hand between us, gesturing at him and me, "This silent treatment thing."

"I am not enjoying it either." He placed the tray on the table but didn't leave immediately after, as he had done yesterday.

Instead, he took his usual wide stance, crossing his arms over his chest. The pose had a certain flare of arrogance, which suited him.

I stood in front of him, trying not to mimic his posture. "I would like to break this silence. Can we please talk again?"

"I would like that, too." He inclined his head as if he were accepting the apology I had never given.

In fact, shouldn't *he* be the one to apologize? After all, I was still the one destined to spend the rest of my life locked up.

I took a long breath in, reminding myself that getting into yet another argument would hinder my plans.

"So," I tried just one more time, as calmly and friendly as I could manage. "Are you absolutely positive that there is definitely no way for me to ever leave this room? Other than once a week, please?"

He dropped his hands to his sides with an exasperated sigh. "Svetlana."

There was something slightly indecent in the way he pronounced my name. It made me think of licking, for some reason.

He obviously wasn't thinking of *that*, judging by his frustrated expression.

"It wasn't a whim of mine, to keep you in here. Anywhere outside of this glass capsule is dangerous." He raked his claws through his fur. "Fuck," he groaned. "Even inside this room, I cannot guarantee your safety."

He frowned, peering past the glass into the dancing lights of the Anomaly.

"They'd drive you mad," he'd said to me once.

His wild expression made me wonder if he had already lost some of his sanity. After having spent who knew how much time in this place, I wouldn't blame him if he had. He definitely seemed to exhibit some signs of paranoia.

"You know your crew," I said, wishing to gauge the severity of the danger he had been talking about. How much of what he feared was a genuine threat? So far, they all seemed to listen to him and obey his orders, at least since the day he had shot one of them.

"I do. I have studied every species here in detail. I've also learned what motivates each individual, by watching them for years." A shadow drew over his features. "I killed ninety-seven of them the day I took over and declared myself their captain. Then I've shot another hundred and fifty-three, re-enforcing my rules and maintaining the order ever since."

He met my eyes, as if waiting for a reaction.

I didn't know what exactly he wanted me to say. That the killings he'd done must have been justified, considering the savage nature of his people? Or that I understood that it hurt him having to commit those murders?

"They are a wild, unrefined bunch of criminals," he continued as I kept silent. "Murderers, rapists, and cannibals. Anyone who had a conscience, manners, or honor had been exterminated long before I took power. Nothing good survives here, Svetlana. Nothing beautiful, delicate or feminine, either."

"Is that how you survived, then? By getting rid of your own conscience and honor?"

His jaw muscles flexed in obvious displeasure at my question. Yet his voice was calm when he replied, "I survived by making myself smarter than them. I've read, I've studied, and I've watched. Then, I've figured out how to overpower them and prevent them from rebelling against me."

Despite our mutual dislike for each other, I sensed some good inside him, buried deep under the hard exterior. Maybe it happened because he had stopped scowling and shouting, and was making an effort to finally explain things to me? For the first time ever, this felt more like a beginning of a real conversation rather than the usual argument.

I held back another snappy reply in response, and instead asked with a genuine interest,

"How, then?"

"Their minds and hands need to be occupied. I try to convert some of their aggression into productive results, by keeping them busy. There is always work to be done around here. My authority is absolute. I ruthlessly eradicate any doubt about that. But it does not go undisputed."

It occurred to me that it might be the only time Vrateus had ever talked to anyone this openly about himself. He was not only explaining *things* for me, he was explaining *himself* to me, as if he cared what I thought about him.

"You think all I need to do is to command and they will obey?" he continued. "Every order I give, I need to supervise to make sure it's executed the right way. I have to be physically present, everywhere at once. Because if I'm not there to check and reinforce, they slack off. Every one of them is just waiting for me to slip up and make a mistake."

He rubbed his face in the now familiar gesture. His exhaustion might be more noticeable by the end of the day but listening to him now, I realized he was *always* tired, no matter how much rest he got.

"Svetlana, I don't know what prior knowledge you have about the species of the Dark Anomaly. You seem to have come from a gentler, better place, where women feel safe on their own. But it's different here."

He held me with his gaze.

"Do you think a release once a week would take care of my crew's sexual frustration? It won't. *Dimos* come several times a day. And that's when they're single. If they catch a scent of a female, they can spend days doing nothing but having sex. Continuously."

He was no longer arguing or even trying to convince me of anything. He was simply stating facts, letting me do whatever I wanted with the information.

"*Errocks* have two cocks each, and they're only truly satisfied when they come from both. Simultaneously. *Ognats* chew the heads off their females during mating. *Kreers* have a birth rate of one male to ten females, because they mate in the water, often drowning the female during sex. Like *ognats*, they are cannibals. They eat everything they kill. *Everything*."

He drew in a long breath, as if talking had exhausted him even more.

"Nothing would stop the monsters I call my crew from satisfying their basic instincts if they got within leaping distance from you while you were walking anywhere alone."

Faced with the horrific nature of the inhabitants of the Dark Anomaly, the argument died in me completely.

"Do you understand me?" he asked, peering at me intently. "Svetlana, do you believe me?"

I had many reasons to mistrust him, but I felt he was being sincere.

"Yes." My knees gave in, and I sank to the floor right where I stood.

Silently, he offered me the cup from the tray. Bejewelled and embossed, it appeared to have come straight from a storybook's pirate treasure. Except that no one here had come from a storybook—from a nightmare, maybe.

"I understand what you're saying." I took the cup from him mechanically. "What escapes me is *why* they are like that?"

"Some of it is in their blood. It's the characteristic of their species."

"No. That's not true." I shook my head. "All of them initially came from the same world I did. And I've never heard of any race being inherently brutal or violent like that. *Errocks* are an intelligent, civilized nation, for example. And that head-eating thing that you said *ognats* do..." I flinched, bringing it up. "It would not be tolerated anywhere in the modern world."

"Then it must be a better world out there now."

"What was it like when they got here?" I asked. "How long have you all been on the Dark Anomaly?"

"It depends. Malahki was the last sentient being to arrive here before you. That was about five years ago. I've been here for over two decades now. That's about six thousand universal years."

"What?" I stared at him, flabbergasted. "Six thousand years? That would be before the beginning of recorded human history!"

"Yours must be a very young race then. Many of the others have been here for much longer than that, twice or even three times as long as I have."

"That would be like traveling through time."

"Except that no one actually travels anywhere." He huffed a bitter laugh. "All of us are staying put."

I took a drink of tea, suddenly no longer feeling like talking.

All of what Vrateus had said was excruciatingly depressing.

He crouched in front of me.

"I have rearranged my schedule for tomorrow. Right after breakfast, I will have one hour to show you around. Crux, Wyck, and Nocc will come with us."

I snapped my gaze to his, shocked by his offer after the speech he had just given me.

"You *will* take me for a walk, after all?"

"With an adequate escort," he said with an emphasis. "You're never to step a foot outside of this room *alone.* Do you understand?"

I nodded, afraid to believe he was giving in.

"There are benefits to familiarizing yourself with the Dark Anomaly. You need to know your surroundings in case of an emergency."

"Thank you," I exhaled with relief and genuine gratitude.

He hovered his hand over my knee for a moment, before tentatively placing it on it. "You're welcome."

I covered his hand with mine, my fingers sinking into the soft fur on the back of his hand.

He blinked, slightly discomfited for once.

"Just, um… Make sure you stay close and do exactly as I say, Svetlana. Please, make it easier for me to keep you safe."

Chapter Nine

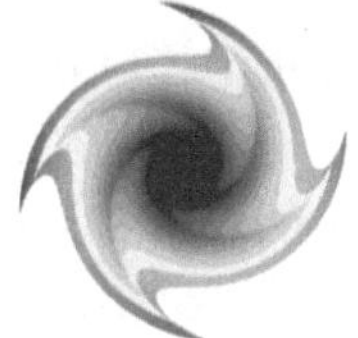

Svetlana

It was only a walk through the rumpled corridors of the junkyard of spaceships compacted together by the unexplained force field in space. Yet from the moment I woke up, I felt excited as if I were six again and my grandma was about to take me to the fair.

Being forced to stay in one room had made me eager to see *anything* outside of it.

"Morning," I greeted Vrateus the moment he walked in with breakfast. "I'll be quick." I grabbed the tray from him.

"Take your time. You have fifteen minutes for breakfast, then an entire hour for the walk."

His days seemed to comprise a string of time intervals, each with a specific task assigned to it.

For the next hour and fifteen minutes the task was me.

"Where are you taking me today?" I stuffed a spoonful of the watery stew into my mouth. The food on the Anomaly lacked not just taste but also variety. I'd had a slight variation of the same thing for every meal.

"We'll take a walk in the opposite direction from the mess hall."

"Oh, good." I wasn't too eager to see the mess hall again, anyway. "What's there?"

"The library and the gardens."

I was hoping for an airlock, the exit to the surface. However, seeing more of the layout of the habitable sector of the Dark Anomaly would still be beneficial. Besides, I might find some information I needed in the library.

"Sounds good."

"Today, we'll go to the library. The gardens will be next week. I also have a visit to the kitchen scheduled, two days from now."

"Really?" I exclaimed, surprised but even more excited now. It appeared I was about to see a lot of this place.

"This won't happen often." He toned down my enthusiasm. "I'll try to find time for more walks in the future, but I can't promise anything definite yet."

"I'd love to be able to walk as much as possible, please," I asked nicely. "Everybody needs regular exercise, right? How do *you* stay physically active?"

He sat down on the floor next to me, and I admired the thick muscles of his thighs, bulging against the dark-brown material of his pants.

"Physical labor." He blinked, following my gaze. "There is always a lot to be done around here."

I finished my stew in record time, drank the bitter-sweet, black tea just as fast, and got up.

"I'm ready."

The relaxed expression he had on his face while watching me eat disappeared at my words. Focus sharpened his features as he walked me to the door and placed his hand on the control panel.

The three members of his personal guard stood just outside the door. Wyck had the end of Lesh's chain wrapped around his wrist. The bizarre creature lowered all three of its heads, hissing at the doors as they slid open.

Neither of the *errocks* offered me a greeting, and I kept quiet, too, deciding it was best not to attract any extra attention.

Wrapping his hand around my upper arm, Vrateus gestured for

Crux to lead. Wyck and Nocc flanked us, each about a step behind Vrateus and me.

I couldn't shake off the feeling of unease while walking down the corridors. This was not a relaxing stroll. The sensation of the *errocks* ogling me prickled my skin. The moist breathing of Wyck's pet heated my ankles.

I focused on where we were going, taking in the dented metal of the ceiling and the bent panels of the wall. Now and then, I spotted a thick round line of melted metal, crudely welded. It circled the corridor—floor, walls, and ceiling. Those must be the places where newly crashed ships were integrated into the Dark Anomaly, adding to the usable space of the metal disk.

I wondered what they'd use my spaceship for. Maybe a storage room, one among many.

"Have you stripped my ship?" I asked Vrateus.

"Yes. Everything we could use has now been taken off and put into storage," he replied, not taking his eyes off Crux's back in front of us.

"How about the spacesuit? And the spare fuel cells I had?"

"All in storage. Along with the other suits we have."

"You have more?"

I doubted any of the ones they had would rival the quality and power of mine. Considering the slower time on the Anomaly, everything Vrateus's people had at their disposal was severely outdated.

"We have several more suits. We wear them to go outside, to do any necessary repairs on the surface."

They *did* get out. There must be an airlock, then.

"What do you need to repair out there?" I asked.

Vrateus flicked his gaze to mine before returning it to the *errock* in front of us.

"Power generating panels. They convert the light of the Anomaly into useful energy."

"How about any antennae? Have you tried to send or receive communication signals from the surface?"

"No antennae. All signals get lost here."

"Yes. In *here*. But have you tried to send one from out there?" I insisted.

"Yes."

His brief answers weren't nearly enough. I wished to see some detailed data. Better yet, I wanted a chance to conduct some experiments myself. The mystery of the Anomaly was what drew me to sign up for the research mission in the first place. I was now inside it and still had so few answers.

Ironically, my main goal right now was to escape this place, not to study it.

"How often do you have to do the repairs?" I asked.

"As often as needed. With each new arrival, things often get banged up on the surface."

Arrival.

He'd made it sound as if they were scheduled—normal things to happen, not the catastrophic events they really were.

I wondered about the number and locations of the exits to the surface. Logic told me that at least one of them should be somewhere close to the storage room with the spacesuits, but I decided against asking him outright, at that moment. I didn't want to give him any more clues about my plans. The look he had given me was already suspicious.

At that moment, Vrateus stopped at the white single door on our left.

VRATEUS

He tapped the code into the door panel. Unlike the lock on his and Svetlana's rooms that had been programmed to open only with his palm print, the one at the library simply required a numeric code to enter. The number was not a secret. Anyone could access this place, though few of his crew ever bothered.

Unlike them, Vrateus had spent many hours here. However, this was the first time he had ever brought anyone along.

"Wow." Svetlana's eyes grew wider as she stepped inside, taking in the floor-to-ceiling shelf units arranged in parallel rows. The room was almost as large as the mess hall. The neatly placed slates of data glowed softly, illuminating the space with multi-colored light. "This is impressive."

Her reaction warmed his chest with pride and an odd sense of pleasure. The library has been one of the biggest accomplishments of his leadership, in his opinion. Sadly, it was also the least appreciated one.

Crux immediately bee-lined for the red-glowing section with sex videos of various species. The other two *errocks* followed him. With his personal guards now occupied by shifting through the data slates, Vrateus followed Svetlana deeper into the room.

"Did all these come from the shipwrecks?" she asked, trailing a finger along the hard edges of the slates that were glowing green. This section contained information on farming and agriculture.

"Yes. Most I've collected during my time as the captain, but some have survived from the prior years."

"They're all in the same format," she noted.

"I've converted everything to one format. It makes it easier to use." He gestured at a crate full of tablet frames. "You can have one if you want."

"Really?" She shot him a guarded glance.

"Sure." He selected a frame for her, in dark brown like her eyes. "What would you like to read or watch?"

"Well…" she rubbed her upper arm. "Since I'm to stay here for the rest of my life, it would be good to learn more about this place. What information do you have on the Dark Anomaly?"

It surprised him how relatively fast she seemed to have accepted the Anomaly as her future. It was good that she had, though, as it made things so much easier for both of them.

"The latest data on the energy field of the Dark Anomaly comes from your own ship." He moved over to the section of slates glowing in faint gray.

"Those would be the results of our research from the outside," she said. "I'd like to learn what I don't know yet. The actual structure where we are. How you've made it habitable and all the ways you keep maintaining it. As well as the information on all the species occupying this place."

"That might be too much for one visit, but I'll get you some to start with." He browsed the units with the gray shelves, selecting a few slates. "Nothing here is in any of the languages spoken on Earth, of course. Some newer articles can be read in the Universal language, though. Do you read Universal?"

She nodded.

"Good," he continued. "Many have an audio version, too, which your implant will translate for you." He then moved on to a much larger section that housed slates glowing in various shades of yellow—from the lightest, nearly white, to the darkest orange, almost brown. "These here contain information on the species, each is color-coded with its own shade."

He pulled out a few, making sure to include a documentary about the life of *themul* on Nofoi. For some reason, he wanted her to know more about his own species, even though he could hardly be considered part of Nofoi culture himself, having left the planet at a very young age.

"Thank you." She took a slate from him, turning it in her hands and examining it closely. "I've heard of this format before but have never held one in my hands until now."

"It must be considered an antique in the world out there by now?" He chuckled.

"Well, yes. It is a severely outdated technology," she admitted, then added quickly as though afraid to have hurt his feelings. "But it works, right? That's what matters."

"This one contains a fictional story from Hexol, the *errocks'* world." He pointed to the slate in her hands.

She'd mentioned she'd had a different opinion of *errocks* before her arrival on the Dark Anomaly. The group of them here were far from their home world, and not just geographically. He had accepted the fact that *errocks*, like all the other species here, had become the product of their environment. All of them have shed layers of civilization under the harsh conditions of life in the Anomaly.

The film he had chosen for Svetlana was a fictional story, but it contained hints of the raw violence he had witnessed in *errocks* over the years. The video would be possibly hard to watch for her at times, but he wanted Svetlana to have no illusions about what kind of people she now had to spend the rest of her life with. The more she knew, the more careful she would be, he hoped.

"Here are the documentaries on *yourlu*, *ognats*, *errocks*, and a few others. The largest groups we have here."

He glanced at the red shelves by the entrance.

Crux had taken a tablet frame and was now selecting slates to watch by ordering the other two *errocks* to pull them off the shelves for him, in no apparent order.

Vrateus made a mental note to reorganize that section after them when he had a minute to spare later. *Errocks* didn't know the *themul* alphabet to do it themselves. He doubted some of them knew any alphabet at all.

"Would you be interested in watching or reading about the mating habits of the various species?" he asked Svetlana, not entirely sure why.

Maybe, it would be good for her to know he hadn't been exaggerating when he told her about the various ways the species here had sex.

Or maybe, he hoped she'd watch the video of the *themul* couple, too.

Maybe, he would have loved to know her reaction to it.

"Mating habits?" She followed his gaze to the red shelf. The *errocks* were leaning over the tablet in Crux's hands. All three were snickering and elbowing each other. "No, thank you," she said quickly, a lovely shade of blush coloring her cheeks. "I think I've got enough here." She tipped her chin at the stack of slates in his arms. "Enough to tide me over until the next visit. We'll come here again, won't we?" She lifted her questioning gaze to his, undisguised hope in her eyes.

There was no reason for another visit to the library. The purpose of today's trip was to help her familiarize herself with the surroundings. Now, she knew the location of the library. He could exchange the slates for her, she didn't need to leave her room for that.

Yet he found himself unable to extinguish the hopeful expression in her eyes.

"Yes. We'll come here again if you want."

Besides, he couldn't deny himself the pleasure of having her here.

It was enjoyable to share this with someone like her, who appreciated the work he had done on the entire spectrum of the library, not just its red section.

Chapter Ten

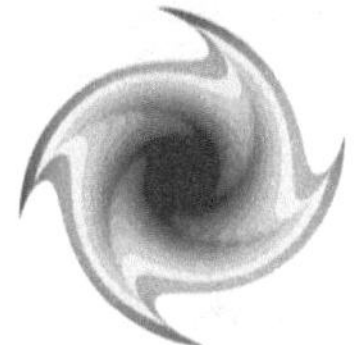

Svetlana

For a couple of days after my visit to the library, I read and watched the info inserts.

Most of the species currently found on the Dark Anomaly came from the sections of the Galaxy farthest from Earth. They had travelled these parts during the early trading days of the Federation, and even before the Federation had been formed.

I found some clues on how they could have ended up here. After analyzing the data found on several ships of different species, I was beginning to believe that the gravity of the Anomaly lashed out, similar to a star's flares, randomly grabbing whatever spaceships might be passing by.

This discovery was eerie and disturbing, but it made sense. That would explain how I ended up sucked in here, too.

The Dark Anomaly spun through space like a giant squid hiding in the depths of the ocean. It shot out its tentacles of gravity to drag ships and their crew to their deaths.

Except that not all were dying on impact with the edge of its disk. I'd survived, as had many others. What killed some of them here was the hopelessness afterwards. Those who survived gave up on civilization, plunging the community into a dark savage state.

While examining the charts and diagrams of the structural improvements done on the body of the Anomaly, I realized that all of it had been done in the past seven years, the same amount of time as Vrateus had been these people's captain.

During this time, he had expanded the oxygen generating facility and improved the efficiency of the air filtration system, which allowed a much bigger portion of the Anomaly's disk to be populated.

Under his leadership, the wrecks of the ships, haphazardly squished together after the many crashes, had been stabilized and secured to create this segment of the Anomaly—rugged and dented, but safe.

A while back, a cargo ship had crashed here with a load of live *vasai*, hideous giant centipedes. Their meat was rich in protein and other nutrients. *Vasai* had escaped the cargo hold after the crash and spread through the numerous tunnels within the Anomaly, hunting and being hunted by others.

By now, most of them had been captured and farmed, their meat and eggs being the principal source of protein for the crew. That allowed Vrateus to outlaw cannibalism, which apparently had been rampant before that.

Cold prickled my spine when I thought about what this place must have been like before Vrateus had brought some modicum of law and order. As wild and crude as it seemed today, it must have been truly feral and brutal before he had come to power.

My sixth morning on the Anomaly was the time of my next trip outside of my room.

Just like the last time, we left after breakfast. Vrateus took me in the direction opposite from the library this time, toward the mess hall.

An uncomfortable feeling scratched inside me as we neared that room. It was very noisy here, with some aliens loitering in the corridor by the entrance. The noise was coming from inside the mess hall—screams, grunts, and dull thuds of flesh hitting flesh.

It sounded like a fight.

I tensed, determined not to look inside, but then couldn't help it and stole a glance as we walked by the entrance.

The mismatched chairs and tables had been shoved to the walls. The occupants of the Dark Anomaly gathered around the cleared space in the middle where two aliens fought. One was a burly humanoid with mottled purple skin and four arms that he sometimes used as legs, moving on all six of his limbs. He pounded with his ginormous fists through the air, occasionally landing a blow on his opponent, a giant black-and-yellow caterpillar with eight pairs of legs and a human-like head and torso.

Both appeared already severely beaten, with blood dripping from the cuts in the one's purple skin and the other's yellow-spotted black chitin.

Always on alert, Vrateus quickly scanned the room and its occupants. He then continued to walk by, not slowing his pace. My arm clamped in his hand, I hurriedly followed.

Crux threw a glance into the room over his shoulder.

"Krakhil will owe me a favor." He spit through his teeth with a crooked smirk on his face. "Remoid is winning."

"Have you made a bet?" I asked him. Despite my severe aversion to having Crux's attention directed at me again, I was curious about the nature of the fight. Vrateus's calm reaction to it told me he must have allowed it.

"I sure did." Crux gave me one of his sliding-down-my-body stares that made me feel like taking a shower right after. "And I'll collect on it tonight, it seems."

His winnings had nothing to do with me. He was talking about whatever deal he had made with Krakhil. Still, the unpleasant feeling inside my chest grew stronger. I vowed never to make any deals or bets with Crux, even if my life depended on it.

We continued down the corridor.

"You allow fights and bets?" I asked Vrateus, keeping my voice down so our conversation would remain private.

"Yes," he replied, looking straight ahead. "As long as they follow the rules."

"What are the rules?"

"No weapons of any kind. No hitting below the belt. No blows that would intentionally lead to crippling injuries. The first to scream for mercy loses and stops the fight. Both the winner and the loser stay alive."

"And they obey these rules?" I asked, sceptically.

He shrugged. "I keep all weapons locked away. They also know that if one of them is injured to the point he can't do his chores, the other one will have to pick up the slack until the first one recovers enough to return to work. If the loser dies, I'll punish the winner."

"What is the punishment?"

"Death."

"Is it always death?" Once again, I remembered him shooting one of his people for touching me on the day of my crash.

"Almost always. The threat of death is the most effective form of reinforcement I've found."

"What if they repent their choices and promise not to disobey? Would you consider their remorse?" I was curious about the way of life here, so different from what I was used to.

"No."

That sounded harsh.

"They don't repent," he explained. "There is never any genuine remorse."

"Ever?" I found this unbelievable.

"They only regret getting caught. If I let them go unpunished, they'd do it again, only more cunningly."

I contemplated his words for a moment as we walked around a bend in the corridor. A multicolored glow on the white paneling up ahead caught my eye. It was a reflection of the Anomaly lights, I realized. And it came from the window in the double-door on the outside wall.

An airlock.

My heart sped up with excitement.

Vrateus moved to turn into a hallway off the main corridor, but I stopped him.

"What is that way?" I gestured down the corridor, at the plain metal door past the glow on the wall.

"An equipment storage room. Beside it is the *vasai* farm, with the garbage sorting room at the back. Nothing of much interest. However, I'll try to find some time to show it to you later, just so you know where everything is. Come, now."

We turned into the short hallway to the right. It ended in a large arched entryway.

"Kitchen," he announced.

Since he hadn't released my arm, we walked in together.

This must be an older part of the Anomaly, an even more outdated ship. The walls here were made of weathered metal, their panels connected by double rows of rivets. The room was almost as large as the mess hall, with a higher ceiling that made it look even bigger. The semicircle of a metal countertop surrounded a huge flameless stove with two enormous pots bubbling hot on it.

About a dozen aliens mingled about, not appearing to be doing anything. It wasn't immediately clear who was in charge here or what exactly was going on.

"Captain." A male who looked like a bipedal cross between a rhino and a hippo covered by brick-colored plating, lifted one of his four giant hands in greeting. Some of the others in the room followed, making the same gesture. "The water is boiling."

"Taste it," Vrateus ordered.

Leading me to the counter, he finally let go of my arm but remained close. The rhino-hippo cross gave me a curious look that quickly turned into a leer.

I briefly considered if I should say anything in greeting but changed my mind, growing increasingly uncomfortable under his stare. It lingered on every part of my body without ever moving higher than my neck.

"Is she here to give us a show?" a smaller alien asked. Sitting on the counter top, he reached with one of his many tentacles into a large jar next to him then smeared the grease from the jar over the fuzzy tuft of hair on the very top of his head, slicking it down.

"No," Vrateus bit off, not glancing at the tentacled alien. "She is here to supervise the food preparation."

It was weird to hear them talk about me in the third person in my presence. However, the last thing I wanted to do was to bring any extra attention to myself. At the moment, I preferred to be invisible, so I kept silent.

"Is that going to be her task from now on?" the larger one asked, perking up.

"Today, it is." Vrateus tipped his chin at one of the pots. "Taste it, I said."

The big alien dipped a large metal spoon into the pot then swallowed its boiling-hot contents without flinching.

Vrateus met his questioning look with a nod.

"Good. Go ahead with the stew, now."

"What was that for?" I quietly asked Vrateus as he closely watched the rhino alien collect some roughly chopped things off the counter and toss them into the pot.

"I make sure no one adds *fuhnid* mushroom juice to the food. It's extremely poisonous."

"Why would anyone want to do it, then?"

"Mostly, to poison me," he replied calmly. "But some would gladly use the mushrooms against others who might have pissed them off during the day—not paid after losing a bet, or for anything, really. Life is cheap around here."

"Do many want to harm you?"

The thoughts about Vrateus suffering from paranoia came back to me. Surely, even these brutes could see how much he had improved life around here. Didn't they appreciate him taking all of this work upon himself? I saw no reason for his crew wanting to get rid of him.

"Most." He shrugged a shoulder. "Maybe all."

"But why?" It made no sense.

"My crew thrive in anarchy. They fiercely detest the order I've been imposing." He exhaled a brief, humorless laugh. "The only reason I've remained their captain for this long is because their dislike for any kind of organization prevents them from organizing against me."

The rhino alien took a blob of the substance from the same jar the tentacled one had used to slick down the fuzz on his head. He sniffed at it, then tossed it into the pot.

My stomach lurched at the sight. The earthy smell wafting from the pot was the same as the stew I'd eaten many times since my arrival.

"This is made for everyone?" I asked Vrateus. "It's the communal food, isn't it? Everyone eats the same?"

"Yes. The food is cooked once a day. Krakhil," he addressed the rhino chef. "Taste the second pot, now."

Krakhil unhurriedly obliged. Upon Vrateus's approval, he then tossed several ingredients into the second pot.

A loud screeching sound suddenly cut through the room. A group of males hauled in something large and terrifying from a side door.

It was a live creature. About six or seven feet long and probably at least a foot in diameter, it had several long skinny legs on each side of its body and a cluster of round eyes on the top of its flat head. With ear-splitting squeals, it struggled against the hold of four aliens, two of them dragging it by its claw-like mandibles.

I sucked in a breath in horror, leaning back against the counter. "What is that?"

"*Vasai.*" Vrateus stepped forward as two of the males dragging the creature yanked at one mandible each, cracking the centipede's head in half. Its long body contracted with its last convulsions then dropped motionless to the floor, a milky substance gushing out of the wound.

"This is just..." I gripped my throat as my stomach churned with nausea.

Staring at the horrific scene in front of me, I hadn't noticed that something was slinking around my thigh, inching in between my legs.

Revulsion shot through me when I realized it was one of the tentacles of the greasy alien on the counter. He met my glare with a smirk. One of his other tentacles moved jerkily somewhere inside the cluster of the rest of them.

"Get away from me," I hissed, ripping the slimy tentacle off my leg, but not fast enough. Glancing over his shoulder, Vrateus saw what was happening. Not saying a word, he threw his right arm up, a gun sliding smoothly out of his sleeve.

The gunshot echoed through the room, the bright flash blinding me for a moment. When I opened my eyes, my offender dropped to the floor with a squishing wet sound. A round hole gaped in his head, the smirk frozen on his face.

"Oh God…" I stepped back, away from the purple liquid from his wound pooling on the floor. "You didn't need to do that…"

The group of males by the dead *vasai* centipede paused for a fraction of a moment at the sound of the shot. They then resumed butchering the dead creature by ripping its body to pieces with their teeth and claws. Krakhil threw the pieces they hurled his way into the pots.

"Can I toss Qen in the stew, too?" he pointed with his chin at his dead buddy, eyeing the tentacles sprawling on the floor.

"No." Vrateus sent his gun back into his sleeve. "Incinerate the body and take the ashes to Malahki for the garden."

Circling my arm with his long fingers, he then led me out of the room.

"Sorry about your man," I said, still shaken by the incident in the kitchen as we returned to my room.

"Qen disobeyed my direct order. He was aware of the consequences," he replied grimly.

It was the second murder committed by Vrateus that I had witnessed. Both times, he acted swiftly and without reservations. Yet I could tell that killing his people was not easy for him.

"Why did Qen still do it then? If he knew you would kill him?"

Sliding the set of black claws out of the tips of his fingers, Vrateus raked them through his fur over the tattoos above his ears.

"Qen was hoping not to get caught," he explained.

"That wasn't very smart on his part."

Did Qen really hope I wouldn't notice him touching me? Or that I might let him fondle me between my legs while he rubbed himself inside the cluster of his tentacles?

A shudder of disgust ran through me at the memory of the slide of the tentacle, and I swiped at my thigh, trying to erase the phantom sensation.

"Obviously, he wasn't very bright," Vrateus agreed. "Most of them are all about the immediate gratification, not thinking past it."

"Could…um," I started, choosing my words carefully. "Do you think shooting him on the spot might have been a little too harsh?"

I sensed it hurt him to shoot his people and wondered if the murders could have been avoided. At the same time, I didn't want to sound as if I was criticizing his actions.

"Would a warning, or something else do in such cases?"

"No." He heaved a sigh. "I could give warnings until I lost my voice. They don't listen. The only things these males understand are actions. Qen knew no one was supposed to touch you but me. He broke the order. He has been shot. Now, the rest of them got a visual demonstration of what will happen if they break this order, too."

"Well, for what it's worth, thank you for protecting me," I said, meaning every word.

He nodded silently in response.

I was expecting him to leave now, but he took a couple of steps farther into the room.

"I shouldn't have taken you to the kitchen." His wide shoulders dropped as he rubbed his face. Again, the thought that he must be exhausted crossed my mind.

Most of the time, Vrateus was enclosed in a hard shell of intense focus and composure, projecting power and strength. Only here in my room with the doors closed had I seen him come out of that shell a little. Then, he always seemed fatigued.

It must be exhausting to run life on the Dark Anomaly. Especially, since he had to do it all on his own, with no help from anyone. Did he ever get enough sleep?

"I'm glad you showed the kitchen to me," I said. "It was good for me to see all of that. Even the disturbing parts."

I had been gaining a better understanding of my new reality. Vrateus's reasons for forbidding me to leave the room on my own also made more sense, now.

"If you think so," he conceded with a tilt of his head, then turned to the door. "I'll bring you dinner when it's ready."

"Thank you," I said, though the thought of the bubbling substance in the pot made my stomach roil.

I continued to stand in the middle of the room long after the doors had closed behind him.

The more I learned about the occupants of the Dark Anomaly, the more I appreciated that Vrateus was among them. He seemed to be the only one who could be reasoned with in this place. I was even beginning to feel respect for him for everything he had done around here and for what he did to protect me.

Except that I shouldn't allow myself to feel anything at all toward this man. I wasn't staying here. There was no way I could live here the way he did. I did not belong here, and I would do whatever it took to leave the Dark Anomaly as soon as possible.

Chapter Eleven

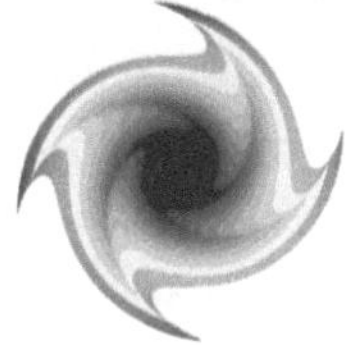

Svetlana

"Get ready," Vrateus told me when he came to pick up my empty dishes after dinner.

As soon as the doors closed after him, I looked at the clothing rack. A week had passed since my last appearance in the mess hall. Tonight, I had to do it again.

A sinking feeling had been in my stomach since the moment I got up that day. The last thing I wanted was to face his wild crew again. Naked.

But that was the condition of my survival. And to escape, I needed to stay alive.

Soon, there would be an end to this.

I now knew where the entrance to the surface was located. By carefully asking just the right questions from Vrateus last night, I had also learned that the storage room next to the *vasai* farm contained my spacesuit. The spare batteries from my ship were stored in the same room, too.

Maybe, he was too tired and preoccupied with other things to question my interest in the spacesuit's location. Or maybe, he trusted me not to betray him.

In any case, I didn't see my escape as a betrayal. When I was finally back in the civilized world, I would send help for the Dark Anomaly's crew and their captain. Eventually, I would get them all out of here, give them a chance at having a better life, too.

I'd gone through the calculations many times. My knowledge, logic, and common sense told me that escape was possible.

All I needed now was to figure out how to get to the storage room with my suit without someone stopping me.

For that, I had to keep on surviving until the right moment came. I couldn't let any suspicions rise. I needed to make Vrateus believe that I'd accepted my fate and was willingly cooperating.

The thought of my future escape helped me approach the clothing rack now.

With a sigh, I slid aside some of the hangers with dresses.

The sooner it started, the sooner it ended.

Only now had I really noticed how exquisite the clothes on the rack were. The jewel-colored fabrics felt soft and luxurious under my fingers. Each dress was elaborately embroidered and encrusted with shimmering crystals. These couldn't have been made to be worn every day. They must be meant for special occasions.

The thought that the collection had been also assembled with care entered my mind. Having gotten to know more about the Dark Anomaly's crew, I knew that only their captain was capable of putting this wardrobe together.

I remembered him insisting on my changing out of my boots. He wanted me to look pretty. As if what I was about to do was indeed some special occasion.

Revulsion prickled my skin. That orgy last week was the biggest humiliation of my life. Even if I escaped the Dark Anomaly, I already knew I'd never escape reliving it in my nightmares.

How did Vrateus not see that him touching me in public brought nothing but shame to me?

How was he not ashamed of himself for what he'd done to me?

What was he thinking when his hands were on me?

What could it possibly bring to *him*?

Vrateus didn't pleasure himself in the mess hall as the rest of them did. That didn't mean he didn't do it later in his own bed, reliving every moment in his mind.

I knew he had an erection when he touched me. But did he do anything about it afterwards when he was alone?

Suddenly, I was trying to imagine him touching himself in the darkness of his room, wherever it was.

He'd always been exceptionally collected and in control. It didn't prove easy for me to visualize him completely relaxed, stroking himself, and coming undone. I wondered what noises he'd make when he came, would his chiselled jaw ever relax, would he melt into me afterwards if I were with him…

Had we met under different circumstances, what kind of lover would he be? Gentle, like his touch on my body? Or wild and unhinged, like the passion of rage I had glimpsed in his orange eyes?

Not that I'd ever find out.

Absentmindedly, I touched the turquoise-blue chiffon of one of dresses, my fingers sinking into the soft cloud of the many layers of its voluminous skirt.

Wrap style, the dress closed in the front with two bejewelled clasps at the waist, draping softly around the chest area. Two long slits on the back, embroidered with gold and pink, might be for the wings or fins the previous owner of the dress had.

What had happened to the woman whose dress it used to be?

Did she die in the crash when the Anomaly had claimed the ship she was traveling on? Or was she among those who were killed after?

Suddenly, I desperately hoped she hadn't been on any ship at all. That she had ordered the dress to be delivered from another planet, but it never made it to her. She had remained safely on her home world and had a long, happy life.

With a sigh, I took the dress off the hanger.

Slipping out of my bodysuit, I got out of my bra and panties, too. There was no need for them, anyway. The less I was wearing the faster it all went. That was one of the reasons I had chosen the turquoise dress. Fastened with only two clasps, it was quick and easy to remove.

The doors swished open a moment after I had closed the two clasps at the waist, and Vrateus came in.

I glanced up, catching him staring at me.

He paused, slowly rolling his gaze over me from head to toe.

"This is the most beautiful thing I've ever seen," he said softly.

It wasn't clear whether he meant the dress or *me* wearing it. My cheeks heated, nevertheless, as warmth of odd pleasure spread through my chest.

I hid my face from him by bending over to rummage through the shoe chest on the bottom of the rack. I caught myself searching for some that would go well with the dress.

Why?

I shook my head.

It almost appeared as if I was trying to please Vrateus by making myself pretty for him.

Ridiculous.

Annoyed, I grabbed the same pair of golden strappy sandals I'd had on the last week and shoved my feet into them.

"I'm ready," I said, straightening my back after fastening the straps.

He continued to stare at me for another moment. His lips parted as though he was going to say something. Then he nodded, taking my arm in his hand and opening the doors.

The *errocks* shuffled out of the way as we exited. Crux and Nocc bounced foot to foot, their eyes greedily undressing me already.

Bringing my shoulders back, I lifted my chin up and kept my gaze straight ahead, trying to ignore their ogling.

The mess hall was packed—filled with undulating, half-naked bodies. The large, brightly lit room buzzed with pent-up energy, lust, and excitement. I quickly focused my gaze at the white floor right in front of my feet, letting Vrateus maneuver me to the spot of his choosing.

He positioned us by the wall again, taking his place at my back.

I tried to block the noise, ignore the lewd greetings and vulgar comments shouted at me from every direction. I needed to find something else—anything—to focus on for the next little while.

"Ready?" Vrateus whispered, sending a flash of irritation through me.

What a stupid question. How could I ever be ready for this? How could anyone?

"Are you?" I bit back.

"Yes," he replied earnestly, my sarcasm lost on him completely.

Letting go of my arm, he moved his hand to my throat again. The soft fur on the back of his hand and forearm tickled my underjaw. I stifled an uninvited giggle.

"Why are you holding my neck?" I brought my head down, getting rid of the tickle by rubbing my chin against his hand.

He shifted behind me, placing his other hand on my waist. "I have sensors in my palm, they enable me to monitor your vitals."

"To make sure I don't pass out before the end?" I made a grim attempt at a joke.

"To help me learn how you like to be touched."

He slipped his other hand into the deep neckline of my dress, pausing for a moment when he found my naked breast underneath. My not wearing a bra must have surprised him. Surely not as much as his words had surprised *me*.

Why did he care about my likes and dislikes?

"I promised them your moans," he'd said a week ago.

Back then he had also told me to pretend, and I had. Why did he bother to learn how I enjoyed being touched? This was all for show, anyway. What did it matter if my moans were real or fake? His crew didn't seem that picky.

I ventured a quick glance around the room. Some males looked like they had already come once without me being even undressed yet. His yellow eyes on me, a sneer on his face, Crux sat on a chair nearby, holding his two humongous dicks, one in each hand.

I promptly closed my eyes, forcing my thoughts back to the only thing in this room that actually felt...nice—Vrateus's hand gently kneading my breast inside my dress.

I fell silent, not wanting him to speak either. This way, I could forget about everything, thinking only about his hands touching me, as if they didn't belong to him or to anyone else at all.

The hands and…that tail. I had almost forgotten about the tail. He snuck it under my skirt, sliding it up my leg, stroking the sensitive skin inside my thigh. The soft brush of his fur between my legs made anticipation tickle deep inside me.

Vrateus didn't open my dress, hadn't exposed me to the room yet, as if he first wanted to steal a moment with me for himself.

His hands moved with more confidence this time, igniting my body with excitement. Somehow, he'd figured out that plucking at my nipple the way he just had would send sparks of pleasure through my body. He must have known that dragging the tip of his tail between my legs would make my inner muscles spasm and my lower belly swell with liquid heat.

How did he learn so much about me so quickly?

He'd spent over twenty years on the Anomaly. Which must be his entire adult life.

Could I be the first woman Vrateus had ever touched, then?

What did all of this mean to *him*?

Suddenly, understanding filled me. For Vrateus, this *was* special.

As much as I detested the idea of what was happening in this room I believed I understood the tenderness—the reverence—of his touch.

For Vrateus, this was not a perversion as I had first thought. This might be the only intimacy with a woman he had ever experienced. This could even be the only physical contact with another person he'd had as an adult. Knowing his crew, he probably had been living without a hug or even a handshake from anyone during all these years.

Surrendering to his touch, I leaned back, relaxing against his strong body.

His hand slipping from my neck, he unclipped the clasps of my dress, finally baring me to everyone's eyes.

The cool air against my flushed skin was sobering, bringing the awareness of all those who must be ogling me.

Squeezing my eyes shut tighter, I forced my thoughts back to Vrateus. His arm under my chest, he slid his other hand between my legs where his tail had already spread the slick heat seeping out of me.

A genuine moan escaped my throat when he slipped his fingers between my heated folds.

I exhaled sharply, leaning my head back against his hard shoulder.

His chest moved with shallow, erratic breaths. It appeared that Vrateus's usual granite composure was finally cracking.

Suddenly, I wished it would crumble completely. I wanted him to unleash the fire I'd sensed inside him. I needed to see the passion burn in those vivid orange eyes of his.

He had been keeping not only his crew but also himself under a very strict control. And I wondered if Vrateus knew his own body as well as he had gotten to know mine.

A part of me wished I had a chance to explore it with him.

Reaching back, I searched for him with my hand. My fingers slid past the point of his ear and dipped into the hair on his nape. It felt soft and luxurious, like the fur of an arctic fox. A swirl of his fingers around the tight nub between my folds made me gasp from pleasure, and I fisted my hand in his fur.

A low rumble in his chest vibrated against my back.

He dipped his head. A puff of hot breath hit the side of my neck. Warm ripples ran down my skin as his sharp canines grazed my skin.

His arms flexed tighter around me. He rubbed harder between my legs, building up the tingling pressure that threatened to explode any minute, now.

The growls of approval and lustful groans reached me through the haze of blinding desire, but they only spurred my arousal.

I got caught up in the lustful frenzy of the room.

Arching my back, I thrust my hips forward, riding his hand. So close now…

A loud grunt came, just to the side of me.

Crux…

The noise yanked me out of the bliss of passion. I wanted to come, so badly. But I didn't want to share this moment with Crux.

This was not about *my* sexual pleasure, anyway.

Grabbing Vrateus's wrist, I discreetly jerked his hand off me.

This needed to end as soon as possible.

I moaned loudly, in a most believable manner I could muster. Digging my fingers into the fur on Vrateus's forearm, I kept his hand away, and he didn't fight me. Then, I ended it all in a few short fake groans and tremors.

Survival.

That was the point of this.

Survival was all that mattered on the Dark Anomaly. So, I did what I had to do to survive. I pretended to come. I faked the orgasm in a most dramatic fashion to satisfy a bunch of dirty aliens.

Vrateus held me from behind. My head down, I opened my eyes, staring at the huge ruby-red stone in one of the golden rings on his fingers.

His chest rose and fell against my back, his rugged breaths fanning across the skin above my ear and moving the fine hairs on my temple.

Our performance was not meant for either of us. Yet his reaction to it seemed to echo mine in its intensity. Uniting us somehow.

"Get me out of here," I whispered. "Please."

My words brought him into action. Shielding me with his shoulder, he quickly retrieved my dress from the floor then wrapped me in its skirts. He swaddled me in it just the way I was, my hands pressed to my chest.

"Come," he ordered, his voice clipped. His hard armour of control slid firmly back into place.

With my arms now buried under the many layers of chiffon, he led me with his hand on my waist—our only escort, Wyck and his pet.

Back in my room, I stopped near the entrance when the doors closed behind us. Vrateus moved to take his arm off me, but I grabbed it, pressing it to my waist.

More than anything in the world, I just wanted to be held at that moment. I sensed some slight fragile connection between Vrateus and me. It might have been forming for some time now, but I'd felt it most acutely in the mess hall tonight. I wanted to hold on to that while he held me in his arms for just a few seconds longer, without anyone else here.

He gazed at me with curiosity and some confusion.

"What?" I asked, not letting him go. "You don't hug?"

"Um…no." Tentatively, he wrapped his other arm around me. "I've had no chance for that."

With a long sigh, I relaxed against his chest, resting my head on his shoulder.

He smelled nice. He felt even better—big, strong, warm.

Safe.

It was wonderful to be held. The lingering sadness and anxiety melted away.

How did one survive for two decades without a hug?

Then, I realized, I hadn't been held like this for a very long time, either.

For a while, I'd had a boyfriend when I was at the Academy. I'd caught him kissing another woman at a party, and left, without ever speaking a word to him again. Months later, I had a number of intimate encounters with another man, but I made sure it never grew into anything more serious than that.

On the space station, I'd stayed away from men entirely. Random connections happened between the staff during missions. But since my parents had me like that, during the one and only project on which they'd both worked together, I avoided any sexual relationships on the station at all. In fact, I had avoided deep connections with people my entire life.

After my parents had left, each going their own way, my grandparents raised me. They were generally cold and distant people, not too pleased with having to raise a child during their retirement years.

My grandfather had been an astronomy professor most of his life. I'd sneak into his study when he wasn't around and pore over the charts on the walls, wishing to travel to the stars one day. My passion had always been exploring the unknown parts of space.

Consciously or not, I had been preparing myself for the same life as my parents. I knew from their experience that it would be a life unsuitable for long-term relationships or for having a family, which suited me just fine. I'd learned early on that the only way to avoid being hurt when people you loved left you was not to love anyone at all. If there were no strong connections, there was no pain in breaking them.

Now, was definitely not the time to think about any form of connection.

But I wasn't *thinking* about anything at all. For a few moments, I simply allowed myself to enjoy being held in a man's powerful arms, to let the feeling of comfort and safety take over me, even as neither was guaranteed around here.

The warmth of his body enveloped me, relaxing…and dangerous. For those few seconds, Vrateus made me forget that I *needed* to leave him. I had to get free from this place, and even more so from him.

"Vrateus," I said softly, prompted by our closeness to try again. "Please, help me leave here. I promise to organize a rescue mission."

If ever there was a person for me to talk sense into anyone here, it had to be him.

He jerked to attention, looking startled by my request.

"Leave?"

"I've done some detailed calculations," I hurried to explain. "I'm confident, it's possible—"

"No," he cut me off.

Instead of releasing me from his hug, he held tighter.

"Please. If you just let me, I could try—"

"No!"

I attempted to free myself from his arms, but he flexed them, forming a vise around me.

"Svetlana." He peered deep into my eyes. "*Trying* always leads to death. Do you understand? Every single attempt resulted in people and ships smashing against the edge of the disk of the Dark Anomaly." He gave me a firm shake, as if trying to get his words to sink into my head. "*Everyone* has died."

Words were not enough to convince me. I had been trained to test assumptions, not to blindly believe them.

"None of them had the most advanced technology, Vrateus," I argued. "Humans can now generate incredible amounts of energy from relatively small power sources. I'm confident it'd be enough to combat even the enormous gravitational field of the Anomaly."

His mouth pressed into a hard line, he combed the claws of one hand through the thick curl of fur hanging over his forehead.

"And what if not?"

I used the moment to twist myself out of his one-armed hug.

"Well, there is always a slight chance of failure in any test. I'm willing to take the risk—"

"Why?" He narrowed his eyes at me. "Why do you want to leave so much? Even risking your own life in the process?"

"Isn't it obvious?" I spread my arms aside, shaking my head in disbelief. "Out there I had the life I chose, the job I loved—"

He narrowed his eyes at me.

"Who is waiting for you there, Svetlana?"

I drew in a lungful of air and...released it, not finding it in me to confess that nobody waited for me out there. I had no one. My grandparents had passed away while I was still in the Academy. And my parents had never cared about where I was, anyway.

"That's not the point," I mumbled, breathing through a sudden tightness in my chest. "I'm not leaving for the sake of someone else. I want to come back to my old life. Don't *you* want to see what's out there, too?"

"No." He retreated to the exit. "Too much risk."

"But the chance of success is also there..." I moved after him.

"No," he repeated over and over, shaking his head, then resolutely slammed his hand on the panel, opening the doors.

"I want you alive," he said firmly before leaving.

The doors closed, shutting me in my room once again.

To live? Not like this.

How about what I *wanted?*

The thought burned through me with rising anger. His stubbornness was beyond exasperating. His curt manner of brushing me off—as if I were a child nagging at him with some trivial request, instead of a trained specialist offering him a chance at a better life out there in the world—was infuriating.

Maybe my earlier guess was right. Vrateus didn't want to be rescued—either out of fear of the unknown or unwillingness to relinquish the absolute control he had on the Anomaly. He might not want to leave behind everything he had accomplished here.

Why would he care how I felt about losing the life I had chosen? About having to play the role of a sex toy for the rest of my existence?

In the eight days I had spent here, over six years had already passed on Earth and my station. My mission contract had ended. Everyone I knew had grown that much older. And every day, every hour I spent here, the life out there kept moving at a much faster pace.

Obviously, Vrateus didn't feel my sense of urgency.

That had been my last attempt at trying to convince him to let me go. Now, I was certain I had to do it on my own.

Chapter Twelve

Svetlana

It had been another week and another public "performance" in the mess hall before Vrateus finally allowed me another tour of the Anomaly.

This time, he was taking me to see the gardens. They were located past the library, along the same long and winding corridor that stretched through the entire habitable area of the Anomaly.

"*Damirian* technology allowed us to grow a variety of plants," Vrateus told me on the way there. "When Malahki arrived about five years ago, it helped me design and build our expansive gardens the way they are today. It's very knowledgeable about agriculture."

It?

"What is Malahki? A robot? AI?"

"No, it's a person."

"Didn't you just refer to him as *it*?" Or had I heard him wrong?

"That's what it is. Malahki is a *damirian*. Its species are born with no gender. They call it the 'neutral sex'. They are neither male nor female until they sexually mature."

That was new to me. Earth had been in contact with *damirians*. We had recently put a program in place, exchanging research findings between our planets. That didn't include an exchange of detailed information about the development of our species. Neither had I ever met a *damirian* in person.

"Referring to them as *he* or *she* before they mature is considered offensive," Vrateus added. "Inconsiderate."

"I'll keep that in mind," I assured him. "How long does it take for them to reach maturity?"

"There is no definitive age for that. Malahki is a full-grown adult. A *damirian* remains neutral gender until it meets the right person. They mate for life and choose the gender opposite of their partner."

"How does it work?" I asked, confused. "If two 'it-s' meet, both of neutral gender, who decides which one of them is to become a 'he' and which one a 'she'?"

"They know. Gender roles are clearly defined in their society. The neutral gender works in all levels of government due to their aptitude for diplomacy and their calm demeanour. The males are more aggressive and dominant, with the females being more playful, easy-going, and creative. After spending some time together, each half of a couple leans one way while the other one takes the opposing role. Then the physical differences form."

The concept sounded fascinating, and I made a note to get more information from the library.

"So, since you told me that Malahki is the only one of his species here, does it mean he…*it* is destined to remain *it* forever?"

"It's been five years since Malahki's arrival to the Dark Anomaly. I suspect if there was a suitable partner for it here, it would have chosen one already."

The fact that Malahki hadn't found a suitable life partner on the Anomaly did not surprise me. Though the fact that it might now be destined to remain alone for the rest of its days carried a certain sadness.

Walking to the gardens took some time. After several turns and curves in the uneven corridor, we finally came to a wide door of opaque glass that folded away to the sides, like an accordion.

The gardens had a very distinct look, different from everything else on the Dark Anomaly. Unlike the glaring white light everywhere else, here it was dimmer, with a yellow softness to it. Vines of every shade of green and purple covered the walls, making the already sizable space appear even bigger.

The air seemed cleaner, rich with moisture and scents of flowers and wet dirt.

"Malahki," Vrateus called out into the labyrinth of greens and purples that dominated the place.

"Yes, Captain," came a calm voice from behind the vines then a tall, lean figure slipped around them and headed our way.

"I want you to show Svetlana everything we have in here." Vrateus gestured for the *errocks* accompanying us to stay behind by the entrance.

"Welcome to the gardens, Svetlana," Malahki greeted me, which made the *damirian* immediately stand out from the rest of the Anomaly's crew, none of whom had ever shown any manners.

According to Vrateus, Malahki got here relatively recently. That might be why it still retained some shreds of civilization.

Tall, with toned muscles and shoulders slightly wider than the hips, Malahki's figure could have equally belonged to a slender male or an athletic female. Its beige skin was smooth and even, like a clean canvas. The same color as its skin, its waist-long hair was braided in plaits of different length and thickness and decorated with vines and flowers.

"It's nice to meet you." I gave Malahki a friendly smile.

At first, I thought the *damirian* was wearing a skin-colored bodysuit, then I realized it wore no clothes at all. Its chest was smooth, as was the area between its legs—no breasts, not even nipples, no distinct genitals, and no body hair.

"Follow me," it invited.

With all its politeness, Malahki's expression lacked emotion. There was no aggression or sneering that I was used to seeing from others here. But neither was there any genuine warmth or strong emotion—just a detached stoic calmness.

I understood what Vrateus meant by saying Malahki was of neutral gender. It truly was genderless, like a basic mold, waiting for the sculptor to add the finishing touches to be complete, both in physical appearance and personality.

We followed the *damirian* down the narrow passages between the long containers with dirt and plants.

"The gardens were completed four years ago," Malahki said, conducting the tour. "Soon thereafter, about ninety percent of the ground had been planted using the seeds and spores we were able to retrieve from the ships. Not all the varieties thrived right away. For the past three years, I have been increasing the yield by rotating crops and improving the soil quality."

The familiar scent of the soap used on the Anomaly wafted through the air as we approached a wide planter with gorgeous umbrella-like plants in it. Their tops were as wide as my hand, vivid burgundy with pink fuzzy lines. I slid the tip of my finger along one of the soft stripes.

"These are beautiful—"

"Don't!" With lightning speed, Vrateus yanked my hand away from the plant.

"Did she touch them?" Malahki hit a button on the side of the planter. A clear cover lowered over the entire container, securely enclosing the plants.

"She did." Vrateus held out my hand to the *damirian*.

It grabbed a bottle with some strong-smelling liquid from under the planter.

"Sorry. I've been fertilizing the soil and needed the cover raised." The *damirian* sprayed the liquid on my palm and fingers then rubbed my hand dry with a soft cloth, cleaning me as if I were a toddler who'd had a messy spaghetti dinner.

Confused and a little embarrassed, I asked, "Was I not supposed to touch these?"

"*Fuhnid* mushroom juice is poisonous," Malahki replied in his even tone. "If swallowed, it would put you to sleep, one you would never wake up from."

"Even touching them is dangerous?" I clenched my hands into fists, taking a big step away from the planter.

"If you touched your face right after or licked your fingers, it could still make you sick."

"Why plant them at all, then?" I asked.

Vrateus glanced over his shoulder at the *errocks*.

Nocc plucked small round berries off a bush, tossing them at Wyck, who laughed trying to dodge them. Standing by the same bush, Crux was stuffing his face with the berries.

"*Fuhnid* mushrooms have no taste or smell of their own," Vrateus said softly, leaning close to my ear. "When added to soap, they completely neutralize all body odors. *Errocks* have an acute sense of smell. They can trace a person by their scent up to an hour after they've passed by."

Malahki had moved ahead, meanwhile, seemingly expecting us to follow. However, I lingered by the planter with the mushrooms, confused by Vrateus's words.

"If they're odorless, what is this smell then?"

"You mean the scent of the soap?" He reached for the bush with white berries nearby, plucking one off it. "The soap is made with *chela* berries. They have a mild scent." He squished one between his fingers, showing me the gel-like substance inside it.

Grabbing his hand, I sniffed at the gel. "No, this smells much milder and different from the mushrooms."

"But mushrooms don't smell," he insisted.

Malahki had noticed that we weren't following and came back, now staring at me, too.

"What is this fragrance then?" I glanced at both of them in confusion, then leaned over the planter with the burgundy mushrooms. Even the glass cover didn't completely stop the pleasant aroma from drifting around. "It's nice. Fruity, with a hint of some… baking spice. Can't you smell it?"

Both stared at me blankly, then exchanged puzzled looks with each other.

"You really can't smell it?" I asked them.

"No one can," Vrateus replied.

"Well, I can." I shrugged, "Must be a human thing, then."

"Must be…" He narrowed his eyes at me, then darted a glance at the mushrooms again. "Would you consider smelling our food every night?"

"Smelling it?" I frowned. "What do you mean by that? Like everyone's plates? Or those huge pots in the kitchen?"

I tried not to sound like I was mocking him, but his request seemed rather odd.

"No, not like that." He rolled his shoulders back.

My gaze slid behind Vrateus. Wyck and Nocc were still horsing around by the berry bushes, now trying to feed some berries to Lesh. Crux, however, was staring at us. The way his eyes glared from under the thick brow ridges made my spine prickle with unease.

Maybe Vrateus's request was not that out of place, after all.

"You want to make sure the food isn't poisoned?" I asked, and he nodded in reply. "How would you like me to do it?" I pretended not to pay attention to Crux anymore, though I could still feel his heavy stare on us.

With the considerable distance between us, he couldn't possibly hear what we were talking about. *Errocks'* hearing wasn't as acute as their sense of smell. Despite that, Vrateus and I both spoke in lowered voices.

"I normally eat in my room," Vrateus said. "After everyone else has had their dinner, including you. From now on, I want to feed you first. If you notice this smell in your food, I'll order the entire pot dumped."

"All right," I agreed. "But what are the chances of anyone poisoning the food? What's the point of killing everyone? No one could survive here on their own. People are needed to run and maintain things."

He rubbed the back of his neck. "It would be just another precaution."

"Okay." I conceded. "I'll do it if it makes you feel better."

"Thank you."

After that, Malahki showed us a variety of edible plants the *damirian* had been cultivating, including some grains and greens.

"Are any of these used in meals," I asked, trying one of the juicy strings from the cluster he had given me. It tasted a little like a banana but with the texture of a watermelon.

"Some." Malahki pressed its mouth into a thin line, displaying obvious displeasure. "Other than grains, the crew prefers meat to plants. And now that they have a whole farm of *vasai*, they can have as much meat as their digestive systems can handle."

The savage scene of butchering the giant centipede came unbidden to my mind.

"The *vasai* also lay clusters of eggs," Vrateus commented. "Which are highly nutritious."

In the meantime, we had circled the gardens, our tour coming to an end. Vrateus stepped aside, talking with Crux about something. I lingered by the last bed with ridged, dark-green spheres that reminded me of a cactus, though they had no needles or spikes.

Idly, I walked around the planter, admiring the round fruit. I wasn't in a hurry to return to the room that felt more like a prison cell with each passing day.

"Watch your step," Malahki warned me.

"Oh. What is this?" I skipped over a pile of dry branches on the ground behind the planter.

"Just some garden waste. I was going to send it to the garbage sorting room." Malahki lifted an armload of the twigs then kicked aside a piece of loose paneling on the wall.

It revealed an opening, large enough for me to fit through. A wide, ribbed strip moved inside it, like a conveyor belt. The *damirian* shoved the branches inside. With rustling and thumping, they moved down, pushed by the belt.

"Is it like a garbage chute?" I asked. "Where does it lead to?"

"To the waste sorting room, near the *vasai* farm. They use these for bedding for the centipedes."

"Does all garbage end up being sent to the same location?" I asked.

"I believe so."

That might mean there were more garbage tunnels accessible by openings in the walls.

"The system isn't perfect," Malahki complained. "You might have seen dead grass and leaves in the corridor not far from your room. There is a kink in the tunnel and debris is often blown out through the wall. I have to sweep the floor there, every time I get rid of garden waste." It shook its head, dumping the rest of the dry branches into the chute.

"Are they steep? The tunnels?"

"In some places they are. But they need to be even steeper, as some garbage, especially the garden waste, ends up getting stuck. I go down the tunnel now and then, to clean or to fix the conveyor belt when it gets stuck. But it's still more convenient to have the tunnels than to carry every armload to the farm myself."

Vrateus returned to us. He took hold of my arm again, signaling it was time to leave. The now-familiar sensation of his large hand firmly circling my upper arm spread with warmth through the rest of my body. I couldn't resist drawing in a long breath, savoring his scent as it filled my lungs.

What was I doing?

I might have just discovered a way to finally escape the Dark Anomaly. Now, was definitely not the time to get distracted by its captain. If anything, I absolutely needed to get out of here rather sooner than later, before whatever it was that kept pulsing hot and cold inside of me in his presence would get out of control.

I no longer felt sad for Malahki possibly having to remain a gender neutral forever. Now, I was envious of the *damirian's* morose serenity. Wouldn't it be a blessing? Not to be affected by hormones at the most inconvenient of times?

As we walked down the corridor, I watched the floor under my feet carefully. A short distance before my room, I spotted a dusting of dirt and some tiny twigs stuck in the cracks between the floor tiles. Passing by, I took a closer look at the wall in that area, noting a gap where a loose panel covered another entrance into the tunnel.

That must be the kink that Malahki had talked about. From

here on, the tunnel went to the waste sorting room by the farm, to the airlock near it, and to the storage room with my spacesuit.

I now had the way to freedom figured out.

What I still needed was a chance to get out of my room.

Alone.

Chapter Thirteen

Svetlana

As soon as Vrateus left after breakfast the next morning, I spent the entire time until lunch studying the door panel.

Using the breakfast utensil, I pried the top cover open but couldn't figure out how to change the program to add my palm print. The technology differed from what I was used to. It was much older too.

At lunchtime, I quickly put the cover back on, then dashed to the bed that Vrateus had found somewhere to replace my sleeping pallet. It was large and comfortable, and aside from the clothing rack and a small table, it was the only furniture I had in this room. I sat on the bed, while Vrateus carried my lunch in and exchanged a few sentences with me.

The moment he left, I continued to work on the panel.

By dinnertime, I'd only figured out the way to disable it, unlocking the door. Before Vrateus returned, I quickly re-attached the cover.

The confirmation light went on and the signal sounded when Vrateus touched the panel outside. However, the lock was no longer functioning. Thankfully, Vrateus didn't notice that, as the doors slid open the way they always did. As he entered my room, his focus was on the two plates of food in his hands.

"This was cooked this afternoon." He handed me a plate. "Can you smell any trace of *fuhnid* mushrooms here?"

I took the plate from him, bringing it to my nose and inhaling deeply. It smelled of wet earth and grease. Not appetizing, at all.

For a moment, I wondered if I should volunteer to make a decent meal for them. Although I wasn't the greatest cook, I was sure I could still whip up something more appealing than this. I would use some plants from Malahki's garden as herbs. Maybe experiment with different grains—try to soak them and the meat in water for a while, to get rid of that musty earthy smell.

The thought of having to cook in that kitchen, though, immediately turned me off the idea. Even if I stayed on the Dark Anomaly for the rest of my life, I'd rather eat the gray, dirt-smelling stew than spend any time in the company of Krakhil and whatever helpers he had there.

"No smell of mushrooms here." I gave Vrateus the plate back then sniffed the second plate. "Or here. Just the usual, meat and grains."

The pleasant aroma of the deadly mushrooms would have actually improved that smell.

"Thank you." Vrateus left one plate on the table, taking the second one back to the door. "Enjoy your dinner."

I stared at his wide back as he departed, noting his posture relax a little after my confirmation. The weight this man had to carry on his shoulders to keep this place from falling apart was enormous.

Having gotten to know the Dark Anomaly and its inhabitants by now, I understood much better the gargantuan task Vrateus had undertaken. I marvelled at his resolve and his ability to keep order here. I even felt sympathy for him, too. He was doing it all alone, saving the people who didn't even realize they were being saved. None of them appreciated his efforts. No one cared or truly helped, either.

Taking a seat on the floor by the door, I propped the big round clock in front of me, watching the time. Guessing that the dinner should be done soon, I calculated the approximate time when life on the Anomaly would finally quiet down. The crew and their captain should settle down for the night at some point.

Then, I would sneak out, down the waste disposal tunnel, and to the spacesuit storage room.

After I had finished the thick stew on my plate, I waited until a significant amount of time had passed.

When I could reasonably assume that most of the crew had gone to bed, I stole to the door and placed my ear to it, listening carefully for any noise. When no sound came, I quietly pushed the door aside. Sticking my head out, I made sure no one was out there.

The corridor seemed deserted. Though, its bright lights remained on. For a moment, I wondered where Vrateus's room was and whether he would be asleep, too. Even the captain needed to rest sometimes.

Once out of my room, I slid the door closed behind me. Unfortunately, with the panel in my room being disabled, I could no longer lock the door from the outside.

With any luck, my disappearance wouldn't be discovered until tomorrow morning when Vrateus would come by with breakfast. By then, I should be far away from here, in another place and even another time.

I ran to the part of the corridor where I'd seen the dust and twigs from the garden on the floor earlier. Tapping along the panels on the wall, I found the one with the tunnel behind it. A ribbed, rubbery strip ran along it on the bottom, moving noiselessly as a conveyor belt.

Quickly, I slid into the tunnel. Lying down with my back on the belt, I let it carry me along.

The space was rather narrow. I pressed my arms to my sides to make sure I didn't get accidently stuck along the way. Malahki had spoken about going down here, occasionally. The *damirian* was tall but slender, only a little wider in the shoulders than me. I doubted Vrateus would fit through here, though. Definitely none of the *errocks* would.

That was good. Even if anyone discovered how I had escaped and where I was heading, they would have to use the corridor to catch up with me, which should take them considerably longer.

A faint murmur of voices came from up ahead, making me realize I must be nearing the waste processing room. I had hoped no one would be there at this hour. Now, I scrambled for a way to slow myself down. Falling out of the chute in front of the undersexed aliens who had used me as a visual stimulus for self-pleasuring for the past three weeks would be a disaster.

Pressing my arms and feet into the walls of the narrow tunnel, I lifted my body off the conveyor belt. The rubbery material of the soles of my boots connected well with the uneven surface of the walls, allowing me to control my climb down this slanted section of the tunnel.

The voices grew louder as I progressed. Several of Vrateus's crew members were there in the room, yelling and arguing by the sound of it.

Keeping my eyes on the tunnel up ahead, I stopped moving as soon as a brightly lit opening came into view.

Judging by the voices, there must be at least four of them out there, but it could be more than that. Not all the males in this place were vocal. Some, like Qen, the tentacled alien who got shot in the kitchen, acted without saying a word.

Even four was too many. I had no weapons to fight them with.

Flexing the muscles in my arms and legs, I hovered inside the tunnel. Suspended over the conveyor belt, I knew I wouldn't last long. Eventually, my legs would give out, and the belt would propel me out into the room.

Although the arguing grew louder, I failed to understand what the four were fighting over. Only a few words reached me in the tunnel, most of them were curses.

My legs felt numb and my arms shook. I prayed no garbage would come from behind and push me out of the tunnel.

A fifth voice joined the group in the room, yelling at the rest to get the fuck out. After that, all went quiet.

Afraid to move, I remained in the tunnel a bit longer, waiting for any noise from the outside. When none came, I relaxed my muscles, letting myself fall back onto the conveyor belt. It took me into the room, dumping me onto a pile of dirt and twigs.

I exhaled with relief, finding the room empty. Picking up a thicker stick from those lying around, I was glad to have at least some kind of weapon.

The room was filled with crates stacked along the walls. Piles of garbage littered the floor. Stepping around them on my way to the exit, I realized that what seemed to be aimless littering must have had a system. The contents of the crates were sorted by the type of material. Unsorted waste piled up on the floor, to be processed next.

The arched doors to the room remained open, and I quietly snuck closer, listening for any voices or footsteps. When none came, I carefully poked my head out.

The small corridor outside the door was empty. It led me to a larger, dimly lit room. Here, there were plenty of noises, but they didn't come from the crew.

Huge cages stood in rows on the floor and along the walls. The giant centipedes crawled inside them. Their hissing and the rustling of their chitin covered bodies filled the air.

This was the Dark Anomaly's *vasai* farm.

Holding my stick in front of me, I carefully made my way between the cages, taking care not to come too close to any of them.

The *vasai* hissed and screeched as I approached. Some lunged at the cage walls, their massive mandibles closing over the thick rusty bars with loud clanking noises.

Heavy clusters of black spheres—each about the size of my fist—hung in some of the cages. These must be the *vasai* eggs Vrateus had spoken about.

A shudder ran across my shoulders when I thought about the horrific centipedes crawling free around the Anomaly, years ago. Vrateus had said that *most* had been captured. Did that mean that some might still be out there, possibly even in the tunnel I had just come from?

Relieved to leave the farm, I exited into the main corridor. My back to the wall, the stick clutched in my sweaty hands, I moved toward the storage room as fast as I dared while making as little noise as possible.

The door across from the entrance to the storage room with my spacesuit had a large glass insert. Behind it was another one, also with glass in it. The brilliant lights of the Anomaly swirled in their timeless dance beyond them.

As I had guessed, this was the exit to the outside, leading to my freedom. There were even bright markings on the wall, from the storage room to the glass doors, to show the way to a person wearing a spacesuit, I assumed. The helmets of some of the older suits limited visibility for the one wearing them, making the markings useful.

The door to the storage room was locked, as could have been expected. I knocked the cover of the door panel off, using my stick. This one turned out to be much easier to tamper with than the one in my room. Instead of a palm print, it was the old primitive technology that required a numeric code to enter. I quickly disabled the lock, bypassing the code.

The suits were neatly arranged along the walls inside the storage room. Some pieces hung off the hooks, some had been laid out on the shelves. My suit stood to the right, its rigid construction supporting it in the upright position.

Tossing the stick aside, I searched for the spare fuel cells that had been taken off my ship. I found them nearby then attached them to the back of the suit, connecting its power supply system to the batteries.

Opening the hatch in the front, I climbed into the suit. Large and clunky with all its systems off, the suit was a self-contained, flexible, and powerful unit when it was fully functioning.

First, I turned the life support system on, quickly checking the performance of the other systems, too. Running the diagnostics, I was relieved to discover that the suit was in a perfect working order. Only the outside sound receptors were malfunctioning, which I didn't need for the escape anyway.

I programmed the trajectory I'd been calculating and re-calculating for days.

It'd been nearly three weeks since my crash. That meant more than sixteen years had passed outside of the Anomaly. The term of my mission had long ended. My team must have reported me as dead, lost in space without a trace.

Most likely, the station was no longer orbiting the Omphi planet. But there might be another station in its place, now. Either way, one of the spacecraft travelling along the trade routes by the water world could intercept my distress signal.

But first, I had to get off the Dark Anomaly.

Unlike most celestial bodies, the gravity of the Anomaly was erratic, making orbiting it impossible. If I didn't gain enough momentum from the start, I risked being sucked back in again. At take-off, the suit's thrusters needed to be at full power to propel me well beyond the gravitational force of the Anomaly.

Powering up the exoskeleton of the suit, I moved out of the room, no longer concerned about anyone seeing or hearing me. Inside the suit, I was unreachable, protected, and stronger than anyone on the Anomaly.

Out in the corridor, I sensed vibrations through the floor. With the suit's noise sensors malfunctioning, I couldn't hear any sound from the outside, but I assumed the vibrations came from the footfalls of someone running my way.

My escape must have been discovered.

I was safe in the suit, though. There was no need to panic.

As I approached the door with the glass insert that led to the airlock, the panel on the wall next to it lit up. The suit's glove glowed the same color as the panel. Vrateus must have programmed it for his use. I placed my hand on the panel, and the door slid open. I moved into the chamber, quickly closing the door to the corridor behind me.

Inside the airlock chamber, I shuffled toward the identical panel on the opposite wall. All I had to do now was to activate the panel for the outside door to open.

I was almost free.

Something hard slammed into my back with enough force to make me stagger, even inside the powered suit. Startled, I took another step forward. It proved difficult, as if something or someone held me from behind.

I activated the three-hundred-sixty vision inside my helmet, to see if the suit had gotten caught on something that was holding me back.

Instead, I came face to face with Vrateus.

Both hands wrapped around the connection of the fuel cell, he held on to me. His expression furious, he yelled something I couldn't hear.

He was the only one in the airlock with me. Holding on to the suit, he couldn't even use any of his weapons. They would probably be useless against the material of the suit anyway, even without me engaging the defense shield.

Despite his significant physical strength, Vrateus was no match for the suit's thrusters. All I had to do was to engage them, open the outer door, and be on my way.

If the emissions of the suit engines didn't burn Vrateus to death on the spot, he would die, blown out into open space with me.

Surely, he understood that. Yet he wouldn't let go.

The man wasn't stupid, but right now he was acting suicidal.

Dammit!

I hit the microphone button inside the suit, hoping it worked even as the sound receptors didn't.

"Let me go," I said loud and clear.

"No," he shook his head. Judging by his expression, he yelled it, too, though I couldn't hear him.

"I will get help," I said, sincerely meaning it.

He shouted back. Unable to hear the words, I could still read his fury as he held on to the suit that would incinerate him at the press of a button. The skin on his sharp cheekbones flushed red. Anger burned in his intense orange eyes, and something else was there, too.

Fear.

Raw terror.

"Please, Vrateus. Please. Let go of me." I was not giving up now, being this close to my escape, with nothing but this stubborn man between me and my freedom. "Go back inside in the corridor or you will die."

"So be it," his hard expression told me.

His determination shocked me.

I realized he wouldn't let go, dead set to keep me here in this vile place.

At that moment, I hated him more than ever.

Then the hatred turned inwards. I loathed myself for being unable to push that damn button. I couldn't send Vrateus to the certain death, even if the success of my escape depended on it.

I couldn't.

His life for my freedom turned out to be the price I couldn't pay.

Self-loathing, I lowered my hand, away from the door panel. Quickly moving to my front, he opened the hatch of the suit then reached inside it to drag me out.

"I hate you!" I spat in his face.

Without a word, he crushed me to his chest in a wild embrace that squeezed the air out of me. I wiggled one arm free, slapping him across his cheek, hard.

Silently, he caught my hand in his, stopping me from hitting him again. Not a muscle moved on his face. It looked like it was set in stone.

"I hate you," I hissed again, anger burning me from inside like acid, stronger than despair or fear.

"You would have died," he finally said, his voice hoarse and repressed.

"I would've been free!" I yelled, struggling against his hold and wishing I could strangle him with my bare hands.

Yet I couldn't kill him just a moment earlier when my freedom had been at stake.

So stupid!

I groaned, hating myself even more than I hated him.

"You would have been dead," he repeated quietly.

"That's what *you* think!" I struggled in his arms. "Your stubbornness, your stupid ignorance has ruined my life."

Something dangerous flashed in his eyes. Keeping an arm around my waist, he shoved me toward the suit.

"Initiate the launch sequence, just like you intended."

For one tiny moment, I believed he was setting me free. Then I realized, he only wanted me to send the empty suit into space.

"Set a one-minute delay," he added.

He was getting rid of my only means of escape.

Swallowing the hard lump in my throat, sorrow threatening to suffocate me, I did what he said. Except that I also secretly added the coordinates of the starting location. Now, if the suit were found, they would know where it came from. Someone would match its serial number to my mission and, hopefully, figure out I was trapped here.

"Come." Vrateus dragged me out of the room after I was done.

A group of *errocks* waited for us in the corridor, along with a few members of other species who were awake. Anything out of the ordinary passed for entertainment around here. Apparently, watching the recapture of the only female on the Dark Anomaly after her failed escape attempt was worth staying up for.

"Watch." Vrateus pushed me against the door, the glass insert positioned right in front of my face.

The thrusters went off the moment the outside door opened. The empty suit launched toward the dancing lights beyond.

Without me.

It grew smaller and smaller the farther it went—a dark, humanoid silhouette against the vivid light show.

My chest hurt watching it go, taking my last hope with it.

Before going completely out of sight, the suit jerked suddenly, sharply changing its trajectory. Swirling off course, it headed back to us, moving exponentially faster than when it had departed.

That was *not* in the program I had inputted.

With a strangled noise of shock, I watched it propel through the distance between us. My hands splayed on the door, I sensed the faint vibration of its impact against the outer hull.

"See this?" Vrateus yanked me from the window to the screen by the door. Punching into it, he brought up images of the outer edge of the metal body of the Anomaly that must have come from cameras they had installed outside.

My spacesuit—made using the latest experimental technology, tested in the bottomless ocean of Olphi, proven to withstand the unimaginable—was smashed against the wreckage of a ship. Its arms and legs bent, its torso twisted in a way that allowed for zero doubt, I would have had no chance of survival had I remained inside. The entire thing squished and dented by the unbeatable gravity of the Dark Anomaly.

I stared unblinking at what would have been my death had Vrateus not dragged me out of the suit just minutes earlier.

I could not accept that all hope was now truly gone.

"My body weight would have made a difference, were I inside," I kept arguing in my head, knowing that it would not, at least not enough to change the outcome. I might have crashed at a slightly different spot, but I still would have crashed.

And died.

My hands trembled, the shakes spreading to the rest of me, as the realization of what this crash really meant descended on me.

I was truly, completely, inescapably trapped on the Dark Anomaly.

For the rest of my life.

Chapter Fourteen

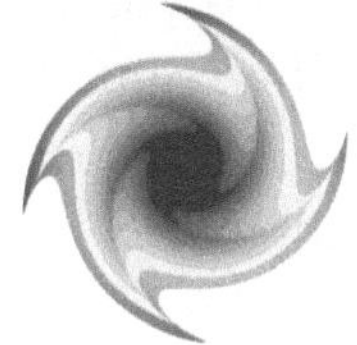

Svetlana

Still in shock and overwhelmed by despair, I was only half-aware of Vrateus dragging me through the corridors of the Anomaly, back to my room.

A group of aliens had gathered in front of it, watching as we approached. They gawked at me and made jokes, mocking my failed escape attempt.

His expression grave, Vrateus hit the panel, opening my door. When he shoved me in, I sensed his hands shake.

"Wine, Captain?" One of his males offered a metal canteen to him.

Vrateus grabbed it from him. Keeping his eyes on me, he took a huge swig from the canteen.

I staggered into the room. The lights of the Anomaly no longer seemed beautiful or mesmerizing. They were mocking me, destined to spend the rest of my life in this inescapable glass prison. I felt like a moth trapped inside a lantern, only with the light being outside of the glass—teasing, enticing, and deadly.

The slam of Vrateus's hand against the door panel was followed by the swishing sound of the doors closing. I idly wondered if he had discovered that I'd disabled the locks. The doors might be closed, but they weren't locked unless he'd fixed the panel, which I didn't think he had.

Suddenly, he grabbed me by my neck, swinging me to the wall and pressing my back against it.

He leaned into me, his face coming close to mine, feral rage distorting his hard features. The orange eyes aglow, his lips stained blood-red by the wine, any shred of his usual composure was blown away. I wondered in an oddly detached way if he would kill me right then and there.

"You could've died," he gritted through his teeth. A flash of unguarded vulnerability flickered through his eyes.

Fear.

For me?

Something clenched painfully in my heart in response. Something I didn't want to feel for anyone.

Terrified of the flames of passion burning higher and higher in his eyes, I searched them for the traces of furry, begging him in my mind, *"Hit me. Hurt me. Give me another reason to hate you."*

The hate for him and this place had been fueling me with energy all this time. The resentment that I cultivated inside me with more fervour that Malahki worked in his garden was dissipating, slipping between my fingers, no matter how hard I tried to hold on to it. Another feeling, just as passionate as hate but so much more dangerous, was taking its place.

Was it lust?

Please let it be just lust.

"You would have been dead if I didn't stop you," he kept saying as if struggling to comprehend that fact.

"*You* would've died, too, had I pushed that button," I bit out.

"Why didn't you?" The fury in his stare settled down as something deeper and darker moved in.

"I couldn't..." I drew in a shuddered breath. The adrenaline receded, leaving deep sorrow behind. "Then we both would have been dead," I said softly. "Not sure about you, but for me… For me, it might have been for the best."

His thick eyebrows drew together, intensity sharpening his gaze. "You've chosen to live," he reminded me.

I swallowed against his hand on my throat, his hold firm but not oppressive.

"Because I had hope, Vrateus. Hope to get out of here, eventually. There is no point, now. What kind of life do I have ahead of me? Being locked up in this room? Used as your sex toy?"

"My toy?" he sounded confused. "From what I know about sex toys, they're used solely for one's sexual satisfaction."

"Exactly."

"That's not what you are to me." His eyes flickered between mine, something warm and intense brewing behind them. "Svetlana, do you dislike me touching you so much that you would rather risk dying than continue with it?" he asked suddenly.

I wished I could lie about that, but his touch was the one thing I enjoyed. As much as I detested being brought into the mess hall on those nights, I started looking forward to the moment when his hands connected with my skin.

Even thinking about it now sent a ripple of pleasure through my chest. Its warmth melted the sorrow away.

"It's not your touching that I dislike, Vrateus…"

How could he not understand that I found being paraded naked in front of hundreds of slobbering, masturbating men degrading?

But then I believed I knew how. Having grown up in the savage environment of the Dark Anomaly, Vrateus simply wouldn't know all the moral implications of some actions.

Only now, after having been immersed in life on the Anomaly for some time, could I see it from his perspective: I was not physically hurt, and his crew was satisfied. As far as he was concerned, he kept me alive and safe by doing what he had to.

He wouldn't know *why* I resented it because I had never really explained the reasons. I had mistakenly assumed he would have the same understanding of morals and values I had. It could never be the same, though, as his background was so different from mine.

Obviously, he believed he had saved me and had been protecting me ever since.

"I like it when you touch me," I confessed. I knew I shouldn't have, but couldn't bring myself to care about the reasons why.

What did it matter now if he knew the truth?

Nothing seemed to matter anymore.

"Like?" My words seemed to send a charge through his body.

I sensed his shudder as he pressed himself closer to me. Another wave of warmth rushed over me, sending tingles over my skin.

Lust. Strong and invigorating desire for a man, for him. Like a powerful drug, it killed the pain of defeat. Completely, even if temporarily.

Needing more of the rush, I pressed my hands to the hard planes of his chest.

"You, Vrateus, turned out to be the most unexpected surprise of the Anomaly, for me," I muttered.

His eyes flashed with heat. His arms shook with strain as he struggled to keep whatever distance still remained between us.

"I don't understand this…what I feel for you, Svetlana" he groaned. "Why are you in my thoughts? Constantly. When you're not around, I need to see you. And when you're near me, I feel like touching you." He slid his gaze to my lips, his thumb stroking my neck. "It's never enough. No matter how close I get, I wish to be closer." His heart thundered wildly against my chest. Sliding his hand up my neck, he cupped my jaw, brushing his thumb along my bottom lip. "And when I touch you, I want to taste you," he whispered, bringing his mouth closer, so close, his breath warmed my face.

I drew in brief, shallow breaths. My body heated under his stare. Desire flooded me. It was so much better than misery.

I focused on the awareness of his hand on my face, his large warm body pressed to mine. My future was dark but distant. This very moment was different—Vrateus was here. The heated gaze of his orange eyes set me on fire.

"Go ahead, then." I slid my hand to the back of his neck. "Taste me..."

Determination flared in his eyes. He wrapped one arm around me, moving the other to the back of my head.

Instead of the brutal kiss I had expected, the brush of his lips on mine was barely there. Truly only a taste, not a kiss. Forever in control, he tentatively slid the tip of his tongue along my lip then peppered my skin with tiny nibbles along my jaw line.

It hit me that Vrateus had never kissed anyone before, never even had the chance. What he was doing to me right now was all him, unskilled but raw and real.

His tenderness melted my heart.

"Vrateus," I whispered.

Taking his face between my hands, I peered deep into his eyes. His pupils, usually in the shape of narrow vertical slits, now widened and rounded, nearly replacing the burnt orange of his irises.

He breathed hard. His lips parted.

"Come here." I took his bottom lip between both of mine, swallowing his sharp exhale.

He tasted of berry wine—tart and heady—with a hint of something fruity and of his very own spice.

He tasted like the only pleasant thing left for me in this life, and I drank him in, never wanting to stop.

I slid my tongue deeper, feeling the muscles in his neck stiffen for a moment. How would a man who had never been kissed react to the tongue of a woman exploring his mouth?

Was he shocked?

Disgusted?

Definitely not the latter, I realized with relief, as he groaned softly then met my tongue with his. He moved one of his hands to my breast, palming my backside with the other. There was confidence in his touch as he kneaded my breast through the material of my suit.

He knew exactly how to touch me.

But there was also some frantic urgency, as if he wanted to caress every part of me he'd never had the chance to lay his hands on before. As if he wished to touch everything, now that it was just he and I, with no one else watching.

The hard ridge of his erection pressed against my hip. Fisting my hand in the fur on the back of his neck, I snaked the other through the opening of his shirt, my fingers skimming the dagger sheath strapped to his chest.

His skin felt flushed, feverishly hot. The fruity flavor of wine on my tongue nagged at my memory, distracting me from the kiss.

I pulled back a little, tearing my lips from his.

"Svetlana…" he panted, reaching after me.

His warm breath fanned across my face. I recognized the fragrance of the soap I used every day.

Fuhnid mushrooms…

"Vrateus?" I grabbed his face between my hands.

His pupils were fully dilated, his eyes glistened dark and wild. From lust?

Or from the poison?

"Do you normally add *fuhnid* mushrooms to the berry wine?"

"What?" He blinked, unfocused. His body still intertwined with mine, he wouldn't let go of me. "No. Mushrooms are poison."

He ducked his head down again, reaching for another kiss, but I shoved my hands against his shoulders.

My mind flashed back to the flask of wine the male outside the door had offered to him. Too upset by my escape attempt, Vrateus hadn't questioned the offering.

He had drunk it.

The one time he had his guard down, his worst suspicions came true.

He'd been poisoned.

Dread prickled with icy needles down my spine.

"Vrateus. The wine you drank was laced with *fuhnid* juice."

His features settled into a frown, focus returning to his gaze. "Are you sure?"

I nodded. "I can smell it."

He raised his hand to his lips.

"How are you feeling?" I asked, cautiously.

"Lightheaded." He rubbed his temple. "My mind is…hazy. But it always is when you're nearby." He gazed at me. "It's hard to focus when you're this close."

"Where do you keep the antidote?" My hands on each side of his face, I directed his attention to my question.

"There is no antidote."

His words exploded through my brain, freezing my insides with fear. I might have been willing to kill him with my own hands a short while ago, but I was not ready for him to die.

Swaying on his feet, he pressed both hands into the glass above my shoulders.

"What happens next?" I asked, my voice shaking. "How long do we have?"

"Next? Dizziness. Muscle weakness. Lethargy…" He closed his eyes for a moment, obviously struggling to collect his thoughts. "By morning, I'll be dead."

"No, you won't," I said stubbornly, having no good reason to make this statement other than the denial of the obvious.

"Svetlana…" He shook his head, as if attempting to shake off whatever fog was clouding his awareness.

The gesture cost him his balance. He stumbled to the side, then slid down the wall to the floor.

"Careful." I grabbed him under his arm, steadying him. "Stay sitting, don't lie down. I'll be right back."

I ran to the bathroom, filling the crystal tumbler left from my dinner with water from the tap.

Back in the room, I shoved the glass to Vrateus. "Drink it. The whole thing."

He obeyed, emptying it in a few big gulps.

"Now come to the bathroom with me." Both hands under his arms, I tried to pull him up, but he proved to be too large and heavy for me to manhandle. "Help me, please. Can you try to get up?"

With a groan through his clenched teeth, he heaved himself up, letting me lead him to the bathroom. I held him around his waist as he lowered himself in front of the toilet.

"Drink this too." I gave him another cupful of water. "Then try to make yourself vomit."

"Vomit?"

"You need to get whatever is left of the poison out of your stomach."

Kneeling by the toilet, he propped his hands on his thighs. "Leave," he growled, glancing from under his eyebrows at me.

I rolled my eyes.

"Fine. Just do it, please. And quickly." I exited the bathroom but didn't close the door behind me, afraid to leave him completely on his own.

Pacing the glass floor, I nervously clenched and unclenched my fists, thinking through everything I knew about poisoning.

"There is no antidote."

Recalling his words paralyzed me with fear, bringing my thought process to a halt.

He couldn't die.

I couldn't let him die.

He had said he wanted me to live. Well, I wanted *him* to live, too.

Besides, what would happen to me here, without him? I *needed* him alive.

Rinse out his stomach. I started to build a list in my mind. *Find charcoal. If they don't have anything like it here, find some hardwood to burn to make some…*

That would take way too much time!

I groaned in frustration.

"I'll be dead by morning."

Time was something we didn't have.

There must be something that would neutralize the poison of the mushrooms. If only I knew exactly what type of poison it was. I had no time to do any tests to determine that, either.

Why would Vrateus allow this stuff to be grown here? Without searching for the antidote? He was always so cautious, so smart about everything.

I was angry at him now, which was nothing new. What *was* unusual was that I felt also terrified for him.

I couldn't let him die.

As soon as I heard Vrateus finish in the bathroom, I rushed back to him.

Resting his forehead on his hand, he crouched on the floor.

"Come." I helped him to get up again. I wanted him to move, afraid that if I left him alone, he'd fall asleep…and not wake up again.

Back in the room, however, he sank to the floor again.

"Tell me what I can do." Grabbing him by the shoulders, I gave him a firm shake as his head started to drop. "Is there anything in the medical kit that would help? Do you even have a medical kit somewhere? How about some charcoal pills? Activated charcoal? Is there anything like that around here?"

With another shake from me, he lifted his head. His gaze focused on me after a moment.

"Svetlana…" he drew out my name, a delirious smile tugging at his lips. "You drive me mad, you know that? And for some reason I love it."

"Vrateus, where can I get help?" I asked firmly, giving him one last chance to point me in the right direction. Time was running out. I needed to do something. With or without his instructions.

"Help?" He blinked, then tightly shut his eyes before opening them again. "When I die, you must go to Malahki," he said quickly, as if rushing it out before his mind plunged into a toxic fog. "Malahki is the only one around here who is not interested in either eating or fucking you." He lifted his hand to my face. "Svetlana…I *need* you to be safe. When I'm no longer here to protect you—"

"Malahki!" I jumped to my feet, filled with sudden hope.

The genderless alien was the one cultivating the damn mushrooms. If there was anyone who knew what to do, it would be the *damirian*.

"Give me a weapon." I knelt in front of Vrateus again.

"To defend yourself," he said, in a distant voice.

"Right. I need something to defend myself if I'm attacked out there."

He shifted, shaking his head. "You can't go out there. Not on your own."

"Well, I'm not staying here, waiting for you to turn into a corpse, either." I slid my hand into his shirt, finding the dagger strapped there.

Before I could pull it out, he trapped my hand, covering it with his. His hold remained encouragingly firm.

"You are the most infuriating being," he said, gazing at me with his eerie, glossy eyes. "The most fascinating and beautiful one, too. I'm glad I lived long enough to meet you."

Was that a goodbye?

I bit my lip, willing my voice not to shake. "You'll live longer than that. I will get help, Vrateus." I wrapped my fingers around the handle of the dagger at his chest.

"I can't stop you." It wasn't a question, more like stating of fact to himself.

"I need to go. I need to do something."

"Here." He allowed me to take out the dagger. From the holster at his thigh, he then took out a device that reminded me of a laser gun I had seen in old movies. "Take this, too. Shoot from a distance, don't let them get too close."

"Thank you." I tucked the dagger into my boot, keeping the gun in my hand. "I'll be right back."

"No." He shook his head several times, as if unable to stop it after just once. "Don't come back here. Tell Malahki to hide you. There are lots of spaces to hide around here. I used them when I was a child. Tunnels, cracks in the hulls, gaps between the walls…"

Sitting on the floor, he tilted to the side as his voice trailed off.

"Vrateus!" I shook him again, sitting him upright. "Stay awake."

I grabbed the tablet he had given me. Finding a video with the most obnoxious music of the last species I had studied, I set it to play in a loop, then turned the volume all the way up.

"Wait for me!" I shouted over the noise. "Please. I'll come back. I promise.

He swayed, his head nodding. There was no way of telling whether it was involuntary or in reply to my request.

With no time to lose, I dashed to the door.

Thankfully, the corridor behind it was empty. Keeping my back to the wall and the gun in my hand ready, I ran toward the gardens, praying that Malahki was there and that it was able and willing to help me.

Chapter Fifteen

Svetlana

All seemed eerily quiet in the gardens when I arrived. Creeping between the planters, I peered through the vines and branches, hoping to glimpse the lithe shape of Malahki nearby. I was also watching out for any trouble, hoping that everyone else would have gone to their beds by now.

Most likely, Malahki would be also asleep at this hour. I hoped that it slept nearby somewhere and that I could find it and wake it up.

I heard nothing but the soft rustling of leaves and the quiet trickling of water from the irrigation system. Then a hand covered my mouth as someone grabbed me from behind, pressing both of my arms to my body.

"What are you doing here?" Malahki's calm voice sounded above my ear. Next, the *damirian* slid its hand to my gun, taking it from me.

I jerked my head to the side, freeing my mouth. "I need your help."

Malahki lifted the gun into my line of sight. "And *this* is to persuade me in case I refuse?"

"No. The gun is to protect me from anyone I may run into on my way here and back."

The *damirian* let go of me, inspecting the gun in its hand. "Probably wouldn't have helped you anyway, human. Most of the males around here would let you shoot their eye out for a chance to fuck a female. A gun wouldn't stop them from trying."

I paid little attention to its words. Right now, I had no time for fear.

"I need your help," I said again. "And I need it quickly. What can I use to neutralize the effects of the *fuhnid* mushroom poison?"

"Nothing." Malahki pressed its colorless lips into a thin line. "There is no antidote." It turned to leave.

"There has to be something," I said, with nothing much but blind faith to keep pushing. "How did you find out the mushrooms were poisonous in the first place?"

"We obtained that information from the ship that delivered the spores."

Delivered. As if it was an order, voluntarily fulfilled.

"Has anyone poisoned themselves with their juice before?"

"Yes." Malahki walked away, and I rushed after it.

"Has anyone died?"

"Also, yes."

I grabbed its arm, yanking the *damirian* to a stop.

"He can't die."

"Who is *he*?" Malahki didn't sound annoyed at my insisting. Though its detached tone of voice didn't offer much hope for help, either.

"Vrateus has been poisoned. I need to counteract the effects before it's too late."

If it wasn't too late already...

I shoved the terrifying thought away. Losing all hope and my mind along with it wouldn't help anyone.

"Make him retch," Malahki suggested with the same calm aloofness that proved extremely irritating right now.

"I did. Would that be enough to save him?"

"No."

Now, I really felt like punching the *damirian*, to knock off its serene composure.

"I need something more effective," I insisted, grabbing its arm again.

Malahki glanced at me, worrying its bottom lip with its teeth, as if hesitating.

"There *is* something, isn't there?" I stepped in front of it. Hope and determination vibrated through me, making my hands shake. "I know you have nothing in common with the savages out there. You don't participate in the fights. I haven't seen you in the mess hall, either. How do you spend your time? Pruning and seeding, sure, but there must be something else. Unlike all of them here, you've been raised and educated outside of the Dark Anomaly. You're smart. Mushrooms would present a challenge for your mind. Please tell me you've experimented with their fascinating qualities. For medicinal purposes, if nothing else?"

The *damirian* remained silent, looking like it was about to turn away from me again.

"Malahki, please," I exhaled a whispered plea.

"Knowledge is the only asset, the only advantage I have over 'the savages out there'," it replied, flexing its jaw. "I work hard to gain it, and I'm not obligated to share it with anyone. No one cares about me here. Why should I care about anyone?"

"Do you think *I* care about this place, about any of them? I don't care about Vrateus, either." Something pinched uneasily inside me at these words, but I kept going, "But I don't want him to die. What do you think will happen if he dies? To you? And to me?"

"Someone else will take his place."

"Who? You are a smart—" I stopped myself before saying "man." "You're a smart individual, Malahki. Surely, you can see that there is no one even remotely as capable as Vrateus to keep this place going the way he has. If he dies, anarchy will prevail. Neither you, nor I will be safe."

"Most of the species here respond to female pheromones in their lust. They have been leaving me alone." It shrugged.

"So, you'll be okay with *me* potentially being raped, without Vrateus's protection?" I fisted my hands at my side, stopping myself from saying more. As outraged as I was by the *damirian's* indifference, I knew that an argument with this person would bring me nothing.

"No, of course not." It frowned.

"Then help me, please," I begged. "Besides, it wouldn't be just rape that we would have to worry about. If Vrateus is gone, none of his laws will stay. The cannibalism will return. Your genderlessness won't protect you from being eaten. Neither you nor I are strong enough to fight them."

Malahki's chest rose with a sigh. "That is true. I am not strong enough to fight any one of them." Its facial muscles twitched. "What will I get if I save the captain's life?" it asked, narrowing its eyes at me calculatingly.

I suppressed a breath of relief. This wasn't over yet.

"What do you want?"

Malahki gave me a long, measuring look. It was unnerving in its intensity, as if the *damirian* had just truly *seen* me for the first time. "I'll need a favor from the captain."

"We'll have to hurry," I snapped, losing my patience. "Otherwise, there won't be a captain to grant a favor."

"Fine," it relented. "I want you to promise the captain will hear me out once he is well and able."

"*If* he is well and able." I bounced on my heels. "Hurry, please."

Malahki demonstratively folded its arms across its chest. "I'm waiting for your promise."

"I promise," I rushed the words out. "I will tell him you saved his life and asked for a favor in return."

Malahki seemed satisfied by my words. Waving me to follow, it headed to the tall planter with the bright *fuhnid* mushrooms.

Raising the clear cover, the *damirian* plucking one out of the dirt. It then squished it between its palms, letting the vivid pink juice drip back into the ground. He then sprayed the now flat-like-crêpe mushroom from the bottle under the planter.

"Here." Malahki ripped a wide round leaf from a vine nearby, wrapping the flattened mushroom he'd rolled into a tube. "Feed this to the captain, with a glass of water. Just one cup of water, though, no more. Wait for ten minutes, then make him throw it all up again."

I stared at the dark green package in its hands.

"Are you saying to neutralize the poison that is killing him, I need to give him more of it?" I asked sceptically.

"Isn't that how many poisons work?"

"No." I shook my head. "A sip of wine, laced with *fuhnid* juice, is about to kill Vrateus. How is feeding him an entire freaking mushroom supposed to help?"

"By drawing the poison out," Malahki replied calmly. Shoving the leaf-wrapped mushroom into my hands, it took the spray bottle again and cleaned its hands, then sprayed my hands holding the package, too. "I squeezed the toxic juice out of the mushroom. If the captain eats it now, it will soak up whatever *fuhnid* juice there is in his body. He would have to get it out of his stomach afterwards, so the poison doesn't seep back into his digestive system and bloodstream."

"Are you confident it will work?" I stared at the package in my hands, afraid to hope. "Has anyone ever tried this?"

"I have. Myself."

That was a relief to hear.

"Only I've had more time for 'experimenting' as you've named it," Malahki added. "I completely dehydrated the mushroom and grounded it into powder first."

"Powder?" I huffed in frustration. "That is very different from what you've just given me. Do you have any of the actual powder left?"

"No. Unfortunately, I don't." The *damirian* pursed its lips. "And *you* don't have the luxury of time to be picky."

That was true.

"Well, thanks for this." I pressed the bundle to my chest.

"Where is Vrateus?" Malahki asked, handing me back my gun. "How far do you have to go, now?"

"He is in my room."

"It's next to his, then."

"Is it?"

"His is the second glass capsule. There are two, side by side."

I had seen the second bubble next to mine, but it had always been dark, and I assumed it was empty. Vrateus had never told me it was his room. Not that I'd ever asked.

"Don't use the corridor to go back," Malahki said. "Take the garbage tunnel from here. It's safer. Just make sure you get out in time. There is an opening in the wall, not far from your room."

I knew about the opening. I'd already used it during my failed escape.

"Thanks. I'll take the tunnel."

Chapter Sixteen

Svetlana

Lying on my belly on the conveyor belt inside the tunnel, I travelled feet first toward my room. Afraid to miss the spot where I needed to get out, I kept my hand on the wall, trailing my fingers in search of the loose panel. When it moved as I passed, I quickly crawled back to it, ready to climb out.

The distant tromping of footsteps suddenly reached me from the corridor, making me pause. I spread my arms and legs wide, removing them from the belt and pressing them into the walls of the tunnel, then froze in place, listening as the footsteps approached.

"We didn't find his weapon storage." I recognized Wyck's voice.

"He hides it somewhere," Crux growled in reply.

The sound of their voices made my knees shake from fear. Nothing good would come if the *errocks* found me here, alone and pretty much helpless. Straining to stay off the conveyor belt, I couldn't even free a hand to use the laser gun tucked into one of the pockets of my bodysuit.

I desperately hoped Lesh wasn't out there with them. Or if he were, that he wouldn't be able to catch my scent. The soap I used made me undetectable to the *errocks'* acute sense of smell, but no one mentioned if it worked the same for Wyck's terrifying pet.

"No matter. He won't be able to do much now, anyway," Crux kept on talking. "Use whatever we have for weapons. Get everyone in the mess hall. Kick them out of beds if you have to. They've got a new captain, now." He guffawed, his voice thick with satisfaction.

My heart dropped.

Was Crux behind Vrateus's poisoning? He sounded as if he was at least aware of his captain's current condition.

No. Crux had just called *himself* the captain. He already thought Vrateus gone.

If Crux was in charge now, I stood no chance. Vrateus was right, the best course of action for me would be to get back to the gardens. I harbored no illusions, Malahki wouldn't go out of its way to protect me. But Crux was cruel and unpredictable. No one could be safe with him in charge. Maybe, I could convince Malahki to be my survival partner. We'd find a place to hide and watch each other's backs.

Meanwhile, the sound of the footsteps faded into the distance.

Carefully inching toward the opening, I peeked into the corridor, making sure it was empty in both directions. Climbing out, I threw a glance back toward the gardens.

I knew Crux would come for me as soon as he had established his full dominance over the Dark Anomaly or even sooner. The way he always stared at me, I knew he meant danger—probably torture and death.

My instincts told me to run straight to the gardens and hide before it was too late.

Yet I couldn't leave Vrateus to his fate. Against all common sense, I ran back to my room.

The doors remained closed but unlocked, just the way I had left them. Icy fear spread down my back when I thought *errocks* could have easily found Vrateus here, weak and unprotected, had they but checked the doors while passing by.

Slipping into the room, I closed the doors, then pulled the cover off the lock panel and slid the part I'd loosened back in to engage the lock from the inside.

The music still blared from the tablet, but Vrateus was no longer sitting upright. His arms tucked under his torso, his legs spread wide, he lay on his stomach, motionless.

"Oh, God, Vrateus…" I rushed to him, praying I was not too late.

He felt cool to the touch, his fur slicked with sweat over his forehead, his eyes closed.

"Vrateus!" I shook him, everything inside me frozen with fear.

Placing my hand on his neck, I found a barely detectable pulse. Weak and uneven, it was still there, easing my horror. Dashing to the bathroom, I filled the crystal tumbler with water then ran back to him.

"Can you hear me?"

I hit the *off* button on the tablet, plunging the room into silence, eerie and ominous after the deafening noise of music.

"You need to wake up. Now!" Rolling him to his back, I slapped his cheek, making his head loll to the side. "Captain!" Straining my muscles, I tried to heave him up into a sitting position. "Your crew won't survive without you. They need you…" His large body, a heavy, solid mass of muscle, was nearly impossible for me to maneuver. Still, I propped him into a reclining position by wedging my shoulder under his. "Fuck it, Vrateus! *I* need you."

His head rolled to his shoulder, with a muffled groan escaping from his throat.

"Vrateus?" I scooted on the glass floor, sliding behind him. My leg on each side of him, I leaned his back to my chest, propping his head with my shoulder. "You need to eat this right now." I yanked the bundle with the flattened mushroom out of the pocket at my hip, then unwrapped it, bringing the mushroom to his mouth. "Dammit, Vrateus. I swear I'll hit you again if you don't wake up, right now!"

Dropping the mushroom into his lap, I grabbed the glass instead. Pressing it to his lips, I tipped it, letting the cold water spill over his mouth and down his bare chest into the opening of his shirt. He winced with a gasp, and I quickly poured some water into his open mouth, making him sputter and cough.

"Good," I murmured. "Now that you're awake, eat this." I ripped a piece of the dry mushroom and shoved it into his mouth. "Chew it." I cupped his jaw. "Or don't chew it. Whatever, just swallow it, please."

Not waiting for him to react, I ripped another piece off, bringing it up to his face. "Here you go," I said when he swallowed, then I quickly shoved more pieces into this mouth. "That's a good boy," I cooed as if he were a baby eating his first solid foods, not a grown man nearly twice my size, dying from poison.

The last piece of mushroom stayed in his mouth when his head dropped to his chest again.

"Vrateus!" I slapped his cheek again. Hard.

"Guh…" he groaned. "That hurt."

"Drink this." I pressed the edge of the glass to his lips. "Or I'll do it again."

I watched his throat bob with each swallow as he emptied the glass. I hoped and prayed that Malahki hadn't misled me, that I hadn't made a colossal mistake by trusting the *damirian* and feeding more poison to our captain.

"You're not only infuriating, you're also brutal and terrifying," he muttered, dropping his head back on my shoulder as if drinking had completely exhausted him.

"Oh, you have no idea how scary I can be," I assured him, trying not to think about how frightened I felt. "Just try dying on me, see how angry I'd get."

His chuckle came out with a cough.

I remembered Malahki had said to wait for ten minutes. The clock was still by the door, but thanks to its huge dial, I could make out the time even from a distance.

Ten minutes.

I wasn't sure if I should try to keep Vrateus awake. Would it be better to let him rest for a few minutes while we waited for the results?

I reined in my fear, letting hope into my heart. Holding Vrateus to me with my arm across his chest, I rested my cheek against his head. The many golden hoops in his pointy ear pressed into my skin.

"Please stay with me, Vrateus," I whispered, not sure if he could hear or comprehend what I was saying. "You said you wanted me to live. Well, I need you to stay alive, too. I'm still not sure if this life is worth living, but it definitely would be so much worse without you." I patted his chest through the soft material of his shirt, feeling the straps and the sheath of the dagger underneath. "I know things haven't always been great between us, but I don't hate you as much as I thought I did." With a sigh, I nuzzled his high cheekbone. "In fact, there are many things I like and respect about you. I hope we can be friends."

What if we could be more *than friends?*

The thought alarmed me, and I chased away the memories of the kiss we'd shared.

Not that it mattered now. Nothing would matter if he were to die in my arms.

A sudden convulsion ran through his body, sending me to my feet.

"Are you okay?" Fear and worry spiked in me. I tried to focus. "You'll need to throw up, now." I attempted to get him up, to lead him back into the bathroom. With no cooperation from him this time though, it proved impossible. He was just too heavy for me to lift on my own.

Bending to the side, he retched on the floor. I stared in horror at the black tar-like contents of his stomach on the glass as the pleasant aroma of the loathed mushrooms rose into the air.

"This is good," I forced the words out. "At least this shit is out of you, now."

Fetching some water from the bathroom, I cleaned up after him, forced another cupful of water into him, then cleaned whatever came out again.

When the shudders of dry heaving stopped wracking his body, I brought the pillow and blanket from the bed.

"Rest now." I tucked the pillow under his head, hoping that everything I had just put him through would be worth it.

I unbuckled the straps around his chest, loosening them to ease his breathing. When I pulled his tall boots off, two knives dropped out of them, clanking to the floor. I also found guns in some elaborate mechanical holders strapped around each of his forearms and concealed by the wide sleeves of his shirt. Those looked too complicated to remove, and I left them, taking off the holsters around his thighs instead.

"You're just like a walking munitions storage," I muttered, tucking the blanket around him.

Vrateus had always seemed tense and alert, always ready to pull the trigger. He acted like a cocked gun himself, ready to strike at any minute.

"It couldn't be easy to go through life while constantly having to look over your shoulder," I said, sitting on the floor next to him.

He didn't respond, didn't even appear to hear me at all. But talking felt so much better than sitting in silence, listening to his labored breathing, and watching the glow of the Anomaly lights reflecting off his white shirt.

"Being alert didn't help you, Vrateus. They still got you." Heaving a sigh, I lay on the floor next to him. "I know it's all my fault. With my escape attempt, I've knocked you off balance when nothing else ever did. When you're better—because you *have* to get better—I promise I'll make it up to you. You know I could be useful if you let me. I am a well-educated, highly trained specialist. I scored in the top ten percent of my graduating class. And I could most definitely cook a better meal than Krakhil. You can also trust me to never add these freaking mushrooms to any of your food or drink."

I didn't tell him I was feeling scared and insignificant, uncertain if I could prevent his possible death, or what to do about *errocks* taking over at this very moment.

Through all of this, a long-forgotten ache grew in my chest—the mixture of warmth, pleasure, and worry for him so intense it brought pain. I hadn't allowed myself to feel any of that for so long,

I'd begun to think I was no longer capable of these feelings—caring, attachments. For me, sooner or later, they all unfailingly resulted in the agony of heartbreak.

Lately, I'd trained myself to run from the people who'd stirred any shadow of affection inside me. Was that at least a part of the reason why I'd tried so desperately to escape this place? I'd sensed I'd have to escape this man before he'd wreaked havoc in my heart?

Even now, my mind urged me to run. To hide before it was too late from him as much as from his crew. It was just a matter of time before they came for me.

Yet I only moved closer to him, unable to leave him to face his treacherous crew alone.

"There's no escaping you, Vrateus. Somehow, you've managed to get a hold of me as strong as that of the Anomaly. And I haven't even noticed when and how it happened."

Laying at his side, I draped my arm around his middle.

"Just get better, please." I buried my face in the voluminous fabric of the sleeve over his bicep. "That's the only thing that matters."

Chapter Seventeen

Vrateus

Every part of his body hurt, as if he had been slammed against the hard edge of the Dark Anomaly without the protection of a spaceship around him.

He tried to move, shifting his legs. A groan tore from his sore throat, hurting on its way out.

Something held his arm down. He rolled his head over, finding Svetlana clinging to his side. She was asleep, and he took a minute watching her, momentarily forgetting about the pain.

With her eyes closed, the frown she often had when she looked at him wasn't there. She appeared relaxed and peaceful, almost childish in her vulnerability. A wavy strand of tea-colored hair had fallen over her face, and he couldn't help himself. He picked it up between two fingers and moved it aside.

She stirred. Her slim dark eyebrows moved together, the usual worry wrinkle forming between them.

"Vrateus?" Letting go of his arm, she patted his chest while blinking her eyes open. "You're up? Awake?" Questions rushed out of her mouth as she jerked herself into a sitting position. "How are you?"

"Um…not sure." He rose on his elbows, and she leaned over him.

"You're alive," she breathed out, pushing the curl of fur over his face back and letting her hand linger on the side of his head.

The caress was unexpected, even more so was the warmth in her dark-brown eyes directed at him and the shy smile on her lips.

"Are you really happy about that?" he asked, skeptically.

"Of course I am." She straightened under his stare, removing her hand from him. He immediately missed the contact. "With you dead, they could've made someone with tentacles or pincers, or lobster claws touch me weekly." Her voices sounded light, cheerful even. "I'd rather it'd be you, with your hands—claws and all."

"So, you like my hands on you?" A smile tugged up a corner of his mouth.

"That was *absolutely* not what I just said." A lovely blush spread on her cheeks in response. He fought the urge to cup her face.

What *did* she say?

He tried to concentrate, but his thoughts remained cloudy. Pushing off the floor, he hauled himself into a sitting position. His head swam with dizziness, his muscles ached, and his throat hurt with each swallow.

"How are you feeling?" She peered at him intently. "Can I get you anything?"

"Water?"

She jumped to her feet, rushing to the bathroom with a glass, then returned, crouching in front of him.

The cold water soothed his parched throat, settling in his stomach with a fresh cooling sensation.

"What exactly happened?" he asked, wishing he could rinse the fog out of his brain the way he had just gotten rid of the thirst. The only thing that remained clear was Svetlana's face in front of him.

"You don't remember?" Her eyes widened with worry.

"I do. Parts. I just need some help organizing them."

She nodded, drawing in a breath.

"Okay. So. You took a sip of wine, from the canteen of someone who looked like a, um… He is lanky, with six arms and a sectional tail that curves up." She swung her arm backwards then over her head. "Like this."

"Tunkrox." The description jolted his memory.

"Right. The wine had been laced with *fuhnid* mushroom juice. It made you sick. You also told me there was no antidote and that I should run and hide in the gardens because you were about to die."

"You didn't run," he stated. Some of what she was saying he already knew. The rest was filling in the blanks as his memory cleared.

"No. Well I did, but I came back. I went to the gardens, found Malahki, and convinced it to help me save you."

"You saved me. How?"

"Malahki told me to feed you a dehydrated mushroom, to draw the poison out. There was also some drinking of water and puking involved, but that's a messy part not worth mentioning. That's pretty much it—about the sick part. Though I do need to talk to you about something else, now."

"There was also a kiss, wasn't there?" The memory of it flooded his mind. He'd seen people bringing their mouths together in videos. Some kissing was friendly, some sexual. When Svetlana had kissed him, though, it was more than anything he could've expected. "I couldn't have dreamed that. I simply wouldn't be able to conjure *that* on my own."

The pink on her cheeks deepened. It went well with the sweet smile that curved her lips.

"It was pretty amazing, wasn't it?" She dropped her gaze to his chest, then slowly raised it back to his face.

He pondered the best way to tell her how he felt but couldn't come up with anything smooth or romantic.

"I want to do that again," he said simply, choosing the most direct route to get his point across. "The kissing. And more. I want to have sex with you, too. Real sex."

Maybe he should have thought about it longer before blurting it out. Something about his words or his tone must have been wrong because Svetlana's expression changed from the sweet and unguarded back to her usual frown.

"Hold your horses, Romeo." She pushed to her feet. "You've just come back from the dead. Plus, there are a lot of other issues."

Not all of what she'd said made sense to him, but the essence was clear. There'd be no sex right now.

"What issues?"

"Crux is taking over your ship as we speak."

"Crux?"

"Yes. I overheard him speaking with Wyck about it. I have a suspicion he's behind the wine poisoning, too."

"Most likely."

He tried to get up. His head swam violently, sending him down to his knees.

"Careful." She grabbed his arm, steadying him. "You need some time to recuperate, get better, and come up with a plan while Crux thinks you're dead and out of the picture."

She was right. He was still too weak. If Crux thought him dead, it could be used to their advantage.

"One thing I'd love to do as soon as possible is to get out of this room." Holding on to his arm, she rubbed her forehead with her other hand. "I have a feeling they'll be coming for me any minute."

"Right." Svetlana was the bounty Crux wouldn't wait long to claim. "We need to leave."

"Your room might be better," she suggested. "If they think you're dead, they may leave you alone for a while. Especially since Crux is not fond of places made entirely of glass and has no interest in taking your room for himself."

"Not the room, but he'd want to get to my weapon storage, eventually."

"You store weapons in your bedroom?" she asked, then slid her gaze to his chest. "That shouldn't surprise me since you store a lot of them on your body, too."

He patted his chest, remembering giving her the dagger and the gun. "You went out there on your own."

"Yes. That's why you're still alive." She brought his boots over, placing them in front of him. "Get ready."

He hadn't even realized he had his boots off. The blanket he was standing on with his knees had been draped over his legs when he woke up.

"Did you…take my boots off?" He stared at them. The only time he'd ever had them off was when he removed them himself. He only ever had a blanket over him when he remembered to cover himself before falling asleep. "No one has ever done things like that for me before…"

"Like what? Looking after you while you're sick?" She gave him her arm for support as he put his boots back on. "Someone had to. I'm glad I was around." She picked up the blanket, taking it back to the bed.

Regret suddenly tugged at his heart. He would have liked to be awake and aware when she had been tucking that blanket around him. For the first time, someone had taken care of him, and he was too out of it to even know what it felt like.

"I'm…um, grateful." He raked his claws through the fur on his nape. "Thank you—"

A screeching noise suddenly came from the door, as if someone scraped it with a metal blade. Or a tool.

Svetlana jerked her head toward the sound, color draining from her face.

"Here they are," she said.

Chapter Eighteen

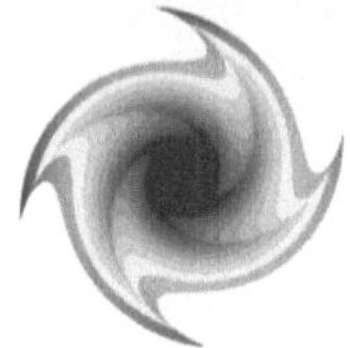

Svetlana

A sickening feeling of déjà vu churned in my stomach. The noise of the tool digging into the door, followed by the sparks of fire and the smell of melted metal, made my mind flash back to the day of my crash on the Dark Anomaly. Only now I knew for sure that nothing good waited for me on the other side.

"Stand back." Vrateus moved to the doors, still unsteady on his feet.

Flicking his wrists, he made both of his guns slide out from his sleeves. I searched around, finding my laser gun on the floor.

Not waiting for those in the corridor to cut through the doors, Vrateus hit the panel, opening the doors himself.

The males, about a dozen of them, stared at him in astonishment, either surprised at finding him still in my room or shocked at seeing him alive, or both.

They recovered quickly.

"Get him!"

Four of them rushed Vrateus.

Lifting his guns, he fired, immediately killing two. Before the rest rushed the room, he leaped into the corridor then hit the panel on the other side, closing the door in my face.

He must have done it instinctively. Because if he *really* thought about it, his going alone against all of them could easily result in him being killed, especially in his condition. And with him dead, it wouldn't take them long to finish what they'd started and break through the door. Locking me in did not save me, but it deprived me of the possibility of helping him.

I huffed in frustration. His protectiveness would get both of us killed.

Vrateus had been doing everything on his own, all his life. Having someone on his side, ready to help, must be new to him.

Hadn't I made it clear I was on his side? Or did he still have doubts about trusting me?

Luckily, since I had tampered with the panel before, he could no longer lock the doors from the outside. All I had to do now was to slide them open, which I did.

About half of the aliens lay on the floor, dead. The other half, however, were swarming Vrateus.

Shoved by one, he fell on his back. A burly alien, with a crown of horns growing on his head and a row of them rising from his spine, lifted the tool they had used to cut through the door.

With the rest of them holding Vrateus down, the one with the tool leaned over him, clearly intending to use the device to cut their captain's throat.

I swallowed a cry of horror, quickly raising my gun.

Aiming at a spot between the horns on the male's head, I pulled the trigger. With a flash of the laser, the alien staggered back, dropping the tool. Vrateus jerked to the side, letting the blade embed in the floor instead of his flesh.

Steadying my trembling hand, I fired again. This time, I aimed at one of the aliens holding him down. Two of them let go of him to rush me. I promptly retreated into the room, taking cover behind the wall. Peeking out, I shot them one by one while Vrateus made quick work of the others.

The last one glanced at me then at the approaching Vrateus, then took off down the corridor.

"Stop!" Vrateus shouted, shooting at the back of the escaping male. He skidded to a stop before tumbling down to the floor, face first.

"Are you okay?" Vrateus hurried to me. Grabbing my shoulders, he spun me around. Patting down my arms, back, and sides, he inspected me for injuries.

"I'm fine," I assured him. "Are *you* okay?"

He nodded.

"No more shutting the doors in my face," I said, grimly.

"Sorry. That was reflex." He had the decency to look remorseful.

"From now on, please, try to treat me as an asset rather than a liability."

He stared at me for a moment. "That will be an adjustment for me. It'll take a while getting used to having someone I can fully trust. I've never had that."

At least he realized he could trust me.

"Well, I got your back." I stared at the floor littered with dead aliens. "We have to get out of here."

He grabbed the nearest dead body by the legs. "We need to lock them all in here. Without the bodies, it will take some time for Crux to figure out what happened."

I shook my head.

"Sorry. I've tampered with the panel. You can't lock the doors from the outside anymore."

Vrateus dropped the legs of the dead alien down again.

"What else have you done?" He stared at me with a mix of shock and admiration.

"Nothing else. Promise. And, Vrateus," I added, desperately wishing to keep his newly found trust. "I will not do anything behind your back, anymore. Okay? From now on, you'll be a part of everything I do."

He gave me a long look, then a brief nod, before retrieving the cutting tool from the floor.

I slid the doors closed, even if they couldn't be locked anymore.

"Come." He took my hand in his, tugging me down the corridor. "We'll need to get more weapons."

More weapons?

I'd say we needed to come up with a plan of action. But sure, why not start by arming ourselves to the teeth?

"So, THIS IS YOUR ROOM?" I TOOK IN THE CAPSULE'S INTERIOR, identical to mine in size, but vastly different in décor.

The floor was bare, just like mine, but he'd plastered his walls with maps and charts. Papers, scrolls, and tablet inserts were piled on every piece of furniture, including the narrow metal bed.

"I had no idea you stayed this close to me." I glanced toward the glass capsule next door. In the lights of the Anomaly, I could clearly see the clothing rack and my bed. "No idea that I was living in a fishbowl all this time, either." I turned to face him. "Have you been watching me?"

His own capsule appeared completely dark from my room—the glass too opaque to see through.

"Yes," he said, obviously not finding anything wrong with that.

"All the time?" I couldn't recall every embarrassing thing I might have done while thinking I was alone, but that was not the point anyway. I thought I'd had privacy, when in fact I had none.

"I watched you whenever I could." He went to the door identical to my bathroom door.

"Why?"

"I had to make sure you were safe."

I folded my arms across my chest. Irritation and embarrassment stirred inside me, but I forced them down. Getting angry with him wouldn't accomplish anything when he clearly didn't understand my take on it. Just like with the weekly sessions in the mess hall, he believed he was doing the right thing.

"The only reason I made it to the airlock in time last night," he added, "was because I noticed you weren't in your room when I was going to bed."

I tried to see this through his eyes. At the same time, I wished he would understand my feelings as well.

"You should have told me I was being watched."

He stopped in front of the bathroom door.

"Why?"

"So, that I knew." How would one explain the concept of privacy to someone obviously unfamiliar with it? "I'm sure I did things I didn't want you to see. Maybe even some embarrassing things. I would have acted differently had I known you were watching me."

"You did nothing embarrassing." He waved me off.

"I'm pretty sure I've walked around naked a few times."

"You have. But you have nothing to be embarrassed about. You look good naked."

Now, my face warmed with blush. It heated even more when I started thinking about *him* possibly walking around naked too, in this very room…

"It's not about that. It's just that…" I rubbed my face, forgetting what I was going to say. "Anyway, spying on people is wrong. Watching them undress when they are not aware of being watched is also wrong. Okay?"

"Okay. So, next time I'm watching you, I'd have to tell you about it first. Would that make it better?"

Well, it was better than nothing.

"Ideally you wouldn't watch me at all. But if you must, yes, at least let me know what you're doing."

He nodded, moving to the wall with charts. "We need to get going, now."

I stepped away from the glass, glad to change the subject.

"Where to?"

"Out of here. Eventually, Crux will send more people to investigate what happened to those who were supposed to retrieve you. If he's been looking for weapons, he may order to search my room, too."

"Where will we go?"

"Here." He ripped one of the large drawings off the wall. "This is the latest map of the inhabited segment of the Dark Anomaly." He pointed at the section along the arch in the drawing. "Here is the kitchen. The mess hall. This is the main corridor. And we are here. See? These shaded areas are the cavities inside the crashed ships. Some formed between the hulls when two or more spacecraft crashed onto each other."

"How often does that happen? The crashes?"

"We get a few a year, all around the outer edge of the Anomaly's disk. As soon as the crash happens in our section, we cut through the hull then weld the new ship solid with the rest. If it's a large spacecraft, I order the oxygen supply and ventilation system expanded into it. If it's a smaller one, like yours, we just cut openings in a way that ensures the best air circulation inside it."

"What happens to those that crash outside of your sector?"

"We use the spacesuits to travel along the outer edge of the Anomaly and collect whatever we can salvage from them."

"So, the gravity doesn't squish you on the outside?"

"Not if you're on the surface, no. Only if you build up some distance from it, it reins you back in with a vengeance."

"Do you know exactly what distance that is?" Even if I never fully explained the mystery of the Anomaly, I couldn't stop trying to solve it. I kept collecting every bit of information I could find.

"I believe there is no exact distance."

"What do you mean?"

"From the data we have from the crashed ships, not all of them travelled at the same distance from the Anomaly when they got sucked in. Some were fairly far away."

"I know I was." I believed I was safe even as the crash happened.

"Right. The Anomaly's gravity acts in a similar way to a star's energy, with flares that reach out into space at irregular intervals."

I'd had the same idea myself. Which meant the reach of the Anomaly's gravity field was even wider than my research team thought.

"So, this…mass is sitting there, like a giant squid deep in the ocean, and it throws out tentacles to capture unsuspecting travellers."

"Not exactly a squid, more like a whirlpool in space," Vrateus said. "It spins, drawing the spacecraft in, compacting them into a disk in the center of its force field. The ships crash along the edge. They then get compressed closer together over time. See?" Vrateus placed the paper in his hands over another similar drawing on the wall. "This one was made by one of the earlier dwellers of the Dark Anomaly, someone who died way before my ship crashed here." I could see the older drawing through the paper of the newest one, backlit by the Anomaly's lights. Vrateus circled a few shaded sections with his finger. "The cavities within the ships have been getting smaller with time." He moved his finger along the radius down to the peak of the segment on the map. "Closer to the center of the Anomaly, all spaces between the walls eventually disappear completely. The ships end up being squished together with no cavities left inside or in between."

He glanced my way.

"I suspect the middle of the disk is compressed so hard that all materials merge. Particles of all substances squeeze between each other, creating a homogenous mass of a high-density material which may be in a liquid state."

"Have you ever gone that way? To the center?"

"Not too far. But when I was little, I climbed through the cavities inside the ships and between them as far as I could squeeze through. At some point, I remember hearing the metal groan, as the Dark Anomaly crushed and compressed the ships deep inside it. I felt the vibrations through the walls, too."

I stared at him, imagining the little boy wiggling his way through the metal body of the Anomaly. It was a miracle he didn't get trapped somewhere.

"And on the surface?" I asked.

"When we go outside, we only travel along the edge."

"You've never explored the rest of the surface of the disk? To see if you could travel to the center from the outside?"

"No. You can see from the edge that the middle is not flat like the rest of the Anomaly. The center of it is bulging out like a sphere. If the material there is liquid, it could also be hot and dangerous. Life around here is all about survival. I can't afford to send people exploring just for the sake of exploration."

"I understand."

He ripped all drawings off the wall. "We better take them all with us, no need to leave Crux a map on how to follow us."

He rolled the drawings together then took a tablet frame and gathered a few opaque inserts from the desk and the bed.

"These, too." He retrieved a long leather bag from a trunk by the wall, packing everything in it, then added a coil of thin rope and a change of clothes. "I'll get us some water."

With two canteens in his hands, Vrateus went to the bathroom.

"Can you grab some blankets, please?" he shouted over the noise of running water.

"Sure." I looked around in search of them.

The fur spread on his bed was soft and luxuriously decadent. Its red color changed to bright orange and yellow in my hands when I picked it up. Despite being thick and fluffy, it took little space when I rolled it into a bundle and stuffed it into the bag.

"You like pretty things," I observed when Vrateus walked out of the bathroom.

"As long as they're also functional." He handed me the filled canteens to put in the bag. "Come."

Taking the bag from me, he picked up the metal-cutting tool then headed back to the bathroom.

"That way?" I asked, confused.

"We need to get more weapons, remember?"

"In the bathroom?"

"Not exactly." He lifted a piece of wall paneling, revealing a hidden door behind it.

"Is that where your weapon storage is?" I gasped. "Crux would love to know that."

"He might still figure it out." Vrateus entered the hidden room, gesturing for me to follow. "Maybe."

The room behind the door was at least ten times larger than the bathroom. Shelves lined the walls, displaying a collection of weapons that would make any museum proud. The earliest models Vrateus had might have been millennia old. Though I couldn't date them accurately, as many seemed entirely unfamiliar.

I recognized a toolbox from my ship standing in a corner.

Vrateus locked the door behind us.

"Let's see." He took a leather belt with holsters from a peg on the wall then turned to me. "This should fit you."

Leaning over, he wrapped the belt around my waist then buckled it in the front. "These go here." He slid a small gun into the holster on my left then put a slim knife into the sheath on the right. "And this will go here." He took a cluster of narrower belts with a sheath. Getting down on one knee, he wrapped the belts around my right thigh.

"I'm not sure how to use any of these."

"You did pretty good out there." He tipped his head toward the corridor that must still be littered with dead aliens. I had shot some of them. The reality of me being a murderer still hadn't settled in. "This gun is similar to the one you've used." He took the small weapon out of its holster on my belt then showed me how to use it, explaining its parts. "Shoot from a distance," he added. "Aim for their face, neck or stomach. Most of the species have thinner skin, smaller scales or a finer chitin layer in those areas."

He placed the gun back into its holster. Sliding his fingers around my leg, he adjusted the straps of the dagger sheath around my thigh next.

The sudden awareness of his hands skimming the inside of my thigh sent a warm shiver up my body. He must have sensed it too, as his fingers stilled on the strap.

His hand splayed on the back of my thigh, he released a shuddered breath, letting his head drop between his shoulders.

"Is everything okay?" I asked, my voice unintentionally breathy.

"Now, more than ever, I need to be fully alert. But you're such a distraction, Svetlana," he groaned.

It didn't come out as an accusation. Still, I felt a pang of guilt.

The image of him chugging the poisoned wine after my failed escape attempt rose in my mind.

"I've been wreaking havoc on your world, haven't I?"

"You have no idea," he growled.

"I'm really sorry about how it all happened. I didn't know that Crux would use my escape attempt as a distraction and strike against you."

"I'm not blaming you for *my* lapse in caution."

"For what then?"

He lifted his gaze, meeting mine.

"For everything that has been happening *inside* me." A storm was churning in his vivid eyes.

"What would you have me do to change that?" I asked quietly.

"I don't want to change a thing, Svetlana. From the moment you arrived, you've scrambled my thoughts, deprived me of focus, and wreaked havoc on my body." He remained on one knee in front of me, his hands splayed on my thigh. "There is a pleasure in this torture, though. I don't understand it, but I don't want it to end. In fact, I crave more of it."

I stared down at his face, confusion visible in his hard features. His physical reactions weren't surprising. If I was the first woman he had ever encountered, some surge of hormones, pheromones, or physical desire on his part could be expected.

What was shocking to me were my own feelings for him. The initial resentment had disappeared, slowly replaced by desire. Now, the genuine attraction was growing strong inside me. It scared me. At the same time, I craved more of him, too.

He slid his hand down, to the back of my knee. My skin inside my suit tingled from the warmth of his palm. Suddenly, I knew what about his touch was so incredible—the gentle reverence with which he treated my body—even when he had touched me for the entertainment of others. I always sensed that, for *him,* every moment with me was special. He had made it intimate, even when we'd been surrounded by hundreds of sex-starved males.

I hovered my hand next to his face then gently placed it on his shoulder instead.

"I like you, Vrateus," I confessed. "I tried not to. I didn't believe it was right for me to have any kind of sympathy or attraction for you. But I ended up having both."

With a long exhale, he pressed his forehead to my belly.

"You can't imagine how good it feels to hear that from you. I've sensed your animosity with my skin."

"It wasn't for *you*, Vrateus, but for this entire situation. I dislike being put on display for your crew. For me, the intimate touch between two people is not supposed to be shared with anyone else. If the intimacy is real, it shouldn't be for the entertainment of others. That was probably why it felt so exceptionally wrong—because with you, it did feel *real*."

"You should have told me that sooner." He gazed up at me.

"I'm afraid I couldn't have properly explained it before."

"It won't happen again." Determination flashed in his eyes.

"But it has to." I cupped his face, gently tracing the sharp ridge of his cheekbone with my thumb. "I understand now why you did it. It's survival, Vrateus. We both need to do what we have to do to survive."

Chapter Nineteen

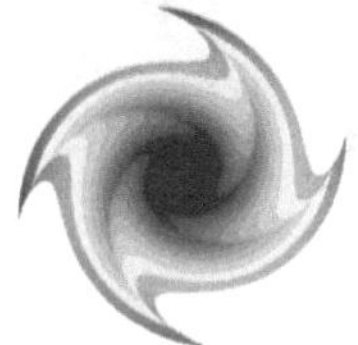

Svetlana

Instead of going back through the doors, Vrateus used the tool to cut out an opening in the back wall of his weapon storage room. We exited into a narrow tunnel behind it then climbed through the crumpled bowels of the Anomaly.

I held up a piece of the thin rope he'd cut from the coil in the bag. As soon as he'd cut it off, the piece glowed bright blue, lighting our way.

Using the tool and consulting the map from time to time, Vrateus cut through the walls that blocked our way, opening a section of a ship or a sealed tunnel between two hulls, allowing us to keep going.

"We should be close," he muttered under his breath, setting the tool down and taking the bag off his shoulder.

"Close to where?" I asked since he still hadn't shared our final destination with me. The habit of being on his own and doing everything alone obviously wasn't that easy to shake off for him.

He pointed at the map. "I slept in this space often when I was younger. It's just behind the library. We'll need to turn here."

He folded the map, then picked up the bag and the cutting tool.

After another turn, we squeezed between two wall panels into a small room with no doors or windows.

No one must have used it since Vrateus. It was empty and clean of any garbage.

"You've slept here?"

"Sometimes." He tossed the tool aside then took the blanket out of the bag. "There was no library back then. Just a storage room full of stuff looted from ships. Right behind here." He splayed his hand on one of the walls.

"How old were you?"

"Eight, when I first got to the Dark Anomaly."

"That small?" My breath caught in my throat. "What happened to the rest of those who were on your ship? Did anyone else survive the crash?"

"Some. But not for long." His jaw flexed. "I'll need to go out, now," he changed the subject. "You'll wait here—"

"Wait, what?" I grabbed his arm. "You want me to stay here, while you're out there alone? Facing hundreds of hostile aliens?"

He widened his stance.

"The *aliens* you're talking about are my crew."

"Doesn't mean they aren't hostile. Didn't some of them nearly cut your head off back there?" I gestured toward my room. "Listen, let me come with you. After all, why dress me up?" I gestured at the weapon holsters strapped to my waist and thigh. "If I don't even get to use these?"

"The weapons are for your protection," he replied, somberly. "In case someone finds their way here."

"Come on, I can be useful, Vrateus." The thought of him going out there on his own filled me with dread. "You never know, you may even enjoy having someone watch your back."

"I..." He raked his claws through the soft curl of fur over his head, pushing it back only for it to fall back down again as soon as he released it. "If you come with me, I'd be terrified for you. It'd distract me, risking possibly getting both of us killed."

His expression was pleading, making me ease off with my demand.

"What are you planning to do out there?" I asked.

"Just a brief reconnaissance trip. I need to know how things are out there before coming up with a plan."

"Promise not to start a war all by yourself."

My words made him smile. "I'm not even planning to show my face to anyone, yet. Promise, no war."

"Good." I nodded, clasping my hands in front of me. "How are you getting out of here?"

Crouching by the bag, he opened the map again, pointing at the place a couple turns back.

"I'll retrace our steps to this spot here. See this corner? Where the hulls of two ships smashed together? If I cut an opening here, this part would hide it from view of anyone in the corridor."

I stared at the map, already silently praying for his safe return.

He picked up the tool again, heading to the tunnel.

"Vrateus…" I stopped him with my hand on his sleeve.

He looked over his shoulder.

Rising on my tiptoes, I placed a quick kiss on the ridge of his cheekbone. "Please be careful."

His eyes glistened fiery orange in the blue light of the string.

"I will."

According to the tablet Vrateus and I had brought with us, it'd been only twenty minutes since he'd left, but it felt like hours.

Sitting in the small room, lit only by the short string of glowing blue light, I cuddled into his soft fur blanket. All seemed to be quiet out there. Unnervingly silent. The growling of the Anomaly compressing the wreckage that Vrateus had told me about didn't reach this far. It must be getting lost in the layers of insulation and paneling, never making it to the outer segments of the disk. Still, sitting alone in this tiny windowless room made me feel claustrophobic and…lonely.

The rustling noise of someone moving inside the tunnel Vrateus had left through sent me to my feet. My heart raced with hope that it was him returning, and fear that it might be someone or something else.

I quickly tossed the glowing string on the floor by the tunnel, illuminating the entrance, it allowed me to hide in the shadows. Grabbing the laser gun from the holster on my thigh, I held it up, ready.

The noise came closer. Then the blue glow fell on the white material of Vrateus's shirt as he entered.

"You..." I lowered the gun. Relief spread through me in a calming wave.

"Has anyone told you that you look fierce with a gun?" A corner of his mouth lifted in an unexpected smile.

"No." I holstered the weapon. "Probably because I've never handled one before."

He entered the small space, immediately filling it with his presence. I stepped back to the wall, though everything inside me urged me to come closer.

"You're a natural, then." His tone was light.

His words brought back the images of the males I'd killed. I hadn't thought twice about pulling the trigger, then. I would have done it again, under the same circumstances. The images of the smoldering holes in the dead bodies, however, stayed in my memory.

"Hungry?"

Only now had I noticed a grease-stained, paper-wrapped bundle in his hands. The smell of cooked meat wafted from it. It wasn't the most appetizing aroma, but my mouth watered. It had been nearly twenty-four hours since I'd last eaten.

"How is everything out there?" I asked, after we both had settled on the blanket, our backs to the wall.

"As I should have expected. Total chaos." Vrateus shook his head, his mouth tightening into a thin line of disapproval. "They are guzzling unmeasurable amounts of berry wine and butchering a month's supply of *vasai*."

"Are they celebrating?"

"Yes. Crux has declared himself the captain and cancelled all my restrictions."

He sounded less upset about the loss of his position than about his crew needlessly wasting supplies and resources.

"Here." He handed me a bone with meat on it. It appeared to be an entire leg of *vasai,* with a meaty chunk at the very top.

I was too hungry to decline.

"Thank you." I peeled a strip of meat off then chewed on it, slowly. "Where did you get it? And how?"

"I stole it from the kitchen. It wasn't hard." He bit a chunk of meat off another bone he had taken out of the paper bundle. "No one is paying attention to anything. Crux has lifted my limits on wine. They're getting drunk out of their minds."

"Sounds like a perfect time to show up and restore the order," I suggested.

"No. Not yet. It's best for us to wait. Alcohol has different effects on different species. *Ognats* have a strong allergy to the berry wine. It doesn't stop them from drinking as much as they can fit in their bellies, though. Most of the *ognats* will die before morning."

"That's awful," I gasped. "They're willingly killing themselves?"

"One of the many reasons I imposed strict limits on alcohol, in the first place." He shook his head. "Those without the allergy have been getting into fights and scuffles. It's not going to end well. *Dimos,* for example, get extremely aggressive when they're drunk. They'll fight anything that moves. When plunged in a killing frenzy, they continue fighting even if their heads get cut off."

"Well." I rubbed my forehead. "It's quite a crew you've got there."

"They are what they are." He shrugged.

"Don't at least some of them come from civilized worlds?"

"All of them came from planets with some form of government. It's just that many had been on the fringes of society even before they crashed here. Most of what we have here now used to be pirates, smugglers, and criminals on the run."

"Those couldn't be the only space travelers in the area."

"Many were," he replied. "Regular trade routes steered clear of the Dark Anomaly. The criminals took risks, by coming closer than they should, to evade being detected or captured. But you're right, not *all* who crashed here were on the wrong side of the law. Some were law-abiding citizens. Most of them didn't survive, though. One needs to be tough and ruthless to make it here."

"Was your family among those who didn't make it?" I asked carefully.

Finishing his meat, Vrateus took the water bottles out of the bag, handing one to me.

"My family were merchants," he said quietly. "Although they didn't shy away from some illegal smuggling here and there as I've learned while examining their log books."

"Do you remember any of them?"

"Vaguely. Everything that happened before the crash is like a dream—foggy and fragmented. The strongest memory is that of my mother patting me here..." Staring straight ahead, he lifted his hand to his temple, touching the tattoos above his ear. "While she sang me to sleep at night, she would trail her fingers here. It felt soothing..." He dropped his hand to his thigh.

"Do your tattoos have meaning?" I asked softly.

He nodded. Sliding his finger along the ornamental lines, without even being able to see them, he named them all, "My name, the name of my clan, the name of our ship, and its home port on our planet. The tattoos tell where I belong... Where I was *supposed* to belong."

Bending his legs, he rested his forearms on his knees.

"*Themuls* live in clans," he continued. "The crew of our ship comprised twenty-eight people, all of them related, either by blood or by marriage. My parents, their siblings and their families. My aunts, uncles, cousins..."

"You said not all of them died in the crash."

He'd mentioned they didn't live long after. That he had survived the cruel world of the Dark Anomaly alone seemed a miracle to me.

"Most died. I was strapped in bed, sleeping, when it happened.

The beds with my cousins were crushed, killing them. Mine ended up wedged under theirs with enough space to keep me alive."

He ran both hands over his face.

"By the time I climbed out, the *ognats* and *kreers* had already made their way onto the ship. The killings of the survivors had started. Then *errocks* and *yourlu* joined them, with *dimos* and the others. That was when the rapes began…"

"Did no one see you?"

"In the chaos that followed, I crawled under wreckage and snuck out."

"You were only eight years old, Vrateus. How on earth did you survive here alone?"

"I hid. Smaller than anyone, I could fit in tiny places no one would bother to look. As a child, I had the same advantage Malahki has. I had neither the scent of a female to excite lust nor the size or attitude of a male to ignite aggression."

"Many would still eat you if they caught you." Even after all my time on the Dark Anomaly, I still couldn't fully imagine the horrors he had lived through.

"True, food was scarce. As was air and water. Without one interconnected air supply system, we relied on the oxygen production equipment of individual ships. The air was thin and poorly distributed. Cannibalism was rampant and widely accepted in those times. The strongest routinely killed and ate the weakest."

"Oh God…It's just awful." I winced, rubbing the pain out of my tightening throat. "What did *you* eat?"

"Whatever I could steal from the others when they were asleep or intoxicated and passed out. A few years later, the ship with *vasai* crashed here. The centipedes got loose, spreading through the body of the Anomaly. By then, I had grown big enough and learned to hunt them. I would corner one, separating it from the rest, then kill it. After a while, I had enough meat to sustain myself and even to trade for things I needed."

"When did you decide to become the captain?"

"Well before that." A crooked smile appeared on his hardened face. "I knew right after the crash that I would kill Raex, one day. The *errock* boasted he'd raped my mother. He was the unofficial leader. I decided when I was big enough, I would take his place to lead them all. Unlike him, I wanted to do it right."

"Did you kill him?"

He nodded. "I knew I needed to be patient, and I was. Biding my time, I learned everything I could about the species populating the Dark Anomaly. Their strengths and their weaknesses. What motivated each of them. I used to sneak onto the newly crashed ships. While everyone else looted them for food and weapons, I'd search for data storage devices. Then I brought them all here." He tipped his chin toward the wall separating us from the library. "I studied everything there was to learn about the world outside and the people we had in here. There was no order back then. But Raex was the leader. I challenged him seven years ago and won that fight."

"You killed him," I exhaled.

"Just as I'd promised myself." An expression of grim satisfaction settled over his face.

"How did the rest of *errocks* take it? Did they defend one of their own?" I drank more water from my bottle, listening to him intently.

"Back on their planet, *errocks* live in tribes. The leader of a tribe can be challenged in one-on-one combat for leadership. I defeated Raex in an honest fight. Not all of them liked it, but they've accepted it."

"Is that what you're planning to do, now?" I asked tentatively, unsure if I'd like the answer. "Are you going to challenge Crux?"

"I'll give him a chance to surrender first." He stuffed his canteen back into the bag.

"Do you see him taking that chance?"

He drew in a long breath. "Probably not. But I want to use any possibility to avoid more violence. Our population will already be drastically reduced when all of this is over. No need to court another rampage."

"Are you planning to talk to Crux?" I cleared my throat, breathing deeply as worry tightened my chest. "When?"

"By tomorrow morning, many of them will have drunk themselves unconscious. Some will be dead. Others hangover. I'll try to talk with Crux then."

"*We'll* try," I corrected him.

He glanced my way.

"Svetlana, it would be best if you stayed here."

"Again?" I stared at him.

He remained silent, shifting his eyes from mine.

I exhaled sharply, calling on my patience. "Listen, I'm not saying I should be out there, slaying men and kicking ass. All I'm asking for is for you *not* to dismiss my ability and willingness to help. If there is any chance for me to be useful, please, include me in your plans."

He reached over and moved a strand of my hair away from my face.

"If there was an absolutely safe place anywhere on the Anomaly to hide you, I would," he admitted. "You have become my dearest treasure, Svetlana. I feel this powerful urge to lock you away and keep you safe."

I blinked at his confession, uncertain how to take it, though something warm and pleasant glowed inside of me from the tenderness in his tone.

"I know that crashing here was a disaster for you," he continued. "But for me, your arrival turned out to be the best thing in my life. From the very first moment, I couldn't get you out of my thoughts. Though, there were some frustration and annoyance too, at the beginning." He smiled.

"*Frustration and annoyance* still sound milder than the emotions I had for you." I chuckled. "I hated you then."

He tilted his head. "How about now?"

The half-grin remained on his face, slightly teasing. However, the intensity in his eyes betrayed how important my answer was to him. He seemed to halt his breath, waiting for it.

"I've already told you, Vrateus, I like you. I just…"

"What is it?" He frowned.

A flicker of enduring hope in his gaze pinched my heart with ache. Vrateus longed for affection, even as he hardly could remember what that feeling was.

Was it specifically *my* affection that he wished for, though?

I was literally the first woman Vrateus had met who wasn't family. Would he have cared just as much about any female who'd crashed here instead of me?

Would he leave if another female came along?

The thought zigzagged with pain along the scars of my previously broken heart.

I crashed here first, I saw him first. He was now all mine to take. And I wanted him so badly.

Could I still stop this, whatever it was between us, from growing any stronger? Could this simply remain all about lust?

"What is it, Svetlana?" he prompted, carefully.

"Nothing." I gave him a smile to mask my thoughts and took his hand in mine.

The soft fur on the top of his hand reached up to his knuckles, leaving his fingers bare. I circled the green stone of one of the huge rings he wore.

"Why don't I believe you?" he insisted, his eyes searching mine.

Because you see through me? You see *me.*

Over the past weeks, he'd learn not just my body, he'd learned to read *me*.

"You've made me feel so many things, Vrateus," I squeezed his hand, afraid to say too much but unable to say nothing at all. "From hate, to rage, to…attraction." And so much more. All the feelings that now bubbled hot inside me, scaring me with their intensity. "No one else has ever made me feel the way you do."

Clasping my fingers in his hand, he shifted closer.

"What are you feeling right now, Svetlana?"

"Now?" I slid my gaze to his mouth. Often pressed into a firm line in focus, anger or disapproval, his lips were slightly parted. Inviting and enticing.

"This very moment…I just want to kiss you again." The words came out, taking my breath with them.

His eyes flashed with heat as he leaned closer.

"Kiss me then," he whispered, his lips brushing over mine. "Use the moment, Svetlana, because on the Dark Anomaly that's all there is. Just this very moment."

Chapter Twenty

Vrateus

He claimed her lips. Remembering everything from their previous kiss, he mirrored her actions. His execution was far from precise. His thoughts were on everything at once as he tried to take her in with all his senses.

Listening and touching.

Tasting and feeling…

She gasped softly into his mouth. Her body stilled, then seemed to come back to life with his touch. Wrapping her arms around his neck, she shifted closer, sliding into his lap. Her scent wrapped around him, and he happily allowed himself to drown in it.

Just like she had, he slipped his tongue deeper, searching for hers. A soft moan vibrated deep in her throat.

Desire jolted through his body like lightning, crushing his self-control.

Letting go of her mouth, he trailed his lips down on the side of her neck, instead. Inhaling deeply, he filled his lungs with her scent, breathing her in. She gasped as his canines grazed her skin. The sound went straight to his cock, making it hard as steel.

Fervently moving his hands, he searched for a way to get under her suit, needing to feel her naked body. His claws sprang from the tips of his fingers, raking along the indestructible material of her suit.

"Here…" She whispered breathlessly, yanking at something in the front. The suit opened from her neck down to her navel.

The claws didn't disappear all the way as he palmed her breasts through her pink harness. She hissed at the prick of the claws, her nipples tightened and hardened under his thumbs.

"Oh God, yes…" she moaned, riding the hard ridge of his throbbing erection through his pants.

Pressing her breasts into his hands, she grabbed fistfuls of fur on his scruff. Intense pleasure coursed down his back from the sting at the roots, making him growl.

More blood rushed to his groin. His cock pulsed hot with need. Hands under her backside, he flipped her down on the fur blanket, grinding himself against her.

Lost in her scent, the feel of her, and her taste, he felt nothing else. Everything ceased to exist. There was just her warm, writhing body under him.

The unbearable, all-consuming need was building up, threatening to explode and tear him apart.

A feral roar vibrated deep in his chest somewhere.

Ecstasy spiked.

Delirious, he bit down on her shoulder, just below her neck, and growled through his teeth as a mind-blowing climax rocked through him.

Again and again.

Brutal pleasure shook his body, rolling through him in waves. He couldn't breathe, couldn't think. When the last spurt of his release burst out of him, he no longer knew his own name.

Spent, he released her from the grip of his teeth, gasping for air and rolling off her into the fur blanket.

"Vrateus?" Svetlana's hand stroked his heaving chest. "Are you okay, sweetheart?"

The tender concern in her voice made him want to cry.

Then, worry chilled the sweat on his back.

"Svetlana…" He jerked his head up, searching for her eyes, afraid of what he might find in them. "I did it all wrong, didn't I?"

For a few blissful moments, he had lost himself to her, forgetting about *her* pleasure.

Her dark eyes glistened in the bluish glow of the light string as she rose on her elbow at his side.

"Not wrong." She gazed at him with a warm excitement. "This was…intense." Her hand went to touch the bite mark on her shoulder. "I knew it would be wild if you let go." She leaned in, cupping his face. "I've seen it in you," she murmured, with a soft kiss on the corner of his mouth. "We haven't even done the whole thing yet, but was it good for you?"

Good?

He still felt like a part of his soul was floating out there among the lights of the Anomaly. He didn't think it would ever come back to reunite with his body. Not when she was stroking his head like that, combing through his fur with her delicate little fingers.

"But I wanted it to be good for you, too," he groaned.

She breathed out a soft laugh.

"It still can be."

Arching her back, she clicked open her breast harness.

Leaning over her, he rolled her onto her back, then pushed the pink material up to her chin. Freed, her breasts spilled out, round and full, tipped with dark pink. The sight of them made his cock throb all over again, but he ignored his own arousal, this time.

"Tell me if you like this." He lowered his head, dragging his long tongue across one of Svetlana's nipples.

Soft and silky, her skin quickly wrinkled around the tip which got hard like a small, perky button.

"I do…" She smiled at his questioning glance, her chest rising faster. "Do you like doing it?"

"I've wanted to taste every part of you for such a long time," he rasped, sucking the nipple into his mouth.

She moaned, stretching under him.

He moved his mouth to the other nipple while stroking the one he had just released with his fingers. Carefully, he slid out the very tip of the claw on his thumb.

She whimpered when he lightly scraped across her skin with it, circling the tip of her breast.

"More...please," she panted.

Releasing all his claws on that hand, he gently dragged their tips over her skin. A shudder ran through her body with her long, shuddered exhale.

"That is so good, Vrateus..."

Good.

The word gave him encouragement. He wrapped his hand around her throat quickly, just to check what he already knew—she was aroused and ready.

He slowly trailed the tips of his claws down her belly, then sheathed them completely before slipping his hand inside the waistband of her shorts.

Touching her there felt familiar. He'd done it several times, now. Except that this time, it was just for the two of them. There were no others.

She gasped, the same way she always did when he circled that spot between her legs.

Rising on his elbow at her side, he watched her face, noting every change in her expression.

She gazed at him with a small, happy smile. Then her eyelids dropped. The smile melted off her face. Her lips parted, letting out a soft moan.

Just for him.

"Faster, Vrateus..." she begged. "Just a little harder...Oh, yes right there..."

Then, she stopped talking completely. Her breathing hitched. Her body tensed; she fisted her hands above her head.

With a long groan, she released her breath that broke into a series of gasps and moans a moment after. Her hips jerked, and she trembled.

He removed his fingers from her. Instead, he cupped his hand between her legs and gently massaged her there, curious how many little shudders he could reap out of her.

Finally, her expression melted into a blissful one. With a sweet, delightful moan, she opened her eyes, meeting his.

"All *these* moans were real," he whispered, happy to see her smile.

"Of course, they were…" She released a shuddered breath, the smile slipped off her face. "This is so not just about lust, is it?"

The sudden fearful expression in her dark-brown eyes made his heart flip.

"No, it's not." He gathered her into his arms. "It's never been just about that, sweetheart."

She closed her eyes tightly, hungrily drawing in another breath.

"Which means it'd hurt that much more if you leave," she whispered, barely audible.

"Leave?" He exhaled a laugh, confused. "Where? There is no leaving here, you know it yourself now."

"People can physically be in the same room, Vrateus, but so far away from each other emotionally, as though galaxies apart."

He took in her beautiful face—the dark eyebrows curved tragically, the bottom lip worried between her teeth. Those eyes—the color of the dark, bitter tea he brought for her with breakfast every morning—glossy with emotion.

"Are you scared that what we have will end before it's begun?" he asked. "Have I given you any reason to feel that way?"

"Not you." She lifted her hand to his face, obvious in her need to touch him. He leaned into it, needing her touch, too. "People don't tend to stick around me. Everyone I've ever loved left, Vrateus."

"Even your family?"

A shadow or hurt crossed her lovely face, making her look younger and vulnerable. Then the words started pouring out, as if they had been piling up inside of her for so long, they couldn't wait to get out.

"I've hardly ever had a family. I lost my parents when I was still a baby. Only they weren't taken from me the way yours were." She stroked his cheekbone gently. "They left on their own and never came back. My grandparents died when I was in the Academy, but emotionally, they'd left me to my own devices long before that. They weren't easy people to love, but still I tried. They were all I had, and I cared for them. My grandmother gave me a hug and a kiss here…" she tapped her cheek, her eyes staring past him somewhere, "every year on my birthday. And my grandfather would shake my hand and pat my shoulder when I brought home a good report card at the end of my school year." A faint smile ghosted her lips. "I tried so hard to have the best grades in my class. And sometimes I wonder if that was because I simply wanted that handshake so badly."

Her chest rose as she heaved a sigh. Her words resonated with his own feelings from his distant past. He had no handshakes and no kisses growing up, but he recognized the longing in her eyes.

"None of my relationships with men have worked out," she continued, dropping her hands in her lap. "And that may be my fault, because after the first one failed, I've never given it my all again. My work has always been there for me, and it's become my one true passion. Until you…" She met his gaze with hers again, and her eyes spoke even more than her words.

"Svetlana…" he half-whispered, afraid to break this moment and the connection that had stretched between them. Only it couldn't be broken that easily, he realized. There was nothing he wouldn't do for her. All he needed in return was for her to be at his side. Always.

"There're so many reasons for me to be afraid right now, Vrateus," she said softly. "There's real danger out there. But right now, my biggest fear is that this…" she waved her hand between them, "is just another heartache waiting to happen. I want to open my heart to you, all the way, but I'm afraid what will be left of it once you're gone…"

"Svetlana," he said again, stretching her name on his tongue like the sweetest of treats. "I'd never touched a woman before you. I'd never held anyone in my arms like this before. The only physical contact I knew was the one aimed to hurt or to kill. I have no idea what I'm doing and how it all works, but I know one thing, there is no *me* without *you* anymore." He tightened his hold on her, feeling every word he said in his heart. "What I feel for you is new, exciting, and unsettling. It's like every nerve in me is exposed, ready to be hurt or experience the highest of pleasure, or both."

"Are you scared, too?" she murmured, raising her large, lustrous eyes to his.

"Terrified," he confessed. Having her in his life made him feel like a part of him now existed outside of his body, beyond his control, extremely vulnerable and painfully precious. "But I want it all. Everything. From now on, there is no parting from you for me."

Svetlana

His words and expression floored me. There was so much tenderness in his eyes, open and unguarded. And there was faith, unshakable faith in *us*.

I breathed deeply, soaking in his words and his strength. It was scary to let him into my heart, but I had no control over it. He'd already made his way under my skin, and I liked having him close way too much to push him away. In fact, I needed him even closer.

Cupping his face in my hands, I kissed him again. Slowly and tenderly, I took his bottom lip between mine then slid my tongue in to meet his, using my kiss to tell him all the things I couldn't put into words right now.

Despite the many horrible things Vrateus had lived through—things that had hardened him, made him strong and uncompromising—he remained innocent in so many ways.

I had the unstoppable urge to kiss and cuddle him.

He welcomed my affection, soaking it in like a desert absorbed the first rain of the season. I realized that all of it was new to him. Every single thing that had happened between us—each touch, kiss, caress, and whisper—was something he had never experienced before with anyone else.

And I wanted to give it all to him—everything he'd missed, stranded in this place with no one capable of any feelings.

I wished to give him my all, but I hadn't expected how much he would be giving back.

With Vrateus, I felt not just wanted, but *needed*, desperately. His strong arms around me made me feel safe in this place filled with danger.

Rolling to his back, he drew me over his chest. I broke the kiss, rising over him on my arms.

He gazed up at me, making me warm with pleasure from the glow of affection in his bright orange eyes. "You make me happy, Svetlana. When I should be stressed and terrified."

"With you, I'm not scared of anything," I confessed. The fear, the dread of what was to come were still there. But all of that seemed manageable as long as he was with me. "Together, we'll be okay, Vrateus. You and me."

Together.

For once, I truly believed it was possible for me to be no longer alone.

Chapter Twenty-One

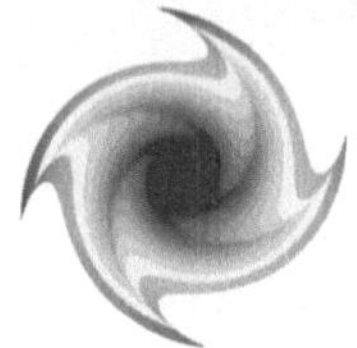

Svetlana

"Here, take this, too," Vrateus said, taking a ruby ring off his pinky and putting it on the ring finger of my right hand.

"A promise ring?" I attempted a joke with a nervous giggle to combat the dreadful anxiety of the looming uncertainty.

This morning, he had taken me to the functioning bathroom on one of the ships near the gardens. Then, we'd had some berries and fruit for breakfast. We had taken care to stay out of sight. However, the gardens appeared deserted. Even Malahki seemed to be gone.

Back in the room behind the library, Vrateus was now getting ready to confront Crux.

"If you press the button here…" He lifted my hand, pointing at a small bead in the setting of the ring. "A needle will slide out. It's soaked in a concentrated *fuhnid* juice."

"It is?" I took a closer look at the tiny button he had indicated.

"Very potent." He nodded. "The needle is too fine to penetrate the skin of every species on the Dark Anomaly, though. If anyone gets too close, aim for the eyelids or lips if you can. It should kill a large male within seconds."

"Wow." I admired the ring with newly found appreciation. "I see what you meant when you said you liked things that are pretty *and* functional."

He checked all my weapons, as if I were the one going out there to face the wild crowd, not staying in the small room behind the library, waiting for his return.

He cupped the side of my face for a moment, then slid his hand down my arm, lacing his fingers with mine.

"I'll come for you in an hour or two."

I squeezed his hand, wishing I didn't have to let go.

"Be careful, please. I need you to come back."

"I will *always* come back to you." He held my gaze. "You understand what you've done to me, Svetlana? It's no longer just about survival for me. You've shown me how to *live*. If I lost you now, I wouldn't know how to go on."

Once again, I was sitting in the dark, waiting. My eyes on the glowing screen of the tablet, I tracked every passing second, counting down the minutes until Vrateus's return.

An hour passed, then another crawled by, and he still wasn't back.

I strained my hearing, listening to every little noise out in the tunnel, but none of them were the sounds of him returning.

At lunch time, I ate some fruit Vrateus and I had brought from the gardens. Unable to sit, I paced in the small space.

Something must have happened. I couldn't shake the dread.

I had no doubt Vrateus would have come for me as soon as he was able. *If* he was able.

Something bad must have happened to him, and I couldn't stay here, not knowing what it was or if I could help.

Adjusting the weapons strapped to my body, I slipped out of the room and into the tunnel, then made a turn to the gardens, the way Vrateus had shown me that morning.

From there, I travelled via the conveyor belt inside the garbage tunnel.

My plan was simple. Stay out of sight, learn what had happened, figure out how to help Vrateus if he needed help.

Keeping my hand on the wall, I felt the loose panel that covered the opening into the corridor not far from my old room. Getting off the conveyor belt, my hands and feet pushed into the walls of the tunnel, I crawled up, then peeked out into the corridor.

No one was here. From what Vrateus had told me, Crux and the crew would either still be celebrating, or recovering after last night's party. Either way, most of them would congregate around the mess hall and the kitchen where the food and the wine were.

Getting back down on the conveyor belt, I kept going in the direction of the waste sorting room.

My destination shouldn't be far now.

I got ready to stop if necessary, listening for any noise up ahead.

Instead, a rattling sound came from behind me.

Was it some large debris going down the tunnel?

It sounded big and heavy enough to push me out into the waste processing room. I had no way of knowing if anyone was out there, and I would get no chance to stop myself before falling out.

I braced my arms and feet into the walls. Maybe, I could at least try to slow down my tumbling out of the tunnel by stopping the debris with my shoulders?

The next moment, the thing behind me rushed down with a sound of a rumbling log. It painfully hit my shoulder, narrowly missing my head, then wedged between the wall and my body.

My stomach lurched with terror when I realized what it was.

A full-grown *vasai* centipede!

It hissed, thrashing violently against me. Its jaws clanked somewhere just above my head.

I shoved at its chitin-covered body as its many legs scraped at my bodysuit. Horror and disgust exploded in my chest. I couldn't scream. My throat closed in terror, choking me.

Tumbling together with the centipede, my limbs tangled with its countless legs, we both flew out of the garbage shoot, landing in a pile of trash below.

The *vasai* seemed really pissed. Sinking its mandibles into my shoulder, it shook its flat head like a fighting dog. It seemed determined to let go only with a piece of my flesh in its mouth.

Rolling down the garbage pile with the nightmarish insect, I frantically patted my side in search of the gun holster. As soon as my fingers brushed by the smooth handle, I yanked the gun out and fired.

I had no time to aim properly. The laser ray grazed the creature's side, not harming it much but enraging it even more. Kicking me with all its legs, it shoved me to my back, knocking the gun out of my hand.

Two brick-brown hands suddenly gripped the centipede's head, twisting it out of its body. A stream of milky-white goo gushed out of the wound, foul and steaming.

My stomach roiled. Then, a fresh wave of terror chilled my spine at the sight of my "rescuer". The burly *dimo* lifted the severed head of the centipede to his mouth, sucking on the dangling tissue and torn vessels.

"God, it's so gross," I groaned, scrambling for my gun.

He tossed the *vasai* head aside, kicking the gun out of my reach.

"Huh!" A *kreer* peeked at me over the *dimo's* shoulder. "Crux's female is here."

Both aliens appeared to be fresh out of a fight. One of the *kreer's* arms hung motionless. The *dimo's* side was covered in blood, his or the *kreer's*, it was hard to tell.

Two more *dimos* were lying by the wall, either death or passed out.

"Go, get Crux," the *dimo* ordered.

"Why me?" the *kreer* whined, his bloodshot eyes fixed on me. "You'll have all the fun with her while I'm gone."

"Go," the *dimo* roared. "Tell him we found her. Crux may let you have her after he's done, for bringing him the good news."

"But you'll have her now—"

"Go, I said!" The *dimo* shoved the *kreer* toward the exit, so hard, the male nearly lost its balance. Spurred into action, the *kreer* jumped to all his feet and ran to the short hallway that led to the *vasai* farm and the main corridor.

At the same moment, the *dimo* lunged for me.

Scurrying around him on all fours, I leaped to my feet and dashed after the *kreer*. This was the only way out of the room besides the tunnel I'd arrived in.

It was quieter inside the *vasai* farm this time. I ran between the cages, many of them empty, their doors open. The clusters of eggs in those were squashed, with the clear contents smeared all over the floor, mixed with the creatures' spilled blood.

My feet slipped in the gore. The heavy footfalls of the *dimo* sounded close at my back.

I sprinted for the entrance.

The sound of other footsteps came from the corridor, then the *kreer* rushed back into the farm, with Crux on his heels.

"Where is she?"

I skidded to a stop, nearly crashing into them. My feet slid in the mess on the floor, and I grabbed on to the bars of the nearest cage to stop myself from falling.

Then the heavy hand of the *dimo* fisted in my hair.

"Finally." Crux smirked, a black flash in his yellow eyes promised nothing good for me.

Fear paralyzed my mind and my body.

The lanky alien, Vrateus had called Tunkrox, staggered unsteadily through the entrance into the farm.

"Hey, Crux…" he hiccupped. "The captain escaped—"

Crux span on his heel, glaring at Tunkrox. "*I am* the captain! You idiot."

"Okay." Tunkrox shrugged, swaying on his feet. "He is still gone, though…"

"How?" Crux roared, hands fisting at his sides. "Lock her in the cage," he threw over his shoulder to the *dimo*. "Fuck! How did he get out? Who was supposed to be watching him? Do I have to be everywhere at once? A bunch of idiots!" he raged, stomping out of the farm.

Unperturbed, Tunkrox stumbled out of the room, following his new captain.

"The cage can wait," the *dimo* growled, flipping me to face him.

Snapping out of the stupor, I punched him in the jaw. The blow didn't seem to affect him, but definitely hurt my knuckles.

He smirked.

"Crux said to lock her up." The *kreer* bounced on the balls of his feet by the entrance to the farm.

"I will," the *dimo* growled, pressing himself against me. "In a minute…"

Glancing out into the corridor then back at the *dimo* assaulting me, the *kreer* seemed to be torn between joining in the fun with the *dimo* or running to rat him out to Crux.

Finally, the fear of the new captain must have won, as the *kreer* ran out the way Crux had left.

Trapping my legs between his, the *dimo* gripped my waist with the two short arms he had growing from each side of his abdomen. He then caught my wrists with the second pair of hands of the arms that grew from his shoulders.

"Now what are you going to do?" He sneered, licking his lips with a wide, meaty tongue, the centipede's body fluids still glistening on his face.

"I guess I'll just let you have me," I said, trying hard not to grimace in revulsion. "If you're good to me, I can be good to you, too."

"I don't need you to be *good.*" He dragged his tongue along the side of my face. The stale stench of alcohol assaulted my nostrils. "I don't even care if you're alive." He guffawed as if he'd just made a funny joke.

"Oh, but you don't know how much more fun I can be alive," I attempted a flirtatious murmur, though it came out more like a strangled croak, as terror pressed the air out of my chest. "Just let me use one hand." I wiggled the fingers of my right hand, playfully. "And I'll show you."

"Just one?"

"Mhm." I nodded, biting my lower lip seductively.

He released his grip on my wrist. "If you try anything funny, I'll make sure it hurts more when I fuck you," he warned.

"Don't worry." I brought my hand up to his cheek. "There is definitely nothing *funny* about this."

Hard plating covered the *dimo's* skull and most of his face. He had no eyelids, his eyes mere slits under the thick brow ridge. His lips seemed just as hard as the rest of him.

"Shove your tongue down my throat," I moaned breathily, trailing the back of my hand down his jaw line.

With an intrigued growl, he stuck his thick tongue out. It descended toward my mouth.

Pressing the small protrusion on Vrateus's ring, I released the sharp needle and stabbed his tongue with it.

He roared in pain then slapped me across my face with his free hand. My head slammed into a cage bar. The blow rang through my head, disorienting me for a moment.

"I want you dead, after all," he snarled, putting his huge hands around my neck.

His enormous body suddenly shuddered. The hands choking me relaxed, allowing me to twist my neck free from his grip.

With gurgling noises coming from his mouth, he collapsed at my feet, thrashing in convulsions.

The *dimo's* tongue had quickly swollen to the size of my forearm, completely blocking his mouth. A pair of his hands clawed at his throat as he struggled for air, the other pair scratching at his chest.

"What did you do?" the *kreer* yelled from the entrance.

He was followed by a group of others. Crux might have sent them to make sure the *dimo* complied with his order of locking me up.

"Get her! Now!"

All of them rushed me.

Jumping over the *dimo's* writhing body, I dashed back to the waste sorting room—there was nowhere else to run.

Swiping my gun off the floor, I shot at the two males who came the closest.

Spinning on my heel, I climbed up the garbage pile, back to the chute. The belt inside moved down when I needed to go up. I'd have to climb up the walls inside the tunnel, careful to stay off the belt. It wouldn't be easy, but I had no other choice.

"Get her!" Someone shouted drunkenly behind me. My stomach dropped with dread. My heart beat so fast, it was hard to breathe.

More of them rushed in.

Frantically, I scrambled into the tunnel. Bracing my boots and my arms against the wall, I climbed up.

Screams and growls reverberated through the room behind me. Then, the sounds of clawing and slamming at the wall began.

Someone must have yanked at the belt with enough force to rip it because it slackened then started moving much faster. The males were pulling it out of the tunnel, probably hoping to get me out this way. They would succeed at that, too, if my arms or feet slipped, and I fell onto the belt.

I clung harder to the walls, afraid to think about what would happen if I fell. The shoulder that the centipede had mauled ached. The mandibles of the creature hadn't been able to pierce through the reinforced material of my suit, but it still hurt.

Something wrapped around my thigh—one of the long, segmented tails of a *kreer.* My heart leaped into my throat. Shoving the loose belt aside, I propped my hand on the floor of the tunnel, then used the other hand to get the knife out of the sheath on my belt.

"Get off me," I hissed through my teeth, slicing the tail off my thigh.

A screeching sound of pain came from outside of the tunnel as the tail limply fell away from me. Clenching the knife between my teeth, I kept moving up the tunnel, eager to get out of reach of all their tails, feelers, tentacles, and other appendages.

My arms and legs shook uncontrollably when I finally came upon the loose piece of paneling in the wall, up the corridor from my old room. There was no way I could make it all the way to the garden by crawling up the tunnel like this. Making sure there was no one around, I climbed out into the corridor, instead.

Like a woman possessed, I ran back to the gardens, and from there, to the small room behind the library.

Chapter Twenty-Two

Svetlana

My heart pounded hard when I made it back to the room. Disappointment, worry, and fear filled me at finding it empty.

Vrateus wasn't there.

From the few words exchanged between Crux and the others, I understood that Vrateus had been captured and escaped. The question remained—had he kept his freedom or had he been recaptured?

Part of me wished I'd immediately run back out there in search of him. The other part held me back out of caution. I was much more useful to Vrateus free and alive, than captured and potentially dead or used as a pawn by his enemies.

Pacing the tiny space, I listened to every small noise while trying to decide what to do next.

A screeching noise outside the wall shared with the library startled me. Sparks flew, and a line formed in the paneling, with melting plastic dripping on each side. Someone was cutting through the wall from the outside.

I darted for the tunnel to hide.

"Svetlana." Vrateus kicked in the piece of the wall he had just cut out.

"You!" Relief spread through me, making me weak in the knees.

He tossed the cutting tool aside and shoved a shelf in the library over, to cover the opening he'd just made.

I threw myself at him, and he caught me in his arms.

"Why cut the wall?" I asked, between the frantic, messy kisses I showered his face with. "Why didn't you use the tunnel?"

"I couldn't get to that section of the corridor," he replied, looking somewhat stunned by my wild affection. "Someone was there, I didn't want to lead them to the tunnel."

"You're alive. Are you okay? I can't believe you're free." I grabbed his shoulders, touched his neck then cupped his face, all the while kissing him wherever my lips would land. "I was so scared for you. What happened?" I slid my hands inside his shirt, needing to feel more of him. "They caught you?"

"Blocked me off, in a dead-end hallway…" He walked me backwards until my back pressed against the opposite wall. "They barricaded me in. I used the laser of the gun to cut through the wall paneling and escaped in the gap behind it. You…" Holding me tight, he blinked and smiled as I kept showering him with kisses. "Did you miss me?"

Missed him? That was the understatement of the century.

Taking his face between my palms, I stared into his bright eyes.

"Vrateus. You are my treasure too, you know? You turned out to be the best surprise of the Anomaly, and I can't let you go."

With a groan, he pressed his body to mine. Digging my fingers into his back, I drew him even closer.

His kiss was hot and frantic. I yanked my bodysuit open, wishing to climb out of it completely. I yearned to feel all of him with every inch of my skin.

We had no time, and it was the wrong place. So much about this situation might be wrong, but I didn't care. Being with him felt right.

He was here, with me, and that was all that mattered.

The glide of his hands over my skin filled me with life. I yanked at the waistband of his pants, and he opened the fasteners for me.

Sliding my hand in, I found his hot, straining erection. Under my fingers, thick grooves swelled and pulsed along his shaft. He hissed under his breath as I stroked the ridges.

"Does it hurt?"

"No, my treasure," he rasped. "But it's a different kind of torture." He lifted my leg to his hip, sliding his hand inside my panties. "There is no way I can stop this now."

"Don't," I replied breathlessly. "Please, don't stop."

I needed this badly. The adrenaline still coursed high inside me. The lingering fear of losing him urged me closer to him. I rocked my hips against his hand between my legs, letting the rush of desire wash away the worry and fear.

"Let me see you," he demanded, leaning back.

One hand on my neck, the other rubbing between my legs, he kept his gaze on my face. I stared back at him, losing myself in the vivid orange of his eyes, until the tide of approaching orgasm made me drop my eyelids.

"Oh, I want you…Vrateus," I panted.

Before the pleasure crested, he entered me, sliding in firmly, in one smooth thrust.

A shudder rolled through his body, resonating through me with another wave of sweet heat.

"Better than I could've ever imagined," he groaned.

His arms pressed into the wall above my head, he moved his hips slowly. The thick ridges on his shaft tugged at my opening, pulsing through my core with pleasure.

I moaned, rolling my head along the wall. My temple touched his arm, and I sensed his body tremble.

"Let it go, honey," I whispered. "Don't hold back."

Even in the frenzy of passion, I trusted him not to hurt me more than I would enjoy.

With a deep growl, he shifted his hand behind my head, grabbing my ponytail. Hiking my leg higher, he brought us closer, plunging deeper.

I slid my hands behind his neck, gripping the fur on his nape. He drew in a sharp breath as my hands fisted tight. A guttural moan came from deep inside his throat.

His thrusts grew faster, more urgent, desperate.

The achy pressure building up inside me threatened to explode any minute.

Yanking my ponytail back, he latched onto the side of my neck, his teeth scraping my skin, without breaking it. The brief pain of his bite skittered with pleasure down to my chest and lower belly, setting off an explosive orgasm.

With a muffled, tortured growl against my neck, he came, taking me with him. Ecstasy rocked me in swells as I clung to him, letting the pleasure consume me.

Our bodies fused together, we remained at the wall, coming down from our climax together.

"You're mine," he murmured into my hair. "I want all of you, Svetlana. Just for me, alone."

"Yours," I echoed, feeling it in the deepest places of my heart.

"Every moan of yours is mine." He licked over the bite on my neck, then hugged me closer, kissing the side of my face. "I'm not sharing your pleasure with anyone else ever again. I'm keeping you all to myself. I don't know how I'll do it, but I *will* make it happen."

VRATEUS GAVE ME A LONG, PENETRATING STARE.

"You're coming with me?" He obviously struggled with the idea of me going out in the open.

Since Crux had been unwilling to negotiate, Vrateus was now going to openly challenge him to a fight.

"Well, I have gone out on my own once already, searching for you." True to my word to share everything with him, I'd told him about my trip to the waste processing room. I'd tried not to get into the gruesome details, but Vrateus was still horrified. "Instead of sitting here alone, dying with worry, I'd rather be out there with you."

"You almost got caught."

"So did you."

His expression grim, he drew in some air to argue with me.

"Listen," I didn't give him the chance to respond. "They caught you unawares this morning. As smart and strong as you are, you don't have a pair of eyes in the back of your head. You could use someone to watch your back. You said you trust me, let me help you." He hesitated, and I added hurriedly, "I can't sit here not knowing if you're dead or alive. I'm armed. I've proven I can handle myself. Let me come with you, please."

I knew Vrateus would rather keep me in hiding while he did everything on his own. A few days ago, I would have probably preferred to wait it out, too. The mess hall was not my favorite place to visit.

As strong as Vrateus had always been, however, I'd also witnessed his vulnerabilities. In the past couple of days, he had been nearly poisoned to death then almost decapitated by his own crew. He needed me, and I needed to be with him.

I closed the distance between us, circling his waist with my arms.

"What if someone finds me hiding here while you're gone? Can't you see?" I rubbed his nose with mine. "Together we're stronger than apart."

His chest heaved with a long breath.

"Stay close." He tightened his arms around me. "Do not let anyone come between us. And if you have to shoot, aim to kill."

"Don't worry about me." I exhaled in relief, glad he was giving in and we didn't have to part again. "Focus on what you need to do. I'll take care of myself."

He moved his hands over the belts and holsters strapped to my body, inspecting all my weapons.

"Don't let anyone close." He stuffed a spare power cell for my gun into my boot.

"I won't."

"There are benefits to keeping you with me, considering the circumstances." He nodded somberly, as if trying to convince himself. "It's best to stay together."

He shoved aside the shelf unit in front of the gap leading to the library, then turned back to me quickly. His hand on the back of my head, he kissed me, fast and passionate.

"Be safe." He leaned his forehead against mine.

"Good luck," I whispered, smiling as encouragingly as I could manage.

Chapter Twenty-Three

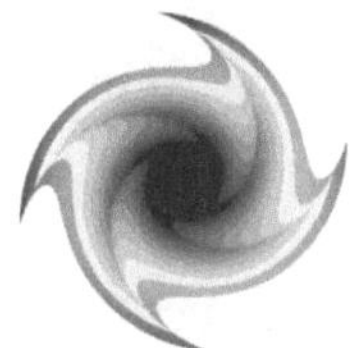

Svetlana

I'd promised to watch his back.

Now, as we walked down the corridor, I paid close attention to our surroundings. We weren't holding hands, keeping them free for weapons. I held my gun in my right hand and a knife in my left. Vrateus had both of his guns out of their arm holsters and in his hands.

The stench of decomposing bodies hit my nostrils as we approached the doors to my room. The dead aliens that Vrateus and I had killed yesterday lay in the same positions we'd left them. No one had bothered to dispose of them, though some bodies showed clear signs of cannibalism.

Vrateus's jaw muscles clenched as he made his way around the corpses. I followed less than a foot behind him, glancing over my shoulder once again.

As we turned around the bend in the wall, the entrance to the mess hall came into view.

It was much quieter here than I remembered. Some males lay

by the wall in the corridor, impossible to tell whether they were alive or dead.

One got up to his feet at the sight of us.

"You again..." he gaped at Vrateus, quickly giving a sign to someone inside the mess hall.

More crew members rose from the floor, joined by a few rushing out to join them. Armed with long, jagged pieces of metal, they menacingly moved our way.

"Keep back, or I'll shoot," Vrateus warned, raising his weapons.

Snarling—their teeth bared, jaws and mandibles snapping—they kept advancing on us.

Vrateus opened fire. I jumped aside, ducking from a piece of metal hurled my way. The sharp edge caught my upper arm. Thankfully, the material of my suit held. The blow hurt but left no cut.

I bit my lip, swallowing the cry of pain, afraid it would divert Vrateus's attention to me. He couldn't afford to be distracted right now.

Two aliens snuck up behind us somehow, rushing us from the back. I aimed and shot quickly, leaving neither of them a chance to throw the long rods they wielded.

"Are you all right?" Vrateus asked over his shoulder, his attention on the entrance to the mess hall.

"I'm fine. Let's go."

Holding both guns up, he moved forward. A few of the males piled by the wall stirred.

"Down," Vrateus ordered, pointing one of his guns in their direction.

Either realizing the threat or out of the habit of obeying his authoritative tone, they froze.

He entered the mess hall. Keeping my gun pointed at those in the corridor, I quickly glanced around him and into the hall.

The room looked like an explosion had taken place. Every piece of furniture had been upturned. Debris, spilled wine, and remnants of food littered the floor, along with puddles of vomit and who knew what else.

The aliens lay and sat everywhere, some still chewing or drinking, others already motionless. A few of the climbing species clung to the walls at various heights.

A huge pile of scrap metal had been erected in the center with a chair placed on the very top of it. Crux reclined in his makeshift throne with the other *errocks* lounging below him. Leaning against the pile, Wyck was chewing on what appeared to be a *vasai* leg. Chained to him, Lesh lay at his feet. All three of his heads were gnawing on a long bone.

Everyone who was still alert snapped to attention as Vrateus entered.

"What a mess you've made, crew." He curled his lip in disapproval. "It's disgusting. You've been without your captain for barely a day and look at this place!"

A few of them shifted uneasily, glancing around the trashed mess hall.

"They have a new captain." Crux rose to his feet.

Due to his massive size, he looked impressive, towering over the room from the height of the metal junk pyramid.

There was no graceful way to climb down it, though. Crux scrambled to the ground, sliding and tripping over his feet. Once on the floor, he stood tall again, his fists on his hips.

"Great to see you here," he smirked. "Now, you'll finally be executed. The female is mine, as she should've been all along."

Other *errocks* moved closer, flanking their leader. The rest of the crew, however, stayed where they were, staring with confusion at the two men who both claimed the title of the captain.

"Relinquish your claim to my position," Vrateus said calmly. "Or deal with the consequences."

"I'm *relinquishing* nothing!" Crux spat on the floor. "Hey boys!" he shouted, "Grab this phoney. As your captain, I give you my permission to do with him as you please." He shifted his weight to another foot. "And bring the girl here. Will you?"

Everyone in the room seemed to freeze for a moment. Back to back with Vrateus, I moved my gun in a slow arch, gauging where the next attack would come from.

One of the *kreers* let go off the wall. With a high-pitched wail, he grabbed a loose cable dangling from the ceiling and swung our way.

I shot. The *kreer* crashed to the floor, blood trickling out of the smoldering wound in his chest.

"You're good?" Vrateus asked me, keeping his gaze on Crux.

"Fine," I bit out, forcing myself to relax my grip on my weapons, since my hands had started to cramp and shake with tension.

He addressed his rival, "You can't just proclaim yourself the captain, Crux."

"Well, *you* did."

"Right. After I'd killed Raex in an honest fight. I didn't *poison* him in secret, like a coward." He swept the room with his gaze, raising his voice to get the attention of anyone who could still focus on what was happening. "You have to earn the title by winning it."

"Do you want to fight me?" Crux folded his arms over his chest.

"Yes."

"Well, you're too late, I'm already the captain."

It surprised me that Crux wouldn't jump at the chance to fight. He seemed to be the one who would welcome any opportunity for aggression. I wondered if he felt intimidated by Vrateus, despite the *errock's* obvious size advantage.

"You're not." Vrateus shook his head. "I'm still here. And I challenge you to fight for the title if you want to keep it." He spread his arms wide, slowly turning around the room. "What say you, the dwellers of the Dark Anomaly? Do you want to watch me fight Crux for the chance to be your leader once again?"

Crux twitched uneasily.

"He'd force you to work again!" he yelled quickly. "He'd lock up the wine and make you fight under his rules. He'd forbid you to eat whatever and whoever you want!"

He said all of that as if those were all bad things. How could forbidding them from eating each other be viewed as a negative?

It boggled my mind.

"I will bring order and discipline back," Vrateus said, loud enough for his voice to carry across the entire room. "With me, you will never have to worry about running out of food or wine. We'll always have lights on and enough oxygen to breathe. If you follow my rules, you will not have to fear for your life or your safety."

Now, *these* promises sounded appealing to me. The males, however, didn't jump at his words. They weren't rallying behind Crux either, which was better than nothing.

"Do you want to see a fight?" Vrateus knew his people better than I did, for they all perked up at that opportunity. Even some of those who had appeared to be corpses piled up by the walls stirred, coming to life. "No rules. The winner becomes the one true captain, with no further challenges from the loser."

This sounded really good if Vrateus won. If he lost, however...I dreaded to think what it would mean for him. For us.

A swell of approving screams and roars rolled from wall to wall. Everyone seemed to be eager to watch a brutal battle with no rules.

I kept my guard up, making sure no one would jump in, in their excitement. Everyone seemed impatient for the fight to start—many might want to join in themselves.

"No weapons." Crux moved into the center of the room, finally accepting the challenge. "I'll rip you to pieces with my bare hands."

I stepped closer to a wall.

"No weapons." Vrateus nodded, backing up to me. Tearing his shirt off over his head, he unbuckled the gun holsters from his thighs and forearms then the dagger's sheath from his chest, tossing them all on the floor at my feet.

With a brief encouraging smile for me, he walked to the center of the room. Broad-shouldered and bronze-skinned, he moved with grace and efficiency.

This was the first time I'd seen Vrateus without his shirt.

The wide strip of white fur peppered with gray and black on his head and nape continued down between his shoulder blades, thinning into a narrow trail along his spine that disappeared into his pants. The fur on his forearms tapered at his elbows, leaving his upper arms and shoulders bare from it.

Three long, rugged scars ran across his left side, parallel to each other. They must have been left by a set of claws some time ago. A crescent of small round scars on his right shoulder could have been from fangs and teeth.

Strangely, seeing the scars on his body gave me some encouragement. They were a reminder that Vrateus was a survivor. He had fought for his life ever since he was a little boy. I had to trust his skills and his abilities.

Still, my heart ached at the sight of him next to the massive form of Crux when they stood facing each other. Whereas Vrateus looked strong and tall, wired with thick ropes of well-defined muscles, Crux was a mountain of hard flesh, capable of crushing a person to death under one of his enormous fists.

"You're dead, *captain*." Crux smirked. "As will be the female when I'm done with her."

"We'll see—"

Crux didn't let him finish, rushing him without waiting for the signal to start.

No rules.

I tightened my grip on the gun, my hands slick with sweat.

Leaping aside, Vrateus narrowly escaped being knocked off his feet by Crux. Leaner than the *errock*, Vrateus was faster on his feet, too. Though Crux still showed some unexpected agility for his size. He landed a blow on Vrateus's shoulder, making him stagger back several paces.

I gasped, my heart speeding up with worry. My attention on the fight, I nearly missed a *kreer* creeping my way along the wall. His hands and feet splayed flat on the surface for a better grip, he snaked one skinny tail my way. A smirk slanted his lipless mouth, drool dripping to the floor from both corners of it.

"Back off." I pointed my gun at him, stepping over the pile of weapons Vrateus had left for me to guard. One of the *kreer's* tails twitched that way, too, and I fired, shooting it off.

He wailed, scurrying away and up the wall. No blood dripped from the stump of his tail, the small wound fully cauterized by the laser blast.

With a loud roar, Crux launched at Vrateus who rolled out of his way at the last second. Following the momentum, Crux slammed into the wall, crashing into the *kreer* who'd tried to attack me.

Enraged by his failure, the *errock* pivoted on his heel, searching for Vrateus with blood-shot eyes.

The night of drinking obviously slowed his movements. I was glad now that Vrateus had been wise enough to get some rest. *His* moves remained quick and efficient.

Lowering himself into a crouch, his tail swaying to aid his balance, Vrateus met Crux's next attack with a well-placed kick to the groin.

No rules. It worked both ways.

Howling in pain, Crux doubled over, both hands pressed between his legs.

Not giving him a chance to recover, Vrateus leaped onto the *errock's* back, hooking his arm around Crux's massive neck.

The *errock* growled. Clawing at Vrateus's arm, he arched his back, attempting to toss him off. Vrateus grabbed his wrist, squeezing his arm harder and crushing the *errock's* windpipe.

Crux's face turned deep burgundy. The veins in his forehead bulged as if ready to burst. His legs shook. With a strangled grunt, he collapsed to his side, crushing Vrateus's leg under his bulk.

A wave of shouts, growls, and roars rolled throughout the room. It was impossible to tell if it was the noise of approval or aggression. Either way, the crowd obviously appreciated the fight, whether or not they cared about its outcome.

Eyes glistening with aggression, a *dimo* moved toward Vrateus and Crux as they wrestled on the floor. He obviously intended to join in the violence.

"Back!" I yelled at him, raising my gun.

He paid me no attention. Cracking his knuckles and licking his lips, he hungrily eyed the fight.

"I said *back*!" I yelled louder. A surge of adrenaline rushed through me with heat and cold.

Getting no reaction from him, I pulled the trigger. The laser blast seared through the plated layer on the *dimo's* shoulder.

Turning his attention to me, his eyes glowing red with rage, the male rushed my way.

"Stay back," I gritted through my teeth, aiming at his face where his plated armour was thinner.

He didn't slow down, and I pulled the trigger again.

The laser blast burned through his eye, incredibly, hardly slowing his advancement on me. I kept pressing on the trigger, holding the gun steady until the ray worked its way through the *dimo's* brain and he crashed to the floor.

"Anyone else?" I pointed my gun at the room, trying hard to stop my hands from shaking. Everything inside me vibrated with tension. No matter how many I'd killed, it didn't seem to get easier.

Thankfully, not that many of those present were paying attention to me, the focus of most was on Crux and Vrateus.

Holding his opponent in the headlock, Vrateus kept squeezing.

The *errock*'s eyes finally closed, and he croaked, "Mercy…"

Vrateus released Crux from his grip, freeing his leg then climbing to his feet.

My heart fluttered with relief and gratitude at seeing him standing tall.

Victorious.

He faced his crew.

"I am your one true captain," he said, slowly moving his gaze across the room. "You live under *my* rules, or you don't live at all."

One thing this bunch of criminals and degenerates seemed to understand better than anything was the pure power of dominance.

Vrateus had no weapons on him. They could rush him, crush him, destroy him—had they had the will to act together. Instead, they remained where they were, held in place by the authority in his voice. Submitting to the winner of the fight.

He knew his people well. He had already made them submit once before. And he had just done it again.

"Now, clean up this mess." He tipped his chin at the garbage littering the floor. "And bring me the key to the wine storage, this instant."

Shifting from their position and peeling off the walls, the crew moved to obey their captain's orders.

Grabbing the holsters with his weapons off the floor, I stepped closer.

Vrateus stretched his arm my way.

"Come here. How are you?" He pulled me in for a firm hug.

"Relieved that we're both still alive." I smiled.

Crux groaned on the floor, rolling to his belly.

Vrateus released me from his embrace, watching the *errock* gather his arms and legs under him.

"What are you going to do with him?" I asked, taking a step back, just in case.

"Accept me as your captain," Vrateus demanded from the *errock*. "Or die."

Crux rose to one knee, rubbing his neck.

"You are my captain." He scowled, tossing Vrateus a glare from under his thick brow ridge.

"You can't let him live," I said to Vrateus, quietly.

A few weeks ago, I would not have believed myself capable of this kind of bloodthirsty ruthlessness, but things had changed. The time I'd spent on the Anomaly had changed me, too.

Keeping Crux alive would be like having a knife aimed at Vrateus's throat. Having been publicly humiliated by his defeat, Crux would strike again. I had no doubt about that.

"He asked for mercy, I have to grant it to him," Vrateus objected, adding, "How can I demand from others to respect my laws if I don't follow them myself?"

He then addressed the room again, "Crux will be whipped for usurping my power. A hundred lashes. Tomorrow morning. He is no longer my second in command." He gestured my way, unexpectedly. "Svetlana is."

The combined roar of everyone thundered through the room. The males paused in their tasks for a moment, eyeing me—their jaws dropped, mandibles slackened, mouths hanging open. Astonished, I turned around to face Vrateus.

"The fuck she is!" With a filthy curse, Crux slammed into me from behind. His meaty arm around my chest, he squeezed my neck with his other hand. "You'll do as I say, or I'll snap her neck in half."

"Don't hurt her!" Vrateus raised his hands, pure horror flashing through his eyes.

My arms pressed to my body, my feet lifted off the floor as Crux crushed me with his brute strength. I couldn't even draw a breath, there was no room for my chest to expand.

The sensation of the gun handle in my hand registered with me.

I bent my arm, wedging the barrel between my back and Crux's front. I angled it at his belly, then pressed the trigger.

He howled in pain. His arms flexed, squeezing the last drops of air out of my lungs, then fell off me. The massive *errock* crashed to the floor at my feet, and I leaped away from him in horror.

"Svetlana!" Vrateus caught me in his arms.

"I broke your rules," I rasped, my throat sore and closing in on itself. Wrapped in Vrateus's embrace, I glanced back at the disembowelled Crux, his legs contracting with their last spasms. "I killed the loser of the fight."

"It wasn't your fight." Vrateus kissed my face, stroking my hair.

He was wrong.

Every fight involving him was now mine, too. Anyone who threatened Vrateus was a direct threat to me. I had a feeling this was not our last fight, either. But at least, there were two of us.

From now on, we would fight all our battles together.

And together we were twice as strong.

His arm wrapped tightly around my shoulders, Vrateus addressed his crew again, "Anyone who dares to touch her again will be shot on the spot. Svetlana has my permission to carry weapons." He met my eyes. "Because she is the only one whom I trust. Completely."

Chapter Twenty-Four

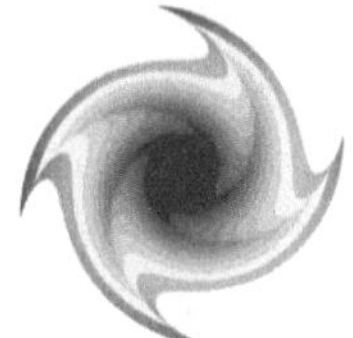

Svetlana

Justice on the Dark Anomaly was swift.

Vrateus ordered some whippings as punishment for disobedience. Those were to be carried out the following morning.

Considering the sorry state of the habitable sector, most punishments ended up being an increased amount of labor for everyone.

Vrateus questioned Tunkrox, the wiry alien who'd handed him the canteen with the poisoned wine. The male confessed that he stole some *fuhnid* mushrooms from the gardens while Crux was distracting Malahki.

Together, they then squeezed the juice and mixed it with wine. Apparently, Crux had promised Tunkrox an unlimited supply of berry wine for the job. And judging by the state and appearance of Tunkrox, the *errock* had fulfilled that promise.

The Tunkrox's execution was ordered for the very next day.

"How about the *errocks*?" I asked Vrateus when we finally returned to his room for a few hours of sleep later that night.

"They'll be whipped," he replied, taking off his clothes then removing all his weapons.

"Do you still want to keep them as your personal guard?"

"They have been very effective in that role."

"*Have been.*" I made a face. "Until they betrayed you. What if they do it again?"

"The better reason to have them close—easier to keep an eye on them."

"So, you want them to resume their positions?"

"Yes. Wyck will be their lead now. I'll announce it tomorrow." He crawled under the covers of his narrow bed and joined me.

I scooted aside, to give him space, but he drew me closer.

"Are you sure about Wyck?" I thought back to the moment I caught the young *errock's* glare after I had shot Crux. Wyck's bright, yellow eyes were full of undiluted hatred for me. I had no illusions I'd made a mortal enemy of him by killing one of his kind.

The better reason to have him close.

"All right. Wyck it is then." I drew in a deep breath. "Tomorrow will be a long day."

"Try to get some sleep." Vrateus kissed my forehead.

The metal frame of his bed cut into my side, and I made a mental note to have the bed from my room moved into his. It was much wider and would be more comfortable for the two of us.

A lot of things still needed to be done, big and small. I remembered how exhausted Vrateus always seemed to be before. Now, I was there, to share the burden and the responsibility of running the Dark Anomaly with him.

And together, we were stronger.

The whippings all took place in the mess hall. Vrateus wanted the entire population present to witness the punishments.

He'd ordered the *errocks* to flog each other. They growled and glared with hatred at those whipping them. That was why Vrateus did it in the first place. By pitting *errocks* against each other, he ensured they wouldn't be as quick to unite against him any time soon.

Maybe, his crew learned their lesson while watching the red welts swell on their comrades' backs after each blow of the whip. Or maybe, they mostly enjoyed another display of violence.

Either way, the punishment had been served.

Afterwards, we all moved to the airlock across from the storage room with the spacesuits. Two of the *errocks* brought Tunkrox out from his holding cell.

"I did it!" he yelled, kicking his long legs out, lashing with his thin tail, and thrashing in the *errocks'* grip. "I drank the wine, ate the mushrooms, and chewed on the flowers… And I'll do it all again!"

"Do you understand why you're being executed?" Vrateus asked at the entrance to the airlock.

I recited the charges, finishing with, "Under the law of the Captain of the Dark Anomaly."

"Captain?" Tunkrox turned to Vrateus with a sly smile. "Fuck you, Captain!" He broke into a series of uncontrollable giggles that turned to loud hiccups after a while. "We don't need a captain here. We need more wine!"

Vrateus gave the signal to proceed, and the *errocks* shoved Tunkrox into the airlock, closing the door behind him. The lanky alien swayed on his feet, glancing over his shoulder once. Then the outer door opened, blowing him out into open space.

I watched the chitin on Tunkrox's body crack and tear as his flesh underneath expanded in the vacuum of space. What was left of him was strewn over the wreckage of the crashed ships. I felt only the slightest tug of sympathy. The predominant feeling was that of relief that with his death there was one less threat to Vrateus and me.

Vrateus's words from long ago rose in my memory, *"Around here, there is no law but mine."*

The Federation had no power on the Dark Anomaly. Intergalactic laws did not exist here. The Federation Forces didn't matter.

Around here, everything was different.

Apparently, I was now different, too.

Chapter Twenty-Five

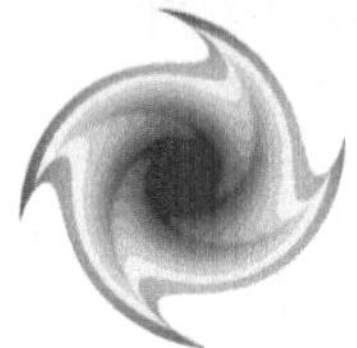

Svetlana

A *month later, Anomaly time…*

I woke up in my old bed that had been moved to Vrateus's room, replacing his narrow metal one. The sound of running water told me he must be in the shower.

It had been a month since Vrateus fought Crux and won. Twenty-five years had passed on Earth. Combined with the time I had spent here before that, it had been nearly half a century since I'd left that world. Every day added another ten months to that time.

Chances were that almost everyone I'd ever known as adults was already dead. That thought didn't feel as crushingly devastating as it had a few weeks ago.

Oddly, knowing that probably no one alive would know about me made me miss life on Earth less. I still dreamed I was running on the grass or swimming in the ocean, now and then. But those were the same dreams I'd had back on the space station during my mission.

I'd said goodbye to Earth long before I crashed on the Dark Anomaly.

By choosing a career in space exploration, I knew I wouldn't be spending much time on the ground for the rest of my life. Just like my parents before me, I had willingly dedicated my life to working off planet, giving up on personal relationships and the potential for a family.

With Vrateus, I had unexpectedly gained some of that back.

He was closer to me than anyone I'd ever had in my life. Our relationship was more intimate—physically and emotionally—than I'd ever had with anyone else.

Stretching under the soft, puffy covers, I rubbed the remnants of sleep out of my eyes.

"There you are." I smiled at Vrateus as he walked out of the bathroom naked, drying himself off with a towel.

I couldn't leave the Dark Anomaly, but I'd gained a different kind of freedom here. I was free to spend the rest of my life with the man I loved. Something my parents never had. Something I'd never thought I could do, either.

"Morning." The fur on his head was still soaking wet, water dripping from the large, soggy curl over his forehead.

"Come here." I sat up, patting the mattress next to me.

When he sat down, I took the towel from his hands, drying his head and shoulders for him. The damp fur stood up in spikes when I finished, and I smoothed it with my hands the best I could.

He smiled at me while I arranged the curly wave over his forehead. The luxurious softness of his fur clashed with the rest of this man who seemed to be made entirely of hard planes and sharp edges.

"Here you go." I fluffed it up a bit, whipping it into its usual shape. "Looks good." I placed a kiss on the corner of his smiling mouth. "Devastatingly handsome. Like always."

"How about this?" He swung his soggy tail into my hands.

"You want me to groom *all* of you?" I tilted my head, raising an eyebrow.

"Could you?" His smile grew teasing. Mischief twinkled in his eyes, brightening their burnt-orange color.

"Well…" I pretended to be annoyed but wrung the water out of his tail with the towel. "If you insist."

He smiled wider. I enjoyed touching him, and I knew he treasured it. Deprived of any physical contact most of his life, he soaked in my attention like a sponge.

From the base of his tail, I moved the towel to his chest, trailing it down his chiseled abs and lower.

The grin slipped from his face as my fingers brushed by his erection. It immediately jumped from half-mast to fully erect.

"Now what?" I glanced up at his face.

He lifted an eyebrow at me, expectantly.

Dropping the towel, I stroked him with my hands. The dark, hard ridges swelled along his shaft, making me tingle with anticipation, for I knew how tantalisingly sweet they rubbed when he was inside me.

"Now, it's my turn to do some *grooming*," he growled, rolling me onto my back. "Only, I'll do it with my mouth."

He dragged his long tongue between my legs, and I rolled my head on the pillow, moaning deep in my throat. Heat flooded me, prickling my skin with pleasure and making my toes curl.

We had things to do this morning. I knew we did. Only I could no longer remember what they were. Nothing seemed to matter.

Even as an inexperienced virgin, Vrateus had been able to make me feel things no one else ever could. Now, after a month of eagerly learning everything about my body, he masterfully played it like a well-tuned instrument.

Easing out his claws, he lightly scraped along the skin of my thighs then up my sides to my breasts. I moaned louder as he found my nipples, squeezing them lightly between his fingers.

He swirled his tongue inside me, and my hips jerked as pleasure rushed through me.

Promptly sliding up my body, he fitted himself between my thighs. I opened my legs wider, lifting my hips to meet him as he fitted himself at my opening then slipped inside.

"It's like coming home, Svetlana..." he murmured in my ear, starting to move. "Every. Single. Time."

I was his home now, and he was mine.

Hugging him closer, I let the pleasure roll through me with his every thrust.

After a few pumps, he flipped me to my stomach. I bent my knees, lifting my hips up for him, and he entered me again, from behind this time.

The ridges along his length tugged and rubbed all the right places inside me. The soft fur of his tail brushed around my thigh. Then the tip slid between my legs, finding my most sensitive spot.

Vrateus growled, gripping a handful of hair on the back of my head. The sting at the roots spread pleasure along my scalp and the rest of my body, making me groan in delight.

He thrust harder. The growls of his pleasure mingled with my loud moans. The intensity was building up as he pumped his hips with increasing speed and ferocity.

"Oh, yes..." I breathed out as the orgasm exploded through every cell of my body.

Throwing his head back, he growled through his clenched teeth as his release rocked us both.

When he collapsed next to me, I held him close. Raking my fingers through his fur, I whispered, "We're going to build a good life here, Vrateus."

At that moment, I truly believed that it was possible. We had found our kind of happiness on the Dark Anomaly. As long as we stayed together, everything was within our reach.

That was how he made me feel—happy, even in the middle of hell.

In the afternoon, Vrateus took me out to the surface of the Dark Anomaly. He needed to check the power supply panels. They converted the Anomaly's lights into energy, which was used to power the life inside it. One of them seemed to be malfunctioning, possibly requiring some repairs.

Dressed in spacesuits, we exited through the airlock, then walked along the surface of the giant disk, just a few feet away from the edge. Vrateus checked the connection of each panel, while I fell behind.

Stopping between two power panels, I took out the two polished metal balls I'd made from some parts collected from my ship.

I made sure that the camera on my helmet was on and that it was connected to the computer on my arm. Lowering myself into a crouch, I set one ball on the surface. With the tool I'd brought with me, I shot the ball to roll toward the center of the Anomaly with a predetermined speed. It bounced and hopped over the uneven surface, rolling to a complete stop about a hundred feet away from me.

The gravity along the circumference of the disk seemed to be the same as it was inside.

I glanced up, toward the bulging center of the Anomaly. Far in the distance, it rose from the disk as a smooth, perfectly rounded dome the size of a mountain, completely black. Not even the vivid dancing lights around us reflected in its hemisphere.

Setting the second ball on the ground, I shot it to follow the exact trajectory of the first one, with a higher velocity. The second ball rolled faster, slamming into the first one and knocking it forward.

Brought back into motion, the first ball rolled toward the center, slowing down again.

When it reached a certain point, however, the speed of the first ball increased again. Speeding up, it rolled faster and faster, until the shiny, silver shape of it blended far in the distance with the bulging mass in the middle.

On the surface of the disk, the Anomaly pulled things to its center. I took a note never to wander past the power panels, lest I be dragged there myself.

I made sure that everything I'd just done had been recorded on the camera on my helmet. I had already inputted the exact mass and dimensions of the two balls. And the computer now calculated the speed and rate of increase in their velocity.

When I got back to the library, I would add all this data to what Vrateus and I had collected so far. I'd also add the new calculations I was planning to do.

I'd left Earth to explore the unknown. Crashing here was a tragedy. But it gave me the opportunity to be closer to the Anomaly than any human had ever been. For as long as I lived, I would study it.

I would never stop exploring.

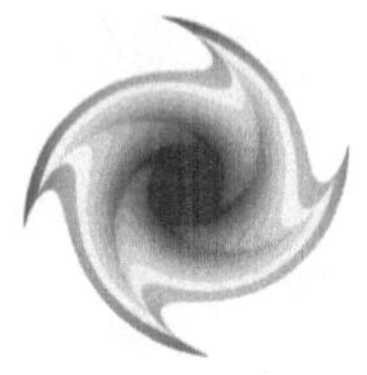

EPILOGUE

Vrateus

"There is the man I love," Svetlana greeted him as soon as he entered their room.

She looked stunning. The bright, flowery dress she wore made the lights of the Anomaly behind her pale in comparison. She had always been the most beautiful thing to him.

A warm trickle of pleasure rippled down his skin at her words. This was the first time he heard the word "love" from her. Judging by the gaze she gave him—her dark eyelashes fluttering like the wings of a bird he'd only ever seen in videos—she knew what she'd said, and she meant it.

"I love you, too." He gathered her into his arms, burying his face in her hair.

She sank her fingers into the fur on the back of his neck, stroking down his spine. The pleasure of her touch flooded his groin with heat. It happened so much more often than it used to before her.

Nuzzling the side of her neck, he nibbled on her skin.

"What took you so long? It's way past dinnertime," she murmured. "I was starting to worry."

Every now and then, he still forgot about dinner, getting caught in one of the many tasks that needed to be done in order to keep life on the Dark Anomaly going.

"Sorry, I lost track of time. How are the gardens?"

"Good. The flour we made from the *laahon* grain worked out amazingly well."

The only reward for saving Vrateus from the poison that Malahki had asked for was to spend more time with Svetlana. The request puzzled Vrateus, but Malahki had explained he needed someone knowledgeable and trustworthy to help with gardening.

Svetlana had easily agreed to that, eager to learn more about plant life on the Dark Anomaly. Vrateus had spent several days with them until he was completely satisfied he could trust the *damirian* to protect Svetlana. He felt comfortable leaving them alone for a couple of hours a day.

Besides the gardening, Svetlana had also taken over meal preparation on the Anomaly, under the condition that no one except for Vrateus or Malahki would be allowed to enter the kitchen.

Taking these two tasks completely off his shoulders and helping him with many others, she'd considerably lightened his workload. Now, he even had some free time, which he always preferred to spend with her.

"Hungry?" she leaned back, smiling. "I made *pizza* for dinner." Delight sparkled in her dark eyes, bringing out the golden specks of happiness he loved seeing in them.

"*Pizza*?" he asked, confused. He wished to share in her excitement, but the translator failed to deliver a word he'd understand.

Svetlana had been gathering various bark, seeds, and roots from the garden. She then used them as ingredients while cooking different dishes and experimenting with flavors.

"Look!" She proudly gestured at the low table she had set with pretty dishes he had collected from various storage rooms for her.

A bunch of large, bright flowers stood in a jewel-encrusted carafe. Berry wine glistened blood-red in two crystal goblets.

“I have been playing with this recipe for a week now, testing different ingredients from the kitchen and the garden.” Svetlana pointed at the flat disk of dough covered with black melted goo that suspiciously reminded him of tar. “It’s a bit scary-looking,” she admitted, with a slight frown. “But it tastes just like a real *pizza* from back home, I swear.”

He must have been staring at the offensive disk a little too long, since she shifted uneasily. “If you don’t like it, I have some stew from the kitchen, too.

“No. I’ll try it.” He drew some air in through his nostrils. “It smells delicious.”

After a lifetime of eating some variation of the same dish, trying all her cooking experiments felt exciting. Even if they turned out truly inedible sometimes.

“Let’s have some *pizza*.” He took her in his arms again. “Just right after I do this.”

He lowered his mouth to hers.

A rush of familiar calm and pleasure descended upon him as he kissed her.

Just like coming home.

“Hey, Captain! There’s another crash!” Valmo, one of the few *akuks* on the Dark Anomaly, panted out of breath and choking with excitement. “Nocc and Wyck are fighting over the female. And they’re not following the rules!”

Immediately, Vrateus thought of Svetlana being the female in question. Wrath and terror flared in his chest, making his heart leap.

He had left her in the gardens with Malahki just a little while ago. Had something happened he’d not accounted for?

“Where are they?” He dashed out of the storage room, leaving Enkail to service the spacesuits on his own.

“On the very edge of the habitable segment, past the gardens.” Valmo was running slightly behind him, struggling to catch up despite the eight pairs of legs on the wiggling bottom half of his yellow-spotted body.

The main corridor seemed endless as Vrateus rushed from one end of it to the other. His heart burned with worry, threatening to burst out of his chest.

"Malahki!" He yelled into the entrance of the gardens as he passed by. The *damirian* was nowhere to be seen, which only intensified his panic.

He rushed further.

Around the last bend in the corridor, he nearly tripped over the cutting tool left on the floor. The outer wall gaped with a freshly cut opening. A couple of his crew members stood by, peeking inside it.

"Svetlana?" he asked, shoving them out of the way.

"She returned to your room a while back," someone said.

"She did?" Vrateus turned to face the speaker, Xoqaek, one of the few *ognats* who had survived the devastating effects of berry wine the day Crux had taken over.

"Malahki said she left," Gahot, a *yourlu*, added, his tentacles splayed on one side of the opening in the wall.

She was safe.

He let the thought trickle through his mind with a calming bliss.

"Malahki? Where is it?"

"Um…" Gahot looked around, confusion spreading on his face. "It was just here…"

Vrateus glanced inside the opening, into the interior of a brightly lit ship he had not seen before.

Only now Valmo's words about the crash had fully registered with him. Then, the understanding for the reason for the fight rushed in.

An unknown human female crouched low by the far wall of the room. Lesh kept hissing, tied to a piece of wreckage nearby. Wyck stood over her, his chest heaving fast and heavy, his gaze unhinged, and his knuckles bloody.

Standing on one knee, Nocc glared at him, blood trickling out of his nose and down his face.

At least two more humans lay on the floor behind them, their heads twisted at unnatural angles. Either they had died during the crash or had been killed shortly after, but they were obviously dead now.

"What is going on here?" Vrateus climbed inside, adjusting the grip on the guns in his hands.

"This does not concern you," Nocc rasped, smearing the blood on his face with the back of his hand. "You already have a female. You can't have them all."

A familiar combination of annoyance and worry rushed over Vrateus.

Another female.

He didn't talk to her. He refused to spare her a glance. A wave of fear and resentment rose in his chest. This female was not just a threat to the barely re-established order, her mere appearance here put the relatively safe existence of Svetlana into danger all over again.

He had managed to force his crew to view Svetlana as their superior. There were no more weekly sessions in the mess hall. With the new arrival, they could easily revert to treating her as an object to relieve their sexual tension—not to mention the disturbance that was already happening.

"So, you have fought, I see." He moved his gaze from Nocc to Wyck. Judging by their positions, Wyck had won the last round. However, if Vrateus didn't stop them now, there could be many more. With the others now coming in, aggression buzzed in the air.

If he let the situation slip out of control now, many more of his crew might end up joining the dead humans on the floor.

"Wyck won?"

Wyck nodded as Nocc leaped to his feet, raising his fists.

"He is not getting her!"

"He *did* best you." Vrateus turned to the two at the entrance. Xoqaek and Gahot had entered, with many more of his crew climbing in or poking their heads through. "Was it a fair fight?" he asked Xoqaek and Gahot.

"Um… Sure." They nodded.

"It's not over yet!" Nocc roared.

"*I* say when the fight is over around here!" Vrateus raised his voice and his weapons. "And I'm saying this one is."

"Wyck can't have her," Enkail rumbled. The *dimo* obviously hadn't stayed behind to finish servicing the spacesuits. Vrateus made a note to discipline him later for not doing his work. "If she is the prize, then we all have to get a chance to fight for her, too!"

That was met with a loud rumbling of approval from everyone.

"No one is getting the female!" Vrateus shouted over the noise, lifting his arm to call for silence. "No one!"

Hostile glares of his crew clashed with his as he turned around the room.

"The rules will stay the same," he said firmly. "The female belongs to no one and to all of us."

"What do you mean?" The same question came from many mouths.

"She will be brought to the mess hall, weekly." The solution had worked well enough before. "You'll be getting your entertainment back!"

Svetlana had disliked the sessions in the mess hall. He had reasons to believe the new female might not be fond of them either. However, the priority was to dissipate the aggression crackling in the air.

And hopefully save some lives.

Another wave of rumbles rolled through the room. To his relief, it was thick with approval for his decision.

It occurred to him that the presence of another female on the Dark Anomaly might work to his benefit. Ever since he had discontinued the sessions in the mess hall, he had overheard plenty of comments and caught enough disgruntled glances tossed Svetlana's way. Having another female to resume the sessions would take the attention from Svetlana and ease the tension.

An unpleasant feeling scratched inside him, as if he were tossing the female to the pack of predators. And in a way, that was very much what he was about to do.

For Svetlana's peace and safety.

He would do anything for her.

"I won't be the one touching her, though," he said to his crew.

"Who will?" the crowd perked up, expectant.

Vrateus gave the new leader of the *errocks* an assessing stare. Younger than the rest of his brutal group, Wyck still shared most of the characteristics of his kind. He was just as aggressive, hot-minded, and rebellious as all the *errocks* on the Dark Anomaly. Since the death of Crux, Wyck had also shown signs of hostility toward Svetlana.

How long would a human female last in his care?

He glanced at Lesh. The ill-tempered *mahdi* had been one of several dozen of the animals, chained and caged in the cargo hold of a *yourlu* ship. It had crashed about nine years ago. All the *mahdi* had been killed and eaten within days. Some had been forced to fight each other—bloody, brutal battles instigated for entertainment. Both winners and losers ended up being butchered afterwards.

Only after Vrateus had taken the power had Wyck come to him with Lesh. He told Vrateus that he had saved the animal, hiding it in one of the side tunnels. He had fed it, trained it, kept it alive, and in return, the *mahdi* gave him his undivided loyalty.

Could Wyck's patience and kindness to the animal be translated into better treatment for the female?

There was no way to tell for sure, but Wyck was the best choice Vrateus had. Wyck had the power and the strength to defend someone in his charge. He would also have Vrateus's full support in doing so.

"As the leader of my personal guard, Wyck will have the honor of taking care of the female," he announced, loud and clear, making sure that none of the doubt he felt made it into his voice.

Nocc growled. Spitting on the floor he threw a heated glare at Vrateus, then stormed out, shoving everyone out of his way.

Vrateus added another mental note to his already longer-than-his-tail list: to watch Nocc more closely.

Wyck shuffled from foot to foot, uncertainly. *"Take care of the female"* obviously didn't make much sense to him in terms of specifics.

"Put her in Svetlana's old room. Bring her meals. Make sure no one touches her." Vrateus rubbed his face. No matter what, every new arrival was his responsibility. He was the captain, after all. He needed to make sure, though, that Wyck understood it differently, in this case. "She is fully under your protection. Do you understand? Her life and wellbeing are your responsibility."

Wyck threw a glare toward the female who sat quietly, a calculating expression on her face.

"Captain…" The *errock* shifted closer, turning his back to the rest of the crew and lowering his voice. "I don't want her."

"What?" Vrateus felt his eyebrows shoot up to his fur line. These must be the most shocking words he'd ever heard from a male on the Dark Anomaly. "Why did you just fight for her, then?"

Wyck rubbed the back of his neck, seemingly unsure about his own motives.

"I found Nocc between her legs. She shrieked and fought… He looked like he would kill her."

"So, you stopped him?"

"He was so much bigger than her. It didn't seem fair…" the *errock* mumbled. His voice trailed off, as if Wyck realized he wasn't making much sense, not enough to continue.

The little he'd said, however, only reinforced Vrateus's conviction to keep the new woman in Wyck's care.

"Keep her safe," he ordered. "If you want someone else to bring her to the mess hall instead of you, let me know by tomorrow night. You don't need to touch her yourself, but you do have to keep her well and alive. Understood?"

Wyck made a half-nod, half-shrug in reply. That would have to do.

"What about the second female?" the *errock* asked unexpectedly.

"What second female?" Vrateus replied sharply. Wyck better not be talking about Svetlana again.

"When I got here, there were two females, at first."

"Two?"

Wyck turned around, scratching his bald head in confusion. "Where did she go?"

"Xoqaek and Gahot. Have you seen another female here? Besides this one?"

Both stared at him with their mouths agape.

"Um… No, Captain."

"Just this one here."

Vrateus took a closer look at the bodies on the floor. There were actually four in total. All four appeared to be male. However, since they all wore the same pale-blue bodysuits as their female, it might be difficult to determine their gender right away.

"Could you have mistaken one of *them* for a female?" he asked Wyck. "This one seems to be as slim as she is." He pointed at one body with the toe of his boot. "Or this one. He has a rather soft, feminine face."

"Maybe…" Wyck frowned, uncertainly.

The female chose this moment to finally speak to Vrateus.

"You're the leader here," she stated, her voice shaky but firm enough considering the circumstances.

"Was there another human female on the ship?" Vrateus asked her. "Where did she go?"

She blinked.

"Another? No. Just me. I'm the only one left alive," she said, quickly. "Listen, I'm appealing to you as the leader—"

"No." Vrateus cut her off, shaking his head. "Wyck is in charge of you. Tell him anything you need." He turned on his heel, already assessing the amount of work that had to be done on this ship before he could call it a night. "Wyck, take her out of here, the rest of you…" he faced the males filling in the space. "You all will have to help me remove the equipment tonight."

"Captain!" the female snapped sharply, demanding attention.

"Listen." Wyck spoke to her directly. "What's your name?"

"I'm not talking to *you*," she bit off.

It looked like Wyck had his work cut out for him. This might be the most challenging task Vrateus had ever assigned to the young *errock*.

Well, they all had their share of work to do around here.

POWER

book 2

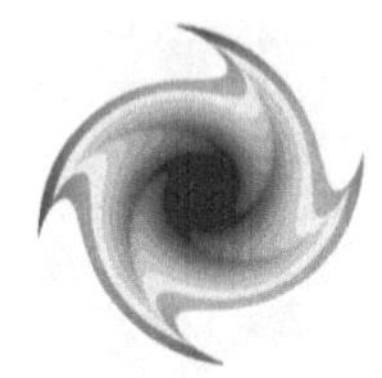

Chapter 1

Nadia

The impact was enormous. Much harder than I'd expected. The hull of our spaceship groaned and screeched. The walls warped and bulged. The panel closest to Val, one of our pilots, caved in, somehow breaking through the protective energy barrier around her chair. She screamed in pain as the armrest snapped, digging into her side.

Jose, the captain, had lost control during the landing, which turned into a crash. I'd caught the moment it happened. His eyes grew larger as he frantically ran his fingers over the control panel. His skin paled, and perspiration beaded on his forehead. No matter how hard he worked, he couldn't prevent our ship from slamming into the edge of the anomaly harder than even the worst of the landings during our training sessions.

Then, all went still and dark.

A moment later, the auxiliary system kicked in, flicking on the lights.

"Val!" Jose climbed out of his seat and rushed to his second-in-command who doubled over in her seat. "Are you okay?"

"I'm pretty sure I broke my rib," she groaned, pressing her hand to her side. "And I think I'm bleeding."

Like all of us, Val was wearing a pale-blue suit, covered with colorful logos from the collar to the boots. I saw no tearing in the material and no blood. It didn't mean she wasn't bleeding underneath it.

Lee, the scientist on board, clicked his seat belt off and jumped out of his chair. "We need to get her into the medical capsule."

Val groaned softly as Lee led her to the wall with the medical bed concealed inside.

"How is everyone else doing?" Jose rose to his feet, surveying the rest of us—two on-board engineers and me, the movie producer.

Yes, that was what I was—the movie producer. My sole purpose on the team was to record everything that could later be assembled into a movie, a documentary, or a series to air for profit. The footage would also provide visual evidence of whatever we discovered here.

The Earth Space Coalition had stopped exploration of the Anomaly GR-A8502 shortly after the disappearance of the scientist Svetlana Kostyk. She had been part of the team studying the mysterious anomaly from a station that orbited the nearby water world Omphi. She'd gone missing during a solo mission a little over fifty years ago. Her ship had lost all communications with the station, and neither the ship nor Svetlana Kostyk had ever been found.

Passionate about her work and new discoveries, it was believed that Svetlana might have come too close to the Anomaly and had been sucked in along with her ship.

Instead of shedding some light on the mysterious Anomaly, Svetlana had only added more mystery to this celestial body. Her disappearance sparked a number of speculations on what might be inside of it.

Five years ago, it had been proven that a solid core lay at the center of the unpredictable force field, renewing keen interest in exploring it further. The mission was deemed too risky by the Earth governments who refused to finance it. Luckily, several private corporations had stepped in, outfitting our expedition.

"Nadia? Are you okay?" Jose glanced my way, not leaving Val's side.

I climbed out of my chair, unsteadily. "I'm fine, I think—"

A screeching noise cut me off, then a fountain of sparks shot from the wall. Another malfunction? Were we not done crashing yet?

Both engineers rushed to the wall but were forced to keep their distance as the spray of sparks fanned in a wide circle. The melting paneling material dripped to the floor.

"Get in the suits, everyone!" Jose ordered. "We have a hull breach."

Lee quickly turned Val toward the hatch where our suits were kept. I ran after them.

With a slamming sound, an uneven oval cut-out of the wall fell in, followed by a smoky cloud with a chemical smell.

"What the—" I heard the confused voice of one of the engineers who was fully enveloped into the smoke. His voice was cut off by a wet crunching sound that I couldn't place at first.

A tall, dark figure emerged from the dissipating smoke that rolled off his shoulders like a cloak.

Then the motionless body of the engineer came into view. He lay on the floor, his neck twisted at an unnatural angle. My stomach roiled when it dawned on me what that wet-snappy sound had been. The monster that had just barged onto our ship had snapped my teammate's neck.

I stepped back, frozen in shock and horror. I'd never witnessed a murder before. Heck, I'd never seen any crime being committed right in front of me. Crime, in general, had been all but eliminated on all the main planets of the Federation, including Earth.

I kept staring at the motionless body on the floor, unable to move a muscle. The man who'd been a living, breathing, thinking individual just moments ago, was nothing but a corpse with its neck snapped.

Jose recovered first.

"We are a peaceful delegation!" He faced the newcomer—the *errock*, I recognized his species.

His yellow eyes narrowed as he gave each of us an assessing glare.

At least a few inches taller than the biggest man of my crew, the *errock* seemed twice as broad. His reddish skin darkened to gray on the hard ridges running along his arms and bald head. Wearing black pants, dark boots, and a wide utility belt, the male was topless.

Errocks were a civilized nation. Yet this individual's behavior was that of a feral, murderous animal.

The second engineer suddenly leaped on the newcomer's back with a laser knife clutched in his hand.

With a grunt, the *errock* grabbed the engineer's head and yanked it, twisting it with his hands. The human's neck snapped with the same wet cracking noise I'd heard earlier. I swayed on my feet, ready to barf.

"Oh, my God…" Val whimpered. She staggered backwards to the wall while pressing an arm to her side. Her face as white as the wall behind her, she slid to the floor.

"Run!" Jose shoved me aside, grabbing a long, heavy tool from the shelf in the suit storage.

Run! But where?

According to the glowing sign over the airlock by the control panel, outer space lay behind it. I had no time to get into my spacesuit. We were trapped on the ship, with the huge, murderous *errock* blocking the only exit he'd created. Where did he come from? Why was he killing everyone unprovoked?

I had no idea, but it was clear he wasn't going to stop. A murderous glimmer in his eyes, lips curved in a menacing smile, he faced Jose.

I anxiously darted my gaze along the walls and the ceiling around me, searching for an escape route, a place to hide, anything. Running to our sleeping cabin would only make it easier for the *errock* to corner me there.

My body shook. Everything inside me vibrated with horror and the need to escape.

The escape capsule!

Tripping over my feet, I dashed for the round door next to the suit storage.

From the corner of my eye, I caught the sight of Jose being hurled against the wall by the monstrous *errock*. Our captain's head dangled awkwardly, only attached to his body with muscles and skin.

Lee ran for the opening the *errock* had cut out, probably hoping to escape that way.

Val was lying on the floor next to the round table in our common area in the middle of the ship.

"Val!" I yelled. "Here!"

Curled into a ball, she didn't move. Was she dead, too? The monster must've gotten her already.

"Lee!" I screamed, stabbing my fingers into the control panel next to the entrance of the escape capsule. The door slid open, and I climbed in.

I poked my head out, searching for Lee. The *errock* held him over his head. He slammed our scientist over his knee, snapping the man's spine in half.

My head spun, terror lodging tight in my throat. I hit the panel on the other side of the door, locking myself inside.

The capsule was designed to take us off the Anomaly upon completion of our mission if the ship failed.

My entire team had been annihilated in seconds. Screw the mission, the documentary I was supposed to make, and the astronomical reward I'd been promised.

With trembling fingers, I strapped myself into one of the six seats inside the capsule and initiated the take-off sequence on the on-board computer.

I was the last survivor of our ill-fated expedition, and I was getting out of here.

A red warning flashed on the control panel in front of me.

"Not enough power to complete the take-off sequence."

What exactly did it mean? I feverishly searched my brain for any mention of this message during my year-long training for this mission.

The capsule was much smaller than the spaceship. Its engines, however, were many times more powerful than the ship's. The sole purpose of this thing was to take us off the Anomaly. Why wouldn't it do just that?

Had something been damaged during our crash landing? I punched more buttons on the control panel, trying to troubleshoot the problem.

The dreadfully familiar sound scraped against the capsule door from the outside.

The *errock*!

He had murdered my crew and was now cutting through the door of the capsule to get to me, too.

Again and again, I re-started the launch sequence, getting the same message.

"Not enough power."

The shower of hot sparks blew into the capsule. The *errock* was cutting through the door, and I was trapped here, like a mouse in a jar, with nowhere left to run.

Panic shot through me.

"How much power do you need? To lift off a capsule the size of a bus?" I yelled at the control panel. Shaking with anger and fear, I punched it with my fists.

I heard a loud thud behind me. The fine hairs on the back of my neck stood up as I sensed *his* presence inside the capsule. His heavy breathing reached my ear.

I didn't want to turn around and face him. Everything inside me urged me to curl into a ball and make myself invisible. Only, there was no place to hide in the capsule.

I'd been cornered.

"Where do you think you're going?" the *errock* growled, mockingly.

Hearing him speak somehow made him even more monstrous. He obviously was a self-aware, intelligent being, not an enraged animal. Yet, he had killed my entire team in cold blood.

His words spurred me into action. I scrambled to the wall, avoiding his hands as he reached for me, then scurried for the opening he'd just made.

If I made it past him, I could get off the ship the way he had come. Fingers crossed, there were no more creatures like him out there.

Tripping over my hands and feet in panic, I climbed out of the opening and back into the spaceship.

"Not so fast." The *errock's* heavy hand swiped me off my feet.

I fell face down. Then the enormous weight of the *errock* crashed on top of me.

Nearly crushed under him, I could barely breathe. Clawing at the floor tiles with my fingers, I attempted to crawl from under him, but that was like trying to shift a tank off me.

"I'll fuck you fast before anyone gets here," he growled in my ear, yanking at my suit. "But I *will* fuck you, even if it's the last thing I do."

He hooked his fingers into the neckline of my suit from behind, and tugged it down, almost choking me. The material held, frustrating him. Painfully grabbing on to my shoulder and hip, he flipped me over.

I came face to face with my attacker. The look in his yellow eyes terrified me even more than his actions. There was no thought in them, no emotion other than the unhinged, feral lust.

Pinning my hips under his pelvis, he straddled me.

The moment his chest lifted off mine, I greedily sucked some air into my oxygen starved lungs.

"Female," he smirked, pawing at my breasts through the suit. Leaning closer, he sniffed my neck. "Smell good, too. Good enough to eat." He dragged his tongue down my throat.

"No. Please…" I whimpered, already knowing that my pleas would make no difference to him. He acted as if he didn't even hear them, sniffing down my body.

Hooking his arms under my knees, he yanked them open and dropped his head between my thighs.

Around my core, I felt the heat of his mouth through the suit. Then a sharp pain blinded me as he bit down.

Anger cut through the terror from the pain. I thrashed in his arms, slamming my fists at his bald head. The three hard ridges running along his skull hurt my hands, but I didn't care. I didn't care about anything other than getting as far away from this monster as possible.

"Yeah, fight me." Satisfaction was thick in his growl as he effortlessly caught my both hands in one of his and fisted his other hand in my hair.

Tears sprang to my eyes at the pain on my scalp as he yanked.

"You didn't wait for me, Nocc," a new deep voice suddenly sounded from above us. "It's against the rules to board a new ship on your own."

Through the blurry film of tears, I saw another *errock* standing by. His arms folded across his chest, he seemed unaffected by the horrors that one of his species had inflicted on my spaceship and my person.

Did he come to join my attacker?

The thought made me wish I'd been killed along with Lee, Val, and the rest of my crew.

"Fuck off, Wyck," the one called Nocc gritted through his teeth. His hand in my hair, he yanked my head back, grinding his crotch against me.

I screamed again at the sudden pain in my neck. It felt like it would snap any minute. Maybe he would kill me sooner than later?

Wyck, the second *errock*, grabbed Nocc around his throat and shoved him off me. I was able to draw a full breath once again.

"What the fuck!" Nocc leaped to his feet with a speed shocking for his size.

Wyck shifted from foot to foot, as if confused by his own action.

"You're killing her," he muttered.

"Not yet. First, I'm going to fuck her!" Nocc bellowed, lunging for me again. "You can stay and watch, but don't you dare get in my way."

I rolled on the floor, scrambling away from him. Nocc tripped over my foot with a long, filthy curse.

Wyck quickly stepped over my legs, placing himself between Nocc and me.

"Kill those who are aggressive," he said. "Let the captain deal with the rest. Those are the rules for each new ship's arrival."

"Since when do you care about *his* rules?"

"There is no need to kill her." It sounded more like a suggestion than a call to action. My defender wasn't that passionate about defending me.

"I'm not killing her," Nocc snarled. "I'm fucking her. Just as soon as I get her out of that damn suit."

"Fucking and killing is the same in your case," Wyck observed calmly.

"In *our* case, Wyck." Nocc shoved at the other *errock's* shoulder. "Don't you forget that. *Errocks* are one and the same around here." He threw a lustful look down at me. "Help me strip her. I'll let you have what's left of her after me."

Thankfully, Wyck didn't seem convinced.

"Vrateus will need to see her first."

"*Him?* You know what will happen once he gets here. Nothing!" Nocc spat through his teeth. "I want my fun. Now."

He licked his lips, glancing down at me again.

"I think you should wait." That came as just another suggestion, though there was a certain power in Wyck's voice.

"Why? Is it because he's made you the leader of his guard?" Nocc scoffed. "Maybe you think he'll give *you* the female?"

Both of them appeared too absorbed by their arguing to pay me much attention. Pulling my legs up, I crab-walked away from them.

A hissing growl behind me sent a chill of dread down my spine. Swinging my head around, I came face to face with a creature that could've only come from a nightmare. All of it felt like a horrible dream.

A three-headed animal the size of a large dog scowled and hissed at me. Each of its mouths possessed several rows of sharp translucent teeth. A wet roar vibrated in all three of its throats.

I choked on my next breath as the monster lunged for me. With a clank, the chain around its middle neck stretched, yanking the beast backwards. It was chained to the railing on the wall I realized with relief as I scurried out of its reach.

Now, I was trapped between the three-headed hissing monstrosity and the two giant *errocks*.

"Get out of my way!" Nocc roared, sending a powerful blow at Wyck's jaw. The other *errock* staggered back, shaking his head.

"Fuck you, Nocc!" he yelled, lunging into a counterattack a moment later.

The two collided like giant boulders crashing into each other with the aftershock of the impact reverberating through the entire ship.

"You're not getting her, boy," Nocc squeezed through his clenched teeth, punching Wyck in the ribs.

"I am your fucking leader, Nocc!" Wyck pummeled Nocc's head, landing one blow after another. How the other *errock* remained conscious and upright after that beating was beyond me.

Frantically, I searched for a way around them. With the escape capsule proven useless, I needed to sneak past them to the cut-out that Nocc had made in the hull of the ship. I had no idea what lay beyond it, but it couldn't be much worse than what threatened me in here.

Stifling my whimpers of horror, I crawled over to Lee's broken body. Jose was lying just a short distance away from him. Both dead. Val was gone, though. Did Nocc move her? Or was she still alive? The hope that she might've survived this nightmare and gotten away rose inside me.

Maybe I could get out of here, too?

My hope was quickly squashed as someone blocked the exit—a group of aliens, it appeared. Though, I had no chance to see who exactly or how many.

"What is going on here?" A tall male entered.

I quickly retreated to the animal on the chain. Ironically, the horrible beast seemed to be less threatening than the men. At least the animal would just kill me quickly. A shudder of fear and misery rolled through me at my utter lack of options.

Hardly sparing me a glance, the newcomer moved toward the *errocks*. He was dressed better than them in a white voluminous shirt, tall boots, and dark brown pants. He had a white stripe of fur on his head and a long, fluffy tail. His species seemed familiar, like I'd seen them in a picture somewhere.

Themul.

I remembered the name for his kind. They came from a small, obscure planet on the fringes of the Federation. I'd never met one in person before.

Brought down to his knees, Nocc smeared blood on his face with the back of his hand. He spoke to the newcomer, "This does not concern you. You already have a female. You can't have them all."

Wyck had pummeled him hard enough to break skin on his lip and possibly the cartilage in his nose. The two had fought like savage beasts. Over me, "the female?" Did I somehow land in prehistoric times? Unfortunately for me, the lives of women weren't great back then.

I searched the floor for anything I could use as a weapon.

"So, you have fought, I see," the newcomer said to the *errocks*. "Wyck won?"

Nocc leaped to his feet. "He is not getting her!"

Other aliens started to climb in through the opening. There were several different species. I recognized a *dimo*, his tall bulky body covered in hard plates similar to a rhinoceros, a few *yourlus* with clusters of pale-blue tentacles instead of arms and legs, and at least one black-and-beige *ognat*, with eight pairs of skinny limbs all along his oblong body.

"He did best you," the *themul* said to Nocc.

My gaze fell on the handle of the laser knife under Lee's foot. One of the engineers had dropped it. Keeping an eye on the males debating who "deserved" to rape me first, I scooted closer to Lee's dead body.

The arguing grew louder.

"No one is getting the female!" the *themul* shouted fiercely over the noise. "No one!"

He lifted his hand, holding a gun. The sight of the weapon sent a new shiver of dread down my spine.

Sliding my hand under Lee's foot, I swiped the knife handle quickly and hid it inside the long sleeve of my bodysuit. The laser utility knife was a tool, not a real weapon. Still, having something to defend myself with made me feel a little better.

"She will be brought to the mess hall, weekly." The *themul* said, making me snap to attention. "You'll be getting your entertainment back."

This man appeared to have authority over the rest of them. The *errocks* had stopped fighting in his presence. Those who had come later kept their distance, remaining close to the opening in the wall.

"As the leader of my personal guard, Wyck will have the honor of taking care of the female," the *themul* announced.

What possibly could "taking care" mean in this place? I nervously balled my hands into fists, expecting Wyck to attack me any minute.

Nocc growled. Spitting on the floor, he threw a heated glare at the *themul* then stormed out, shoving everyone out of his way.

The man in the white shirt definitely was in charge here. Now, he was giving instructions to Wyck.

"What about the second female?" Wyck asked.

"What second female?" the *themul* replied sharply.

"When I got here, there were two females, at first."

Two?

Wyck had seen Val, then. Where did she go? I hoped for her sake that she'd managed to hide on the ship somewhere.

One of the aliens called the *themul* "captain," confirming my assumption that he must be the figure of authority here.

I took a bracing breath.

"You're the leader here," I addressed the captain.

"Was there another human female on the ship?" he asked me. "Where did she go?"

"Another?" I stared at him. There was no way I would tell him about Val. If she had managed to hide, she'd be better off staying hidden. "No. Just me. I'm the only one left alive," I said quickly. "Listen, I'm appealing to you as the leader—"

"No," the captain cut me off. "Wyck is in charge of you. Tell him what you need. Wyck, take her out of here, the rest of you..."

he faced the males filling in the space. "You all will have to help me remove the equipment tonight."

Everyone seemed to be moving on, leaving Wyck, the *errock* who had just fought for the right to rape me, "in charge" of me.

Panic spiked hot inside me. "Captain!" I scrambled to my feet.

"Listen," Wyck spoke to me. "What's your name?"

"I'm not talking to *you*," I dismissed him quickly, moving after the captain who had already started to organize his crew.

Wyck strode to me. I'd never realized how massive *errocks* really were. Maybe because I'd never stood next to one this close before. Or maybe this one was especially huge, even for his kind.

Much taller than an average human male, Wyck towered over me. His chest was above my eye level, his bulging muscles partially concealed by a short leather vest that was open in the middle.

"Fine," he said. "Don't talk to me, then. I don't care about anything you have to say, anyway."

He wrapped his enormous hand around my arm, dragging me toward the opening in the wall as if I were nothing more than a fly.

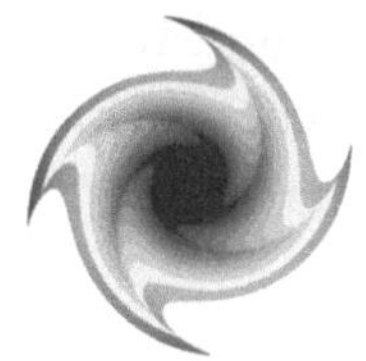

Chapter 2

Wyck

"Let me go!" The female thrashed in his grip as he took her out into the corridor.

Her scent, maddeningly tantalizing, assaulted his senses. Warm and feminine, she smelled…sweet, like the pollen sugar Svetlana used in her baking. Suddenly, he wondered if the female's skin would also taste sweet if he licked it…

"Get your filthy paws off me!" She made another attempt to yank her arm out of his hand.

The males, crowding the corridor, snickered and leered. Some laughed openly.

Wyck closed his eyes for a moment and quickly exhaled the air rich with her enticing sweetness. Reining in the wild urges her presence had caused wasn't easy, but he needed to focus. He was the newly appointed leader of the captain's personal guard, and he would be damned if he'd let this woman humiliate him in front of the crew.

"Move it." He clenched his jaw, shoving her ahead of him.

The crew parted as he walked her down the corridor, but he

lacked the authority of Vrateus to command their respect. They didn't remain quiet.

"Hey, Wyck, are you going to have fun with her?" Someone shouted from the back of the crowd.

"Can I get in on it, too?" Another one chuckled eagerly.

"Listen, you lost a bet three days ago. I want her to pay for you." Krakhil, the *dimo*, unceremoniously reached out and grabbed her thigh, making the female squeal and jump.

"Out of the way," Wyck growled low, shoving the *dimo* aside with his shoulder.

He didn't ask for the female to be placed in his care. Now that this task had been assigned to him, however, he couldn't fail. He already sensed that looking after her would bring its share of trouble.

The female made another attempt to twist out of his grip.

"Let me go, I said." She even stomped her foot. Cute. But useless, nevertheless.

He didn't waste words on her, dragging her along, past the crowd.

"Do you hear me at all?" she raised her voice. "Are you too dumb to understand? I'm not going anywhere with you, or with anyone of your kind. Not after what happened on the ship."

She shoved her elbow into his ribs, hitting the flashlight in the pocket of his vest. The pointy end of the flashlight's handle painfully jammed into his side, sending a flash of irritation through him.

"Stop this." He yanked her arm sharply.

She cried out. The high-pitched sound brought him to a stop.

"You dislocated my shoulder!" she yelled, grabbing onto her arm with her other hand. "It hurts like hell!"

Was she really *that* fragile?

He let go of her, just in case, then stared, unsure what to do next.

She stopped screaming abruptly. Spinning on her heel, she bolted down the corridor, away from him.

A sly, little liar.

He stalked after her, being in no particular hurry. She disappeared out of sight, running around a bend in the corridor, but there was nowhere for her to run. She wouldn't get far.

The corridor lay inside the outer layer of the Dark Anomaly's disk, stretching along the entire habitable sector. It was long but not endless. The female wasn't familiar with the layout of the Anomaly. She'd never find a place to hide where he wouldn't find her. Besides, her scent trailed in a strong alluring tendril behind her, guiding him.

The female's sharp cry made him move faster, though. It seemed she hadn't made it far after all.

As he turned around the corner, the female came into view. Lying on the floor, she kicked her feet at Kex and Tezul who both tried to climb on top of her.

Instead of rushing to her rescue, Wyck slowed his pace.

Kex was a *yourlu.* The purple, four-armed Tezul was a *bretoin.* Both were horny but not hungry. Had she been attacked by one of the inherently cannibalistic types like *ognats* or *kreers,* he'd be worried about her being bitten and—depending on the location of the bite—seriously injured or even killed.

These two would simply try to get into her pants. Since Nocc's actions hadn't taught her to be cautious, Wyck decided to fall back and let these two teach her another lesson.

He was far less articulate than Vrateus, the captain, to eloquently explain to this female the dangers of running around the Dark Anomaly on her own. He also lacked the captain's patience. *Showing* her what awaited her was much more efficient than telling, in his opinion.

He sauntered toward the trio rolling on the floor. Tezul used his six limbs to catch and immobilize the legs of the female, while Kex slithered his tentacles into the opening of her neckline, yanking the closure of her suit down. The two sides of it fell open.

The sight of the delicate globes of her partially exposed breasts momentarily stopped Wyck in his tracks. The impact of rushing desire felt like a physical blow to his groin. He swallowed a groan as both his cocks throbbed in the tight confines of his pants. Her sweet scent seemed to have permeated his entire being.

With a grunt, the female arched her back, freeing her arm. Something bright flashed in her hand, then half of one of Kex's tentacles dropped to the floor with a wet, sloppy sound.

The female had a weapon!

And she'd sliced Kex's tentacle off.

Alarm jolted him out of the stupor that his raging lust had plunged him into.

Kex wailed in pain. Tezul didn't seem to notice anything at all, busy with fitting himself between her legs while ignoring her suit.

Grabbing Kex by the scruff of the short, tattered shirt he wore, Wyck tossed him aside. Next, he kicked Tezul off her. Whimpering and glaring at him, both scurried away.

"Come." He reached for the female's upper arm again, but she kept brandishing the knife in her hand.

Sitting up jerkily, she suddenly stabbed the blade into his side.

The pain zigzagged through him, all the more acute as it was unexpected.

"What the fuck!" he roared, shock and anger rolling through him in swells. To his relief, however, at least his desire had subsided. "Why me?"

"Why not?" she bit out, her breathing ragged, her expression startled, as though her jamming the laser between his ribs surprised her as well. "Are you any better than them?"

She yanked the closure of her suit back up.

He certainly didn't believe himself to be *better*—or worse—than anyone else on the Dark Anomaly. He was simply a part of the crew. One of them.

"Give it to me!" He wrestled her back to the ground.

Stradling her thighs, he pressed her arm to the floor then forced her fingers open to release the knife handle.

"No!" She slammed her free fist into the side of his head.

The blow was more infuriating than painful. The wriggling of her lithe body under him rushed blood to his groin, all over again.

"Will you stop!" He leaped off her, shoving the laser handle into a pocket on his vest.

"Give me back my knife." Propped on her elbows, she glowered at him from the floor.

Her suit was primly closed all the way up to her throat now. But there was something about her position—her bent legs open, her breasts thrust upward—that made him momentarily lose focus.

She jumped up to her feet, going for the pocket where he'd put her knife. "I need it back!"

"And I need you to listen to me!" He caught her arms and gave her a shake.

This was not going well. His ability to concentrate around her was severely impaired, and he needed all his mental power to keep her safe. It didn't help that she seemed to be dead set on getting herself in trouble.

Immobilized in his grip, she glared at him, her eyes wide open, wild and...green, like the plants in Malahki's garden. Fear shone vividly through her expression. He sensed her body vibrating with it. Fear often made people make irrational decisions and act rashly, didn't it?

Maybe he should try to calm her down first before attempting to talk any sense into her.

"You *need* to listen to me," he said again, softer this time. Closing his eyes for a moment, he inhaled deeply. Her scent rushed in, filling his lungs, but he ignored it the best he could and loosened his grip on her arms somewhat. "What's your name?" He asked again, keeping his voice low and calm.

She blinked, releasing a shuddered breath.

"Nadia." Her voice trembled.

"My job is to keep you safe, Nadia. Don't make me fail at it."

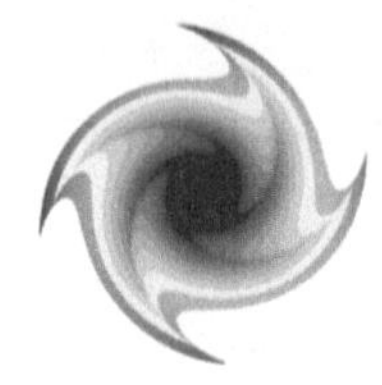

Chapter 3

Nadia

"*My job is to keep you safe.*"

It took a moment for his words to register. "Safe" should mean I was in no immediate danger, shouldn't it? Of course, it largely depended on Wyck's definition of danger. It didn't escape me that he hadn't been in a rush to help me fight off my assailants.

It felt like from the moment I landed in this place, someone had been trying to assault me. Wyck ended up helping me, every time. Unhurriedly, almost reluctantly, but he had stopped them. Other than manhandling me and taking my weapon away, he hadn't tried to harm or assault me himself.

"What do you mean by 'safe?'" I had to clarify.

"I need to keep you alive." He shrugged. "Not eaten."

"Eaten?" Surely, I didn't hear him right. Sentient beings—humans or aliens—didn't eat each other.

"A few of us here might eat you if you're not careful."

His casual tone must mean he was joking. Wasn't he?

The individuals in this place appeared crude and rough, less civilized than any species I'd ever encountered. I got the impression, though, they were after my body to satisfy their carnal needs, not their hunger. Their actions had been despicable. However, cannibalism would be a whole new level of savagery.

"Would *you*...be one of those few?" I watched him closely.

He made a face, giving me a once-over, as if accessing a supermarket package of meat.

"No. I don't eat humans," he finally said to my relief. Though the fact that he'd taken some time for deliberation before giving me his answer unnerved me.

"Would you do anything else to me?" I asked carefully.

"Right now," he wrapped his huge paw around my upper arm once again, "I will deliver you to your room and keep you there."

"What for?"

He tugged me along the corridor once again. The movement made him wince. He pressed his other hand to his side, over the wound I'd inflicted.

"Come," he bit out sharply.

I moved promptly alongside him. Dark blood welled between his fingers. The knife's blade would have cauterized the edges of the wound. However, I must have made the gash long enough or deep enough or both for the blood to seep through.

"You'll need to get someone to look at that." I gestured at his side.

"Who?" He gave me an incredulous glance, as if I'd suggested something utterly ridiculous, like he'd hop on one foot around me.

"Don't you have a doctor here? Or something like a medical capsule?"

I could tell him about the one we had on our ship. It was meant for humans, but it might have a program to assess and treat other species as well.

Thinking about the medical capsule brought the memory of Lee and Val who never got to use it. The thought of my entire crew left lying dead on the floor stabbed through my heart with pain. Over the year of training, I'd gotten to know those people well. We hadn't been close friends, but we'd gotten along well. I knew they all had dreams they'd hoped to fulfill after completing this mission. Now, most of them were dead. Their dreams gone.

"No. There're no doctors here." Wyck let go of his side, wiping the blood from his hand on his pants. "I'll be fine."

Fine.

Why should I care about his wounds if he didn't? I had other things to worry about. Things that concerned me, personally. Scary things.

"What's going to happen to me, now?"

"You'll stay here." He stopped in front of a set of dark-gray double doors and shoved one side open.

"For how long?" I didn't go through the doors, didn't even so much as glance inside. I had the feeling that walking in would signal my acceptance of my fate before I even knew what it was.

Letting go of me, Wyck crossed his arms over his massive chest, staring at me expectantly with the most bizarre yellow eyes.

"For as long as you shall live," he replied.

For the rest of my life? It didn't even matter how long or short it was going to be. If I were to spend it all here, in this place, it meant my life might as well be over already. I stared at him in a stupor as the seconds ticked by.

"I…I can't," I muttered finally. "I need to get back."

"Back where?" He sounded confused.

"Back to Earth, where I came from."

"That's impossible. So, the sooner you stop thinking about it, the better it'll be."

"There has to be a way." I shook my head.

"There isn't," he bit out. "Now, get in and stay there." He gave me a shove, pushing me through the door backwards.

"How did all of you get here?" I rushed out, holding onto the door frame. "How long have *you* been here?"

"All of my life." He closed the door in my face, leaving me alone.

Trapped.

"Wait!" I tried to slide the door open, pushing at it with my hands. It wouldn't budge.

I leaned my forehead against the cool material of the door. The horror of my situation descending on me.

"That's impossible."

Wyck's words echoed in my mind.

I had no reason to trust anything he said, but could I prove him wrong? Even if I managed to somehow fix the cut-out in the escape capsule door that Nocc had made, I had no idea what to do about the system malfunction.

"Not enough power to take off."

I distinctly remembered the warning message on the control panel, but I didn't know what had caused it or how to fix it.

Our team had been carefully selected. The distinct skill set of each individual was meant to add to the combined knowledge base we had as a group. My expertise, sadly, appeared to be the least useful for the current situation.

As a movie producer, my sole purpose on the team was to obtain appealing footage to create a documentary that would showcase the achievements of our expedition in the best light and make our sponsors look good. The cameras I had installed around the common areas of the ship would've recorded the carnage upon our arrival and the demise of my entire crew—nothing for the sponsors to brag about.

I had no idea how to fix any of the complicated space travel technology that had gotten me here. I'd spent nearly a year in training, learning how to *use* it. It would take years more of studying to learn how to *repair* any of it.

The people who could do something about it were now dead. My chest tightened as the image of the motionless bodies of my teammates rose in my mind's eye again. The horror of their murders churned painfully in my soul.

A little flicker of hope burnt through the darkness of my despair. Val wasn't among the corpses on the floor when Wyck had taken me off our ship. I hadn't witnessed her being killed. Could she have survived and made it out of there undetected? And if she had, how long would she be able to survive in this place?

According to Wyck, being anywhere on the Anomaly on your

own meant risking being raped or eaten. After everything I'd experienced here in the short time since our landing, I was inclined to believe him on that one.

The horror of it all crept up my throat, making it hard to breathe and bringing tears to my eyes. I pressed my eyes shut quickly, refusing to let the tears flow. As long as I was still alive, I had to keep going.

First, I needed to talk to Wyck—or anyone who would speak to me—to find out more about this place and those who occupied it.

Letting go of the door, I finally turned around. My breath caught in my throat at the sight of the room Wyck had put me in.

It'd been made entirely out of transparent material. Attached to the pewter-colored wall with the entrance doors, the glass bubble extended out into the open space beyond. The bottom of it was flat, serving as the floor, the rest arched around me, surrounded by the rolling waves of multi-colored light. It ebbed and pulsed in an endless cosmic dance, impairing my sense of reality.

The space beyond the glass room was both beautiful and terrifying in its vastness. Staggering back, I pressed my hands into the door behind me, letting the sensation of cool solid metal ground me.

One didn't need to be an expert to realize this light show was not a normal occurrence. For all the wonders of space I'd witnessed on my journey here, I'd never seen anything like this before. The mesmerising beauty would've beguiled and excited me had Wyck not made it clear—this was now my prison.

Beautiful and terrifying.

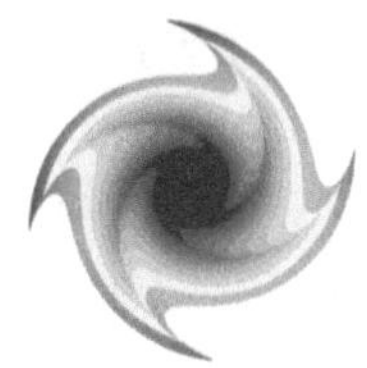

Chapter 4

Wyck

He punched the code into the newly mounted panel to engage the lock, then leaned against the closed doors, grateful to have the female and her scent finally concealed behind them. The urgent throbbing in his cocks subdued somewhat, resuming the normal blood flow to his brain.

Now what?

"Take care of her. Feed her…" Vrateus had instructed.

She must be hungry. He needed to get her some food.

Since Vrateus's woman, Svetlana, had taken over meal preparation on the Dark Anomaly, the crew was no longer allowed to come and go in the kitchen whenever they pleased.

Three times a day, Krahkil served the crew the food Svetlana cooked. Outside of the meal hours, snacks were available in the mess hall.

Lunchtime had passed, and there was still some time before dinner. He should get something for the female—Nadia—from the mess hall, but first he needed to get Lesh.

He'd left the *mahdi* chained in the humans' spaceship. Lesh could take care of himself, but Wyck didn't like leaving him alone for long anywhere but in his room.

Pushing away from the doors, he turned right, heading in the direction of the human's spaceship.

Three *errocks*—Nocc, Trox, and Gler—were working on stripping the ship of equipment.

Chained in the spot where he'd left him, Lesh lay on his belly. However, his posture was far from relaxed. His paws drawn under him, all six eyes trained on the *errocks*, the animal was ready to pounce on anyone who came too close.

"There you are," Gler growled as soon as he'd sighted Wyck. "Get your beast the hell out of here. He's in the way."

Lesh leaped to his feet the moment Wyck entered. He refrained from petting or even greeting the animal in the presence of the others, silently unwinding the chain from the bar on the wall, instead.

"Where is Vrateus?" he asked Gler.

"Took some boxes with weapons over to his storage."

Weapons.

He remembered about Nadia's knife in his pocket. It was resting right above the wound she'd made between his ribs.

Crazy female.

A warm thrill tickled inside his chest at the thought of her.

Vrateus didn't allow anyone but Svetlana to carry weapons. Although the laser knife was more of a utility tool, Wyck was certain his captain would classify it as a weapon and would demand Wyck surrender it to him. Any of the *errocks* present would love to get their hands on the blade, too.

He didn't always obey his captain, but he'd never concealed anything from his family before. Except for Lesh. His grip tightened on the chain connected to the *mahdi's* middle neck.

Wyck had found Lesh in one of the narrow passages that were plentiful around the Dark Anomaly, in which only the *mahdi* pup could fit. He'd been not much bigger than Wyck's forearm back then, whimpering in fear, his three heads pressed tight to each other.

The youngest on the Dark Anomaly, Wyck was only fourteen

back then. Finding someone younger than himself had intrigued him. Having someone small and defenseless, who wouldn't order him around, had felt refreshing.

"Hey!" Nocc stomped out from a side compartment, hauling out an armload of spacesuits. He dropped them on the floor. "How is *my* female doing?"

Wyck's neck muscles stiffened, and his jaw tightened at the word "my."

"*Ours*," he corrected. "That's what the captain said."

"Fuck the captain." Nocc came closer and wrapped his arm around Wyck's shoulders.

Just a hand-width shorter than Wyck, Nocc was two decades older than Wyck's twenty-four years of age.

"The captain put you in charge of the female, didn't he?" Nocc said in a conspiratorial tone. "Whatever you do with her now is up to you, right?"

"That's not what he meant—"

"Since when do you care about what he means?" Nocc snapped. "All *errocks* are a family. Here, we're all brothers. And family comes first."

Wyck had been raised with this motto hammered into his brain—the *errocks* are one large family. His father had died in the crash. The remaining *errocks* raised him, with Crux taking the role of his father.

As one of the *errock* family, Wyck had even gone against the captain's authority before. Only a few weeks ago, Crux had poisoned Vrateus, intending to get rid of the captain. Wyck helped Crux and the others to bring the crew under their control. Had Vrateus and his woman not wrested back the power, things would've been very different right now. Nadia would've ended up in the *errocks'* possession. In which case, she might be dead already.

He'd heard *errocks* fucked in savage ways. Ever since Wyck grew big enough for his cocks to get hard, Crux showed him plenty of videos depicting sexual acts. Crux accompanied them with even more graphic comments, describing the gruesome details no video had.

"If you're that scared about upsetting your precious captain, there're many ways we could cover it up," Nocc kept talking while hugging Wyck's shoulders like a brother. "We can let the *kreers* eat her after you and I are finished with her—"

"Hey! How about me?" Gler had obviously been eavesdropping. "If you're sharing the female, I want some of her pussies too!"

"Human females only have one pussy, I've heard," Trox chimed in, shifting closer.

"Just one? What a waste of a warm body," Nocc spit through his teeth with disgust. "Anyway, we're a family, Wyck, remember? Whatever one of us has belongs to everyone."

"I don't *have* her." Unease crept up his back at the thought of any of his family coming near Nadia again.

"But you can *get* her. Let's do it tonight. We'll come in with you when you bring her dinner."

"She's in the glass room."

"What?" Nocc winced.

The mention of the glass room made Wyck cringe inside, too. The way the clear walls exposed the open space beyond made his head spin. Terror had filled him at a mere glance at that crazy room.

The sensation was typical for *errocks*. However, the glass room didn't seem to bother any of the other species on the Anomaly.

"Why did you take her there?" Nocc snarled, huffing a breath through his nostrils.

Wyck decided not to reply to that one. Telling Nocc that he'd obeyed the captain's orders would bring nothing but more scoffing and mocking.

"You can get her out, though." Nocc's voice filled with new hope and promise. "Tell her she needs to go to the mess hall for dinner, then bring her over to my room. I give you my word, she'll be yours after I'm done with her. I'll also let you watch what I'll do to her." He smirked, glancing over his shoulder at Trox and Gler. "It's about time, the boy got a real-life lesson on how to fuck."

Gler didn't seem amused. "To make the lesson worthwhile," he growled. "I'd have to go before the boy.

"Not a chance!" Trox shoved him aside. "I'll never go after Gler again. Remember what you passed on to me the last time? A piece of dead meat, unusable in any way."

Wyck had heard about "the last time" before. Before Svetlana's ship, the last time a spaceship with live females crashed here was over two decades prior.

He was too young to remember that night, but he'd heard plenty from the others. The *errocks* bragged often about the "great time" they'd had, though most of them admitted they'd been too drunk to remember much. Their accounts often contradicted themselves, leading Wyck to believe that a lot of what they said must be made up.

True or not, the idea of Nadia turning into a piece of "dead meat" sickened him. He hadn't asked to be tasked with the job of looking after her. In fact, he'd tried to decline "the honor." Now, that she was his responsibility, however, he refused to put her in harm's way.

"She is taking the place of Vrateus's woman in the mess hall." He shrugged Nocc's arm off his shoulder. "We'll all get to see her naked, more than once."

"That's not what I'm asking you to do, boy." Nocc stepped in closer. "Are you going against your family?"

Lesh released a warning hiss, and Wyck tightened the grip on his chain.

"That's not it, Nocc." He tried to recall some of the words Vrateus had used to convince them all before. "It's a chance to use the female in any way you like, but only in your imagination. As long as it's in your head only, she'll last longer."

"Are you protecting *her*?" Nocc scoffed, the expression of utter disgust distorting his face. "If so, your father must be rolling in his grave, laughing his head off, boy! Females are disposable. The Great Scodr changed his women more often than he did his clothes. He liked his females fresh every night. If they pleased him, he'd set them free on the next planet we'd come upon. Those who crossed him in any way were sent the fuck out the airlock."

Gler roared with laughter. "The human with her *one* fucking vagina would've been tossed out into the space, for sure! The good old Scodr wouldn't have put up with that."

Nocc and Trox guffawed at that, too.

Wyck didn't always find their jokes funny, and this one fell especially flat.

"Well, there you go." He shoved past them, tugging Lesh along. "Father wouldn't have approved of her, anyway. No need to bother."

"Hey!" Nocc yelled as Wyck exited the spaceship. "We'll make do with her. We don't have the fine choice of females that Scodr had—"

"Exactly," he snapped. Usually, he felt pride when hearing about his father, the Great Scodr, who once had a fleet of fine ships and led an army of free men, submissive to no law but his own. Now, irritation grew in his chest. "We can't be like my father. We only have *one* female. If I let you have her, we'd have none at all."

He didn't pause to listen to their objections, heading down the corridor and away from the humans' ship.

Vrateus was striding his way.

"How is she?" the captain asked quickly, passing him by.

"Good."

Vrateus nodded, disappearing into the opening of the humans' spaceship.

Wyck pressed his hand to the pocket with Nadia's knife. He was not surrendering the weapon. He sensed he needed it more than Vrateus did.

He took Lesh with him to the mess hall. The *Mahdi* needed some food, too, and with the female in his care, Wyck now had twice the responsibilities.

Once there, Wyck quickly grabbed a few of the hard, round disks Svetlana called *cookies*, and stuffed them in his vest pockets, promptly leaving the room right after. There was always someone mingling in the mess hall, and he had no desire to answer any question about the new female or to ward off any more mocking comments.

Out in the corridor, he fed three of the *cookies* to Lesh, and popped one in his mouth. The sweetness of the pollen sugar covered his tongue with every bite, reminding him of Nadia once again.

The wound in his side ached, bringing to mind the image of her fighting him in the corridor. He remembered her fear-filled eyes. The horror and desperation in them reminded him of the look Lesh had when he'd found him. The *mahdi* would've died had Wyck left him behind nine years ago.

Nadia wouldn't last long, either, if he allowed Nocc to have his way with her.

"Show the boy how to fuck."

Nocc's words followed him.

In all honesty, he would've *wanted* to see that. Even more so, he would've liked to *do* that to her himself. Nadia's sweet, tantalizing scent seemed to have soaked his lungs and permeated his clothes. Even with her no longer around, the mere memory of her scent teased his cocks like a stroke of a hand… Her hand.

He knew that Vrateus and Malahki added something to the soap on the Dark Anomaly that neutralized their scent, making them practically undetectable to *errocks'* acute sense of smell.

Before reaching Nadia's room, he made a sharp turn toward the closest storage, instead. He needed that soap for Nadia so she could wash off her tormenting scent.

The door to the storage room was open. He poked his head in to find Svetlana rummaging through one of the boxes on the shelf unit by the wall.

He cursed under his breath. He didn't expect to find her here, though it made sense that he would—they all used the same supplies stored in the same rooms.

Her shoulders jerked, and she stilled for a moment before turning to face him, laser gun raised in her hand.

"Oh, hi Wyck." Her voice was friendly enough, though she

didn't put away the gun at seeing him. In fact, she adjusted her aim, pointing it straight at his head. "Looking for something?"

"Soap."

"Here." She stepped aside, gesturing at the box she'd just taken two soap bars from herself. "All yours."

She slid closer to the door, waiting for him to move so she could exit.

A whiff of her scent reached him. From this distance, even her daily showers didn't mask it completely. In addition, Wyck could clearly smell Vrateus's most recent kisses on the skin of her neck. The two scents mingled in an alluring, enigmatic combination, stirring tantalizing reactions inside him.

He hated having his cocks twitch in response to Svetlana. The fact that he had no control over it left him feeling powerless. He reached deep inside his emotions, searching under the thick layer of arousal for the resentment he had been breeding and cultivating toward Svetlana ever since she'd murdered Crux, the man who had been his father figure.

According to the customs of his family, the murder of one's father could only be avenged by the death of the killer. Crux might've been only his *adoptive* father, but he'd taught Wyck everything he knew.

Svetlana deserved to die, by his hand.

He wasn't sure why he hadn't done what the family honor demanded of him. Vrateus trusted him enough to have him guard Svetlana on occasion. Sure, Svetlana had always been careful and carried a gun on her at all times. However, there were ways for him to ambush her despite that. He'd had opportunities to kill her.

Of course, Vrateus would've ripped him limb by limb and fed him alive to the *vasai* centipedes if he so much as made a hair fall off Svetlana's head. But Crux would've been avenged.

"Well, um…" She edged closer to the door, keeping her distance, her gun trained on him. "I'd better go."

He stepped into the room and to the side, getting out of her way.

Her expression relaxed a little at having a clear escape route.

Then her gaze slid to the wound on his side.

"You're hurt." Her dark eyebrows slid close together into a frown of concern.

Concern—the last emotion he wanted her to feel for him.

"It's nothing," he dismissed gruffly.

"It's from a fight," she stated, confidently. Plenty of injuries on the Dark Anomaly resulted from the nightly fights between the crew members. "I can treat it for you. If you let me—"

"No." He needed her touch even less than he needed her concern. "I'm fine."

"Okay, then. Well, there're some medical supplies right here, in this box." She pointed with the hand holding the soaps at a metal crate behind her. "I have more in our room if you need them. Come see me anytime if you change your mind."

She slipped out the door promptly. The sound of her light footfalls moved away down the corridor.

He guessed Vrateus hadn't told her about Nadia, and Wyck had absolutely no reason to tell Svetlana about her either.

Grabbing as many soap bars as he could fit in his hand, he was about to leave the room, too. The wound on his side twitched with a sharp pain as he twisted his torso on his way out. A few drops of blood oozed out, trickling down the ridges of his abs.

Fucking Nadia and her blade.

He paused in irritation. The fact that the new female was of the same species as Svetlana added to his annoyance. Obviously, human females brought nothing but trouble.

The wound seemed clean and would probably heal on its own. Yet even with the slightest chance of an infection setting in, the fever would impair his abilities to take care of those in his charge.

Normally, he fussed little about his injuries. However, he'd never had as many responsibilities as he had now. He simply couldn't afford taking any time off to fight an infection.

With a grunt of displeasure, he reached for the crate. Finding some antiseptic and sterile gauze, he cleaned and bandaged his wound the best he could, then took the *cookies* and the soap to the human in his charge.

Chapter 5

Nadia

I was pacing my prison cell of glass when the doors swished open and the three-headed animal ran in, its chain rattling.

With a startled noise, I leaped back.

Covered in black shiny scales with red stripes on its side, the thing was terrifying, a true creature of nightmares. All three of its mouths hung open, saliva dripping from its sharp teeth, with three black tongues dangling out. Its long tail slithered behind it like a snake.

"Lesh, back," Wyck commanded in a quiet voice, and the beast obediently trotted back to its master.

"You trained it well," I said, with a genuine appreciation.

A corner of Wyck's mouth lifted in a half-smile.

"It took me a while to teach him who the boss was. Now that he knows it, he doesn't forget." With a flash of affection in his gaze, he placed a hand on one of the beast's heads.

The doors slid closed behind them. Wyck remained in the doorway, his feet firmly planted on the metal plate that covered the floor by the threshold.

"Here." He stretched his arm my way, holding a handful of flat, black disks. "*Cookies* for you."

"What did you just call them?" I couldn't believe my ears.

Shockingly, he'd used the English word for "cookies," carefully articulating each obviously foreign-to-his-ear syllable.

"Where did you hear that word?" I took the disks out of his hand and turned one between my fingers. It looked hard and glossy, like a flat hockey puck.

"From the woman who made them." He took one out of the pocket on his vest. "Eat." He shoved the whole cookie in his mouth. "See? Safe to eat."

My empty stomach tightened. With all the worry and adrenaline, I hadn't realized how hungry I was. I tentatively bit into one disk. Hard and crunchy, it tasted very much like the sugar cookies from back home.

"Who made them?"

"The captain's woman." He winced, as if mentioning her left a bad taste in his mouth.

"This woman is from Earth, isn't she?"

"How do you know?"

"She speaks one of the Earth languages I do." I lifted the half-eaten disk in my hand. "*Cookies*. That's English, one of the many languages from Earth, my planet."

To my knowledge, Svetlana Kostyk was the only Earth woman who'd come anywhere near the Dark Anomaly. She was of Ukrainian background but spoke fluent English. All of my spaceship's international crew had also spoken English to some degree, in addition to Universal. Though most were more fluent in the latter.

Back in Svetlana's time, however, Earthlings had just been introduced to the Universal language. Not many spoke it back then, and not on the same level as we did now.

It'd been assumed that Svetlana was long dead. Could she have been living on the Dark Anomaly, for the past fifty years? Baking cookies for these savages? Or was it someone else?

"Where is the woman who made the cookies? Can I meet her?"

"No." Wyck shook his head, evading my gaze. In fact, he'd been avoiding looking into the room ever since he got here. His body angled sideways, he persistently kept his gaze on the metal side of the doorway.

"Why not?"

His jaw muscles twitched. "It's not necessary."

"But I'd love to—"

"What you'd *love* is irrelevant," he snapped abruptly. "It's up to the captain to decide who meets her. She is *his* woman."

That was puzzling. The only Earth disappearance I knew of that had happened in this area was that of Svetlana Kostyk. It happened over fifty years ago, though. If Svetlana survived here somehow for that long, she'd be an elderly woman now.

"What exactly do you mean by her being *his?*"

"It doesn't matter." He shrugged, jerkily. "It's not *her* you should be worried about, anyway."

He wasn't wrong. I should be asking questions about my future. But this topic was too remarkable to give up. After all, I'd come here to find out what had happened to Svetlana. Now, there appeared to be another woman from Earth, which was a completely new mystery to me.

"Have you ever heard of a human woman named Svetlana Kostyk?" I asked. "She might have crashed here about fifty years ago. I know it was long before you were born…" Wyck appeared to be about my age, maybe even younger as *errocks'* massive size often made them look older and more mature than their age. "But maybe you've heard something from the others?"

Finally, he turned his head to me. His eyes narrowed to slits as he stared at me in some odd calculating way, not saying a word.

I took another bite of the cookie in my hand. "These taste similar to the ones we have back home."

"Don't all baked goods kind of taste the same?" he replied. "There's just so much one can do with eggs, bark flour, and some pollen sugar."

Clearly, he'd never been to an international bakery on Earth and hadn't been exposed to the vast variety of flavors different nations gave to the same ingredients.

"Could you at least tell me the name of the 'captain's woman?' How did she get here?" I insisted.

He shook his head resolutely. "What difference would that make to you?"

"I *need* to know. Is there anything at all that you could tell me about her? Who is she? How long has she been here? What else does she do, other than bake cookies?"

He made a face as if he'd bit into something bitter. Clearly, the "captain's woman" was not one of his favorite subjects.

"The only thing you really need to know," he said curtly, "is what *you'll* be doing here."

I vaguely remembered bits of what the captain had said back at the ship—something about entertainment.

"What is it?" I asked carefully.

He kept staring away from me, rubbing the back of his neck. The edge of his vest lifted up with the gesture, revealing the clean bandage on his side. Someone at least had taken care of his wound, I noted with relief. The sight of the blood-oozing hole I'd made in his flesh had been unnerving.

The medical capsule on our ship would treat a flesh wound within seconds and significantly speed up the healing. It might've gotten damaged during the crash, though, or the captain had ordered it taken apart, by now.

"Tomorrow night, I'll take you to the mess hall," Wyck said, bringing my attention back to him.

"Why? What is the mess hall here?"

"A room for large gatherings, among other things." He stared at the wall again.

"What am I to do there tomorrow night?"

"You'll have to take your clothes off. In front of everyone."

"What?" I nearly choked on the last bit of the cookie. "That's a joke, right?"

Please let this be a joke.

Alarmingly, after everything I'd seen of this place, what he'd just said seemed entirely possible. Dread gripped my heart with icy fingers.

"What are they going to do to me?" I asked, swallowing hard.

"They'll look at you." His casual tone sent a chill down my back. He obviously didn't think what he was saying was wrong.

"Why?"

Wyck had saved me before. Every time someone had tried to assault me, he'd put a stop to it. Was it because he'd been saving me for *this*?

"Because seeing you naked would excite them. And excitement feels good."

"Why should I care about them feeling good?" I raised my voice. Fear made it sound squeaky. "And who are *they*, anyway?"

"The crew of the Dark Anomaly." He pressed his hands into the wide metal stripe of the threshold, leaning into it as if for support.

Something was bothering Wyck. Sadly, it didn't seem to be the subject matter of our conversation.

"They'll want to see you naked, and they'll want to watch you come."

"Co… What?" Horror and shame rolled over me in a suffocating swell. "You've got to be kidding me. That's just—"

"You can do it yourself," he said without a shred of humor in his tone. I couldn't fool myself; he wasn't joking. "Touching I mean. Or like the captain said, you can choose one of the males to touch you instead."

"In front of everyone?"

"Yes."

It was simply ridiculous, except that he spoke of it earnestly.

"Do you even realize how absurd you sound?"

He glanced my way but quickly diverted his eyes again, staring back at the metal in front of him. I couldn't see his expression clearly, and it unnerved me.

"It can't happen." I breathed faster, as the room suddenly appeared to be short on oxygen. "You know it's wrong—you can't even look me in the eye when you say it."

What was up with that? What was so fascinating about that wall that he wouldn't take his eyes off it?

"I'll bring your dinner soon." He shoved away from the wall.

"Tonight, you'll rest. Tomorrow, you'll do what you're supposed to do if you want to stay alive."

"Is that a threat?" Fear shook through me. "Is it a live-or-die thing? Are you going to kill me if I don't disrobe and let one of you touch me? Is that it?"

He finally leveled a stare at me. Heavy and cold, it made my skin crawl.

"I won't have to kill you," he said gravely, his every word falling into the room like a stone. "There're plenty of others who will if you don't give them what they want."

"And you'll do nothing to stop them?" I asked, my voice low and thin. I could have guessed the answer already—he didn't care.

"I hope it won't come to that," he said evasively.

"You *hope*? Why do you even think I'll go ahead with your plan?"

"If you have any brains in that head of yours, you will."

"Brains are the last thing required for what you want me to do," I muttered, glaring at him. "I'm not going to do it."

"You will. If you want to live."

He held my gaze with his, his yellow irises especially bright and unnerving.

"Or you'll starve." He suddenly snatched a cookie from my hand.

"Hey!" I leaped back, hiding the remaining two cookies behind my back.

Turning to fully face the room, he kept his gaze on me. His gloomy expression had smoothened out, giving way to calculation and…interest.

"You'll get to eat only *after* you cooperate." He suddenly looked annoyingly pleased with himself.

"Are you serious? You're going to starve me until I comply?"

He shrugged. "Whatever worked for a *madhi*, should work for a human, too, I imagine."

"Did you starve your pet, too?"

"Starve? No. I used food as motivation to train him. Lesh proved to be smart enough to learn quickly what's best for him—to do as I say. He never starved."

"So, you're hoping to force me into obedience, too?"

He shrugged.

"I can only hope you're as smart as a *mahdi*?"

I seethed with resentment at the indignity of it. He stared straight at me now, but I remembered the signs of his unease ever since he'd entered this room. I stepped aside, and his gaze followed me, as if glued to my face.

"How about these two?" I waved my hand with the two remaining cookies in front of me. "Aren't you going to take these away to increase your bargaining power?"

His gaze shifted, and his focus seemed to slip along with his composure. His self-indulgent smile disappeared. Confusion, mixed with genuine fear momentarily distorted his strong features. He grabbed on to the metal panel, turning sideways again.

The warm umber of his skin paled on his cheeks. His chest moved rapidly with shallow breaths.

Understanding dawned on me.

"You're afraid of this room, aren't you?"

"Afraid? Don't be ridiculous," he scoffed.

Afraid might not be the most accurate word, but something about staring straight into the glass room or the lights beyond it made Wyck uncomfortable, and judging by his reaction, severely so.

"Yeah? Then prove it." I took another step back, holding a cookie out to him. "Come and get it, big guy."

He wouldn't look at me.

"Come on," I taunted, dangling the cookie in my hand. "You want to starve me. Start now. Take this away from me."

He didn't move. His huge hands balled into fists at his sides, his jaw muscles tensed. The rest of his body stilled, as if packed with compressed power that threatened to explode.

Suddenly grabbing the metal corner strip, he roared, the deafening sound rolling under the glass ceiling. Muscles bulged like boulders in his arms. He yanked off the metal rail that protected the corner of the wall in the entryway and bent it in his hands.

His deep roar rocked the room and reverberated through my chest. The cookie dropped from my fingers, weakened by the terror of witnessing the crushing power of his temper and the graphic demonstration of his strength.

Now, I hoped whatever it was that prevented him from entering the glass room was strong enough to keep him from lunging after me in retaliation for taunting this beast of a man.

He yanked on Lesh's chain, threading it through the loop he had bent the metal strip into, then tied it to it.

"Lesh is staying here." He tossed a glare at me over his shoulder. "No more food for you from now on." He shoved the door open, tipping his chin at the last cookie in my hand. "Make that one last."

The door slid closed behind him.

Lesh's left head quickly swiped the cookie I'd dropped off the floor.

"You're in it with him, aren't you?" I narrowed my eyes at Lesh as his left head gleefully chomped on my cookie. The central head licked the crumbs off the muzzle of the left head.

"A bunch of thieves," I mumbled under my breath, moving away from the beast just in case, though he didn't look that threatening at the moment. My cookie, settling in their joined belly, must've felt nice, mellowing the fierce expression of all three heads. "You're no better than your master," I told him.

My stomach still rumbled hungrily, and exhaustion weighed me down, along with a depressing feeling of utter hopelessness. I wandered off to the far end of the room.

"I'm not looking after your dog!" I yelled toward the door. Not that Wyck would hear me, but yelling seemed to release some of the frustration pressing heavily on my chest. "I'm not giving him any water either!" I turned to Lesh again. "I bet that cookie made you thirsty, didn't it? Too bad your owner doesn't care about you."

Wyck obviously didn't care about anything or anyone.

I glanced at the very last cookie in my hand.

"Make it last."

What for? With the future that awaited me, it might be better to starve than ration this last pathetic little bit of sustenance.

Taking a big bite of the cookie, I examined the contents of the room.

A clothing rack with ridiculously bright, embellished long gowns and a small table on gilded rollers were the only furnishings. Behind the rack, I found a roll of blankets. They seemed clean enough, though I was so tired by now, I wouldn't have cared much even if they weren't. I took them as far away from the door and Lesh as I could and set up a bed for the night.

Wyck's beast sat down on his haunches, bringing to mind Cerberus with his three heads. All three moved in sync, following my every move. The three pairs of black beady eyes watched me intently.

The fact that the animal made no sound creeped me out. Completely silent, he appeared even more like an eerie creature from the underworld.

"You want water?" I asked. The middle head growled at the sound of my voice while the other two hissed. "You know, you three should be in an agreement whether you're thirsty or not—you look like you share a stomach after all."

I walked to the bathroom, getting a drink for myself. The cookie had made me thirsty, too. Thankfully, there didn't seem to be a water shortage in this place. It ran freely from the faucet in a wide continuous stream. I filled a large, empty soap dish then brought it over to Wyck's pet.

He got to his feet as I approached. All heads lowered to the ground with a joint hissy growl as the eyes glowered up at me menacingly.

"Great, *now* you're in agreement," I mumbled, setting the dish down. "All three of you unanimously hate me."

The chain clanked as Lesh strained to reach the dish, but it turned out to be just a little too far. All that growling from him had scared me from placing it any closer.

He glanced up at me.

"Hey, don't look at me like that. It's not my fault your master dumped you here."

He sat back on his haunches once again, and I shoved the dish a little closer with my foot. There was no way I'd come any closer to this beast than that, especially while he was watching me with his sharp, translucent teeth bared in warning.

Only once I'd stepped back to my sleeping pallet did Lesh lower his left head to take a sniff at the water. The other two kept watching me, unblinking.

"Are you picky or just mistrusting?" I threw him a glare of my own. "Well suit yourself, I'm going to bed." I climbed under the blankets.

The slurping sound of Lesh drinking reached me as I closed my eyes.

"If you need to go to the bathroom," I mumbled through the warm, heavy haze of the approaching sleep, "hold it until your master is back. There's no way I'm going to clean up after you."

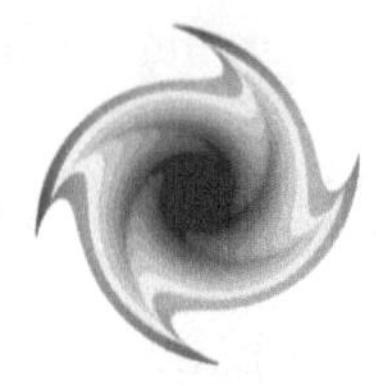

Chapter 6

Nadia

I woke up to a vomit-inducing stench.

"For the love of all that's holy, Lesh!" I groaned, burying my face in the blankets. "What the fuck did you do?"

What had Wyck been feeding him?

The cookie couldn't have caused that smell, could it?

"No, no, no," I moaned into the blankets. "No way. I'm not cleaning that. Wyeeeeck!" I yelled in desperation. It was unlikely that the broody *errock* would hear me or rush to my rescue.

I had no idea what time it was. The lights outside the glass moved in the same chaotic pattern as they did when I went to bed. I still felt tired, needing more sleep. But not in this stench.

Cursing and groaning, I rolled out of the sleeping pallet and climbed to my feet.

Lesh's chain clanked, but he remained lying by the door. All of his heads were wide awake, six glimmering eyes watching me intently.

On the glass floor between me and the hound from hell, a huge steaming pile lay.

"I can't believe this." I speared my fingers through my hair then shook my hands out. "I told you to wait for your master, didn't I? What am I supposed to do with this?"

There was so much of it, too.

Lesh tilted all of his heads to the same side. They moved simultaneously like a synchronized swimming team.

"Don't you stare at me like that," I snapped at him. "Like you're proud of what you've done."

I paced the floor in front of the offensive pile, pressing both hands to my nose and mouth and trying not to gag. It smelled like something huge had died in here, then had been baking in the sun for months while its decomposing corpse had been used as a place to go to the bathroom by every space creature imaginable.

"Wyck is insane!" He must be crazy. Only a man with an intense, unhealthy attachment to the animal would keep it around and clean after it regularly.

I had no idea how long the stinky Cerberus was supposed to stay with me. However, there was a good chance I wouldn't survive this stench long enough for Wyck to starve me.

"I hate him! I don't have anything to clean up this shit with." I stomped my foot. "Nothing!"

No automatic cleaning machines like we had on the ship. No soap, no rags, no hot water.

I stomped over to the rack that held the shimmering evening wear. The clothes were less useful to me than the bedding. If I had to rip something for rags, it had to be one of the dresses.

It hurt to ruin the gorgeous outfits, but they were out of place here, and I needed to do something about the gallon of alien poop on the floor.

Using my hands and teeth, I managed to rip off two long, voluminous sleeves of a velvet dress, then to tear one of them in half. I tied one long strip over my nose and mouth, using it as a face mask.

"Gaaawd, this is so, so gross." I crouched by the pile of Lesh's waste as he kept staring at me, not moving a muscle. Despite his lying position, he appeared tense, like he was ready to pounce on me if I made a wrong movement. I knew his chain was long enough for him to reach me. After all, it'd been long enough for him to take a dump in this very location.

At this point, however, the risk of a vicious animal attack seemed irrelevant when faced with the dire need to breathe some fresh air.

Holding my breath, I quickly scooped the mess with the pieces of fabric then tossed it into the toilet. I had to do several trips, scooping and tossing, before most of it was gone. Then, I filled the empty soap dish with the water from the bathroom faucet and scrubbed the floor the best I could.

I rinsed out and dumped the dirty pieces of fabric into the waste basket in the bathroom, then washed my hands thoroughly and shut the door.

The place still smelled awful, but at least the sharp edge of the stench was now gone.

"I'm going to kill your master with my bare hands," I vowed to Lesh afterwards. "Even if it'll be the last thing I ever do."

"Did you have a good night?" Wyck's voice woke me up. There was an uncharacteristically warm note in his tone.

I lifted my head off the pallet and opened my eyes. Wyck wasn't talking to me, which explained the affection in his voice.

Lesh's front paws planted onto Wyck's chest, the heads of the scaly monster fought over the patting that Wyck was generously shelling out to them. Having not enough hands to pat all three at the same time, Wyck did his best to give an equal amount of attention to the flat heads of his pet.

"How did it go, my friend?" he cooed, scratching the side of the right head's neck. The animal literally smiled in response, baring his teeth, his three tongues dangling out. His heads leaned toward Wyck's hand, the snake-like tail wound around one of Wyck's short boots. "Did she give you any trouble?"

I huffed, dropping my head back to the sleeping pallet.

"*I* gave him trouble?" I asked curtly, my voice hoarse from the lack of sleep. "He took a huge dump in here! What on earth do you feed him, it reeked like decomposing flesh."

"It still does." He wrinkled his nose.

Whatever air filtration system they had in this room had done its job, in my opinion. I couldn't smell anything anymore. I'd heard that *errocks'* sense of smell was superior to that of humans, though. Also, I might've gotten used to the smell and no longer noticed it even if it lingered.

Whatever the case, the disgusted expression on Wyck's face irritated me. It wasn't my fault the air in the room was not entirely to his satisfaction.

"You know what…" I got up and stomped to the bathroom.

A nauseating wave of stench assaulted my nostrils the moment I opened the door. The soiled rags in the waste basket had done a great job at overpowering any efforts of the air filtration system.

Pressing my nose into my shoulder, I grabbed the basket then went back to Wyck.

"Here" I shoved it into his chest as he stumbled back, astonishment mixed with deep repulsion on his face. "Get rid of this, will you? Make yourself useful instead of just complaining."

He stared at the offensive basket, his full, shapely lips curved in disgust.

"Take it!" I urged.

He shoved at the door behind him, sliding it open, then tossed the basket out into the corridor and closed the door quickly.

"Now, get out." I heaved a long breath. "And take your pet monster with you. I need to get some sleep if I still can."

Wyck glanced down at Lesh who stood at his side, keeping an eye on me. I was well inside the reach of his chain, I realized. He didn't attack me, and I felt too tired to care if he still could.

"Lesh stays here." From the hip pocket of his pants, Wyck produced a long meaty bone wrapped in a piece of plastic.

"No, he is not," I protested.

Wyck calmly unwrapped the plastic and tossed the bone on the glass floor. Lesh lunged after it, his three mouths soon gnawing at the meat with gusto.

"I'm not cleaning after him again." I glared at Wyck from under my brow.

"He's trained to use the bathroom."

"How much good does it do if he can't *reach* the bathroom? He's chained."

"Lesh," Wyck called, quiet enough. The animal heard him. Immediately letting go of the bone, he trotted back to his master. "Here you go." Wyck unclipped the chain off the black leather collar around the middle head's neck.

"What are you doing?" I gasped, instinctively stepping closer to him as Lesh ran back to his bone.

"Releasing him, so he *can* use the bathroom next time."

"What next time?" I fought the panic rising inside me at the prospect of sharing the room with Lesh *unleashed*. "I don't want him here. He'll chew my head off in my sleep."

"Do you want me to stay and watch him while you sleep?" Even with my eyes to the three-headed monster, I could tell by the smile in Wyck's voice that he was teasing me.

"I want you here even less than I want him," I snapped. "Both of you need to get out."

"Someone else may come in, then."

"Who?"

"Anyone."

"You lock the doors, don't you?"

"Yes. But the palm-reader panel was broken a few weeks back. It's been replaced with a numeric code one. Who is to say it won't be broken again by someone. Or hacked." He gave me a suspicious glance. "How good are you with technology?"

"Me?" As far as technology went, I had the expertise of a user. Any kind of hacking or tampering was way out of my skill base. "Rest assured, I won't be able to get out of here when the doors are locked. There is absolutely no need for you to leave your guard dog here."

"*Dog?*" He gave me an incredulous look. "Lesh is a *mahdi*."

"Whatever." I waved him off, stumbling back to my pallet. "I've had a rough night. I need some sleep. And you need to get out and leave me alone."

"Lesh will stay here," Wyck reiterated in a firm tone. "For your protection."

"No. Please." Dread washed away my sleepiness. "Don't leave me with him. He's unchained."

The creature appeared calm enough, occupied with his bone. However, the scraping sound of his teeth against it was unnerving enough to drive me mad with fear.

"He won't touch you if I tell him not to," Wyck assured me casually. "He's had some time to get used to your presence by now and will be calm, unless you irritate him in some way."

"*Me* irritate *him*?" I screeched.

"Yes." He turned to leave. "That shrieking voice you just used, for example, may set him off."

"What? Wait!" I rushed after him.

"I'll be back at lunchtime," he tossed over his shoulder as the doors closed, shutting me in the room alone with the three-headed beast gnawing on a bone.

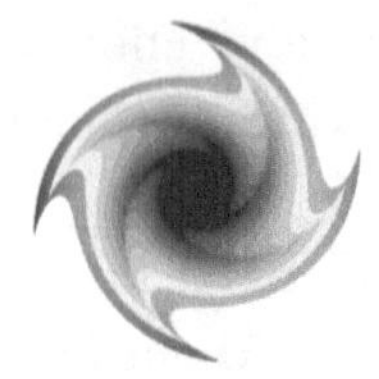

Chapter 7

Nadia

Lying on my pallet, I could no longer sleep, despite being tired. I couldn't relax enough to fall asleep while Lesh freely roamed the room.

He took his bone to the door. Lying across the entranceway, he kept chewing on it, even as there no longer seemed to be a shred of tissue left.

The smell of cooked meat had replaced the earlier stench of his excrement in the air. This one was at least pleasant and increasingly more appetizing to me.

My stomach growled. The sound rivaled that of the scraping of Lesh's teeth.

He lifted his heads in alarm, staring at me.

"Yeah, well, if you wanted complete peace and quiet, you should've shared that bone with me, you know, back when it still had some meat on it."

The sound of my voice, snarky as it was, oddly appeared to pacify the beast. He turned his attention back to the bone.

After what felt like an eternity, the doors finally slid open again.

Lesh leaped to his feet at the first sound of them moving and pivoted to face the entrance. The bone completely forgotten, he lowered his heads to the ground and made a loud hissing noise.

For what it was, I had to admit he did make a good guard.

The beast relaxed as Wyck entered. The tip of Lesh's tail brushed by Wyck's ankle, as if in greeting.

"Hungry?" Wyck murmured, lowering himself to the floor.

The large plate in his hands irresistibly attracted my attention. It was huge, the size of a tray, piled high with weird looking but probably delicious things.

Wyck sat by the door, his back propped against one side, his long legs stretched across the entire entranceway. Lesh made himself comfortable alongside him, resting his heads on his master's knee.

"How has it been?" Wyck's gaze remained on his pet, but I knew he was talking to me this time. The tone of his voice had changed, lacking the note of affection it held when he spoke to Lesh.

"Splendid." I pursed my lips, trying and failing to tear my gaze away from the food.

He lifted a piece of what appeared to be a stew meat and tossed it to Lesh. The center head snatched it from the air, its teeth snapping loudly.

Swallowing the saliva that had gathered in my mouth at the appetizing smell of cooked meat, I schooled my features into what I hoped was a casual expression before meeting Wyck's gaze. He'd been watching me, with a knowing look in his eyes.

I shifted on my pallet, annoyance muffling my hunger.

"It's tonight," he said calmly.

"All right."

"'All right' means you'll do it?"

"'All right' means 'I know' and 'fuck off.'"

"*All right*, then," he said pointedly, rising to his feet.

My eyes moved back to the food, completely against my will.

"Wait!" I yelled as he bent over to place the plate down for Lesh.

"Yes?" He straightened, the plate still in his hands.

"I'll think about it, okay." I couldn't even remember the last time

I'd eaten. It must've been a ration bar, back on the spaceship right before our failed landing.

"You had enough time to think." He lifted another juicy chunk of meat off the plate and tossed it to Lesh's left head. I couldn't help but follow it with my eyes. "I need your promise, now."

"Why do you think I won't break the promise once I've eaten?"

"I suspect that's possible." He paused for a moment, eyeing the food on the plate. "I'm gambling on the belief that you're a person of honor. And if you're not..." He shrugged. "I can always resort to dragging you to the mess hall by force."

"Why don't you just do that?" I scoffed. "Why pressure me for a promise?"

"I'd love to have some cooperation from you." He shifted his weight to his other foot. "I want you to have whatever choice I can give you. Because *I am* a person of honor."

"I don't believe there is any *honorable* way to deal with this fucked-up situation." I sighed. "Whose idea was this anyway?"

"The captain's. If you have one female and over six hundred males who want her—"

"Six hundred!" I gasped.

He nodded.

"There used to be over seven hundreds of us just over a month ago."

"What happened to the rest then?" I asked mechanically.

He shrugged his wide shoulders before replying evasively, "Power struggle." Gazing at me with curiosity, he asked, "Does the size of the crowd bother you? Is there a smaller number that you would prefer?"

"Yes!" I exhaled sharply. "How about zero?"

"That's not going to happen. They want you."

"But why?"

"Isn't it clear? They all want to fuck you. Only if they do, you will die, and they'll be left with nothing. Vrateus gave them the next best thing—they'll *watch* you and pleasure themselves. They'll get their fun, and you'll live."

From the captain's perspective that might be a win-win situation. Except that no one took my personal feelings into consideration.

"And if I refuse?"

"You'll die." He huffed a breath, his thick brow ridges twitched in annoyance. "Listen, I don't have much patience, and long explanations bore me. So, you either go out there and do it on your own or I'll drag you to the mess hall myself and—"

"You'll molest me?"

He stared from under his heavy brow.

"It doesn't have to be me. In fact, I'd prefer if you choose someone else but me."

"Oh, it'd better be *anyone* else but you," I said quickly.

His jaw muscles flexed again, the way they tended to do when he was irritated or angry. I'd learned some of his tells already.

"I'm sure Nocc would love to give it a go," he gritted through his teeth. "Or Kex and Tezul, the two males who tried to climb on top of you yesterday."

The recent memories of that made my stomach churn with nausea, which must be what Wyck had been hoping for when he'd brought it up.

"You're not helping by scaring me." My voice came out gravely hollow.

"I need your promise," he insisted, stubbornly.

The promise to allow someone to assault me in front of hundreds of over-sexed aliens. Or to die.

There had to be another way.

"So… They need entertainment?" I asked, slowly. "Of…a sexual nature?"

"Right."

I bit my lip, mulling over an idea in my head.

"What if I gave them that—something like that. But without, you know, the whole touching and coming part."

"What are you talking about?" He shook his head.

I raised my hand, as if about to make a vow.

"I'll give you my promise that I'll provide entertainment for your buddies." I waved my hand in the air. "But on *my* terms."

"I'm asking again." He frowned. "What's that supposed to mean?"

"I'll be needing a few things…" I glanced back at the clothing rack. It held enough dresses for me to make a costume. "Do you have something that plays music?"

"Why music?" He stared at me, clearly dumbfounded.

"I'll dance, okay?" I explained. I'd taken dance lessons for years in school and then in art college. I'd even won a few competitions, back in the day. Not that any of that mattered much to a group of males searching for stimulation to get themselves off. "I'll take my clothes off too," I added, reluctantly. "Some of them."

I stifled a sigh. Sadly, I wouldn't be the first woman in history pressured into stripping by necessity.

"Dance?" Wyck scrubbed his hand over his face, not looking convinced at all. "How is a dance supposed to be exciting?"

Clearly, he'd never seen a striptease before. That could work to my advantage: they'd have nothing to compare me with. I'd have the sense of novelty on my side.

I really hoped that would be enough.

The idea could be tested right here, I realized.

"Oh, Wyck. Dance can be so many things," I said in a deliberately low, raspy voice, moving toward him. Swaying my hips, I gave him a sultry look. "It can also be very, very sexually stimulating."

I hoped *errocks*—as well as the rest of the aliens here—responded to body language similarly to human men. Because that plate with steaming stew looked and smelled more amazing the closer I got.

Wyck's nostrils flared as I approached.

"Hungry?" he asked, his voice came out rougher than normal.

"Very." I held his gaze, licking my lips.

His thick eyebrow ridges shifted together, his bright eyes glaring with menace and heat. At this distance, I spotted grass-green spots floating in the yellow-gold of his irises—a touch of calm amongst the wild light.

"Come and get it, then." He took a piece of meat off the plate, holding it out between his fingers. The same way he'd done when he'd tossed food to Lesh.

I was sure he intended to insult me, but I was too hungry to care. Stepping closer, I rose on my tiptoes, tilted my head back, and opened my mouth.

"That's a good girl." His voice rumbled with approval. He sounded almost delusional, as if caught in a surreal dream with me.

This place certainly felt like a dream—teetering on the edge between a nightmare and a hallucination.

He dropped the meat between my lips, quickly withdrawing his hand, not giving me a chance bite his fingers. This might not be the best meal I'd ever had, but it certainly felt like it. I quickly chewed and swallowed the piece of meat right there.

"More." I reached for the plate in his hand, but he lifted it up higher.

"Not so fast."

"I've given you my promise." I stepped on the toes of his boots, to get higher. I'd never thought of myself as short, but Wyck would dwarf any human with his height and bulk. Next to him, I felt petite, and the plate remained out of my reach.

"Not exactly the promise I'd asked you for." He moved the plate even higher.

Hooking one arm around his massive neck, I pulled myself up, straining to get to the food. "Who cares? As long as you get the same results?"

His other arm wound around my waist, holding me in place.

My attempts to get to the plate suddenly halted, the awareness of our position rushed in.

I was hugging his neck, my face at his eye level, my body pressed flush to his so tight I could feel the firm beat of his heart against my chest. Every breath I took was filled with his scent—strong and masculine like him.

"That hungry, are you?" The velvet rumble in his voice gave his phrase a whole new meaning.

He dipped his face to the place where my neck met my shoulder, and his wide chest rose with a breath so deep, it lifted me up.

"I want you to *listen* to me," he growled against the skin above the collar of my suit. "And *obey*."

"Keep dreaming, buddy." My voice came out breathy. For whatever reason, I kept clinging to his neck and shoulders instead of letting go and retreating into the safety of the room where I knew he wouldn't follow. Despite my upbeat words, the closeness of his massive body appeared to subdue if not paralyze me completely. "It's not going to happen."

He yanked his head back up. His yellow eyes glistened bright like two flashes of lightning.

"You *will* listen to me," he said with force. "You'll do *what* I say, exactly *when* I say it. Or you'll end up as a piece of 'dead meat.'"

His nostrils flared as he drew in the air around me again. The look in his eyes turned from wild to outright feral, and he shoved me away from him.

Startled by his words and his actions, I still managed to snatch the plate from his hand the moment he lowered it. I then scurried backwards into the middle of the room.

Whatever kept him at the door restrained him more effectively than Lesh's chain. He didn't follow me. He didn't even appear to notice the plate was gone. Closing his eyes, he kept breathing deeply, a pained expression on his face. It was as if he were eager to fill his lungs with the drug he knew would hurt him.

"Take a shower before I come back," he finally growled, tossing a small rectangular package on the floor next to me. "Make sure to use the soap."

Then, he was gone.

Chapter 8

Nadia

Fighting was not in my nature. The confrontation with Wyck had drained me. It had done something else, too. For whatever reason, I could no longer think about him without an odd feeling fluttering in my stomach.

The sensation of the hard as rock muscles in his neck and shoulders stayed with me. The brutal power I sensed in this man could be frightening if directed against me. Yet there would certainly be some comfort and reassurance in his strength, were he on my side.

The feeling of his presence lingered in the room, even after he was gone. I couldn't forget his scent—warm and heady, with a hint of some exotic spice. I found it pleasant and…invigorating.

He obviously thought that I stank, though.

Resisting the urge to sniff my armpit, I threw a resentful look at the bar of soap he'd tossed to me.

My suit was made from an experimental self-cleaning material. It kept a pre-determined shape, requiring no undergarments. It also absorbed impurities, leaving only a thin layer of body oil to maintain healthy skin but eliminating dirt and offensive odors.

While wearing the suit, I could go without taking a shower for weeks. It helped reduce water consumption in space. None of my crew had ever complained about my smell. Neither had I ever noticed any of them stinking.

But then again, *errocks* did have a superior sense of smell. And something about my body odor must have offended Wyck.

Not that I should care about offending the man who had intended to starve me into obedience. Chasing the thoughts of Wyck away for now, I focused entirely on my bounty—the plate full of food.

As hungry as I was, it filled me up quickly. With still more than a half of the meat, grains, and bread left on the ginormous plate, I offered the rest to Lesh.

The beast eyed me suspiciously when I placed the plate on the floor in front of him. I stepped back to give him space to eat in peace. Slowly, he crept toward the plate. His central head keeping its eyes on me, while the other two salivated over the leftovers.

"You have more control than they do over that stomach of yours, don't you?" I asked the central head, which somehow seemed to be in charge of the other two. Although Lesh was one animal, there were subtle differences in the behaviour of his heads.

The left one, the most impatient of the three, lunged for the food first, snatching the dark dinner roll. The right one gave me a once-over then calmly started eating as well. The middle head watched me intently for a few moments as the other two ate.

"I'm not planning to attack you or to snatch the food from you," I assured it.

My presence obviously unnerved the creature. I decided to follow Wyck's advice—more of an order, really—and take a shower. Not because I worried about offending Wyck's sensibilities with my body odor, of course, but because the chance to have a soothing shower felt enticing.

Picking up the bar of soap off the floor, I headed to the bathroom.

There was nothing soothing about the brief, cold shower I ended up having. The water was barely room temperature, and it stopped running before I even managed to properly rinse all the soap out of my long hair. I ended up using the sink for that. Even as there wasn't a shortage of drinking water in this place, the water consumption must still be regulated.

The cold shower, however, felt invigorating. It woke me up and brought me into action. Since I had no plan beyond surviving tonight, I put all my energy into that.

Selecting a few dresses off the rack, I lay them out on the floor. I wished I had a pair of scissors or at least my utility knife. Since I had neither, I used my teeth and hands to rip sleeves off some of them, separate bodices from the skirts and shorten their length the best I could.

It wasn't easy. My fingers hurt after a while.

"I could use your teeth here," I said to Lesh, who had finished the food, licked the plate clean, and now was resting in his usual place by the door. His two heads were taking a nap while the middle one continued to watch my every move suspiciously.

I wasn't quite finished with my work when Wyck returned with an armload of flat, opaque tiles that glowed in different colors.

Lesh greeted him as enthusiastically as ever.

"Here, here." Wyck patted his pet.

Taking a cookie from his pocket, he tossed it to Lesh. The animal paid little attention to it. His left head licked the cookie once or twice before Lesh settled down on the glass floor by the wall. All three heads sleepily dropped to the floor, one by one.

Wyck's gaze landed on the empty plate on the floor.

"We shared," I explained before he had a chance to ask. "He seemed hungry."

"You're not to feed my beast." He glowered at me.

"Well, you've never told me that before. And it's too late, now."

At the sound of Wyck's grumpy voice, "the beast" gave us a sleepy glance with only half of his eyes open. He then went back to his nap, the long, scaly tail forming a circle around his body.

"What are those?" I pointed at the stack of tiles under Wyck's arm, diverting his attention.

His brow still furrowed in displeasure, his lips pressed tight, Wyck followed my gesture with his gaze.

"Data slates," he bit out curtly. "You've asked for some music."

"Oh, yes!" I jumped to my feet. "Let's see what you've got."

He shuffled back a little as I approached, then tentatively drew in some air through his nose, his chest rising.

"What?" I winced. "Do I still stink?"

From the impression I got of this place, the air around here wasn't pristine or completely odorless. His excellent sense of smell aside, I couldn't possibly smell worse than anyone else in here.

"Stink?" He frowned. "Who said you do?"

"You keep making faces whenever I'm near, as if my smell offends you." I snatched a few slates from him. "How do these work?"

He shuffled through the remaining stack of slates, producing a black frame.

"Slide a slate in here, it'll light up for you to use." He handed the frame to me, then added in a softer voice, "And you don't stink, never did, even before you took the shower."

Something in his tone made me look up at him. His eyes on me, he appeared absolutely serious, genuine.

"How do you know I took a shower?" I brought a hand up to my slightly damp hair. "Can you smell it?"

"Yes. And it's…nice, either way." He shifted foot to foot, tipping his chin at the slates in my hand. "Tell me which color has what you need, I can bring more."

Color?

I turned the slates. Two of their spines glowed yellow. Two were gray. The remaining few that Wyck was still holding were green.

"What do the colors mean?"

"The data slates are organized by color in the library."

"You have a library here?"

He nodded.

"The captain put it together."

I quickly ran my gaze over the words etched into the glowing spines. These were in Universal, with a line of text under it in a language I didn't recognize—*themul* most likely, since that was the species of the captain.

According to the titles, the yellow slates contained documentaries on the lives of indigenous tribes of some distant planet. These wouldn't be the obvious choice in search of some fast, catchy music to strip to, but I'd have to see the videos on them first.

The gray ones had words "The Dark Anomaly" imprinted on them. There were even less likely to contain the music I needed, but the words piqued my interest.

"Let's see this one first." I slid one of the gray slates into the frame, and it came to life, its surface turning into a touch screen. "I've heard about this technology in my Interplanetary History of Film class in college. I can't believe you're still using it."

Holding the frame in my hands, I sat down on the floor right where I stood. Wyck sat in his usual spot in the entrance way, and I scooted closer to him, so he could watch with me.

"Tell me about this place."

Humans had learned about the Anomaly having a solid core inside, but we weren't sure whether it was a planet or something else. Finding life existing in its core was a complete shock.

"The Dark Anomaly is a disk, made of crushed ships it has been sucking in," Wyck started, somewhat hesitantly. "They used to crash here more often in the past, but we still get a few a year. Most of them unmanned."

"So, there is no solid planet here at all? No atmosphere?"

"No."

"You don't go outside?"

"Only for maintenance purposes. While wearing a suit with an oxygen supply."

That would be like spending an entire life inside a spaceship. A sickening feeling of claustrophobia tightened my chest.

I pulled up a chart, or possibly a map, on the screen.

"What's this?"

He leaned closer, peeking over my shoulder at the device.

"That's the habitable sector of the Dark Anomaly, by the look of it. We're here." He pointed at a spot on the map with a thick finger, tipped with a smooth nail. His skin, the warm color of reddish clay, darkened to charcoal-gray on the protruding ridges over his knuckles. "This is the main corridor," he continued sliding the tip of his finger along an arched line. "It runs from the place where your ship crashed, all the way here, past the *vasai* farm and the airlock on the other end."

I read the labels, following the movement of his finger. The gardens, the library, the captain's room, numerous storage and utility rooms along the way. The mess hall.

I had yet to see most of that with my own eyes, but from the map, this looked like a fairly large area, equipped not just for survival but for a lifestyle allowing for some recreation. This place had been built to live in long term.

Wyck had mentioned that he'd spent his entire life here.

"How did all of you get here, Wyck?"

"Crashed, the way you did."

Except that I didn't crash. We had deliberately come here. Our landing, as rough as it was, was not an accident.

"Why have you never left?"

"You can't leave the Dark Anomaly," he stated simply.

"Why?"

"It won't let you."

Despite his casual tone, his words sounded ominous, like a line from a horror movie. What he had said made the Anomaly appear alive, like a being with a mind of its own—a dangerous mind.

"But has anyone tried?" I asked, refusing to accept it.

"Many times."

"And they ended up staying?"

"They ended up dead."

The dreadful feeling grew stronger, prickling cold down my spine. Instinctively, I leaned even closer into the warmth of Wyck's large body at my side.

"Why?" I ventured another question, already wary of the answer. "What happens?"

"Every ship that has tried to take off ended up crashing back, killing everyone."

"So, you're all stuck here for life?"

"As are you." He gave me a side glance.

I wondered if I should tell him about the true purpose of our expedition. Could I trust him to help me get off the Dark Anomaly? Or would he try to stop me?

"You see. Ours wasn't exactly a crash," I started carefully. "We came here on purpose."

He shrank away from me, catching my gaze, his expression shocked.

"How? Why?"

"This was a planned mission."

"Why?" He stared at me in bewilderment, obviously unable to comprehend why anyone would voluntarily travel to this place.

His expression gave me hope that he might not be entirely opposed to the idea of getting out of here.

"Ever since the solid mass inside the Anomaly was discovered, there have been talks about sending a ship here."

"But what for?"

"To see what it's like. It's a mystery, you know? Kind of like a modern-day Bermuda Triangle—" I cut myself off, realizing the analogy would be lost on him, since he most likely had no idea what the Bermuda Triangle was. "Anyway, there was a lot of interest from the public. All our unmanned probes have disappeared without a trace, so the Earth governments were reluctant to send a live crew. Especially, since Svetlana Kostyk had gone missing…"

A muscle in his face twitched when I mentioned Svetlana's name again.

"Do you know what happened to her?" I asked him.

He sat quietly for a moment, assessing me the way I had assessed him minutes earlier. Slowly, he reached into a pocket on his vest and pulled out one of the black, glossy cookies.

"Did she end up crashing here, after all?" I prompted since he kept quiet.

"She is the one who makes these," he finally said, staring at the cookie in his hand.

"It is her!" I stared at it, too, as if it were an object from another dimension, or at least from another time. "Is she here, then? Alive?"

"She is very much alive." He heaved a sigh then bit into the cookie with a vengeful expression. "She's Vrateus's woman."

"The captain's?"

Hearing that the human scientist, whose disappearance hadn't left the news for decades, ended up as someone's "woman" felt so wrong. Was she his property? Had she been forced to submit? By the same means Wyck had been coercing me into stripping—do it or die?

Of course, I didn't know Svetlana Kostyk personally, but I believed this would not be the life she would've chosen for herself.

"I can't believe she survived here all this time," I muttered to myself.

Svetlana would be about eighty years old, now. The captain appeared to be around thirty.

"In what way is she *his* woman?" I asked.

Wyck shrugged. "In every way there is."

"Do you mean like…sex, too?"

"Sure. I smell them on each other all the time."

"Oh God," I looked away. "All the time? Are you sure it's consensual on her part?"

The thought of the captain molesting the helpless elderly woman made me sick to my stomach. What would be unimaginable on my world, seemed to be plausible around here.

Wyck's mouth twisted in a sarcastic smile.

"Not that Svetlana would ever confide in me about her sex life, but she seems content with the captain."

"How long has it been going on?"

"Pretty much since she got here. Why is it of any interest to you?"

I wondered if that was the way to avoid the sex sessions in the mess hall—being claimed by one of the males here as his own. Not that I personally wanted to be claimed in any way.

"Did Svetlana ever have to do what you want me to do tonight?"

"A few times." He nodded. "At the beginning."

"Fifty years ago?"

"Why fifty? Svetlana got here just about two months ago."

"What? Where has she been for the fifty years that she's been missing, then?"

He shook his head.

"She couldn't be missing for that long. She isn't much older than you or me. Vrateus's age, maybe."

I sat up straighter.

"It can't be the same Svetlana, then. The one we've been searching for disappeared over fifty years ago. She'd be at least eighty, now."

He gave me an incredulous look. "How many Svetlanas have your people lost around here?"

One, that I knew of. The things didn't add up.

"Are you sure this Svetlana is a human?" I asked. "Does she look like me?"

He gave me a long assessing stare then said with something oddly like regret, "She does. Well, her hair is darker than yours and her eyes are brown not green, but she is most definitely a human."

"I need to talk to her. Wyck, please. Does she even know I'm here?"

"I don't think the captain told her."

"Well, can *you* tell her?"

He grimaced again, as if the very idea of him talking to Svetlana repulsed him.

"I'll ask the captain," he promised reluctantly. "Is that why you came here? To take Svetlana back?"

I shook my head, still reeling from his revelations.

"We never thought we'd find her alive. The most we hoped for was to learn what happened to her. Her age doesn't make any sense, though. Unless there is some kind of a time warp—"

"Probably."

"Do you know anything about it?"

"Not much." He shifted into a more comfortable position. "When Malahki got here about five years ago, it said it'd been thousands of years since my father's fleet traveled space. There is a difference between a year on the Dark Anomaly and a year out there." He waved a hand in the direction of the lights outside the glass, without looking up from the tablet in my hands.

"Who is Malahki?"

"The last sentient being who crashed here before Svetlana. You won't see it much. It works in the gardens and keeps to itself."

"It?"

"It's a *damirian*, without a gender. It probably won't even be in the mess hall tonight."

"Thousands of years..." I thought about Malahki's words. "How old is your father?"

"*Was*," he corrected. "My father died during our crash here, twenty-three years ago. I was still a baby."

Two decades on the Dark Anomaly equaled thousands of years out there in the galaxy. Yesterday, I'd had a thought about landing in pre-historic times. It turned out I hadn't been that far off.

"What kind of fleet did your father have?"

"A fleet of fine ships led by the crew of free men," he said somewhat mechanically, like the words had been repeated so often, their meaning had lost its luster to him. "The men who answered to no law."

"Pirates, you mean?" I exhaled slowly. I'd heard about the cosmic pirates of the past. Brutal, unruly, and bloodthirsty, they used to terrorize this part of the Galaxy millennia ago.

"Pirates, mercenaries, free traders..." Wyck ran his fingers over one of the raised ridges on his head. "They had many names."

"How about your mother?" I asked carefully. It couldn't have been easy to be a woman back then.

His expression hardened.

"She wasn't on the ship when it crashed," he replied evasively.

From his tone, I understood he wasn't willing to elaborate, and I decided to leave it at that for now.

"So, the other *errocks* raised you?"

"Yes. Crux, Nocc, and the others. We are a *family*," he said with emphasis.

Nocc would be the last person in the Universe whom I'd want in my family, but the obvious pride in Wyck's voice stopped me from saying anything out loud.

"Would you mind if I kept these?" I pointed at the gray data slates, changing the subject. "I'd like to read some more later, after..." The thought of what was supposed to happen in the mess hall tonight sent anxiety vibrating through me. "I need to get ready."

I quickly searched through the remaining slates. Neither of them had any even remotely suitable music I could use. The green slates contained detailed information on *damirian* best practices for cultivating some crops. Which made me wonder why would Wyck bring them here at all.

"None of them will work," I exhaled in disappointment.

"I'll get you some more, then." Wyck climbed to his feet, and I followed, getting up, too. "What color do you prefer? Green or yellow? Or should I grab different colors? There are some in blue, pink, and purple, too."

I stared at him in some confusion.

"It's not about the color. I need music—human or of any other race—a track I can dance to. These have some music, but not what I need." I pointed at the documentaries on tribal life. "And these have no music at all." I gestured at the rest.

"Okay." He brushed the cookie crumbs off his pants. "I'll get more yellow ones, then."

"But what do the pink and the blue ones have on them?"

"I don't know." He shrugged, not meeting my eye.

"Well, make sure you read the titles first. Something with words like 'music,' 'dance,' or 'concert' could be it."

He just stood there, shifting foot to foot.

"Is there a problem?" I asked, confused by his hesitating.

Suddenly, understanding dawned on me as if someone dumped a bucketful of ice-cold water over my head.

"You can't read, Wyck, can you?"

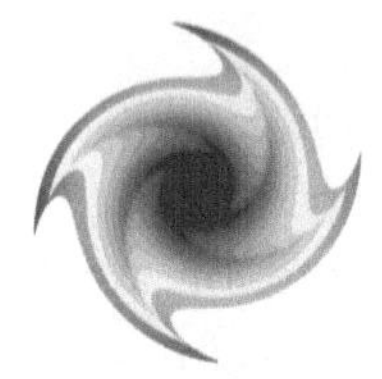

Chapter 9

Nadia

I couldn't believe it. Did Wyck really not know how to read? There wasn't a civilized person—human or alien—out there in the Universe who didn't know how to read and write. Even the most isolated tribes on remote planets, who actively refused technology, had advanced written languages, and some read and wrote in Universal. The use of translator implants by the general public had been declining because so many spoke the same language now.

I knew for a fact that most *errocks* on Hexol, their home world, spoke Universal just as well as their native language.

Maybe things used to be different back when the *errocks* of the Dark Anomaly had been on their home planet last?

"Can you read Hexolian?" I asked. "The *errocks'* native language?"

With a furtive glance at me, Wyck reached for the slates in my hands. "I'll take these back."

"No one has ever taught you how to read?" I had to clarify, shocked and shaken by this discovery. "In any language?"

He didn't reply, refusing to meet my gaze, which was an answer of its own.

Wyck was a grown man, raised by his own kind, and he couldn't so much as read the few words of the title on a data slate.

Something inside me twitched—compassion with a hint of pity. Not being able to read could be considered a form of handicap in the modern world. It greatly impaired one's quality of life and independence.

"I'll get you some more slates." He turned to leave.

"No. Wait a second." I stopped him by placing my hand on his forearm.

There was no point in sending him to fetch something he wouldn't be able to find.

"Is there someone…" I intended to ask if he could bring along one of the crew to help him, then realized that if no one had bothered to teach him how to read all his life, there probably wouldn't be anyone who'd want to help him with reading labels now, either. "Is there a way for me to come with you?" I asked instead.

"No," he said resolutely before the last word even left my mouth. "Not safe."

I realized that, I hadn't forgotten the attacks by the crew on me.

"Is there a way to sneak in undetected? You'll be with me. We'll make it quick."

"No." He sounded just as resolute, but it took him a little longer to say the word "no" this time. I hoped it meant he might be considering taking me along.

"Are there lots of people around here this time of the day?"

This time, he took a considerable pause, definitely thinking about something.

"What time is it?" he asked.

"How am I supposed to know that?"

He silently pointed at the tablet in my hand.

"Oh, is it connected to a network?" I turned it on again.

"No. There is no network on the Dark Anomaly. But the clocks of all devices have been synchronized. Makes it easier to keep a common schedule."

"Okay. So…"

He glanced at the tablet screen. "Lunchtime."

"Which means?"

"Most of the crew will be in the kitchen where Krakhil is serving food."

"So, we can go, then?" Despite, the potential danger, I was looking forward to getting out of this crazy room with its restless dancing lights. Having Wyck with me made me feel safer.

Wyck took the tablet out of my hands and placed it on the floor. "We'll leave all the slates here for now. I'll pick them up later, when I'm on my own."

I guessed that meant I was coming with him.

"I'm ready." I clasped my hands in front of me.

He gave me a long measuring look, as though assessing my worth in battle. It wasn't much, I had to admit. At five feet five, I had less than average muscle tone. My self-defence strategy would be kicking my opponent between the legs and running as fast as my legs would carry me. That obviously hadn't worked during the previous attacks.

Wyck had already gotten a preview of my limitations—he'd thrown enough males off me yesterday.

"Stay close," he said grimly, probably thinking about the same thing right now. "Keep your hands free. If something happens, don't get in my way."

"Got it." I chose not to clarify what exactly he meant by "something."

He slid my knife handle out of his pocket and clutched it in his right hand, then opened the door. Making sure no one was out in the corridor, he grabbed my arm and dragged me out of the room with him.

"Lesh," he called back into the room.

The animal leaped out of the door before Wyck closed it. All three of us were going, then.

"Watch our back," Wyck said to me, not letting go of my arm.

I glanced over my shoulder as we promptly moved down the corridor in the direction of the crash site of my ship. Fear rose the fine hairs on the back of my neck. I half-expected someone to leap at me any minute.

Wyck kept me a little ahead of himself, shielding me with his shoulder from the back, and I shifted even closer to him. The enormous size of his body felt comforting, it was like having a fortress wall move along with me.

Lesh followed us closely, his warm breath reassuring against my calves. I knew the animal didn't have any particular loyalty or attachment to me personally, but I hoped the mere presence of the fierce-looking beast would make anyone think twice before attacking us.

A little while later, Wyck stopped in front of an opaque-glass double door. Tossing a glance up and down the corridor, he punched in the code in the panel by the door and poked his head through when the doors slid open.

"Come." He ushered me inside then promptly closed the doors behind us.

Once we were in the room, his shoulders relaxed a little.

"That's the library?" I took in the large area filled with floor-to-ceiling shelves with glowing data slates neatly arranged on them. "Impressive."

"Is it?" Wyck cast a glance around the room as if seeing it for the first time or from a new perspective.

I walked over to the closest shelf unit by the door and slid my finger along the red-glowing spines.

"The captain did all of this? On his own?" It must have been a long tedious task.

"Yes." Wyck cleared his throat, standing close behind me. "The red ones have sex videos, not much music there, other than in the background in some."

"Oh." I jerked my hand away. "How about the rest of the colors?"

The collection was clearly color-coded. From what Wyck had brought to me earlier, I assumed the gray-marked slates contained data on the Dark Anomaly itself. The yellow ones must have something to do with history or studies of various alien ethnicities, and the green ones were on agriculture. There were more colors here, though.

"I'm not sure," Wyck confessed.

He'd sounded rather confident about the red section earlier.

"So, you're only familiar with that part of the library?" I waved back at the shelves glowing red.

"I'd watched most of those by the time I was fifteen years old." He didn't appear embarrassed or uncomfortable admitting that. "Crux brought me here."

"Crux is one of those who raised you?" I skimmed over the titles of the slates in the blue section then moved on to the pink one.

"Was. Crux *was* the man who raised me after my father's death."

"Has he passed away, too?"

"Yes." His features shifted into a stern expression.

"I'm so sorry to hear that."

"Why?" He narrowed his eyes at me.

"Why am I sorry?" I blinked, staring at him for a moment. How easily did people say these words when a tragedy happened? What exactly did they mean when they said they were sorry? "Because I believe you're hurting, Wyck. The loss of a loved one is always painful, no matter how long ago it happened. If you loved the person, it hurts when they're gone."

"Avenging their death is supposed to ease the pain," he said grimly, not meeting my eyes.

"Was Crux murdered?"

He nodded.

"And you believe that killing his murderer would make you feel better?"

"Vengeance is an honorable thing," he replied mechanically, as if reciting something he'd learned by heart.

"Vengeance doesn't always give you closure. Justice does. Have those who killed him been brought to justice? Was their punishment equal to their crime?"

His brow furrowed, he appeared to be deep in thought, then his expression turned troubled, confused. Something bothered him, deeply. Without knowing his entire situation, I couldn't tell what exactly it was.

"What do *you* know about vengeance and justice?" he asked.

"Personally, not much," I admitted. "But I do know loss. My parents died when I was a teenager."

My dad passed away from a heart condition when I was sixteen. Mom died from cancer two years later. Both were in their eighties when it happened.

They'd spent most of their lives building their careers. I was conceived from a frozen egg when they were in their late sixties. By then, they'd decided their lives were comfortable enough to start a family. They knew they might not live long enough to see me graduate college or even high school and had made sure I had the means to complete my education when they were gone. Financially, I had been okay without them. Emotionally, however…

"I miss them every day." Our happy family time had been cut short by my parents' weakened health in their later years and then by their deaths, yet I'd always treasure every minute spent with them.

It was comforting to know that they had accomplished a lot and had done everything they ever wanted to do. They'd shared a long, happy life together. I just wished I'd been there for a much bigger part of it.

That was the main reason why I'd decided to start my own family early. I wanted to spend as much of my life as possible with my child. With my parents taken from me so early, I couldn't wait to start my own family. The fact that I hadn't found a man I'd consider a suitable life partner wouldn't stop me.

I'd had a sperm donor selected and a clinic appointment booked for the scheduled end of the mission. The financial reward promised to me upon the completion of this mission was supposed to supplement the money left to me by my parents. It would ensure a more than comfortable future for me and my baby. If I ever got back, I'd be a wealthy woman who no longer needed to work and could dedicate her entire life to raising her child.

I had so much waiting for me back on Earth.

Aware of Wyck's large figure looming over me, I thought back to the conversation we were having.

Loss and grief were the things I knew way too well.

"What has been helping me deal with the pain is all the good memories we'd made when we were together," I said softly. "Before I fall asleep, I often think about a trip we took together or our family celebrations. All moments are precious, even the smallest ones—like the many times my dad made me laugh or when my mom held me close while I cried over a scraped knee. Keeping my parents alive in my memories helps me deal with them no longer being here."

Wyck held still, and I looked up to see his reaction. He stood over me, watching me like some kind of a novelty, as if the concept of honoring the loved ones through memories was entirely new to him.

"Tell me about a good moment with Crux," I asked, hoping that talking about the one he had lost would help ease his grief, too. "Something you two did or shared that made you feel happy."

The furrows on his heavy brow grew deeper. His features hardened in concentration, then he winced, not saying a word.

Were there no good memories of the person who had been like a father to him?

The most recent thing Wyck had said about Crux was that he'd introduced him to all the sex videos in the library. Yet Crux didn't seem to show him any of the other ones in this large collection.

What kind of a parent was Crux if he hadn't even bothered to teach Wyck how to read in all those years?

The silence that stretched between us threatened to remain infinite.

"Well," I spoke first since it didn't appear Wyck would say anything any time soon. "I think some of these slates might work." I crouched by a shelf at the wall farthest from the entrance. It contained purple glowing slates with titles suggesting the subject of arts and entertainment.

I accidentally pushed a slate with the side of my hand while taking a few others out. Instead of stopping at the wall, the slate disappeared somewhere behind it, landing in the darkness beyond with a thud.

"What's there?" I asked Wyck.

"Where?"

"There's no wall behind this shelf."

"Really?" Pressing his shoulder into the corner of the unit, Wyck easily shifted the whole thing aside, revealing a dark cut-out in the wall.

"What is it?" I moved to poke my head in, but Wyck stopped me quickly with a hand on my shoulder.

"A sure way to lose your head on the Dark Anomaly is to stick it into unknown places."

He got a flashlight out of his pocket and flicked it on.

The beam of light fell inside a windowless room beyond the wall.

"Is it someone's hiding place?" I ventured a little closer since the place seemed completely deserted. "Why is it here?"

"There are a lot of hidden places all around. When ships crash into each other, pockets of space end up being created. We don't know about all of them. Many aren't easily accessible."

"Well, the access to this one has been created by someone." I slid my finger along the edge of the cut-out. The paneling had melted around it, as if it'd been cut through with a tool that produced heat.

Lesh released a hissing sound, and Wyck stilled suddenly. A moment later, the sound of footfalls out in the main corridor reached me.

"Someone's coming."

"Maybe they just need some slates?" I suggested.

"Maybe, but they may want something else if they see you. Here." He shoved me into the space behind the wall.

Wyck then quickly got in with me, too, and called Lesh to follow us as well. He then yanked the shelf unit back in place from the inside.

The footfalls stopped at the entrance to the library as the person entered a code in the panel.

Lesh hissed in warning again.

"Quiet." Wyck placed his hand on the animal's middle head.

Crouching by the opening, I peeked out through the gap between the slates on the shelf.

The tall boots of Vrateus, the captain, came into my view as he entered. He headed to a unit that held gray glowing slates and added the two he'd brought with him to the shelf.

I felt air stir as Wyck lowered into a crouch at my side. His thigh brushed by my knee—the contact cost me my concentration. I kept staring at Vrateus, watching him browse the shelves. My mind, however, was momentarily overtaken by the awareness of Wyck next to me. I had to shift away from him a little, to regain my composure and focus on what was going on in the library.

After selecting a few slates of various colors, the captain headed for the door. He paused just before the exit. Bending down quickly, he pulled out a slate from the red-glowing section then left.

"Did the captain just take a sex video?" Wyck's eyebrow ridges rose in shock.

"Looks like he wants to have some fun tonight," I let out a short giggle. "To spice up a date, maybe?"

He gave me a questioning look.

"What's a date?"

I gazed back at him. "You really don't know what it means?"

"I suspect it has something to do with sex." It wasn't exactly a question, however his voice sounded uncertain.

"A date is when two people who are interested in each other romantically get together to spend some time. Back on Earth, that would often be a dinner or a trip to a movie or a show. And yes, if they like each other enough, there may be sex, too."

"Why would he need a video if he has Svetlana?" Wyck appeared genuinely puzzled. "They share a room."

"Maybe they'll watch the video together?" I was just speculating here since I didn't know either the captain or Svetlana that well.

"People do that?" he squinted at me, curiosity and disbelief evident on his face.

"Well, some couples do, I guess. It makes sense when you think about it," I tried to explain. Not that I had that much experience in that department myself. A high school boyfriend and a few casual dates in college were all I had in terms of romance in my past. "If you're watching a sexually stimulating video, it's nice to have someone nearby to turn the fantasy into reality, don't you think?"

He tilted his head to the side. "Have you had a date?"

"A few."

"With a sex video?"

"Um, I don't recall watching porn with a guy," I admitted. "But I'm sure my ex and I have watched movies with love scenes in them, at some point."

"Does 'ex' mean he is no longer your man?"

"That is exactly what it means."

"Did he die?"

"What? No. We both went to different colleges, and the long-distance thing didn't work out after a while. Why would you think he'd died?"

He shrugged. "That would be the only way I'd ever give up something that's mine."

"Something? You mean a woman?"

He gave me a long look.

"*Especially*, a woman."

He kept his eyes on me for a moment longer. "*Errocks* don't keep women for long, but—"

"That's not true," I objected. "*Errocks* form long-term family units very similar to humans. They get together for procreation, but many remain as couples for life. If you like each other's company why separate, right?"

Wyck shook his head. "That is not the *errocks'* way."

"Here on the Anomaly, maybe," I argued. "But the world is so much bigger than this place."

He seemed to ponder my words, then shoved the shelf aside, clearing the exit for us.

"We should go back." He took my hand in his, leading me out and back into the library.

Only when we were already walking down the corridor had I

realized that he kept holding my hand, instead of dragging me by my arm the way he'd done on our way to the library.

My thoughts went to what lay ahead for me tonight, and I felt betrayed by the comfortable feeling I got in Wyck's presence. At the end of the day, he was still the man who was forcing me to strip for the entertainment of strangers.

I carefully worked my hand out of his. With a glance my way, he took a hold of my arm once again then led me down the corridor like the prisoner that I was.

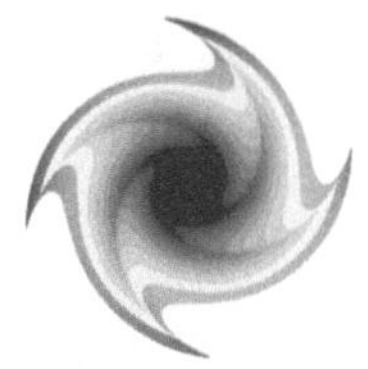

Chapter 10

Wyck

On his way to Nadia's room that night, he fought a feeling he'd never had before—he was extremely worried…about a woman.

He'd allowed Nadia to go ahead with her plan to dance instead of being touched.

Frankly, he had no idea what to do if he were to touch her in front of everyone. That might be the main reason why he'd agreed with her plan in the first place. The thought that he might do something so wrong it would upset her, make her dislike him, or laugh at him filled him with anxiety.

The closest he'd ever come to that level of intimacy was when he watched Vrateus and Svetlana in the mess hall during those few sessions.

Unlike the rest of the crew, Wyck hadn't touched himself, then. He'd been fascinated by what had been happening in front of him. Svetlana, always distant and on guard with everyone, had melted into Vrateus's touch, becoming soft and pliable in his hands. Their calm and collected captain had nearly come undone when he held her in his arms.

After that, Wyck became intrigued, watching the connection grow between the two, week after week. All of it was so new to him —a woman willingly committing to a man, not just in body but in spirit and soul. He saw the way Svetlana looked at Vrateus, as if she were ready to cuddle him or to die for him or both.

She'd ended up fighting for Vrateus and even killing for him—both things that, according to Wyck's upbringing, only a family would do for each other. For as long as Wyck knew him, Vrateus had always been alone. Until Svetlana became his family.

The *errocks* on the Dark Anomaly abhorred and ridiculed this kind of connection between a male and a female. Yet Wyck found it…enviable.

Why didn't he feel the way the rest of his kind did? There must be something wrong with him. He wished he could talk to Nocc or any of his brothers about it. He'd venture speaking with Crux had he been alive. Except that Wyck was absolutely certain he'd only be laughed at, provided he could even find the right words to express what he felt.

The best way he knew to touch a woman would be to copy Vrateus's hands on Svetlana's body. As much as the idea of feeling Nadia's bare skin excited him, he wouldn't like having to recall Svetlana when touching her.

At the same time, the idea of letting someone else touch Nadia filled him with a rage so strong, it burnt through his insides like acid, urging him to punch something.

He drew in a long breath, fighting the feeling of worry and unease about Nadia's performance tonight. He'd never seen a woman dance before and was actually looking forward to experiencing something new. He just hoped the rest of the crew would find the dance an acceptable substitute for the entertainment they were expecting.

He punched the code into the door panel, bracing himself for the onslaught of panic that always hit him the moment he faced the glass walls of the room and the open space beyond.

Lesh slinked around his legs in greeting the moment he'd entered.

"Ready?" He asked…and froze, speechless.

It wasn't the lights that shocked him this time but the sight of the smiling Nadia, standing in front of the clothing rack. She was wearing something so beautiful it could've only come out of a dream.

Her outfit consisted of several layers made of the dresses she'd cut to various lengths. The top one was trimmed with yellow feathers along the edge of the long skirt. The material of different colors was light and transparent, each layer slightly visible through the rest, giving the entire outfit the iridescent effect of a rainbow. With the most layers being over her breasts and hips, he couldn't see all of her body through the fabric—just a teasing whisper of her curves underneath it.

Her scent was only a slight tendril at this distance. Combined with the sight of her in this outfit, however, her scent had the effect of a punch to his chest, leaving him breathless.

"Do I look okay?" She smoothed a hand over her straight, light-brown hair she'd let down for the night.

The dancing lights of the Anomaly cast streaks of gold on her long tresses. The fear in her green eyes was softened by the smile on her lips.

"Yes, um… You look…okay," he mumbled as soon as he'd found his voice.

His insides twisted at the thought of taking her out there to be gawked at by hundreds of males. Everything in him urged him to hold her tight, to keep her to himself. He closed his eyes and clenched his hands into fists, fighting the unexplained wave of possessiveness.

"We should go," he croaked.

Before I change my mind, take you for myself, and get us both killed.

"Okay," she said softly. "Let's do it."

He opened his eyes, finding his worry and anxiety reflected in hers.

"I'll keep you safe," he vowed, fully intending to keep his promise, no matter the cost.

She picked up the frame with a purple slate inserted in it. He took her arm and opened the door.

They headed down the corridor, with Lesh walking slightly behind them. The *mahdi* remained unchained. Wyck needed his hands free and Lesh ready to leap to their defence if needed.

Nadia hugged the frame with the slate to her. Her chest rose rapidly with shallow, uneven breaths.

"I'll keep you safe," he reiterated.

Even if it's the last thing I do.

He could almost sense her fear. The soft, layered outfit made her look exceptionally vulnerable. He had the urge to grab her and hide her away from everyone.

Would she fit in the small room near the *vasai* farm where he had kept Lesh for years before Vrateus took over and Wyck thought it was safe for the one surviving *mahdi* to join the crew? But no one had known about Lesh's existence back then, no one had searched for him. If Nadia went missing, every male out there would be tracking her, hunting her.

"She belongs to all of us." Vrateus's words came to mind.

Irritation at his captain rose in his chest. Vrateus had cleverly avoided sharing Svetlana with anyone. Nadia had been thrown to the crew in place of her. And she was scared.

As they approached the mess hall, some members of the Dark Anomaly crew came into view. They lingered by the entrance to the room, glancing down the corridor impatiently.

Nadia tensed at the sight of them. She slowed her steps and moved so close to him, he nearly tripped over her feet.

From the corner of his eye, he noticed someone reaching for her. He threw his elbow out, shoving them out of the way.

"Stand back," he gritted the warning through his teeth, leading Nadia into the room.

It appeared that the entire population of the Dark Anomaly had gathered here, except for Vrateus and Svetlana. Even Malahki had shown up and now lingered casually at the back of the crowd. Curiosity must have brought the genderless *damirian* out tonight.

The tables in the room remained the way he had them arranged about an hour ago. Pushed close to each other, they formed a long line in the middle of the mess hall, just as Nadia had told him she needed them arranged.

"Where to?" he asked her.

Her face had paled, the green eyes open wide, as she stared at the half-naked males who filled the space.

The crowd was agitated, charged with anticipation and energy.

He slid his hand from her arm up to her shoulder, "Where do you want to start?"

"Oh." She snapped from her fear-induced stupor and gestured at the line of tables. "Either end is fine."

With shaking fingers, she fumbled to turn on the frame in her hands. The sound of an upbeat, sultry song filled the room.

"Could you hold this, please?" She handed him the frame, approaching the first table in the long line.

He placed the frame on a corner of the table. "Do you need help getting up?"

She nodded quickly.

His hands under her arms, he lifted her up onto the table. In his arms, she felt light like one of the feathers from the top layer of her clothing. In her multi-colored outfit, she truly reminded him of the rainbow-colored bird he'd once seen on a poster in one of the ships.

Now, she was positioned above the crew.

A few *ognuts* and most of the *kreers* were clinging to the walls, some of them hanging off the lighting cables dangling from the ceiling. However, most of the males sat in the haphazardly arranged chairs all over the room. The first crooked row of chairs was a few paces away from the line of tables—and from Nadia.

"Are you ready, boys?" Her upbeat voice startled him.

Forgetting all about the room and the expectant males, he snapped his gaze to Nadia.

Her fear was still there, he sensed it. Her fingers never stopped trembling. Her eyes remained open so wide, the entire room could drown in them.

Yet her back was straight, her head held high. She had a smile on her lips—a wide, inviting smile.

"What the fuck is she doing?" he muttered under his breath.

An excited roar rolled through the room. The rest of the crew appeared to be just as surprised as he was, though they seemed to recover quickly, shouting, clapping, and stomping their feet.

Nadia tilted her head playfully.

"Let's start then." She stomped her foot as the music picked up with the next beat.

Pinching the side of her skirt between two fingers, she lifted its top layer up and cocked her hip. Before he had the chance to fully appreciate her sassy stance, Nadia waved her skirt with a flourish and lunged along the line of the tables, moving in rhythm to the music. Her feet fluttered deftly along the hard surface of the tables. Her skirts billowed like the clouds of shimmering colors as she twisted, twirled, and turned.

He stared, mesmerized by the vivid show of the young woman jumping, swaying, and spinning, within the iridescent swirls of fabric. As the pace of the music increased, so did the speed of her dance—her feet but a blur beneath her skirts.

Suddenly, the clasp of the wide gold-tone belt around her waist clicked open and the upper, pale-yellow layer of her outfit slid loose —the one with the longest skirt trimmed with feathers.

She shrugged it off her shoulders in a slow, seductive gesture, then tossed it off into the crowd. The crew roared, growled, and hissed, fighting over the garment.

He watched in horror as the fabric was ripped to pieces in seconds. For one terrifying moment, he imagined it being Nadia herself.

She did not belong here—delicate, beautiful, and vulnerable—like a bright flower tossed into a dirty fighting pit. He had to get her out of this room and lock her up again—safe.

He balled his hands into fists so tight, his fingernails dug into the skin of his palms, but he ignored the pain.

"Nadia." He moved along the tables, keeping himself between her and the males who were devouring her with their eyes.

She didn't skip a beat in her dance. Her movements light and easy, she leaped into the air as if taking off to fly through it. He had never seen anything more spectacular in his life. Nadia was now his definition of beauty and magic.

Deliberately slow, she unwrapped the next layer of fabric from around her. Crimson red, it fluttered through the air like a wisp of the Anomaly light, landing among another group of males who immediately shredded it, too. Nadia followed it by yet another layer, without stopping her dance.

As she revealed more of her body, the movements of her limbs had become more apparent and even more fascinating to him. Her legs propelled her through the air. Her arms undulated smoothly, like wings, as if the music gave Nadia the power to conquer gravity and levitate.

He couldn't take his eyes off her, enthralled by her dance. Reality ceased to exist. She no longer appeared as a person but a magical being from another world.

Eventually, the music slowed down then faded away. With a graceful sweep of a leg to the side, Nadia lowered herself into a deep bow.

Her chest heaved. Her eyes shone with life and excitement when she rose and glanced around the room. The wide smile on her lips was genuine.

His consciousness slowly floated back from the blissful feeling of awe her dancing had plunged him into. A new kind of pleasure rolled through his body, warming his chest. He wanted more of this, so much more. At the same time, he was afraid his heart would burst from emotions he couldn't name.

Raising his hands, he clapped—the only way he could remotely express his deep delight and appreciation for her performance. The noise of his clapping seemed to grow and multiply, as others joined in his applause.

Whistles, stomping, and roaring took over.

Nadia looked around nervously. Her gaze landed on him. Then, she smiled again, just for him this time. He nearly staggered from the charge of pleasure rushing through him at the sight of recognition in her eyes.

He had to get her back to her room, the sooner the better.

"Hey!" Nocc's voice cut through the noise of the crowd like a rusty knife. "How come she's still wearing clothes?"

A short purple skirt and a narrow matching scarf tied around her breasts were all that remained from Nadia's outfit. Yet it proved too much for Nocc and some others who started joining him with growls of disapproval.

Nadia raised her hands in front of her as if trying to stop an approaching disaster.

"Step back, everyone!" Her voice rang high with fear, though she visibly made an effort to remain calm and to calm down the crowd. "Stay were you are if you want to see more."

She moved a hand up to the knot of the scarf around her breasts.

Judging by the musty smell of semen saturating the air in the room, most of the males had already come during her performance. Wyck guessed that seeing her naked might satisfy them further, but it wouldn't stop their demands. The more she gave, the more they'd want.

Tossing a glance back to the door, he estimated the number of steps it would take him to reach the exit with the weight of Nadia in his arms—too many—especially with the agitated crew between him and the door.

Someone crashed into his back as a scuffle broke out behind him. Lust came hand in hand with aggression here. A massive fight was brewing. He flicked the laser blade on, stabbing without looking. Enkail, the *dimo* rushed him, the hard-plated skull painfully ramming into his shoulder. He shoved Enkail aside.

"Nadia." Wyck twisted in her direction just in time to see Nocc leap onto the table next to her. He ripped the end of the scarf from her fingers and yanked at it forcefully. Nadia spun around as the scarf unwound from around her, freeing her breasts.

At the sight of her naked flesh, wild roars ripped from hundreds of throats. The lust-crazed males rushed to Nadia, shoving the chairs and tables aside and trampling each other.

"Nadia!" Wyck yelled at the top of his lungs.

She swung her head toward his voice, her arms pressed to her breasts, her expression terrified.

"Come here!" He punched a *kreer* out of the way, crashing through the crowd to her.

Lesh launched himself at someone's throat. He left him to it.

There were at least as many tables as fingers on his hand between Nadia and him. The males filled the space separating him from her quickly, punching each other to get closer to her as she stood on a table, hugging herself, terrified.

He couldn't get to her fast enough. She needed to be moving, too.

He opened his arms for her, and she ran.

Those light feet of hers leaped from table to table even as the pieces of furniture were moved and shoved aside by the thickening crowd. Her strong legs propelled her forward as she evaded the greedy hands reaching for her from all sides. Jumping in the air from the last table, she briefly landed on the back of Enkail who had fallen to the ground in a scuffle.

The *dimo* grunted then tried to turn around to catch her, but she had already jumped up and into Wyck's arms before anyone else could get to her.

"I've got you," he exhaled. As soon as she was in his arms, something loosened inside him, allowing him to breathe freely once again.

"Lesh!" he called the *mahdi*. The animal had been gnawing on some tentacles that were still attached to a *yourlu* who was writhing and screaming in pain. "Lead," he ordered.

The *mahdi* dropped the whimpering *yourlu* and plowed through the crowd separating them from the entrance. His three heads snapped, bit, and ripped to pieces the flesh of those who stood in their way.

Wyck held Nadia to him with one arm. Her limbs wound tightly around him, she buried her face in his shoulder, surrendering all control to him. With the knife in his other hand, he slashed through the air, deterring any attempts to attack them from the side.

Once in the corridor where the crowd had thinned, he ran. Lesh fell behind slightly, snapping at anyone who tried to pursue them.

When all three of them made it back to her room, he allowed himself to release a long breath, feeling the tension drain from his muscles and letting the worry finally ease in his chest.

His back to the closed doors, he slid to the floor, settling Nadia in his lap.

"Nadia?" he called softly, stroking her long, mussed hair.

She wouldn't move.

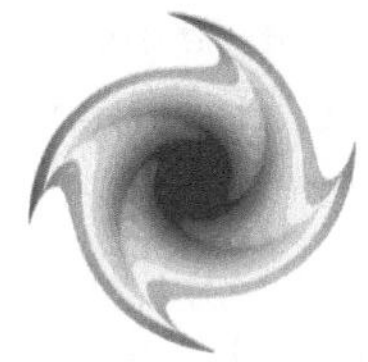

Chapter 11

Nadia

If I kept my eyes closed—the wild faces distorted by madness, the fangs dripping with saliva, and the hands grabbing for me wouldn't come back. There would only be the warmth of Wyck's large, hard body and the safety of his strong arms around me.

Forever.

Among the sea of scowling faces and hulking figures, Wyck had stood out as the biggest and the most intimidating. Yet as soon as he had yelled my name, I'd run to him. I'd run so fast, I practically threw myself into his arms.

"Nadia." His voice filtered through the dark fog of terror, like a ray of sunshine breaking through the storm clouds. "Are you okay?"

His wide, callused hands rubbed my back—my *naked* back. My front was bare, too. The scarf had been ripped off my chest. My naked breasts pressed directly into Wyck's chest as the sides of his vest had fallen apart.

I shifted in his lap, realizing that my body was practically plastered to his, head to toe, while the short, flimsy excuse for a skirt was the only piece of clothing I was wearing.

He must've become aware of that, too, as his erection started to harden and grow against my core.

I peeled myself from him.

"I'm fine. Thank you. For getting me out of there…" I leaned further back, wrapping my arms around my chest. "I'll need to get changed."

"Stay," he rasped, flexing his arms around me. Trapping me.

His erection kept growing. How huge *was* this guy?

His green-speckled golden eyes pinned me in place, the expression in them increasingly more unhinged, wild, so similar to what I'd just seen in the eyes of the others.

Alarm lanced though me.

"Wyck…" Covering myself with one arm the best I could, I pressed my other hand into his chest. "I—I should go."

He yanked me to him. My heart sped up. I desperately tried to hold back fear.

"Please," I begged. "Let me go."

A pained groan rose from his throat. He buried his face in my neck.

"Just give me a moment," he growled against my skin, the short dark stubble on his jawline prickling lightly.

This very instant, he appeared more tortured than dangerous.

"What for?" I asked, tentatively placing my arm around his shoulder.

He inhaled deeply, then again, and again.

"If I smell you long enough," he said, without lifting his head, "if I let your scent fill me inside and out, without holding back for once, then maybe there is a point when I can say I've had enough of you for a while."

His hold on me was as firm as ever, but he didn't let his hands wander. He simply held me close.

I managed to relax a little against him. Placing my hand on the back of his neck, I soothingly trailed my fingers along the three gray ridges. They ran all the way along his head. The one in the middle went down his spine, disappearing under his vest. The two on the sides split at the base of his neck, running along each of his shoulders then down his arms to the knuckles on his hands.

"I thought this might make it easier letting go of you," he said, uncharacteristically softly. "I was wrong, it doesn't." He unwrapped his arms from around me, setting me free. "But go on, get changed."

I wasn't sure what all of that meant exactly, but he did appear calmer after our hug. The wild expression in his eyes didn't entirely disappear, but it had softened somewhat, turning wistful.

Climbing out of his lap, I found my suit then took it to the bathroom to change.

Tonight's events wouldn't leave my mind. My hands still shook and the anxiety about next week had already started to build.

"Why are they like that?" I asked Wyck upon my return from the bathroom. He remained sitting sideways in the doorway, his eyes focused on the metal panel ahead of him. "So...brutally feral?"

"The crew?" He shifted, making some space for me in the entranceway. "That's what they are, what all of us are by nature."

"That's not true." I sat opposite him, my back pressed against the panel he'd been staring at. He had no choice but to look at me, now. "Violence and disrespect are not inherent characteristics of any nation in the modern world. They might've been prevalent in some places, at some point in history, but that's not how things are anymore."

I studied his features for a while, really *seeing* him for the first time.

The three gray ridges on his head met in a peak over the bridge of his nose. The typical for *errocks* heavy brow gave him a fierce expression. The bright yellow eyes glistening underneath appeared almost glowing in the shadows. His proud, angular nose and high sharp cheekbones with dark stubble clashed with the sensual shape of his mouth. The shapely upper lip had a defined curve of the cupid's bow, and the full lower one seemed to be made for kissing.

Wyck was a handsome man, I realized. I had no way of knowing whether an *errock* woman would find him good-looking, but I was positive that many human women would.

He flinched under my scrutiny, and I promptly shifted my stare away from his face.

"Sorry," I mumbled. "I've never spent so much time in the company of a non-human before. I've never even been this close to one of your species. It's all still new."

"*Errocks* and humans don't get along out there?"

"Oh no, we do. There are many joint projects between Hexol and Earth, your planet and mine. Most of them are done remotely, though. Earth is just so far away from the rest of the planets in the Federation. We're also still the newest member."

"You're saying *errocks* out there—people in general—are not the same like they are here?"

"Absolutely not." I shook my head. "Believe it or not, I could be completely naked in a room full of men and no one would dare to touch me without my explicit permission."

He lifted a brow ridge.

"Have you done that?"

"Um, no," I blinked, then gave him a smile. "That is not a common practice. It was just an example."

"Then how can you be so sure no one would touch you?" He gazed at me inquisitively. "You said you haven't been this close to an *errock* before—clothed or not."

"Because I know a lot about the larger nations of the Federation, including the *errocks*. I studied their art and culture. I know the *errocks* nation has been an active member of the Federation, instrumental in making the organization what it is—a safe, peaceful place where all nations live and work together in harmony. Their laws protect personal freedom of all individuals, and they strictly enforce them."

His brow furrowed, Wyck stared at me with suspicion.

"One of the most esteemed politicians in the Federation government is an *errock*," I continued. "His name is Krix Kussur. He came to Earth as part of a delegation, about a year ago. I was sick that day, but my friend went to the welcoming rally and got to meet him in person. He shook her hand and gave her a hug." I crossed my stare with Wyck's. "He did not attack her. Trust me, Nocc's way is *not* an acceptable way of treating women."

"It's not…" he sounded as if thinking out loud.

It blew my mind that personal freedom and respect—something that I'd taken for granted—were a complete novelty to Wyck.

Did he really think that what was happening on the Dark Anomaly could be the norm anywhere else in the Universe?

But then again, had he ever had a chance to learn the truth, before now?

"You only know what the others told you," I said, realizing just how isolated Wyck's life had been in here. Their library was the only window into the world, and he couldn't even use it fully because he didn't know how to read.

Most of his life knowledge came from men like Nocc. I'd never met Crux, but I had a feeling he couldn't have been much better than Nocc. This group of *errocks* had last seen the world outside of the Anomaly thousands of years ago. A lot had changed in the Universe since then.

What had happened out there since *my* arrival here? I'd been on the Dark Anomaly for over a day now, which must be close to a year out there. A dreadful feeling slithered down my spine. Aside from a few close friends, I had no one left on Earth to mourn my disappearance. However, I knew that the rest of my team had families who must be frantic to learn about their fate.

Since I might be the only one who'd survived, I owed it to everyone and to myself to find a way to get out of here.

Once again, my thoughts went to the ship and the damaged capsule. I needed to get out of here, and I might have the means to do that, but I needed help.

I moved my gaze back to Wyck.

"Would you like to see what the world is like out there?" I asked tentatively.

He shot me a glance, and I glimpsed a spark of curiosity in his expression. As grim and unaffected as Wyck tried to behave, I believed he was thirsty for new experiences. It couldn't be easy for him to be cooped up in one place all his life. He had been soaking up every word I'd said about the world beyond the Dark Anomaly.

"No," he said quickly, the light in his gaze dimming. "There is no leaving this place. Dreaming about what's out there only leads to disappointment or death."

Obviously, I wouldn't try to get off the Dark Anomaly without making sure it was safe to do so. Yet Wyck didn't believe it was possible to escape, at all.

I had to find another way to approach this.

"Can I get more slates from the library?"

"It's not safe for you out there, even less so after what happened tonight." He tipped his head in the direction of the mess hall.

"Would you bring me some, then?"

"You need more music?"

"Actually, I'd like to read more about the Dark Anomaly, please. Here..." I grabbed one of the slates lying around. We'd left the frame behind while escaping the mess hall, and without the frame, the slate wouldn't work. I blew a breath on the smooth surface then drew two words in the condensation with my finger. "This is how Dark Anomaly is spelled in the Universal language."

He threw a sideway glance at the words.

"What is it that you need to know about this place? Knowledge won't affect your life in any way."

In some ways, he was right. My life here was not much different than that of a caged animal, let out only for the entertainment of others. However, knowledge was power that could potentially enable me to change things.

There could be a way for me to make Wyck more interested in those changes, too.

I wiped the slate off with my sleeve, then blew on it again.

"Have you ever seen your name in writing?" I asked, tracing the letters in the fog on the slate. "Here, this is how it looks in Universal."

This time, he studied the slate a little longer.

"That's my name?" He took the slate from my hands to take a closer look at the word.

"Yes." I nodded. "These are letters—the written record of each sound in your name. By rearranging the letters, we write words."

"What does *your* name look like?" He handed the slate back to me.

"Here is mine." I wrote it quickly. "See? We have the same sound in yours and mine, which in the Universal language corresponds to the same letter. There it is." I pointed at the letter that in Universal stood for both sounds that the letters *y* and *i* made in his and my names, respectively.

"We share a letter?" He seemed especially pleased by that fact.

"Right." I smiled.

"Is it the same in *my* language?"

"I don't know." I rubbed my forehead. "I don't speak Hexolian. There might not be. There are no common letters in our names in either English or Russian—the two Earth languages that I speak. Both have more complicated structures. But that's the point of Universal—it simplifies things. It was created to unite people of many planets by making communication easier. That's why it's one of the easiest languages to learn, if not *the easiest* one of all."

He kept staring at the slate until the condensation evaporated and the letters disappeared.

"I can teach you how to read," I offered quietly and held my breath in anticipation of his answer.

"Why?" he said after a short pause.

To me, his inability to read was an impairment that could be easily fixed. There was no downside to it. Wyck didn't need to continue going through life in ignorance. I sensed a keen interest about the world in him. He wanted to learn more about it, but he couldn't do so independently.

"Because we have some time to kill," I replied casually. "And being able to read is handy, even around here."

He slid his gaze aside, biting down on that plump lower lip of his.

"I don't think I can learn. Crux used to say I was too dumb for that," he said it simply, without bitterness, as if stating a fact.

Suddenly, I wished Crux was still alive, so I could slap him.

"Crux obviously had no desire to bother teaching you."

Knowing what I did about the men responsible for Wyck's upbringing, there might be more to it. Having Wyck grow up unable to learn things for himself must've made it easier for them to control him. The only truth he'd ever known was whatever they'd told him.

"Knowledge is a kind of power, Wyck."

He rolled his shoulders back, flexing the bulging muscles in his arms.

"I've got enough power as it is." He gave me a crooked grin.

"Physical strength is only part of it. Your captain is not as big or as strong as an *errock*, yet he holds the authority over all of you."

"Because he is smart," he replied slowly.

"See? Knowledge *is* power," I said with conviction. "It'd give you the ability to think for yourself and to make your own decisions based on the information you'd be able to access on your own if you could read."

He kept quiet for a little while. I could almost *see* the thoughts running through his mind.

"You may think you're one of them," I continued. "But you are your own person, first and foremost. And you're not like them."

He stirred, ready to protest, but I wouldn't let him.

"When they all lunged at me back there, ready to rip me to pieces, you got me to safety. You've held me, almost completely naked, in your arms and you let me go without causing me any harm. Would any one of those over six hundred males have done the same?"

Maybe I was wrong. Maybe I had too much faith in him and not enough in the others, but he no longer tried to argue.

"You're not like them, Wyck. You don't have to be."

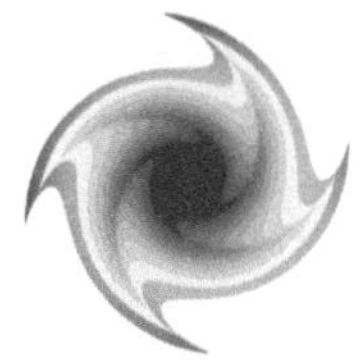

Chapter 12

Nadia

"So, this guy here…" Wyck shifted into a more comfortable position on the floor, in his usual place in the doorway. The tablet frame with an orange slate was in his lap. "He invented the medicine that cured a large portion of the population of a *themul* country on Nofoi."

Leaning against his side, I nodded. "Hundreds of thousands of lives were saved. More than that, though, the process the *errock* Professor Lercur created has been used to make life-saving medicine for other species, too, not just the *themul.*"

"And that's why he is celebrated as a hero everywhere."

"Right."

It had been three days since I started teaching Wyck how to read Universal. His nearly photographic memory allowed him to memorise entire words, which proved a hindrance sometimes. I had to force him to break the words into letters, so he could then learn to read words yet unknown to him, too. Despite some slight setbacks, once he had grasped the concept, he was moving forward with astounding speed.

Wyck had been spending most of the days here with me, leaving only to get us food and to exchange slates from the library. I'd noticed he was especially eager to read biographies of famous men. I believed he loved learning about the many ways in which a person could distinguish themselves in the modern world. At first, he listened with fascination and admiration when I read the stories to him. Now, he had slowly started reading them himself.

"Has Professor Lercur ever visited Earth?" he asked.

"No. I don't believe he has."

"Do you know anyone who has been to Hexol?"

"Not personally. No." I shook my head.

"Would you like to go there one day?"

I snapped my gaze up to his face. It was impossible to tell whether his question was purely hypothetical. I hoped he might be considering the possibility of traveling beyond this place one day.

Other than this mission, I hadn't travelled much. Until now, my life plan had focused on settling down, then creating and raising my family. Now, when I imagined myself taking a trip to Hexol, in Wyck's company, it seemed extremely appealing.

"I'd love to see Hexol," I replied sincerely then added, "If it were possible, that is."

We sat in silence for a while, each lost in our own thoughts.

"Did you have to learn how to dance?" Wyck spoke first, changing the subject, for which I was grateful. "Or are humans born knowing how to do that?"

"No, that's not a born ability. I took dance classes for many years. Though, I did love dancing probably from the day I was born."

"Why?"

I blinked at him in confusion. Why did people like dancing? Or art in general? How could I best explain it to him? And was an explanation even possible?

I often had to adjust my way of thinking around Wyck. He questioned many things I took for granted, forcing me to look at the world from a different perspective. For him, so many things I grew up with were new as he learned about them for the first time.

Dancing seemed to be one of them.

"I always loved it." I shrugged. "While in school, I considered becoming a professional dancer, but when I got a little older, film production attracted me more as a career. Dance just stayed a hobby for me."

"Do you dance at home, when you're alone?"

"Sometimes," I confessed. "But I also go out with friends. I've done a few dance competitions, too. It's been fun. You see, dancing is both my way to relax and revitalize."

It didn't escape me that we both were talking about my life in the present tense, as though I still *had* that life.

"How so?" he asked. "I'm sure it's a strenuous exercise, though you do make it look easy."

I smiled wider.

"True, after a performance I feel tired, but also energized. There is a sense of accomplishment—satisfying and fulfilling. Don't you wish you could express yourself through something bigger than words, sometimes? Don't you ever feel so full with emotions that no words would do? None seem good enough. That's when dancing becomes a necessity for me."

"When I'm *full of emotion*?" He arched an eyebrow ridge, a corner of his mouth lifting in a half-smile. There was a genuine desire to understand behind his amused expression, though.

So, I continued.

"Yeah, like…" I searched for words to describe that mix of longing and energy that grew and bubbled, threatening to explode if I didn't move—the *need* to dance. "I believe it's in everyone, the desire for another form of self-expression. Everyone has something that brings them happiness while they're doing it. It doesn't need to be dancing, of course. It could be any form of art—music, painting, singing—or crafts, creating something with your hands—carving, sewing, knitting."

"You think everyone has that?"

"Sure. Sports could be that, too, for some. Any physical activity."

"Like fighting?"

I bit my lip. The type of fighting that took place on the Dark Anomaly, I suspected, was not what one would call "relaxing and revitalizing."

"Do you feel satisfied after a fight?" I asked.

"If I win. Which I always do." He gave me a cocky grin.

I thought back to the fighting he'd done in the mess hall the night of my performance. He threw punches and maimed people with a sole purpose of allowing us to get away, not because he enjoyed it.

He couldn't be talking about that.

"Do you have some kind of sparring here?" I clarified. "When you fight without the intent of seriously hurting your opponent?"

"There are one-on-one fights organized, nightly. There is always plenty of intent to hurt, but seriously harming each other is not allowed during those fights. Vrateus has strict rules against intentionally inflicting serious injuries." His face lit up with a wide smile. "It's still fun, though."

"Well, I guess fighting without injury could be seen as a form of couple dancing," I mused. "One person attacks, another parries. One leads, another follows."

He tilted his head, as if considering something.

"Sex then could be viewed as a dance, too," he said, unexpectedly.

"Um…"

How exactly did it come to talking about sex?

"One partner attacks," he explained, "the other submits."

I felt I owed it to every woman who might have sex with him one day to correct him on that one. Then, I winced at the thought of Wyck with another woman. It was not a pleasant one, and I chased it away like an annoying fly.

"The goal of having sex, other than for procreation, is the pleasure of both partners," I said to him, "which means it shouldn't be approached like a fight, where there could only be one winner."

"Why not?" He slid his gaze to my lips as I spoke, and I found myself staring at his mouth, too. "Doesn't one person lead and another follow in both cases? Isn't there also some power involved?"

I forced myself to look up from his sensual lips and into his eyes. "Power? Are you talking about something like the power of passion?" I muttered.

His eyes lit up, making me warm inside.

"You see," I cleared my throat, dropping my gaze into my lap, "unlike a fight, there are no losers in good sex. If it's done right, both partners end up winning. That's what so great about it."

"Women also experience pleasure." It wasn't a question. His statement sounded as though female pleasure was not an entirely new concept to him.

"Yes." I glanced up again. "Women do experience pleasure, Wyck. With the right partner, the sex is like a most wonderful dance, with a beautiful finale for both the man and the woman."

He licked his lips, his eyes on me, and I followed his tongue with my gaze.

If I kissed that full bottom lip of his, would his taste have the same flavor as his scent?

The thought was sudden and wrong.

I'd been spending so much time with Wyck, hoping to eventually convince him to assist me in getting off the Anomaly, not to be seduced into daydreaming about the taste of his kiss. The way he was looking at me right now—the glowing gold of his eyes making my insides melt like warm butter—didn't help, either.

"So many wonderful things have happened since your arrival," he said softly.

Had anything *wonderful* ever happened on the Dark Anomaly? For me, it had been nothing but fighting off various aliens and a constant struggle for survival.

That would be Wyck's regular life, I imagined—both rough and monotonous. For him, my arrival here *had* brought some changes to that life, and probably some new excitement along with them.

Turning at the waist to face me, he lifted his hand to my face, and I halted my breath in anticipation of his touch, unsure where it would lead but not willing to stop him.

With a soft whimpering sound, Lesh scooted closer to us from his spot by the wall. He placed all three of his heads across my legs and onto Wyck's lap.

I froze in alarm as the animal's long scaly necks stretched across my thighs, his black curved claws resting on my shin. His right head, the more outgoing one, nuzzled my hand.

"He wants you to pet him." Wyck huffed a laugh, dropping his hand down without touching me after all.

"This one wants it, maybe." I tentatively stroked the red stripe of scales on the side of Lesh's right head. "I'm not so sure about the middle one, though."

In the past three days, as I'd worked on taming his master, Lesh and I had also grown closer. The animal had been staying in my room all this time. Wyck had brought us both food, and all three of us had eaten every meal together.

Unchained, Lesh was free to roam my room, but he appeared to respect my space, sticking mostly to the area along the wall and near the door. He was guarding me when Wyck was not around. And for that, I was beginning to feel a real appreciation for him.

Wyck wasn't lying when he'd said that Lesh had been toilet trained. Ever since he'd unchained him, Lesh had been using the bathroom without fail, which had gained him a new level of respect from me. There hadn't been any more stinky incidents.

Yet until today, Lesh hadn't allowed any physical contact between us.

"The middle head looks like it wants to move away from me as soon as possible." I continued gliding my fingers over the hard, smooth scales on the side of the left head. Lesh's left head also appeared relaxed, but the central one kept watching me with its shiny, black eyes. "It has a rather suspicious personality, doesn't it?"

"What are you talking about?" Wyck petted the middle head then scratched under its jaw. Lesh closed all his eyes, releasing a soft hiss of pleasure. "They're all one animal."

"They are," I agreed quietly. "But if you look closely, each head has its own personality. The middle one is obviously in charge, I'm going to call him Lesher. This one is Leshic." I scratched under the right head's chin, the way Wyck had done to

Lesher. Leshic let me do it, its thin lips stretching into a blissful smile.

This was the most amazing ability of Lesh's, in my opinion—he could smile. With his razor-sharp teeth now on display, the smile wasn't far from a scowl, but I could tell the difference.

"You're a mellow fellow, aren't you?" I murmured, petting the smooth flat top of the right head. "That one, on the left, is cuddlier than the rest. That's how he gets away with much more, too. You are a troublemaker. Right, Leshy?" The left head opened an eye at my question, as if responding to the nickname. I'd seen him demanding and getting more attention than the rest from Wyck.

Wyck watched me intently as I spoke. I wondered if it annoyed him that I'd gotten to know his pet this well and even was taking the liberty to name his heads.

"I call them Boss, Calm, and Cuddly," he finally confessed, his expression a little sheepish. "You're the first one to notice the difference in their behaviours. Normally, I keep Lesh away from everyone."

"Why? He can be friendly once he gets to know you."

He exhaled sharply, shaking his head.

"There is no need for others to know that. Being friendly and approachable may get him killed."

"That's horrible." I hugged Leshic with both hands. "Why kill a friendly animal?"

Wyck shrugged his shoulders, with a somber expression.

"For fun."

I could point out that there was no fun in murdering anyone, let alone an animal. Sadly, I'd gotten to know the dwellers of the Dark Anomaly well enough by now to agree that most of them would possibly derive a perverted kind of pleasure in murder.

"Lesh arrived with the ship that was transporting a large group of *mahdis*," Wyck explained. "All of them were killed within days. He must've escaped the cage somehow because I found him hiding in a short, narrow passage near the *vasai* farm. I was fourteen at the time, and he was only a pup. I hid him away from everyone and kept him alive until both of us grew big enough to protect each other. When Vrateus became the captain, I told him about Lesh. He made Lesh part of the crew, which gave him the same rights as everyone else. Under the captain's rules, Lesh can't be killed without punishment for the murderer. That doesn't mean some still wouldn't try to end him if they got a chance."

He rested his hand on top of the middle head of the animal.

"Lesh needs to be vicious and scary in order to survive and to protect you and me. Deep inside, however, he is still the cuddly playful pup he's always been. We'll just keep your happy side a secret from everyone, right Lesh?" He patted his pet.

Being the only one who was let in on their secret made me feel even closer to both of them, as if I was now officially included into their tiny group.

Stroking Lesh's smooth scales, I snuggled into Wyck's warm side. These few square feet of space by the door might be the only place in the entire Dark Anomaly where both of us felt the most comfortable.

"I'll tell you what," I said. "You'll finish reading this chapter, then we'll take a break from learning. This afternoon I'd say let's watch a movie together. There are a couple you got from the library last time. One even looks like it may have some dancing in it."

He wrapped his arm around my shoulders and settled the tablet between us, re-opening the biography he'd been reading.

I listened as he read out loud, still haltingly and tripping over some long or unknown words. His perseverance was admirable, though, and the speed with which he soaked up everything new simply astonishing.

Sitting like that, cuddling next to Wyck under the blanket, I could almost forget where I was and what lay ahead of me.

Almost.

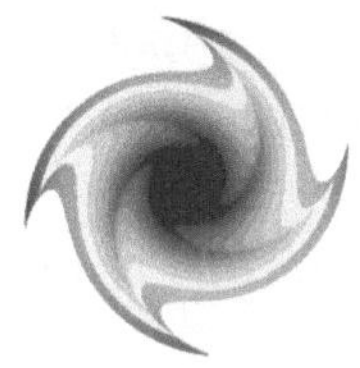

Chapter 13

Wyck

"Hey, boy," Nocc stopped him outside of Nadia's room. Trox and Gler were with him, as they often kept together. What surprised Wyck was that Krakhil, a *dimo*, was also standing nearby, looking as if he were a part of their group, too.

"How is the female doing?" Krakhil asked, a smirk stretching the lipless mouth on his hard-plated face.

"Fine." Wyck started walking towards the mess hall.

It'd been eight days since Nadia landed on the Dark Anomaly. Another session in the mess hall was scheduled for tonight. He had left Nadia in her room because he needed to set up the tables for her dance. He also had to get some lunch for her and Lesh.

The four males who'd accosted him in the corridor were too close to Nadia's room, which troubled him. He walked faster, eager to get them as far away from her as possible.

Thankfully, all four followed him.

"You've been selfish, Wyck." Trox elbowed his way closer to him. "One of the only two females available is in your reach, and you've been keeping her all to yourself for the entire week."

"I'm keeping her safe, for all of us." The statement sounded wrong even to his own ears.

Vrateus had said that Nadia belonged to them all. By now, however, she was more Wyck's than anyone else's.

Only his.

Mine.

The powerful urge to proclaim that out loud vibrated through him. His muscles ached to be put to a good use. He balled his hands into fists, ready to strike.

"If she is ours how come *you're* the only one who smells like her?" Trox growled.

Did he?

Nadia had been taking showers with the soap regularly, making her scent barely discernible. There hadn't been any sex or even kisses between them, of course. The scent Trox was talking about must be coming simply from him being in her proximity daily.

She'd sit next to him in the entryway, the only portion of that room he could tolerate because it had a solid floor instead of glass. He loved the feeling of her body pressed to his—one of the reasons why he'd been spending so much time in the room he hated. He'd often wrap his arm around her shoulders, to get her even closer.

It wasn't much, but they would spend hours siting side by side—enough time apparently for her scent to transfer to his clothes and skin.

Knowing he had her scent on him pleased him, even as Trox continued to harp at him, "We're a family, Wyck. What yours is ours."

"How about *him*, then?" Wyck tipped his chin at Krakhil. "Is *he* a part of the family, too, now?"

"Hey!" the *dimo* roared, the fingers on all four of his hands twitching. "Why do *you* get to fuck her all the time while the rest of us only see her once a week? And even then, she wouldn't spread her legs for us to see or do anything!"

Wyck's temper flared.

"Listen you!" He pivoted into the *dimo's* direction. "No one is fucking her. Definitely, not *you*." He raised his fist, searching for the least armored place on the *dimo's* face to land a blow.

"There, there, now." Nocc stepped closer, draping his arm around Wyck's shoulders. "Krakhil is a friend. A family friend. Okay?"

"He is *not* family." Wyck glared at the *dimo*, keeping his fist aimed at the male's face.

"No, of course not." Nocc patted Wyck's arm in a gesture that felt more patronizing than calming. "But *you* are." He led Wyck down the corridor again, with the rest of the group catching up. "We're a family, Wyck, don't forget that. We live together. We fight together. And we die together. Our loyalty to each other is what has kept us alive all these years—here on the Dark Anomaly and out there before that."

Nocc slowed down, making the two of them fall behind the rest of the group.

"Women are whores to be fucked and tossed out," he continued casually.

Wyck had heard these words often. Never before, however, had they made his skin crawl with revulsion as they did now. His mind and his heart rejected the notion.

"That's what your father did to the female who gave birth to you," Nocc kept going. "He left her in the filthy brothel he'd found her in. It's your luck you were born a boy, so he brought you on his ship. One day, you would've taken over his entire fleet. You're the true leader of this family, Wyck. And the leader is always just and generous to his people. The human girl is our bounty. And as such, she should be shared fairly among all of us. That's what the Great Scodr would've done. It's your legacy, Wyck."

"If I am the 'true leader' of the family," Wyck had chosen a portion of Nocc's speech to focus on, "then I want you to help me carry out this task."

He stopped outside the mess hall, gesturing to the rest of their group to carry on walking.

Krakhil folded his arms across his chest, taking a stance that said he was not moving anywhere. Trox and Gler also paused, glancing at Nocc for directions.

So much for Wyck being their leader. After the death of Crux, Nocc had been the one who held the true power in their group.

Nocc waved his hand, making them all move away, then turned to face Wyck again.

"You don't need to be afraid of Vrateus, boy," he said in a conspiratorial tone. "His days are numbered. He and his woman are as good as dead. I promise I'll let you have the final round with Svetlana, so you can fuck her to death and have your vengeance."

Wyck knew it was his obligation to avenge the death of Crux, but *that* wasn't how he'd do it. When he finally killed Svetlana, he'd do it the way she killed Crux, by shooting her in the belly. That was the reason he kept taking his time, Wyck told himself, he needed to get hold of a gun first.

"Nocc." He diverted the male's attention to what he felt was more important than vengeance at the moment. "I don't want any harm to come to Nadia."

"Who is Nadia?" Nocc made a face, as if the sound of any female name was offensive purely because it was female.

"The woman in my charge."

"You know her name?" Nocc slid him a suspicious glance, his expression sour.

"I have to call her something, don't I?" Wyck snapped.

Nocc shrugged instead of an answer, and Wyck made an effort to rein in his temper.

"We are a family," he used Nocc's own words. "I have a task to complete, and I'm asking for your help."

"Which is?" Nocc narrowed his eyes at him.

"To keep the female safe. I can't do it alone," he added as Nocc curled his lip in disgust. "You saw what happened the last time."

Nocc tilted his head. "Did you hear anything of what I've just told you, boy?"

"I heard every word, Nocc." Keeping his rising anger and frustration at bay was proving harder by the minute. "And I'll tell you the same thing I've told you before—no one harms Nadia. She's here to entertain six hundred males, and the only way for her to do that is if I— if *we*—keep her well and alive. I need to know you're with me on that. Can I count on my family to support me?"

Nocc gave him a long, penetrating look.

For the first time in his life, Wyck felt that the *errocks'* loyalty to each other was not a given. Nocc had spoken the truth when he'd said that the *errocks* on the Dark Anomaly had stood up for each other. Until now, Wyck had always felt the support of their entire group behind him. His strength stemmed from their collective power. The feeling of being on his own lately had been destroying him from the inside. He needed the loyalty of his people, he wanted them on his side. Yet, he also felt that it was *he* who had been drifting away, going against the group.

"You want all of us to help you keep her alive?" Nocc's expression turned calculating.

"Yes. I want you to protect her with me."

"Did Vrateus say something about this?"

"No," Wyck replied firmly. His task had grown way past Vrateus's orders. Keeping Nadia safe had become Wyck's personal mission. "It's because *I* want her safe. And I need you—all of you—on my side."

Nocc shifted his weight to the other foot, his expression finally relaxing. "What exactly do you want us to do?"

Wyck released a short breath. It was too soon to breathe with relief, but Nocc's words gave him hope.

"I want you to keep the crew at bay tonight, away from her. Let her do her dance and let me get her out of there without anyone laying their hands on her."

"Her dance?" Nocc folded his arms across his chest. "She'll need to do more than that tonight."

Wyck's heart hollowed with dread.

"You didn't like her dancing?" he asked flatly.

"It was…*lovely*," Nocc spat the word out as if it burnt his mouth. "But I barely caught a glimpse of her tits before you hauled her away. That was hardly fair, boy."

His thoughts drifted back to that night. The moment Nadia had run to him something had snapped in his heart. Since then, she'd been becoming his main reason to wake up every morning. By now, he felt he would die to protect her. Except that his death would leave her completely on her own. And he might need help to stay alive.

"If you want to see her naked," he said to Nocc, slowly, "you'll have to make it safe for her to do so. No one touches her, no one even comes close enough to breathe on her. Do you understand?"

Nocc chewed on the inside of his cheek, taking a pause that was too long for Wyck's comfort.

"It's a deal," he finally said, and Wyck was able to inhale deeply.

"Promise she won't be harmed," he demanded, needing to hear it said out loud.

"Promise." Nocc nodded.

Getting Nocc's word on it was as good as securing a promise from their entire group. Having his family fully behind him again took a load off Wyck's shoulders.

Errocks were the largest group on the Dark Anomaly, both in size and in number. Vrateus recognized their power, giving them the honor of being his personal guard. Even after Crux had taken over the Dark Anomaly, naming himself the captain, and Vrateus had fought him to get his title back, he'd kept the *errocks* as his guards. The captain needed their power.

No one dared to mess with *errocks*, and Wyck loved that. He enjoyed being a part of something bigger than he could ever be on his own.

Feeling somewhat lighter at heart, he got some food for Nadia, Lesh, and himself. Then the three of them had lunch together. It was easy to forget about the world outside of their glass bubble when he was talking with Nadia.

She smiled, telling him another story about the outside world that was beginning to truly fascinate him. Lesh lay at his side, gnawing on a bone. And Wyck didn't want to think about anything beyond the present moment.

Once he finally forced himself to leave her side, he turned right from her room, not left. Then, he headed toward Vrateus's room instead of his own.

"Captain!" He slammed his fist into the set of double doors, identical to those of Nadia's.

Vrateus had occupied this room ever since he'd become the captain of the Dark Anomaly. Wyck was sure that the reason the captain had selected this space out of the many available on the carcases of the crashed ships that made up the solid body of the Anomaly was its glass walls the *errocks* found unnerving.

Wyck harbored no illusions. The captain used and tolerated the *errocks*—that didn't mean he liked them or trusted them in any way.

Yet he had to make the captain trust him this one time.

"Captain!" He slammed his fist into the door once again. "It's me, Wyck. I need to talk to you."

The door slid aside a little, the gap not big enough for Wyck even to slid his hand through. He wasn't planning to get in anyway, even if he'd been invited.

"I need a gun," he blurted out as soon as Vrateus's face came into view through the gap.

"No."

Wyck wedged the toe of his boot into the gap, afraid the captain might shut the door in his face.

"You told me to protect Nadia, the human female," he rushed out. "I need a real weapon to do it effectively."

"Who is it, honey?" Svetlana's voice cooed from somewhere deep in the room.

Her tone was warm and soft, the words swaddling Wyck's heart like a fuzzy blanket. He knew she wasn't talking to *him*, but that didn't lessen the wonderful effect of the love in her voice.

"It's Wyck, my treasure," Vrateus replied softly over his shoulder. "Just give us a minute." He slid the door open a little wider and slipped out into the corridor.

Suddenly, Wyck knew *why* he'd never honored the ancient tradition of his family and hadn't killed Svetlana. This feeling between her and the captain that he'd sensed weeks ago had captured his curiosity. He'd never witnessed anything like that between a man and a woman. It was like a puzzle, an enticing mystery to him.

He'd let her live, while he'd watched them together, day after day, trying to decipher whatever this relationship was that they shared.

What he'd seen and heard had bred a new feeling inside him.

Envy?

He wondered how it would feel if *he* had someone to speak to him the way Svetlana did to Vrateus. He wished to have someone he could *treasure*, too.

Well, he did have someone he needed to protect like the dearest treasure there was.

"I'm not leaving here without a gun," he said stubbornly, giving the captain a glare.

Vrateus folded his arms across his chest, leaning back against the closed doors.

"Whom are you going to use it against?"

"Against anyone who tries to hurt her," he replied earnestly.

Vrateus gave him a long stare, and he firmly held it with his own.

Resentment rose inside his chest, heating up the anger he'd carried since the day of Nadia's nearly tragic performance. Under the captain's scrutiny, his temper rose higher with each passing second—Vrateus was the one who'd put her in the situation that had nearly led to a disaster last week.

"How do I know you won't turn the weapon against me?" Vrateus asked calmly. "Like you did a few weeks ago, with Crux."

That was a valid question. Vrateus had every right to be cautious. However, Wyck didn't care about his precautions right now. The thin film of his composure broke, and the anger boiled over.

"You did this!" He grabbed handfuls of Vrateus's pristine white shirt at the captain's chest and shoved him against the wall near the door. "You threw Nadia to the crew to protect your own woman, didn't you?"

Vrateus's facial muscles barely twitched. With a sharp click, one of the guns he always carried on him slid out of his wide sleeve. The cold metal of the tip pressed against Wyck's temple. "Cool your temper, Guard Leader," the captain said slowly.

Wyck's temper had caught on fire, though, even the cool metal of death at his head failed to stop him.

"You know that human women find it disgraceful and terrifying to undress in front of the hundreds of males here," he gritted through his teeth, scowling into the *themul's* face.

"I do." The focus sharpened in the captain's bright orange eyes, the vertical slits of his pupils narrowed. "But how did *you* learn about that?"

"I saw it last week," Wyck seethed. "She was scared. She is outright panicking right now."

"And you care?"

"Yes!" He gave the captain another shove, ready for a fight. Blood coursed hot in his veins, pumping his muscles with energy to punch and crush.

Shockingly, Vrateus lowered his gun in response.

"Good. That means I didn't make a mistake by assigning you to her."

The captain's calm reaction left Wyck with no opponent. Confused, he relaxed his grip on Vrateus's shirt.

"If you really care for her," the captain said. "Then you should understand better now what I did back then. If you had to choose between protecting your woman or Svetlana, which one would you have sent to the mess hall?"

Wyck dropped his hands, releasing the captain, and took a step back. The realization rushed him—were he in Vrateus's place, he would've done exactly the same. He'd sacrifice others to keep Nadia well and happy.

"I didn't simply replace Svetlana with Nadia," Vrateus continued. "By the time the human ship arrived here, I'd already found a way to keep my woman away from the crew. If you care about yours, find a way to keep her out of their reach, too. Your chances are even better than mine because you're not alone. As one of their own, you have the *errocks'* loyalty. No one would dare go against you while you have your brothers by your side."

That should be true. Why did the unwelcome doubt scratch inside him when he was reminded about his family's loyalty to him?

Vrateus must have caught something in his expression.

"How is Nocc?" he asked.

"Fine."

He would never admit to Vrateus that he had to talk Nocc into helping him. Vrateus didn't need to know about the inner dealings of the *errock* family, definitely not about any rifts between them. Wyck had gotten Nocc's word, that should be as good as gold.

"Whatever you decide to do to protect her," the captain continued, "you'll have my support. I can order the end of the sessions in the mess hall any time, but my orders are only as good as their enforcement. Can you and your brothers contain the rest of the crew when they learn you'll be keeping the female away from them? Are you confident you can stop them from rushing her room or ambushing you on your way to her or attacking all of you in your sleep?"

Listening to the captain, Wyck realized how much worry this man must be living with every day. Protecting a woman was not a battle but a constant war on the Dark Anomaly.

Vrateus briefly placed his hand on Wyck's shoulder. "Think about it, then let me know."

"For now, I just need a gun," he said. "Nadia was attacked last week, I won't let it happen again. You've put me in charge of her, give me the means to do my job well."

After another long, assessing stare, the captain finally nodded.

"Just one?"

"I only have two hands, and I prefer to keep one free and ready to punch." Besides, more guns potentially meant more chances for them to be stolen.

"Wait here." Vrateus went back into his room and when he returned, he had a black leather holster with a laser gun in it.

Wyck grabbed it, but Vrateus held on tight.

"Promise me you will only use it for her defense."

"I promise," he said sincerely. "I need it for tonight only. You can have it back first thing tomorrow morning."

"Find a way to keep her out of their reach," the captain had said, and that was exactly what he intended to do. He needed some time to

figure out how, but he vowed right then and there that tonight would be Nadia's last dance for the crew.

"Keep it." The captain released his hold of the holster belt. "I hope you won't have to use it."

Vrateus might be right. With his family at his side, managing the mob should be much easier.

"Captain?" he said as Vrateus turned to go back into the room.

The *themul* glanced his way, his long furry tail whipping across the tops of his tall boots.

"Is there something else?"

"Yes." Wyck rubbed the back of his neck, unsure how to word his other request. "Nadia has been asking about Svetlana."

"What?" the captain growled. His tail lashed wildly and the orange in his eyes darkened. "Why?"

Wyck shrugged.

"She wants to talk with her. The two of them are the only humans here."

For him, Nadia's desire to see someone of her own species made perfect sense. However, he had no idea if as a *themul*, the captain shared the same sense of family.

"The only surviving women, too," he added.

Vrateus heaved a long breath, leaning back against the door again.

"You haven't told Svetlana about Nadia, have you?" Wyck asked, already knowing the answer. He wanted to find out the reasons for the captain's silence.

"No."

"Why? Are you afraid they'd plot another escape plan?"

Vrateus glanced up at Wyck from under his dark eyebrows. "You know there is no way to *escape* here." He raked his claws through the wide stripe of long, thick fur on his head. "I'm not afraid that Svetlana would leave. Fuck, I'd go with her if that were possible. What scares me is that she would try again."

"She *has* tried," Wyck reminded. "She knows she'd die if she tries again."

"She does." Vrateus heaved another sigh. "However, the risk of death wouldn't stop her, I'm afraid. Svetlana is a scholar, with an unquenchable thirst for knowledge. She is willing to risk her life in the quest for more knowledge, in the name of research."

Still a week ago, the meaning of this would've been lost on Wyck. Now, he realized he understood it well. Moreover, he could *relate* to Svetlana. He, too, had developed a thirst for knowledge, looking forward to every new chapter and each new book. He asked questions and searched for answers. Except that so far, he'd been able to find answers to most of his questions. How far would he go to get answers to the yet unanswered ones?

Vrateus shifted his weight to his other foot. "If Svetlana learns about a human ship crashing here, with significantly more advanced technology—"

"They didn't crash," he blurted out.

"What do you mean?"

"It was a controlled landing," he explained, there was no point in holding this information back now. "They planned to eventually take off and leave."

"Leave? They thought they could do that?"

"That's what Nadia says. Yes."

The captain huffed a sad laugh.

"They might have *planned* it. Doesn't mean they would've succeeded." Vrateus furrowed his brow. "More reasons not to tell Svetlana about it. I'm worried she would be tempted to test their theories."

"So, how long are you planning to keep the new ship a secret from her?"

The human vessel had landed at the very edge of the habitable sector, at the end of the corridor past the gardens. There might never be a reason for Svetlana to wander that way. The crew rarely spoke to her—the possibility of someone telling her about it was low. Unless she somehow accidentally discovered the cut-out, she could remain ignorant about its presence for a very long time.

"Will you ever tell her?" Wyck asked.

"I don't know. Maybe. One day." The captain flashed him a warning look. "Don't you dare tell her yourself."

"I won't," he promised. He hardly ever spoke to Svetlana himself. Keeping her informed was not on the list of his duties. "Thanks for this." He swung the holster on the belt the captain's way.

"Take good care of it," Vrateus said, on his way back to his room and to his woman. "And take good care of your female."

Your female. Wyck loved the sound of it, and he no longer needed the captain's orders to care for Nadia.

Chapter 14

Nadia

"Ready?" Wyck walked into my room.

I knew it was time for my next performance. But I was *not* ready.

I had changed into a new outfit with a floor-length, purple gown for the top layer. I'd put on a pair of golden sandals I'd found in the trunk under the clothing rack. I had been standing in front of the door for a few minutes now, waiting for Wyck to take me to the mess hall.

But I was not ready to go through with it after what had happened the last time.

"Yes," I said, pressing the tablet with my music to my chest. "Let's get it over with."

Because it would be over soon. Tomorrow morning, we'd be having breakfast together. And I wouldn't have to dread taking my clothes off in front of a wild crowd for another week.

"Nadia." He placed his large hands on my shoulders, peering into my eyes.

I nodded quickly. "I know. They'll want me completely naked this time."

They'd made their preferences very clear last week. My artful half-disrobing hadn't been enough for them.

His fingers flexed on my shoulders, digging in to the point of pain.

"This is the last time, I swear," he gritted through his teeth.

I winced, and he eased his hold on me.

"I've made sure you'll be safe."

"I know." I nodded again, my voice clipped from nerves. "I trust you."

I did. I trusted Wyck. Last week as I'd been surrounded by the crowd of lust-crazy males, he stood out as the largest and the most intimidating of them. Yet I had run to him for safety. Instinctively, I'd known then that he would rescue me from them. I believed he would protect me tonight, too, if it came down to it.

"We'll be fine." I patted his hand on my shoulder, trailing my fingers over the hard ridges on his knuckles.

His expression was grim and focused, but concern warmed the gold of his eyes. With the last encouraging squeeze, he let go of my shoulders, then produced a device from the holster under his arm. It took me a few moments to realize that he was holding a weapon.

I only had some theoretical knowledge of guns. To me, they were mostly costume props we used when filming historical movies. I knew just enough to distinguish between the projectile shooting handguns that the captain had used to threaten his crew the day of my arrival on the Dark Anomaly, and the slightly more modern laser gun that Wyck was now holding in his hand.

Both kinds of weapons had been long eliminated from use by civilians back on Earth. I'd never had a chance to see a real gun until I got to the Dark Anomaly.

"Are you planning to use it against your own crew mates?" I asked. My hands started to tremble from the anxiety caused by that thought.

"Let's hope I won't have to," he replied with an ominous note in his voice.

Clutching the tablet so hard my fingers hurt, I nodded silently, following him to the door.

Wyck clipped the end of Lesh's chain to his belt, holding the gun in one hand while he took my arm with the other.

As we walked down the corridor, his hand gradually slid down my arm. By the time we stopped in front of the entrance to the mess hall, his fingers were laced through mine.

I gripped his hand tightly. It was large and rough, warm and strong and most importantly, unlike mine, it did not tremble. That alone was more comforting to me than anything.

The air in the room was rich with sweat and charged with lust. I tried to avert my eyes from the half-naked male bodies. It was challenging to find a safe place to rest my gaze, however. Every chair in the room was occupied. Some of the crew were reclining on the floor, leaning against the walls. Others clung to the walls or the pipes and cables under the ceiling.

The mass rippled and stirred with excitement as Wyck and I entered. I felt the weight of their attention on me, their gazes sliding down my body, their nostrils flaring to suck in my scent.

"Show us what you've got, sweet thing!" someone yelled.

"Yeah but give us more to see this time!" another one warned.

I stopped myself from raising my eyes to search for them. The less I saw, the less I'd remember and the fewer nightmares I might have later.

Letting go of Wyck's hand regretfully, I turned on the tablet. The upbeat music of my selected song filled the space, drowning out the noise of the crowd.

"I'm ready," I said to Wyck quietly.

Hands on my waist, he lifted me up onto one of the tables that had been pushed next to each other to form a makeshift catwalk-style stage. I glanced back at him, getting some comfort from having him here.

His yellow eyes focused on me with wonder and anticipation.

Was Wyck just as excited as the rest of them to see me strip?

What would it matter if he were? He was one of them after all.

I drew in a deep breath, letting the music take over my senses.

The dancing part was easy. I hadn't practiced the choreography beforehand, it just came to me as I went. Letting my heart guide me freed my mind. After having spent a week locked in a room, I found any movement liberating. I twirled, leaped, and glided, wishing I could simply keep dancing like this, lost to the world.

Except that *they* were waiting—the world of the Dark Anomaly.

Blindly, I found the tie of the top layer of my outfit and tore at it. The long, wrap-style dress fell away. Someone snatched it out of the air before it had a chance to flutter to the ground. I was left in another long, flowing skirt and a cropped, sleeveless top.

A roar rolled through the room.

"Too many clothes!"

They didn't want to be teased. They demanded *everything*, and they wanted it *now*.

I glanced Wyck's way. His expression momentarily made me forget about the restless crowd. Wonder and appreciation shone on his face—the expression that every artist longed to see on the faces of their audiences.

Out of the hundreds of individuals here, Wyck was the one who truly appreciated my dancing. He appeared happy to watch it even as I remained fully clothed.

I gave him a smile, just before someone's arm or tail lashed against me, knocking me off balance.

Fear slammed at me full force as I fell, my knees painfully hitting the hard surface of the table. Hands, tentacles, and other appendages reached for me. They tore at my clothes, slithered under them, groping for my body underneath.

"Nadia!" Wyck's voice was like a lifeline in the ocean of chaos. I crawled toward it, making my way through the mass of male bodies fighting on top of me. They shoved and punched each other out of the way in their strife to get to me first.

Thin, crackling sounds of laser shots pierced the noise of the crowd, followed by the stench of burnt flesh.

"Wyck!" I yelled, frantically kicking at someone's hand gripping my ankle.

Another rough hand grabbed my arm, and I was yanked out of the pile of gyrating bodies on top of me.

"And there she is," an *errock* said with a smirk, my arm painfully clammed in his massive hand. "Our bounty, at last."

"Trox, let her go." Wyck's voice sounded strangled.

He lay on the ground. A *dimo*—Enkail, I remembered his name from the day of my landing—had his hard-plated knee planted between Wyck's shoulder blades. Another huge *dimo* sat on Wyck's back, behind Enkail. A whole swarm of *kreers* held down Wyck's legs and arms. His knuckles were bloody. One side of Enkail's face had been smashed in despite the plated armor that *dimos* were born with.

A *yourlu* lay on the ground with his head twisted aside, motionless. Quite a few other males littered the floor. Bearing laser wounds, some of them remained unmoving, others writhed in pain.

Wyck had fought hard before they'd all swarmed him and wrestled him down.

"Let's see what she's got." Nocc stepped from the crowd, making my skin crawl at the memories of his hands on me.

Enkail handed Nocc the laser gun they had taken away from Wyck. Nocc already had my knife in his other hand.

A growling hiss from the middle of the room made me glance that way. Poor Lesh was tied to a cable dangling from the ceiling. A bunch of *yourlu* taunted him with their tentacles. They slapped him from all sides then leaped out of his reach before he could bite any of them.

Nocc pressed the gun into my belly, snapping my attention to him again. Lust burned bright in his yellow eyes—lust for both my flesh and my life.

I halted my breath, even my heart seemed to stop as terror spread in cold tendrils through my chest.

"Nocc!" Wyck growled. "You promised!"

Nocc narrowed his eyes, his jaw muscles twitched in annoyance.

"I know," he barked over his shoulder. "I'm not going to *harm* her." He slid the gun higher up my belly, between my breasts, then stuck the end of it into my neckline. He smirked, keeping his eyes on me. "She'll live." His words sounded more like a threat than reassurance.

I shrunk away from him, but Trox yanked me back in place.

"Nocc. Fuck!" Wyck roared and bucked, shaking the hulking *dimos* off his back as if they were bowling pins. "Get off me!" He rose to his feet.

His massive figure towered over the scattered males—imposing and intimidating. Hands fisted at his sides, eyes glowing with rage, nostrils flaring, the sight of him was sure to send fear into the hearts of anyone.

"You promised!" he bellowed, moving on Nocc.

A foolish *kreer* stumbled in his way, and Wyck swiped him aside with his fist. The *kreer* screeched, flying through the air, then wedged under one of the tables behind me.

Nocc promptly pointed the gun at Wyck. Faced with the approaching menace, Nocc's expression changed from smug to worried.

"Stand back!" he yelled. "Or I'll shoot!"

"Go ahead. Shoot." Wyck slammed a fist into his own chest, taunting. "Or would you rather do it when I turn my back to you? You backstabbing puddle of slime."

Nocc leaped to me, jamming the gun under my chin.

"Or maybe, I'll shoot her first." Some confidence returned to his voice. "Kill your pretty little toy, then no one gets to play with her."

Wyck halted abruptly, as if he'd hit a brick wall.

"Don't."

Nocc smirked, no doubt feeling the power over Wyck.

"That's better." He tipped his chin at the youngest *errock*. "You stay where you are, and I'll let you both live. I'll keep my promise, it's the *errocks'* way after all. I know we're a family, it's you who keeps forgetting it, boy."

He took a pause, for emphasis, then continued, "You're the one who's been acting like a slimy softy around this one." He shoved the gun harder against my throat, making me cough. "Your father would've been long done with her. He was just and always shared his women with his crew, too. If there was anything left to share, that is."

Moving his stare away from Wyck, Nocc slid it down my body in an assessing way.

"I'll tell you what." He licked his lips. "I'll show you just how kind and generous I am. I'll let *her* choose her first fuck."

"No one is fucking her!" Wyck lunged my way. Two *errocks* grabbed his arms, aided by two *dimos*, straining to hold him back.

"Stay where you are, boy." Nocc grabbed a handful of my hair, tipping my head back. The cold metal of the gun trailed a chilling path along my throat. "Or I'll change my mind on being kind and generous tonight."

"We had a deal." Wyck glared at him.

"The deal was for her to entertain us. And none of us find her fancy moves entertaining enough."

"I'll touch her, no one else." Wyck shrugged his shoulders, making those holding him stagger. "Like Vrateus touched Svetlana."

"Too late, boy. I don't care about touching. I want to see some real fucking."

"No!" His teeth clenched, Wyck yanked his right arm free then punched the *errock* on his left in the jaw.

Nocc jerked the gun Wyck's way again. Two more *errocks* leaped from the crowd and onto Wyck. Someone kicked the back of his legs, sending him to his knees.

"Don't hurt him." A sob ripped from my throat, warm tears rolled down my cheeks as my entire body shook from shock and terror.

How did it all go so wrong so fast?

"I said stand back!" Nocc pressed the gun to Wyck's head, between two bony ridges. "I swear on the memory of the Great Scodr, I'll burn a hole in your brains, my promise be fucked."

Nocc's threat charged the air with a new level of brutality. The room stilled, everyone watching the *errocks* going against each other. The tension grew so thick, I could hear it ring in my ears. It seemed a drop of a pin could set the fire off, resulting in the murder of an unarmed man.

"I'll do it!" I said, barely realizing myself what I was doing. My voice sounded high but strong enough to carry through to the far walls of the room. "I'll do what you want me to do. Put the gun down."

If Nocc shot Wyck, I'd be on my own. I didn't dare imagine what would happen to me then, but it wasn't the reason why I'd stopped Nocc. At that very moment, I didn't think far enough ahead to worry about myself. I simply couldn't let Wyck die.

The two men broke their stares from each other to gaze at me—Nocc with an obvious triumph, Wyck with utter shock.

"Nadia." There was so much in Wyck's voice—warning, regret, sadness…

"Unlike you, the girl has some brains." Nocc beamed with satisfaction that quickly turned to eager anticipation.

"Or maybe she's horny, too!" Trox snorted, shifting closer to me.

I'd come here tonight fully expecting to be degraded. What they wanted from me, however, added an entirely new level to it.

"You said I can choose," I hurriedly reminded Nocc. Panic pulsed inside me as I'd seen how little weight Nocc placed on his promises.

"Do you have someone in mind already?" He gave me another one of his leering stares.

I bit my lip, holding back a curse and a slap to wipe that repulsive smirk off his face. Unfortunately, he was the one with the gun at Wyck's head, and therefore the one with the power over both of us.

"I want Wyck," I said firmly.

Nocc's brow ridge rose.

"Him?" He released a roar of laughter. "You want the boy?"

Trox growled low at my side, his grip on my arm tightened from bruising to agonizing.

"Did you hear that, Wyck? Your newest pet wants you to fuck her." Nocc kept guffawing. "The hassle of looking after her might be paying off for you."

I dropped my gaze to the floor, dreading to look at Wyck. Whatever camaraderie we had shared before, whatever fragile friendship might've developed between the two of us, I felt it would now be crushed by the brutality of this situation.

Wyck was the last one I wanted to see me as nothing more than a sex object. His was the only opinion that mattered to me here. I didn't want any intimacy between us to happen this way.

Yet there was no other choice. The thought of being touched by anyone else in here made my stomach churn with revulsion.

"Well, what do you know," Nocc mused, stepping aside. "The boy will get to fuck for real, after all."

"About time!" Trox scoffed, finally letting go of my arm.

I rubbed the soreness out of it, keeping my gaze down.

"Go get her!" Nocc slapped Wyck's back as he rose to his feet. "Then, we'll all show you how the real men do it." He howled with laughter again, the rest of *errocks* joining him. "Here." Nocc shoved the laser knife into a tentacle of a *yourlu*. "Make sure she doesn't do anything funny."

I stepped back, away from all of them, until my backside hit the table behind me.

How much could a woman go through?

How much could *I* take?

Since I'd landed in the Dark Anomaly, I'd seen my colleagues brutally murdered, I'd been assaulted and humiliated. Every time I thought I'd reached the limit of what I could take, more had been thrown at me. Every time, I went through it, my limits grew. And here I was now, about to have public sex in order to survive for just a little bit longer.

Was this life even worth living? Any struggle to prolong this existence suddenly seemed useless. I closed my eyes—the fight, the light, and the energy draining from me.

I recognized his warm, spicy scent and knew he'd come closer.

His chest touched my forehead, and he put his hands on my waist.

I didn't want this to happen this way.

I wanted to tell him. My throat tightened too much for me to speak. The words weren't strong enough to convey the anguish I felt, anyway.

He lifted me up onto the table behind me then stepped closer between my legs.

Everything inside me tensed. I no longer felt the relaxing comfort I'd grown accustomed to in his presence. Right now, even Wyck's touch felt foreign and invasive.

He lowered his head to my ear and whispered, "I have no idea what I'm doing."

My heart leaped with a loud thud in my chest, and I blinked in shock. I'd been expecting to be ravaged publicly, hoping that with Wyck, it would be more bearable somehow.

I did not expect this confession.

Slowly, I lifted my gaze to his. His warm, golden eyes were on me, a light smile curved his full lips.

Relief flooded me. There was no resentment, no cold hostility I'd dreaded to see, not a trace of any violent lust in his expression. Though, the burning desire was prominently there, but it was softened by kindness and affection that melted my heart.

I wasn't alone, the Wyck that I knew was still with me.

"Come here," I said softly, cupping his face.

The music was still blasting out of the tablet, the same upbeat song playing on a loop. It helped with drowning out the noise of everyone else in the room.

"Keep your eye on the gun and the knife," I whispered into his ear before planting a kiss on the side of his neck. "I'll do the rest."

"I—I'll try..." he breathed out, wrapping his arms tighter around me.

Nocc sat in a chair nearby, the gun in his hand still trained at Wyck's head. The *yourlu,* with my laser knife clutched in one of his tentacles, took a place on the table right behind me. The blue-flame blade was hovering just above my shoulder.

I focused on the music for a moment, thinking only about Wyck. Sliding my hands up the hard planes of his chest, I savored the sensation of his warm skin under my palms. I hooked one arm around his neck, to bring his head lower. Using the moment, I finally did what I'd wanted to do for so long now—I kissed him.

I gently took that plump lower lip of his between mine, and he released a soft gasp into my mouth. The spice of his scent was in his taste, pleasant and familiar. I slid the tip of my tongue between his lips, and he yielded, parting them for me.

He splayed his large, warm palms on my bare back between my top and the skirt. The sensation tingled with warmth along my arms and thighs.

This could be so good.

Being with Wyck could be amazing, it dawned on me—had this been for real.

But it wasn't, this was all for show.

"What the fuck is she doing?" Nocc's rough voice yanked me out of the soft, blissful haze of kissing Wyck. "Spread your legs and take his cocks in. Now!"

The blade of the knife in the *yourlu's* tentacle jerked closer to my neck, searing a lock of my hair off.

I whimpered in terror, dropping my hands away from Wyck.

"Ssh." He cradled my head to his shoulder. His other hand went for the clasp on his pants. "I won't hurt you, promise."

I knew I could trust *his* promises. This did not ease my anxiety, though. It spiked even higher when his erection came into view. The same reddish brown as most of his skin, it had a slight greenish undertone where the thick veins protruded all along his length. Incredibly, it appeared longer and thicker than my forearm.

Errock males had two penises, I remembered something I'd heard back in college and recently from Nocc. Their females had two vaginas, too. I didn't. I couldn't even begin to think what to do with one of those, let alone two.

I stared at it in horror.

"This will never work," I mumbled, cold with dread.

"Why?" Wyck asked innocently.

"Too big…" was all I could manage, swallowing hard.

He took my hand in his and placed it on his massive shaft, wrapping my fingers around it.

"Make it smaller, then."

"How?"

He felt hot and hard in my hand. The smooth, silky skin

stretched thin around his massive girth. The thick veins bulged and pulsed under my palm as he slid my hand along his length.

Wyck pressed my fingers tighter, and miraculously, the hard flesh in my hand squeezed smaller.

He hissed, his expression pained.

"Does it hurt?" I asked quickly, trying to yank my hand away.

"Somewhat." He wouldn't let me remove my hand, pumping it along his length with me. "But in a most wonderful way."

As I squeezed and moved my hand, a thin layer of slippery moisture seeped between my fingers. "What's this?"

He shrugged. "Makes the rubbing easier."

"I see." I smiled at his words. I could actually smile in this situation. How? I had no idea, only that with Wyck's wide back shielding me from most of the room, breathing had become easier.

"Does it feel…right to you?" he asked.

Right? Nothing about this felt right.

But that wasn't what Wyck was asking about, I understood. He wondered how I felt. He cared about my feelings. And that was the one thing that actually *was* right.

He asked because he had no frame of reference whatsoever. He'd told me that after Svetlana, I was the only woman he'd ever seen in his life. I realized I must be the first woman he'd ever touched.

More than that, his earlier confession could also mean that he'd never even seen two people making love. He'd seen people fucking in the videos that the men who raised him had made him watch. Consciously or not, however, he didn't want to repeat what he'd seen in the videos with me. Right now, Wyck was trying to do something entirely new to him with me—he wanted to be gentle. Something he had never been taught to be.

"We'll make it right, Wyck," I whispered, kissing the ridge of his cheekbone. "We'll make it right for *us*."

Shifting back on the table a little, I lifted my legs, planting the heels of my feet on the edge. The long, mint-green skirt I was wearing draped between my raised knees, concealing me from the lewd stares of the others.

"Come closer." I tugged him to me.

His erection in my hand had shrunk to a much more manageable and far less intimidating size by now. Holding him in my fist, I slid my hand under my skirt and positioned him at my opening.

"Closer…" I whispered.

He bucked his hips, his well-lubricated length sliding inside me effortlessly.

I buried my face in the base of his neck and closed my eyes. This moment was for Wyck and me only, even as hundreds of others were witnessing it.

He inhaled a shuddered breath. "Fuck…Nadia…" His arms clamped tight around me. No one would be able to pry me away from him now.

"I need to move," he groaned.

"Mhm." I nodded as he began to pump his hips.

With each smooth slide, he grew inside me, filling me entirely. A slight flicker of pleasure low in my belly grew brighter, spreading in hot tingles along my thighs.

"Is this right?" he asked.

"This is perfect…" I murmured, griping his vest below his shoulders and tugging him to me.

I did not expect this. I was not prepared to enjoy any of this. I'd braced myself to get over tonight and hoped to still be alive in the morning. Now, as Wyck moved inside me in smooth tantalizing thrusts, pleasure kept growing, spreading through me in waves.

My reply must have given him more confidence. Gradually, he had taken over. With one hand, he continued to cradle my head, the fingers of the other dug into my hip, holding me in place as the power of his thrusts increased.

A low growl vibrated in his chest, resonating through me. His arms slid around me once again, as he pressed me to him so tight I could barely breathe. His massive body convulsed with his release, pushing the table back with a loud screech against the floor.

I ventured a peek over his shoulder, quickly sweeping the place with my gaze.

Nocc remained in his chair, with Trox sitting on the floor next to him. Both held their enormous dicks in their hands.

Though Wyck was only using one of his, the rumors were true, *errocks* did have a pair each. With a dick in each hand, Nocc had no hands left to hold the gun. It lay on the corner of the table I was sitting on, a little too far for me to reach in one move. I believed I only had *one* move, one chance at it while Nocc was still coming, spurts of shimmering green goo shooting all over his hands.

Wyck leaned his head on my shoulder, spent after his orgasm. I slid my hand up, trailing my fingers along the bumpy line of ridges on the back of his neck.

"The gun," I whispered so softly only he could here. "Can you get it?"

Wyck's arms were longer than mine. While standing, he also had a wider range of motion.

His muscles tensed at once, all post-orgasmic softness completely gone from his body. Tucking himself in with one hand, he dashed sideways, going for the gun.

The knife over my shoulder dipped, slicing through my hair and scorching the skin at the base of my neck. I squeezed the tentacle that held the knife handle and leaped off the table. Twisting my wrist, I flipped the blade back, toward the tentacle.

"You filthy whore!" The *yourlu* scurried to the edge of the table after me, his other tentacles lashing at me as I cut through the one that held the knife.

"*Filthy*?" I snapped at him, yanking the knife from his loosened grip. "Do you consider yourself *clean*?" I wrinkled my nose at the soiled, greasy shirt he was wearing.

He scurried back, away from my knife. The cluster of tentacles he had for legs undulated under him, sliding and slipping along the surface of the table.

I saw Wyck point the gun at the two *errocks*, their limp dicks draped listlessly over their thighs. He was in control, now. Knife in my hand, I dashed to Lesh.

He hissed and growled as I made my way to him, dodging the males. Some of them still had their pants around their ankles.

His teeth snapping at everyone around us, Lesh didn't so much as nip at me. Grabbing his chain, I sliced with my knife through the cable it was attached to.

"Good boy." I patted Lesher. "Now, let's go get your master."

With the vicious *mahdi* clearing my way, moving through the crowd proved much easier. However, there were still too many of those who wanted a piece of both of us.

"Wyck!" I yelled over the crowd, hoping that he'd be able to meet us halfway.

He was easy to spot, towering over the rest. His head snapped in my direction, then he shoved aside at the aliens surrounding him, parting the crowd like the sea on his way to me.

He reached me in a few wide strides, firing at those who were too slow to move away in time.

"Come here." He hugged me to him with one arm. Without slowing down his pace, he swept me off my feet, half-carrying me out of the disgusting mess hall.

"She's dead meat, boy!" Nocc's voice shot from the room like a bullet at our backs.

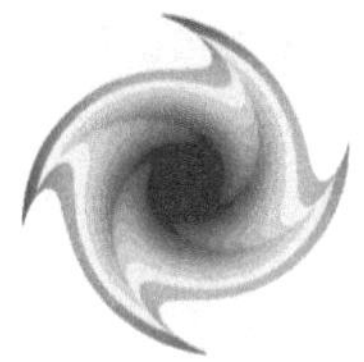

Chapter 15

Nadia

"Never again," Wyck hissed under his breath when we got back to my room.

A storm raged in his eyes, his chest heaved with heavy breathing, his expression dark—he was furious.

Never again?

God knew, I agreed with him. But what could we do to stop this? What could anyone do in this lawless place forsaken by the rest of the world?

His gaze fell on me.

"Nadia." He took a step closer.

He wanted to hug me, and I quickly stepped back into the safety of the glass room where I knew he wouldn't dare follow me. My body retained the memory of him being inside me, and my mind was still reeling at how it'd happened.

We'd been forced, both of us. They'd used us to violate each other. The last thing I wanted right now was to have anyone's hands on me, again. Not even Wyck's.

"This was not how it was supposed to happen," I said quietly in reply to his questioning stare, backing all the way to my sleeping pallet by the far wall.

"We'll make it right," he said resolutely, repeating what I'd said to him earlier.

He swept a glance around the room then winced and quickly averted his eyes.

"You'll need a better place than this." He made the doors open again. "I'll be right back."

Lesh hissed with a whimper as the doors closed behind Wyck. My legs gave in under me, and I sank onto the sleeping pallet.

The animal trotted to me. After restlessly pacing in a circle for a minute or two, he lay down on the floor next to me, his tail snaking in a circle around him. Lesh fixed all of his eyes on the door behind which Wyck had gone.

I found myself staring at it, too. I worried about how my thoughts and my heart trailed behind that man, refusing to leave him even as he was no longer with me. I didn't want him to touch me, yet I hated when he left. I *needed* him to be here. No place on the Dark Anomaly felt safe unless Wyck was there with me.

The future seemed grim. I knew I had to keep faith that things would get better if I wanted to hold on to my will to survive. Yet faith was so hard to come by.

Wyck

He slowed down his pace, walking along the corridor.

His lower cock, the one that hadn't known the bliss of being inside Nadia, remained painfully hard. Every step added to the agony. The only way to get rid of the pain was to make himself come, but his thoughts weren't on it.

As long as everyone knew where she was, Nadia was not safe. That thought was like a thorn in his chest. He needed to find a better place for her. He wished to hide her, lock her up, chain her in somewhere she wouldn't be able to escape from and where no one would ever find her.

The hurricane of feelings for her raged inside him—new and confusing. Ironically, the only person whom he could talk to about them was her. No one else would even begin to understand.

He'd gone against his family over her. When he thought back to the moment he'd held the gun pointed at Nocc, he felt he was ready to kill one of his own kind for her. How did she become so important to him that he would go against everything he'd been raised to believe in, against everything he'd been taught he was supposed to be?

His room was on an ancient ship behind the mess hall. He shared the space with the rest of the *errocks*, his bunk separated from theirs by just a curtain. There was barely enough space on the floor for Lesh's dish and sleeping mat.

Living in the tight quarters had never bothered him before. For the first time in his life, however, he didn't feel entirely safe spending the night here. The memory of Nocc's betrayal burnt through his heart. His own family turning against him made him look over his shoulder everywhere he went.

Thankfully, the ship was empty right now. He grabbed all the blankets off his bed and left promptly before anyone showed up.

Passing by the mess hall, he realized why the *errocks* weren't back in their sleeping quarters despite the late hour. A number of fights were taking place. The crew had decided to deal with their lingering lust by physically releasing aggression against each other.

"Hey, Wyck." Krakhil, a *dimo*, sauntered from the room, a tattered rag draped over his shoulder. "Wonna fight? Place a bet?" he asked casually, as if nothing had happened just a short while ago. As if Krakhil wasn't one of those who'd held Wyck down while the rest threatened to violate his woman.

Wyck gritted his teeth, reining in his rising anger. His muscles ached with strain and tension. He'd love to throw a punch or two or even let a few land on his body. A fight might bring a welcome distraction to the mess happening in his head.

He had other priorities, though.

"Busy." He snatched the rag from the *dimo's* shoulder and shoved it in the pocket of his pants.

"Hey!" Stretching his four arms, Krakhil reached for the corner of the rag sticking from the pocket. "I need that to wipe blood and stuff."

"Use your shirt." Wyck swatted his hands away.

"I'm not wearing one!"

Ignoring Krakhil and the curses he was throwing at his back, Wyck headed toward the *vasai* farm.

There, behind a row of centipede cages, was a wide crack in the wall. Making sure no one was around to see him, he squeezed his large body between the two ragged edges of paneling and into a room with a low ceiling behind the wall.

At the far end, there was a short passageway. It was narrow. Even at fourteen years of age, Wyck had had a hard time wiggling through and into another small room with a window behind it. Now, that he had doubled in size since, he could only get his arm through, up to his shoulder.

It was just as well. The room on the other end of the passage had a small window, and he'd seen enough of the dizzying lights of the Anomaly to last him a lifetime.

He shoved the blankets through the passage into the small space behind it. This was where he had kept Lesh as a puppy, many years ago. And this was where he now intended to bring Nadia.

The place was not ideal. There were no bathroom facilities. He'd have to take Nadia out to use the bathroom in the farm a few times a day. It would mean a higher risk of being discovered for her, but she needed to take daily showers to avoid being tracked by scent.

Unlike the hated glass room, however, he didn't experience any discomfort from being here. Since other species on the Dark Anomaly weren't bothered by the glass room, he'd always worried that someone might find their way in when he wasn't around.

The narrow passage to the room with the window was too small for any male to fit through. Nadia's slender dancer's figure should be able to fit, though. That put his mind at ease somewhat.

Sitting down on the floor next to the entrance to the passage, he opened his pants. Taking care of his throbbing erection had become a necessity. The agony of lust had been clouding his mind, making it difficult to focus on anything else.

His second cock had swollen by now, too. Both pulsed hot and hard when he took them in his hands.

His mind flashed to the moment when Nadia's small, delicate hands held one of them, kneading and reshaping it to her liking. The memory of the sensation shot through his core like lightning, bringing an intense pleasure.

Both cocks prickled and ached as he squeezed them in his hands and slid his fists up and down, spreading the sleek moisture that seeped through his skin.

Ecstasy raged through his body, the memories of Nadia fueling pleasure into an inferno.

She'd kissed him. Her lips had been as sweet as the pollen sugar collected from the *endoi* flowers in the gardens.

Her warm hands on him, so gentle and…loving. He'd never experienced anything like her touch in his life.

The unforgettable sensation of being inside her…

There'd been fog after that—the hot, sticky haze of desire and ecstasy mixed into an explosion of climax. The feeling of complete bliss he'd been plunged into was incomparable to any orgasm he'd brought himself to.

His climax hit him now, bringing physical release. The long spurts shot out of both cocks simultaneously, and the pain of the pressure had finally dissipated, draining the tension from his body.

He wiped off the mess, using the rag he'd snatched from Krakhil, then tugged his pants back up.

There was no energy to get up right away, and he allowed himself to rest for a moment. The thoughts of Nadia wouldn't leave him, even as the lust had subsided. Now, he wished to feel her relaxing against him, imagining holding her soft body in his arms.

An achy feeling seized his heart—the longing for having her at his side. He could no longer truly rest when he was away from her. A feeling of loss tormented him, as if something was missing and he needed to go search for it.

Restless, he crawled out into the *vasai* farm and got to his feet.

A sudden tremor ran through the walls and floor, making him sway on his feet. He got a hold of the nearest cage to steady himself, feeling the receding vibration through his palms.

Shakes and tremors happened on the Dark Anomaly. Sometimes a spacious cavity deep in its bowels compressed, causing the aftershock to rumble through. Every now and then, it reached as far as the outer edge of the habitable sector.

Other times, it happened when a large, heavy ship crashed on the surface nearby.

It wasn't unusual. He knew it from the lifetime spent here and from what he'd learned while reading with Nadia. Held together by the incredible gravity, the structure of the Dark Anomaly was fairly stable.

An inexplicable worry, however, nagged at him to hurry to Nadia.

The last of the crew were clearing the mess hall as he passed. It should be all empty by the time he brought Nadia here on the way to their new hiding place.

The corridor seemed endless. The feeling that something was wrong gripped his heart. He kept increasing his pace, finding himself practically running the last few paces.

Lesh lay in the threshold inside the glass room. He didn't move when the doors opened.

"Lesh?" Wyck dropped to his knees, lifting the animal's middle head...*Lesher*, Nadia had named it. "Are you okay? What happened to you, buddy? Where is Nadia?"

Lesh didn't respond. His eyes remained closed.

Alarm spiked higher. *Mahdis* lived as long as *errocks* did. Lesh had always been healthy.

"Lesh!" He shook the animal, in desperation. Lesh released a soft hiss, it sounded like it came from all three of his heads at once. "You're alive."

"Nadia." Wyck darted a glance around the room. His head swam with dizziness at the sight of the lights behind the glass. Even while he was sitting on the solid floor in the entranceway, the unsettling feeling of floating churned his stomach.

There was a reason why the *errocks* of the Dark Anomaly never went on spacewalks to repair the battery panels outside. None of them could stand the sight of open space. Solid walls grounded him and brought the comforting sense of normalcy.

An unknown massive dark shape outside obscured the lights on the right. This must be the newest ship that had just crashed, causing the tremors he'd felt earlier. The side of it touched the glass of Nadia's room.

"Nadia!" he called into the room.

Squinting against the lights, he made out her shape on the sleeping pallet by the far wall.

"Nadia!" he roared as loud as he could.

She didn't move, and his heart dropped into the hollow of his stomach. Dread chilled his insides, making it hard to breathe.

"Nadia, wake up!" he kept yelling, but she didn't seem to hear him and wouldn't come to him.

What the fuck had happened here?

Fighting the dizziness, he examined the dark shape leaning against the glass on the right—the newly crashed ship. Even judging by the small part he could see, it must be massive. A fine web of cracks spread through the glass from the point of its contact with the side of Nadia's room. The clear material from which the room had been constructed was infinitely stronger than any regular glass. Yet it obviously wasn't indestructible.

Wyck realized that his difficulty breathing didn't come merely from his worry and stress. The air inside the room was thin—the oxygen must be steadily escaping through the cracks.

From Nadia's safe haven, the room could quickly turn into her grave.

Lesh sucked in a long breath, releasing a choked coughing noise.

At least he was most definitely alive, which Wyck couldn't say for sure about Nadia.

Chilling anxiety buzzed through him with urgency. He needed to go to Nadia to get her out of the death trap this room had become. With the oxygen seeping out, this place was slowly killing her if it hadn't already.

There was no time to get help, provided there even was anyone in the entire Dark Anomaly who would help him without asking for something in return.

He needed to get her out as quickly as possible, only he couldn't fathom the thought of entering this place. The idea of stepping off the metal floor panel and onto the clear glass felt like diving head-first into the abyss from which there'd be no return.

His breathing turned shallow, his lungs straining to draw in enough of the receding oxygen. Fear suffocated him even more effectively than the lack of air.

He ripped his vest off and tossed it on the glass. With a bracing breath, he took his first step onto the vest.

The room seemed to sway around him. He spread his arms wide for balance, as if he were treading a tight rope suspended in nothing.

The lights swirled, assaulting him with a new bout of nausea. His stomach churned, and his vision narrowed to a peep hole.

The small figure of Nadia curled under the blanket on her sleeping pallet became his only focus. He stared at her as he reached for the clothing rack on the right and ripped from it the first garment his fingers touched.

The voluminous skirt of the dark green dress puffed out, spreading on the floor when he tossed it in front of him. The material covered the clear glass, giving him a point of stability—small and unreliable, but stable enough for him to continue.

Quickly, he leaped onto the dress, then crouched down to move his vest from behind to ahead him. All while keeping his eyes glued to Nadia.

One more flip of the clothes on the floor, and he made it to her.

"Nadia." He dropped to his knees by her pallet.

She appeared to be sleeping peacefully but didn't wake up when he shook her shoulder.

"Please, don't leave me, now." It was a half-plea, half-threat as anger and desperation both took over.

He picked her up, blankets and all.

A screeching noise came from the right as the crashed ship

leaned heavier against the glass capsule. The Dark Anomaly tightly gripped its newest acquisition, pulling it firmly into place.

There was no time to lose. He had to get out of here before the glass gave in completely.

Step after step, he moved back toward the exit, along the vest and the dress he had spread on the floor. The clothes only reached into the middle of the room, though. With Nadia in his arms, shifting them farther up the floor would take some extra time he might not have.

Drawing the thin air in through his nostrils, he closed his eyes and ran.

The sound of his boots hitting the uncovered glass filled him with panic. The sickening feeling made his blood pound in his ears. His chest tightened. His throat felt sore, each particle of oxygen seemed to scratch it from the inside on its way to his air-starved lungs.

Dashing through the exit and into the corridor, he placed Nadia on the floor then punched in the code to seal the doors behind him.

That was all he'd managed to do before a violent bout of nausea sent him crashing to his knees. His stomach twisted in agonizing knots then emptied itself onto the floor tiles between his knees.

Lesh whimpered, crawling to him.

He placed a hand on top of one of his heads, leaning back to catch his breath. His heart thundered in his chest, wildly beating against his ribs. He panted loudly, greedily sucking in lungfuls of air, again and again, until some clarity of thought returned.

Nadia.

He darted a worried look her way.

He'd been ready to kill for her. Now, he'd nearly died for her. There was no way back for him—this woman owned him. And he wouldn't have it any other way.

"Nadia..."

He crawled on all fours to her, afraid he'd get sick again if he tried to get up.

Her eyes remained closed.

He stroked the side of her face tenderly, just like she had touched him before.

Dying was one sure way to leave the Dark Anomaly.

"Stay with me, my sweet human woman." He leaned his forehead to hers, breathing in the tendril of her irresistible scent he now loved more than feared.

A faint breath puffed against his lips—Nadia's exhale.

"Breathe," he pleaded in a whisper, afraid to hope. "I'll get you out of here."

Gathering whatever strength he could muster in his shaking legs, he rose to his feet, holding her in his arms.

With a sad whistle, Lesh crawled after him, too weak to get up yet.

"Stay here," he ordered. "I'll come back for you."

Instead of going left, to the new place where he was planning to hide Nadia, he turned right in the direction of the captain's room. Just like Nadia's, it was a glass capsule. There might still be the danger of it being crushed next.

With his hands occupied, he slammed his boot into the captain's door.

"Captain! Get up!"

The alarm must be apparent in his voice, as the door opened within seconds.

Sleepy and completely naked, Vrateus looked ready to jump into action, nevertheless.

"What is it, Wyck?" he asked, his voice clipped, his eyebrows pinched together in a frown.

"A ship crashed. Broke the glass in Nadia's room. You may want to get the doors to it permanently sealed shut, now."

Svetlana's worried face appeared behind Vrateus's bicep. She darted a confused gaze at Nadia in his arms.

"What... *Who* is this?" she moved around the captain while clutching the blanket she had wrapped around herself to her chest. "What have you done?" She raised an accusing glare at Wyck.

She saw him holding a motionless woman and assumed it was his fault she wasn't moving. Of course, Svetlana would think that.

She must have heard about what the *errocks* of the Dark Anomaly did to women. After the way Crux and the others had treated her, it was no surprise she'd assume the worst about him.

He had no time and no desire to explain himself, though.

"The new ship hasn't settled yet," he said to Vrateus, turning to leave. "Your room may not be safe either."

"Hey, where are you taking her?" Svetlana yelled at his back.

Where hopefully no one would find her.

"Vrateus, who is that woman?" Svetlana wouldn't give up.

"Wyck!" Vrateus's commanding tone made him pause for a moment. "Is she okay?"

"She will be," he said over his shoulder, heading down the corridor in wide strides.

She'd better be.

He let Vrateus explain to Svetlana the things that the captain should've probably explained long ago.

Wyck had something else to worry about. Someone else.

Nadia *had* to be okay.

As he passed her old room, Lesh rose to his legs, all four shaking. Unfortunately, the animal still wouldn't be able to keep up with him, and he had no time to wait.

"I'll come back for you Lesh." He kept going.

As he'd hoped, the mess hall was almost empty by now. The few crew that still lingered around were too far away to notice his precious cargo or to even pay attention to him as he quickly sneaked by the entrance on his way to the *vasai* farm.

Once safely in the room behind the cages, he carefully laid Nadia down on the floor. A faint light filtered from the farm, barely enough for him to inspect her face. She was breathing. It took him a few moments to detect her pulse, but it was there.

"Nadia," he said softly, touching her cheek. Her skin felt cool and soft under his calloused hand. "Please, wake up." He gently slid his thumb along one of her eyebrows, the short hair rather coarse but silky. She parted her lips, and the hope in his heart grew. He never forgot the taste of her mouth when she kissed him—sweet and intoxicating. "Open your eyes, my sweet pollen sugar," he cooed in a voice softer and more tender than he'd ever thought he was capable of.

Her features crinkled into a frown. She rolled to her side.

"How are you feeling?" he asked, shifting closer. "Anything hurt?"

"My head..." she groaned.

He sympathized, despite feeling almost hysterically happy at finally hearing her voice.

"And my throat... Thirsty."

"I'll get you some water." He moved to leave.

She caught a hold of his wrist.

"Wait... What happened?" She blinked her eyes open. "Where are we?"

"In a safe—" He winced and corrected himself, "well, *safer* place. Your room got destroyed by a ship crashing into it."

"Why don't I remember it?"

"You went to bed. There was a crack in the wall. A small one, but it sucked out enough oxygen to make you pass out."

"How did I get out, then?"

"I got you."

She blinked again, taking a moment before replying.

"You got me? From my bed? I thought *errocks* couldn't enter that room."

"It wasn't fun," he admitted, cringing inside at the memory of that nauseating place. "But I had to enter, to get you out."

She studied his face for a second, then closed her eyes and rubbed her forehead with a grimace of pain.

"I'll get you water." He shifted toward the exit to the farm. "I'll need to get Lesh, too. Would you wait here for a few minutes?"

She nodded, without opening her eyes.

"While I'm gone, you'll need to wait there." He touched her shoulder, prompting her to look at him, then gestured at the narrow passage that led to the small room with the window. "None of the crew can fit through there. You'll be safe until I come back."

She nodded again, gingerly as not to aggravate her headache, he guessed. She then crawled to the tunnel, without arguing or questioning his request.

He waited until she was safely on the other side before leaving her.

There was no door to lock. The only protection was the smell of the centipedes that overpowered Nadia's scent and the noise of their chitin-covered bodies as they scurried in their cages that drowned out other sounds.

He hoped that would be enough to keep Nadia safe and undetected until he came back.

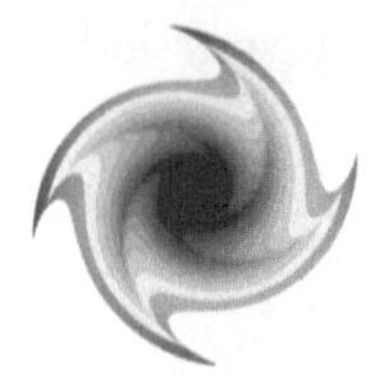

Chapter 16

Nadia

The headache was unbearable, as if a million jackhammers rammed against my skull from the inside. The undulating lights of the Anomaly outside the small window didn't help.

With my eyes half-closed, I found some blankets on the floor, wrapped them around myself, and settled down to get some rest, completely exhausted by the effort.

The blankets smelled like Wyck. From him, my thoughts went on to everything that had happened in the past few hours.

Pain and exhaustion weakened whatever hope and resolve I had left. Everything I'd been forced to do here and all the emotions it had caused that I'd tried to burry now rose to the surface. Hiding my face in the blanket, I let the tears out.

The flood didn't last long. I was too tired to even have a proper meltdown. Before the sobbing convulsions had fully subsided, I was asleep.

Brutal thirst woke me. My throat felt like sandpaper. Even my chest and my stomach hurt. In the multi-colored glow cast by the lights outside the window, I spotted a large tumbler of water at the entrance to the passageway between the two rooms. Grabbing it, I drained it in huge, greedy gulps.

The sleep and the water made me feel more like myself again, and I explored the new place a little.

The room was small—just long and wide enough for me to stretch out on the floor in either direction. The ceiling was only high enough for me to stand up on my knees. Initially, it must have been a part of a larger room before a section of the ceiling prolapsed, possibly during the crash, separating it from the rest of the space.

At this point, it was more of a cage or a holding compartment than a livable space. I felt more like a trapped animal here than ever before—a creature kept for entertainment, with absolutely no rights.

I feared this was not the existence I could survive for long without losing my mind. Anguish and sorrow threatened to suffocate me with tears once again.

Crawling to the passageway, I peeked out into the adjacent room.

Wyck lay on his side on the floor there, his back to me. The bulk of his massive body blocked the exit out of the room—even in his sleep, he was protecting me.

Lesh stretched on his feet. The animal raised a head, probably having sensed my movement. Realizing it was me, he relaxed again, lowering the head down and closing his eyes.

The two looked so comfortable out there, despite laying on a bare floor with no bedding. Wyck didn't even have his vest on, his bent arm tucked under his head instead of a pillow.

Dragging a blanket behind me, I crawled through the tunnel to him.

His bare back was warm. I pressed myself to him, drawing the blanket over both of us. His deep, even breathing halted for a fraction of a moment.

"It's safer for you in the other room," he muttered softly, his voice rough from sleep.

"Where are we?"

"Just behind the wall of the *vasai* farm."

"The giant centipedes?"

I've seen *vasai,* the wild creatures that had both an internal and external skeletons, in the movies. On screen, they seemed terrifying.

Wyck must have felt me tense.

"We're safe here," he assured me. "But you should be in that other room."

"Do you want me to go back there, then?" I held my breath, dreading that he would send me away.

"No," he said, after just a moment of hesitation.

I exhaled in relief, snuggling closer.

"Thank you," I whispered, pressing my face to his back, next to the hard, gray ridge over his spine.

I wasn't sure what exactly I was thanking him for—too many things made me feel grateful for having Wyck in my life. His warmth and strength gave me comfort. It melted the shaky wall of defense inside me, making silent tears trickle down my cheeks once again. Then, the sniffles came.

"Nadia." Wyck turned in my arms to face me. "Are you still in pain?"

"No." I shook my head, wiping my tears away only to have the new ones roll down faster.

He gazed at me, his eyes the warm tint of lampshade yellow in the semi-darkness of this room.

"Come here." He draped his large, strong arm around me, pulling me closer.

"I'm so sorry, Wyck. I thought I could change things," I sobbed into his chest. "That I would entice them into accepting a dance instead of…" My words drowned in another bout of tears.

"It's not your fault. I've made a mistake trusting someone more than I should have," he said somberly.

Images of the events in the mess hall came flashing back, like a slideshow of nightmares.

"They could've killed you." A shudder ran through me at the thought of how close I'd come to losing him tonight. "I should've stuck with what worked before…like Svetlana did. Just like you told me to…"

"I don't believe it would've made a difference, to be honest." He stroked my back soothingly. "They always want more, no matter how much you give them."

"How do you know that?" I sniffled, though the tears had slowed down somewhat.

"Because I'm one of them," he said softly into my hair. "I'm just like them, Nadia." He slid his hand up to my nape, his fingers caressing the skin of my neck. "The more I get from you, the more I want. I've just been inside you, and I still want more."

I tilted my head back, finding his eyes with my gaze. There was no threat, no menace in it. The heat of desire simmered in the background, but longing was the overwhelming emotion on his face.

"What is 'more' for you, Wyck?" I asked.

"I want *all* of you, Nadia, my sweet sugar. Every little thing. I want you to come to me whenever you need a hug—only me. I wish all of your kisses to be mine from now on. And I want a *date*, just like in that movie we saw—with a dinner and a movie." He nuzzled the top of my head as I buried my face in his chest.

"I'd love to go on a date with you, Wyck," I confessed, even as sorrow tightened around my heart—so many of the things I used to take for granted weren't possible on the Dark Anomaly.

Freedom. Safety. Going out with a man I liked. Simply walking down a corridor without having to look over my shoulder in fear of an attack was not possible here.

He kept stroking my hair, the tension slowly draining from my heart and my body. Warm and comfy in his arms, I stopped crying. With a long sigh, I drew in another lungful of Wyck's warm, spicy scent. To me, it was now associated with safety. It relaxed me enough to start drifting to sleep again.

Over the course of the past several days, Wyck had become my true safe place, not just on the Dark Anomaly, but in the whole of the Universe.

I WOKE UP TO NOISE OUTSIDE THE ROOM—TALKING, YELLING, THE screeching of the rusty cage doors being opened and shut, and the stomping of feet.

"What…" I lifted my head to meet Wyck's eyes directed at me.

He pinched both his lips between his thumb and his forefinger in the Federation's gesture of a call to silence. I made a sign that I understood, without saying a word.

His gesture, however, had led my gaze to his lips, and I let it linger there. The memory of our kiss and his taste on my tongue made my mouth water. I swallowed hard, unable to tear my gaze away.

The expression in his eyes heated. His arm flexed around me, and he shifted closer. Shutting my eyes, I moved forward, searching for his lips with my mouth.

He met me in a kiss with a soft groan.

Warmth and longing flooded through me. The pain, shame, and despair of this place ceased to exist as long as Wyck kept kissing me.

I slid my hand to his face, the short stubble on his cheek tickled my palm. He rolled me to my back, leaning over me. I trailed my fingers down his chest, through the soft dusting of hair there then over his side to his back.

Tentatively, he slid the tip of his tongue past my lips, and I met it with mine. My response seemed to give him reassurance. He was exploring my mouth, diligently and reverently. His movements quickly became more confident and more urgent. Passion started to take over the insecurity and even the caution.

The weight of his body on top of me and the feel of his hard muscles under my palms were invigorating, making me want more of him. Gliding my hands down his back, I slipped my fingers under the waistband of his pants.

He moaned into my mouth as I shoved my hands further down. I trailed my fingers over the hard half-globes of his backside. He jerked his hips, rocking against me with another tortured, muffled moan.

"Nadia…" He tore his mouth from mine. "We can't…"

The noise outside had calmed down, but someone was still moving around out there.

I nodded, reluctantly withdrawing my hands from his pants, but I wouldn't move away. Even as he rolled off me, I scooted closer, snuggling into his chest. The need to be next to him was stronger than anything.

His bicep under my head, he placed his other arm on me. I took his hand in mine, tracing the curved lines of the hard ridges over his knuckles.

"The feeding must be over, now," he whispered as the noise outside our room quieted down.

"You raise the centipedes here?"

"Yes, for meat and eggs." He tipped his head back toward the exit. "They're fed twice during the day. This was the morning feeding."

I would've never considered eating centipede meat back on Earth. Here, however, things were different. Unknowingly, I must've been eating it all along ever since I arrived.

"It should be safe for you to go out soon."

I held on to his hand tighter. Sooner or later, I knew I'd have to go out, to use the bathroom at least. At the moment, however, I was glad to escape the harsh reality of the outside world for just a little bit longer.

I laced my fingers with his, rubbing the tips over his hard knuckles. "These would do some serious damage in a fight," I said thinking about the many times he had used his fists to defend me.

"Mmh," he hummed in response. "Crux used to say that most species have to wear a special brace around their knuckles to match my punch. *Errocks* are born to fight."

"Do you believe that's *all* you were destined to do?"

"What else is there for me?" he glanced down at me.

"The world is so much bigger than this place. Out there, you can be anything you want to be, Wyck, do anything you wish."

He shook his head.

"The world outside of the Dark Anomaly doesn't exist for us, Nadia, just as we don't exist for it."

I rose on my elbow to see his face better.

"What if there was a way out of here?" I said, carefully watching his expression. "Would you consider leaving?"

"There is no way out," he said stubbornly. "Don't even think about it. Escape ideas will drive you mad. Trying to get away will kill you."

I searched his face, gauging whether I could really tell him everything.

"We came here intending to leave once our job was done. Our mission's plan included our departure."

"How?" He sat up.

I trusted him with my life; I decided to trust him with my one chance at regaining my freedom, too.

"Our return capsule is attached to the ship."

"And do you think it'll work?" he asked suspiciously, but I noticed a spark of interest in his eyes. His natural curiosity and the enduring hope of youth challenged his deep-ingrained belief that the Dark Anomaly was inescapable.

"No," I replied honestly, wishing so badly I could give him more than that. "I tried to use it when that ass…when Nocc attacked me, but something is wrong with the capsule. It didn't have enough power for the takeoff. I'm not an engineer or a pilot, though. In fact, I have no technical skills beyond those needed to operate the equipment. My purpose on the mission was to film a movie."

"A movie?" He gaped at me.

Suddenly, my role on our crew seemed as useless and trivial as our entire mission to the Dark Anomaly had proven to be. We didn't come here to rescue Svetlana, she'd been believed long dead. We didn't even come for research or to get any specific data for science, certainly not to give any assistance to the sentient beings stranded in this place—we had no idea about their existence. We came only to get information that would sell well back on Earth. My sole purpose was to preserve and present that information in a nicely done, professionally produced package. Nothing more.

"There has been a big interest—public curiosity—on Earth about the Dark Anomaly," I tried to explain this to Wyck. "Svetlana's disappearance put an end to the government sponsored in-person exploration of it. However, the private sector managed to outfit an expedition of their own…" I heaved a sigh, thinking about my dead team mates again. "Looking back, it was a stupid idea all along. But I was so excited when I got selected to participate in it."

"You *volunteered* to come here?" he asked, his eyes growing bigger with shock.

"I was one of thousands who volunteered." I nodded. "Simply being selected already felt like an achievement. The promise of a huge reward, of course, didn't hurt. I had big plans and needed the money."

"What for?"

I paused, thinking how much I should reveal in my confessions. I'd never told anyone about my plan, it felt too personal. My future family was meant to be all my own, there was no need for anyone to know.

Wyck was no longer just "anyone," though.

"I wanted to start a family," I admitted. "You know, to have a baby…"

"And you need money for that?" His dark eyebrow ridges rose in confusion.

"Out there, you need money for everything once the baby is born. But in my case, I had to pay even for getting pregnant."

"Why?"

"Because I didn't want to waste my life, waiting for the right man to come along. What if he never came? How long would I be waiting? Neither did I want to have sex with a stranger or a casual partner just to get pregnant."

He kept staring at me, clearly confused, so I continued explaining, "My parents had me very late in life. Both were gone before I even reached adulthood. I want to spend as much time with my children as possible, to be there for them when they start their own families, and to meet my grandchildren. With the reward money I was supposed get for this mission, I'd be able to afford a nice place without having to work five days a week. I could stay at home and raise my children. I could have the family time I got so little of with my own parents."

"So, you don't need a man to have a baby on your planet?" Wyck looked shocked by the fact.

"No…I mean yes, technically, there is still a man involved. Except that I've never met him, and I wasn't going to. He anonymously donated his sperm. The clinic kept it until they sold it to me. A doctor would insert it…um, inside me, to get me pregnant."

"There is no joy in that," he stated flatly.

"The procedure is not about joy. It's about having a baby without being involved with the biological father. It's easier that way, you see."

"Maybe, but a family is so much more than just the people you give birth to. You don't even need to share blood to be a family. My brothers and I are not related by blood but—"

He cut himself short. A dark shadow moved over his features, and I wondered if it was from the memory of one of his "brothers" almost killing him last night.

Feeling the need to comfort him somehow, I placed my hand on top of his.

"True. One doesn't need to be related to be close like a family. But what if you don't meet anyone you want to be close to?" I released a long breath. "One has to start somewhere, right? Some people start with a partner. I decided to start with a baby."

He sat in silence for some time.

"Is that why you want to go back to Earth?" he finally asked. "To get pregnant and start a family?"

"Not just because of that, of course. In my world, I have the freedom to lead the life I like. Here, I'm trapped…"

"You said the return capsule doesn't work."

"But it could be fixed. I think. I don't know for sure, but…" What harm could there be in telling him about Val too, now? Maybe he could help me find her? I knew now I could trust him not to hurt her. "There was another woman on my ship when we crashed."

“There was?” He straightened his back quickly. “I knew I saw and smelled someone else.”

Smelled.

“Have you caught the same scent anywhere else since?”

“No. Why did you lie about being the only one?”

“Why do you think?” I spread my arms. “By then, most of my crew had been annihilated. I’d been nearly raped by one of you. If Val somehow got a chance to run and hide, I wasn’t going to send all of you on a hunt for her.”

He regarded me for a moment. “Why are you telling me now?”

I squeezed his hand tight.

“Because I trust you, not just with my own life but with hers, too.”

“What do you think happened to her? I haven’t heard anyone speak of another female. I’m sure if someone found her, they’d brag about it.”

“So, that’s a good sign then, right? I hope she hid somewhere and…is still alive.”

To survive all this time, Val would need some food and a source of water. With all resources on the Dark Anomaly being controlled to some extent, those things wouldn’t be easy to come by.

“Promise me, you won’t tell anyone about her,” I begged Wyck. Even with his constant protection, I never felt completely safe anywhere on the Dark Anomaly. I dreaded to think what would happen to Val if she were discovered by the crew while on her own.

“It may be a good idea to tell the captain,” Wyck suggested. “He would assign her a protector and ensure she is looked after if she is found.”

“Is there any man in here who would protect her the way you’ve protected me?” I challenged.

His expression grew blank.

“Protection” had a different meaning for the rest of the crew. Nocc had made it clear last night that his idea of “not harming” me would be not killing me after a gang rape. That was as much mercy as a woman could count on from him. The rest of them weren’t any better.

I doubted that any of them had Wyck's willingness to learn and his ability to change. Being so much older than Wyck, they all had come here as hardened criminals already. Brutality was the only thing they knew. It was also what they chose to live by.

"I can help you look for Val," I offered.

"No." He shook his head resolutely. "You will need to remain here, in safety. I'll search for her myself."

I thought about the cameras I'd installed throughout the living area of our ship. They were to capture the daily routine of the crew on our way to the Dark Anomaly. Now, I wondered if I could use the footage to find out more about Val's fate, provided the captain or the crew hadn't removed the cameras and destroyed or damaged the recordings.

"What happened to our ship?" I asked Wyck. "Is anyone occupying it?"

"No, not yet. Its location is inconvenient, being on the very edge of the habitable sector, away from everything—" he cut himself short, a sudden understanding spreading on his face. "Do you think she would sneak back on it?"

I hadn't thought about that, but it was entirely possible.

"It would make sense." I perked up, feeling hope rising inside me. "The ship has everything for her to survive for weeks if needed, even months."

"All the supplies have been taken from it," Wyck pointed out.

"I doubt *all* have been. One would only take what he *thinks* can be taken."

"What do you mean?"

I shifted to face him fully, eager to explain.

"Until recently, spaceships had to bring all their food and water on the journey with them. The latest technology allowed us to make most of it onboard. We didn't carry canisters of food and water. We have built-in replicators that create them both on demand, from ingredients that take up just a fraction of the space and weigh much less than the final product."

"Are such things even possible?" he gazed at me in wonder.

"They are now." I smiled, patting his knee. "If Val has made it back to the ship, she might be okay. That's where we should start looking."

My excitement was reflected in his eyes.

"I'll go check on my own, first," he said. "But I'll take you to the bathroom first. You'll need to take a shower to wash off your scent."

"That's right. It's been almost twenty-four hours since I showered last. I must be gross and dirty." I winked at him, teasing.

He cupped my chin, bringing our faces closer.

"Not dirty. Sweet." He brushed the tip of his tongue along my bottom lip before taking it in a kiss. "Sweet like sugar," he whispered against my mouth. "And so irresistible to all of us here."

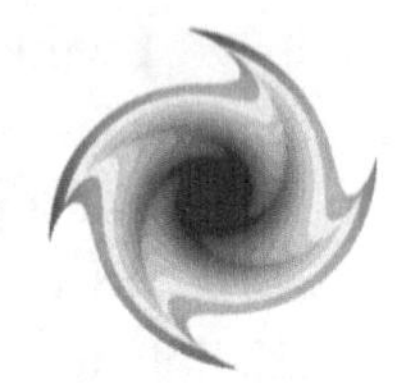

Chapter 17

Nadia

I lay on the pile of Wyck's blankets on the floor of the small room behind the *vasai* farm. He wasn't here, and bouts of worry and terror wracked me.

Tonight would be my third scheduled "performance" at the mess hall. The captain had officially cancelled my appearance days ago. Deprived of their "entertainment," the enraged crew had started a hunt for me. Hundreds of males had been raging through the Dark Anomaly, crushing everything and everyone in their way.

Wyck had forbidden me to leave this room out of fear that the crew would find me. I'd begged him not to go out tonight, either, afraid for his life more than mine.

"I need to know what's going on out there," he'd explained. "I'll lead them away from here if necessary. As soon as it's safe again, we'll go to your ship." He'd kissed me before leaving.

During the past week, Wyck had made a couple of excursions to my ship on his own, sadly finding no trace of Val's presence or scent.

Only I could open the locked doors to our sleeping cabin on the ship where Val still might be hiding. However, Wyck had been reluctant to let me go because I'd have to walk along the entire length of the main corridor of the Dark Anomaly to get there. With the crew actively looking for me for days, it'd been more dangerous than ever.

Wyck's other concern had been the safety of our ship. The cutout that Nocc had made in its hull needed to be repaired. On his last visit to the ship, Wyck had brought along a large slab of metal that he used to block the entrance.

Now that the unrest had finally started to quiet down, we planned my move to the ship.

Wyck wanted to do it early in the morning when most of the crew would be hopefully passed out, exhausted after wreaking havoc all night.

I waited for him to come back soon and, hopefully, confirm that it was safe to finally leave our small hiding place where we'd spent the week.

Afraid to breathe, I was listening carefully to every little noise reaching me from the outside. The now familiar sounds of the centipedes scurrying inside their cages and the clanking of their mandibles against the metal bars didn't scare me. Straining my hearing, I tried to pick out any sound of the rioting crew.

My only defence against them was to remain undiscovered. I had no weapon on me. The large, unmanned cargo ship that had crashed last week ended up completely destroying the glass room, along with Wyck's vest and my knife. Thankfully, to defend himself, Wyck still had the gun and, of course, his fists.

I knew he'd been getting into fights and scuffles, though he wouldn't talk about it when I'd asked. Throughout the past week, I'd spotted blood on his knuckles on more than one occasion. There had also been fresh claw and teeth marks on his arms and back.

The thought of what might be happening to him right now made my stomach churn and my hands shake. I wished to get out of here, to be next to him, but I knew that my presence out there would only make things worse for both of us.

Instead, I was laying here, shaking in my suit, afraid to even get under the blanket in case someone showed up and I'd have to fight for my life. Hiding, I barely breathed, making as little noise as possible.

This had been my existence for the past week—sneaking out to use the bathroom, quickly eating the food Wyck smuggled in for me, lying low, afraid to move, day after day.

Wyck's hugs and occasional kisses were the only things that kept me sane in this nightmarish place. Only in his arms could I get any rest.

Every night, however, I crawled through the short tunnel into the tiny room with the window, leaving him alone to guard the exit. I knew that unless I was safely on the other end of the narrow tunnel, Wyck wouldn't relax enough to fall asleep. My safety had become his mission in life.

Aside from my parents, I'd never had anyone who cared so much about me. In turn, I began to genuinely care about him, too. He meant more and more to me with each passing day. Here, on the Dark Anomaly, Wyck had become my entire world.

Come back to me, please.

I didn't dare say these words out loud, not even in a whisper, for the fear that one of the crew might hear me. But I pleaded for his safe return in my mind.

Come back to me.

The stomping of feet out in the farm made me halt my breath.

Someone crawled into the room on the other side of the tunnel —someone very large by the sound of it.

"Nadia," Wyck's whisper reached me, and I exhaled in relief.

Lesh's soft hissing announced that Wyck's pet had made it back with him, too.

"You're back…" I crawled through the tunnel and into Wyck's arms.

He had a split lip and there was a wide smudge of blood on his temple.

"Wyck, what happened?" I reached back into my room to grab the glass with water. "Are you okay?"

I dipped the end of a blanket in the water then gently dabbed at the blood streak below his lip.

"I'm fine." He attempted to smile then winced instead.

"Hurts?"

"A little." He shrugged.

"How about that one?" I pointed at the smudge on his head.

He brushed his hand along his temple then stared at his bloodied fingers in some confusion.

"That's not my blood."

"Good." I cleaned his face with the wet corner of the blanket while he sat still, gazing at me. "Did you…kill someone?"

"A few." He nodded somberly.

One thing I'd never witnessed in my life before coming to the Dark Anomaly was murder. So many had been killed since. The only thing I was grateful for was that Wyck remained alive.

"Thank God you made it," I said firmly.

"I had help."

Did the other *errocks* finally come to his aid?

"Vrateus helped me get out of there when things got wild at one point."

No *errocks* then. It saddened me because I knew Wyck was hurt when his family had turned against him. And it was all because of me.

"So, the captain was out there, too?"

"If he didn't come, many more would've died. He is the captain, the crew eventually listened to him, for now anyway. It helps that he always carries a lot of guns and shoots fast. As a punishment for the riots, he is making the entire crew scrub the sector clean tomorrow."

"Well, that should keep them busy and out of trouble." I released a short breath.

Wyck's frown didn't ease, however.

"I hope it doesn't cost the captain another mutiny."

"Is there a high chance of that?"

"The crew is a volatile bunch. They're hard to control and quick to get angry. One never knows when an explosion may happen," he replied, rather enigmatically. "We're moving out of here tomorrow night, instead of the morning."

"Why night?"

"It'll be easier to do while everyone is busy cleaning and doing chores."

"While they're all awake and moving about, you mean? How is that easier?"

"Vrateus gave me the code to the lock of the spacesuit storage room. It's the one that's next to the *vasai* farm, very close to here. I'll get a large crate and a dolly from there to transport you to the ship, pretending I'm doing a task for Vrateus like the rest of the crew."

As much as I wished to leave this cage of a room, getting out there felt terrifying. Wyck must have sensed my fear and cupped my face gently.

"We'll be okay, my sweet."

"We'll be fine," I replied, forcing a smile. I was so sick of being scared all the time.

WYCK TOOK A QUICK LOOK INSIDE THE SHIP THAT HAD BROUGHT ME to the Dark Anomaly weeks ago, which seemed like another lifetime, now.

"Come, quickly." He helped me climb out of the crate I'd hidden in while he transported me across almost the entire habitable sector of the Anomaly. "Get in, now." He nudged me toward the cut-out that served as the entrance to the ship.

Despite the late hour, the lights were on. Wyck had told me that the lights were never off on the Dark Anomaly. I wondered if the captain knew that someone was always ready to attack, and he wanted to make it easier for everyone to watch their backs.

"Val?" I called softly as soon as I climbed in.

Wyck had gone through the ship before, finding no trace of anyone occupying it. Yet I still hoped that Val would magically appear when I got here.

No one replied. The place stood bare and desolate. The images of the gruesome murders that had happened here assaulted my memory.

"Vrateus promised to keep the crew away from here." Wyck

promptly followed me in, dragging the crate behind him. "But there's always a risk of someone wandering by unexpectedly. We'll need to be careful."

Clinking with his chain, Lesh leaped in through the opening, too, and Wyck leaned a large round slab of metal against the cut-out, blocking the entrance from the inside.

"This is nearly impossible to roll away from the outside," he assured me. "If anyone wants to enter, they'd have to push it in, and we'll hear it crash as it hits the floor."

He stood next to me, turning around to take in the large open space of the common area of the ship—beige walls, the wide control panel far ahead with the six crew seats in front of it; the dining area in the middle; the storage hatch and the medical niche to the left; the wall with the crew cabins behind it to the right. "You said there're places to hide in here?"

"Yes, the sleeping cabins…" I replied distractedly.

The day of our ill-faded arrival kept replaying in my mind. I wandered over to the spot where Nocc had climbed on top of me before Wyck confronted him. The positions of the other members of my crew came to mind. Lee, Jose…all dead.

Val…

"You said you saw Val the day we landed here. Do you remember where she was when you came?"

He rubbed the back of his head.

"I'm not sure, now, if it was her. It could've been just one of your men. Humans are rather puny, male and female."

"Right…" I'd argue with that statement if I weren't so distracted by my thoughts.

I walked over to the main control panel.

"Is something wrong?" Wyck had caught on to my lack of attention.

"I have several cameras installed around this area." I turned on one of the screens on the panel. To my relief, it came to life immediately. "One is between the medical chamber and the space suit storage hatch, two over the dining table next to them, two right here." I pointed at either side of the main control panel. "See those little dark spheres? They've been here all this time. They're off now, but the recording was on during the landing. That was an event I definitely wanted to get on camera. The last time I saw Val, she was lying by the wall near the storage hatch. The camera over there by the cabins should've caught her."

Running my fingers over one of the screens of the control panel, I pulled out the folders containing the footage. It was organized by date and camera number.

"Look." I tapped on the date of our arrival, bringing up the footage from the camera over the cabins.

The echo of that day's horror rushed over me again as the images came to life on the screen. Wyck's back came into view as he stood over me, his shoulders squared, his hands fisted at his sides. I'd been on the floor, too close to the wall, only my legs were in frame. The full frontal of Nocc, however, was visible. The broken body of Lee on the floor behind him. And further back, behind the round table…

"There she is!" I pointed at Val's figure curled on the floor, the bright sponsor logos on her uniform suit glowing in the shadows.

"I knew I saw a woman!" Wyck exclaimed triumphantly.

The two *errocks* on the screen threw punches at each other, and the small figure by the wall stirred. Slowly, she crawled under the table, then behind one of the chairs, and out of camera range.

"She was alive! There must be more videos. There has to be…" I opened every single folder marked with that date, closely examining the images taken by each of the cameras.

Unfortunately, I had no camera pointed on the exit from the ship. Back then, before Nocc cut the hole in the hull, it was just a boring wall with some storage cabinets. There had been nothing to film at that angle until that day.

"No…" I groaned, disheartened. "What happened to her?"

Val had been injured during the landing. Even perfectly healthy, a woman had a slim chance of surviving this place for long.

"I hope she's okay, that she's still alive, somehow." I bit my lip as it began to tremble. Tears prickled behind my eyelids.

Wyck hugged me from behind. "If the worst has happened to

her, sugar, we would've found something by now. A body part, some of her clothing, blood—something." He kissed the side of my face. "No one has seen anything. That has to be a good sign."

That had to be because I refused to lose hope of finding Val alive one day.

"We're here now," he continued. "We'll be here if she comes back."

I nodded, drawing in a shuddered breath. "Maybe we could figure out a way to put a camera outside the entrance, in the corridor? That way we'd see her even if she can't push the slab away to get in."

"Good idea. It'd be helpful to see who comes to the door. Now..." He released me from his arms, turning around to face the room again. "I need to hide you better than this. Where did you say those cabins were?"

"Right here." I walked over to the wall covered with beige, textured paneling, the same as the rest of the ship's interior. The two vertical slits running up from floor to ceiling could easily be mistaken for seams between two pieces of the wall material. However, a small square screen at my eye level lit up when I waved my hand in front of it. I pressed my palm to it, and a wall panel slid aside, revealing our cabin inside.

"That's sleek." Wyck clicked his tongue with appreciation, following me in.

The cabin was large enough to comfortably accommodate Val and me on our nearly two-month-long journey to this part of the Galaxy.

Unlike the main area, this room hadn't been raided—all my things remained intact. Which must mean that neither the captain nor the crew knew about the cabins.

I promptly closed the doors behind Wyck. Here, we were safer than anywhere else on the ship, right now.

"This is where I lived on our way here." I swept the place with my arm.

The entrance was right in the middle, with the room divided in two equal parts on each side. My area was on the left, Val's on the right, with the common space in the middle. A narrow bunk bed folded out of the wall in each personal area. We each had a desk and a chair, too.

I walked over to Val's part of the room and pressed the button on the wall. The grey, solid privacy partition lowered from the ceiling, hiding from view what used to be Val's personal sleeping and working space.

"This is Val's," I muttered, rubbing my upper arms with my hands. "We shouldn't go there."

The sitting area in the middle of the cabin had a small breakfast table, a couple of chairs and a very comfy couch. Here, we used to have our meals on those days when we didn't feel like going out into the common area to eat. The two of us would watch movies while sitting on this couch. When Val had to work elsewhere on the ship, I used to like reading here.

On the wall to the right of the entrance was a wall-mounted food station with a narrow counter below it and a small sink. To the left was the bathroom with a toilet and a shower.

"As I said, it's self-contained." I brushed my fingers over the food station screen with lit-up pictures. "There should still be enough supplies to create food for two human females for at least two more months—the duration of our journey home if we had managed to take off in the ship. Though, the escape capsule was considered to be our most likely means of return."

There was another food station in the common area, but I had no idea how long the supplies there were supposed to last.

Wyck walked around the space, inspecting the equipment and the furniture.

"This will do for now." He gave me a smile, visibly relieved. "You can take the bed, I'll sleep on the floor." With a long exhale, he brushed his hand over his face, his slumping shoulders evidence of his exhaustion.

"Um…" I followed his gaze from the bunk bed to the floor next to it.

I'd spent way too many nights alone, listening to him breathing in the other room and wishing he were holding me while I slept.

Here, we were in relative safety. There was no need for us to sleep separately. Yet it didn't feel entirely right for me to demand that we sleep together.

Wyck had been doing so much for me, and it'd cost him. The job of looking after me had damaged his relationship with the rest of the crew, including his family.

I'd been taking so much from him—his time, his attention, his support, and protection. Demanding his presence in my bed, now, would be like asking for more of all of that when I felt I had nothing to give him back.

Wyck deserved so much better. He deserved everything.

He noticed my hesitation. "Is something wrong?"

"No… It's just that…" I clasped my hands in front of me. "I can sleep on the floor, too."

He tilted his head, giving me an inquisitive look.

"With me? Or alone?"

Now that he'd asked me directly, I couldn't pretend.

"With you." I dropped my gaze down. "If you don't mind, of course."

He stepped closer. So close, I could feel the warmth of his body, but he wouldn't touch me. Instead, he drew in a long inhale.

"You should take a shower, then." He took a bar of soap out of his pant pocket.

"Okay." The relief that he'd agreed to sleep together made me ridiculously happy. "Let's just make the bed first," I offered, not giving him a chance to change his mind.

I took the mattress pad off my bunk bed. The two of us then stretched it to more than double its original width.

"That's amazing how you can simply change its size," Wyck mused, pushing with both hands on the thick and comfy pad.

"It's made from the same material that's currently used to make mattresses on Earth. It goes from single to double size and even bigger. Which is much more practical than the old way of manufacturing and storing all possible sizes of mattresses," I chatted, grateful for the distraction.

There was a certain tension in the air, the awkwardness I hadn't experienced in Wyck's presence lately, and I didn't know how to deal with it.

We put the sheets on the mattress on the floor then spread the blankets we had brought with us. At the end, it turned out to be a perfect bed, much more comfortable than anything I'd been sleeping on since the day I got to the Dark Anomaly.

A corner of the top blanket happened to be bent over, and we both reached for it to straightened it out. Our hands touched. A spark of sensation, hot and intense like lightning, shot up my arm. I jerked my hand away quickly, darting my gaze to Wyck's face.

He was crouching next to me, his thigh touching mine. His expression mirrored my confusion.

We'd touched many times before. We'd kissed. Never before, however, had we been in a place that felt this comfortable for both of us. With no immediate danger to worry about, my attraction to him bloomed brighter. The hunger in his eyes burned hotter than ever.

Since he'd lost his vest, Wyck had been wearing nothing but the gun holster on his torso. The wide, ornately embossed leather belt crossed his massive chest. I balled my hand into a fist to stop myself from reaching out to touch it.

"I better go have that shower," I mumbled.

Quickly rising to my feet, I escaped to the bathroom.

I slid the door panel closed behind me and yanked the closure of my suit down. Usually barely noticeable, the material of the suit seemed extremely irritating right now, too hot and confining. I couldn't wait to get rid of it, peeling it off quickly.

Naked, I drew in a long breath. The air in the room seemed to be hot and heavy, too. It stroked along my bare arms and breasts like a caress, making my skin tingle. Leaning over the shower control panel on the wall, I started to program the water temperature and flow. Judging by my body's reaction, I needed a cool shower tonight, especially if I wanted to share a bed with Wyck—an ice-cold shower.

Suddenly, the bathroom door slid open.

"You forgot the soap." Wyck stood in the doorway.

His gaze roamed greedily over my naked body. He squeezed his fists so hard, the bar of soap cracked in his hand. Yet he wouldn't cross the threshold.

My heart thundered in my chest but not from fear, for once. With Wyck, I didn't need to be afraid. The streams of warm water rushed down from the ceiling, caressing my skin. I wished it was Wyck's rough hands instead.

"Bring it here," I said, stepping back to make space for him.

The shower area was just enough for one person. As Wyck entered the bathroom, his huge body nearly filled the entire room.

Pressing the buttons on the control screen, I made the toilet slide into the floor. The sink folded into the wall, and the streams of water rushed from the openings along the entire surface of the ceiling. The whole bathroom had now become one much larger shower with smooth, metallic walls and a fine mesh over the floor.

Water sluiced over Wyck, drenching the material of his pants and running into his boots. His pronounced eyebrow ridges kept the water out of his eyes, diverting it around his face. Wyck wiped it off with his forearm.

"Soap?" He handed me the bar.

I placed the soap on top of a dispenser nearby and took his hand in mine. There was no blood on his knuckles this time, but the size of his hand and the fierce hardness of the ridges on it left no doubt, this hand could be and had been used as a weapon.

"Do you still believe that *errocks* are born to fight? Do you think you're inherently brutal by nature?" I lifted my gaze to his. "Do you want to hurt me, Wyck?"

He stepped to me, leaving his hand in mine. There was but a hair-breadth of space between us, yet he wouldn't close it, ravaging me with his gaze alone.

"I want to fuck you hard," he growled. "I want to see your hair tangle and your skin drip with sweat. I want to hear you gasping for air as I pound into you. But I don't want to hurt you, Nadia. I want you to enjoy it all as much as I would."

The warmth of the water seeped through my skin into my

muscles. The heat in his gaze reached all the way through to my core.

Wyck towered over me. He was so much bigger and stronger than me. Yet I felt *I* had the power over what would happen here, now. He'd given it to me freely.

An overwhelming sense of gratitude for this man flooded me. He had been my one and only ray of sunshine for so long. No one and nothing could spoil this for us.

"We will make it right," I whispered as a mantra, closing the distance between us.

Everything about him felt *right*, even his wrongs.

I slid my hand around his back, unbuckling the gun holster from around his chest.

Sinking his fingers into the wet hair on the back of my head, he kissed me, deep and hard. The familiar taste of his kiss thrilled and relaxed me at the same time.

"Does it hurt?" I asked when he let me come up for air. I hovered the tip of my finger over the cut on his lip.

"The pain is worth the pleasure I always feel when I kiss you." He gave me a happy smile. "Do you like kissing me, Nadia?"

His kisses had been like shots of medicine against the festering sickness of my mind during the darkest time of my life. I'd been using Wyck to help me cope and now, he had become the addiction I could no longer quit. I didn't want to quit. But I wished to try giving something back to him.

If he felt pleasure from kissing me, I wanted to make him feel more.

"Let's get you out of these wet pants," I murmured, clicking the front closures of his waistband open.

The smile slipped off his face when I reached inside, my fingers sliding along his hard-as-rock erection—one of them.

"Do you really want this, Nadia?" His tone sounded almost like a threat, a warning. "Because once I start, I won't be able to stop."

The sound of his deep, low voice made my skin tingle with anticipation. I wished to give him pleasure, but I sensed I'd enjoy doing it. Wyck deserved it all. We both had earned this moment of time together, away from everyone else.

Instead of an answer, I resolutely shoved his pants down his legs. I sank to my knees in front of him. Opening the heavy buckles on his boots, I made him kick them off.

"You're all mine now," I whispered, sliding my hands up his long, muscular legs.

His two enormous dicks were positioned about an inch or two apart, one over the other. Both were so hard, the higher one pointed straight up, nearly touching his stomach.

I'd never seen a naked *errock* before, not even in a picture. I knew of the scientific and cultural exchange between our species. To my knowledge, however, there'd been no collaborations in terms of reproduction yet.

There was no point in asking Wyck about the *errocks'* cultural norms in terms of sex. All he knew would be mostly the customs of the group of *errocks* on the Dark Anomaly. Whatever little information he got had been filtered for him by those who had raised him.

He and I would have to discover our own ways.

"Tell me if you don't like something I'm doing," I told him, gliding my hands up the insides of his bulging thighs, thick with ropes of muscles.

His hard abs rippled when I took both of his massive dicks in my hands. He hissed, spreading his arms to grab onto the walls.

"Are you okay?" I asked, trailing my fingers along both his lengths.

He nodded quickly, sucking in another breath.

His girth—either of the two—was too thick for one hand. I let go of the top one and focused my attention on the lower one for now. Wrapping the fingers of both hands around it, I slid my hands up and down. When I squeezed my hands tighter, it got thinner, the clear, shimmering moisture beading along the entire surface. The moment I loosened my grip, he slowly grew bigger again.

It felt like having a thick roll of dense clay in my hands, and I couldn't resist playing with it. I squeezed, patted, and rolled.

"Do you like this?" I slid my hands up and down once more,

then leaned in and flicked my tongue over the tip. The slick liquid seeping from his skin had a taste, I discovered. The flavor reminded me of cloves and nutmeg, a bit spicy and unexpectantly pleasant.

He threw his head back with a long, guttural groan.

"Tell me if you want me to stop." I wrapped my lips around the tip then slid my mouth along his length, taking more of it.

"Don't..." he rasped. "Do whatever you want to me, but do *not* stop."

I hummed in agreement, flexing my lips and pumping my hand along what I couldn't fit into my mouth. I swirled my tongue around the tip.

His abs flexed and his thighs shook.

"I—" he managed before his hard, throbbing length spasmed in my mouth. A hot, spicy stream hit the back of my throat.

Not expecting so much of it and so soon, I gagged, coughing. He slipped out of my mouth. Spurts of vivid green with a pearly sheen, kept shooting out as I pumped him with my hands. Mixed with water, they swirled around my legs before being sucked into the floor.

I took my hands off only when he stopped coming. He swayed then dropped to his knees in front of me.

I cupped his face. "Was it good?" I searched his eyes. His expression was a confusing mix of torture and bliss. "Better than the last time?" I asked with hope.

"Every time with you is simply amazing," he groaned, wrapping his arms around my waist.

He lowered his mouth to mine, sliding me into his lap.

My core connected with another hard thickness between us. His second penis remained as erect as ever, throbbing urgently between us.

"I never got to learn what *you* like," Wyck said softly, placing a kiss on my shoulder next.

"Generally, it takes time for human women." I felt the need to warn him after having witnessed, twice now, how quickly he came himself. "Our bodies need some... um, longer stimulation to reach an orgasm."

"I've got time," he murmured against my skin, moving his kisses up to my neck. "I don't have to be anywhere until breakfast, which is in about eight hours. Would that be enough? Or shall we forget about breakfast tomorrow?"

The stubble on his chin tickled against the skin on my collar bone, making me giggle.

"It shouldn't take *that* long," I said. "If we do it right, we may even have some time left for sleep, out of those eight hours."

Judging by the way my body already buzzed with desire, it might not even take long at all.

"Remember I don't know what I'm doing." He slid his hands up my back then slipped one between us to cup my breast. "You'll have to teach me."

His thumb grazed my nipple, and I inhaled sharply as ripples of pleasure fluttered through my chest to my lower belly.

"You liked that?" He took my other breast in his other hand, rolling the tip under his thumb. "Does this feel good?"

"You're… an excellent student," I breathed out.

Sweet pressure swelled hot between my legs, and I rocked my hips against him, needing to move.

"I want to taste you," he whispered, catching my mouth with his once again. His tongue found mine quickly as he kissed me with passion and confidence.

The taste of him still lingered in my mouth—spicy, pleasant, and clean. He released my breasts, and I pressed myself closer to him.

"I want you inside me," I begged, grasping for the erection between us.

He was so huge, and I was too impatient in my desperate desire for him. Sliding my hand just once or twice along his length, I didn't make him much smaller before impaling myself on him.

A deep roar vibrated deep inside his throat as I lowered my hips into his lap. Despite the intense urge to have him in me, I had to do it slowly. Tightly stretched around him, I inched down, each tiny slide shooting sparks of pleasure through my entire body.

"Nadia, you look—" Wyck gazed at me intensely. "Am I hurting you?"

"No, sweetheart…" I rose over his thighs, letting him out a little, then lowered my hips again, taking him deeper. "This is *everything*. Having you inside me is…wonderful."

Wrapping my arms tightly around his neck, I kissed him, putting everything I couldn't express in words into that kiss.

Wyck had been my survival. He'd always made me feel safe. But for the first time since I came here, the joy of life was seeping back into my heart. He didn't just help me survive, he was bringing me back to life.

"Take me, darling." I slid all the way down into his lap, taking all of him.

With a groan, he rose to his feet, lifting me up, too. His expression turned from tortured to wild as he pressed my back to the wall.

"I'm *taking* you," he growled, thrusting his hips into me. "You're mine." He pumped harder, rubbing just the right spot in this position. "*My* woman."

His speed increased. He rutted wildly, violently. I felt his power with each brutal thrust. It spread through me with ache and pleasure, claiming me for him.

He came, just as fiercely, with a growl and gritting of teeth.

The moment his cock slipped out of me, his hand was between my legs.

"How?" He cupped me there, sliding a finger in and out of me and trailing it around my opening. "How do I make you come? Show me where?" he demanded.

Pleasure skirted and pulsed around my core from his touch. I rocked my hips against his hand, needing all of it and more.

I found his finger with my hand and pressed it to that one spot where I needed him most. "Right here."

"This here?" He circled the tight, throbbing bud, and I gasped as my hips bucked. "So small?" he muttered in amazement. He pressed harder, watching me writhe in ecstasy against his hand. "And so very powerful."

I hooked my arm around his neck. He rubbed, caressed, and

rolled, playing with me the way I'd played with him just a little while ago. Each movement of his exploring fingers was taking me higher. With another press of his hand, the orgasm finally hit me.

I gasped with a moan, hugging him tighter. My hips jerked as an intense pleasure spasmed inside me, blinding me to the rest of the world.

"There you go," Wyck murmured, his voice thick with satisfaction. He lightened his touch, gently stroking the last ripples of the orgasm out of me. "It didn't take long at all."

I smiled against his neck, slowly drifting down from the crest.

"I guess you're right." I sighed, relaxing in his arms under the warm streams of water rushing over us.

It'd been a while since I'd had sex, but that wasn't what had made it so incredibly amazing this time.

"It's because I really like you, Wyck. I like you so much."

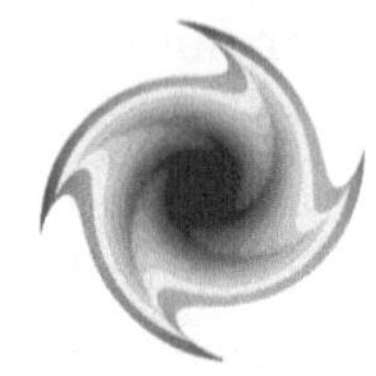

Chapter 18

Nadia

I woke up to the caress of lips and to the slight prickle of stubble along my skin.

Wyck trailed soft, tender kisses up my shoulder.

I stretched with a moan. The achy feeling through my body reminded me of everything Wyck and his two glorious dicks had done to me last night.

"How does it happen for you?" he asked, his warm breath fanning along my chest as he moved on to my left breast. "When do you start feeling desire?" He licked my nipple then sucked on it. "What are you feeling right now?"

He was learning, I realized. Everything he'd ever been taught about sex he needed to re-learn because all of that knowledge was warped.

"You care about what I feel?" He obviously did, but I wanted him to express it in words. I needed to hear it. "Why?"

"It brings me joy to know you feel what I'm feeling," he replied simply. "My pleasure is not complete without yours."

I trailed my fingers down the familiar dips and elevations of the three ridges on his head. Between them, the skin of his scalp was completely smooth, unlike the stubble he had on his cheeks and chin. The stubble never grew into a beard, though. I'd never seen him shave. It was always the same length, just like the slightly longer and softer hair on his chest.

"Sex really is like dancing, then." I smiled. "A couple dance works the best when both partners are equally into it. For me personally, the desire starts like a fire. It begins with a spark from a touch, a word, or even a thought. Then it grows with more touching until it bursts with release. How does it happen for you?"

He exhaled a laugh, resting his head between my breasts.

"For me, it's always there, my sweet sugar. Pain and pleasure—both urgent and intense. The real challenge is to wrestle it under control, to hold it back long enough to be able to think and function. Every day."

I cradled his head to me with one arm, wrapping the other one around his massive shoulders. "Thank you for wrestling it and for holding it back until I was ready."

He raised his head to catch my gaze.

"I want *your* desire for me to match *mine* for you, as wild and crazy as it is. Do you think it's possible?"

I could see it all in his eyes—the raging desire he spoke about, the desperate struggle he led to contain it, the intense hope in anticipation of my answer.

"I believe it is possible for me to want you as desperately as you want me, Wyck. In every way. You're firmly in my heart already, and apparently it doesn't take long for my body to catch up with my heart. We saw it last night." I smiled wider.

"Your body likes being touched," he stated it as a fact.

"By *you*," I clarified. "The person who is doing the touching makes all the difference."

He seemed to contemplate my words, gliding his hand over my ribs to cup my breast then back down again. He repeated the motion a few times, as if lost in thought. The sensation of his palm against my skin spread warm tiny ripples through me. On his next slide up, his thumb slightly brushed over my nipple, making me gasp softly. The sound seemed to bring him back into the moment.

He slid a gaze down my body, all the way to the blanket that was covering me up to my waist.

"I want to learn all the places you like me to touch you, Nadia. Here?" He kissed my shoulder again.

A shoulder wouldn't be considered one of the most exciting erogenous zones. But Wyck had often kissed me there. By now, it had become a sign of his affection to me. His caress now fanned my anticipation.

"Do you like it when I do this?" he asked, trailing his mouth further along my collar bone.

The warmth and softness of his lips, along with the prickle of the short stubble along his jawline, created a unique sensation inside me. A series of tingles scattered down my bare arms.

"I do," I admitted. "I like it very much."

"How about here?" He kissed my throat, and I tilted my head back, giving him more room to keep kissing.

"Definitely," I agreed. Feather-light pleasure stroked my skin at his caress, and I hummed in delight.

He continued to tantalize me with his touch, kissing up my neck.

"I know for a fact you like this," he murmured before sliding his lips over mine and taking my mouth in a deep, ravenous kiss.

His alternating between gentle and passionate teased and ignited me. I had no idea if he'd ever had a chance to build a fire while living on the Dark Anomaly, but he sure knew how to stoke the flames inside me.

Arching my back, I squeezed my right breast, pinching the nipple, and he immediately followed my gesture, replacing my hand with his. The sensation of his hands felt so much better than that of my own. My breast all but drowned in his large hand, his rough palm rubbing against the tip in a most delightful way.

I moaned into his mouth through the waves of growing pleasure.

"More," he exhaled, tearing his mouth away from mine. "I want to taste more of you."

Sliding down my body, he sucked the tip of my right breast into his mouth. All the pinching and rubbing had made my nipples hard, hot, and highly sensitive. The heat of his mouth and the smooth glide of his tongue now sent a new charge of desire through my body.

The building pressure between my legs throbbed with heat. I kicked off the blankets, spreading my legs open. The cool stroke of air against my heated folds felt more thrilling than soothing. My need flared higher.

I reached down, between my legs. My gesture served as another guiding sign to Wyck in his exploratory journey along my body. Before I could touch myself, he beat me to it.

His thick finger slipped inside me, probing, swirling, exploring in and out.

"Oh yes, Wyck…" I pressed my legs together, trapping his hand between them.

He rubbed his hand against my most sensitive spot, and I moaned, rocking my hips against him.

Pumping his finger in and out of me, he rested his head on my chest.

"I wonder if you taste as deliciously sweet as you smell, sugar," he said with a crooked smile and a glimmer of heat in his gold-yellow eyes.

I was not in a position to reply, moaning wildly from the onslaught of intense pleasure with his hand on me and with his finger inside me.

Thankfully, he didn't wait for a reply. Shifting smoothly down my body, he threw my legs over his shoulders and fitted his head between my thighs. The hot slide of his tongue between my folds made me buck my hips.

"Hmm," he hummed, his mouth hovering over my sensitive flesh. "More delicious than I could've ever imagined."

The puff of his breath felt simultaneously hot and cold, the need for him spiked higher. I fisted my hands into the bedding, pressing myself against his tongue as he lapped at me.

"How much do you want this, Nadia?" he asked between the

brief nibbles and long sucks that drove me wild with lust. "How much do you want *me*?"

"More than anything, Wyck…" I panted. "More than anything in the world."

"As much as I want you, then," he said softly before sucking at me again.

One firm swirl of his tongue set it off. I grabbed on to his head with both hands, riding the most intense orgasm of my life. His mouth turned from relentless to gentle, tenderly guiding me down from the crest.

I let my hands fall away as the last tremors of bliss had subsided. My legs dropped to the mattress, my body heavy and warm.

"How are you feeling right now?" Wyck shifted back up to me.

His mouth glistened wet and enticing, and I couldn't resist placing a small kiss on his bottom lip.

"Happy," I replied honestly. "This very moment, I feel completely happy, Wyck." I threw my arms around his neck. Happiness inside the Dark Anomaly was nothing short of a miracle, and I had no one but Wyck to thank for that. "I want to make you feel happy, too."

"I'm already—" he started.

"You're in pain, aren't you?" I cut him off.

The slight furrowing of his brow, the barely contained lust in his eyes, the way he held his lower body angled away from me—all told me that I was right in my assumption. He was highly aroused and…hurting.

"Pain is a part of desire," he said calmly. "It always hurts when I'm hard. And I'm hard more often than I'm not."

I wondered if having two erections at once only made it twice as painful for him.

"Doesn't it get better when you come?" It was an easy solution in my mind.

"Usually," he replied evasively.

"Why not always?"

The idea of Wyck hurting in any way while he made me feel so blissfully happy pained me.

"My pleasure is not complete without yours."

His words from earlier made even more sense now because I also didn't feel completely satisfied without him feeling the same.

I slid my hand down and wrapped my fingers around one of his hard-ons. He tensed next to me, a shudder running through his body.

"Do you like this?" I asked softly, sliding my hand up and down along his slick length.

He closed his eyes, thrusting his hips into my hand. Yet his expression remained tortured.

"What is it, Wyck? What am I doing wrong?" I was doing the same thing I'd done last night. He'd seemed to fully enjoy himself, then. But had it been truly *fully*? "Does this feel good?"

"It does," he groaned, rolling onto his back. I shifted after him, not letting go unless he told me to. "The cock you're holding feels amazing beyond belief. The other one, however…" He groaned again, but this time it was filled with agony.

"The other one?" I moved aside the one I held in my hands, bringing the one under it into view. Thick and swollen to almost twice the size of the one in my fingers, his lower cock visibly pulsed with tension, a bluish tint mixed into the warm earthy tones of its skin. "It looks like it's ripping at the seams," I muttered with concern.

"It feels that way, too." Wyck heaved a long, shuddered breath. "Like it's about to explode, and not in a good way."

"What can I do?" I asked, gently stroking along his second length. It jerked under my fingers.

Wyck gritted his teeth.

"Was that better or worse?"

"Better," he croaked. "More. Please."

I circled both of them, one in each hand, even though my fingers on either hand were way too far from meeting the thumbs.

"Last night, you came from both. Was it not enough?" I asked, sliding my hands up and down simultaneously and making sure I was giving an equal attention to both of his huge members.

He stretched, spreading his arms, his expression relaxing somewhat.

"One at a time doesn't work as well," he explained, his eyes closed and his voice a bit dreamy. "When I come from one only, the other one gets harder. And hurts more."

"So for you, the orgasm from one penis is never a complete orgasm?" I said, not slowing down the glide of my hands on him. "I've heard that *errock* women have two birth canals."

"Two vaginas? Yes."

"Hm." I pursed my lips. It made sense for the males to have two penises, then. Combined, the double amount of semen must be intended by nature to increase the chances of conception.

In my case, however…

"There is something we could still try," I said tentatively, fully realizing the risk of potential mortification in what I was about to offer. "I've never done this before, to be completely honest."

With Wyck, I was willing to try anything. I trusted him fully and completely. I'd even risk the potential embarrassment because I believed he would not make me feel bad if my attempt failed.

"What are you talking about?" He opened his eyes and rose on his elbows.

"Do you trust me?" I asked, straddling his thighs.

He watched me closely for a moment as I increased the pressure of my left hand, the one that was wrapped around his lower erection. The tighter I squeezed, the thinner it got.

"I do, my sweet. I trust you." His voice was soft and breathy, his expression intrigued, and his eyes full of anticipation.

I blew out a breath, calming my nerves. I cared about this man, and I knew he cared about me. This was worth a try.

Kneading and rolling, I shaped his lower penis as thin as possible. I only managed to shorten it to about the length of a hotdog, though.

"Stay on your back," I instructed, rising on my knees and positioning myself over his pelvic area. "Ready?" I asked more for my benefit than his. Panting hard, the blankets twisted in his fists, Wyck had appeared very *ready* for a while now.

"Here we go," I said in an exaggeratedly cheery voice as my heart pounded and the skin on my arms prickled with nerves. Positioning each of his cocks against both of my openings, one in the front, the other—the tighter one—at the back, I slowly lowered my hips down.

Even though I'd made the lower penis so much thinner, I felt the invasion from the back more acutely. The deeper I took him, the more the sensation of being filled thoroughly and completely overwhelmed me.

"Oh God…" I swayed, sinking onto the top of his thighs and fully taking him inside me.

He sat up promptly, catching me in his arms.

"How… how is it possible?" he asked, his eyes open wide in wonder. "I thought human females only had one vagina."

I wished he wouldn't speak about it, at all. Even hearing the word "vagina" right now made me cringe inside. But he was learning, and I needed to teach. As far as human women went—or any women, really—Wyck still knew so little.

"The vagina is at the front." I wrapped my arms around his neck and whispered straight into his ear, hiding my blushing face. "And at the back… Well, the opening there is not used for procreation purposes, at all. Though, humans still use it during sex, sometimes."

"Do some human males also have two penises, then?" he asked innocently.

"No. If a woman wants two penises on Earth, she has to, you know, be with two men at once."

Leaning back, he regarded me for a moment. "Have you ever been with two men at once?"

"No!" I slapped him lightly on his shoulder. "I told you I haven't done any of this before…" Having this conversation, with both of my orifices filled, started to feel rather awkward. "You know what, let's just get on with this, okay? Before I completely freak out and bail on you."

"Don't bail," he pleaded with a soft kiss on my temple. "Tell me what to do."

"Lie back down."

Pushing against his shoulders, I made him sink back to the mattress. Hands pressed into his hard chest, I lifted my hips off his lap. His long moan of pure pleasure rewarded me for my efforts. The slick sliding of him inside me sent warm ripples through my body.

He rolled his head on the pillow.

"I want you to enjoy this, too." His voice sounded slightly delirious after another pump of my hips.

"You know what? I just might," I murmured as another wave of pleasurable shivers rolled though me.

The sensation of being filled to the limit, combined with the tingling pressure from being stretched so very tight, fanned my arousal brighter every time I moved over him. The fact that I had a complete control in this position gave me confidence. Gradually increasing the pace, I moved faster.

I slightly shifted my hips, finding the perfect angle and hitting just the right spot with each glide against him.

Pleasure rippled and ebbed, flooding my lower body with heat. Just a little bit longer… I could already sense the first tantalizing wisps of the approaching orgasm.

Wyck's long, pained groan reached me. I snapped my gaze to his.

He sank his teeth into his bottom lip, his expression strained, his thighs trembling under me.

"Come for me, Wyck," I whispered.

"Not without you," he gritted through his teeth.

Sitting up, he grabbed my hips. Bringing me closer, he made the contact between our bodies tighter. The increased pressure released my climax. The pleasure unfurled like a tightly wound spring, shooting through me in spasms of ecstasy.

I gripped his shoulders, the bumps of his ridges there digging into my palms. My gasps and moans mingled with his roars and grunts as he joined me, our bodies rocking together through our orgasms. Swept into the hurricane of pleasure, I clung to him. My own climax felt that much more intense because Wyck shared it with me.

He breathed hard, drawing in air in big, hungry gulps. His arms tight around me, he buried his face in the place between my neck and my shoulder.

I stroked his nape, tracing the dips and protrusions along his spine, and wishing I never had to let go. If there was a way for me to ever leave this place, I vowed then and there to beg Wyck to come with me. The world outside, my carefully planned life on Earth—none of that would be complete without him anymore.

"Nadia?" he asked softly, not lifting his head from my shoulder. "Is love a good or a bad thing to a woman?"

Love?

Hearing that word from him made my heart skip a beat. It then resumed its beating in loud thuds.

"Generally," I started tentatively, my fingers hovering over his back motionlessly. "Being loved is considered a good thing, both by men and women. A *very* good thing."

I leaned back a little, making him lift his head. I needed to see his eyes.

"Why do you ask, Wyck?"

His expression was serious when he met my gaze straight on.

"In that dancing movie we watched together," he said. "When the man told his woman he loved her at the end, she cried."

"Those were happy tears." I smiled, stroking the side of his face. "After everything the two of them had been through together, she was so happy to hear those words from him, the feeling overwhelmed her to the point of tears."

He seemed to mull my words over for a moment.

"The man didn't cry, though, when she said it to him."

"He probably was already expecting her to say it back and had been better prepared?" I gave him a small shrug. "Why are you asking?"

"It's just…confusing." He rubbed his chest then pulled me into a firm hug. "All of this. The emotions…"

There was so much in what he and I shared. The wide array of feelings I held for Wyck had confused me too, at times. Lately, however, it all appeared to make more sense—my own emotions merged into something strong and bright for him, giving me some clarity.

"You'll sort it all out, darling." I gently stroked his cheek. "With time."

And time was all we had in here, on the Dark Anomaly.

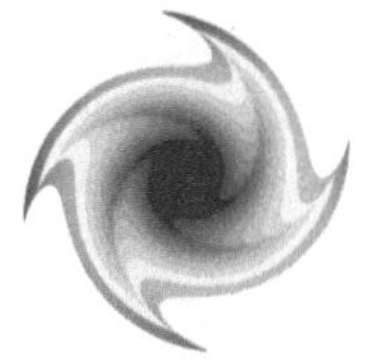

Chapter 19

Nadia

The crashing noise of the metal slab blocking the entrance to the ship made me jump in my seat inside our cabin. It wasn't Wyck returning. He had enough strength to roll the slab aside quietly.

Everything inside me immediately froze with dread. My fingers tightened on the frame of the tablet I held in my hands, and I felt momentarily paralyzed with fear.

Wyck had gone out right after breakfast that morning. In addition to taking care of me, he had other tasks to do on the Dark Anomaly, like everyone else on the crew.

It'd been a week since we moved to the new place—a blissfully uneventful week. We'd spent it talking, making love, reading, and watching movies together—getting to know each other in every way.

Together, we'd also managed to move a camera outside and mounted it over the entrance. However, I was still trying to figure out how to transfer the feed to a tablet in the cabin. For now, all footage was transmitted to the control panel in the main area.

Today would be the time of my next "session" in the mess hall had the captain not cancelled the "entertainment." I knew the crew had been severely upset by the cancellation. Their mutiny had more or less been suppressed by now. But what if the crew had managed to find me here, after all?

Wyck had taken Lesh along, but he left his gun with me, for my protection.

It appeared I might have to use it.

The sound of someone moving around in the common area of the ship filtered through the wall. The person must be smaller than Wyck, their footfalls sounded lighter. That didn't mean much, everyone here was smaller than Wyck. They might still be able to cause a lot of harm to me if they found me here.

Setting the tablet aside, I got up from the couch as noiselessly as I could. Drawing the gun out of its holster loosely draped over my shoulder, I pointed it at the door panel.

Chances were the intruder would leave soon. No one had discovered the cabins so far. Most likely, all I had to do was remain quiet and wait for them to go.

The footsteps moved closer, then stopped. It appeared the person now stood right at the door, on the other side of the wall.

I held my breath, half-expecting the dreadfully familiar spray of sparks from a cutting tool to shoot through the wall any minute. Raising my gun higher, I tightened my grip on it, ready to fire. I was not going to let them catch me off guard. Nocc was not going to touch me ever again.

Instead of the sparks, the beeping noise of the lock screen came. No one could open the doors, not even Wyck. The lock had been programmed with my and Val's palm prints only. The cabin was our private area.

The door slid open, revealing a woman standing behind it. To my disappointment, it wasn't Val, though she looked eerily familiar. Shock flashed on her face when she saw me. She leaped back, training her own gun at me.

"Svetlana? Svetlana Kostyk?" I mumbled, lowering my weapon.

She was exactly the same as in the pictures taken of her over fifty years ago—completely unchanged by time. Goosebumps rushed down my arms.

"You?" She stepped inside, quickly tucking her gun back into the holster at her belt. "So, that's where he's been hiding you?"

"You know of me?" I gaped at her, flabbergasted.

With a wide smile, she came up to me promptly and unexpectedly enclosed me in a hug.

"I can't believe I've found you," she muttered, holding me close, as if I were her long-lost relative. "I can't believe you crashed here."

She leaned back, holding me by my shoulders, and gave me a once-over, friendly excitement on her face.

I stared at her, too. Upon closer look, there actually were many differences between the woman who now stood in front of me and the official pictures of Svetlana Kostyk that I'd seen back on Earth.

Just like in the pictures, she had her long, wavy, chestnut hair pulled back into a ponytail. However, it wasn't the sleek, tight, high ponytail in her official portrait. Now, it was low and loose, with tendrils of fly-away hair framing her lovely face.

Instead of the white uniform suit, she was dressed in a knee-length, flowery tunic with long sleeves and a pair of black pants.

The smile on her face smoothed out the severe wrinkle of focus and concentration she had on her brow in all the pictures I'd seen back on Earth.

"I did not expect to see another human here any time soon!" she gushed in a very girly way. Then, the excitement on her face dimmed. "I mean I'm sorry about the accident that brought you here."

"It was no accident." I shook my head. "The expedition was planned."

"It was, wasn't it?" She nodded slowly, not appearing surprised by my statement. "I wondered about that."

"Why?"

"I've analyzed all available data of the past crashes. The one from your ship didn't follow the usual pattern. At least not until the very end."

"That's when we lost control." I sighed.

"So I thought."

"Listen…" I took a nervous look at the door she'd left open. The sight of the gaping entrance filled me with anxiety. "We should lock it. And block the entrance to the ship, too."

She followed my gaze then nodded with understanding. "Right."

Together, we managed to prop the metal block against the entrance to the ship again. Then, Svetlana lifted the opaque cover of the electronic lock from the floor by my cabin.

"Did you break it?" I stared at it in alarm. Broken things scared me, I had no clue how to fix them. In this place, a broken lock was more than an inconvenience, it could be a matter of life and death.

"I've disabled it. Temporarily." She deftly adjusted something inside the lock panel then fixed the cover back in place. To my relief, the soft glow immediately returned to the screen. "I've finally figured out how to reprogram palm readers, but not this one. The technology has sure advanced. Is it programmed with your handprint?"

"Mine and another woman's who used to live here with me."

She tilted her head, regarding me with interest. "Where did she go?"

"Disappeared. Shortly after our landing here."

She stared at me for a bit longer. "You need to tell me everything."

"What's your name?" Svetlana asked, sitting on one end of the couch in our cabin.

I took two cups of freshly brewed coffee out of the food station compartment. "Nadia."

"Are you Russian?" she asked, switching from English to Russian.

"My parents were," I kept speaking Universal.

I hadn't spoken the language of my parents since they'd passed away. Generally, when talking about work, using Universal was so much easier for me. It didn't matter what language either of us spoke anyway, since we both had our translator implants.

I handed her the cup, and her dark-brown eyes lit up with delight.

"Mmm." Through her nose, she drew in some of the steam that was rising from the cup. "Coffee… How I missed you!" She took a small sip then closed her eyes, a blissful expression spreading across her face. "This must be the most amazing invention of the past fifty years—the food replicator."

"Um…" I rubbed the back of my neck, trying to recall all technological advancements of the past half century. "There have been quite a few more."

"I'm sure there have." With a sigh, she swept the cabin with her gaze. "How long did it take you to get here?"

"Two months. Approximately."

"Fast. It took my team nearly a year." She took another sip of her coffee.

I tried to imagine what it would feel like for Svetlana to have the world as she knew it gone.

"Did you leave a family behind?" I asked softly. "Friends?"

"Not many." She heaved a sigh. "Colleagues, mostly. I suppose all of them would be gone by now. Their work surely contributed to the progress of the past fifty years." She glanced up at me. "That was what mattered most to many of my team—to leave our mark on the scientific world."

Talking with this woman, who was born many decades before me yet looked just a few years older, made me feel like time travel was possible. Though, it remained unclear who exactly had time travelled in our case. Had Svetlana moved ahead into the future? Or had I slid back into the past.

Probably both. Time hung suspended inside the Dark Anomaly, allowing for the meeting of the future and the past.

I took a seat on the opposite end of the couch.

"Are you with the Earth Space Coalition, too?" she asked, regarding my suit with interest.

The colorful patches of sponsor logos shimmered with a metallic sheen all over my arms, legs, and torso. Compared to the old plain-white Coalition uniforms, my outfit was more decorated than a Nascar driver's racing suit.

"No." I fingered one of the patches that had been molded into the fabric on my sleeve. "After your disappearance, the Coalition stopped their exploration of this part of the Galaxy. All countries' governments refused to finance it. Our expedition was sponsored and outfitted by the private sector."

She frowned. "Did it have any scientific purpose at all?"

"Mostly commercial," I admitted.

"Then you are..."

"*Not* a scientist." I took a long drink of my coffee. It had cooled off a bit by now, warm enough without scalding. I inhaled the pleasant aroma, savoring it. "My mission was to produce a movie. Except that I haven't filmed much while being here," I huffed a short laugh.

There were no regrets in me for not collecting any footage at all other than whatever had been recorded automatically by the onboard cameras of the ship. Most of what I'd seen here so far would be horror-movie worthy. I wouldn't wish to relive any of it other than the moments with Wyck, and those were too private for others to see.

"A movie?" She gazed at me, confused. "For entertainment?"

"A documentary, of sorts." More like a reality TV of the past, if I were to be entirely honest with myself. "Something of commercial value for our sponsors."

"And how were you supposed to get the movie to them?" She tilted her head. "You're aware that no signal travels past the force field of the Anomaly?"

I inhaled deeply.

"The plan was for us to leave here."

"I see." She pressed her lips into a slim line.

"Our landing was harder than expected," I hurried to explain. "Some of the equipment might've gotten damaged. I don't have the necessary knowledge to accurately assess the damage. However, I believe the escape capsule is salvageable."

"Is it the one with the hole cut in the door?"

"Right." I nodded. "Nocc did that..."

Svetlana sat quiet for a moment, gazing at me with compassion.

"Vrateus told me about the murders of your crew. I'm really sorry about your friends and colleagues." She frowned again. "What else did Nocc do?"

"Nothing good," I said, my reply clipped.

She waited for a second or two, but I didn't elaborate. Recounting the details of that day felt like it would release too much hurt at once. I wasn't sure I could deal with all that pain yet.

She nodded somberly, as if she understood even without me saying anything.

"I'm really sorry about all of it, Nadia." Her chest rose with a sigh. "Vrateus didn't tell me about you right away. He means well and strives to do the right thing, but his understanding of what's *right* is still a bit skewed. He thought he was protecting me by keeping your arrival a secret from me. On your landing day, he didn't tell me that your ship had a crew on board or that it came from Earth. I had no idea there was another woman on the Anomaly until I saw you with Wyck."

"When?" I had no memory of ever seeing her until today.

"A week ago. You seemed to be asleep or unconscious. Wyck took you away before I could stop him."

"That must've happened when the newest crash destroyed the glass room where I'd been kept," I explained. "I passed out from lack of oxygen."

"I made Vrateus tell me everything, right then and there. He didn't know where Wyck took you, but he assured me you were safe. I've been searching for you ever since." She gave me a long look. "Are you okay, Nadia? Have you been hurt? Is there anything I can do?"

Nothing about this place had been okay. However, Wyck had managed to keep the worst of it away from me.

"I'm fine," I said. "I haven't been hurt. Thanks to Wyck."

"Wyck?" A note of surprise rang in her voice. "He's been difficult for me to figure out. However, as a protector, he'd be my first choice over the rest. Not that the rest are any good at all. I believe Wyck severely dislikes me, though. Has he been treating you well?"

"Yes." I quickly lowered my gaze to the coffee cup in my hands, hoping she wouldn't notice the blush that heated my cheeks. "Wyck has been very nice to me," I mumbled, before raising my eyes back to hers. "He's a good man. Why do you think he doesn't like you?"

"He has good reason to dislike me. I killed one of his kind," she said simply. "I shot an *errock*—Crux."

"You did?" I stared at her in shock.

"It was self-defence, but I'm afraid that's not how Wyck sees it."

"Crux was the closest Wyck had to a father growing up," I said softly.

Her slim dark eyebrows knotted into a deep frown. "I didn't know that."

"From what I've learned, Crux sucked at parenting," I pointed out.

"That doesn't surprise me. The Dark Anomaly is not a nice place. It's filled with brutal people. The fact that Wyck has managed to grow into a 'good man,' as you say, is a miracle."

It was a miracle. If nurture were a hundred percent responsible for the kind of a person he'd become, he wouldn't be what he was. From what I'd heard, Wyck's biological father hadn't been much different than Crux. I wondered if everything that was good and wholesome in Wyck had come from his mother. He didn't talk about her, and I believed it might be because he didn't remember much of her and didn't want to repeat what the others had told him about her.

"It definitely is not the best place to grow up," I agreed then added tentatively, "Would you consider leaving here?"

She nearly spilled her coffee at the question.

"Consider?" she laughed. "I'd die for a chance to get off the Dark Anomaly. In fact, if it wasn't for Vrateus, I would've died already, trying to leave."

"The captain wouldn't let you?"

"He saved my life by stopping me. The force field that had

brought all of us here would've crushed me against the hull of a ship along the edge of the Anomaly disk."

I set my empty mug on the table and leaned a little closer toward her. "What if there was a way to fix the capsule? Some of the best minds of our century have been involved in the planning of this expedition. They believed the departure from here *was* possible."

"No one," she lifted an eyebrow, leaning closer to me, too. "No one in the Universe knows the Dark Anomaly better than I do now. And, I'll tell you that there is no sure way to leave it. Any attempt would carry some risk, to an extent even I cannot predict."

Hope was evaporating from my heart with her every word.

"Yet I would still try," she added unexpectedly.

"You would? Even knowing you'd be risking your life?"

She nodded with an easy smile.

"There is little I wouldn't do to solve the mystery of the Dark Anomaly. I've dedicated my life to this research. I've risked it before, and I'd do it again in a heartbeat if the results gave humanity answers to the many questions I have." She paused, taking a long breath in. "However, I would *not* risk Vrateus's life for any of that."

"Vrateus? The captain?" I asked, wondering what exactly she meant by that.

The warm expression lingering on her face explained it all—Svetlana loved Vrateus. She hadn't become "the captain's woman" out of the need to survive. She truly cared for him, so much that she was prepared to spend the rest of her life in the place she despised—because of him.

"If there is the slightest possibility of harm coming to Vrateus, I'd rather spend the rest of my life here than search for a way out," she confirmed my assumption. "You see, I love him and would never leave without him. He loves me, too, and he trusts me enough to follow me anywhere I choose to go. It places an enormous responsibility on me. I'm in charge of his safety in this case, and I can't bear the thought of hurting him in any way."

"So, you'd stay here, just because leaving may carry some risk? Not to you, but to him?"

"Exactly."

I leaned back against the couch, trying to make sense of it. Svetlana was sacrificing her chance at a better life because of a risk to another person? She appeared to have made that choice all by herself. Vrateus hadn't coerced her.

Then, my thoughts drifted to Wyck. At this point, I wouldn't want to leave him behind, either. Would I choose to stay in this hell forever because of that, though?

Svetlana straightened in her seat.

"Well, that doesn't mean I don't want to explore any new opportunities presented by the technology of your ship and its equipment. All of it is new and exciting. I do want to get that capsule fixed, even if just to run an unmanned test. Would you like to help?"

"Of course. I'll do my best. 'My best' isn't much, though, I have to warn you. Val would've been much better help here than me. She was… She *is* a pilot."

Is or *was*? That was the scary question.

"Val? Is it short for Valya? The full name—Valentina?"

"Yes. It's the name of the woman who disappeared."

"So far, without a trace," Svetlana said slowly, her expression contemplative.

I didn't want to think about what the phrase "without a trace" could mean in a place with a recent history of cannibalism.

"Yeah. Wyck has searched for her, but so far without any luck."

"I'll talk to Vrateus about her. He knows the habitable sector much better than I do. He knows his crew, too. He might be able to figure out what has happened to her."

She released a breath and pushed up to her feet.

"I should go. Vrateus dropped me off at the gardens, to work with Malahki. He'd freak out if he came to pick me up and didn't find me there. Would you mind if I told him I've found you? I hate keeping secrets from him, even though he kept you a secret from me. I need to teach him by setting a good example. I want to be completely honest with him."

"I suppose there wouldn't be any harm in him knowing—"

The slamming noise of the entrance block crashing to the

ground made my words stick in my throat. Svetlana's face turned as pale as a bedsheet. She yanked her gun out of its holster, spinning to face the closed door to the cabin.

Panic spiked high inside me, and I fumbled for my gun, too.

"Nadia!" Wyck's voice bellowed from the main room.

"It's Wyck!" I rushed to the door of the cabin.

Svetlana touched my shoulder in a gesture of caution.

"Be careful. You don't know who might be with him."

Wyck pushing the slab in was unusual. Normally, he'd roll it away, making little noise.

"Nadia! Are you there?" He slammed a hand into the panelling outside the cabin. The worry reverberating in his tone made my heart melt.

"He can smell you," I said, moving to the door past Svetlana. "And he's concerned for me."

Svetlana stepped aside and got into a position, aiming her gun at the entrance. I placed my right hand on the screen to unlock it, holding the gun in my left hand, just in case.

The door slid open, and Wyck barged in.

"You okay?" he exhaled, grabbing me in a one-armed hug, his other hand balled into a fist, ready to strike. His roaming gaze fell on Svetlana, sliding to the gun she had trained on him. "What is *she* doing here?"

Chain rattling, Lesh leaped into the cabin, too, making Svetlana stagger out of his way. I pressed my hand to the screen of the lock again, sliding the door closed—leaving it open even for a few seconds unsettled me.

"Why is she here?" Wyck glowered at Svetlana, drawing me closer to his side.

She lowered her gun.

"I mean no harm to you or Nadia."

"That remains to be seen," he snapped reproachfully.

I jumped to her defence, "Svetlana learned about me and searched for me. She wanted to meet me. We're from the same planet, Wyck. The only women here. We have a lot in common."

"Your own kind can betray you, too," he said gloomily.

My heart pinched with compassion. Family loyalty meant so much to Wyck. Yet I'd seen the *errocks* turn against him, because of me.

"I didn't come to betray, to fight, or to argue." Svetlana holstered her gun. Only then did Wyck unfold his fists. "I wanted to make sure Nadia was well and alive."

"Keeping her well and alive is my job, not yours." He glanced my way. "She is safe with me."

Svetlana followed his eyes, carefully regarding both of us for a moment or two.

"I'm glad to hear that. Wyck…" She turned to face him fully. "I know you don't like me much—"

"Don't like?" he scoffed. "I *hate* you." He put so much emphasis on that one word, it made me wonder if he did it as much for his own benefit as for hers. "Had I done the right thing as I was supposed to, you would've been long dead."

"Wyck…" I took one of his large hands in mine. His body ridged with tension so strong it appeared to bleed into the air and vibrate between the three of us.

"Do you truly believe that killing me is the right thing to do?" Svetlana challenged him.

"That's what the honor demands from me."

"What honor would there be in murdering a woman who stood up for herself against her attacker? You know that the only reason Crux didn't kill me first that day was because he wanted to use my life as a bargaining chip against Vrateus."

"It doesn't matter—"

"But it does. It makes all the difference, and you know it. You know there is a dissonance between what you've been taught and the way you really feel. That's the reason why I'm still alive, why Vrateus believed that Nadia would be safe with you, and that's why she *is* safe. Anyone else from your 'family' would've done to her the same horrible things that Crux wanted to do to me. Wouldn't they?"

His chest heaving, Wyck flexed his arm tighter around my shoulders and remained silent.

Svetlana stepped closer and carefully placed her hand on his forearm.

"You're not like them," she said softly. "And that's *not* a bad thing, Wyck."

We said goodbye to Svetlana at the exit to the main corridor.

She glanced at the heavy slab that Wyck and I used to block the opening in the wall. The floor panels by the entrance had shattered and cracked from the impact of the slab when Wyck had shoved it forcefully on his way in.

"This could be done better," Svetlana muttered. "We should make a sliding door here, with a proper lock or two."

"How long would that take?" Wyck asked. His tone remained guarded when speaking to her. However, the open hostility had disappeared from his voice and his glare.

"It depends if Vrateus finds some time to help us. He's been busy searching for a new room for us."

"You're moving?"

She nodded. "We have to. Vrateus is getting increasingly worried that our room may be destroyed with another ship crashing on the Dark Anomaly. It's always just a matter of time. But since the latest crash, he fears time is running out."

I worried my lip with my teeth, moving my gaze from Wyck to Svetlana then back again. I liked them both, but would inviting her to live under the same roof be asking for trouble?

"You can move here if you want," I suggested after a little consideration. "This way, we can fix the door, the capsule, and whatever else needs to be fixed here much quicker."

"Here?" Svetlana glanced around the main area of the ship.

"*Where* exactly?" Wyck frowned.

"There is another cabin right next to ours."

"There is?" Both of them turned to stare at the wall with the door to our cabin. Another narrow slit ran along it, a short distance to the right.

"That's the one where the male part of our crew used to live," I explained. "Their cabin is even bigger than the one where Wyck and I are because it was made to house four people instead of two. I can't open their door, the panel is not programmed for my palm print, but since you know how to disable them..." I turned to Svetlana.

"This might work," she muttered under her breath, taking a closer look at the wall and the panel.

"It has its own bathroom and a food station. If we make a proper main door, the whole ship would be safer, too." I glanced up at Wyck, feeling his worry and suspicion. "It may be better for the four of us to stick together. Don't you think?"

"Vrateus living here would give away your location to the rest of the crew," Wyck pointed out. "There is already a risk of someone tracking me to this place, no matter how careful I am. With two—" He glanced at Svetlana. "With *three* people coming and going as they please, someone would figure it out quickly."

"They would," Svetlana agreed. "Two women being in the same place will make this an appealing target for everyone."

"We may need to fortify it even better, then. Maybe all of us could limit our trips outside? This ship is entirely self-contained. We can make enough food and water to sustain all of us for a while, even if we lose access to the food supply of the Dark Anomaly for any reason."

"And, there is coffee." Svetlana smiled with a wink at me.

"Exactly." I grinned back. I really could use a friend in this place. The idea of her and the captain moving in appealed to me more and more.

"I'll talk to Vrateus," she assured me then turned to face Wyck. "Trust me we don't want to jeopardize Nadia's safety, but it's just a matter of time until the crew finds out about her whereabouts. In which case, it's best to be prepared. Together, we'll be stronger."

Chapter 20

Nadia

"I have something for you." Svetlana hopped off her seat at the table and rushed to the men's cabin, which was now her and Vrateus's room.

Vrateus and Svetlana had officially moved in last night, less than a week after she'd first found me here.

After Svetlana had left that day, Wyck and I talked for a while about the four of us living on the ship. His main concern was safety. Though, he agreed that he would feel better having someone with me while he was gone, even if the someone would be Svetlana.

She had her tasks on the Dark Anomaly, but Vrateus had been cutting them down lately, reducing the amount of time she spent outside of their room. The captain was obviously concerned about the unstable situation with his rebellious crew.

"Are you sure you'll be okay sharing the ship with more people?" I'd asked Wyck. "It's not that much space around here."

He'd only laughed at that. "Sugar, I've had nothing but a bunk bed and a curtain to my name, my entire life. And even that I had to share with one pretty large *mahdi*. Despite my size, I don't need that much space to be comfortable."

During their move, Wyck had been civil to Svetlana and even carried a few things from their old room over to our ship for her when Vrateus happened to be busy elsewhere. I still sensed some tension on Wyck's part toward her, though to my relief, there was no obvious resentment in his behaviour.

I watched him shoot a brief glance her way as she left the table now. He then calmly returned to eating his breakfast—*vasai* eggs and dark bread rolls Svetlana had brought from the kitchen.

Vrateus laid his food utensil down the moment Svetlana moved away, his eyes focused on the door behind which she'd disappeared.

Overall, the captain had exchanged only a handful of sentences with me since the move. He always appeared to be lost in thought, an expression of severe concentration on his face. I could almost hear the wheels spinning in his head, whirring and humming as daily plans constantly rolled through his mind. Running the life of hundreds of people on the Dark Anomaly couldn't be easy. As focused as he seemed to be on that, though, he also appeared to be aware of Svetlana's whereabouts at all times.

"Here." She came back into the room, carrying a large bejewelled pot.

It looked like a kettle, with four ornately curved spouts spread out equally around it. Made from gold-tone metal, it was decorated with swirls of green and blue enamel, the intricate designs inlaid with shimmering crystals.

"A housewarming gift, kind of." She smiled setting the kettle on the table in front of me. "Thank you for having us here."

"Wow, thank you. It looks so pretty." I trailed my finger along the relief of the design on its surface. "What is it?"

"According to an article I found, it's a family tea pot. I'm sure you could use it for coffee, too. It works like this."

She lifted the kettle by its ornate handle then placed all of our mugs under it, on the table. Rotating each of the four spouts to point down, she positioned the kettle so that each spout ended up directly over one of the cups.

"See? You can pour a cup of coffee for all of us at the same time, and it all comes from the same source. It eliminates a chance of poisoning each other," she added abruptly.

"Poisoning?" I asked, confused.

She winced and scratched her ear.

"Sorry, that last part has absolutely nothing to do with the four of us. I'm not even sure why I said it. Vrateus has been poisoned once, but it has nothing to do with this gift, of course." She awkwardly thrust the kettle to me. "Anyway. I'm not good at this social…um, friends and family stuff. Vrateus found this pot in one of the storage rooms a while back. I thought about you and the coffee as I was packing things for the move. I looked it up. It comes from the planet Hexol, the *errocks'* world. It seemed a fitting gift…"

She cast a quick glance at Wyck, who stared at the pot in my arms with a new interest.

"It belonged to the Roohala dynasty, which ruled around the same time your ship crashed here," Svetlana said to him.

"It came from my planet?" He took the kettle from me, turning it in his hands. "An *errock* made this?"

"Probably more than one *errock*." Svetlana stepped closer. "After the metal had been forged and shaped, a more delicate hand would've been required to paint all these designs, you see?" She leaned over his shoulder, tracing the delicate curve of one of the lines with her fingers. "And to lay these tiny crystals, too. Your nation has always excelled at producing items that require high precision and craftmanship."

"All of this was made by hand?" Wyck asked, continuing to inspect the ornate surface of the piece.

"Most of it. The Roohala dynasty era marks a unique time in Hexol's history when space travel on some parts of the planet happened alongside a relatively simple lifestyle of manual labor and low-technology in the others. I can give you the slate with the article I read about it," she offered. "It's written in Universal. Can you read in that language?"

"Yes, I can." Wyck met her gaze.

I simply loved the confidence and the pride in his voice when he said that. I felt so proud of him, too.

Vrateus lifted one of his thick eyebrows.

"Really? You can read Universal?" he asked. "A while back, Crux told me not to give you any written instructions. He said it wasn't possible to teach you anything, including reading."

Wyck's jaw tightened. Blood rushed hot to my face with a stab of indignation for him through my heart.

"Crux just didn't want to bother with teaching Wyck anything good or useful," I snapped. "Wyck is an incredibly capable student. He is smart and quick, with an amazing memory and perseverance. He works hard. And he *can* read."

The captain stared at me, his eyebrow arched even higher. My passionate defence of Wyck must've amused him, especially since no one was actually attacking Wyck at the moment. I had jumped into a fight that wasn't there, punching the air instead of an opponent.

"Looks like I got you a good defender," Vrateus said with a spark of humour in his orange cat-eyes.

"Yes. He is good at defending too," I said earnestly.

"I was talking to Wyck, this time." The captain's firm lips twitched, his severe expression melting into a smile. "You're *his* defender. A very passionate one, too."

"Oh…" I shifted in my seat.

A ramble of laughter suddenly erupted next to me. I spun in my chair to find Wyck laughing heartily. Svetlana's soft chuckle joined the roaring sound. She leaned over Vrateus's shoulder, hugging him from behind.

"Come here, my vicious defender." Wyck dragged me out of my chair and into his lap. "Thank you for standing up for me, sugar." He said with a warm kiss on my lips.

The merry mood at the table caught on like a wild fire. I let out a burst of happy laughter, too, hugging Wyck's neck.

"You're worth fighting for, darling."

He leaned back, catching my gaze. "I've never heard you laugh before. And now I never want to stop hearing the sound of it."

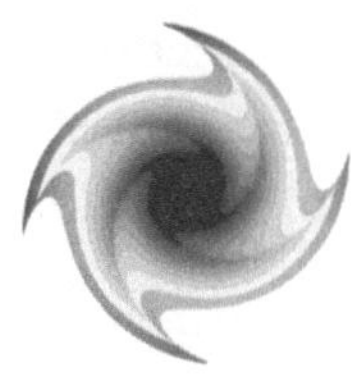

Chapter 21

Nadia

Apparently, a human being could get used to anything, even life on the Dark Anomaly. Or at least, I could. It helped that the four of us had managed to create a pretty decent life for ourselves here.

After a week of living with Wyck, Vrateus, and Svetlana on the ship, we all fell into a routine.

The thick slab of metal that blocked the entrance had been mounted on tracks and fitted with several locks. This way, it made for a sturdy, secure sliding door. Vrateus also made sure to bring on board all tools that could be used to cut through it, making our living here that much safer.

Vrateus, Wyck, and Lesh left the ship right after breakfast. By now, Wyck had become not just the head of the captain's guard, he was also the only *errock* guard Vrateus fully trusted. Together, they did what needed to be done to keep the Dark Anomaly running and all of us inside it alive.

Both men were firmly against Svetlana and me going out on our own, even if the two of us were armed and went together. They were convinced that two women would present a doubly attractive target for the crew—too tempting not to attack.

With Wyck and Lesh for escort, Svetlana would leave for the kitchen in the afternoon, to cook enough food for the crew to last for the next twenty-four hours. I stayed behind with not much to do.

I ended up rearranging the remaining cameras in the living area. Then, I set them up to record at certain times of the day. Taking videos of some of our mealtimes or conversations felt like making a family movie. I didn't do it for sponsors or for anyone else out there. I simply had more happy moments in my life that I wished to keep a record of.

Before their move, Svetlana also used to work in the gardens in the mornings, helping Malahki, the *damirian* gardener. However, Vrateus had cancelled that task. He said Malahki had informed him that her help was no longer necessary, and I knew the captain was relieved she now spent most of her time securely locked on the ship with me.

I liked having Svetlana to keep me company. I waited with excitement for Wyck and Vrateus to come home in the evening. All four of us often had dinner together.

There was a feeling of normalcy in this routine. Sometimes, I had to remind myself that nothing about this situation was normal. I wasn't spending my time behind the closed doors because I liked it that way. I kept hiding from what awaited me outside if I stuck my head out.

Every night after dinner, all of us had been working on the escape capsule. We had managed to patch up the door to our satisfaction. However, Svetlana had some upsetting news after reviewing the data of the capsule's system.

"This one is more sophisticated than the one on my suit was," she muttered under her breath, scrolling through pages and pages of data on the console inside the capsule. "This system measures the fluctuations of the gravity field around the Dark Anomaly. It calculated that the engines didn't have enough power to break free from it after take-off. So, it didn't even launch."

"Is that what the error message meant?"

Not enough power…

It'd flashed on the screen as I desperately tried to escape Nocc's clutches the day of our arrival.

Svetlana rested her hand on my shoulder. "The capsule's system saved your life, Nadia. If it took off, you would've crashed and possibly died."

"So, the escape capsule can never be our *escape*?"

"I'm afraid not."

My heart dropped as our last hope disappeared. Was I destined to spend my life here, on the Dark Anomaly? The thought chilled me with dread. My carefully planned future had disappeared into the dark fog of fear and uncertainty.

Wyck came up silently and enclosed me in a tight embrace.

I cried into his chest, and he made sweet love to me that night. He masterfully used everything he'd learned about my body. Each tender touch of his soothed the pain a little, as if he tried to prove that not everything about being stranded on the Dark Anomaly was horrible.

In that, he was right. Wyck coming into my life had turned out to be the best thing that had ever happened to me. He was my safe place, the one bright ray of light that pierced through the dark, scary gloom of the future.

As calm as our life on the ship had been in the past week, the rest of the Dark Anomaly was far from stable. From the brief conversations between Vrateus and Wyck, I'd gathered that the situation outside of our sanctuary was heating up.

Although the captain had been able to control the outbreaks of mutiny so far, the crew hadn't forgotten or forgiven my sudden disappearance, and they blamed Wyck for it. Their hostility had spread to include the captain and Svetlana, too.

Living in the confinement of the ship might not be the best. However, there was no safer place for me anywhere else. The times I'd been forced to spend with the crew were still giving me nightmares. For now, I was happy to remain behind locked doors.

"Well, I better go." Svetlana took the last long drink of her tea after we'd finished lunch. "Are you sure you're okay doing the dishes?"

"Yes." I got up to take our empty lunch plates over to the cleaning unit. "It's not like I have much else to do around here."

"I'll try to finish early in the kitchen today." She followed me, carrying her mug to the unit. "You and I can cook something fun for dinner tonight. The crew sure loves their stew. Their tastes don't leave me much room for experimenting."

"I'd love that. Let's do a dessert, too. I've been craving a cake—a simple vanilla cake. Can we come up with something like that? Even if it ends up looking tar-black?"

"I guarantee it will turn out looking black." She laughed. "The bark flour is black, remember?"

She smoothed the long skirt of the red-and-gray dress she wore over a pair of pants. I'd noticed she always wore several layers of clothing when leaving the ship. The captain kept the air temperature mildly warm on the Dark Anomaly for the comfort of the majority of the species here. Svetlana didn't dress in layers to keep warm, I suspected, but to add any extra barrier in case of an attack.

I liked the colorful dresses she wore but decided to stick with my suit for the time being—its material was nearly impossible to tear. My clothes' most important value to me was in how difficult they'd be to rip off me—a sad and scary fact.

Svetlana walked over to the main control panel in the front of the ship. She turned on the screen with the feed from the camera mounted in the corridor over the entrance to our ship.

"Is Wyck there?" I asked.

"Nope. Not yet."

It was unusual for Wyck to be late for picking up Svetlana to escort her to the kitchen each afternoon. Vrateus maintained a strict schedule, running our daily routine like clockwork. Wyck barely had time to give me a long kiss before rushing off when picking her up every day.

"Why would he be late?"

I tried not to worry. Things happened; people got delayed. Except that the things that happened in this place were never good.

"And there he is!" Svetlana pointed at the screen then hurried to the door. "Since he's late, make your kiss quick this time," she said with a wink as she passed me.

A blush warmed my cheeks. When we were alone, Wyck never held back on his displays of affection. He'd quickly grown comfortable with having Vrateus and Svetlana around, too, hugging and kissing me in their presence whenever he felt like it. Not that I fought him on that. The closer to him I was, the happier I felt.

Svetlana threw the locks open. I slid the heavy door aside, eager to see his handsome face again.

A muscular arm with the familiar bony gray ridge along it quickly reached in from the corridor. It hooked around Svetlana's neck and roughly yanked her out.

"Wyck?" I frowned, leaning out of the door. "What are you d—"

The question stuck in my throat as I came face to face with Nocc. He was wearing Wyck's leather holster and was holding Wyck's gun as he dragged Svetlana out and into the corridor.

She managed to twist out of his grip, and he lunged for her. She gritted her teeth, reaching for the gun at her hip. "Run, Nadia!"

"Get that one, Krakhil," Nocc barked out the order, tipping his head my way.

A huge *dimo* stomped around them, heading in my direction.

I leaped back into the ship with a squeak of terror and quickly rolled the door shut. With trembling fingers, I threw a lock on before my legs gave out and I slid down to the floor. My knees shook, and my heart beat so hard, I felt it all the way up in my throat.

The old, sickening fear washed over me, making it hard to breathe or think. Panic urged me to run and hide, like I had done all this time. Hiding and waiting it out had always been the wisest choice for me. The safest one.

Except that Svetlana was getting murdered out there while I sat in here.

Not even trying to get up, I scurried on all fours to the holster with the gun that Vrateus had brought specifically for me. He'd showed me how to use it, and it'd been hanging on the back of my chair at our dining table, ever since. I hadn't used it, not even once. Until now, I'd been relying on everyone else to keep me safe.

Now, it was my turn to help someone. Svetlana needed me. And Wyck…

I tried not to think about what could've happened to him and how Nocc had come into the possession of Wyck's things. Grabbing my gun, I finally scrambled to my feet.

There were two choices before me now—to stay here and hide or to open that door. And there was only one choice I could live with without being ashamed of myself for the rest of my life.

Heaving a bracing breath, I opened the door.

Nocc and Krakhil had been joined by at least two dozen more of the crew members, now. Even more of them were rushing down the corridor, like a rolling wave of menace.

To my surprise and relief, Svetlana was far from defeated.

Her back to the wall, she fired her gun at whoever came the closest, a pile of dead bodies forming on the floor around her. In the space constraints of the corridor, only a few of the males could advance on her at once. It limited the number of her immediate attackers, allowing her to singlehandedly hold defence.

Holding Wyck's gun in his hand, Nocc stood back. Hiding behind the others from Svetlana's fire, he wouldn't shoot at her, possibly hoping to capture her alive or maybe having difficulty getting a clear shot in the scuffle.

"You! Get here!" Enkail, another *dimo*, launched for me, shoving others out of his way. His elbow knocked the gun out of Nocc's hand, but the *dimo* didn't seem to notice it.

Raising my gun in my shaking hand, I pressed the rounded trigger in the handle, just like Vrateus had showed me. A blast of blueish light shot out, scorching a black line across Enkail's armoured shoulder.

"You…" he gritted through his teeth, stomping inside the ship after me.

The laser ray hadn't caused him much harm.

"Press and hold, Nadia!" Svetlana's voice rang high from the corridor. "Press and hold to burn through his armor!"

"Good advice," Enkail smirked, stalking my way. "Not that it'll help you."

I shot again, aiming at his face.

He charged me, moving faster than could've been expected from someone that large with limbs enclosed into hard shell.

I jumped back, out of his reach, but tripped over my own feet in fear and panic and fell backwards. Landing on my ass, I scurried away, crab-walking.

"Where do you think you're going?" he scoffed, advancing on me.

Where *was* I going?

Panic had deprived me of logic. I kept moving further inside the ship, leaving Svetlana to fight for her life out in the corridor.

My goal should be getting Enkail out of here and helping Svetlana to get back in.

Enkail out, Svetlana in.

Gathering my legs under me, I jumped up and aside. "Come and get me, tough guy!"

Holding the gun in my hand, I ran around the table and back to the exit.

With a grunt, Enkail followed.

Someone, a *yourlu*, poked his head into the ship. His tentacles snaked in, trying to block my way. I pointed my gun at his narrow forehead, right under the purple tuft of hair on the top of his head and fired. A smoldering hole formed in his bluish skin, then he crashed to the ground.

"I just killed a person!"

The thought shot through me, not unlike the laser blast. Only I had no time to freak out or even comprehend the full meaning of it. Someone else took the *yourlu's* place, and I shot again, then again, blasting my way out of the ship.

"Nadia!" A deep roar reverberated through the corridor.

Wyck!

Far down the corridor, his massive figure towered behind the crowd. Lesh's chain was wound around Wyck's torso, binding his arms to his sides. A group of *errocks* held him back as he fought against them, shoving at them with his wide shoulders.

Having no slack in the chain, Lesh tangled at his master's legs. Leshy and Leshic snapped at the ankles of his attackers. Nearly strangled by his collar on a shortened chain, Lesher seemed to be fighting for air.

I'd just taken the shortest glance at them, but it cost me a split second of concentration. Enkail gained on me. Grabbing my foot, he knocked me to the ground.

Wyck's roar shook the corridor, spreading through the bowels of the Dark Anomaly. Pure horror distorted his beloved features.

"Get off her!" He thundered.

His huge body strained. Blood rushed to his face, turning his skin from the warm color of reddish clay to flaming red, like a volcano ready to erupt. Veins in his thick neck swelled, and the muscles in his arms bulged. A link in the chain gave in under his enormous physical power. It bent and snapped, sending two ends of the chain flying open.

Enkail crawled over me, pressing my hips into the floor and reaching for the gun in my hand. Twisting aside, I held the gun with both hands and fired straight into his face, between his eyes.

"Press and hold," Svetlana's words rang in my head as I kept the trigger pressed.

Enkrail roared in pain and jerked aside. I moved my arms, aiming the laser ray at the exact same spot on his face. The laser burned through the plating between his eyes. The wound got deeper and wider, the nauseating stench of burnt flesh filling the air. The *dimo's* hard, heavy body slacked, still partially on top of me, yet I kept pressing—my finger froze in place as terror paralyzed me.

"He's dead." Svetlana yanked on my arm. The ray had made its way through the *dimo's* skull, leaving a scorch mark on the opposite wall. "Let go, Nadia."

I drew in a gasping breath, filling my lungs with the smell of the burning flesh of the male I'd just killed. My arms shook and my teeth chattered.

"Come." Svetlana helped me up. Tugging me up with one hand, she held her gun in the other, shooting at anyone who dared to approach us. Raising my gun in my shaking hand, I shot, too.

Wyck was working through the crowd to us. Pieces of the chain dangled off him. He swung his fists left and right like a pair of maces, crushing the bone and skulls of those in his way.

"Wyck!" Nocc leaped in front of him and thrust a long piece of a thick metal rod at him. "Stop this right now, boy."

"Get out of my way." Wyck kept moving ahead, ignoring Nocc and his makeshift weapon. "Nadia!"

"Is that your choice, boy?" Nocc yelled, pressing the jagged end of the rod into Wyck's chest so hard, a trickle of blood formed where it dug into Wyck's skin. "You choose some pathetic female over us, your family? You're betraying your own kind!"

"*My kind* is larger than you, Nocc," Wyck growled wildly. "There're billions of *errocks* out there, and they're better than any of you."

"What's *there* doesn't mean shit when you're *here*. Your father—"

"I'm *not* like my father!" Wyck shoved Nocc aside. "I *choose* not to be like him."

"Then you're no good to me, boy," Nocc spat through his teeth, charging Wyck.

The rod entered through Wyck's chest, like a spear.

A scream of horror lodged in my throat, blocking my next inhale.

Shock registered on Wyck's face—an utter disbelief at the betrayal. He clamped his large hands around the rod then yanked it out of his flesh and from Nocc's grip. Dark blood gushed in pulsing spurts from his chest. In one powerful movement, he speared the rod through Nocc's throat, then collapsed to his knees.

Everything inside me froze in terror. The world around me seemed to slow down, shrouded in thick fog.

I was only half aware of Svetlana holding back the feral crowd of males, drunk on blood, lust, and violence.

Of Nocc writhing on the floor in the last convulsions before stilling for good in the puddle of dark blood.

Of Vrateus suddenly rushing down the corridor, his guns drawn and firing.

Of the only *damirian* on the Dark Anomaly, Malahki, running with the captain, then skidding to a stop at the entrance to the gardens.

My vision shrunk, obscuring the view of all of them completely. My mind, my thoughts, the focus of my entire being at that moment narrowed on the hulking figure of my beloved giant tipping over to the floor. Cut down and crashed, like a hundred-year-old oak tree, he lay on his side. Without Wyck, existence on the Dark Anomaly suddenly made no sense to me. The entire world turned cold and lonely without him.

"Wyck!" Climbing over Nocc's motionless body, I scurried to Wyck's side.

I pressed both my hands against the deep wound in his chest. The stream of his hot blood pulsed through my fingers, uncontainable.

"My sweetness…" he whispered. His golden eyes glossed over before closing completely.

Svetlana's slender hand came into view as she pressed it to the side of his neck then to his chest over his heart.

"Let's go, Nadia." She tried to drag me away.

"No." I clung to his arm, my hands bathed in his blood.

"He is…dead, sweetie." Her voice broke, and my heart shuttered. "We can't help him."

"No…" I doubled over in horror, pressing his hand to my forehead. The hard ridges of his knuckles dug into my skin. The pain of that was nothing compared to the burning agony of loss in my chest.

"Quickly!" Vrateus rushed to us, urging both of us toward the ship. "There're more coming, and they're armed."

"Armed?" Svetlana gasped, her voice brittle with fear. "With guns, you mean?"

"Krakhil discovered the storage in our old room. They took the weapons that I'd left there. Come, Nadia. Or we'll all die."

"No!" I shifted closer to Wyck. My hands under his arms, I tried to drag him to the ship. "I'm not leaving him here."

It was like trying to move a mountain. Wyck's massive body wouldn't budge.

"We don't have much time," Vrateus's voice rang with urgency.

I dug my heels into the floor and kept trying to pull, afraid he would make me leave Wyck out here, in the corridor, at the mercy of the wild beings who could hardly be called "people" at all.

Nervously glancing down the corridor, Svetlana lifted Wyck's legs. "Nadia is right. We can't leave his body for them to desecrate."

Dragging the remainder of the broken chain behind him, Lesh limped our way. He whistled and hissed wistfully at Wyck's side then got hold of his master's pants on the side, helping us pull him along.

"Quickly then." Stepping over a few dead aliens, Vrateus came to my side and grabbed on to Wyck with me.

My vision blurred as we dragged Wyck over to the opening to our ship. Tears dripped down onto my arms, washing paths through the layer of blood—Wyck's blood. There was so much of it…

"Close the door," Vrateus told Svetlana as soon as all of us were finally inside the ship.

She dropped Wyck's legs and slid the heavy door back into place. Vrateus rushed to help her engage all the locks.

"Nadia, sweetie…" Svetlana returned to my side, compassion warming her voice.

I wouldn't have it, though. Evading her embrace, I stumbled to the niche in the wall opposite of our cabins and activated the flat screen mounted there. A long, padded panel slid out of the wall.

"What's that?" Both Svetlana and Vrateus stared at it in confusion.

"Medical capsule," I sniffed, whipping the tears out of my eyes with my shoulder. "Help me get him up here."

I punched commands into the screen, lowering the padded bunk to the ground.

"Nadia," Vrateus said carefully as he helped me heave Wyck's body onto the padded surface. "He has no pulse, no detectable breathing."

"It may be too late," Svetlana added softly.

I realized that. My brain—the logical part of it—understood it all, but my heart wouldn't accept it.

"Well, let's hurry then," I mumbled stubbornly, swiping the commands on the screen.

The bunk-gurney slid back up along the wall, lifting Wyck with it. A clear rounded canopy descended over him, its edges fusing with the perimeter of the gurney.

"A patient detected. Species errock. *Male. Please confirm,"* a metallic voice demanded impassively.

"Yes!" I yelled. "Help him!"

"Assessing..." the voice continued. *"The patient is clinically dead."*

Blinking the rushing tears away, I frantically swiped though more commands, trying to remember everything I'd been taught during training. The medical capsule was Lee's area of expertise. The rest of us had only gone through the basic steps of operating it in case of an emergency. No one could've imagined back then what exactly the *emergency* would be.

"Select 'resuscitate,'" Svetlana came to my assistance, reading the commands for me as the words and letters on the panel merged into a blur in front of my eyes—the fog of tears obstructing my vision. "Then 'life support.'"

"Right." I wiped at the tears with my sleeve, entering the series of commands as she kept reading them to me.

Tubes and probes launched into motion inside the capsule, prodding and sliding along Wyck's body. Two slim tubes snaked into his nostrils. One slipped between his lips and into his mouth.

"Tissue and organ damage detected," came from the machine. *"Recommendation—repair the physical damage while on full life support, before the following functions of the body can be fully restored."*

A list scrolled down the screen, and I glanced at Svetlana, unable to focus enough to read it.

"Yes." She nodded. "Repair the damage."

"Please confirm the voice command," the machine demanded.

"Do it!" I punched the screen buttons to confirm. "Just do it, dammit!"

Svetlana gripped my shoulders from behind as I sobbed, my hands splayed on the glass of the capsule.

The metal tools hovered in a cluster over Wyck's gaping chest wound. Some clamped onto the rugged edges of it, holding it open, while hair-thin wires descended inside.

Several agonising moments that felt more like centuries passed while the robotics did their work. I moved my gaze from them to Wyck's face.

The warm glow had disappeared from his skin, making it look dull and ashen. Droplets of blood dried on his cheeks, a few clinging to the lips I loved kissing so much.

"Please, please, please…" I prayed to every deity out there. *"Don't take him from me. He's all I've got. He is my everything."*

Most of the tools withdrew. A few were still working on the skin around the wound. The muscles underneath it had been fused together. A dozen tiny pincers pulled the cleaned edges of the skin to each other. Then, a healing ray sealed the wound, the sides of it knitting together into a flat, pale scar.

Wyck's chest rose with an inhale but I kept the hope at bay. In full life-support mode, the machine was doing the breathing for him, as it did everything else at the moment.

"How is he?" I croaked, my throat dry and painful.

"What's the patient's status?" Svetlana asked in a much stronger, clearer voice than mine.

"The patient has been resuscitated and stabilized," the life-saving machine replied impassively.

"What is his prognosis?" She squeezed my shoulders in a reassuring gesture.

"Undetermined."

"Why?" I cried out.

Wrapping her arms around me, Svetlana held me closer.

"How long until you can *determine* it?" she asked the machine.

"Approximately twenty-four to forty-eight hours."

Svetlana's chest rose with a sigh, pushing against my back as she kept hugging me from behind.

"All we can do is wait," Vrateus said somberly, standing next to us.

Svetlana rubbed my arms gently.

"He'll be okay."

I nodded, drawing in a tight breath.

Wyck had to be okay. He needed to get better. Because without him, my life had no meaning on the Dark Anomaly or beyond.

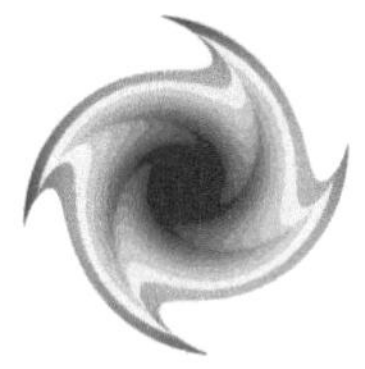

Chapter 22

Nadia

"Did you sleep out here again?" Svetlana asked, entering the common area with a mug of coffee in her hand.

I hadn't moved our mattress back to Wyck's and my cabin yet. The evidence of my spending yet another night on the floor under the medical capsule was right there for her to see.

"I don't want to miss any changes," I mumbled, drawing circles with my finger on the smooth surface of the glass canopy.

It was the second day of Wyck being enclosed there. And every day, the system kept repeating the same thing about the "twenty-four to forty-eight hours." It was driving me mad with worry. I didn't trust the machine. There was no way for me to tell if it even was functioning properly or if it'd suffered some damage during the landing. I'd run the diagnostics on the main control panel; however, no damages had been reported. Yet there'd been no progress and no updates on Wyck during these two long days.

"Come have some breakfast with me," Svetlana said, her voice warm and caring.

From the food replicator, she carried a second cup of coffee for me and two pieces of plain toast, one for each of us.

The atmosphere outside our ship remained volatile, forcing all of us to stay inside since the last attack. Cut off from the resources of the Dark Anomaly for the time being, we'd begun to ration the food supply available from the replicators on board. There were no more lavish meals for us.

"Come, Nadia." She set our modest breakfast on the table.

"I'll need to get my bed out of here, first." I toed my mattress with my bare foot. I'd slept in my suit, but I'd taken my boots off for the night and didn't bother putting them back on yet.

"I'll help you move it back after breakfast," she said. "You'll need to eat something. Please?"

I took a seat next to her at the table and bit into the toast. The smell of coffee was oddly nauseating, so I didn't touch the mug. I felt ravenously hungry, though, and polished off the toast in a few huge bites.

"Is Vrateus still asleep?" I asked, attempting to converse, even as all my thoughts remained on that capsule.

"Yes." Svetlana glanced at the door to their cabin and lowered her voice. "He stayed up late last night, analyzing the situation."

"And?"

She inhaled deeply, hugging her coffee mug with both hands.

"It's not the first time that Vrateus has had to deal with mutiny on the Dark Anomaly."

I nodded. Judging by the wild nature of his crew, it didn't surprise me they'd proven difficult to control. I'd heard of other mutiny attempts before.

"He'd been able to make them submit, every time," she continued. "But now, he's doubting if it's worth the price."

"What do you mean?

"Every time there is a power struggle, a lot of people die. And Vrateus has grown to care about some of the people here too much to risk their lives." She smiled. "I'm talking about you, me, and Wyck, of course. He wonders if he should even bother fighting for power at all."

"He doesn't want to be the captain anymore?"

"His main goal, now, is to keep the four of us safe and well. And it's getting harder and harder to do so out there." She gestured at the entrance to the corridor. "The life out there carries a constant risk, and it's not just about surviving hardships. The crew are actively killing each other. Nothing would stop them from killing us, too."

I understood the problem. The solution remained vague, however.

"What does Vrateus want to do?"

She bit her lip.

"There aren't that many options, sadly. We could start a smaller community with just the four of us and whoever else would want to join on the condition that everyone works hard and respects each other. That would mean of course that the rest of the crew would be left to their own devices. It pains Vrateus to abandon them. He's cared for their wellbeing for so long."

"While they've been trying to overthrow and murder him, constantly." I scoffed.

"True." She scraped her hand over her face. "Anyway, we'll have to discuss it together when Wyck gets better…"

We both turned to the medical capsule at her words.

A soft-yellow light lit up on its control screen. It hadn't been there before. Shoving my chair back, I got up quickly, worry spiking in me.

"Something's happening." I hurried to the capsule, yelling at it, "Patient's status update!"

"The life support is no longer necessary for the following functions and systems…"

A long list scrolled down the screen as the robotic voice read it out loud.

"Breathing, heartbeat, blood production…" The list went on and on.

"What exactly does it mean?" I demanded. "Is he getting better? When is he going to be well again?"

"Initiating the sequence of returning the patient to full consciousness," the system announced instead of replying to my questions.

"He'll be waking up, now." Svetlana stood next to me as we both gazed at Wyck lying under the glass.

I sucked in a breath and gripped her hand.

"What is the patient's prognosis, now?" she asked.

"Full recovery," the mechanical voice replied with zero emotion.

A wall of feelings rushed through me, I swayed on my feet, nearly knocked over by relief, hope, and worry. All tubes were removed from him and disappeared back into the wall.

Wyck's chest rose with a breath he took all on his own. His eyelids fluttered, then his eyes opened.

A loud sob tore from my throat at the sight of his luminous eyes—bright yellow with calming specs of green.

The transparent canopy lifted.

"Go to him." Svetlana softly nudged me.

By "go to him" she might have meant a hug, hand holding, or maybe a kiss.

None of those seemed sufficient at the moment. I needed all of that and more. I wanted all of him, at once.

Sobbing, I climbed on the bed to him as Svetlana left the room, going to tell Vrateus the news.

A knee on each side of Wyck's hips, I braced my legs to keep my weight entirely off him. I leaned over him, cupping his face.

"Wyck..." I gently kissed his lips. "My love..."

I couldn't stop kissing his face, every touch of my lips against his warm skin being another reassurance of him finally coming back to me.

"Love?" He blinked in the bright light of the room and slid his hands up my hips to my waist. "I know exactly what that means, my sweet sugar. I love you."

Tears streamed anew, and I didn't bother to wipe them away. They dropped on his chin, getting lost in his stubble.

He lifted a finger to my face, tracing a tear from my eye down my cheek.

"Are those happy tears?" he asked.

"A new patient detected..." the system suddenly announced.

I paid it no attention, lost in the moment with Wyck.

"Happy tears," I whispered, staring into his eyes. "Those are very happy tears, Wyck. *My* Wyck. I love you, too."

He slid his hand behind my neck, then lowered my head down to his mouth for a kiss.

"Human female…" the system kept talking.

I raised my hand, blindly searching along the wall for the screen to shut it up. I was not going to break our kiss even if…

"Gestational age of the fetus is estimated at five weeks…"

I dropped my hand down, sitting upright abruptly.

"What is it saying?" I gaped at Wyck as if he had an explanation.

"Mixed species— errock *and human. Gender male. Development normal for this stage of pregnancy…"*

Shock rolled through me.

"A fetus?" Wyck sat up, too, shifting me into his lap.

"A baby?" I mumbled, and we both stared at my stomach area.

"Is that possible?" he asked me. "Are there babies of mixed species out there?"

"A few. To my knowledge, all of them have been created by artificial insemination. In a lab. Not like…this. And no human-*errock* ones yet."

"Five weeks?" He looked just as utterly confused as I must have.

"They calculate the gestational age in a weird way. The fetus…" I touched my belly, with trembling fingers. "The baby has actually been there only for two or three weeks of that time."

It must've been conceived shortly after Wyck and I moved here over three weeks ago.

"There is…" He covered my hand with his. "There is a baby in there?"

"That's what the medical capsule says, and I have no other way of confirming it." Other than my rather sudden aversion to the smell of coffee. "Could the system be malfunctioning?"

"Is it the same system that has just patched me up?"

I nodded, shaken and overwhelmed.

He rubbed the faint scar on his chest. "Seems to be functioning pretty good. I feel great." He splayed one hand on my stomach, sinking the fingers of the other into the hair on the back of my head. "Are we starting our very own family, then?"

"I guess we are," I breathed out, staring at his golden eyes full of life and love. "How do you feel about it?"

"Nadia." He leaned his forehead to mine. "You are *my kind*. You and…he, the baby. I'd die for you."

"You already have." I took his face in my hands, finding his eyes with mine again. "You've already died once. You've just come back from the dead. No more dying, my darling. We need to live, now. All of us."

His eyes shimmered, glistening brighter than ever. Then a tear rolled out, trembling on the end of an eyelash. I leaned closer, kissing it off. "Don't cry, sweetheart," I whispered, my heart overflowing with tenderness and love.

"These are all happy tears, promise," he laughed and cried, holding me closer. "Sugar, I've never been happier in my life."

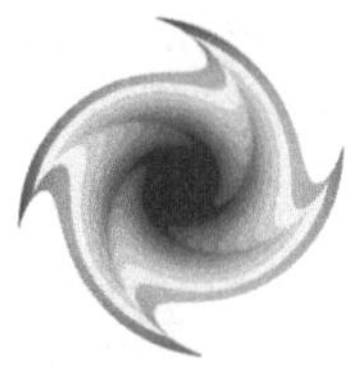

EPILOGUE

Wyck

"Hmm," Nadia hummed softly, rolling his cock between her palms while straddling his thighs. "What shall we do this time?"

He didn't know what she had in mind, and that made the whole thing so much more exciting.

"There are so many variations with you, you know," she giggled quietly. He loved that happy sound of hers. He loved every little thing about her.

The way her golden-brown hair, mussed from sleep, was framing her lovely face.

The way her green eyes glistened mischievously from under the few tangled tresses hanging over her face.

The way her lips curved with a teasing smile, just begging for him to kiss them.

The way her breasts swayed enticingly as she rolled and kneaded his cock between her hot, little palms...

He strained, pulsing with need. The thought of her tight channels made him ready to beg or charge forward and take. He knew, she'd welcome either action from him. Nadia liked it both ways, either rough or gentle.

He chose to go with gentle this time. His body shaking with anticipation, he caught her breasts in his hands and stroked her nipples. He wished for her to feel the desperation that was torturing him. He was going to make *her* beg him.

Bending his knees, he made her slide down his thighs, until her slick core pressed hot against his bottom erection.

She inhaled sharply, rubbing herself against him.

"On second thought…" she rasped, her voice breathy. "Forget searching for variations. I want you, right now." She leaned over him, sliding his bottom cock inside her. "I want you, Wyck," she groaned softly as he plunged deeper. "So, so much."

The top cock got trapped between them as she slid up and down along his body. The tandem pleasure in both was driving him wild.

"You feel so good, my sweet," he moaned with a rumble vibrating deep inside his chest. He'd chosen to be gentle, and he strained his muscles to restrain himself.

Slow meant he could savour every glide of their bodies against each other.

She leaned closer to his chest, grinding her hips against him. "This is…*perfect*," she exhaled, pressing her forehead to his shoulder.

And…he was done with being gentle. Holding her in his arms, he rolled them over, taking control.

She squeaked with surprise and delight.

He angled his hips, aiming for that spot he knew would drive her mad with desire and pleasure. Rising over her, he pounded hard as the approaching climax rolled closer. A surge of pleasure tightened the muscles in his thighs and lower belly, ready to explode if he let it.

His eyes on her, he watched for the familiar signs of her orgasm nearing. He'd learned to read her expressions as well as a book.

Her eyes closed tight, her lips parted, her brows drew into a frown of both torture and rapture.

He thrust one more time, both of his cocks strained to the limit and ready to erupt. His skin gliding smoothly against hers.

She tilted her head back, her neck flexed, and a shuddering wave of orgasm rocked her body. Her climax set his off. His release exploded, flooding him with ecstasy and blissful relief.

"Your pleasure is mine…" she muttered, with her eyes still closed, her hips undulating under him. She couldn't see him, but he knew she felt him with every cell of her body, because that's how he felt her.

"And yours is mine." He kissed her deeply—his sweet, delicious woman.

She was his home, his one true family.

Next to her was the only place where he belonged.

A gun in each hand, he walked along the corridor, trying to step as noiselessly as his size and weight would allow.

Vrateus and he had been taking turns patrolling this portion of the corridor and the adjacent hallways next to the human ship.

While staying on the ship, the four of them were safe. They had their own water, air, and light, separate from the grid on the Dark Anomaly. The food supply, however, was limited. The occasional trips off the ship remained necessary.

Every now and then, one of them would sneak out to get some supplies from a storage room that hadn't been fully raided by the crew yet, or to hunt an occasional *vasai* centipede for meat.

The added purpose of these expeditions was to assess the current state of the Dark Anomaly.

Judging by the many signs he had passed, the situation wasn't great. Bare bones of *vasai* centipedes littered the floor, mixed with debris and an occasional mangled body part of one of the crew.

The order Vrateus had maintained on the Dark Anomaly was gone within hours once the crew had taken over. Complete and utter anarchy had reigned ever since.

Wyck snuck into the gardens—a desolate and abandoned place, now that Malahki was no longer there. The *damirian* had been last seen the day Krakhil had locked the captain in a storage room while

Nocc and the others overpowered Wyck and tied him with Lesh's chain. The rogue *errock* and the *dimo* then tricked and attacked the two women.

Malahki had helped the captain escape that day, alerting him to the attack on the human ship. The *damirian* disappeared shortly after that. Wyck hoped for its sake that Malahki had managed to hide somewhere. Though chances were, it'd been attacked and eaten sometime during the past weeks of anarchy.

Vrateus was concerned about Malahki's fate. He'd instructed Wyck to watch for any trace of the *damirian* whenever possible.

Neglected, the gardens had been slowly deteriorating. Some parts had been growing out of control, wild and unkept. In the others, the plants withered and died—the planters here stood almost bare of green already and overhung with dead foliage.

Walking between them, Wyck collected some of the fruit that had survived, then ripped off an entire vine of edible leaves, withered but still green. Not finding any signs of the *damirian* here, he headed back.

A small nook behind a planter by the entrance caught his attention when a faint whiff of an old scent reached him.

He snuck around a large planter, staying close to the wall. Clicking a flashlight on, he shone its ray into the nook.

A rusty smear on the floor must be what had left the scent. Someone appeared to have bled here. Considering the state of things lately, it could've been any one of the crew.

He turned to leave. Then the ray of the flashlight illuminated a short string of characters on the wall, just above the spilled blood on the floor.

It wasn't written in Universal because Wyck couldn't read it. Though, he believed that the characters had a meaning. They reminded him of letters forming words. The lines and swirls had an order and had been drawn in that deliberate way he'd come to expect from written language.

Back at the entrance to the human ship, he tilted his head back to clearly display his face to the camera above the door then knocked.

The door slid open, revealing Nadia's beautiful face, a gun in her hand pointed at his chest.

"Come in." She stepped aside promptly, aiming the gun behind him.

As soon as the door was closed and locked, he hugged her to him. The feeling of her warm, soft body in his arms and her sweet familiar scent made everything right with the world, even in the middle of the chaos they called the Dark Anomaly.

"I got some fruit," he said, when he'd gathered enough willpower to tear himself away from her.

"Fruit?" Her eyes lit up.

She'd had a healthy appetite lately, which pleased him greatly. However, she'd also been craving odd things. Most were from her home planet, Earth. He didn't always know what they were, but he wished to get them all for her. Nadia was his family, the future mother of his son. She deserved to have anything she desired. It frustrated him that he couldn't get everything she wished for her.

"Do you want some?" he asked, happy to fulfill this one wish of hers.

"Yes, please." She smiled, and he couldn't resist stealing another kiss from her.

Svetlana took the mesh bag out of his hand. "I'll get it washed and peeled. You just keep kissing there." She waved her hand at them.

Wyck thought about the letters on the wall, breaking the kiss.

"What is it?" Nadia frowned, sensing his concern.

"Nothing to worry about, my sweet." He kissed the tiny wrinkle that had formed between her slim eyebrows. "I just need to ask you something.'

He walked over to the table where Svetlana had already unpacked the fruit.

"How are things?" Vrateus asked, setting the tablet he'd been reading aside.

"Wild." Wyck leaned over the table, propping his hands against it. "I've found something."

He picked up Vrateus's tablet. Recalling the characters he'd seen, he recreated them on the tablet's screen from memory, by gliding his finger over the lit surface of the slate.

"Do you know what this means?" He turned the screen to the captain.

"No." Vrateus stared at it closely. "What language is it?"

"Let me see?" Nadia peeked around his arm.

Svetlana was plucking the leaves off the vine, placing them into a wide dish. She took a glance at the screen, too, from across the table.

Both women's faces paled.

"Do you know this language?" he asked, now absolutely certain this was a language, and the characters represented words or letters.

Svetlana nodded.

"It's English, one of Earth's languages. Do you think it's from Val?" She turned to Nadia.

Nadia kept staring at the screen, her green eyes larger than ever.

"It must be from her. And it could only be meant for me. She didn't know about you being alive. And she didn't want anyone from the crew to understand it, that's why she wrote it in English, not Universal."

"What does it mean, sugar?" he asked. "What does it say?"

"It says 'Help Me.'"

EXPLOSION

book 3

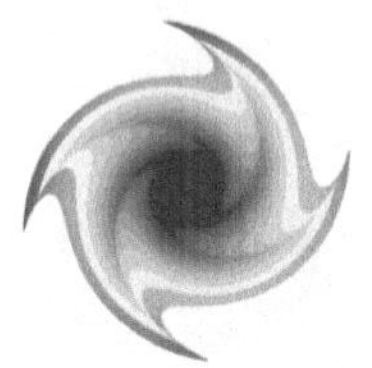

Chapter 1

Valentina

The armrest of my seat snapped off, its sharp end jamming into my side. Blinded by pain, I doubled over. The seat belt yanked me back against the seat, jolting my injury. The lightning of agonizing pain shot through my side, making the world around me fall away for a moment.

Blood, warm and sticky, trickled down my skin. The material hadn't been ripped however, so no blood marred the outside of my pale-blue bodysuit covered with holographic patches of sponsor logos.

"Are you okay?" Jose rushed to me to help me out of my seat.

"I'm pretty sure I broke a rib," I groaned, holding onto the side that hurt like hell. What if it was more than just a broken rib? "I'm bleeding."

Lee, our scientist, said something about a medical chamber. Jose checked with the rest of our team of six, making sure no one else had been injured during the landing that felt more like a crash.

Something had happened when Jose was piloting our spaceship in for a landing. The anomaly in space we'd come to hadn't been well explored. We'd expected differentiations from the landings we'd done while in training. As one of the pilots, however, even I couldn't tell exactly what had knocked us off the carefully calculated trajectory. Jose had obviously lost control during the approach. We needed to discuss this in a briefing…

A screeching noise cut through the air.

Were we not done crashing yet?

"Get the suits on, everyone!" Jose shouted. "We have a hull breach."

Lee helped me to the hatch where our spacesuits were kept.

An oval cut-out from the wall of our spaceship fell in, then the interior filled with smoke. I coughed, jolting my wound with mind-blinding pain.

A massive *errock* emerged from the smoke, tossing a lifeless body of one of our engineers to the floor. I hadn't seen the engineer being killed, but I knew the man was dead when his body hit the floor, his limbs dangling like those of a rag doll, his head bent at an unnatural angle.

Without pausing, the *errock* murdered our second engineer by snapping his neck as if it was a twig.

"Oh, my God…" I whimpered. My knees went soft, pain and horror made my head spin. Staggering back to the wall, I slid to the floor.

This must be a nightmare, a hallucination brought on by the pain from my injury and by the loss of blood. It just couldn't be real.

"Run!" Jose shoved Nadia out of the *errock's* way, then grabbed a long tool from the shelf in the suit storage.

Brandishing it over his head as a weapon, he charged the murderer.

The *errock* took the blow on his thick, wide shoulder. Lifting his enormous fist, he smashed it into Jose's arm, against the elbow joint.

With a harrowing crunching sound, my captain's arm overextended and broke. Jose cried out in pain, his weapon dropping to the floor from his weakened fingers.

The *errock* trapped Jose's head between his huge hands and yanked it with a twist.

I watched in horror and disbelief as my captain, my friend, the man I'd hoped would be more than a friend one day was murdered right before my eyes.

And I couldn't take it.

"No…" I tried to crawl to Jose when the killer tossed his limp body on the floor, just a few feet away from me.

My head swam, a bout of dizziness sending me into darkness.

God, please let it all be just a nightmare, or don't let me wake up at all.

When I came to, it became clear, the nightmare was real.

Another *errock* joined the first one. They now argued over Nadia. Our poor movie producer was lying on the floor, with one of the *errock's* standing over her.

I searched the place for anything I could help her with. The long tool that Jose had dropped was to the right of me, on the floor. If I stretched my arm…

The pain in my side sent me back into the fetal position, both arms pressed to my middle. Hot searing agony spread through my chest. Every breath hurt. I wiped my mouth on my shoulder, it left a red smudge of blood on my suit. The material quickly absorbed it, but it was clear, the injury had caused some internal damage.

A soft noise reached me, like someone was clicking their tongue. It came from the cut-out in the wall. I glanced that way, finding a person standing there, just outside of our spaceship. A *damirian*, I recognized the beige skin and hair of that species.

At first, I thought it might be a hallucination. Tall and lithe, the newcomer wore a serene expression, so out-of-place with the carnage and violence inside the ship. Then I realized, the *damirian* was of the neutral gender, which explained its enviable composure in the middle of hell.

It made another clicking noise with its tongue, gesturing me to get out.

"Kill those who are aggressive," the *errock* standing over Nadia said to the one who'd murdered Jose and the rest of our team. "Let the captain deal with the rest. Those are the rules for each new ship's arrival."

Was he *protecting* Nadia?

I glanced back at her. She looked terrified but alert, watching both *errocks* intently.

A large, three-headed animal leaped in from the opening in the wall. I stifled a scream of horror as it sniffed, turning one of his heads my way. It then, thankfully, headed to the *errocks*. The two didn't pay me any attention, either unaware of my presence or thinking me dead.

The *damirian* at the exit energetically gestured for me to get out.

I had no idea what waited for me outside the ship. *Damirians* were a peaceful nation, though. Their species were born as a neutral gender and became male or female when they met their partner. I'd only ever seen the *damirians* of neutral sex, and even then, only on TV. Those of the neutral gender served in the government and came to Earth with delegations from Ak'ae, their planet.

The one gesturing to me to get the hell out right now was definitely of the neutral gender. Its body lacked the colors that I heard the other genders developed.

Compared to the *errocks* inside the ship, the *damirian* definitely seemed a safer choice.

Gathering my strength, I crawled toward the exit. My arms shook and my knees trembled. Dizziness disoriented me. Consciousness threatened to leave me again, but I kept moving, pulling myself with my elbows toward the table that stood between me and the exit, then over to the wall with the cut-out.

A sound of footsteps came from the outside. Someone was rushing this way.

The *damirian* raised its hand, urging me to stop moving. It then pinched its lips between its thumb and pointer finger, in the universal sign of silence. Clearly, the *damirian* didn't want the attention of the others on me. It wanted me still and silent.

Too hurt and exhausted to figure out its reasons, I simply did what it wanted of me. Muffling a groan of pain, I lay still by the wall next to the cut-out.

"Hey, what's going on here?" A voice sounded from what seemed like right above me.

"Another ship!" someone exclaimed excitedly.

They spoke different languages, but my translator picked up both, flawlessly conveying the meaning to me.

"Holy fuck!" the first one yelled. "Is it a female?"

I drew my head into my shoulders, afraid they'd spotted me.

"Of course, the *errocks* got to her first," he added with disappointment, and I realized he was talking about Nadia.

"The captain's female?" another one asked.

"No, it's a new one. Look, over there."

"The captain's woman went back to her room a while back," a calm voice which I assumed belonged to the *damirian* replied. "This is a new female. Just arrived. Hey," it added casually. "Vrateus still doesn't know about this. Whoever tells him first would most likely get a reward. What do you think, Valmo?"

"A reward?" One of the other aliens sounded intrigued. "Like what?"

"Well, I don't know. Maybe relief from your chores tomorrow. You could sleep in then play cards all day."

"Shit! I'm in!" Valmo hurried away, with the scurrying sound of several sets of feet. Whoever Valmo was, his species must have had a lot of legs.

"How about you, Gahot?" the *damirian* continued. "Don't you want to earn a favor from the captain?"

"Nah," the other male replied. "The *errocks* are about to fight. I want to watch."

I ventured to angle my head a little and saw the pale-blue tentacles slinking over the edge of the cut-out in the wall. Gahot must be a *yourlu*, another alien species of the Federation.

All nations currently in the Federation were civilized and peaceful. Wherever we'd landed, however, I wasn't sure I could trust any of them, not after all the murders I'd witnessed. I probably shouldn't be trusting the *damirian* either. But what choice did I have?

I was about to pass out from pain and exhaustion. I'd rather be away from the murderous *errocks* when that happened.

"Oh look! Who is it there?" the *damirian* said loudly, frantically gesturing to me to climb out at the same time.

"Who?" Gahot asked stupidly, turning to look down the corridor where the *damirian* was now pointing.

Pressing an arm to my side, I awkwardly climbed out through the cut-out and crouched behind the *damirian's* legs. It had its arm wrapped around the *yourlu's* shoulders, directing his attention away from the cut-out and from me.

"Not there." The *damirian* turned the *yourlu* back to the ship. "A fight right there. See?" It pointed inside the ship where the argument had escalated to shouting. Then, the sound of flesh punching flesh came. The fight had started.

"Yeassss!" Gahot released a satisfied hiss. "My bet is on Wyck. He's so damn big!" There was an undisguised appreciation in Gahot's voice, the *yourlu* obviously placed a huge importance on physical size.

Trying to make as little noise as possible, I scurried along the wall in the direction the *damirian* discreetly gestured for me with his hand behind his back.

Outside of the ship, the indoor space had the shape of a long corridor, with uneven floors and dented, mostly white wall panels. There were no windows here. The illumination came solely from the lit cables loosely draped along the ceiling.

How far did the *damirian* want me to go? I had no strength to get up and walk. Crawling over the dips and cracks of the floor aggravated my injury. I pressed my arm to my side, but that didn't stop the warm sticky blood trickling down my side inside the suit. I was losing too much blood for the suit's material to absorb it all.

A sound of thundering footsteps rushed up ahead, coming closer.

Were those made by a friend or a foe?

Most of my crew had been murdered violently. I harboured no illusions and dreaded the worst. Not waiting for them to come closer, I scrambled for a place to hide. There was a set of white doors, shaped like an accordion, on my right. With no time to think, I shoved one half aside and slipped in.

Air, rich with moisture, hit my nostrils on the other side of the doors. The place I found myself in appeared to be a botanical lab or artificial gardens. Raised pots formed passages through the large space, which was illuminated by bright white light. Plants of all shades of green and purple grew in neat rows in the planters. Some were tall enough to form dividers throughout the room, which made it impossible to accurately judge the size of this place.

The sound of the footfalls filtered through the doors to me. Not knowing if the newcomers were on their way to the gardens, I crawled behind the nearest planter, trying to hide out of sight.

Thankfully, there was a small alcove in the wall behind the planter, and I climbed inside it. With my legs drawn up to my chest, my entire body fit inside the alcove.

The effort of crawling through the corridor had drained me of energy completely. Stifling a moan of pain, I leaned against the wall.

The flesh around my ribs throbbed and burned. Gingerly sliding open the front closure of my suit, I examined the injured area. Blood had been collecting inside the suit. It splashed out, leaving a bright red puddle on the floor. How much had I lost so far? My head swam with dizziness, and my limbs felt cold.

The entire left side of my chest and stomach, between my breast and the hipbone was generously smeared with blood. Through the long rip in my skin and muscle, I saw the white of a bone…*my* bone.

The sight made me nauseous.

I threw my head back, leaning it against the wall. My mind teetered on the fringe of consciousness. I clung to the last shreds of my awareness. If I passed out, I would bleed to death, alone.

I thought about Nadia, the last surviving member of my ill-fated crew. What would happen to her, now? With the two brutal *errocks* fighting over her?

The *damirian* had sent someone to get the captain, which sounded like a person of authority. Hopefully, the captain would stop the *errocks* from harming her. Maybe, he'd punish the one who'd killed Jose, Lee, and the others. There must be some kind of order around here, whatever this place was.

Maybe, they could help me then, too?

My hands shook, covered in blood. I touched the wall with my finger, leaving a smear of it on the dirty white surface. No one would see me here, behind the planter if I fainted.

Reaching as high as I could, I wrote, *"Help Me,"* on the wall, using my own blood. I wrote in English which the aliens were unlikely to understand. The only person I trusted not to harm me if they found me unconscious and completely defenceless was Nadia. And I desperately hoped she was safe and sound herself.

For a moment I just sat there, staring at the red letters. I wondered whether it was hope that made me write it or the desire to leave a mark on this world—the last mark before I left it myself.

Then, the swell of dizziness rose higher, shrouding my mind in absolute darkness.

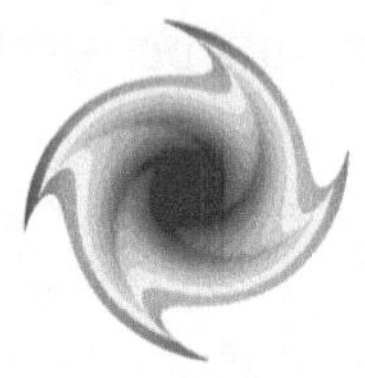

Chapter 2

Valentina

A song filtered through to my awareness. It had no words, but it had a melody to it—soft humming pleasantly buzzed in my ear.

The pain ebbed and rose with its rhythm. Each wave of agony came slower and smaller than the one before, as if the humming took some of the pain away. I let my mind ride the sound, the darkness inside me growing smaller with each crest of the soothing melody, until it took me away, luring me into a sleep where there was no pain at all.

Something smelled nice. Like herbs. Italian seasoning? And coriander? Not quite the same, but just as pleasant.

I shifted on my back, turning toward the smell. The movement painfully echoed in my side, but it was no longer the sharp, mind-blinding agony as it used to be.

"Stay still, lest you crack your ribs again and make another hole in your lungs," a calm voice warned.

"Who's there?" I tried to raise my right arm. It worked for a few moments. Then, my muscles trembled and my arm dropped back to my side. "Where am I?" I mumbled, opening my eyes.

"At my place," the same voice replied. "I said don't move," it added sternly. "You don't have the strength for it yet."

I stared straight up above me at a piece of tapestry draped like a canopy over the bed where I lay. Embroidered with weird plants and unfamiliar animals, the tapestry also had garlands of beautiful strange evergreens suspended under it. Their leaves had the shape of snowflakes.

"What is this place?" I winced, trying to remember anything that happened after my journey to what they called the space anomaly GR-A8502.

"Like I said, it's my room." A note of pride slipped into the voice this time. "It's warm, clean, and safe, which is something to be treasured on the Dark Anomaly."

Very carefully, I turned my head toward the voice. The *damirian* sat in a chair at my side in the room with sunny-yellow walls. On the low table next to it, a painted clay pot steamed with something fragrant in it.

The *damirian* took a wide cup in its hand, then spooned some dark liquid into it from the pot.

"How long have I been here?" I asked, trying to collect the broken pieces of my most current memories.

"For sixteen days now. You have no strength left in your muscles. To regain it, you'll need to eat." It leaned closer to me, holding the cup in one hand and lifting my head with the other.

"What is it?"

"Vegetable broth." It brought the cup to my lips.

Pieces of black gelatinous mass floated in the dark liquid, though it smelled rather appetizing.

"What are those?" I wrinkled my nose at the sight of the blobs. "Something is swimming in it."

"Swimming?" The *damirian* tipped the cup its way, taking a look inside. "It's an egg, you dummy. You need protein to recover your muscle strength, and boiled meat stinks too much for me to allow it anywhere near my quarters." It pressed the edge of the cup to my lips. "Drink."

I closed my eyes to get rid of the nauseating visual of the black blobs, and took a sip. The solid pieces of the egg slipped past my lips, making my stomach roil. The delicious taste of the warm, flavorful broth, however, made up for the unpleasant sensation.

"It's…good," I said softly, when the *damirian* lowered my head back to the pillow. I inhaled slowly, as not to aggravate the pain in my side, the tiny effort of taking a drink had exhausted me. "Did you say I've been unconscious for over two weeks?"

"Well, not *entirely* unconscious, but I did keep your mind in a twilight state."

"What exactly does that mean?"

The *damirian* glanced inside the cup with a dissatisfied frown. Clearly, it didn't like how little I'd managed to drink.

"You had some broken ribs," it said. "One of them punctured your lung. You lost a lot of blood. Grave injuries like that are best to treat without the mind's involvement."

"So, you knocked me out?"

"I kept your mind from interfering with the healing process of your body," it corrected tersely. "Your bones and lungs didn't need your brain sabotaging their recovery with grief and mourning."

Grief and mourning…

The pieces of memories suddenly snapped together, forming the horrifying picture of our landing.

"They're dead…" I whispered, closing my eyes again.

Now, I wished so badly to return to that blissfully numb place, with nothing but someone's humming in my brain.

"Yes. They're dead." The *damirian's* voice sounded somber but lacked any true sorrow or compassion. It was like it accepted my grief but couldn't feel it.

Dead…

The pain, a million times greater than any physical injury,

crushed my heart. They all had families, friends, loved ones who'd never see them again.

I'd never see Jose…

My eyes burned with unshed tears, and I briefly turned my head away from the *damirian,* needing a minute to collect myself. Its actions toward me had been kind, but I didn't believe it'd done it simply out of the kindness of its heart. I was not going to cry or mourn openly in front of it.

Instead, I swallowed past the tightness in my throat and asked, "And Nadia?"

The *damirian* shot me a glance, its eyes the same beige color as its skin and its long, braided hair. The green and purple vines, the *damirian* had woven in its many braids were the only bright colors on its figure.

"All dead," it reiterated. "Nocc killed them all."

All dead.

The words crushed me, blocking my throat and settling heavily in my chest. I groaned, throwing my arm over my eyes to hide the tears I could no longer hold back.

"I shouldn't have left her there, alone," I wailed, guilt and regret rocking through me.

"Then, you would've been dead, too." The *damirian's* even voice grated on my nerves, even if what it was saying was true.

"What is this place?" I exclaimed. "Is there no order? No justice here?"

"Not much." It shrugged.

I rose on my elbows, grinding my teeth against the renewed pain in my side.

"The murderer must be held accountable. I have to talk to the captain—"

The *damirian* slammed the cup down on the table, its irritatingly perfect composure finally wavering.

"I said you need to stay still," it snapped at me. Pressing both hands on my shoulders, it forced me down on the bed. "No sudden movements, or you'll stay in bed forever. My healing skills aren't limitless, you know. There's only so much I can do if you don't help me by taking care of yourself."

"But I have to—"

It pinned me with its stare.

"There's nothing you can do. Not one damn thing, got it? If you try, you'll die." Its voice was sharp as steel, the serene expression blew away from its face. "I saved your life. Do not throw it away now. No one but me knows you're here. Keep it that way."

"You didn't tell anyone?"

"No, I didn't. And you can't leave here without my permission. If anyone, I mean *anyone* in this place finds out about you..." The *damirian* inhaled deeply then released the air slowly, as if trying to gather its composure once again. "They will kill you," it said in a somewhat calmer voice. "But they'll make you their sex toy first."

"They, what?" I gulped the air in one shaky breath.

The *damirian* leaned over me, keeping its hands on my shoulders.

"There are no women on the Dark Anomaly—"

"How about the captain's woman?" I recalled him mentioning her in his conversation with the two other aliens at the cut-out entrance from my ship.

He blinked, pausing briefly.

"She is dead, too," he said quickly.

"Why?" I gasped.

"Because that's what happens to females around here," he bit out. "Like I said, there're no women on the Dark Anomaly. But there're hundreds of males. Most of them belong to the species that react exclusively to females, which means they can't even have a satisfactory sexual relationship with each other." Its colorless eyes held mine. "Hundreds of males who haven't had sex with a female for decades. How long do you think you'd last?"

I closed my eyes, unable to bear the *damirian's* stare. It couldn't be true what he was saying. People couldn't be this cruel. These things didn't happen anywhere in the world anymore, not on any of the Federation planets.

This wasn't a Federation planet, though. Murders in cold blood didn't happen out there either. Here, however...

No one had known that life existed on the Dark Anomaly before we came here. But now, I knew, and I wasn't going to be silent. I'd report the atrocities that had taken place here, and I'd bring justice to this place myself. I owed that much to the families of my crew.

I had to get well, if only to get out of here.

The new resolve helped smother my grief like a heavy blanket would put out a fire—for now, anyway. I still felt like crawling into a hole somewhere and screaming until my lungs burned and my voice was gone. But in the *damirian's* presence, I wiped my tears away and managed to compose myself.

"For what it's worth, thank you for saving my life," I said, my voice only slightly shaking.

The *damirian* let go of me, sitting back in the chair.

"You're welcome." It accepted my gratitude with a dignified tilt of its head. "What's your name?"

"Valentina." I managed to hold back a sniffle. "My friends and family call me Val or Valya."

Well, my friends stuck to Val. Only my parents and my brother had called me Valya. Both of my parents had been dead for years now. My brother had married and moved to another country. He had two daughters now, my baby nieces. I adored them, though I didn't get to see them nearly as often as I would've liked.

The *damirian's* forehead wrinkled.

"Your friends and family don't like you enough to bother pronouncing all syllables of your name?"

I blinked, wondering if it was its usual sarcasm or just genuine confusion.

"It's a nickname, a form of endearment..." I tried to explain then just waved my hand its way. "It doesn't matter. I really don't care what you'll call me. What's your name, anyway?"

The *damirian* pressed an arm across its chest, inclining its head in a stately, elegant bow.

"I'm Malahki."

"It's nice to meet you, Malahki." I tried a bow, too, which wasn't easy since I was still lying on my back. "It's a pretty name," I said genuinely admiring the sound of it.

Its brow furrowed at my compliment. Had I said something wrong?

"Pretty?" it echoed, a muscle in its jaw ticked.

"Um, I meant it in the nicest way possible," I clarified, wondering if there might be something wrong with the *damirian's* translator.

Its elbows on its knees, Malahki leaned forward, gazing at me intensely.

"Instead of gratitude for saving your life, may I ask you for a favor?" it asked.

"Of course," I nodded. "If there is anything I can do—"

"Can you think of me as a male, please?"

"A male?" I stared at it, confused.

"Yes. I'm a *he*, not an *it*."

I'd never met a *domirian* in person before. I'd only seen them on TV, and I read a little about their technology and their political and social structure. To my knowledge, it was considered insulting in their culture to attribute a person to a wrong physical sex. That included the pronouns.

Did I get Malahki's sex wrong? I'd only ever seen *damirians* of the neutral gender. Maybe the male sex wasn't that different physically as I'd thought?

"A *he?*" I asked again.

As if on its own, my gaze slid down to between its…*his* legs. In Malahki's current position, I had the unobstructed view of his groin. And since he wore no clothes, I could plainly see the smooth surface of his skin between his thighs. A slightly darker, barely visible line marked the vertical seam behind which the base for his reproductive organs lay dormant, completely invisible from the outside.

He was most definitely of the neutral sex.

Malahki followed my gaze with his eyes and cleared his throat. However, he didn't cross his legs, not trying to hide or deny the obvious.

"Will that be difficult for you? To think of me as a man, even if I'm not one, physically?" he asked, the same intense expression on his face.

"No, of course not," I protested. "Back home, people often decide for themselves what gender they belong to. What's between your legs doesn't have to define you," I blurted out, then tried to explain my initial hesitation, "It's just that I thought it was different for *damirians*. Once you choose your identity, the corresponding... um, physical attributes of the sex grow quickly.

His eyes narrowed slightly.

"And who told you that?"

"Well, no one. That's just what I've gathered from some articles I've read. There isn't that much information on your sexual development or customs, to be honest," I admitted.

"No." He pursed his lips, disapprovingly. "We don't advertise our species' gender specifics to everyone. Unlike humans, we don't send pictures of our naked bodies, complete with reproductive organs, all over the galaxy."

"What are you talking about? We don't do that."

He lifted a tablet off the floor and presented me with the picture on its screen.

"This has been sent from your planet, has it not?"

It was a drawing of a human male and female side by side next to the pulsar map.

"Oh," I rubbed my forehead. "That was a part of the message humans sent into interstellar space long ago, before our planet had been discovered by the Federation. Did we have it on the ship along with other historical documents? Why do you even have it?"

"I found it in the library when I searched for information on how best to treat your injuries. This particular picture proved useless for that." He tossed the tablet aside. "You don't even look like this woman."

I followed the tablet with my gaze, looking at the image from his point of view. I definitely didn't have the curvy hips or even the fairly average breasts of the woman in the picture. Mine were much smaller. Visually, I was probably closer to Malahki's body shape than to hers. Taller than average, I'd often been called "sporty" based on my looks. However, I didn't really do that many sports. I liked jogging early in the mornings. And I played beach volleyball with a group of friends, back on Earth.

"I do have long hair like hers," I muttered, dragging my gaze away from the screen. Though, the woman's hair appeared blonde on the drawing. Mine was dark-chestnut, with faint reddish highlights. The length was about the same—somewhere between the shoulders and the waist.

"So do I." He shrugged. "I have long hair, too. That doesn't make *me* a woman."

"True." I shifted on the bed again, very carefully. My side hurt less, but lying in the same position made my back muscles ache.

"Well, whatever you've done worked, I definitely feel better." Physically, at least, I did.

"You have to drink all of this." He lifted the cup of broth again.

Closing my eyes, I did as he said, taking a few big gulps.

As my stomach filled with the warm aromatic broth, my mind kicked into gear. I needed to contact Earth, inspect my ship, find a way to take the bodies of my teammates back home…

"What is the best way to send a message from here?" I asked when Malahki took mercy on me and let me take another break from drinking.

"There *is* no way," he said simply, setting the cup down. Taking a piece of soft cloth from the table, he wiped the corners of my mouth with it.

"Well, maybe I could sneak back on my ship, just to use its communication system, then—"

"You can't." He stopped my attempt to argue with another hard stare of his. "First, communication signals don't go through the Dark Anomaly's force field. Second. Remember what happened on the ship? It's not safe. You can't go there. You can't leave the gardens. In fact, I prefer you didn't leave this room at all."

He leaned over and fluffed the round pillow under my head.

"Malahki," I said quietly, but firmly. "I need to inspect my ship, fix what needs to be fixed, and go back to Earth."

He heaved a sigh, sitting back in the chair.

"This is going to upset you," he muttered under his breath.

"What? What is it?"

He bent over, picking up the tablet again.

"Let me tell you more about this place, Valentina." He changed the slates in the tablet frame then turned the screen with a blueprint on it to me. "We call it the Dark Anomaly. And there is no leaving it."

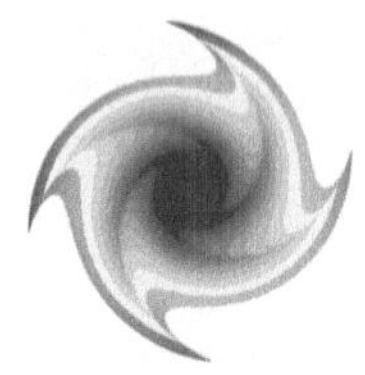

Chapter 3

Valentina

I cried. These were the ugly tears I hadn't wanted Malahki to see but now no longer cared about hiding.

It had taken me a while to fully comprehend what Malahki had been saying when he showed me pictures, diagrams, and numbers. Once the meaning of them hit me, it all came crashing down on me at once.

The phenomenon we called "the space anomaly GR-A8502" turned out to be nothing more than a junkyard of crashed ships, smashed together into a disk by an inexplicable force. It was hurtling through space, sucking in all powered objects with the live beings still on board.

It had done it for thousands, millions, or maybe billions of years. Entire lives had been lived here. With no escape.

Time was warped on the Dark Anomaly. In the sixteen days I'd spent recovering, over thirteen years had passed back on Earth. No one had come looking for us. In another month or two, our expedition would live only in history books—just another unsolved mystery of space travel…

Our friends and family had mourned our disappearance and had most likely declared us all dead, including me. They had plenty of time to move on by now—all while I was lying in bed in a semi-conscious state. Even if I had been fully conscious all this time, according to everything Malahki had shown to me, I couldn't have done anything to leave here or even let the Earth know of our fate.

"This can't be true," I sobbed, my arms thrown over my face. My tears kept running from my eyes to be soaked up by the embroidered pillow under my head. "I need to go home."

He stroked my hair soothingly.

"This is your home, now." There was no real emotion in his voice. He wasn't trying to calm me because he cared, but because my crying probably made him feel uncomfortable.

"There has to be a way…" In my mind, the numbers and graphs Malahki had shown to me made sense. In my heart, I just couldn't accept any of it. "There could be a mistake in the calculations."

"The latest data came from one of your own. She—" he cut himself off, as if having said more than he'd intended.

"One of our own? A human, you mean?" I wiped my tears with my hands, peering at him between my fingers. "Who is *she*?"

"She? No." He shook his head quickly. "There is no 'she.' I meant the most accurate data we've collected came from the probes sent here by humans and from your own ship's landing records." He leaned closer, taking my hand in his. The spark of emotion I hadn't seen before flashed through his colorless eyes. "I'm sorry you're hurting, Valentina. But we can't afford to have hope on the Dark Anomaly. I don't want to watch your spirit die slowly over the years to come."

"You'd rather kill all hope in me, now?" I bit off.

He released a long breath, squeezing my hand tighter.

"The sooner you learn to accept your fate, the faster you'll be ready to fight for your survival in this place. Because sooner or later, all of us will have to fight to survive."

"I don't want to fight." I turned my head away from him. At that moment, I wasn't sure if I even wanted to survive.

He sat in silence for a few seconds, drawing small circles on my hand with his thumb.

The sensation grounded me. I focused my mind entirely on that one small movement of the pad of his thumb along my skin, because if I let myself think about anything else, I feared I'd lose my mind.

"Your fate is better than that of many who have come here before you," he said softly. "I've saved you from the worst. Stay with me, and together we may have a chance at surviving what's to come."

I STAYED IN BED FOR A FEW MORE DAYS, FULLY CONSCIOUS THIS TIME and acutely aware of every second passing by. It was exceptionally painful letting the time pass, when each day translated into ten months back on Earth and each moment took me further into oblivion for everyone back home.

Malahki came and went during the day. He said he had chores to do out in the garden. At night, I listened to his even breathing as he slept on the pallet on the floor next to my bed. The purple vines in his hair glowed soft blue in the darkness, and I tried to come to terms with never seeing sunshine or moonlight ever again.

One morning, after breakfast, Malahki came in holding a bowl of water in his hands.

Since the day of our first conversation, he'd started wearing clothes—or something like it. Two long pieces of brown fabric hang off his belt past his knees, covering his front and his back from my view.

"Time to take off the dressing from your wound." He set the bowl on the painted-wood table next to the bed. "Then, you'll have to take a shower."

"Do I stink?" I asked, opening my suit for him mechanically.

"You smell strong enough for *errocks* to catch your scent," he replied.

Opening my suit wider, he exposed me from the waist up, including both of my breasts.

His attention remained firmly on the healing scar on my side, and his gaze didn't stray upward once. The touch of his fingers on my skin was light and efficient as he cleaned off the dark-green paste he'd applied before.

His complete and utter disinterest in me as a woman had made it easy for me to relax under his touch and let him do the job of my nurse that he'd assigned to himself.

He dipped a piece of cloth into the warm water then washed the green residue off around my scar.

"The mark will stay," he observed. "But it'll get smaller and will pale with time."

"I don't care, either way." The emotional scars bothered me so much more than the physical. Only they would take much longer to heal, and I feared I would never be completely whole again.

He pressed his mouth into a tight line of disapproval but continued in a lighter tone, "I'll help you to the shower now. You have to use the berry soap to make sure *errocks* don't smell you."

Errocks…

The image of the two of them towering over poor Nadia on the day of our landing, rose in my mind again.

Malahki had told me about the various species they had here on the Dark Anomaly. He'd told me about Vrateus, their *themul* captain. All of them had been stranded here for years or decades, but had been missing for millennia to the outside world. Just like I would be, too.

"You can't keep thinking about that." Malahki guessed the course of my thoughts. "You'll drive yourself insane, which would kill you more effectively than anything else around here."

"How long have you been here?" I asked, as he started taking off my bodysuit for me.

"Over five years." He helped me free my arms from the sleeves.

"What helped you stay sane?"

"Work." He dragged the suit down past my hips then carefully lifted each of my legs to take it off completely. "I left Ak'ae, my planet, to operate a botanical laboratory in space. As a technician, my job was to maintain the equipment, collect seeds and seedlings, plant them, and record all stages of the plants' life cycle in space. I was on route to Omphi, the large, water world planet in this area, to collect a few oceanic plant species from there when the Dark Anomaly sucked me in."

"Were you alone in your laboratory?"

He nodded.

"That must be hard, to travel through space all by yourself," I said.

The vastness of the interstellar space had often made me feel small and insignificant on our way here. Having my crew helped retain the feeling of normalcy during the two long months of traveling.

"I never minded being alone," Malahki replied. "In fact, the reason I took that job in the first place was to be on my own."

"Why?"

His gaze slid off me, focusing on something only he could see.

"I always liked the peace and quiet of solitude. The clear thinking with the insight that's only possible when one is on their own and their mind is unimpeded by the erratic urges of the body."

"What urges are you talking about?"

"To reproduce, for one," he said, with a grimace of distaste.

"Wait a moment, are you saying you went away because you didn't want having to select another sex eventually?"

I didn't know it was even possible for *damirians* to remain of the neutral gender forever.

"Many of us wish to remain the way we're born," he replied evenly. "The alternative means losing the blissful calm to rage, lust, and other unstable emotions of either males or females."

"Is it even possible for a *damirian* to remain of the neutral sex? For the rest of their live?" I asked.

"It's possible, but the chance of it is slim if one remains in society. Sooner or later, relationships happen and attachments form. The urge to mate triggers the change."

"So, without a potential partner, there is no urge at all?"

"Absolutely none." He gave me a serene smile, helping me off the bed. "The bliss of calm is the hardest to gain and the easiest to lose. I treasured it."

I stood on my own two feet for the first time in weeks. My knees shook and my hands trembled. I would've fallen had Malahki not held me firmly under my arms.

"This way." He led me behind a brocade curtain, through the narrow passage, and into a metallic bathroom. Cold and unadorned, this must be a part from a different ship than the one where Malahki's bedroom was located, but it looked so different from his colorful room that it seemed to be from another world entirely.

Supporting me with one hand, Malahki unclipped his belt, taking off his loincloth and hanging it by the entrance. He then turned on the water from a cone-shaped spout in the ceiling.

"It's cold!" I gasped as the barely lukewarm water hit my skin.

"Energy preservation, on the captain's orders," Malahki replied, calmly. "You only get five minutes a day, so we need to hurry. This is the soap you'll have to use daily." He made me sit on a stool under the stream then lathered my body with the small brick of soap.

He was thorough, washing my hair and lathering every crook and cranny of my body. Just like when removing the dressing from my wound, his movements remained quick and efficient. He made no difference between touching my breasts or my elbows.

"The bliss of calm…" he'd said earlier, and I believed I understood him well.

I'd never been truly in love, but I knew the yearning for love very well. Ever since I met Jose, I wished he'd notice me not just as a friend and colleague but as a woman, too. He never did, which had cost me a lot of sleepless nights of tossing and turning in sweaty sheets—alone.

Maybe having no desire at all would be a blessing as compared to the torture of wanting what one couldn't have?

"I wish it was possible for humans to be of neutral sex, too," I said.

Malahki spread the water rushing from the spout with his hands, rinsing the soap off me.

"I can see the benefits of not suffering from emotions," I added. Sadness and grief had been hanging over me like a dark shroud ever since I'd regained consciousness, making me long for the oblivion of earlier.

The water stopped, and Malahki put a wide, knitted towel around my shoulders, drying me off.

When he helped me up to my feet again, his expression was no longer neutral. A frown settled over his face.

"What is it, Malahki?" I asked.

"There are advantages that other genders have over the neutral sex," he said slowly.

"What are they?"

He'd asked me to think of him as a male, though he didn't have the physical features of that sex. From what I'd gathered about him, Malahki didn't mentally associate with the male gender, either.

"The main advantage of the *damirian* men is their physical strength," he said.

I exhaled a laugh.

"That's it? Brawn is hardly an advantage by itself."

"Around here, that is all that matters," he said firmly.

"Is that why you want to be male?" I guessed.

He flexed his jaw, his mouth settling into a hard line.

"In the world where physical strength can mean the difference between life and death, yes, I've made the decision to become a male."

Holding me by my shoulders, he settled his eyes on mine.

"Sadly, just wishing for it is not enough, Valentina, neither does simply spending time together, I've tried that. It didn't work. I need a partner who is willing to enter into a relationship with me."

"A woman," I said quietly as understanding of his past actions came to me.

"Yes. The partner needs to be of the opposite sex—"

"And as you've said," I added quickly, "there're no females on the Dark Anomaly, but me."

He blinked, momentarily shifting his gaze aside.

"Right. No one but you."

I swallowed hard, my knees shaking.

"Is that why you saved my life?"

"Yes..." His eyebrows twitched, moving closer together. "Well, no. Either way, I couldn't leave you out there to be brutalized by the *errocks*."

"Well, thanks..." I nervously tugged at a strand of my wet hair. "Apparently, you wanted to keep the *brutalizing* part for yourself."

Malahki's "noble" act of saving and keeping me safe somehow no longer seemed that honorable, since he'd had a hidden agenda all along.

He winced.

"I'd prefer not to go about it in any aggressive way. No brutalizing, please," he assured me. "Can't the mating be done in some more civilized manner? I admit I don't know much...or anything about physical relationships, but I have been thinking about a slower, more natural approach."

I gaped at him in disbelief.

"You're honestly planning to mate with me?" A queasy feeling tightened my stomach as I listened to him speak.

"Eventually, yes." He didn't deny it. "As soon as you're feeling well enough, we'll be sharing the bed every night. You'll sleep naked, as will I. You will show me how you like being pleasured, and I will do it regularly."

I might not have known love, but I knew affection—even if unrequited affection—very well. This wasn't it. There was no attraction toward me in Malahki. There'd been more longing in his eyes when he'd spoken about the serenity of working and living alone in space than he had when he looked at me.

"We can start right now, with a kiss." He closed his eyes and lowered his face to mine.

Malahki was generally a good-looking person. His features were symmetrical and straight, his skin smooth and soft to the touch. His long hair, with several long braids and vines of flowers woven through, framed his face, giving him a flare of artful fantasy. I admired his appearance as I would admire a beautiful picture on a wall.

His body had none of the definite male or female features of his species, but that only meant that both men and women would possibly find him physically attractive, in my opinion.

His looks were not what made me recoil from him. His absolute lack of even the slightest spark of attraction for me made his words sound clinically cold, his proposition revolting, and a kiss between us impossible.

"That's not how it works," I said softly.

Twisting out of his grip, I wished I could run away. My weakened legs betrayed me. I only managed one unsteady step to the wall, then had to brace myself with both hands against it.

Malahki didn't seem to be offended by my rejection. Coming closer, he supported me under my arms again.

"We need to start going for walks in the gardens daily, to build up your strength," he observed calmly, leading me back to the bedroom.

Once there, he helped me into the chair by the bed then lowered himself into a crouch in front of me.

"Like I said, I don't know much about relationships, Valentina, but I'm willing to hear any suggestions you may have."

There was no passion in him, not even close. But I sensed genuine desperation in the way he gripped my hands.

"Malahki," I took a long breath. "You are a strong, capable person as you are. More than that, I believe you're happy with who you are, too. Is it really that important to become someone you don't really want to be, for just a little bit more muscle power?"

He briefly closed his eyes. His chest rose as he inhaled deeply. "Have you ever met a *damirian* male, Valentina?"

"No… I'd never met anyone from Ak'ae at all, other than you."

He opened his eyes again.

"Well, trust me then when I say we're not talking about 'just a little bit more' strength and brawn. A *damirian* male is a weapon on his own, which makes our army one of the best in the Federation. But there is a reason why none of our males hold any position of power on Ak'ae, not even in the upper levels of the Military. Their physical power, combined with almost reckless courage and aggression, makes for a dangerously uncontrollable combination when political governance and military strategy require a cool head and calm logic."

He massaged my hands in his as he spoke.

"I used to find physical strength vulgar, Valentina, especially when combined with recklessness. I still do. But here, on the Dark Anomaly that's what rules—the explosive combination of power and aggression. Until now, I've been lucky to survive by what I am here. My neutrality didn't trigger either the aggression or the lust of the males on the Dark Anomaly. So far, they've let me be. But things are changing. The order among us is shaky. It had crumbled before, and I'm afraid it will collapse for good, soon. When it does, it'll be every person for themselves. Even if no one wants to fuck or fight me, many here wouldn't stop to think twice before killing me for food when they get hungry."

"Really? They would?" A breath lodged in my throat at his words. How many horrors could one place hold?

He wrapped his fingers around mine, slightly tugging my hands to him.

"From what I've observed, those who form groups have a better chance at survival here than those who stay on their own. There aren't many people here I would trust, but I've decided to trust you. I figured you are a civilized person. I've studied everything we have at the library on human culture and values, and I believe your gratitude to me for saving your life would facilitate the mutual respect between us." He fixed his imploring gaze on me. "Help me go through the change, Valentina, and I'll be able to protect both of us much better."

I understood what he said, but what he demanded from me still didn't seem possible. This wouldn't even be sex without love. What Malahki wanted was sex without desire. I knew he felt nothing for me in a physical sense.

"That's not how it works, Malahki," I repeated.

His expression hardened with determination.

"Tell me *how*, then?"

How was I supposed to explain this to him?

"You see, you want me to let you touch me, but you have no actual desire to touch me. This may be even worse than demanding sex for money."

He squinted at me.

"You'd prefer to be paid?" he asked, horribly misunderstanding me. "Do you want money for this?"

"What? No! God, no." I shook my head energetically. "That's not what I meant at all. Listen, I thought *damirians'* transformations are triggered by mutual attraction between the couple that develops over some period of time. Not by any amount of regular…pleasuring."

The last word left a bad taste in my mouth. I didn't dislike Malahki. His touch didn't repulse me when he changed the dressing on my wound or helped me in the shower. But I just couldn't imagine him touching me with any passion or intimacy. And without that, how could there be any real pleasure?

He shifted uneasily.

"First of all." His voice held an edge of annoyance, this time. "We may *not* get to have any long 'period of time together.' Time is a luxury on the Dark Anomaly. One has to earn it first. Second, I have tried to simply spend time with a woman before, and it didn't work…"

"You've tried? Who was she?" I remembered now he'd mentioned something about trying to trigger the gender change before.

He waved me off. "It was a long time ago."

"When? Back on Ak'ae?"

"A long time ago," he said firmly, without elaborating any further. "Tell me, Valentina…" He stared at me for a moment, his eyes narrowed with suspicion. "Did you already have a man back home? Is your heart not free? Because I believe that was what impeded my change the last time. The woman was not free."

The memory of Jose tightened painfully in my chest. He'd never been "my man." Though, I always had a place for him in my heart.

"The man…" I started then exhaled, without finishing the sentence. "I don't have a man. My heart is free, but that's not what it's all about, Malahki. I don't know what to say to make you understand. You know what? Come here." I scooted to the edge of the chair, cupping his chin. "I'll show you."

He'd asked for a kiss, back in the bathroom. So, I drew his face to mine and placed my lips on his.

His mouth felt warm and supple. He dutifully parted his lips, allowing me full access, but I didn't take the invitation. The sensations of touching him never went past my skin. There was no warmth in my chest, no butterflies in my stomach, none of the painfully delicious pull of desire in my lower belly, either.

"Do you see now?" I leaned back. "A touch is just a touch. It's the emotions, right here…" I took his hand and placed it on his chest against his heart. "That makes it special. That's where the real pleasure starts."

He moved his gaze from our hands at his chest up to my eyes. His crestfallen expression and disappointment tugged at my compassion. I wanted to help him, I just knew I couldn't.

"I'm speaking as merely a human here, but I believe you have to feel something in your heart first, Malahki."

He appeared to ponder my words.

"Just me? Or both of us have to feel it?" he asked.

"Both would be the best, of course. But mutual attraction has to start somewhere, right? Sometimes, desire can be contagious. If you know the other person likes you, it may ignite an interest on your part in response." I thought back to Jose and me, and finished, a little deflated, "But it doesn't always happen that way, either."

He let go of my hand and swiftly rose to his feet.

"So, you're telling me you've spent all of your life as a woman, and you can't clearly explain to me how the attraction between sexes happens?" The frustration in his voice came from disappointment, but it also sounded like he blamed me.

"Listen," I said. "I wish I could be more helpful here, but nobody really knows exactly how and why people fall in love."

His lips pressed together, turning nearly invisible. He grabbed another loincloth from the chest by the wall and wrapped it around his hips, hiding from view what wasn't there to hide in the first place

He appeared to view his "sexlessness" as a sign of failure to become in form what he had decided to be in his mind. Except that I believed he wanted it for all the wrong reasons. Malahki didn't really wish to be a male. He just wanted to be stronger than he was.

Maybe that was where his failure lay?

Stripping the sheets off the bed, he started changing the bedding.

"Have you ever been in love?" he asked, in a calmer, more usual for him tone.

"No," I replied. "But there was a time when I longed for it."

He paused with his back to me.

"Did you want to have it with Jose?"

Hearing his name out loud twisted the knife of grief lodged in my chest. I inhaled deeply, taking a moment.

"How do you know about Jose?"

"You said his name many times while I was healing you. Was he one of your crew?" He glanced at me over his shoulder.

I nodded, clasping my hands together.

"My captain," I whispered around the tight lump that nearly blocked my throat.

He came closer.

"I'm sorry you lost him in such a brutal way."

I lifted my eyes to his, surprised by the genuine compassion in his voice.

"You can feel emotions?" I blurted out in shock.

He took the towel from me then helped me back to bed, into the fresh sheets.

"Of course I can," he said, indignantly. "I'm a person, not a machine. I have a heart and a brain to feel and understand. What I also have is the ability to process emotions inside gradually, without letting them explode outwardly. The uncontrolled explosion of emotions is dangerous and can be devastating both to you and others."

He tucked the blankets around my naked body then lifted my bodysuit, holding it between two fingers.

"You've had it on for weeks. I'd better soak it overnight."

I smiled as he wrinkled his nose, holding my suit at arm length from him.

"It's fully self-cleaning material," I assured him. "It doesn't need to be washed."

"It doesn't?" He squinted at it suspiciously. "Well, maybe at least air it out a little."

He shook the suit out, then draped it over the brightly painted, wooden trunk by the wall.

"Thank you, Malahki," I said softly. "I really wish I could help you, and I'm very sorry that I cannot. Unlike yours, my emotions are very much out of my control. I know I could never fall in love or even feel an attraction to anyone at will."

He lowered himself in the chair by the bed again. Propping an elbow in the armrest, he placed his chin in his hand.

"You just get well, Valentina," he said after a long sigh. "Two of us are still better than one. We'll manage."

"Can we still try to be friends?" I offered.

He gave me a small but warm smile and nodded.

"If that's all we're destined to be…"

Chapter 4

Valentina

As of the next day, I started walking regularly. In addition to bathroom trips, I added a few steps around the room at first. Eventually, my walks got longer. With Malahki's help, I soon ventured into the gardens. We started with a trip around a planter, gradually increasing the distance every day.

At the beginning, Malahki almost carried me, my arms draped around his neck. After a few days, however, my body grew stronger under his care. Eventually, he only needed to support me around the waist with one arm, to steady me.

Malahki chose the early morning hours for our walks in the gardens. He said that was when "the others" were still asleep.

The still largely unknown to me world of the Dark Anomaly had been divided in two parts in my mind. One part was the comfortable, colorfully decorated room where I felt safe with Malahki at my side. Beyond it lay the dangerous, colorless space, with dented walls, bent floors, and equally warped people—"the others." I didn't see them, but I sensed their menacing presence out there, beyond the gardens.

One morning, Malahki pointed at the neat rows of shaggy-looking lavender-colored plants. "This here is the *xaevoe*. That's the grains we had for dinner last night."

Despite the relatively limited variety of food, I couldn't complain. Malahki had been using a range of fragrant herbs to flavor the dishes of grain and greens, making our meals not just nutritious but also very tasty. Now and then, he would use black-shelled eggs that came in a cluster, but no meat.

He'd explained that the meat on the Dark Anomaly came from *vasai* centipedes, seven-feet long creatures with a multitude of chitin-covered legs. Their description alone had made me lose appetite even before he added that their meat stunk when cooked.

"*Xaevoe* is much prettier in its plant form," I commented. The grain looked muddy gray when cooked.

"Aren't all plants most beautiful when they're growing, lush and fresh?" he murmured, plucking a yellow flower off the vine from the planter we were passing by. "That's their best stage of life." He tucked the flower in the braid over his ear.

Surrounded by life he'd planted and maintained, he truly appeared to be in his element. Malahki had enough patience to nurture a plant, enough insight to spot any subtle changes in the seedlings, and enough knowledge to intervene when it was necessary. He obviously enjoyed the peace this place offered him in return.

As we rounded a corner of the next planter, his arm around my waist stiffened. I heard the sound of muffled voices coming from the corridor outside the gardens.

"We need to hide, Valentina," Malahki whispered.

The peaceful atmosphere of our walk shattered into pieces by the alarm in his words.

"Where?" I asked quickly, gripping his hand with both of mine.

I wished to be back in the safety of Malahki's room tucked behind a broken piece of paneling far at the back of the gardens. But it was too far for us to get back in time at my current speed. The voices kept coming closer, fast.

"Right here." He stepped between two planters, each holding

long vines that climbed up the thick lattices to form walls. Now, I understood the strategic placement of the planters throughout the space. That was how Malahki created hiding places all over the gardens.

"Hey! *Damirian!* Where the fuck are you?" a thick voice bellowed from the entrance to the gardens.

The sound of heavy footsteps followed. Then, a tall, armor-plated figure showed up. A *dimo*, I recognized the species, watching him through the gaps between the leaves. Every part of the *dimo's* gray-brown body was covered in hard plates, reminding me of a rhinoceros.

A group of other aliens followed him into the gardens—a pale-blue *yourlu* with clusters of tentacles for arms and legs, three chitin-covered *kreers* with a bunch of long, segmented tails each, and one of the other species, which took me a while to remember their name as I'd only ever seen them in a picture once—*remoid*. His skin was covered in purple pigment spots, and he had two legs and four arms.

The males fanned out from the entrance. Some plucked and ate seeds and berries off the plants while passing by the planters. Others obviously weren't here to snack. They just uselessly ripped leaves and branches off vines and shrubs.

"Urkril," Malahki whispered. "That's the *dimo's* name. The *yourlu* is Xid. The *remoid* may be Leephron, I'm not sure, I don't know the male that well. And I can't recall the names of these *kreers*."

"What do they want?" I asked him in a barely-there whisper, too. Some of the group had come closer, and I didn't want to attract their attention by making any noise at all.

"Where is that *thing*?" The *yourlu*, Xid, asked in a whiny voice. "Where did the *damirian* go?"

"Spread out, let's search this place." Urkril ordered.

Malahki squeezed my hand briefly.

"Stay here." He moved to get out from our hiding place, but I wouldn't let go of him.

"No…" I gripped on to his bicep. I wasn't sure if I was scared more for him or myself, but I wanted us to stay together, come what may.

He gently freed his arm from my grip then squeezed my shoulders, looking into my eyes.

"I have to talk to them," he said. "Otherwise, they'll start sniffing all around here. Whatever happens, don't let them see you. Do you hear me?"

I forced down a whimper of protest and nodded instead.

"If they find you, you're dead... Or worse." He frowned, glancing back at the unwelcome visitors.

My hands grabbed on to the empty air as he slipped out of my reach. I bit my bottom lip to stop myself from crying out.

Malahki stepped into the open.

"How may I help you, gentlemen?" he enquired calmly.

"There it is!" the *yourlu* squealed in delight, pointing with all six of his tentacles that his species had for arms—three growing from each shoulder.

"Hey." Urkril strode toward Malahki. "We need *irsen* flowers." He bent over, grabbing a wide silver bucket from under the nearest planter. "As much as you can fit in here." He slammed the bucket into the dirt in the planter, crushing the pale-green herbs that grew there.

Malahki tilted his head, casting but a glance at the ruined sprouts he'd so carefully planted and maintained.

"I can't do that," he said. "Not without personal permission from the captain. You know the rules."

Malahki had told me about the *irsen* flowers. They had some properties that made them useful for medicinal purposes. They also had strong narcotic qualities, which made them addictive and dangerous in large large quantities.

Most of the flowers had been ripped out during the last mutiny by the crew. Since then, Vrateus, the captain, had ordered the planters with the flowers Malahki had re-seeded to be hidden.

The new *irsen* plants had sprouted and bloomed since. Malahki had used them sparingly, for medicinal purposes, including brewing the tea he'd given to me while my injuries healed.

"Fuck the rules!" the *remoid* yelled, swaying on his feet unsteadily.

He had to prop two of his four arms on the floor to regain his balance.

"We have the permission," Xid waved him off, shoving aside a *kreer* to get closer to Malahki.

"I need to hear it personally from the captain, then." Malahki crossed his arms over his chest, widening his stance. "Where is he?"

"He's in his fucking room, where else?" a *kreer* snarled, his long, black tails lashing about.

Urkril jabbed him in the ribs with his hard-plated elbow, making the *kreer* whimper and bend over in pain.

"If you don't give us the fucking flowers, we'll get them ourselves," the *dimo* growled, menacingly advancing on Malahki.

"You will never find them on your own," the *damirian* replied evenly.

Compared to the *dimo*, Malahki was so much smaller and leaner. He stood his ground, however, seemingly unafraid.

"...I have emotions. I'm a person, not a machine..."

I recalled his words. Just because he didn't show fear, it didn't mean he wasn't frightened when faced with the massive *dimo* towering over him.

"Where are they?" Urkril roared in Malahki's face.

The deafening sound made me shake behind the planter, yet Malahki didn't waver.

"I said I need the permission—"

Urkril jerked up his elbow, smashing the hard, serrated nob of the joint into Malahki's temple.

I jammed my fist into my mouth to stop myself from screaming in horror as I watched Malahki stagger to the side.

Next, Urkril raised his massive fist then slammed it into Malahki's jaw.

Panic shot through me. I choked on my unreleased scream, shoving my fist so far in my mouth, I could barely breathe.

Malahki's knees gave in and he dropped to the ground.

I hadn't witnessed this kind of cold, brutal, unnecessary violence in my life. Even the murders on board of my ship had been different. Then, I could pretend the *errock* was a deranged man on the loose, who might've been triggered by the fear of the unknown.

Here was an act of deliberate cruelty that had no reason and no purpose other than the demonstration of one's power over a physically weaker being.

"Fucking *it*!" Urkril spat into the bucket he'd failed to fill with what he'd come here for. "No cock, no pussy. Good for nothing."

He spun on his heel, stomping to the exit.

Giving the motionless Malahki a slap with a tentacle, the *yourlu* yanked a vine from the *damirian's* hair. The braid it'd been woven in had come undone, Malahki's long, sandy-colored hair falling over his face.

I wanted to rage, punch, and harm those who'd hurt the person I cared about, my friend—because Malahki had absolutely become my friend. He'd cared for me, talked to me, protected me…for as long as he could.

Suddenly, I understood perfectly clear his desperate desire to change. I, too, wished to be stronger and bigger. I wanted to be ruthless, hurting those who'd hurt us. What could I do, though, if I could barely stand upright, still so weak and sick?

"What are we going to do now?" The *yourlu* hurried after the *dimo*, chewing on the vine he'd plucked out of Malahki's hair. "Nocc said not to come back without the *irsen* flowers…"

The rest of the aliens followed the pair out of the gardens, too.

"Fuck Nocc!" I heard the disgruntled voice of Urkril in the distance.

I didn't wait until the sound of their footfalls and voices had quieted down completely. Ducking behind the plants and containers with dirt, I scurried to Malahki.

He lay on his side, his face turned upwards, his eyes closed.

"Malahki," I called in a loud whisper, taking his face between my hands. "Please, Malahki. Get up. We need to get out of here."

Here on the floor in the fairly open area of the gardens, the danger of being discovered pricked my skin with dread. The fear that he wouldn't get up or even open his eyes overshadowed any concern for myself, though.

"Please, Malahki." I brushed aside the long strands of loose hair from his face.

I would run back to the room to get some water to splash in his face, but I was so scared to leave him lying here alone. What if Urkril came back? I'd recognized the name Nocc, too. That was the *errock* who'd murdered my entire crew.

Malahki's eyelids finally fluttered open.

"Oh, thank God, are you okay?" I kept petting his face, afraid he'd close his eyes on me again.

He grimaced in pain, and my fingers came back smudged with red when their tips brushed by his temple.

"I'm so sorry, Malahki," I gasped, covering my mouth with my hand.

Tears burned in my eyes at the sight of blood where the *dimo's* rugged armor tore through Malahki's skin above his ear. A bright red spot was spreading under his skin along his jawline, where Urkril had punched him. The skin here wasn't broken but a huge bruise was forming already.

"This shouldn't have happened," I sobbed. "They shouldn't get away with this."

"They will," he gritted through his teeth, propping his hands into the floor to sit up. "They always do."

Always?

"Has it happened before?" I asked, feeling hollow in the pit of my stomach.

He looked at me, pausing his eyes on mine for a long moment. A corner of his mouth suddenly rose in a smile.

"Only once or twice." The tone of his voice lifted. "I'm too smart to let it happen too often."

Was he trying to cheer *me* up?

"Oh, Malahki." I grabbed him under his arm, fully intending to help him up.

"No." He freed his arm from me gently. "The last thing we need is you cracking your ribs again. I'm fine."

Gathering his long legs under him, he got up on his own, only slightly swaying on his feet.

"Come. Before any of them return." I took his arm again, tugging him toward our bedroom. The effort cost me my balance, and I steadied myself by grabbing on to one of the containers along our path.

The bright pink and purple plants in it were enclosed under a tall rounded glass dome. My hand slipped down the smooth surface of the cover. The tips of my fingers wedged between it and the edge of the container, sinking into the dirt inside it. I yanked my hand out and moved to wipe them on the side of my suit.

"Wait." Malahki gripped my wrist. "Don't touch anything with this hand."

He produced a spray bottle from under the planter and a clean cloth.

"Why? What are these?" I asked as he sprayed my hand with the liquid from the bottle then whipped my hand dry with the cloth.

"The *fuhnid* mushrooms." He jerked his chin at the wide purple umbrellas with pink fuzzy stripes growing under the dome. "The captain adds their juice to the soap. It makes our scent undetectable to the *errocks*' highly-sensitive sense of smell. But the mushroom juice is also highly toxic."

A faint, pleasant scent wafted around the planter.

"Is it lethal?" I inspected my hand carefully, seeing or feeling nothing out of ordinary. Of course, my fingers hadn't really come into contact with the mushrooms, just with the dirt they grew in.

"If swallowed, even a tiny amount, it's most certainly deadly. But the mushrooms can also kill if they simply come in contact with your mouth or eyes. In other words, don't ever touch them without wearing protective gear. Come now."

He steadied me with his arm on my waist, and I had my arm wrapped around his middle, too. That was how we made it back to the room—two hurt, broken people, supporting each other.

"Sit down." I gestured at the chair when we got inside. "It's my turn to take care of you."

He gave me a sad smile, but didn't argue. His shoulders relaxed, he appeared relieved to be back in the room where we both felt safer.

I filled a cup from the carafe of drinking water Malahki liked having on hand, then took a washcloth from a shelf by the curtain next to the bathroom passage.

"If you tell the captain what happened, would he punish them?" I asked, gently dabbing at the blood on the side of his face.

"Probably."

"Then why don't you tell him?"

"He has other things to worry about." He shrugged.

"He's your captain. Your wellbeing should be on his list of things to worry about."

I rinsed the cloth in the cool water then placed it against the swelling on his jaw, the place where the hard fist of Urkril had planted a blow.

"Valentina, if there is one thing you'll get out of what happened this morning, please, let it be that we're the only ones responsible for our own wellbeing on the Dark Anomaly, no one else." He took the washcloth away from me. "Besides, if Urkril and his thugs get punished because of my complaints, what do you think they'd do to me the next time they visit my gardens?"

I didn't want to think about that, but he stared straight at me, obviously expecting an answer.

"They'd do…something worse than a couple of punches," I muttered.

"That's right." He rose from the chair to get the jar of green substance he'd used to treat my wound. I wondered how many times he'd had to use it on himself before.

"Here." He handed it to me. "I can't see that spot well myself. Would you apply it, please?" He sat back in the chair.

The muscles in my legs started to tremble from the strain of standing for so long, and I lowered myself onto the edge of the bed. He scooted closer with the chair then leaned over the armrest toward me.

I opened the jar, dipped a finger into it then started dabbing with it over the tear in his skin. Setting the jar aside, I took a handful of his hair, holding it back while I worked.

"It's done." I wiped my hand on the cloth he'd handed to me. "How do you feel?"

He beamed an unexpected smile. "Better already."

I personally didn't feel better at all. The hurt and indignation for him burned as painful as ever.

"Why didn't you just give them the damn flowers?" I asked.

Who cared about some stupid rule by the captain who obviously couldn't keep his own people in check.

The smile slipped off his face.

"During the last mutiny, the crew gained access to the *irsen* flowers. Some had too many and died. Others got too aggressive due to the effect of the flowers and started killing each other. I didn't want to be responsible for more carnage," he replied simply.

Whatever his gender, Malahki proved to be a better man than any of the males in this place. He cared about their lives more than they did.

"Why not let them search the gardens like Urkril threatened he would? Chances were they would've never found them, anyway."

I didn't ask that question out loud, because I already knew the answer. If Malahki had let the thugs search, they would've found me. Instead, he distracted them by allowing them to beat him up.

Subdued, I ran my fingers through the locks of his ruined braid. "Do you want me to fix this for you?"

He arched an eyebrow with a glint of interest in his eyes. "You can braid hair?"

"Not as elaborately as you do, of course." I looked closely at his other braids. To replicate their intricate pattern, I'd need some above average weaving skills. "But I could try to do something simple. If you don't mind."

He slid a critical gaze down my messy ponytail. "Only if you allow me to fix that disaster for you."

"A disaster?" I touched my straight, long hair that I'd hastily pulled back into a ponytail. "Is it that bad?"

"No." He shook his head, with another cheerful smile. "I just want to see how a *damirian* hairstyle will look on you."

Malahki's lean figure stood by the planter in the garden. There was sky above the lush green-and-purple space he'd created—the real blue sky, with sunshine and clouds. I tilted my head back, letting the sunrays warm my face, and laughed.

A sickening sound of flesh hitting flesh cut my laughter short.

"You are nothing," a huge dimo roared, grabbing Malahki's head, the same way the errock on the spaceship had with Jose. "Fucking ***it!****" he yanked Malahki's head to the side. His braids whipped, and his neck snapped with a cracking sound that I felt all the way through to my bones…*

I sat up on the bed with a gasp.

No, no, no…

Not again.

I breathed hard. Cool perspiration gathered on my forehead and trickled down my spine. Fear shook my body.

Not Malahki, too…

I was in his room. All was quiet. The luminescent garlands under the colorful tapestry over the bed softly glowed blue. Malahki lay right there, on the sleeping pallet by the bed. I'd offered to take the pallet myself before, feeling uneasy about kicking him out of his own bed, but he'd refused. He'd said the mattress was softer and easier for my healing ribs.

"Malahki?" I whispered.

He was so close, all I had to do to touch him was to lean over the edge of the bed and reach down. I patted his shoulder.

"Mmm?" he groaned, sleepily.

"Could you get in bed with me? Please?" I asked tentatively.

Spurred by the fear from the nightmare, I didn't have the time to think it through. The moment my request left my mouth, however, I worried about his potential rejection.

He rubbed his eyes. "What? Why, now?"

His words about us sleeping naked together and his pleasuring me came to mind, warming my cheeks with blush.

"No. I don't mean it like *that,*" I mumbled. "I'm wearing my suit, you don't have to touch me." Saying that made my face feel even hotter with mortification. "There is a lot of space here for both of us. It's a big bed..."

Maybe I should've practiced the words first, but I just wanted him next to me, so that if I dreamed about him being killed again, I could feel his heartbeat and hear his breathing the very moment I woke up.

"Oh, all right..." He nodded, and I exhaled in relief.

He climbed from his pallet into my bed. I scooched over to make room for him then drew the blankets over both of us.

"I had a dream about you," I explained as he lay on his side, his eyes wide open, now. "It wasn't good. The *dimo* killed you."

He gave me a small comforting smile, petting my shoulder.

"Don't worry. I've survived this long. I'm not going anywhere."

I longed to believe him, but the unsettling feeling after the nightmare wouldn't leave me.

He lifted a braid he'd made in my hair earlier. It had dark-green leaves of evergreen from his planet, Ak'ae, woven through it. Shaped like snowflakes, they glowed softly in the night.

"This looks even prettier in the dark," he said softly.

I now had the same hair-do as him—five intricately braided pleats on top of my head, two of them framed my face on each side, with the rest of the hair left to fall free under the braids. One of Malahki's braids, the one made by me, was plain and boring compared to the rest. He had insisted on keeping it, anyway.

One arm under his cheek, he blinked lazily, the ghost of a smile lingering on his lips. Then his eyes closed, and his breathing deepened as he fell asleep.

The dark, crusted with blood scar on his temple was clearly visible in the soft glow of the vines in his hair.

I heaved a long, heavy breath at the sight of it. Finding his hand under the blanket, I wrapped my fingers around it.

He didn't need to be big and powerful. He didn't need to be male. Malahki had saved my life, being just the way he was. And he was still finding ways to protect me. Even if it hurt him.

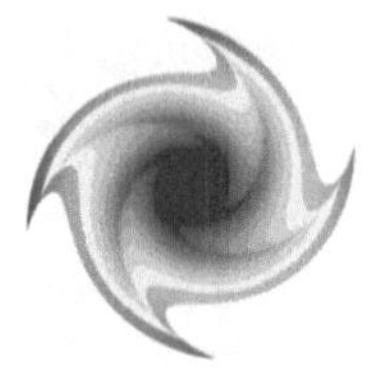

Chapter 5

Malahki

He woke up with Valentina's leg draped over his middle, her face pressed against his upper arm.

It'd been over two weeks since she'd first invited him to share the bed with her. He was still getting used to waking up with her limbs thrown all over his body, her warmth sending a trickle of perspiration down his back and along his inner thighs.

At first, he'd expected having someone in his sleeping space to be uncomfortable. And physically, it kind of was. He would often wake up when Valentina turned and tossed through the night. Sometimes, she'd groan and mumble things in her sleep. He had woken her up too on a few occasions, by tossing an arm or a leg aside, unaware in his sleep of her presence.

The benefit was that he no longer had to get up to check on her. Whenever he opened his eyes, she was right there, next to him. He could listen to her breathing and see her face, peaceful in the soft light of the glowing plants.

He glanced at the lit dial of the clock on the shelf in the corner.

It was time to get up and make breakfast. He had *pherli* leaves soaking in *orkok* juice overnight. When rolled and fried in *gruzo* oil, the leaves became crisp and salty on the outside, but remained soft and mild on the inside. Valentina loved when he made them for breakfast.

He moved to get up, but she shifted closer, throwing her arm over him in addition to the leg and hugging him tighter. She hadn't talked about having bad dreams anymore, but he'd felt her waking up with a start every now and then.

This morning, she was clinging on to him like a lifeline, and he realized he liked the feeling when she held him like that—he felt *needed.*

He'd never cared about being needed by anyone before. In theory, it'd always seemed like a burden to be responsible for anyone other than himself. But Valentina made him feel important, without him having to do anything at all. Just his being there seemed to calm her, bringing back the peace of sleep.

The fresh evergreen in her hair tickled his nose when she put her head on his chest. He felt the sudden urge to kiss her hair, and he didn't fight it. Lifting his head, he buried his lips in the fresh fragrance of her dark hair.

The silky strands tickled his face, making him smile. He felt even hotter with Valentina's entire body now wrapped tightly around him. But the positive sensations of her embrace far outweighed the discomfort of a little perspiration.

"Is it time to get up already?" she muttered sleepily, her lips moving against the bare skin of his chest.

"No. You can sleep for a bit yet." He made a point of keeping a schedule, whether it was on his one-person-crew space lab before or now on the Dark Anomaly. But what would be the harm in letting Valentina stay in bed for a few more minutes if that was what she desired?

"Sleep," he murmured, soothingly gliding his hand up and down her upper arm.

Generally, Malahki preferred the gardens to anywhere else on the Dark Anomaly. Having Valentina here, made any desire to get out into the common areas even smaller. However, he had to keep an eye on what was going on in the rest of the Dark Anomaly.

The last time he'd left the gardens was a few days ago, and he didn't like the mood of the crew then.

He'd overheard that Wyck, the *errock* in charge of the other surviving human woman from Valentina's ship, Nadia, had taken the female all to himself.

In a way, that was what Malahki had done too, with Valentina. Except that Malahki tried to keep her existence a secret, sparing her the disgrace of performing naked in public, when Wyck had to display his woman to the entire crew.

Wyck had come by the gardens, screaming Valentina's name. It terrified Malahki that her presence on the Dark Anomaly might have been discovered. Once, Wyck even brought Nadia with him, as a bait for Valentina, no doubt. Nadia must have been coerced to disclose Valentina's name to Wyck.

Thankfully, Valentina had been too weak back then. She had slept more often than she'd been awake, and she'd missed them coming to the gardens.

After that, Malahki had gone out and listened to the crew talk among themselves. No one else mentioned Valentina's name or even the possibility of a third female on the Dark Anomaly, which had calmed him somewhat. Wyck and Nadia had no way of knowing that Valentina had survived. They must have wondered what had happened to her, but they wouldn't search forever. If they didn't find her, they would eventually give up looking, he hoped.

Of course, he never said anything to Valentina about the others looking for her. Unlike Wyck, Malahki knew he wouldn't be able to physically defend a female from hundreds of males. He had to employ other tactics. He kept her hidden. And if it meant resorting to lies to keep Valentina safe, then so it had to be.

"I'll need to leave the gardens again," he whispered in her ear.

She jerked her head up, alarm flashing through her eyes that were a pretty shade of dark blue like the midnight flower from Ak'ae.

"Why?" She asked.

"I need to see what's going on out there."

He used to get updates from Svetlana, daily. Ever since Valentina had started to recover, however, he'd told Vrateus he no longer needed Svetlana's help in the gardens. The risk of the two women seeing each other would've been just too great.

Malahki had enjoyed spending time with Svetlana while the two of them had worked together. But he didn't trust her not to tell Vrateus if she learned about Valentina. And then, well, Malahki had seen what Vrateus did with Nadia. The captain gave her to Wyck to do whatever the *errock* wanted with her. Malahki had heard that *errocks* had even forced the poor woman to have sex with Wyck in public.

Unlike the captain and the rest of the crew, Malahki arrived on the Dark Anomaly as an adult from more modern times. He understood better than any of them that a woman, regardless of what alien race she belonged to, would not appreciate being turned into a sex toy for hundreds of crude, raunchy males.

As long as he lived, he would not allow such treatment of Valentina.

Now, without Svetlana keeping him up to date, if he needed to know what was going on out there, he had to leave the gardens and go see for himself. Even if Valentina's eyes told him clearly, she wanted him to stay.

"It's important, Valentina." He moved a braid over her shoulder. "We need to know what the others are doing. So we can be better prepared for whatever comes next."

He'd lived through the first mutiny of the crew. He'd witnessed some really disturbing things then. Things that had proven to him how fragile peace and order were on the Dark Anomaly.

Last time, the captain had been poisoned and nearly died. For a while, his power had fallen into the hands of the *errocks*, a brutal group. During those few days, Malahki had seen murder, abuse, and more violence than he'd ever seen in all his life prior.

"When will you leave?" Valentina sat up. Sleep had completely left her eyes, replaced by worry.

"Right after breakfast." The crew would be lingering in the mess hall, chatting while finishing their morning meal—a perfect time to gauge their mood and find out what was brewing in their midst.

"Can I come?" she asked tentatively, not with much hope in her voice.

"Of course not. It's not safe."

"Will it ever be safe?"

What could he tell her? That he sensed the things were actually getting worse? That the safest future he could envision for her on the Dark Anomaly would be her spending the rest of her life right here, in this room, unseen by the others.

He didn't have the heart to tell her that. Instead, he chose to lie. Again.

"One day, things will get better, I'm sure."

They had breakfast mostly in silence. He sensed Valentina's subdued mood. She didn't like being on her own. But he also knew that she worried about him.

She walked him through the gardens, all the way to the last planter with *almai* vines. They rose up to the ceiling then draped down over the pipe up there, creating a safe alcove to hide from the eyes of anyone who might walk into the gardens unexpectedly.

Unlike the captain's, Malahki's safety measures weren't the metal doors and an extensive arsenal of weapons. He used stealth and plenty of hiding places.

"I'll be back before you know it," he told Valentina.

"When?" She gripped his forearms.

"Soon. Before lunch, most likely."

He didn't plan to linger out there. All he wanted to do was a quick reconnaissance.

She raised her face to his. Her eyes glistened, the intensity in them took his breath away. He couldn't physically walk away from her when she was looking at him like that, as if he were the only person in the universe.

Instead, he brought his face closer to hers.

Her eyes flicked to his lips. His mouth felt dry, and he licked his lips.

Her mouth opened, just a little.

He didn't have one single thought in his head when he lowered his face all the way down and touched her lips with his.

With a soft whimper of surprise, she rose on her tiptoes and gripped his head, keeping his mouth on hers. Her kiss felt like her hug, warm and natural.

He'd sensed she needed a stronger form of connection with him before saying goodbye, and he gave it to her.

A warm feeling rose in his chest from the sensation of her soft lips sliding over his. It grew, bubbling and getting warmer. When he felt like his chest was about to explode from that growing heat inside him, he panicked and drew back, breaking the kiss.

Her eyes were open wide, worry floated in them along with fear and something else he couldn't name. Her lips glistened like freshly plucked *lornee* berries.

She kept holding his head between her hands.

"Please, hurry back," she whispered.

THE THOUGHTS OF VALENTINA WOULDN'T LEAVE HIM AS HE WALKED down the corridor toward the mess hall. The memory of her kiss still tingled on his lips. The odd tightness in his chest wouldn't let go, making him unusually lightheaded.

At the same time, everything around him appeared more acute somehow. The warped panels of the corridor walls seemed whiter than normal. The light from the cables above shone brighter. And the noise of the crowd inside the mess hall as he approached was sharper, each sound separated from the rest.

The morning meal was almost over. Svetlana cooked food once a day in the afternoon. Krakhil and a few others warmed up the dinner leftovers for breakfast.

The gray stew with the foul smelling *vasai* meat had almost been finished by the males. Oddly, Malahki didn't find the smell of meat that disgusting today. It was strong, but not as nauseatingly repulsive as usual.

The crew paid little attention to him, as was the norm. He

preferred it that way. Staying close to the walls and away from the groups, he lingered among the males, listening to their conversations and gauging the mood of the crew.

There were the usual complaints about the captain and his rules, which was normal. No matter what Vrateus did, someone was always displeased.

Most of the crew had been on the Dark Anomaly for decades. They'd been sucked in from the outside world millennia ago, back when the interstellar space was a wild place, rife with crime and filled with delinquents.

Even when *he* got here, five years ago—Dark Anomaly time—which roughly translated to about fifteen hundred years in the world out there, one of the popular options to avoid the law of the Federation had been to take off into the dark, unexplored corners of the galaxy. The crew of the Dark Anomaly comprised former criminals, unhappy to live under any rules but their own.

This time, however, there were different notes in the usual disgruntled buzz. Some complaints were new and much more specific.

They got even louder after Vrateus, the captain, came through the mess hall for an inspection accompanied by Wyck, the *errock* from his personal guard.

"They each have a female to fuck whenever they want…" Malahki heard.

"We got nothing…"

"We should've had a fair fight," the dreadfully familiar voice boomed nearby.

Malahki tossed a glance in the direction of the voice, spotting Urkril, the *dimo* he was beginning to hate with the passion he'd never thought himself capable of before.

"A fight! Whoever wins gets the female," the *dimo* roared, surrounded by a group of males charged with anxious energy.

"Or we all could share them," someone else chimed in.

A heavy premonition chilled Malahki's heart when he saw another group enter the mess hall. This one was led by Nocc, the *errock* who'd murdered most of Valentina's crew. Krakhil, another *dimo*, walked shoulder to shoulder with him.

The two groups merged like two dark clouds, and Malahki feared they would create a storm the Dark Anomaly might not weather well.

Ever since the last time, he'd expected another mutiny. The crew had always been volatile. The sudden tossing of the females into their midst could only be the catalyst of an explosion.

Teasing the males with the sight of females then denying them any access to them was a mistake on the part of the captain. It could bring nothing but trouble. Malahki long knew it, but only recently had he begun to understand the captain's actions. As far as Svetlana was concerned, Vrateus obviously hadn't been driven by logic, but by a desperate desire to keep her alive and later to get her away from the others.

Malahki would never let the crew touch Valentina, either. For as long as he lived, he'd do anything to keep her safe.

"How come Wyck ended up with a female all to himself?" someone snarled in the crowd.

"He stole her," Krakhil growled. "From us!"

"Well then maybe we could steal them both back?" Nocc hissed. "You want a fight? We'll force them to fight!"

His words acted like fuel splashed on an open flame. Caught by the crowd, Nocc's call to fight echoed under the ceiling as the crew raged.

Malahki had promised Valentina to be back by lunch, and he wanted nothing more but to rush to her, to touch her hand, to see her smile, to make sure she was still safe and sound, hidden far away from the disaster that was about to happen.

First, he had to try to warn the captain. Vrateus had established control over this mismatched crew of delinquents not once but twice already. If there was anyone who had any chance at stopping the mutiny with its devastating consequences, it would be the captain.

Nocc grabbed a table and slammed it into the floor, smashing it to pieces. The crashing noise drew delighted cheers from the crowd.

Wielding the metal leg of the table as a weapon over his head, Nocc stormed out of the mess hall.

A few crew members lingered. Some were still picking pieces of food from the dishes on the tables. Many were so pumped from Nocc's words, they started picking fights with each other.

Carefully avoiding the brawls breaking out all over the room, Malahki slipped out of the mess hall.

Around midday, the captain should be finishing his rounds. Though his schedule often changed, Vrateus would normally be visiting the *vasai* farm early in the afternoon. Malahki turned right from the mess hall, heading to the *vasai* farm first.

Here, large, mismatched cages lined the space. The giant centipedes crawled and screeched in them.

He detested this place probably more than anywhere else on the Dark Anomaly. Poorly lit and noisy, it stunk of *vasai* excrement, no matter how often the captain ordered the cages cleaned. The creatures threw themselves against the bars, their chitin-covered bodies scraping against the metal. Black clusters of eggs were suspended in the corners of some cages. Along with the grains he grew in the gardens, these were the main protein source in his personal diet. He found the food eaten by the rest of the crew repulsive and had long started making his own, using a small flameless stove he'd managed to salvage from his own ship that had crashed here.

Many of the cages remained empty as the centipedes had been needlessly butchered, their meat often getting wasted during the last riot. Because of that, in those terrible days when the *errocks* were in control, food had become scarce. Fights over the remaining supplies broke out, all over the Dark Anomaly. He'd seen the crew attacking and killing each other then devouring the flesh of those who had lost.

He knew that despite his superior intelligence over nearly everyone of the crew, he'd most likely lose a fight against any of them. When it came to physical strength, he'd be the one who'd end up being eaten.

His first thought when he'd seen Valentina back on her ship—the vulnerable, injured woman—was to get her away from the *errocks* fighting over Nadia, the woman he could no longer save. The *errocks* hadn't spotted Valentina yet, and he saw the chance for her escape.

The idea that she might be useful to trigger his change had come to him later, after he'd found her passed out in the gardens.

Obviously, he'd been naïve thinking that simply having a woman in his proximity would get him what he wanted. Valentina had lived with him for almost six weeks now, two of which they had been sharing the bed. Yet the place between his legs looked as smooth as ever.

At the same time, that didn't feel like a complete failure, somehow. There was so much he'd gained since she came into his life. During the past four weeks since she'd been conscious, the two of them had become inseparable. He grew to enjoy having someone to share his meals with, to talk to, and to spend time with.

Not finding the captain anywhere in the farm or in the waste sorting room behind it, Malahki quickly checked the equipment storage room by the airlock next to the farm. It was locked, and no one replied when he knocked.

After that, he headed back to the mess hall. It was almost completely empty now, save for a few males of various species who were passed out on the floor.

The nearly deserted state of this section wasn't unusual for this time of the day. However, Nocc's words from earlier made him worry.

Speeding up his pace, he hurried along the corridor toward the captain's room.

He was still a long way away from the room when a *yourlu* poked his head from a side hallway. Malahki recognized Xid, who'd been there when Urkril had attacked him last time. Normally, Malahki would give him a wide berth. Out of all the species on the Dark Anomaly, *yourlu* were one of the most annoying on the crew.

"Keep moving, *damirian*," Xid hissed, gesturing with all six of his arm tentacles for him to pass.

The air of self-importance that Xid emitted made Malahki pause.

"I said keep going, asshole!" The *yourlu* bounced with the eagerness of someone doing something important.

The insult scraped against Malahki's nerves unexpectedly, causing a flare of irritation.

"What if I don't?" He widened his stance, crossing his arms over his chest.

A new thrill zapped through his muscles. He found himself wishing for the *yourlu* to accept the challenge.

Xid didn't disappoint. Tossing a shifty glance at the door at the end of the side hallway, he moved on to Mahlaki.

"Then, I'll make you. Get out of here!" He lashed out with a tentacle.

Malahki grabbed it, yanking hard.

Obviously not expecting the resistance, Xid staggered on the cluster of tentacles *yourlu* used for legs, losing his balance.

"You fucking *damirian*," Xid cursed under his breath, scrambling to his tentacles. "This time, you're dead!" he yelled, charging Malahki.

Malahki leaped aside, evading the attack.

Avoiding the confrontation didn't feel enough, though. Being "a bigger person" by walking away didn't appeal to him as much as it used to. He craved the satisfaction of a well-placed blow. His fists itched to wipe that arrogant smirk off Xid's face, who expected him to turn his back on him and leave. And normally, he would have.

Not today, though.

Xid whipped around. His bottom tentacles undulated under him, propelling him forward.

Instead of ducking from the incoming blow, Malahki lunged ahead. He grabbed the *yourlu* by his scrawny neck.

"What the f…" Xid croaked.

Startled by Malahki's attack, the *yourlu* hardly offered any resistance. Using the momentum, Malahki threw him backwards and to the floor.

"You've been asking for this for years," Malahki gritted through his teeth.

Blood boiled in his veins. His muscles tingled and ached,

begging to be used. He struggled to hold back from punching the life out of Xid.

"Fight me, now!" He gave the stunned *yourlu* a shake.

The air in Xid's throat gurgled as the male strained to pass a word through Malahki's grip. His tentacles lashed around them, whipping Malahki's bare arms and shoulders. The suckers on them attached to his skin, tearing at it, but Malahki barely noticed the pain.

He forced his hand to relax only when the watery eyes of the *yourlu* swelled and bulged out of his skull.

"Let me go..." Xid pleaded, in a voice he'd never used with Malahki before. "I have a job to do. Nocc will be furious—"

He glanced back to the door at the dead end of the hallway and cut himself short, his eyes shifting away again.

"What's behind that door?" Malahki demanded.

"Nothing," Xid replied quickly, way too quickly.

"Is it locked? Where is the key?" Placing his knee onto the *yourlu's* chest, he squeezed his throat once again.

"What key?" Xid croaked, his tentacles tightly wound around Malahki's arms. A couple of them made it for his neck, but Malahki swiped at them. Twisting a bunch of tentacles into a bundle, he shoved them under his other knee.

The *yourlu* whimpered as Malahki put his weight on that knee, pressing down on the pale blue cluster of flesh.

"Key!" he ordered. "Give it to me."

"Fine." A tentacle emerged from the quivering mass of them. On the tip of it, a rectangular piece of metal with bumps and indentations dangled on a ring—the key to the storage room.

"Nocc will kill you both," Xid hissed, each word soaked in undisguised hatred.

"But who will tell him?" Malahki tilted his head, enjoying the flush of terror in the *yourlu's* eyes right before Malahki punched him. He held back, controlling the force of his blow, aiming to neutralize, not to murder.

With a brief, strangled noise, the *yourlu* jerked, his tentacles jolted and twitched. Then his body stilled, his long, twisty limbs spread motionlessly over the floor.

A rush of excitement rolled through Malahki with that blow. He craved to hit again, to feel the flesh give in under his fist. At the same time, the realization that he'd just extinguished the awareness of another being filled him with horror.

Sliding the key off the unconscious *yourlu's* tentacle, he climbed from the male's motionless body.

"Nocc will kill you both."

Malahki wondered what Xid had meant by "both." For a moment he feared that Valentina had been discovered.

When he neared the door, however, he heard a sound of someone moving behind it. Then, a faint scratching noise came through the door panel.

He briefly considered leaving the key and whoever was behind that door to their own devices. He didn't get involved in the crew's scuffles if he could help it. However, he feared that today's conflicts involved more than just isolated fights.

Sliding the flat rectangle into the slot on the door, he unlocked it.

"Malahki?" Vrateus stood on the other side of the door. A laser gun and a long piece that appeared to be a part of one of the shelves in his hands.

A chunk of the door with the lock dropped to the floor with a loud clunk, nearly missing Malahki's foot. The captain had been well on his way to freeing himself.

"Thanks," he said, moving past Malahki and out into the corridor. "Where is that traitor Nocc?"

When Malahki turned around, Xid was no longer there. The *yourlu* must've come to while he wasn't looking then ran away either to hide or to complain to Nocc.

"They all went that way." Malahki gestured down the corridor, in the direction toward the captain's room, the library, and the gardens.

"Who all?" Vrateus tossed aside the long metal piece and made a gun slide out of his sleeve instead.

"Almost the entire crew." Malahki discreetly picked up the discarded piece as Vrateus headed up the corridor. Having any kind of weapon appeared a necessity at this point. "What happened? Why were you in the storage room?"

Vrateus winced, his bronze skin darkened on his cheekbones with obvious embarrassment. His long, furry tail lashed angrily against his boots.

"They attacked Wyck while I was in there, getting supplies. Have you seen Wyck?" Vrateus asked.

"No. But he may be that way, too, because I haven't seen him either in the farm or the mess hall."

Vrateus glanced at Malahki over his shoulder, his expression even more severe than usual.

"Something is brewing, captain. I overheard them talking about taking the women—"

"Svetlana!" Vrateus took off in a mad dash, his weapons at the ready.

Malahki ran after him. He told himself there was no reason for him to worry about Valentina. She would be safe in their bedroom deep inside the gardens. No one usually went to that part of the gardens. He'd arranged the planters around it, in a way that made people pass it by, without noticing. The unpleasant feeling wouldn't leave him, though.

The noise of the crowd reached them as they came closer. The wild rumble reverberated between the warped walls of the corridor. Something was happening up ahead.

They passed by a few crew on the way, all of the males restless and agitated.

As they came around another bend in the corridor, the battle scene opened fully to his view, Wyck and Nocc both falling to the ground. The crew literally crawled over each other to get closer to where the entrance of the human ship was. Laser shots fired, joined by the bullets of the captain's much louder projectile weapons.

Malahki had no time to watch and no desire to linger, worry about Valentina suffocating him.

At the double-doors to the garden, he slowed down.

The anticipation of seeing Valentina rushed over him. He rubbed his chest, trying to ease the growing bubble of heat inside it, but it only seemed to grow bigger, slowly descending down into his belly.

Maybe what he'd wished for and dreaded was about to happen, after all?

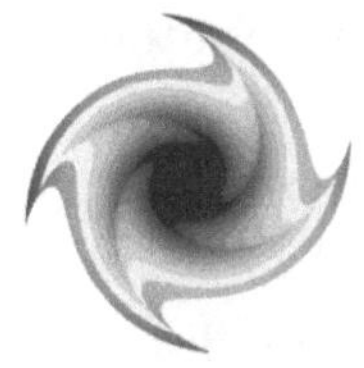

Chapter 6

Valentina

Lunchtime had passed, and Malahki was nowhere in sight. I anxiously paced in circles inside our bedroom, listening to every sound from the gardens.

What if something had happened to him? What if he needed help while I sat here, waiting for him in vain?

I searched the small kitchen area Malahki had set up in a recess in the wall in the bedroom. Grabbing the long, narrow knife he used to peel vegetables, I poked my head from behind the wall paneling that separated our room from the gardens.

Caution warred with the burning desire to find Malahki. I grew up in a crimeless society. Never in a million years would I worry about walking on my own outside of my apartment building back on Earth, no matter the time of day.

I would've never been able to comprehend the extent of danger Malahki had warned me about had I not witnessed the violence of this place with my own eyes. On the Dark Anomaly, I knew I could be attacked without provocation. I could be killed, too.

All seemed to be quiet out in the gardens, though. The irrigation system trickled quietly. The delicate leaves of *almai* vines trembled and rustled as I passed by.

For now, all I wanted to do was to get to the entrance into the main corridor of the Dark Anomaly and take a look in both directions for any sight of Malahki.

I'd never been outside of the gardens, but I knew the layout of the entire place well enough from the maps and charts that Malahki had shown to me.

It was a very simple design, too. The entire habitable sector of the Dark Anomaly consisted of one long corridor that ran along a section of the outer edge of the disk. Smaller hallways and corridors branched out from it, but not too far. Since the gravity created in the centre of the disk compressed the ships crashed on the Dark Anomaly—the closer to the center one went, the higher the pressure. The older ships had been compressed too much for live beings to occupy them. Whatever empty space remained there threatened to collapse under the ever-increasing pressure closer to the center.

I wasn't worried about getting lost if I left the gardens. My biggest concern was being spotted by a member of the crew. Malahki had been adamant, I could not trust anyone here. So far, I'd had every reason to believe him. Going out into the corridor was not my intention.

The noise of footfalls and loud, agitated voices reached me as I made it closer to the entrance. The corridor outside of the gardens seemed to be filled with life today. Could that be what delayed Malahki?

I stilled, holding my knife in a sweaty hand. If I had to use it, I wasn't sure I could. I'd never stabbed a person before, never so much as slapped one even.

"But isn't the *damirian* going to be there?" A voice reached me from the corridor.

I flattened myself against a wall, hiding behind the vines of the nearest planter.

"So?" another voice replied, much closer. "Who cares about the fucking *damirian*. What is it going to do? Run to the captain to complain?"

By the several snorting and snickering sounds, I realized there were significantly more than two males speaking.

Darting my gaze back to the bedroom, I gauged the distance and whether I had enough time to get back. I didn't, as they entered the gardens at that very moment.

There were six of them. Two *yourlu*, two *kreers*, an *ognat*, and an *errock*.

My throat tightened at the sight of the massive *errock*. From the distance, peeking through the vines, I couldn't tell for sure whether it was one of the two I'd seen on my ship. Just the sight of his massive figure, confidently strolling through the place that had been my sanctuary for the past six weeks felt like an invasion. The bounce of energy in his step didn't promise anything good.

"Should I search for the *damirian*, Trox?" one of the *yourlu* asked the *errock*.

"The *damirian* isn't here," the other *yourlu* said, rubbing his neck. "He's with the captain. Busy."

I recognized this one as Xid, the *yourlu* who'd been with Urkril when the *dimo* had assaulted Malahki here, in the gardens.

"How do you know?" the first *yourlu* asked.

"Trust me I do." Xid rubbed his neck with another tentacle.

"The fuck do we need the *damirian* for?" The *errock* spat through his teeth. "Search this place for the *irsen* flowers. Izcigs, you get some of the mushrooms. They could be handy, too."

One of the *kreers* headed for the planter with the pink and purple *fuhnid* mushrooms under the transparent dome. The rest spread through the gardens, shoving aside the planters and knocking on walls.

I crouched in my hiding place, closer to the exit to the corridor than to the bedroom. With the other *kreer* heading in the direction of our room, my not being there, might be a good thing after all.

"Trox! The planter is locked." The *kreer* Trox called Izcigs slammed his fist into the clear dome over the *fuhnid* mushrooms. After the incident when some of the mushrooms had been stolen and their juice had been used to poison the captain, Malahki had put strong hinges and a lock on the dome as a precaution.

"So?" Trox grabbed a metal planter with *xaevoe* grain plants. He lifted the entire thing over his head then tossed it into the glass dome, smashing it to pieces. Most of the mushrooms got crushed, dirt flew out and all over the floor.

"There you go." Trox smirked. "Get them." He gestured at the few pink-and-purple umbrellas of the mushrooms still standing. "Did anyone find the fucking flowers yet?"

"Hey Trox! There's a room here," the other *kreer* yelled from behind the vines that concealed our bedroom.

My heart dropped. Our hiding place had been discovered.

Malahki had done a great job making it look like the gardens ended before it. However, by knocking on walls, the *kreer* found the loose piece of the paneling concealing the entrance to our secret sanctuary.

Both *yourlu* rushed that way, reaching the vine curtain before Trox.

"Ha! That's where the *damirian* sleeps. Look that's his bed," Xid said, followed by the noise of shoved furniture and breaking dishes.

"Not a bad set-up it's got here!" the other *yourlu* exclaimed. "Look at these pretty curtains." He erupted in a loud laughter.

"Well, are the fucking flowers there? Is that where it keeps them?" Trox barged in after them.

The noises of them trashing our living place grew louder.

I sat in my hiding spot, listening as they vandalized the one place on the entire Dark Anomaly where I'd felt relatively safe. The sound of things being broken painfully reverberated through me, making me feel personally violated.

Finally, the nose quieted down.

"They're not here, Trox," Xid stated the obvious.

"Wait, I smell something…" Trox replied.

I stiffened in my crouch, wishing I could make myself completely invisible.

"The *irsen* flowers?" the *kreer* asked with hope.

"No, something else… Much sweeter." The thick glee in Trox's voice made my skin crawl with dread. "Guess what? The fucking *it* isn't living here alone."

A whimper of terror stuck in my throat, and I slammed my hand over my mouth, stopping the whimper from escaping.

"So, who cares—" Xid started.

"Shut up!" Trox snarled. "Did you check all the walls here? Any hiding places?"

"Checked, and no, the walls are solid."

"How about the bathroom?" Trox insisted.

"Nothing."

"She has to be here somewhere."

"She?" several voices exclaimed excitedly.

"Yeah, I smell a female. She must be still around. The *damirian* wouldn't have killed or eaten her. And there is no leaving the Dark Anomaly."

I'd been taking showers with the berry soap daily, like Malahki had instructed me. He'd said the juice of the *fuhnid* mushrooms in the soap neutralized my scent. However, spending as much time as I did in our bedroom must have made the overall concentration of my smell there high enough for the sensitive nostrils of the *errock* to pick up.

Now, that they'd learned about my existence, I had no doubt they wouldn't stop searching until they found me.

My heart thundered in my chest. My hands grew cold as my fingers trembled. I needed to get away from them but where? The commotion outside in the corridor intensified. The sounds coming from there spoke of a real battle taking place, with laser blasts, cries of pain, and shouting.

Here in the gardens, the males rushed out of our bedroom, spreading between the planters in the enthusiastic search for me. Sooner or later, they'd find me.

I was trapped.

Aware of every step taken my way, I kept my gaze at the entrance to the gardens, clutching the kitchen knife in my sweaty hand. If I dashed for it now, I could possibly make it out of here faster than any one of those in the gardens, but then what? With the fighting in the corridor, I risked jumping out of a frying pan and into the fire—getting away from six males only to end up in the middle of a battle of possibly many more.

The heavy stomping of the *errock* closed in on me. I pressed my body into the side of the planter I used for a cover, wishing I could simply become a part of it, invisible, insignificant, and safe.

"Fucking shit! There she is!" Trox bellowed right above me.

A lash of panic spurred me into action. Leaping to my feet, I ducked under his thick arms that reached for me and sprinted for the white folding doors to the corridor.

With no time to think, I took my chances with whatever waited for me out there rather than falling into the clutches of Trox. After the murders of my entire crew by an *errock*, I'd developed a deep ingrained fear of his entire species. And nothing about Trox eased it in me.

My arms pumping, my heart leaping high into my throat, I ran as fast as I could. The doors were almost there, another step or two and I'd be out of here, come what may then.

"Ha!" Trox's burly arms whipped around me, tripping me.

I slammed both hands into the exit doors. So close!

"Nope," he growled into my ear. "You're not going anywhere."

"No!" I panted in terror, my tightened throat hurting with every breath.

"Oh yes." He dragged his tongue along my neck. "Whoever the fuck you are, you're mine for the next little while."

"Hey, Trox! How about us?" the others rushed to us, tripping over their feet, tentacles, and each other.

"I'll hold her for you," the *yourlu* who wasn't Xid eagerly offered, slinking closer. "I know how to open her suit, I did it once on that other female from her ship—"

"Fuck off, Kex!" Holding me with one arm, Trox threw his other fist out, punching the *yourlu* out of the way. "Who cares about the suit? I'll peel the fucking thing off her with my own teeth if I have to."

Holding me from behind, he shoved his big, grabby hand between my legs, squeezing me there so hard I cried out.

"See? She wants it." He ground his crotch against my ass.

Terror choked me, clouding my vision and my mind. Through the fog of panic, the sensation of the hard handle of the kitchen knife still clutched in my hand registered.

My first impulse would be to stab the blade into the rough hands groping me, but I held back, taking a moment to think of a better target. I had but one blow, one chance and I needed it to be effective against the massive *errock*.

At the same time, I couldn't think too long, lest they notice my weapon and take it away. So far, they'd been too excited about finding me to spot it.

"I'm going to fuck you good." Trox flipped me to face him.

There was nothing of a sentient being in his yellow eyes. Unseeing, they seemed to stare past me as he grinded against me forgetting all about getting me out of the suit first.

"No!" I threw my right arm back and up. Swinging my entire body forward, I jammed the long, slim blade of the knife into the *errock's* thick, clay-red neck.

His huge body jerked against mine, his delirious stare jolting back to awareness with a flash of shock.

"What the—"

He loosened his grip on me, and I didn't wait for him to finish the sentence. Yanking my knife out of his neck, I twisted out from his hands. A gush of dark blood shot out of his wound, spraying red over the pale blue of my suit.

"The bitch has a knife!" Xid wailed.

There was no time to run around them and make for the door again. Instead, I dashed between Xid and the *kreers*, heading for the back of the garden. I had no plan other than to put as much distance as possible between us.

I hoped my wounding Trox would delay them. However, all five lunged after me, leaving the *errock* to bleed alone. Falling to his knees, he clutched his neck with both hands in an attempt to stop the blood and life from leaving his body.

"Get back here, you sweet delicious thing," one of the *kreers* hissed, gaining on me. Lashing with one of his long, segmented tails, he swiped me off my feet.

Crashing face first to the floor, I barely managed to break my fall with my arms. Both wrists screamed in pain taking the weight of my body. The knife fell from my fingers.

"Sweet, sweet meat," the *ognat* squawked, using all eight pairs of his skinny limbs to crawl closer to me.

"Hey!" Xid yelled, scurrying over on his lower cluster of tentacles. "No eating her until I fuck her, do you hear me?"

With Trox out of the picture, Xid's confidence grew tenfold.

"Get the knife away from her, first," he ordered to the others.

The *kreer* quickly grabbed my knife off the floor with his black as kohl, skinny fingers.

"As long as we get to fuck her, too." He rolled over to his back, exposing his dirty-white belly. A slit opened in the pouch in his crotch and a cluster of black, wiggly appendages unfurled from it. Glistening with slime, they swarmed, straining toward me.

My stomach roiled with revulsion and horror. I clawed at the hard, metal floor, trying to crawl away from all of them, but the *kreer's* tail held my legs firmly like a rope wound around my ankles.

"Me first!" Xid announced, spreading his leg tentacles in a circle to reveal a thin, undulating one in the middle.

A long, strangled growl rolled through the gardens, then a strong arm hooked around the *yourlu's* scrawny neck.

"I should've killed you before," Malahki gritted through his teeth.

Xid's expression turned to an intense mix of hatred and terror, but he didn't get a chance to say a word. Yanking *yourlu's* head aside, Malahki stabbed a long metal piece into his neck.

Kex, the second *yourlu* jumped on Malahki's back, wrapping him in his tentacles.

I grabbed a handful of the wiggling mess of the *kreer's* genitalia. The slime coated my hand, seeping between my fingers as I squeezed and twisted my fist.

Tossing his head back, the *kreer* squealed as if being murdered. The noose of his tail finally loosened around my ankles. Kicking my feet, I tossed it off and crawled backward.

Malahki reached back and grabbed the head of the *yourlu*

attacking him. Throwing him over his shoulder, he snapped Kex's back over his knee.

I couldn't even begin to process the horrors of everything that was happening. My concentration narrowed. Every single male in the gardens beside Malahki was a threat to him and me. And my entire being focused on eliminating the threat.

As the *ognat* and the second *kreer* closed in on Malahki, I lunged for the knife in the first *kreer's* hand.

"You nasty female!" he cursed, yanking it away from me. "I'll chew your head off while I fuck you, like the *ognats* do!"

The pouch low on his belly closed, however, hiding his genital cluster from view. When he lunged after me again, there was more murder than lust in his black as bullet hole eyes.

I crab-walked away from him, struggling to get up. He wouldn't let me regain my footing, grabbing my right leg with his hand, all of his tails curling around my left one again.

My shoulder hit a planter behind me, and I reached for the edge of it to haul myself up. Straining the muscles in my arm so hard they hurt, I tried to get up to give myself a fighting chance with the male.

"Let's see how you taste." He slashed at my calf with the knife. The suit fabric held, protecting my skin, though it didn't make the blow of the blade much less painful.

I groaned, trying to kick my feet free. My fingers sunk into the dirt in the planter as I gripped its edge.

"Valentina!" Malahki punched the *ognat* away, on his way to me. However, the second *kreer* had his tails wound tightly around Malahki's chest and waist. One of them inching dangerously close to his neck.

Sharp pain cut through my finger as I dug my hand into the dirt. Glancing back, I realized this was the planter with *fuhnid* mushrooms. A shard of glass from the dome destroyed by Trox sliced through my skin.

Grabbing one of the surviving mushrooms, I squished the delicate umbrella in my hand. The deadly juice beaded bright between my fingers.

"Eat this!" I shoved the whole thing into the *kreer's* half-open mouth.

He choked, spitting it out. But I jabbed my juice-soaked fingers into his eye sockets. He bellowed in pain, recoiling from me.

I ripped another mushroom from the planter, shoving my knee into the *kreer's* belly. He swayed on his feet. Losing his balance, he crashed backwards. I quickly jumped on his chest, not giving him a chance to recover. Though, judging by his bulging eyes and puffed up skin around them, his recovery was questionable at best.

"You want to eat me?" I growled wildly, not recognizing my own voice. "How do you like this?" I shoved the mushroom into his mouth, cutting off his screams of pain.

My hands shook. Everything inside me vibrated with terror and adrenaline. I had no coherent thoughts, no other emotions but aggression and fear—aggression against those who wanted to hurt me, fear that I might prove weaker than them.

Wet, garbled noises bubbled up from the *kreer's* mouth, muffled by the crushed mushroom gag I'd stuffed in it. His body arched and stiffened under me. All eight pairs of limbs scraping against the floor in agony.

Then, he stilled.

I darted a glance at Malahki. Baring his teeth and straining his muscles, he ripped to pieces the tails restraining him. The second *kreer* screeched as green blood sprayed from the remnants of his tails.

The *ognat* was already lying on the ground, his head smashed in, his black-and-beige body convulsing with its last tremors.

The knife dropped by the *kreer* I'd just killed lay on the floor at my boot. I kicked it Malahki's way. He grabbed it and slit the last *kreer's* throat, giving him a quick death.

Still sitting on top of the male I'd killed, I leaned back against the planter.

The feverish energy that had been fueling me during the fight was draining now, but no relief came. Only emptiness moved in on me.

"Valentina." Malahki rushed to me. "Are you hurt anywhere?"

Taking my chin in his hand, he peered at me intently. Red, orange, and purple swirls swam in his eyes, beautiful and bizarre.

I lifted my hand, and he caught my wrist.

"Wait. Don't touch anything yet." He grabbed the familiar spray bottle from under the planter.

I hissed when the liquid hit the cut on my finger, the cut left by the shard of glass.

"Is your skin broken anywhere?" Concern rang in his voice as he turned my hand over.

The small cut on the inside of my ring finger was bloated and angry red. The skin around it swelled and turned purple.

"It acts fast," I mumbled, my tongue barely moving as my mouth turned dry.

"No. Hold on. Valentina. Please." Malahki hurriedly sprayed my other hand then wiped them both, using the cloth from under the planter. "Don't close your eyes," he pleaded, lifting me in his arms. "Talk to me. Say something, anything."

I threw my arm over his shoulder as he carried me between the planters to our ransacked bedroom. His familiar scent and warmth of his body pressed to mine made everything right with the world, even if just for one moment.

"I'm…so glad…"

I wanted to say I was glad he'd returned. I wanted to tell him how I waited for him to come back, how much I missed him and worried about him. But my tongue refused to obey me.

My thoughts scattered. Then my mind drifted away someplace much darker than even the Dark Anomaly.

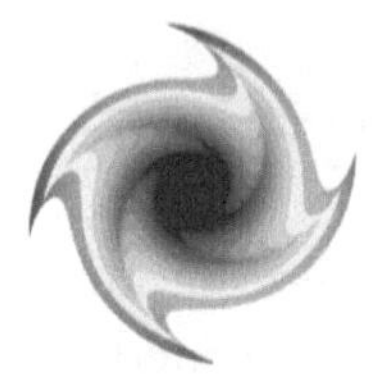

Chapter 7

Malahki

Valentina muttered something in her sleep, and he placed a cool, wet cloth on her hot forehead.

He'd made the decision to give her some tea with just a drop of the *irsen* juice again, to make her sleep while her body fought the poison of the *fuhnid* mushrooms and its aftereffects.

And she fought hard. It'd been a week now. Her skin still flushed with heat, delusions bothered her judging by her screams, but her breathing was strong, and her heartbeat stable.

She remained alive.

For the tenth time that morning, he said thanks to the higher spirits for helping him heal her again. Taking her unbandaged hand in both of his, he pressed her palm to his face, breathing in her familiar delicate scent.

"One more day," he whispered against her skin. "Tomorrow will be the time to wake you."

Bursts of excitement pulsed in his chest. He'd spent most of his life alone, feeling no need for a companion. Now, he couldn't wait to see Valentina open her eyes and to hear her voice again. The anticipation warmed his heart, making it so full, he thought it might explode.

"Soon," he murmured as a promise, kissing her hand.

A tinkle of a tiny bell alerted him of someone entering the gardens. He'd installed a simple mechanical system of ropes and springs recently. It triggered the bell in the bedroom when the doors to the gardens were opened—a warning system that alerted of the intruders.

With a last quick kiss, he let go of Valentina's hand. Taking the two biggest knives he had, he slid one in the sheath at his belt that he'd made, keeping the other one ready in his hand.

He'd heard that Nocc was killed on the day of the last unrest, along with many others. The population of the Dark Anomaly had been steadily shrinking due to fights even before that.

There had been over seven hundred of the crew just a few months ago. After the two mutinies that had taken place since, no one bothered to count the number of survivors. By Malahki's estimate, there were just over half left, and that number kept going down daily. Those alive, however, remained dangerous.

As he had dreaded before, order on the Dark Anomaly had been weakening. Malahki hadn't seen the captain doing his rounds anymore. Neither did Svetlana come to the main kitchen to cook the crew's meals as she used to.

He believed Vrateus had retreated into hiding with her, possibly locking themselves in his room. The captain had given up on his treacherous crew, choosing to protect what was most important to him—Svetlana. And Malahki had done the same, keeping safe at all cost the one person in the world who'd become more precious to him than any other—his Valentina.

As noiselessly as possible, he stepped to the entrance from the room to see who had come to the gardens this time. The place had been raided a few times in the past two weeks. As the order crumbled, hunger had raged among the crew. Though most of them preferred eating meat, they'd been coming here to comb through the planters for anything edible at all.

Peeking from behind the remaining vines, Malahki saw an *errock* come in. He was alone, which was good. Malahki could fight him if needed. Lately, the possibility of a fight didn't disgust him as much as it used to. He found himself wishing for it, even with someone as huge and intimidating as the *errock*.

As the male circled the gardens, Malahki recognized Wyck, the one who got the human woman Nadia in his charge. Malahki's fists itched even more for a fight now.

The *errock* had come here before, looking for Valentina, but as long as Malahki was alive, he wasn't going to get her.

Adjusting the grip on his knife, he quietly followed Wyck. The *errock* collected some of the leftover plants and fruit, then stopped at a planter by the exit.

Malahki froze, motionless. He wouldn't shy away from a fight, but the caution dictated it was best not to pick one either.

Finally, the *errock* headed out the door.

Malahki creeped after him into the corridor, too, then followed him as Wyck turned right. There was nothing at that end but the crashed human ship. The cut-out that served as the entrance to the ship was now blocked with a piece of metal. The dead bodies left behind after the last mutiny and the battle that had taken place here had been moved away or eaten by now. Everything dead served as food lately.

Wyck stopped in front of the blocked entrance to the human ship and tilted his head back. The metal part slid aside, letting Wyck in. From his vantage point, Malahki couldn't see the person who opened the door, but it most likely was another *errock*. The *errocks* always stuck together on the Dark Anomaly. The entrance then closed again, followed by several hard clicks, which must be the sounds of the locks sliding back in place.

All surviving *errocks* must be behind that door with Wyck. Knowing that, Malahki made a metal note to stay away from this part of the corridor.

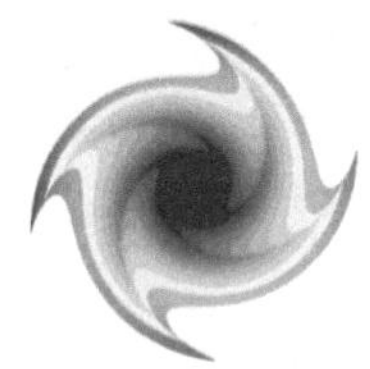

Chapter 8

Valentina

"Wake up, Valya," a familiar voice said softly.

Latching on to it, I followed the voice out of the darkness.

"There you are." Malahki smiled when I opened my eyes. He lightly stroked my forehead. "The fever is finally down. How are you feeling?"

I blinked in the soft light of the vines under the ceiling. The beautiful canopy that used to hang over the bed before was now gone.

"I'm good," I croaked, my voice low and rough.

"Here." He shifted closer, holding a small cup of tea to my lips. "Drink this."

I did as he said. The warm, slightly sweetened tea refreshed my mouth, making my tongue easier to move.

"Here we go again." I gave Malahki a weak smile. "You keep nursing me back to health, and I can't stop getting hurt."

He placed the cup back on the upturned plastic crate nearby but didn't release me from the half-hug he had me in. His arm around my shoulders, he sat on the bed next to me.

I leaned my head against him, my neck too weak to hold it up for too long.

He stroked my hair. "I need to do a much better job at keeping you from harm in the first place."

I lifted my right hand up. My ring finger was tightly bandaged with a piece of yellow cloth. The skin on my hand had a light bluish tint. My finger felt warm and tingly under the bandage but there was no pain.

"How long have I been under, this time?" I asked.

"Today is day eight."

Another week had passed by. But did time really matter anymore?

"And how have *you* been all this time?" I shifted to see his face better and paused.

He looked hardly like the Malahki I knew. I leaned further back, taking in his appearance.

His features seemed harder and more angular somehow. His eyebrows thickened and darkened from their previous sand-blond to the current sable-brown. Thick strands of the same darker color were sprinkled through his hair, too.

"You're changing." I frowned, cupping his face. Unsure of the reasons for the changes, I couldn't tell whether they were good or bad, which worried me.

"Am I?" He rolled his shoulders uneasily, glancing aside. I suspected he might not be comfortable with the changes.

"How are you feeling?" I stroked one of his sharpened cheekbones. His jawline seemed harder and more prominent, now. The vines in his hair had withered, most of their leaves gone. He hadn't replaced them in days. "Malahki, are you okay?" I turned his face to me, forcing him to look me in the eye.

The swirls of vivid color I'd noticed in his irises the day of the last attack were no longer there, though his eyes weren't their former serene beige either. Uneven splashes of brown and burgundy spread through them like ink spots.

"I'm fine." His words were clipped. He pressed his lips together as he often used to do before. Except it looked different now, on his barely familiar face.

"Were you hurt? That day?" I asked, concerned.

"No. Nothing like what you got." He took my bandaged hand in his and started unwrapping the yellow strip of fabric.

My mind went back to the day I got attacked, to the massacre in the gardens, and to the people I'd killed.

"Did all six of them die?"

He nodded, understanding what I was talking about without questions.

"What happened to the dead bodies?" I had to know.

"Gone."

"How?"

He spoke, without looking at me, "I loaded them into a wagon I use to transport the garden waste that's too large for the garbage chute and took them down to be incinerated."

"Were there any questions? Did someone come looking for them? I'm so sorry you had to deal with all of that on your own." I sighed.

He removed the bandage from my finger, revealing the dark purple powder caked over the cut.

"There is no one to look for the dead, Valya," Malahki replied somberly. "Those still alive are busy killing each other."

The new, steel-cold expression made him even less familiar—almost a stranger.

Unable to bear the look in his eyes, I dropped my gaze down to his lap, noting that he was wearing a pair of black pants. A little loose around his trim waist, the pants were held up by a wide leather belt with handmade sheaths that held knives. The pants weren't his. I saw them last on Trox. Malahki had stripped the dead body before disposing of it.

"What are you saying, Malahki?" I kept staring at the pants of the dead *errock*. "What's going on out there, outside of the gardens?"

"The captain abandoned the crew after they almost killed him—again. There's no order, now. We're on our own."

"On our own…" I echoed, staring straight ahead and afraid to think what exactly that meant.

"We're fine here. For now, anyway," Malahki added in a softer voice, as if sensing my dread and wanting to reassure me. "I have some food collected. And I replanted the *xaevoe* grains. The crops will be ready in a few weeks."

He gestured at the long narrow planters hanging on the wall in rows, right here, in the room. I swept the place with my gaze, taking in other changes. The colorful rugs and tapestries were gone. The painted ceramic dishes had been replaced by a few metal containers. Malahki's artfully decorated trunk, where he used to store clothes and bedding, was also no longer there. The room appeared harsher and more utilitarian, very much like its owner looked now, too.

I remembered the intruders trashing this place. Malahki either hadn't been able to replace all the beautiful things they'd broken or simply didn't care about replacing them.

"I killed two people," I said, my voice hollow just like everything inside me at that moment.

"One," Malahki corrected. "The *errock* was still alive when I got here. I finished him for you."

I darted a glance to his face, but his focus was on cleaning and re-bandaging my finger.

"I'm sorry I had to kill, but I don't regret it," I said, to eradicate any doubts he or I might have on the subject. "If someone, anyone comes back here with the intention to harm you or me, I won't hesitate doing it again."

Kill or be killed. Never before had the meaning of this phrase been this clear to me.

"I don't judge you for murders," I continued, wondering if guilt or trauma of what we'd done might be the reason for the hard expression in his eyes. "I hope you're not judging me, either. We did what we had to do. It didn't mean we enjoyed the murder or wished for it to happen in the first place."

He settled his heavy stare on me, the weight of it pressing down on my chest.

"Except that I did, Valentina." Each word of his came out as if laden with lead.

"What do you mean?" I swallowed hard.

"Fighting them thrilled me. I reveled in watching life leave them. I did enjoy the murder." He spoke in short clipped sentences, like flipping a play card with each one to reveal what he'd been hiding all this time.

Had he always been this cold-blooded and ruthless? Did the changes to his body bring it up? The change of our circumstance, maybe? Or both?

I thought I'd gotten to know Malahki well during all the time we'd spent in close proximity. Now, he seemed a complete stranger to me, and it was not just his altered appearance. I felt I had to start getting to know him anew, and I feared what kind of a person I might discover.

He turned his back to me, lowering his feet to the floor. Placing his elbows on his knees, he rested his forehead on his hands, his fingers spearing through his hair.

"What is happening to me, Valya?" he exhaled.

Air rushed out of me in a breath. Compassion squeezed my heart so hard, I could cry. I was merely watching him change. What was it like for him, having to go through it all?

"Oh, Malahki…" I walked on my knees to him and hugged him from behind as he sat on the edge of the bed. "It's happening, isn't it? That's what you wanted. You wanted this change."

To be bigger, stronger, ferocious. To be able to defend himself and to protect me better.

"I know I did. But it's like having everything that I am—everything I've ever been—slowly slip away. And I'm not sure I like the pieces that are left behind."

"Don't say that." I kissed his cheek then buried my face in the side of his neck, my chest pressed to his back.

Whoever he had become, whoever he was still becoming, I could never abandon him. I was with him in it to the very end.

"We'll figure it out somehow. Okay?" I said. "We will find a way to put all your pieces back together again. You and I."

Chapter 9

Valentina

"This is just…" My sentence broke off as I was unable to put into words the devastation that lay in front of me.

The seeds that Malahki had carefully planted and scrupulously nurtured into plants had been ripped out, their fruit destroyed before it had a chance to ripen. Most of the planters had been moved around or upturned. Their careful order dismantled, dirt spilled everywhere.

"We have to fix this," I said resolutely. It would take a long time for just the two of us, but we could restore the gardens if we worked hard every day.

To my surprise, Malahki shook his head.

"We'd be only wasting our time. The gardens will get raided, again and again. We'll never get a chance even to finish planting anything."

"Is that why you've moved the little we have left to the bedroom?"

He nodded. "The smaller the area, the easier it is to hide and protect."

I glanced around the destroyed gardens again, seeing them in the new light. Some plants had withered and all but died. Others, on the contrary, took off, sprawling out of their planters in a wild unkempt fashion.

The entrance to our bedroom had been camouflaged with dead vines then hidden behind the wild, overgrown bushes. There was a purpose in all this chaos, I realized. Others might have destroyed the gardens, but Malahki had directed the destruction in the way that suited him—us.

"You've watered some and let others die, haven't you?"

He nodded again.

"The dense shrubs deter most from getting too close to our room. The dead vines behind them tell those who make it past the bush that there is nothing to look at there. So, they wouldn't go through the effort of searching closely, hopefully."

The six aliens who had seen me were now dead. My existence on the Dark Anomaly remained a secret. All because of Malahki.

"Thank you," I said. "Thank you for saving me—again—and for keeping me safe."

He took my hand in his silently. Despite everything that had happened, stubborn hope clung to my heart that together, we may still make it here, no matter what.

Instead of trying to fix what would be inevitably broken again sooner or later, Malahki and I focused our energy on our personal survival.

With my hand healed fully in the next few days, he taught me how to dry and preserve the plants, berries, and vegetables we still had. For days, we'd dried, pickled, and salted, accumulating food to sustain us for even harder times that Malahki was convinced lay ahead.

I helped him to hide our preserves around the gardens, in places that only he and I knew about. A few containers, Malahki took out of the gardens and hid them elsewhere on the Dark Anomaly, just in case we might be driven out of this place.

I dreaded to think about a situation that might force us to abandon this piece of the Dark Anomaly—even destroyed, the gardens had been our safe haven.

Between all the food preservation activities, we worked on a plan. A part of it was to create as many hiding places as possible throughout the gardens. After having been caught by the *errock* once, I made sure each of our small hiding spots had at least two escape routes—one had to be a direct path back to the bedroom; the other one, a way to get to the exit from the gardens. Preferably both of those routes had to be concealed from view, too, so that we could sneak away undetected.

One morning, after breakfast, Malahki helped me move yet another planter to the spot I thought would be a good hiding place. One of the handmade knife sheaths I had strapped to each of my thighs caught on a branch.

"Do you think we should start stockpiling some weapons, too?" I asked, freeing the strap from the bush.

"That wouldn't hurt," Malahki replied calmly. In addition to a knife at his hip, he had several smaller ones on the belt he'd made to carry over his shoulder and across his chest.

Danger had been hanging in the air so thick, I could never dismiss it or even forget about it for a moment anymore.

"I'll see if there is anything left in the storage rooms that we could sharpen to use as blades," he said.

To raid the storage room, Malahki would have to go out again. He refused to let me accompany him whenever he went out. And I agreed to remain behind only because he said I would attract attention and bring danger on both of us if spotted. It was safer for him to get around on his own.

Instead, I stayed behind, worried sick whenever he was out, and counted seconds until his return.

He frowned in thought.

"I'll see if I can repurpose—"

The loud thumping and screeching noise cut him off mid-sentence. I whipped around, frantically searching where the noise was coming from. Malahki grabbed me with his left arm around my middle. His other hand went to the largest of his knives, the one he carried on his right hip.

"Up there!" I yelled, realizing the sounds were coming from the ceiling. The height of it was at least thirty feet in this section of the gardens.

"Watch out!" Malahki leaped away with me in his arms as something dark and large dropped from an air vent high above.

It hit the ground next to the planter we had just moved.

"What is this?" I gaped at the creature wiggling on the floor.

At least six or seven feet long, it had a cylindrical body, with numerous skinny legs along each side. Its round, multifaceted eyes bulging out, it kept snapping its mandibles with a clunking noise.

"It's a *vasai* centipede." Malahki held me closer to him. "The crew used to breed them in cages, in the farm close to the kitchen. The farm has been ransacked with all of the *vasai* now gone. This one must be a wild one. There're a few of them around."

He and I had eaten *vasai* eggs often before the farm got destroyed, but I certainly had never seen a live centipede before.

"Do they just drop down like that?" I asked, snuggling closer into the safety of his body.

The creature had stopped screeching when it fell. Its movements now turned to erratic convulsions.

"Never," Malahki said. "This is the first time I've seen this happen."

Moving me to the side and behind him, he stepped toward the centipede.

"Careful." I touched his arm.

But he sheathed his knife and crouched at the centipede's side. The poor thing looked like it was dying.

"It's no longer dangerous," he assured me, though his dark eyebrows moved together into a frown.

"It must have hurt or broke something on impact," I offered a possible explanation.

Carefully avoiding the sharp mandibles that could cause damage even through the last contractions of the creature's muscles, Malahki took the *vasai's* head in his hands then turned it, inspecting. The light in the gardens broke up into rainbows in the thousands of facets of the centipede's large, round eyes.

"I think it was unwell before it hit the ground," he said. "That's why it fell out of the vent in the first place."

The long body stopped contracting, the dozens of skinny legs curled and stilled. I ventured to come closer, too.

"How did it get up there?"

"There're a number of wild *vasai* around here. A load of them was on a ship that crashed here a while back. Most were captured and farmed. But some managed to hide in the many tunnels and openings of the Dark Anomaly and survived on their own."

"How?"

He shrugged.

"By eating scraps, each other's eggs or the garden waste. I run into them every now and then in the garbage disposal chutes when I climb in to maintain the conveyor belts or clean a blockage. They're vicious and energetic, always alert and ready to attack. Not like this one." He dropped the creature's head, getting up to his feet.

"What do you want to do with it?" I asked.

He eyed it critically, from a distance.

"We can't eat it." He touched one of its legs with the toe of his boot. Ever since I woke up from my last injury, Malahki had been wearing black leather boots along with the dead *errock's* pants. "We don't know what it died of. Its meat could be contaminated."

The Malahki I knew from before would've never even considered eating meat, contaminated or not.

"If we leave it here, the scavengers will find it," I noted.

We'd been getting visits every now and then. The crew came, combing through the gardens in search of food, even as there was nothing left to take. I had no doubts, most of them would grab the dead centipede for meat. If the *vasai* died from a disease, they might get ill, too.

He nodded.

"The scavengers will find it, no matter where we put it. But we have to get rid of it before it starts to rot." He bent over, grabbing the centipede by its head. "Can you get its tail, please?"

I lifted the bottom end of the *vasai* by the last pair of its legs. Hard and shiny, they proved to be also smooth and slippery, making carrying it a difficult task.

Together, Malahki and I managed to get the body to the nearest garbage chute. As I held the panel over the opening up, he shoved the long body of the *vasai* through, bit by bit. The moment the textured conveyor belt connected with it, it dragged the rest of it through and out of sight.

A heavy feeling pressed on my chest. The unexplained death of the creature bothered me, adding to the general anxiety of day-to-day life on the Dark Anomaly.

Malahki squeezed my shoulder, and I leaned into his body, seeking the comfort I always got from our contact.

Lately, however, things had been different. We continued to share the bed, and he would hold me in his arms as I fell asleep. But when I woke up, he always lay away from me, with as much distance between us as the size of the bed allowed.

After that kiss on the morning of the latest mutiny of the crew, there hadn't been any more kisses. He never even fully hugged me anymore, giving me instead just a one-armed half-hug every now and then, like the one he was giving to me now.

I missed the easy camaraderie we'd achieved earlier and somehow had lost now. I wouldn't even mind his former snappy attitude, if only the gloomy cloud that seemed to perpetually hang over him would disappear.

"We should get back in for lunch," he said, taking his hand off me, and I immediately missed the contact, leaning after him.

We had barely made a few steps across the gardens on our way back to our room when the crashing noise of the entrance doors made me jump. Malahki stiffened at my side, his knives in his hands again.

I didn't even realize how my knives ended up in my grip as well. Living constantly on edge, I acted automatically. I jerked my head his way, and he pinched his lips between his fingers in a call to silence. He noiselessly stepped behind a planter with an outgrown shrub, taking me with him.

Growling and scraping noises came from the entrance. They grew louder, increasing in numbers, not just volume.

I moved a branch aside, peeking through the bush in that direction.

At first, it appeared to me a large group of animals crashed into the gardens from the outside corridor. Wild beasts I'd never seen before. Peering closely, I realized these were some of the crew of the Dark Anomaly.

Dozens of them crawled in, mostly *kreers*, with a few *ognats* and some other species in between. They didn't walk or run. They *crawled.* They scurried on all their limbs, low to the floor, like a dark, glistening mass, tails lashing, teeth snapping at each other.

A *kreer* whipped one of his tails around the neck of another one, closest to him. The second *kreer* screeched, sinking his sharp teeth into the segmented tail around his neck. Dark green blood burst in a spray from the wound, dripping between his teeth. The first *kreer* snarled, lunging on the one biting him. Blood stained them both from the bites and scratches they shelled out to each other.

The rest of the group crawled over the two on their way further into the gardens. Some lingered to take a bite from either one of the fighters. Both were eventually trampled and consumed by the crowd.

My stomach churned, bile rising high in my throat. Despite the loud screeching, growls, and yelps, not a single discernible word came from the advancing mass. It was as if they had lost either the physical ability to speak or the mental ability to form the words. Just like they had obviously given up walking upright.

Afraid to make a sound, I glanced at Malahki. His expression was as confused as mine. Taking my hand, he backed away from the half-beasts that were invading the gardens.

My confusion was quickly replaced by horror as the snarling crawling creatures spread through the gardens. They tipped over planters, chewed on the vines and dried branches, and dug through the dirt.

Every now and then, a fight would break out. With both opponents ending up injured, the rest would then move in to gnaw on what was left of them.

The horror of the scene choked me. The knives squeezed in my hands, I crossed my arms over my chest, afraid I'd scream or vomit.

A tug on my shoulder almost sent me into a panic attack before I realized it was Malahki, silently urging me to retreat toward the wall with the chute, away from the crowd spreading through the gardens like vermin.

To move away, however, meant to abandon our cover. It wouldn't serve as such for long, anyway. The *kreers* and the *ognats* swiftly moved through the space, upturning and sniffing everything. By staying in our hiding spot, we risked being discovered and surrounded, cut off from every escape route.

A loud screech slashed through the air, assaulting my hearing. One of the *kreers* had spotted us. Scurrying over the others, he climbed over the planters, upturned and upright, on his way to us.

"Run!" Malahki turned to the wall with the chute, shoving me ahead of him on our dash to escape.

Afraid to look back, I sprinted through the open space. An ear-splitting squeal behind me, forced me to glance back in concern for Malahki.

He slashed with his knife, cutting across the face of the *kreer* pursuing us. The male whimpered in pain, falling back. Several others swarmed him quickly. The green blood splashed on the floor as his body was ripped to pieces, the crew feasting on the flesh of one of their own.

Others moved in our direction.

"Valya, fast!" Malahki yanked me to the garbage chute. "Go first," he ordered.

With dozens of the wild things swiftly approaching and even more of them pouring into the gardens, there was no time to argue or debate.

Shoving my knives back in their holders, I broke off the panel that covered the entrance to the tunnel as Malahki slashed and sliced the *kreers* chasing us.

I gripped the edge of the opening, swinging both legs in and onto the conveyor belt. It caught grip on my boots, tugging me further in. The slope of the tunnel made it easy for me to let go and slide in, but I propped my boots into the walls slowing down my progress.

"Malahki!" I screamed over my shoulder.

There was no way in hell I'd leave him to fight the horde of feral *kreers* on his own. I'd find a way to climb back up and out if I had to.

"I'm here!" He slid into the tunnel behind me, and I let go of the walls traveling further down to give him space.

His shoulders must have gotten wider since the last time he'd come into the tunnels to fix the belt. They spanned across the entire width of the tunnel, wedging him in place.

"You don't fit," I breathed in horror, slowing down my descent again to grab on to his boot. The belt screeched, scraping against both of us.

With a grunt, Malahki shifted to the side, curling his shoulders to make himself smaller. The belt jerked again then moved, dragging both of us along.

The screeching of the *kreers* echoed through the tunnels. They were way too big to fit through to follow us. They fought at the entrance of the chute, shoving each other away until I lost them from view with a bend of the tunnel.

"Valya, listen." Malahki's voice sounded strained and urging, not allowing me to relax even for a second. "There is an opening coming up on your left. Try to feel for it with your hand. A piece of loose paneling. That'd be the exit into the corridor, roughly across from the captain's room. I want you to try to stop. Can you?"

"Okay." I let go of his boot reluctantly, feeling the wall with my hand on my way down.

When the piece of the panel clapped under my hand, I braced my boots into the walls, slowing down. I wasn't fast enough, however. The opening slid past me. I grabbed onto Malahki's boot again as he curled his fingers around the edge of the opening, forcing both of us to stop.

"Here," he said confidently.

Muffled growls and shuffling filtered through the wall.

"Careful," I half-whispered, holding my breath as he lifted the panel to peek into the corridor.

A pale-blue tentacle lashed through the narrow slit. Malahki shrank back with a startled sound. Growls and screeching grew louder, reaching a deafening volume. A black segmented tail of a *kreer* whipped around the *yourlu's* tentacle, yanking it back into the corridor. Blood sprayed into the tunnel, staining Malahki's shoulder with the dark red blood of the *yourlu*, not the green of the *kreers*.

"Keep going." Malahki let go of the opening, letting us continue to slide downwards, along the slope of the garbage chute.

Mayhem appeared to be taking place all over the Dark Anomaly.

"Where exactly will this tunnel take us?" I asked, shaking from fear and adrenaline.

What was happening out there? A massacre? The crew, deranged and unhinged, were brutally murdering each other.

My chest tightened, making it hard to breathe.

"The chute will take us to the waste disposal room," Malahki said. His voice sounded deceptively calm, but I knew he must be freaking out, too. He just didn't want to scare me any more than I already was. "There is always a pile of debris on the floor under the drop-off. The crew never managed to clean it off in time even when the captain was there to make them do it regularly. You'll land in it. Watch out for anyone who might be there. The room is next to the *vasai* farm. The cages may be empty now, but the crew are hungry. Someone may still be lurking around."

The crew were hungry. And we were nothing but food for them. Not unlike the centipedes.

Cold fear gripped me as I bent my head, staring ahead while we kept moving. My breathing grew heavier. Every drag of air required an effort.

When a pale light showed up at the end of the tunnel, I slid one of my knives out again, keeping the other hand free to guide and brace myself if needed on the way out.

The tunnel slope tilted more sharply down, speeding up our descent.

The fall wasn't as high as I'd expected. I hit something soft before Malahki rolled out of the tunnel and on top of me.

The air reeked of rotting meat. The hand I used to break my fall with slipped in something.

"Watch out!" Malahki warned, leaping off me.

Slipping and sliding, I managed to sit up and look around. I was sitting on top of a pile of…dead bodies. I screamed, scrambling off it. These weren't even whole bodies—pieces of decomposing flesh and half-eaten carcasses littered the small room. They were piled up high in the middle, judging by the condition of the rotting flesh, no one bothered to bring anything fresh here for days. Or maybe anything fresh was simply eaten out there, without ever making it here anymore.

Disgust racked me. Revulsion brought up the remnants of my breakfast. I vomited at the bottom of the grisly pile of rotting flesh.

The sounds of a fight with grunts, screeching of teeth, and flesh hitting flesh brought me back to my senses. Spurred into action, I climbed over the bones and rotten meat around the pile, finding Malahki on the other side of it.

He hadn't had a chance to draw his knives. His fist covered in green blood, he pummeled a *kreer* in the head. Another one lay dead on the ground already, next to the body of the dead centipede Malahki and I had dumped down the chute just a little while earlier. Two more *kreers* were feasting on the flesh of both the centipede and their dead comrade.

I could throw up again or simply faint from it all, only worry for Malahki kept me upright. With a knife in my hand, I lumbered through the mess on the floor to him.

He smashed through the head of the *kreer* he was fighting, killing him instantly. Without so much as taking a fresh breath, he grabbed one of the two who were eating and punched him in the face, too.

The *kreer* hissed, baring his sharp teeth and slinking his long black tongue out. Grabbing the *kreer's* head with both hands, Malahki twisted it, ripping it off the males's shoulders.

I gasped, pressing my hand to my chest as the green blood gushed from torn vessels.

He tossed the head aside and kicked the lifeless body out of the way, before going after the last remaining *kreer*.

"Malahki," I said softly, hardly recognizing *my* Malahki in this person who hit and murdered relentlessly, without stopping.

He killed the last *kreer* with a punch in the head then kept on punching again and again, spraying the blood in green bursts all over the corpses and himself.

"Malahki," I called louder, as he didn't seem to hear me, lost to the no longer needed violence. "He's dead…Stop it."

He wouldn't listen, pummeling the body of the *kreer* into a bloody mess.

"Malahki!" I yelled. "Stop it!"

He stilled, as if suddenly deprived of the energy to make another move.

"Stop it," I said softly, tentatively touching his back.

His muscles stiffened under my hand. A long shudder rolled through his tense body, his hands still fisted at his sides.

"We need to think about what to do next." I carefully dragged my hand down, stroking his back.

His shoulders lifted with a deep breath.

"Right." He stepped over the dead *kreer*. Shaking out his hands, he finally unclenched his fists.

I was afraid to look him in the eye, but I had to see his expression. It wasn't as easy for me to read him now as it used to be.

Glancing up, I caught his eyes in my gaze. The remnants of bloodlust still glowed in them, swirling red, orange, and purple in his irises. Eerie and terrifying.

I removed my hand from him, taking a step back. Pure aggression radiated from him, barely contained.

Yet when he reached for me, offering me his hand, I took it, sticky and covered in blood as it was.

"That's the farm." He pointed with his chin at the only entrance from the gory waste disposal room to our left. "There may be more of them out there. Stay close."

Chapter 10

Valentina

"Stay behind me," Malahki instructed, punching the code into the lock panel to the storage room, located not too far from the airlock. He'd said the crew kept the space suits collected over time from the crashed ships here.

We'd gone through the farm and the nearby section of the corridor, finding the same devastation everywhere. Remains of *vasai* centipedes littered the floors, mixed with bones and body parts of the sentient beings who once populated the Dark Anomaly. The stench was unbearable, forcing me to cover my nose and mouth with my elbow. Thankfully, there was a bathroom in the farm. So, we'd been able at least to wash the gore and blood off our hands and faces.

The storage room was the last place at this end of the habitable sector that we hadn't checked yet. Malahki hadn't explicitly stated so, but I knew what he was looking for—survivors.

Something horrible had been happening on the Dark Anomaly while the two of us huddled in the relative safety of the gardens.

The crew's self-extermination and the cannibalism were a part of it. Or maybe the consequence.

Like Malahki, I wanted to get answers, hoping to find someone who could still speak.

The door to the storage room screeched, shifting off its hinges when Malahki opened it. The room had been raided. Most shelves here were empty. Some of their contents had been swept to the floor. Five or six spacesuits remained upright, attached to the walls, the rest had been knocked over.

Two large figures lay on the floor on their sides.

"*Akuks,*" Malahki said.

I recognized this lesser-known species, visually at least. I knew little about them, despite having studied everything I could get my hands on about the species of the Federation while getting ready for our expedition to the Dark Anomaly. Their lower bodies reminded me of giant black caterpillars, complete with dozens of small skinny legs. Their heads, arms, and torsos appeared more humanoid, the black blotches on their backs turning to bright yellow on their bellies.

"They don't look like they were murdered," I pointed out, covering my mouth with my arm again. The air inside the storage room was stifling, the stench of decomposing bodies unbearable.

I stepped back, closer to the exit.

"No one has eaten them, either." Placing his hand over his mouth and nose, too, Malahki crouched by one of the bodies.

The *akuks* had no visible wounds. They lay in natural poses as if having fallen asleep.

Malahki got up to his feet again. Tilting his head back, he surveyed the vents positioned around the room, under the ceiling.

"Is it me or is it exceptionally hard to breathe in here?"

"It stinks." I pointed at the bodies.

"Not just that." He heaved a breath. "The air seems to be low on oxygen."

Now that he'd said it, I had a hard time getting enough oxygen into my lungs. My breathing was deep and fast, yet I felt suffocated.

"Let's get out of here." I tugged at Malahki's arm. Quickly checking the corridor first, I hurried out of the storage room.

Malahki followed me. He leaned the broken door against the entrance to the room, not quite closing it completely since it was now partially off its hinges.

I kept thinking about the two *akuks*, who appeared to have lain down for a nap to never wake again.

"Do you think someone killed them by cutting off the oxygen to the room?" I asked Malahki as we carefully moved along the corridor back to the farm.

He shook his head.

"The door can be unlocked and opened from the inside. They would've had no trouble getting out."

"Why didn't they, then?"

"They didn't know they were in danger of suffocating. They just went to sleep."

"And never woke up," I finished for him. Silent invisible death was hanging over this place, making my skin crawl.

"Did you notice the air was thin in the garbage chute as well?" Malahki asked unexpectedly.

"I thought I couldn't breathe because of fear and worry, but now that you mention it…" I let my voice trail off, pondering his words for a moment. "Is something wrong with the air supply system?"

Dread slithered cold down my spine. If the oxygen production system had failed, there was no hope for any of us.

Malahki knew it, too. He drew in a long breath as if savoring the fact he still could.

"If the central system's air supply drops, the oxygen levels would be reduced in the harder to access places first, those that do not have the direct vents to it, such as the garbage chute, and any other areas of space trapped between the walls and ceilings of the ships. The centipede of this morning must've fallen out of such a place, not out of an air vent."

"You think it was suffocating when it fell."

"Possibly. That would explain why it fell in the first place. *Vasai* are good climbers otherwise."

I considered that for a moment.

"The storage room has vents, though," I said.

Malahki rubbed his forehead.

"The supply to it might've been cut off, intentionally by someone or accidentally, due to poor maintenance. No one has been looking after the system for weeks, now."

He stopped in his tracks abruptly. The sound of scuffling and grunting came from up ahead in the corridor.

"Come here." He hurriedly ushered me into the closest room, which was the farm again.

All cages stood empty. The doors on many of them were missing. A thick layer of dried blood of various colors and the content of broken eggs covered the floor.

Malahki took me behind the cages, along the wall to the left from the entrance and out of sight from anyone entering.

Emitting short, panicky screams, a *yourlu* rushed in, the lower cluster of his tentacles practically vibrating from the effort to move fast. It wasn't fast enough as a *kreer* scurried after him. With a loud screech, the *kreer* lunged on top of the *yourlu*.

The sharp teeth of the *kreer* closed over the *yourlu's* head. The *yourlu's* tuft of bright purple hair disappeared in the *kreer's* mouth, red blood dripping down his face as the *kreer* sunk his teeth into the *yourlu's* skull, crushing it.

I whimpered, covering my mouth with both hands. Wrapping his arm around me, Malahki dragged me down to the floor to hide behind the cages.

My back pressed into the wall, and the wall gave in. Losing my balance, I would have fallen through it backwards, had it not been for Malahki's arm. He pulled me to him.

The *kreer* must have noticed the commotion. Letting the dead *yourlu's* head drop out of his mouth, he peered our way intently.

My heart dropped into the pit of my stomach in horror as the *kreer* shifted off the dead body, visibly getting ready to head in our direction.

"Stay here," Malahki whispered, getting a knife out.

Before he had a chance to make a move, however, something launched from the entrance. Long and shiny, it speared through the *kreer's* head, dropping him dead.

"Got him!" a deep voice exclaimed with glee.

I grabbed on to Malahki's wrist, silently urging him to stay in place, hidden with me.

A large *errock* entered.

"Gler," Malahki exhaled, barely audibly.

I understood Gler was the *errock's* name. Dressed in a dark pair of pants, similar to the ones Malahki himself was now wearing, Gler headed for the *kreer* he'd just killed by hurling the metal rode at his head.

"I'll take this one," he said to the *akuk* who followed him in.

"The *akuk's* name is Ivall," Malahki said softly.

Gler heaved the dead *kreer* up and draped his long body over his shoulder.

"You get the other one," he said to Ivall, tipping his head at the body of the *yourlu*. "Let's go back to the ship." He then turned to leave. "We'll have enough to eat for a few days, now. As the only *errock* on the ship, I'll get the first pick of the piece of meat I want."

"Meat."

The *yourlu* and the *kreer* were on the same crew as the *errock* and the *akuk*. All used to live and work together. Chances were Gler knew their names. Yet all they were to him now was "meat."

I hugged myself watching the two haul their "kill" away.

"What 'ship' did they go to, you think?" Malahki said with a thoughtful expression on his face. Unlike me, he managed to focus on practical parts among the horror of the chaos.

"A spaceship?" I offered.

"Yes, but which one?" he asked, rubbing his chin.

Obviously, I couldn't give him an answer to that. Besides, my attention honed in on something else.

"Gler spoke," I said, the full significance of the fact dawning on me. "The rest of them look like they've lost their minds, but he acted normal. Well, normal for an *errock*."

The *akuk* hadn't said anything, but he hadn't behaved crazy or deranged, either.

Malahki nodded, thinking out loud, "The air on the Dark Anomaly is supplied through a combination of a central system and individual ones of the ships that have them. Gler and Ivall must have moved to one of the ships with its own autonomous air supply. That's why they weren't affected by the malfunctions of the central system."

"The malfunction might've affected different species differently, too," I added. "Do the gardens have their own system as well?" I felt grateful that Malahki and I had escaped the fate of the *kreers* and *yourlu*—so far, anyway.

"The gardens have both. I found the central air supply inadequate from the very beginning and incorporated an axillary system in their design, for the improved air flow for the plants."

I drew in a lungful of air. The stench of death was a little less here than in the waste processing room. There were no decomposing bodies in the farm, and the layer of grime on the floor was old and had crusted over.

"The air appears okay in here," I said tentatively.

Malahki's chest rose with a deep breath, too.

"It does, doesn't it?" he agreed. "I wonder if the malfunction was temporary, or if it just affected certain areas."

It could have been both. It also didn't mean that there wouldn't be more malfunctions, and not just with the air supply system. No one had maintained anything around here for weeks.

"Did the crew all just go crazy simply from the lack of oxygen, then?" I speculated.

"I don't know how the lack of oxygen affects each species, but there might be more than that involved. I wish we could talk to someone who was here when things started to change."

"Someone who could still speak at all," I added, fighting a heavy feeling in my chest. I couldn't detect any unusual smells in the air. But the stench of decay had penetrated these walls so thoroughly, it was hard to smell anything beyond that. "Can we find the problem and fix the system?"

Malahki blew out a breath.

"I'm afraid there might've been more problems than one. And more may still happen as the system is deteriorating. In any case, we don't have something like a central control room here. The things have been created over many years. New parts have been added as new ships crashed. We'd have to thoroughly inspect the entire system, vent by vent, pipe by pipe to find what is wrong. That would take time."

The time we didn't have, surrounded by deranged crew and those who might still have their mental capacity intact but chose to use it for murder.

Malahki let go of me, getting up.

"Come." He offered me his hand. "I have some pickled *caur* hidden in the ceiling near the kitchen."

"You do?" Despite our bleak situation, I couldn't hold back a smile at his resourcefulness.

He grinned, too, wiggling his eyebrows.

"You know I'm good at finding hiding places. I've stuffed food all over the Dark Anomaly. We'll eat, then figure out whether to try making it back to the gardens or find a safe place here, instead."

"Are there any safe places left on this smashed tin can in space?" I muttered under my breath. Today was the first time I'd ever left the destroyed, ravaged gardens and so far, everything else I'd seen of the Dark Anomaly had been even worse.

I leaned back, ready to get up to my feet, too. My shoulder blades pressed against the wall panel again, and it gave in behind me. With a strangled cry of surprise, I grabbed on to Malahki's hand.

"What's back there?" He crouched next to me.

"A loose panel. I nearly fell in twice already," I explained, feeling silly for forgetting about it.

"Let me see." He peeked in the gap between two panels. "There's light," he said softly.

"What?" I brought my face next to his, trying to get a look, too.

"Stay back," he warned, lifting a knife and getting ready to strike if attacked.

Bending back the loose panel, he revealed a dark open space behind it. It could barely be called a room, more like a large closet with a prolapsed ceiling. A pale reflection of shimmering, undulating light filtered from the narrow opening on the opposite wall, which appeared to lead to an adjacent room.

"There is no one here," I said, in a whisper for whatever reason.

"You don't know for sure." Malahki fitted his shoulders between the panels. Holding his knife in his hand, he crawled in.

He couldn't stand up all the way, the ceiling was too low for him. In a crouch, he approached the opening to the tunnel on the opposite wall and carefully looked inside it.

"There is another room here, with a window." He gestured for me to follow him as I still sat outside in the farm.

Glancing around the farm to make sure no one had seen us, I slipped into the closet-room with him.

He poked his head into the faintly illuminated tunnel. His shoulders bumped into the edge of the opening on each side. He swore under his breath.

"I can't fit through here," he said. "Not anymore."

"Not anymore."

I took a closer look at him. Malahki's proportions had changed. I wasn't sure how long it had been happening. The physical changes didn't seem to happen smoothly or gradually. Or maybe they had been so slow that I didn't always notice them right away. His shoulders indeed appeared significantly wider now. He was taller too, I could tell as he bent over next to me to avoid hitting the ceiling with his head.

"Let me try." I crouched down by the opening.

"Be careful." He grabbed my hand.

I nodded, taking out one of my knives. From here, the room on the other end of the tunnel appeared empty. I saw or heard nothing. But one could never be too cautious on the Dark Anomaly. Holding the hand with the knife ahead of me, I moved in.

My head and shoulders went through without problems, the rest of my body followed in.

The new room was even smaller than the one I'd just crawled

from. But there was a window here—the round porthole with the view of the spectacular lights of the Dark Anomaly.

"Wow," I whispered in awe, unable to take my eyes off the magnificent colorful tendrils of light that curled and undulated, following the pattern of some invisible power. "This is…mesmerising."

"Don't stare at the lights for too long," Malahki warned from the other end of the tunnel. "They say it'll drive you mad."

"Apparently, you don't need the lights to go crazy on the Dark Anomaly." I sighed, thinking about the madness that took over so many of the crew, bringing them a tragic end.

"True," he agreed. "There're many ways to lose one's mind and life around here. How is the air in there?"

I drew in a breath. It wasn't any harder to do than breathing in the *vasai* farm. The air felt even cleaner, since the stench didn't reach in here as much.

"Good," I said, turning away from the window, ready to go back to him.

"Stay there," he stopped me. "If I can't fit through, no other male can. You'll be safe there while I go get the food."

I exhaled a brief laugh, peeking at him through the tunnel.

"I hate to break it to you, Malahki, but you're no longer the smallest man on the Dark Anomaly. Have you looked at yourself lately?"

His dark eyebrows twitched as he rolled back his shoulders.

"I did get bigger," he muttered under his breath, rubbing his upper arm, which I'd just noticed also had significantly bulked up.

"That said," I continued. "I believe you're right, I barely squeezed through myself, so no one else around here would probably make it."

I reached for him through the tunnel, and he grabbed my hand in his.

"Please be careful," I begged, my worry for him never left me. I hated parting from him even for a little bit. Would there ever be a time when the two of us could walk freely everywhere together?

"I won't be long." He squeezed my hand tightly. "Please stay there."

Then he was gone.

I stood on my knees in the tiny room with the low ceiling and with the dancing lights behind the window. I hated watching Malahki go, hated waiting for him alone while I measured the time with my heartbeats until his return. I worried for him every second of every minute he was out there on his own.

On the other hand, I understood that if I went with him, my presence would be like an open invitation for an attack. Malahki might be turning into someone more dangerous and even lethal, but he was not invincible. I didn't want to make this trip any more dangerous for him.

I had no way to tell how long it had been since he left. Every moment without him seemed like an eternity.

When the panel cracked and the rustling noise of someone crawling through reached me, I felt more excited than scared. It could be a mad *kreer* coming for me. But my heart leaped with anticipation, making me lean closer into the tunnel.

"It's me," Malahki's voice sounded from the other room.

Not losing a second, I quickly slinked through the tunnel to his side.

"I got some food and water." He chuckled as I covered his face with kisses. He had to hunch over under the low ceiling, which made his head easier for me to reach. Hugging his neck, I placed one last kiss on the edge of his jaw, before finally letting go of him.

"Here." He sat down on the floor, placing two containers between us.

"How did it go?" I asked, sitting next to him. "Is it quiet out there?"

"Mostly," he replied evasively, wiping a green smudge off his right hand on his pants. A *kreer's* blood? I didn't want to know. "I had the *caur* in double containers, to better conceal their smell from the others. I filled the second container with water from the tap in the bathroom here. Thirsty?"

I nodded. "Did you have some?"

"I did." He opened the smaller container with the dark green leaves of the *caur* plant. Like round, chubby cactus, the leaves had soaked up the marinade we'd preserved them in, tasting juicy and simply delicious to me right now. After all the horrors of today, I hadn't even realized how hungry I was.

"Thank you," I said, stuffing my face with the *caur* and washing it down with the water he'd brought.

Malahki ate a few, too. His eyes seemed even darker in the dim lighting of the room. His hair had turned to dark-brown with streaks of ink-black through it and with no beige left at all.

"How are you feeling?" I studied his body for more changes that seemed to happen all the time now.

He brought his gaze to my eyes, and I knew he understood exactly what I meant.

"Different," he said softly.

"In a good way?" I asked, hopefully.

He stretched his neck awkwardly, breaking our eye contact.

"I'm not sure yet," was all he said.

He obviously didn't want to discuss the changes he was going through.

"I'm here whenever you want to talk," I said softly. If he needed some time, I just wanted him to know that I had enough patience to wait until he was ready.

"I know. Thank you." Stretching his long legs, he bumped his boot into a long, silver canister I'd just noticed by the exit to the farm.

"What's that?" I asked, changing the subject.

"Oxygen tank," he replied, visibly relieved to be talking about something else. "With two masks. I found them in the spacesuit storage."

"The one with the two dead akuks," echoed in my brain.

"We'll stay here for now," Malahki continued. "There're still some crew scavenging in the corridor around the kitchen and the mess hall."

"How long do you think we should stay here? Is there no other way to the gardens other than the main corridor?"

He shook his head, his expression contemplative.

"You could try to climb up the garbage chute. It'd be more difficult than going down, though. I'll have to cut the belt, to stop it from pulling you in the wrong direction."

"*Me?* But how about you?"

He laughed.

"I doubt I'll fit in the tunnel, Valya. I'd need to use my arms and legs to climb up, but there's just not enough space for me to do that."

He appeared to have grown bigger even since the last time I saw him. His shoulders now were much wider than that morning. I didn't think he'd fit in the garbage chute tunnel at all.

"Then, I don't want to go that way, either," I said.

"I don't want to send you up there alone." He wrapped his arm around my shoulders, drawing me closer to him.

I leaned my head against his upper arm.

"Is that what we're doing then? Trying to get back in the gardens?" I asked.

He tugged at the braid that fell across his chest, looking lost in thought for a moment.

"That's the place we both know best," he finally said. "We have the most food stored there. And now that we know what we're up against, we'll take the necessary precautions to make our life there safer."

"Like reinforcing the entrance doors?" I took another chubby *caur* leaf out of the container.

"I'm thinking about blocking them permanently. Shutting them closed, barricading and reinforcing them so that no one from the corridor could ever open them again."

That would isolate us from the rest of the Dark Anomaly and any other survivors for good. A lifetime spent with only Malahki for company was not the worst thing in the world. Never seeing another enraged *kreer* again seemed appealing.

I heaved a sigh.

"We could replant the gardens, then, without the threat of them being ruined over and over again. But we'll need to do something about the air supply, to make it completely independent from the central system, which will probably completely fail soon, anyway," I thought out loud. "I'll help you with that. I'm pretty good with tools and stuff."

"We'll need to have our own oxygen production, just for us," Malahki agreed. "The same goes for water and light."

"It'll take time to get it all done."

"Yes, but we'll have to hurry before things start falling apart."

I chewed on the *caur* leaf, which had lost its taste to me as I tried to imagine the future we faced. With the doors shut and blocked, we'd be completely isolated from the rest of the Dark Anomaly. A world within a world. There'd be a lot of hard work to make it happen, and that would be if we didn't get killed or eaten first...

We were already isolated from the rest of the world here. However, further sealing ourselves away in the gardens felt even more extreme, like walling in during the medieval times.

"Are you absolutely sure no one else has survived this?" I asked softly. "No one else worth rescuing, I mean?"

Malahki bit his lip, looking as if considering something.

"We'll need to stop by the captain's room on the way back to the gardens," he said, with not much hope in his voice. "Vrateus is the one who I hope has managed to survive. Though, he's always been the first target of the crew during every mutiny."

I drew in a long breath, thinking I should consider myself lucky that I could even breathe still. I'd survived the crash, the murders of my entire crew, the many attacks by those who craved to hurt me. I was with the person who cared for and protected me. That was so much more than anyone who'd come to the Dark Anomaly with me got.

As if sensing my troubled thoughts, Malahki drew me even closer into his side, kissing my hair.

"We're safe here for now," he said firmly. "We'll make it, Valya. You and I. We'll keep on surviving."

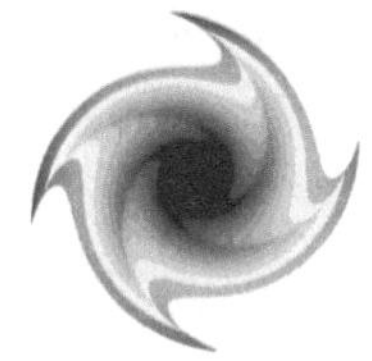

Chapter 11

Malahki

Valya danced in the clearing of the purple forest on Ak'ae, his home planet. The soft grass of the clearing shone pink in the bright morning light of the large, orange sun. She twirled, throwing her arms open wide. And she laughed, tilting her head back and turning her face up to the light.

She was naked, no suit, no boots. Nothing. Only garlands of bright red and purple flowers woven through her straight, dark-brown hair.

Smiling, she faced him as he approached.

"You've changed, Malahki," she said. Her slim, black eyebrows twisted into a frown, and her blue eyes darkened to violet.

He slid his gaze down her body, taking in the small perky breasts with dark nipples, the expanse of her pale skin, the triangle of dark hair between her thighs.

The sight of her made his own body buzz with something he couldn't name and had never experienced before. Heat coursed from his chest down through his stomach, pooling and throbbing in that one spot low in his belly.

"I can't even recognize you anymore," she said wistfully and lightly touched his chest.

The contact of her fingers sent a rush of thrill along his skin. The hot mound between his legs swelled so much, it ached. It was an unfamiliar, tingling kind of pain that begged to be touched, stroked, rubbed…something.

She turned around, getting ready to leave.

He couldn't have that.

"Come back." He grabbed her shoulders, but it wasn't enough. He needed to touch more of her. Sliding his hands down, he found her breasts. They filled his hands perfectly, the nipples turning hard as he pinched them between his fingers.

She gasped—a breathy sound between a moan and a cry of surprise.

He pressed himself to her, needing to feel her body with every inch of his. Still it wasn't enough. He needed to get closer, to crawl inside her, to make her a part of him.

Desperately, he ground his pelvis—the part where the bulge between his legs grew and throbbed—against her ass. The stronger he pressed, the more contact he craved. The harder he rubbed, the faster and harder he needed it to be.

"No…" she pleaded as he used her body, unable to satisfy the need that consumed him and deprived him of any sense or thought. "No!" She fought against him, trying to pry his hands off her.

Yet he couldn't stop, he couldn't even slow down.

He couldn't…

He woke up with a start. The air swooshed out of his chest as the forest of Ak'ae vanished, the metal and plastic of the worn walls came into view. In the faint reflection of the multi-colored lights of the Dark Anomaly, he remembered where he was, in the small room behind the wall of the *vasai* farm.

The rest of his dream remained. Valentina was here with him. Her back turned to him, she curled into a ball in her sleep, breathing softly. He had his hands on her hips, his fingers digging into the fabric of her suit, his pelvis still grinding against her ass.

Mimicking the lights outside, the skin on his hands glowed with red and purple swirls. The colors pulsed, echoing the throbbing pain in his groin.

He grunted in mortification, forcing his fingers to uncurl and release her.

"Malahki?" she murmured in her sleep, making a move to turn around.

Spirits, he couldn't face her! Not after waking her up like that. Not while he yearned to ravage her with each cell of his body and every fibre of his soul.

Scrambling away from her, he crawled out into the farm.

His hands shook, swirls of red burning his skin. The pain between his legs spread through the rest of his body, making him shake as he stumbled between the cages, unseeing. Every step made it worse, yet he couldn't stop.

His muscles tingled and ached. His bones groaned. He had to stop this madness, but he didn't know how.

Passing by a cage, he slammed his fist into the bars, bending them. His knuckles hurt, but it diverted his mind from the longing in his chest and the burning between his thighs.

His shoulder bumped into the door frame on his way out of the farm. He looked at it with surprise. When did his body become not his own? So much larger than it used to be, it felt like borrowed clothes or the living quarters he occupied but did not own.

His new body demanded a price. His hands fisting tight, he needed to do something or he'd go mad. He'd crawl on all fours back to Valya, begging her to either fuck him or slit his throat with her knife.

The corridor was disappointingly empty, but there were noises coming out of the kitchen. Loud clanking of pots. Whoever made the noise obviously believed they had no reason to be afraid of attracting anyone's attention. Well, now they attracted *his*.

He stomped into the kitchen, finding a *dimo* in front of the flameless stove. A large pot of water boiled on it, with a pile of butchered meat on the floor.

The *dimo* lifted his head as Malahki approached.

"Who the fuck are you?" he snarled.

The male didn't recognize him, but he knew exactly who the *dimo* was.

Urkril.

"You've tormented me enough times to remember who I am," Malahki gritted through his teeth, stalking closer.

"*Damirian?* What the fuck has happened to you?" Urkril gaped at him with disgust and some trepidation.

"The question is what is going to happen to *you*, now." Malahki growled.

With a sweep of an arm, he swiped the boiling pot off the stove. The hot metal singed his arm, but he hardly noticed the pain. The boiling hot water splashed over the butchered meat, steam rising into the air in a cloud of stench.

"Hey!" Urkril roared, infuriated. "Fuck off! Or I'll cook you with them!" He jerked his chin at the steaming pile of meat.

Malahki silently fisted his hands. Blood pumped through his muscles with a tingle of energy and strength.

Grabbing the empty pot off the floor, the *dimo* heaved it over his head, charging at him.

Malahki blocked the blow with his forearm, the hard metal of the pot painfully bruising against his bone. The pain rushed through his body in ripples of aftershock, agonizing and energizing.

"Yesss," he hissed, riding the wave of thrill as he slammed his fist into Urkril's plated face. The hard shells cracked, the ragged edges tearing the tissue underneath and bursting the *dimo's* blood vessels.

The sensation of the warm blood misting Malahki's fist made his head spin.

Urkril staggered back with a roar of pain.

The sound pushed Malahki's bloodthirst surge higher. He threw another punch then another. The *dimo* crashed to his knees first, then slumped to the floor into a motionless heap. Still Malahki couldn't stop punching.

Blow by blow, he turned the *dimo's* head into a bloody mess, and still it was not enough. Growling like a beast possessed, he clawed and tore at the hard plates on the *dimo's* chest. Ripping them off, he tore through the sinew and tissue underneath, broke and wrenched out bones until he made it to the warm heart of Urkril.

Insatiable hunger rolled through him—the hunger that no plants could satisfy. With a triumphant roar, he ripped the still quivering organ out of the *dimo's* chest then sank his teeth into it.

As the warm blood trickled down his neck and chest, a faint thought fluttered in his mind like a fragile moth in the night.

"What have I become?"

The answer came unbidden but clear—a monster.

Chapter 12

Valentina

"Malahki?" I patted the empty space around me.

I could have sworn he was just here. He'd held me as I fell asleep. And he was still holding me tight just a little while back. I faintly remembered feeling him move. And now, he was gone.

We'd slept fully clothed. I'd just removed the knife sheaths from around my thighs before going to sleep. Taking a knife out of its sheath now, I crawled to the exit and peeked out into the farm.

All seemed the same out there. The broken, rusty cages arranged haphazardly throughout the space, with not a movement in sight.

I ventured to stick my head out, carefully surveying the entire room, wall to wall. Still nothing.

Where did he go? To get more food? We had enough left for breakfast. The water container was also still half-full.

Worry that something might have happened to him slithered into my heart.

Afraid to attract unwanted attention, I didn't call out his name, carefully moving along the wall toward the exit to the corridor. I had no intention of strolling along the corridor on my own. I wanted to simply take a look in both directions as far as I could see to orientate myself. If he wasn't there, I'd go back to the room and wait for him. Again.

The heavy stomping of feet made me freeze in my tracks. Someone was coming, and they didn't care about being stealthy.

If they weren't afraid of anyone, chances were I had to be afraid of them.

I started backing along the wall to return to the room where we'd spent the night.

Someone walked in, and I stared at him in shock, my feet refusing to move.

My heart knew it was Malahki, but my eyes could hardly recognize him. He'd grown even more, being at least a head and a half taller than me now. His shoulders all but blocked the doorway. His long hair had fallen out of the braids. Ink-black now, straight, and glossy, it streamed down his shoulders, reaching his waist.

Bright red, glowing swirls of color curled and curved along the skin of his bare arms and torso, reaching his face, too. They blended with the thick layer of blood that covered his entire front from the lower part of his face all the way down his pants. His arms looked like he had dipped them up to his elbows in blood.

It must be someone else's blood, since he didn't appear to be injured, though there was suffering in his gaze. His eyes shone as he slowly moved them across the room, stopping on me.

Breath caught in my throat, I was unable to stir a muscle, caught in his stare like a fly.

With a low growl, he lunged my way.

There was so much power and menace in his large figure charging at me, I screamed, terrified. At that moment, there was nothing of Malahki that I recognized.

Spinning on my heel, I dashed back to the room. If I could make it through the narrow tunnel, he wouldn't be able to get to me.

I weaved between the cages and the wall, running as fast as I could. Afraid to look back over my shoulder, I heard the slamming and crashing noise of the cages being shoved out of his way.

Reaching the crack between the panels, I dropped to my knees to crawl in, to safety.

A heavy hand landed on my shoulder, hauling me up to my feet, instead. Afraid to face him, I kept my face to the wall.

Slamming his hands in the wall above my head, he caged me in with his massive body, pressing his pelvis to my back. Something throbbed and bulged between his legs, something that wasn't there before.

"What's the matter, Valentina? Why are you running *away* from me not *to* me this time?" The bitter sarcasm in his voice as well as the use of my long, formal name brought the memory of the old Malahki back. The one who saved my life and cared for me. I'd never been afraid of him.

Did I have any reason to be afraid of him, now?

His entire body was pressed against me, his breathing ragged and heavy, but he didn't touch me anywhere otherwise.

I panted hard, struggling to catch my breath after running. My heart still pounded fast in my chest. The heat of his body surrounding me seeped into my muscles.

"Do you no longer want to see me?" he growled, nuzzling the side of my face.

His familiar scent enveloped me, putting me more at ease. Ever since our one and only real kiss, I craved being closer with him. But he'd been keeping me at arm's length ever since, caring for me and protecting me, but nothing more.

"Does the look of me disgust you, now?" Hand on my shoulder, he flipped me around to face him.

I sucked in a breath and held it, staring at him smeared with blood, the bright swirls of color blending and curling all along his skin and in his eyes.

"Malahki…" I exhaled, tripping over his name as all other words deserted me.

He leaned closer, reaching for a kiss, but I turned my face away from his blood-stained lips.

"What's the matter?" He rasped in my ear. "You no longer want my kisses?"

"I do," I whispered, so quiet, I could barely hear it myself.

I missed his kisses so much it hurt. I wanted Malahki's arms around me, his lips on me. I just didn't know who exactly this wild beast of a man in front of me was. His behaviour sent chills of trepidation down my arms. I was afraid to breathe, to move, to speak, but I was *not* afraid for my life with him. Whoever he was, whatever he had turned into, I just didn't believe Malahki would ever hurt me.

Slowly, I raised my gaze to his, meeting his terrifying eyes. Terrifying, but also beautiful, I found. The bright colors swam in his irises, spreading and disappearing like drops of paint in water. Mesmerising.

The wild desire—so new and exciting—in his gaze sent another charge of heat down my body. At the same time, something sad and broken deep inside his eyes made my heart ache.

Lifting my hand to his face, I gently wiped the blood off his lips.

"I always want your kisses, Malahki," I said, louder. I just needed a moment to gather my courage to receive them. Some strength to return them. I heaved another breath, placing my hands flat to the wall behind me, willing the cool surface to help me control the feverish heat coming awake in my body.

Instead of being relieved, however, he seemed to get angry.

"You do?" He shoved away from the wall and from me. "Do you want *this*?"

He unclipped his belt, yanking his pants down.

A cry of shock lodged in my throat as I gaped at the place where there had been absolutely nothing when we met. His genital slit was now wide open, turned inside out. A massive, fully erect penis sprouted from the center. Tapered at the end, with a pointy head, it looked thicker than my wrist at the base. Pulsing red, it seemed to glow from strain and heat.

Instead of hair, a cluster of thin, flexible antennae circled it. A little shorter than his shaft, they were almost as thick as a pencil each. Also erect and bright red in color, they vibrated as if charged with electrical current.

"Is that what you want?" he asked again, with a bitter note.

"I…" I swallowed hard. The thought about how that amazing cluster of his would possibly feel between my legs made me squirm.

So much about this barely familiar man felt strange and intimidating. Yet… I'd craved intimacy with Malahki for some time now. It'd been a soft desire that had glowed gently under my skin, keeping me warm in this cold hostile place. I'd always doubted he'd ever want me back, though.

There were no doubts any longer. He practically shook with need, devouring me with his stare.

"Desire can be contagious," I once told him.

And in our case, it proved true. My body caught his fever, fueled by nothing but his hungry stare. My breathing grew shallow. My suit that I'd barely ever noticed before now chafed against my flushed skin. My breasts tingled. The nipples pebbled, pushing hard against the thin fabric.

His hands propped into the wall next to my head, he leaned his forehead to mine.

"I'm a true monster now, Valya."

Lifting a trembling hand to the suit's closure at my neck, I slid it all the way down in silent invitation for him.

"Be *my* monster, then," I said softly.

His wide chest expanded with a deep breath as he stepped back. Sliding a long, heated stare down my body, he lowered his head, reminding me of a bull about to attack. Without another word, he grabbed the edges of my suit and yanked it off my shoulders.

Dropping to his knees, he kept peeling the suit off me. I swayed on my feet, freeing my arms from the sleeves, as he licked and nibbled my skin down my belly, shoving my suit all the way down to my ankles.

His nose pressed to my skin, he inhaled deeply then sprang to his feet.

"Is that what you want?" he repeated, sounding delirious.

Spinning me around, he kicked my legs open with his knee.

"You want to be fucked?" Curling his arm around my hip, he dipped his hand between my legs, pressing my ass to his hard, pulsing length.

Biting down on my shoulder to keep me in place, he slid his fingers between my folds, already slick for him.

"Fuck." He sounded shocked. "You do want this."

My entire body trembled, and I no longer knew whether from trepidation or need.

His mouth firmly latched to that place where my neck met my shoulder. He found my breast with his other hand, pinching my nipple. I whimpered, grinding my hips against the fingers that kept moving between my thighs.

"You want me to fuck you," he growled against my skin.

He thrust forward, sliding inside me. The tapered tip of his shaft entered me smoothly. The base stretched me wider and wider for him as he thrust deeper.

The little antennae—or feelers or whatever blessed things they were—trembled all around the place where our bodies connected, charging my every nerve with thrill.

"Oh yes, Malakhi…" I panted, bending over to take him even deeper.

One arm around my middle, he gripped my hip with the other hand, slamming hard inside me again.

I braced myself on the wall with both arms as he rutted in me from behind.

With a loud roar, he came, but hardly slowed down. Taking a long breath, he kept going, frantically thrusting inside me.

Another climax rocked his large body. Sliding out of me, he turned me over to face him.

I threw my arms over his shoulders to support myself as my legs shook and my knees threatened to give out. Where my bare arms touched his skin, more colors flared to life. Deep purple, magenta, and iridescent green joined the red and orange swirls. They spread in tendrils along the dips and valleys of his muscular arms and torso like spilled paint.

"Beautiful," I breathed out, tracing the colorful swirls with the tips of my fingers, which appeared to create more and more tendrils.

"You like that?" he grunted, shoving his hard length inside me again.

How was he hard again already?

I got no time to ponder that. At this angle, his body hit my sensitive spot as he started to move. The tender, flexible antennae caressed between my thighs, like fingers.

My entire body pulsed with heat, in rhythm with his swirling colors. Pressure built inside me, teasing me with the approaching orgasm. With another hard thrust from him, pleasure exploded through me. I threw my head back, ready to scream, unable to keep it all in.

He caught my mouth in a kiss, swallowing my screams of pleasure while pumping his third climax into me.

Breaking the kiss, he curled his body around mine, spent. We stood like that for a few moments. Being pinned between Malahki and the wall was the only reason I remained upright at all.

"You like it," he'd said. And I still had no idea what I'd reply to that.

No one had ever taken me like this, fully and completely before, with so much need and desperation. I felt both used and thoroughly loved.

Every muscle in my body vibrated with the aftershocks of the most intense orgasm I'd ever had. I realized I would not want to go on without this anymore. Anything I'd had before with anyone else paled in comparison with what we'd just had.

"I did like it, Malahki," I murmured, pressing my lips to his shoulder in a kiss.

"You did," he said, a note of wonder in his voice. "You. A human."

"I'm a woman first, I guess." I shrugged.

And as a woman, I felt very satisfied at the moment.

Letting go of me, he leaned with his back to the wall then slid down to sit on the floor. Without his support, I lowered to the floor too. My body felt boneless, my trembling muscles too weak to keep me upright.

Placing his forearms on his bent knees, he flexed his fingers, staring at his blood-stained hands. I slid a glance down my naked body, there were plenty of red smears on my skin, too.

"Whose blood is it?" I asked, relieved it didn't appear to be his.

"Urkril's." His voice sounded hollow.

"Is he…"

"Dead." He nodded, running his hand over his face.

"Serves him right," I said firmly, remembering Urkril's senseless beating of Malahki many weeks ago.

He slid me a curious look, as if seeing me for the first time.

"What? I'm not going to feel sorry for that one." I pulled up my suit, threading my arms into its sleeves.

He glanced back at his blood-covered hands then stared at me again.

"Did you really like what I just did to you?" he asked.

I shifted on the floor, tugging the two sides of my suit together over my chest.

"I enjoyed it. Physically. It was different." I was not going to apologize or feel bad about how I felt. Not about Urkril, not about the sex.

"How do you feel about me?" His frown deepened as he awaited my answer, but there was a faint glow of hope in his expression, too.

"I've always liked you, Malahki." I took his hand in mine, wiping the blood off it with my sleeve.

His skin returned to its previous color—smooth beige, like the color of prairie sand or unbleached canvas. When I stroked his hand with a finger, however, the multi-colored swirls came back to life in its wake. They spread along his hand, fading away and disappearing the moment I removed my finger from him.

"You like the monster I've become?" he insisted, gazing at me intently.

"Did you really change that much?" I met his eyes, the colorful storm in them slowed down, settling into a pretty pattern of brown, purple, and red.

He huffed a bitter laugh, dropping his head between his shoulders. His pose reminded me of the one he had when I'd woken up after being poisoned by the *fuhnid* mushrooms. Back then he asked me what was happening to him.

Just like then, I couldn't even pretend to understand what it would be like to have one's identity completely changed like that, mentally and physically. But when I thought about that now, I wondered if the change had been as drastic as he feared.

"Malahki," I started, squeezing his hand in both of mine. "You're still you. It's not like you disappeared anywhere. There have been certain…um, additions to you, physically and mentally, but do you feel like anything has been taken away? Do you have a feeling of loss? Or do you think you've lost more than you've gained?"

He stroked my knuckles with his thumb, staring at the floor straight ahead of him.

"Well, I've gained you." He moved his gaze to me and paused as if giving me a chance to argue or disagree, though he looked like he hoped I'd confirm.

I smiled.

"You've always had me. Only now, you can have me in some *other* ways, too."

His frown eased a little. I studied him carefully—all the new things about him. His increased height and width. The bulky muscles on his arms and thighs.

His hair was so glossy and black, it even seemed heavier now. His high cheekbones looked as if carved from a stone—hard and sharp. The thick black eyebrows furrowed over his bright eyes. The serene beige didn't return to his irises, and I didn't think it ever would again.

There were many changes, but I spotted the old and familiar pieces of him, too. They were mostly in the intonations of his voice, his expression, and his body posture.

"There are changes, for sure," I said. "But fundamentally, I don't feel like I lost you. You're still there, despite all the muscles and that, um…spectacular thing you grew between your legs."

I moved my gaze aside, determined not to stare at the bulge

between his thighs. He'd yanked his pants back up, but his belt was still undone.

"I'll need to learn how to walk again," he said suddenly.

A laugh burst out of me. "Does *it* get in the way?"

"No!" He laughed, too. "Well, a little. But I mean I'll have to get used to my bigger size, overall. I keep bumping into things." He rolled back his shoulders, demonstrating how massive they'd grown.

I loved hearing him laugh again.

Now, that the frenzy of sex had calmed down, however, anxiety returned to me. The constant feeling of danger surrounding us urged me to nervously scan both the entrance to the waste processing room and the exit to the corridor on the opposite end of the farm.

"We should probably get back in, to hide." I gestured at the crack in the wall. "Someone might come."

Malahki just shrugged.

"Let them come." He jumped to his feet, fastening his pants. "No more hiding."

"What? You just want to walk around? In the open?"

His sudden carelessness puzzled and worried me.

"Let's have a shower," he said.

When we used the bathroom yesterday, we'd done it quickly, looking over our shoulders all the time. Now, Malahki scanned both entrances to the farm calmly, looking ready to fight, not to run.

"Come." He gave me a hand, helping me up. "I made a mess." He rubbed at the smudge of blood on my chest in the opening of my suit. "Let me clean you up."

"But what if someone sees us?" I asked nervously.

"Who?"

"Well—"

"I'm bigger than anyone of the crew, now, Valya. Gler said he was the only *errock* left, and I can fight him with one arm tied behind my back."

For as long as I knew him, Malahki had always been confident. When he was smaller and weaker, he had a cooler, more calculating type of confidence. Now, it was hot and careless, bordering on arrogance.

"It's not just about the size, or strength, or even the weapons, Malahki. A little bit of caution never hurt," I objected.

"All right." He headed for the bathroom with an easy swagger. "Let's be cautious. We'll close the door to the bathroom when we shower. I'll even lock it, okay?"

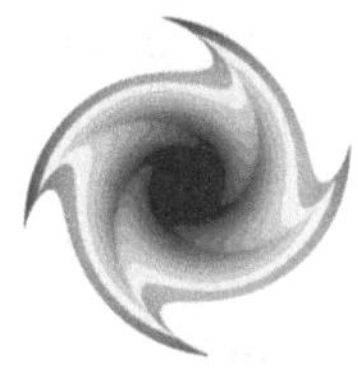

Chapter 13

Valentina

In the bathroom, he fucked me again. Because of the five-minute shower limit, we hadn't even turned on the water until Malahki had come twice.

Washing off the blood and the evidence of sex from me, he caressed my body with his hands under the stream of the shower.

"I dreamed about this so often." He bent his knees and lowered his head to lick a drop of water off my nipple. "I feel so sorry about all the showers I've wasted on just washing you, instead of doing this."

He sucked the tip of my breast in his mouth, twirling his tongue around it.

I wouldn't call any of our time together as being "wasted." Every moment I'd spent with him, we learned more about each other. Because of all that time before, I knew now that I could trust him completely. With him, I felt safe, even when he fucked me hard, like the monster he thought he'd become.

He seemed calmer now, his caresses decadently slow. Slipping his hand between my legs, he circled my opening, my flesh still highly sensitive from his earlier touch.

I moaned, leaning back against the wall for support. He dropped to his knees, draping my leg over his shoulder.

Burying my hands in his thick, silky hair, I rode his face as he nibbled and sucked. The water had long stopped running, yet he wouldn't let go of me until the orgasm hit me. A shuddered moan escaped my lips as my hips jerked against his mouth.

When my tremors finally subsided, he kissed his way up my body back to my lips.

"Showers are definitely much more fun, now." He beamed at me before kissing my mouth again.

"So, you just want to go back to the gardens in the open?" I asked, needing him to confirm it again. After weeks of striving to be invisible to everyone on the Dark Anomaly, I couldn't fathom just strolling down its main corridor in plain view of whoever might come along.

"That'd be the easiest." Already fully dressed after the shower, Malahki wrung the water out of my hair, divided it into sections, then deftly braided it as I pulled up the closure of my suit.

"How about something less dangerous?" I argued.

"Like what?" He shook his hair out then braided it into one thick plait that almost reached his waist.

My thoughts flickered to the garbage chute again. The cover it provided appealed to my sense of caution. Malahki wouldn't fit in the tunnel, being nearly twice his initial size now. My taking it would mean I'd have to separate from him, but I didn't want to let him out of my sight ever again, no matter how terrifying walking out in the open felt.

Sensing my hesitation, he placed his hands on my shoulders.

"There's hardly anyone left around here, Valya," he said softly. Hearing the name my parents and my brother called me felt comforting. He rubbed my shoulders gently. "The survivors are holed up in their ships. There might be some deranged males scurrying in the corners, but I'll deal with them if they decide to attack. All right? Don't be scared. I'll protect you."

I'd trusted him to protect me before, and I nodded now.

We took the canister and the oxygen masks with us. As we passed through the farm, Malahki grabbed the dangling door of one of the cages and wrenched it off its hinges.

"Here," he yanked out one of the thick bars and wielded it like a spear over his head. "See? A weapon." He grinned at me. "We're even better armed, now. Do you feel safer?"

I gave him a tight smile in reply. Seeing him break the thick metal bar out of the door frame was reassuring. It was also a shocking demonstration of the pure physical strength that Malahki now possessed.

He strolled out of the farm in long, confident strides as I slid my knives out of their sheaths, constantly scanning the space around us.

"How many survivors are left, do you think?" I asked.

"No idea. It really depends on how many ships we still have with fully functioning air supply systems."

"My ship would be one," I said. "As far as I know the air system still worked when we landed. You said someone occupied it already."

"The *errocks*." He winced, with dislike.

I grimaced, too, sharing his resentment for that particular group on the Dark Anomaly. His frown was suddenly misplaced by a calculating expression.

"What is it, Malahki?" I wondered.

He blinked. "Gler said he was the only *errock* on the ship."

"Yes, but the *akuk* was with him. There may be other males, too."

He waved me off.

"The others don't matter. I can take them all. I can fight the *errock*, too. If there were more than one that might be a problem, but if he's the only one."

Malahki walked with an added bounce to his step, as if eager for the fight.

"How do you even know what ship he was talking about?" I asked.

"Yours."

"Why?"

He turned to me.

"I saw Wyck, another *errock* enter it a few days back."

"So? Gler may be on another ship, with another group—"

"No." He shook his head resolutely. "*Errocks* always stick together. If Wyck was on that ship, the rest also would be there. If Gler was the only one left, then the rest are all dead."

I pondered his words for a moment.

"Gler didn't look that upset about losing his entire tribe."

"The *errocks* on the Dark Anomaly are…*were* a brutal bunch. They called themselves a family, but I always had a feeling they'd end each other over a piece of meat if it came down to it. They stuck together for power and intimidation, not for any real attachment or affection for each other."

Two sets of pewter double doors came on our left. One had been welded shut and sealed. The other, not far from the first, was partially open.

"Wait." Malahki touched my arm.

I stopped in my tracks, nearly tripping over my feet. Being on edge made me jumpy. My heart leaped to my throat.

"What is it?" I looked around wildly.

"The captain's room." Malahki moved to the partially open doors, gesturing to me to fall back behind him for safety.

I noted he stepped lightly. The sense of caution hadn't completely deserted him. He glanced inside then slid his hand along the edge of one of the doors. It appeared to be stuck half-open. It wouldn't budge either way even under Malahki's newly-found incredible strength.

The edge of the door was jagged and chipped. As if something sharp had been used to open it in the first place.

"Is anyone there?" I asked. "The captain?"

"No." He shook his head with a gloomy expression. "The room is empty."

"Do you think he's survived?" I came a little closer.

Malahki threw a glance in both directions along the corridor, then squeezed his large body between the doors, gesturing for me to follow. I slid into the room after him.

The room was made entirely out of glass. The bright lights of the Dark Anomaly moved outside of it in their eternal dance.

"It's gorgeous." I wondered what it would be like to live in a room like that. Mesmerising at first, but it would probably cost me my mind at the end.

"The lights will drive you mad," Malahki had said.

For me, the most infuriating would be looking *outside*, while knowing I could never get there. All of us were trapped in this place. At least when I was in the gardens, I could fool myself that they were my "outside," with all the plant life, greenery, and space.

Malahki inspected the room. Aside from a narrow metal cot and a few pieces of broken plastic that littered the floor, the space was completely empty. Unlike so many other places on the Dark Anomaly, there weren't any decaying body parts in here, no signs of blood, either.

"He could be hiding elsewhere," I offered, knowing that despite his strong disdain for the crew, Malahki held a true respect for his captain.

"Maybe," he said, slowly circling the room. "If he is dead, he wasn't killed here."

After leaving the glass room, we continued down the corridor toward the gardens. When we reached the white doors of the gardens, however, Malahki paused, not entering.

I wondered if he was thinking about the *kreers* and the others who had driven us away from the gardens yesterday. The fine hairs on the back of my neck stood up when I thought about those creatures. Behaving worse than wild animals, they couldn't even be called sentient beings, anymore.

"Do you think they're still there?" I asked, shifting closer to him.

"Maybe." He shrugged.

Malahki certainly didn't look scared, but his thoughts appeared to be elsewhere.

"What are you thinking about?"

"I'm not afraid of the crew," he said. "Especially of those who can no longer even think for themselves. What worries me is that the central air supply system is unreliable. It can fail at any time. What if the supplementary system proves inadequate?"

"We have the masks." I touched the device strapped around my neck.

"We can't wear them forever. What if the system fails when we're asleep? Or anything else fails without us knowing? Whatever happened to the crew may happen to us, too."

I released a sigh, thinking about the dead *akuks* in the storage room. It could have been us, had the malfunction happened in the gardens. Expanding the auxiliary system would take time, each minute of which would be like sitting on a timebomb, dreading another breakdown that could happen any time. Malahki was right, other life-support systems could fail, too.

"We need a safe place to stay while we modify the air supply in the gardens and get ready to seal them off," Malahki concluded. "Your ship is right up ahead." He headed in that direction.

"But you said the *errocks* are there." I hurried after him, a heavy feeling pressing on my chest.

"*One* errock." He kept going.

"And who knows how many others!" I didn't necessarily disagree with his idea, but I wished he would think it through first, instead of barging head first into the danger.

I grabbed his arm, forcing him to stop.

He could have shaken me off like a fly, but he faced me. Drawing in a long breath, he patiently explained, "You said your ship has a functioning air production and filtration system. It must be true since the *errocks* have been living there, obviously unaffected by the malfunctions of the central system—you saw Gler, he functions well. You and I will need a safe place to live while we're working on fixing and improving the gardens. Your ship is safe. So, we will go and get it."

"What makes you think they will just let us take it?" I propped my hands on my hips.

He gave me another one of his nonchalant shrugs.

"I won't ask. I'll just take it from them."

"And if they fight back?"

"Then, I'll kill them," he said simply.

"What if they kill you?"

He lifted an eyebrow, giving me a lopsided grin.

"Malahki," I exhaled, worry shooting through me, sharp and painful. "Please, think about it first. There're others there, not just the *errock*. We have no idea how many—"

"Couldn't be that many, after all the fighting that has happened here lately." He proceeded up the corridor again, leaving me no choice but to follow.

I hadn't been in this section since the day of the crash. As if on their own, my feet slowed down as the memories rose in my mind. Last time I'd been here, I'd crawled, stricken by panic and grief. Had it not been for Malahki, I had no doubt I wouldn't be here today.

He took my hand in his, pulling me to a stop at his side. The opening that the *errock* had made in the wall to get on our ship had now been solidly blocked.

"I want you to stand over there," Malahki said in my ear softly, pointing at the wall opposite from the entrance.

"Me? Why?"

"There is a camera right above the door, I want them to see you."

"You what?" I tripped over the words. After doing everything possible to keep me out of sight before, he was willing to display me for the others to see, now. "You want to use me as a bait." It dawned on me.

"Yes," he said, with an easy smile. "Don't worry," he added quickly as I just stood there, gaping at him. "I'll never let any harm come to you. I need them to open the door. Once they see you on the camera, they'll come out to try to catch you.

"You think?" I huffed a nervous laugh.

"That's when I'll get them." He adjusted his grip on the makeshift spear in his hand.

A spark of anticipation flashed in his eye. A muscle moved in his jaw as he shifted his weight to the other foot, impatiently.

Not only was he not afraid, he yearned for the fight.

"Have you ever seen a damirian male?" he'd asked me long ago.

Now, I completely understood his earlier reservations and concerns. Malahki had known all along what would happen. He knew *what* he would become, from the beginning. For someone inherently detesting any kind of violence, it must've been especially disturbing to know he'd crave it one day.

"Okay," I said softly. "I trust you."

"Oh, Valya," he murmured. Coming closer, he lowered his head to me, shielding me from the world with his wide shoulders. "Don't worry, please. No one will get close enough to touch you. I won't let that happen."

I nodded, drawing in a bracing breath.

"I know, honey. I trust you."

He brushed my lips with his in a soft, comforting kiss.

"Let's do it." I marched over to the entrance, not waiting for my courage to waver.

Coming to the metal piece that had been fitted over the cut-out in leu of the door, I firmly slammed my fist into it a few times. Clutching a knife in my other hand, I hid it behind my back.

"Hey, boys!" I yelled, lifting my face to the camera. "Come and get me."

I had no doubt they'd bite. From what I'd learned about them, the crew of the Dark Anomaly rarely exercised caution or even common sense, letting their instincts guide them more often than their brains.

Sure enough, it took but a second before the sounds of clunking and clicking of what must be locks and chains came through the door.

My heart leaped high with trepidation. I didn't have Malahki's reckless bravery or even any affinity for confrontation. Backing all the way to the wall, I forced myself to stare straight ahead. Even the quickest glance in Malahki's direction would be risking giving away his presence prematurely.

The door slid open.

"Val!" A familiar feminine voice exclaimed, rendering me speechless.

A woman?

Nadia!

She rushed to me from the opening.

And Malahki struck.

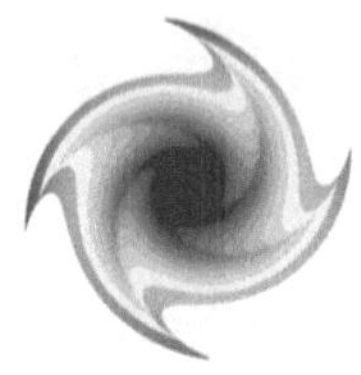

Chapter 14

Malahki

He didn't waste time to see who it was. The person moved toward Valya, and he charged at them. Considerably smaller than an *errock*, or any male for that matter, they didn't present much of a challenge, crashing to the floor the moment his chest collided with their body.

A whimper, followed by a small cry of pain, made him take a closer look at whom he'd tackled. Green human eyes, open wide in terror, met his gaze. The feminine scent and feel of her small body under him doused his urge to fight, like a rain putting out a wildfire.

"Nadia!" Valya rushed to her friend.

"Um…" He tried to scramble off the woman without causing her any more damage with his weight or weapons.

"Get off her!" Someone bellowed, before attacking him.

The impact felt as if a spaceship crashed into him or he had gotten into the path of a humongous meteorite.

His new opponent was definitely an *errock*. Malahki's bones groaned from the shattering blows of the male's hard knuckles. The two of them rolled away from the females, the *errock* furiously pummeling his face and shoulders.

Malahki's blood boiled. His insides heated. His muscles swelled with energy. The thrill of the fight bubbled in his chest with effervescence, causing him to feel drunk on violence.

He laughed with joy, though the sound came out more like a threatening snarl. Ducking from another blow of the *errock's* massive fist, Malahki landed one straight into the male's temple.

The *errock* grunted, his eyes growing glossy. Malahki shoved the male's heavy body off his.

"Wyck!" the female, Nadia, cried out.

Malahki made a move to get up, but the *errock* grabbed him around the middle, tossing him back on the floor.

"Malahki! Stop it!" Valya's voice broke through the fog of excitement and violence.

"That's enough!" Vrateus shouted.

What was the captain doing here? The question flickered through his mind faintly as his fists pounded Wyck's hard, muscular chest. The *errock* unfailingly returned his punches, matching them blow by blow, neither of them willing or able to stop.

Ice-cold water suddenly crashed over Wyck and him. The deluge rushed over his face, flooding his mouth and nose. He splattered and choked, his thirst for fight immediately quenched for the time being.

"What on earth is going on here?" Svetlana glared at the *errock* and him, an empty bucket in her hands.

Lesh, Wyck's three-headed monster pet, hissed, letting go of his ankle. Malahki hadn't even realized when Lesh appeared. Absorbed by the fight, he didn't even feel his boot had been trapped in the animal's jaws.

"Get up, Malahki," Valya said softly, casting a cautious glance at Lesh as Wyck called his pet off. "These are friends." She glanced at Nadia, and the other woman nodded.

"Malahki?" Svetlana's eyes opened wider. "Is that really you?"

She came closer as he climbed to his feet. Svetlana and he used to be almost the same height a few weeks ago. Now, her face was somewhere around his chest area.

She tilted her head back to look him in the eye, then took in the rest of his face carefully.

"I'm so happy you're alive, Malahki. But I can't believe how much you've changed." She shook her head.

"Nice to see you again, Svetlana," he said. "Captain." He inclined his head in greeting of Vrateus.

Svetlana's presence brought the memories of the calm times when working in the gardens with her, further helping him regain control of his bloodthirst. He moved his gaze from her to Vrateus then back again, his heart swelling with gratitude at finding both seemingly well and alive. He had no idea how the two of them ended up here, in the company of an *errock* and the human woman who Malahki believed would've been long dead, but he was really happy to see them unharmed.

"Wow!" Svetlana gasped, walking around him in awe, as if he were a rare exhibit. "You look so different. I wouldn't have recognized you if I didn't hear your name."

For someone who had only seen him as neutral gender, the physical changes in him would be sudden and dramatic.

He was at least a head and a half taller and probably twice as broad as before. The pants he'd taken off Trox a while back—the ones that used to be so loose on him, he'd needed a belt to hold them up—now felt almost too tight around his buttocks and thighs.

He knew his facial features had hardened and sharpened. His hair, eyelashes, and brows had turned completely black.

And his eyes…

He'd had no chance to examine his eyes lately, but he suspected they'd be even brighter than his skin, which was still flaming hot with the battle colors of red, orange, and pink.

"What happened to you, Malahki?" Svetlana asked. "Are you okay?"

"I changed." He spread his arms aside.

His attention then snapped to Valya, who regarded the two of them with a confused frown.

"You know each other?" she said, and his heart dropped into the empty abyss of his stomach. "You said there were no other women on the Dark Anomaly, but you knew Svetlana Kostyk was here. Alive."

STAYING OUT IN THE OPEN WHILE HAVING AN EMOTIONALLY CHARGED discussion was never a good idea on the Dark Anomaly. Once all six of them got inside the human spaceship and locked the doors behind them securely, Nadia hugged Valya tightly.

"We've been looking for you. Everywhere. We thought you were dead," she sobbed.

Valya turned an accusing stare at him, and he couldn't hold it. He knew they'd been searching for her–Wyck was. But Malahki had been convinced the *errock* was abusing Nadia. And, spirits may damn him, but Malahki would've never let Wyck know about Valya. He still was shocked that Nadia turned out to be alive and appeared well after what he'd heard the *errocks* of the Dark Anomaly had done to females in the past.

The hurt expression on Valya's sweet face floored him.

"You lied to me?" she said softly.

"Valya, please." He forced himself to remain in place, even as everything inside him screamed to grab her in his arms and kiss her until she forgave him everything.

"You told me there were no other women on the Dark Anomaly. You said *all* of my crew were dead." She breathed rapidly.

Grabbing a chair from the table in the middle of the large open area of the spacecraft, Nadia put it behind Valya. As if her knees wouldn't hold her, she plopped onto it. Her dark-blue eyes remained on him, accusations floating in them, demanding an explanation.

How could he explain what he'd done? He'd been led mostly by fear—fear that if Valya knew about Nadia or Svetlana, she would try to make contact with them, likely revealing her presence to the crew in the process.

Until recently, stealth had been his most effective weapon

against the brutalities of this place. He stayed out of sight of others to avoid conflicts with them. He kept Valya away from everyone, too, for the same purpose.

"I didn't want any harm to come to you," he said, trying to keep his voice even, though his heart pummeled so hard, his chest felt like one huge bruise inside.

"They wouldn't harm me!" She gestured wildly at the four people surrounding them.

Rubbing her forehead, Svetlana swiftly walked over to a raised panel with a screen on the wall. She filled a metal cup with water then brought it over to Valya. With a deep breath, Vrateus went to the front of the ship and took a seat in one of the crew chairs by the control panel.

"Maybe they wouldn't." Malahki measured with his gaze each of the four people who watched them carefully. "But they wouldn't do much to protect you, either."

"That's not true!" Nadia bristled.

Wyck stepped closer to Nadia's side in silent support. Malahki had no time to ponder why the *errock* was here and not with Gler and the likes of him.

"Isn't it?" Malahki addressed Nadia. "How much have any of the crew protected you? Tell Valentina what the captain made you do. Tell her what the *errocks* did to you."

Valya shot a questioning look at her friend, but Nadia didn't meet her eye. Blinking rapidly, the woman turned away, blush spreading thickly over her face.

"Leave her alone!" Wyck boomed, stepping forward.

"I need Valya to know what fate she's escaped by staying with *me*, not with *her*." He gestured at Nadia, who lowered herself into another chair by the table, wrapping her arms around her.

"What are you talking about?" Valya moved her gaze from him to Nadia then to the *errock*.

"Tell her, Nadia, how he paraded you naked in front of everyone!" Malahki pointed an accusing finger at Wyck. The indignity of what had been done to the woman he'd hardly knew spurred another wave of aggression to rise to the surface. "Her too!" He pointed at Svetlana who quietly stepped aside.

Vrateus leaped out of his seat. "I had reasons—"

"Reasons!" Malahki scoffed, outrage bursting from him. "Hear that, my sweet Valya? If you stayed with them, he'd find *reasons* to make you undress for the crew, too."

Her eyes open wide, Valya sank her fingers in her hair, wildly shifting her eyes from one person in the room to another. "Is that really what's happening here?"

"No—" Svetlana stirred, but he wouldn't let her speak.

"Then, he'd force you to touch yourself in front of everyone, and if you refused, he'd get someone to do it for you, so they all could jerk off while watching you. Now tell her, everyone, that's not what happened here. Tell her I'm lying!" he demanded, moving his gaze from one face to the next, daring them contradict his words.

Valya had paled so much, she almost looked blue, like her suit.

"Nadia?" she half-whispered, her eyes pleading with her friend to reassure her.

Nadia hid her face from her, shaking her head with a quiet sob. Wyck placed his hand on her shoulder, hurling a glare at him, sharp like a dagger.

Malahki was beyond any warnings, however.

"The captain would've made you have sex with someone like *this one* here," he moved his finger to the *errock*.

"Fuck you!" Wyck took a step forward, swinging his fist at him.

Malahki ducked, evading the blow then shoved the *errock* aside.

"I protected you, Valya," he kept talking, with the desperate hope she'd understand and forgive. "None of them would've protected you from that."

Without any further warning, the *errock* turned on his heel and punched Malahki in the back of his head. His teeth clanked from the blow. The echo of it reverberated inside his skull.

The captain leaped to them, rushing to break up the fight. Malahki swung his fist, without looking, knocking Vrateus in the face. The captain staggered on his feet, then drew out a gun and punched Malahki in the jaw with its handle.

Aggression took over again. He growled, trying to hold back. His aim was to clear a path to Valya, not to kill anyone.

"That's it!" Giving the three men an assessing look, Svetlana hurried to Valya. "Come, you can stay in our room until these hot heads cool off."

Valya still looked shocked from his revelations. Sadly, he couldn't tell what she thought about him from her stunned expression. Svetlana helped her get up then led her to the open door in the wall to the right.

Wyck twisted Malahki's arm, making him bend over. His attention fully on Valya, he didn't fight back.

"Where are you taking her?" Alarm shot through his system.

Nadia joined the two women, opening a second door next to the first. "Her bed and her things are here, Svetlana. Val, I put the divider up in your area. No one has been there since."

The women were ignoring him, taking Valya away from him.

"Valya, wait!" The aggression sharply shifted into rage. Punching the men who tried to stop him out of the way, he lumbered after her.

She turned in the threshold to the room.

"You have to calm down, Malahki, and let me think. Please," she said softly, her voice trembling, her eyes glistening with unshed tears.

Nadia ushered her through the door, and the panel slid closed, separating him from his woman. Svetlana stayed on this side of the door. She quickly jumped aside as Malahki charged the wall.

"No! Valya!" He slammed into the panel at full force.

"Fucking *damirian!*" the *errock* growled, getting to his feet after the last blow of Malahki had sent him to the floor. Grabbing the closest chair, he smashed it over Malahki's head. "I think I liked you better when you were beige."

Malahki staggered on his feet, his vision momentarily cloudy.

"Stop it. Now." Vrateus's voice was cold like metal. Something hard pressed to the back of Malaki's head—a gun. "Or I'll shoot."

He swayed, his head swimming from the impact with the chair.

"Do you think these may be the effects of the *kronite* leak into the air supply system?" Svetlana asked, keeping a safe distance from the men.

"Maybe," Vrateus replied grimly. "If so, then it would be best if I shot him sooner rather than later."

Taking a leather belt from around her waist, she handed it to Wyck. "Let's just tie him up for now."

"Is Val all right?" Vrateus asked, moving to Malahki's side. The cold barrel of the gun now pressed hard at the side of his neck.

Svetlana nodded. "She's safe."

Valya was safe with *him*, no one else. He'd kept her well and alive all these weeks on his own.

"Let me go to her," he gritted through his teeth, forcing himself to remain still to prove to the captain that he was not a threat and didn't need to be shot. He even let the *errock* bind his wrists with Svetlana's belt, every muscle in his body vibrating with strain and the need to fight.

Svetlana ignored him, talking to Vrateus. "I'll have to examine Val to confirm she's okay, but if they didn't spend every day together, he might've gotten a dose while she didn't."

What were they talking about? He couldn't focus on anything else but the horrible fact that Valya had been taken out of his sight, that she willingly walked away from him.

"Take me to her," he growled, lowering his head and squaring his shoulders. He could hold back for just so long, though. His body felt tight like a wound spring, ready to unfurl to bring menace and devastation.

As if sensing the threat, Vrateus pressed the gun more firmly to Malahki's neck.

"This may be just the way he is," the captain said, his expression contemplative. "The *kronite* leak may have nothing to do with this. I read *damirians* turn vicious when they change to males."

"His transformation is incredible. But I hope it didn't change his mind or his personality too drastically." Svetlana heaved a sigh, giving him a compassionate glance. "You'll have to calm down and get some rest, Malahki, so I can test you for *kronite* exposure later."

He couldn't stand it any longer.

"Valya!" he bellowed, tossing his head back.

The captain jammed the gun hard into his skull. "That's the opposite of calming down, my friend."

Friend? A friend wouldn't keep him away from the only person he needed to be with right now.

"Where is Valya?" He shoved his shoulder into the *errock* who held his arms, then launched for the door again.

"Fuck." Wyck jumped on his back, knocking him down.

With his hands tied, he crashed to the ground like a cut down tree.

Vrateus stood over him with a gun at the ready. "I'm locking you up. Until you calm the fuck down!"

"We could put him in the escape capsule, maybe?" Svetlana suggested, rushing to him with a small cylinder in her hand. "I'm so sorry, Malahki," she said softly. Then a cool mist with a sharp chemical smell hit his face.

He gasped, drawing a lungful of mist-rich air. The walls around him seemed to liquify, the edges of the paneling softening and curving. The floor and the ceiling wavered, with dips and swells. The faces of the people surrounding him distorted into soft, fuzzy circles.

Then, everything disappeared.

"Valya!" was the last thought echoing through the vast, dark emptiness of his mind.

When he came to, he was lying in a reclined seat inside what appeared to be a small spacecraft. The lights had been dimmed, and one of the six seats had been converted into a bed for him.

Valya wasn't there.

Svetlana had sprayed him with a sedative, he guessed. Then the rest of them had hauled him in here.

He jumped to his feet. Too fast. The aftereffects of the spray made his head spin, sending him down again. He missed the chair, landing on the floor. Scrambling up again and holding on to the backs of the seats on the way, he made it to the round door at the back.

It was closed and locked.

He slammed his fists into the door, clawing at the plastic and metal and calling her name until his throat hurt and his voice turned to croak. Until his muscles ached, and despair and exhaustion descended on him.

It'd been a while since the last time he'd slept alone. He'd had Valya next to him every single night lately, and he couldn't rest until he got her back. She had to be with him, *needed* to be where he was.

His swollen cock throbbed painfully. The feelers vibrated from strain. Back on Ak'ae, his home world, the newly mated couple would stay in their bedroom for days after the transformation. They would take short breaks for food only, spending the rest of the time satisfying their new burning need for each other.

Here, he was alone. And it wasn't just his body that craved her, his heart twisted in agony at the thought she might never again want to share his bed or his life with him. He'd lied to her. She had every reason to hate him.

Gathering whatever strength he had left, he slammed into the door separating her from him.

"Valya!"

He needed her more than food, air, or water. He had to get back to her.

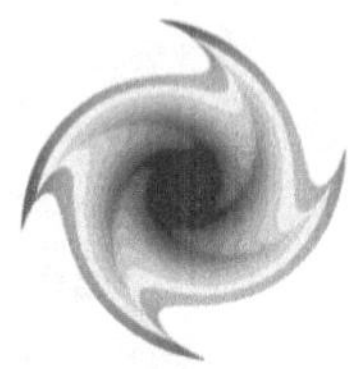

Chapter 15

Valentina

The clock above my bed told me it was morning. Most of the night I'd spent tossing and turning, worrying about Malahki.

Svetlana and Nadia had come to my area after dinner. They'd talked to me a little about how they survived and about the last attack of the crew, when Wyck had been nearly killed. The four of them had gone into full lockdown mode on the ship after that.

It was surreal to find Svetlana Kostyk, the scientist who'd been missing for decades, alive and physically unchanged. But then again, more than five decades had passed since our expedition left Earth for the Dark Anomaly, when it'd been just barely over two months for me here. All of us were now trapped in the bubble of warped time, forgotten by the rest of the galaxy.

I'd cried and kept hugging Nadia. Seeing her well and alive was like having her come back from the dead. I was so grateful that she'd survived, unharmed.

To my shock, she'd said she was in love with Wyck, and that they were expecting a baby. I had a hard time wrapping my mind around that after viewing all *errocks* of the Dark Anomaly as brutal and heartless. Though, I had to admit that Wyck treated Nadia with nothing but love and adoration in my presence.

Nadia's eyes shone with excitement when she'd told me about her pregnancy. However, I'd spotted worry deep inside them, too. There were many reasons to worry. I'd never heard about a naturally conceived *errock*-human baby. Besides, life on the Dark Anomaly had been all about survival. What parent wouldn't be extremely worried about bringing a baby into this harsh and unforgiving world?

After Nadia and Svetlana had left, I'd lain in bed, thinking about everything that had happened.

Finding more survivors made me feel optimistic—we were not entirely alone in this godforsaken place. At the same time, spending the night on my own, made me exceptionally lonely. My thoughts kept drifting to Malahki.

Svetlana had said he was staying in the escape capsule tonight. I knew it was best for both of us to spend some time apart. Ever since we'd met, we'd been inseparable, and I needed to step back to sort out my feelings for him. Maybe he needed to do the same, too.

He'd lied to me. I'd asked him, and he'd said to my face that all my crew was dead. He'd told me there were no other women around, that I had to stay hidden because the crew wanted me and they would kill me in some brutal way if they found me. They would've done worse things before killing me, too.

Stunned and angry after discovering his lies, I'd spent the evening talking to Nadia and Svetlana to discover the truth on my own.

I understood that some of what he'd told me was true. Had I known about Nadia or Svetlana, I would've certainly wanted to get in touch with them. But I wouldn't necessarily run out there recklessly, putting myself in danger. There had been other ways for us to reconnect, but I had to know that they were alive.

The problem was that Malahki didn't trust any of the men on the Dark Anomaly. He might have respect for the captain, but he didn't trust even him with my safety.

Malahki knew he could only protect me if I remained hidden. I hated that he resorted to lying to me instead of talking to me, but I realized that my ability to fully comprehend the danger in this place, so different to what I was used to, might've been limited back then—because he, Malahki, had sheltered me from the worst.

My head full of worrisome thoughts and my heart heavy, I sat up in bed.

"Knock, knock." Nadia poked her head behind the partition separating my personal area from the rest of our room. "Are you up? I brought you breakfast."

She slipped onto my side of the partition with a tray in her hands.

"Hungry?" She put the tray with a mug and a plate on my work desk that also served as a night table. "Sorry, it's nothing fancy. We've been rationing food," she said, gesturing at the plain toast and a cup of coffee.

"No, it's great. Thank you." I took the cup from the tray.

"Are you okay? Did you sleep well?" Nadia took a seat next to me on the bed.

"Yes, I… How is Malahki?"

Nadia bit her lip. "Still locked up."

"Locked up?" I stared at her.

Nadia's gaze flicked aside.

"Well… He gave Wyck and Vrateus some trouble last night."

"What do you mean?" Setting the cup aside, I rose to my feet. "What kind of trouble?"

"He was difficult to talk to. So, they locked him in the escape capsule to give him some time to cool off." She shifted uneasily before adding, "I have it recorded if you want to see it, with his permission of course."

"Recorded?" I echoed numbly. While I slept in my comfy bed, Malahki had spent the night locked up, like a prisoner?

Nadia blew out a breath, twisting the end of her light-brown ponytail between her fingers.

"I should've told you last night, but there was so much to talk about. Remember the cameras I had installed around the living area? I have them working again."

"Why?"

"I'm not sure." She shrugged with a sigh. "This was my one purpose on this expedition, you know, to make a movie…"

I snapped my gaze to hers.

"Nadia," I said somewhat harshly. "There is no expedition anymore. No one out there cares about us any longer. No one will ever see your movie."

She dropped her gaze down, twisting her fingers in her lap.

"I know…" she said softly. "It just gives me something to do, takes my mind off things."

I couldn't stand her defeated expression. My heart twisted and ached. Who was I to tell her how best to deal with what all of us had been going through? I shifted closer to her and hugged her so tight she squeaked.

"Do it if it helps, then," I said softly, kissing the hair over her temple. "Do whatever helps, Nadia."

She patted my hand.

"Do you want to see the recording of last night?" she asked.

"No." I released her from our embrace and headed to the partition. "I need to see him."

Nadia made a move to stop me. "Val. What if he attacks you? Svetlana wants to test him for *kronite* exposure."

"For what?" I paused.

"*Kronite*, the toxic gas that leaked into the air supply in the mess hall a few days ago. Most of the crew had a terrible reaction to it. Wyck and Vrateus were attacked when they went out to the supply room after that."

"Is that what she tested me for last night?" We were in the middle of the conversation when she'd asked me to breathe in some tube. I'd been too distracted by so many other things to ask for details at that point.

That was what had caused the crew to lose their minds—*kronite*.

Nadia nodded. "Yours came back negative, but if Malahki was in the mess hall when the leak happened—"

"No." I shook my head resolutely. Malahki was nothing like the beast-like creatures who'd attacked us. "He is not like them. He will never hurt me."

He might've called himself a monster after his transformation, but even when he fucked me, delirious with lust, I knew I could make him stop any minute if I wished. I just happened *not* to want to stop him. Malahki's way of "lovemaking" was not something I would ever consider before, but I had enjoyed being with him. I craved it even.

Maybe whatever changes Malahki had been going through somehow had affected me, too. My feelings and emotions had synched with his so easily. We ended up resonating in love as well as we had in friendship before.

I missed him.

"Nadia, I need to see him. Now." I stepped behind the partition, heading for the door out of our room.

She caught up with me, taking my hand in hers.

"You have every right to be angry with Malahki," she said, misunderstanding my intentions. "He lied, and he kept you away from us all this time. But things really could've been worse if you stayed on the ship with me the day of the crash. Other than Vrateus and Wyck, there was really no one else. Vrateus did what he could to keep the crew under control. Wyck had to fight them off me. If there were two of us to protect, I'm not even sure if anyone could stop the males if they rushed us in a free-for-all stampede. And then…who knows where we would be."

Dread slithered cold down my spine at the thought of how much worse things could've been for both of us.

I drew her into another hug.

"I'm so, so sorry about what happened to you, Nadia."

She hugged me too, patting my back soothingly.

"I'm lucky, I got my Wyck out of this," she said, with a sigh. "But I'm glad you avoided facing the crew altogether. Don't be too harsh on Malahki. Okay?"

"I won't," I promised as she released me from our embrace.

She nodded with a smile. "Let's go see if he's tame enough this morning to have visitors."

Svetlana was having breakfast in the main living area of the ship, along with Wyck and Vrateus.

"Morning." She waved her hand, smiling.

Both men nodded in greeting.

"Morning." I gave them all a smile in return. It was nice to have people around—people who wouldn't try to bite your head off, literally.

Each of the three had a cup and a plate in front of them. A tray with tea and toast stood on the side of the table, untouched.

"Is that for Malahki?" I asked.

Wyck grunted, stretching his neck. "I'll take it to him." He made a move to get up.

"I can do it." I stopped him.

He gave me an incredulous look.

"He'll rip you apart," he warned me. "He tossed a cup at Vrateus's head and punched me in the face when we tried to deliver his dinner last night." He rubbed his jaw where Malahki's last blow must've landed. "Svetlana still didn't get a chance to test him for *kronite* exposure, but if you ask me, he must've taken a huge gulp of it."

"He didn't. He's spent almost all of his time with me." Other than a few trips to hide food, Malahki hadn't left the gardens before our trip down the garbage chute. The last part of his transformation, including the sudden surge of aggression, happened just yesterday, after the leak. "I'm so sorry, guys." I scraped a hand over my face, feeling guilty for leaving them to deal with the enraged *damirian*. "Malahki... Well, he's just been a little unstable after his change."

"A little?" Wyck scoffed, still rubbing his jaw.

"It's the transformation," Vrateus agreed with me, taking a sip from the mug in his hands. "I've read about *damirian* men. They're unstoppable in battle. In the early days of interplanetary conflicts, other nations always sought an alliance with Ak'ae, to have the *damirian* army on their side."

"If that's what he wanted to be, I'm happy it worked. But a part of me will always miss the old Malahki," Svetlana said wistfully. "I liked working in the gardens with him. His unaffected calm had always been so soothing in this crazy place."

Her words felt like a knife through my heart. Was Svetlana right, though? Were some parts of Malahki gone for good? Irrecoverably lost? I loved all his pieces, every single one—from the inferno of his passion to the serenity of his calm.

"No. He is still there," I protested, clasping my hands so tight, my fingers ached. "Malahki is…well, Malahki. He hasn't changed. He's just…evolved. All of him is still there, old and new. I—" I picked up the tray from the table. "I'll have to go to him."

"I'll come with you." Wyck grabbed a metal rod from a shelf in the corner.

I glared at him. "That won't be necessary—"

"Go with her, Wyck," Vrateus cut me off. "Make sure he's stable."

Wyck took the tray from me, heading to the escape capsule door. I had no choice but to follow. The door appeared as if it had been cut through before and then fixed after. Wyck shifted the metal rod under his other arm then turned the handle.

I touched his arm quickly, begging, "Please don't hurt Malahki."

He glowered. "Let's hope he won't give me any reasons."

I tripped over Malahki when Wyck opened the door. My *damirian* lay on the floor in the threshold.

"Valya," he croaked, catching me in his arms before I could hit the floor.

Tension that had been seizing me since our separation drained from my muscles the moment his arms wrapped around me.

"Hey! Watch it." Wyck deposited the tray on one of the seats and moved to my "rescue," wielding the rod over his head.

"No, Wyck." I shielded Malahki with both arms. "I'm fine."

"Get out, Wyck," Malahki growled menacingly, pressing me to his chest like the most cherished treasure.

Wyck took a wider stance, crossing his arms over his chest, demonstrating he wasn't going anywhere without making sure I was safe.

"Are you sure, Val?" he asked.

"I'm good, Wyck. Honestly." Malahki's burly arms crushed me to him without leaving a sliver of space to move, but he was careful not to squeeze too hard for his embrace to be painful. "He won't hurt me." I wholeheartedly believed that.

"Leave!" Malahki ordered in a deep, raspy voice.

Wyck tossed him a glare before moving his gaze my way again.

"If you need anything, just knock on the door," he told me before leaving.

Malahki shoved the door closed behind the *errock*. I noticed the door paneling was shredded and torn off on the inside. Had Malahki been clawing at it?

Sitting on the floor with me in his lap, he buried his face in my neck, rocking us softly. Sweet, achy tenderness swelled in my heart.

"Are you okay, baby?" I ran my hands through his hair. It was tangled, his braid undone.

"Valya," he groaned. "Don't ever leave me like that."

"I needed some time—"

He shook his head wildly.

"Yell at me. Get angry with me. Punch me if you must. But don't just walk away, without talking to me first. Please. Don't leave me alone. I've nearly gone insane, thinking you may never come back, that you may never even want to look at me again."

Compassion tightened around my chest, as firm as his hug.

"I was going to talk, Malahki. But I had to think about all of it first."

After the initial excitement at seeing Nadia well and alive, I'd had a sharp feeling of betrayal by Malahki. Disappointment and hurt came right after. I felt sorry for all the time I'd spent hiding, dreading for my life and safety, when I could've been with Nadia on my ship, all along. I'd had no idea that Nadia had been hiding, too, that they had moved to the ship only recently.

"I had to talk to Nadia and Svetlana," I said to Malahki. "I needed to hear their side of the story to get the full picture."

"I'm sorry. I'm so, so sorry," he murmured against my skin. "Please stay with me."

I threaded my fingers through the long strands of his hair, smoothing the tangled tresses.

"I'm not going anywhere, Malahki," I whispered in his ear, then kissed the corner of his mouth. "I understand the decisions you've made and appreciate what you've done for me. But you have to trust me, too."

His shoulders relaxed a little, though he still gripped on to me desperately like to a lifesaver.

"At first, I didn't know you well enough to trust you not to rush to see Nadia, risking your life," he said. "If I told you what was being done to her, I feared you might plot to help her behind my back, and I knew you wouldn't succeed. Later, I hadn't seen Nadia for a while, I thought she truly was dead. Telling you that no longer felt like a lie."

He took my face between his large hands, peering deep into my eyes.

"I'm sorry, Valya. I promise never to lie to you ever again."

I linked my hands behind his neck, breathing in his warm familiar scent.

"I missed you, Malahki," I whispered. "So, so much."

He groaned, spearing his fingers through my hair. "I can't sleep without you, Valya, can't think clearly without you. I need you." He kept kissing my neck, my face, my hair. "I've never needed anyone so much before. I didn't know if you were sad or hurting, and it drove me mad. I need to know you're happy and if not, I want to do everything to make you happy."

Basking in his affection like in sunshine, I shifted my hips a little and made him groan again. His erection was trapped between us, I realized, hard like a rock.

He jerked his pelvis back, away from me, sliding me back toward his knees.

"Does it hurt?" I murmured in his ear.

"You have no idea." There was so much longing in his raspy voice.

"Can I do something about it?"

"You are the only one who can." He glanced at me.

I lifted my hand to the closure of my suit.

"It's a good thing I'm here, then." I smiled.

His eyes flashed with heat. Sliding his hands inside my suit, he slipped it off my shoulders and down my arms. I stood up as he peeled it off me. Getting down on his knees, he unbuckled and took off my boots, leaving me completely naked for him.

My feet on each side of his thighs, I stood over him as he slid his hands up my bare legs. Grabbing my thighs, he yanked me closer and buried his face between them.

I gasped, grabbing on to the backs of the two seats behind him to keep my balance.

His long hair tickled the inside of my thighs, his tongue sliding between my heated folds. The intense need for him that had been simmering under my skin all night, exploded in desire impossible to contain.

"Yes, Malahki," I whimpered as he feasted on me. "Please…"

Pleasure rippled through me, building higher and higher. I gripped the padded seat backs, riding his face with abandon.

My knees trembled and bucked as the orgasm hit me. If he hadn't held my legs, I would've fallen. After squeezing every single shudder of pleasure out of me with his dexterous tongue, he released my thighs, letting me slide down into his lap.

"When did you learn how to do that?" I murmured into his shoulder as he glided his hands over my body in sweet, soothing caress.

"Yesterday."

"Just yesterday?" I thought back to all the amazing things he'd done to me at the farm and then in the shower.

"I kissed your sex, and you liked it," he said simply.

"I did," I confessed, gazing into his eyes. They glowed with swirls of the brightest tints of orange and red.

"I feel acutely every reaction of your body, Valya, and I learn. If you like something, I do more of it. If your body doesn't explode with pleasure when I do something else, I change that."

I didn't think there had been any time for "learning" when he ravaged me against the wall yesterday. Apparently, he'd managed to note and memorize things when I thought he'd been too desperate for a release to even think.

"I'll still need to learn a lot." He moved one of my braids behind my shoulder. "But I'm looking forward to it."

I smiled, playing with a long strand of his hair.

"How about you?" I asked. "Will you teach me what *you* like?"

He released a short laugh. It came out strained. His body grew even more rigid.

"Spirits, that'd be a short lesson, Valya! I'd like anything and everything you do to me or let me do to you."

I slid my hands down the hard planes of the muscles of his chest. The bright colorful swirls on his skin came to life under my touch, following the tips of my fingers.

"You're holding back."

"Valya," he groaned. "Lately, all I want is either to fight or to fuck. And I'm not interested in *fighting* you."

"All right." I let my hand travel down the ridges of his flat belly toward the closure of his pants. "Let's not fight, then."

He leaned back, giving me a better access to the waistband of his pants. I opened the closure then dipped my hand lower. The soft touch of the thin appendages that grew around his shaft made me smile.

"What are these?" I asked, moving my fingers among their cluster.

"Feelers." He exhaled in a gasp the moment my fingers brushed his hard length.

"What are they for?"

"To give you pleasure." He panted.

"Me?"

With a strangled groan, he nodded, then lifted his hips to yank his pants down. The tapered length of his erection sprang free, the feelers around it straining toward my hand.

"Is that all they do?" I asked.

"That is their only function." He got up, lifting me in his arms. "Their sole purpose is to caress you while I'm inside you."

My inner muscles spasmed at the idea of having the gentle sensation I'd just experienced on my fingers on my most intimate place. Yesterday morning, I hadn't fully appreciated that. It all had happened so fast and so suddenly. My first time with Malahki remained but a wild swirl of need, passion, and ecstasy in my mind.

He placed me on the padded seat that had been fully reclined into a single bed.

"Right now, giving you pleasure is the only purpose of *my* life, too," he said softly, bringing his large body over mine.

My skin tingled from anticipation.

"You're holding back," I whispered again as he hovered over me, our bodies barely touching.

"I want to savor every moment with you, even if it's the moment of tormenting need."

No one had ever looked at me with so much tenderness and adoration. My heart beat wildly as my insides melted with an enormous feeling for him that bubbled and grew in my chest.

"Oh, Malahki. I need you, too. So, so much." I raked my fingers through his black-as-night hair.

He lowered his lips to mine in a kiss as he entered me.

A gasp of pleasure escaped my lips, and he swallowed it, devouring my mouth.

I hooked my legs around his middle, anchoring him to me. The tender feelers stroked me as he began to move. They caressed me gently at first, their touch like a silky glide of flower petals. The faster Malahki thrust however, the firmer their touch became. They rubbed against me, tightly winding the coil of pleasure inside me and making it ready to explode.

I moaned wildly as the orgasm rolled through me in swells of ecstasy. Clinging to Malahki's strong shoulders, I sensed him going still for a moment before his release rushed through him, too. He pumped it into me in deep, powerful thrusts.

"Spirits take me…" he groaned, rolling to his side and taking me with him. "Stay with me, Valya." He kissed my hair, pressing me tight to his chest again. "Stay with me," he repeated like a mantra.

The warm feeling inside me expanded so much, it appeared to fill the entire capsule.

"I'm here, sweetheart." I caressed his back in long, soothing strokes. "With you is the only place I ever want to be."

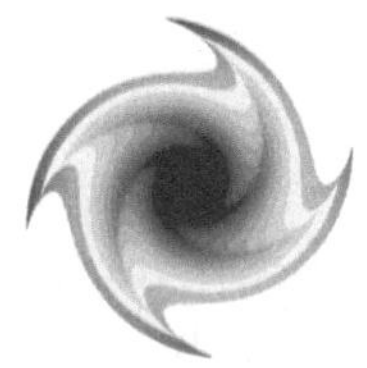

Chapter 16

Valentina

"Be careful, okay?" My fingers wrapped around the belt with weapons that Malahki wore around his shoulder, I couldn't bring myself to let go.

It was two days after we'd come to the ship to fight its inhabitants but found the only four friendly people on the Dark Anomaly instead. With Malahki and I joining them, the supplies in the food generators of our ship had to be stretched even thinner, now. Vrateus and Malahki were leaving to pick up the preserves that we'd hidden in the gardens and other places of the Dark Anomaly.

Malahki took my face between his hands.

"I'm not going to war, just to get some food," he said softly.

Vrateus brushed by, adjusting his weapons. "Isn't going for food just like going to war?" he asked.

"You're not helping, captain," Malahki snapped, then turned to me with a much gentler expression. "I'm better equipped to fight a war, too."

"That's not helping much, either." I shook my head with a faint smile. "I don't want you to get in any situations where there is a risk to your life or health."

He arched an eyebrow.

"We're in the wrong place for that. There's always some risk on the Dark Anomaly. Even while staying here behind locked doors, you're not as safe as I'd like you to be. I hate parting with you." He gave me a long kiss.

"We won't be long," Vrateus assured me when Malahki finally released me from his arms. "Wyck is staying with you, just in case."

Malahki glared at the *errock*, who met his glare with an equally reproachful stare. There obviously was no love lost between these two. Malahki had a lingering hostility toward the entire group of the *errocks* of the Dark Anomaly. And Wyck couldn't forget my *damirian's* recent punches and blows. The dark bruises on Wyck's clay-red skin would still take some time to disappear completely, especially since being the proud man that he was, Wyck refused to use the medical capsule to speed up the healing.

"Be careful," I said again as Malahki and Vrateus stepped out into the corridor. Each carried an empty bag over his shoulder to collect the food containers. Both of them wore oxygen masks around their necks connected to tubes linking them to the air tanks on their backs.

"We won't be long." Malahki waved to me before Wyck rolled the thick metal block on rails, closing the entrance to the ship. Nadia helped him lock all the chains and deadbolts.

Despite immediately missing Malahki, I felt the safest I'd ever been since our landing on the Dark Anomaly. For once, I didn't need to listen carefully to every noise around me or get ready to bolt and hide at the first sign of danger. It felt comforting to have friends in this hostile place.

"Val." Svetlana touched my shoulder. "Malahki undid some of the repairs we've done on the capsule door—"

"Oh, I know I'm so sorry." I rubbed my eyes. "I'll fix it."

"Can you look at it now, please?" She gestured in the capsule's direction. The subtle urgency in her expression made me pause for a moment.

"Sure." I followed her as she took her tablet off the table and headed for the capsule.

We climbed in.

"Svetlana," I started apologizing again. "I'm really sorry about the damage. *Damirian* men—"

She closed the door behind us quickly, then turned to me.

"It's not about the door," she said hurriedly. "I mean, we do have to fix it eventually, and I know you will do a much better job than we did, since you know so much more about this spacecraft. But I need to talk to you about something else."

"Okay." I sat in one of the chairs. "What is it all about."

She rubbed her eyes, and I realized how tired she looked.

"Did you sleep well?" I asked.

She shook her head with a faint smile.

"I haven't slept for a few nights now. I've been thinking…" she let her voice trail off, as if unsure how to proceed, then lifted her dark-brown eyes to mine. "Can you give me some numbers in terms of speed, range, and engine power of both your ship and the escape capsule? I may need their weight capacity, fuel consumption… And a few other things, like how do you think the spacecraft would perform under certain conditions."

"Why do you need all this information?" I asked.

She hesitated, but understanding slowly dawned on me.

"Are you planning to travel some place?" I asked tentatively, afraid to voice my guess out loud.

"Maybe," she replied, just as cautiously.

My mind had been so consumed with survival that I hadn't thought about escape at all lately, not after Malahki had convincingly proven to me, using charts and graphs, that it wasn't possible.

Was he wrong? And if so, was it deliberate?

A doubt about my man slithered inside me. I hated it, hated to think he might've lied to me about that, too.

I cleared my throat.

"Malahki says leaving is impossible," I said, with a hollow feeling in my stomach.

"He's right." She nodded confidently.

Despite it being disappointing news, something inside me lifted at her words. Knowing that Malahki hadn't lied this time.

The problem with someone having lied to you once was that even if the lie was forgiven, trust didn't come automatically anymore. It would take some time for me to stop doubting Malahki.

"If you can't leave here, where do you want to go, then?" I asked Svetlana.

She inhaled slowly, leaning against the mutilated door.

"I'd love for you to look carefully at the door repair we've done. It's conveniently exposed now that Malahki ripped all the siding and insulation off it." She pursed her lips in an amused accusation.

"He was just trying to get to me." I felt the need to defend him.

"Talk about going lust-crazy," she wiggled her eyebrows. "I hope he made it worth it for you afterwards."

"Oh yes, he did," I said with a soft giggle, and she smiled broadly at me.

"Thankfully, a few of the males of the Dark Anomaly make it worth landing in this place, don't they?" She laughed, and I joined her, happy that after everything she'd gone through here, Svetlana could still laugh the way she did, cheerfully and carefree.

"Okay," I said, still with a smile lingering on my lips. "I can do it right now. I'll just need to get the tools back at the ship. Are you planning to disconnect the capsule from the ship at some point?"

"Yes." She lowered her voice as if afraid that Wyck or Nadia would hear us from behind the door. "Nadia told me she tried to take off in it, right after your landing, but she got an error message. Though she doesn't believe there was a malfunction with the system, she says she doesn't have enough knowledge to accurately diagnose it if it was. Can you look at it?"

I nodded. Part of my training for the mission was studying in detail both the ship and the capsule. Unlike the onboard engineers, I wouldn't be able to perform many major repairs on either, but I knew their systems explicitly and could identify and troubleshoot a long list of malfunctions if needed.

"I can run the diagnostics, but what good would it do? Even if both craft are in perfect shape, it's impossible to leave here, isn't it?"

Svetlana sat down in the seat opposite of mine. Her fingers drummed a nervous rhythm on the surface of the tablet in her lap.

"I wonder if we've tried everything yet," she said, her eyes focused right ahead of her.

"What do you mean?" I shifted closer to her. "Are you saying there is a way to get the fuck out of here?" My heart raced as my mind reeled at the idea.

"Listen." She placed her hand on mine. "I don't want anyone to know anything about this conversation, do you hear me? Vrateus would freak if he knew. I tried to escape here once, and I'd be long dead if he hadn't stopped me. I don't want Wyck or Nadia to have any false hopes, either."

"But do you really think there's a way?" I stared at her imploringly. Hope flickered in my heart, refusing to leave now.

"No, that's not what I said." Svetlana shook her head. "But there is one possibility I haven't fully explored yet. I need those numbers for more accurate calculations on my theory. That doesn't mean the calculations would end up giving us any viable results. It could end up being just another discarded theory. I have at least a hundred of those by now. So…"

"I see." I heaved a long sigh.

My hope was crushed before it even had a chance to take root, but it was still painful to let it go. I understood why Svetlana wanted to spare the others this disappointment.

"Okay, tell me exactly what you need, and I'll see if I can get it." I moved to the seat in front of the control panel and brought it to life.

Screens with familiar displays lit up. Everything looked in perfect order, deceivingly convincing me that all I had to do would be to take off and fly free wherever I wished.

"Okay, so…" Svetlana sat into the co-pilot's seat and turned on her tablet. "First give me the numbers, please. Then, I'll give you the parameters of the conditions, and you explain to me exactly what your spacecraft is capable of."

"Which craft are we talking about? The main ship or the escape capsule?"

"Both. They each have their strengths and weaknesses, I presume?"

"Yes, the capsule is more powerful and agile, while the ship is more suitable for interstellar travel."

"I'll look at both," she concluded with a nod.

"From what I see right now, though, neither of them would combat the gravity of this place," I exhaled heavily, scrolling through rows of data on the main screen. "The latest numbers come from the system analysis of our landing, and it says here—"

"No." Svetlana shook her head with a confident smile. "*I* have the latest analysis and the most complete data. No one knows the anomaly GR-A8502 as well as I do—no one in the world. I've been studying it very closely for months now. In and out."

A FEW DAYS LATER, SVETLANA AND I SAT IN THE PILOTS' SEATS OF the capsule again. This time, we were about to take the craft for a ride—a test drive of sorts.

"Well, so far so good." I glanced back at the door while disconnecting the capsule from the main ship.

All the preliminary testing I'd done on it after the latest repair told me the door was solid. The instrument displays on the control panel said that it held fine, too. But the visual confirmation of seeing the door closed gave me the most satisfaction.

"You did a great job on it," Svetlana agreed.

"Thanks. Am I going straight from here?" I asked, turning to face forward again.

Though Svetlana and I had planned and mapped the route beforehand, I felt apprehensive. I didn't need the confirmation as much as just hearing someone's voice to reassure me.

"Yes." Svetlana sounded a bit too cheerful herself, nervously so.

Or maybe she was just excited to go on a "road trip." It wasn't every day that we got to go outside of the habitable sector of the Dark Anomaly. For me, this was the very first time ever since coming here.

I drove the capsule away from the ship manually, along the uneven surface of the disk's edge. With the transparent front of the capsule, the lights of the Dark Anomaly surrounded us.

"It's beautiful," I couldn't hold back my appreciation for the visual spectacle all around us.

"Absolutely gorgeous," Svetlana agreed with a short laugh. "I would love the lights if I didn't hate them so much."

I'd spent less time here than Svetlana, most of it in the gardens, with no windows, but I shared her feelings toward the lights. To me, the Dark Anomaly appeared like a cruel trick, a trap—mesmerizingly beautiful on the outside and deadly on the inside.

"Well, let's see if we can leave here, one day," I muttered under my breath.

Svetlana shot me a glance.

We had an unspoken rule. After our very first conversation, we didn't speak about the final purpose of all the work the two of us had done in the past several days. As Svetlana had said, there was no reason to give hope to the others. By avoiding talking about it ourselves, we also tried not to let our own hope grow. At the back of my mind, however, I knew the ultimate purpose of all of this was to leave this God-cursed place. Despite my best intentions, the hope remained in my heart.

"Do you want me to take it over the edge onto the surface, now?" I asked Svetlana to confirm the next point of our travel plan.

"Yes, please." She gripped the armrests, her gaze firmly ahead.

I steered the capsule to the left, maneuvering it from the edge onto the rim of the disk's surface.

"Just make sure to stay within the zone." Svetlana pointed at the yellow-lit area on the screen of the control panel.

"Sure." I adjusted the controls, staying on the route we'd worked out before.

"It looks great," Svetlana said hesitantly, as if needing my confirmation, too.

The escape capsule's systems performed without an issue. I'd expected that after running the tests and diagnostics on them. Still, it was a relief to see the engines in action.

"So far so good," I agreed quietly, afraid to jinx it.

When our expedition was planned, people on Earth had just discovered that the Dark Anomaly had a hard disk at its center. No one would've thought about driving on it, though. Despite Svetlana's thorough calculations, things always could go wrong.

"Is she okay, then?" Svetlana tipped her chin at the control panel where the screens and dials of the instruments displayed the continuous analysis of the spacecraft's systems.

I nodded silently, concentrating on keeping the capsule on course on the uneven surface.

"Let's take her in?" she suggested.

"Okay." I bit my lip, steering the capsule more to the left. The map on the control panel shifted into the orange area now, several hundred feet closer to the center of the Dark Anomaly's disk.

Svetlana's knuckles turned white as she gripped the armrests tighter.

"Do you feel it? The pull?" She gasped.

According to Svetlana, the gravity of the Dark Anomaly was stronger at its center. It pulled objects from its rim along its surface.

"Yes." I sharply adjusted the steering to stay on route.

"Do you think the engines would handle one more increase?" she asked, her voice breathy.

I didn't reply, just shifted the controls to take the capsule slightly left again, another three hundred feet closer to the center. Our path remained parallel to the rim of the disk but shifted closer to the center as I entered the red zone.

The pull was even stronger here. I flexed my arms to keep a firm grip on the controls.

"This isn't normal." Perspiration misted my forehead from effort and concentration.

Nothing was "normal" about this godforsaken place.

Svetlana quickly punched in her tablet, periodically glancing at my control panel.

"Actually, this is very much within the range I expected," she said.

My arms ached, and my hands started to cramp from clamping

onto the controls so hard. Svetlana might have expected this, but the readings on my screens shifted very much outside of the range I preferred them to be.

"Listen, I need to get out of here." Even my lips hurt because I'd been biting them so hard.

Svetlana nodded quickly. "Okay. I'm good. I have enough data to work with, now."

I swerved back into the orange and then into the yellow zone, relieved to be away from the power that had tried to wrestle the controls from me. Maneuvering the capsule from the rim to the edge of the disk again, I glanced Svetlana's way as she furiously punched in the numbers and scrolled through calculations on her tablet.

"So, what do you think?" I asked her softly. Despite striving not to hope, I did anyway. I desperately hoped her theory would work.

"Well." She placed the tablet into her lap and folded her hands over it. "I guess it's time to share this with the others."

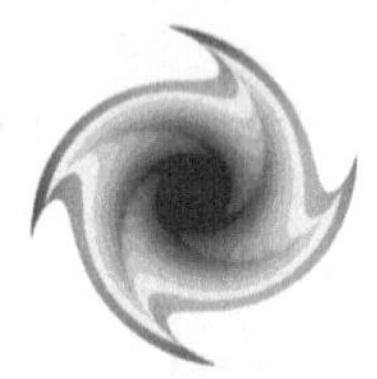

Chapter 17

Valentina

"Fuck, yes!" Malahki exclaimed so loudly that Nadia jumped in her seat, and Lesh woke up from his nap, hissing in warning. "I volunteer!"

"Honey." I took his hand in mine and placed it in my lap.

All six of us sat around the table laden with tablet inserts. Svetlana had very carefully mentioned her plan for escaping the Dark Anomaly, which got Malahki so excited. The other two men seemed just as agitated. Nadia had a huge smile on her face.

"It's not that easy." Svetlana lifted her hand. "The risk is…well, huge."

"Send me first," Malahki insisted. "I'll test it for you."

"That's not how it works," Svetlana explained patiently. "It's not possible to do it one by one. We'll all go, or no one does."

Malahki shifted his gaze to me. Concern replaced his enthusiastic expression. As eager as he'd been to put his own life on the line, he obviously wasn't as willing to risk mine.

"What exactly are our chances for success?" he asked Svetlana, not taking his eyes off me.

She rubbed her face, placing her elbows on the table. I knew she hadn't been sleeping well. I had trouble sleeping myself lately. After the first night spent in my old bed, I'd moved with Malahki into the escape capsule. We had the back two seats converted into a bed. With him next to me, I'd been able to fall asleep easier, but I woke up often through the night.

Whenever I would go back to the ship to get a cup of tea when I couldn't sleep, Svetlana would be sitting at the table, surrounded by tablet inserts and going over her calculations again and again.

"I can't tell you the exact chance of success," she replied to Malahki. "It's impossible to calculate that precisely because the power field of the Dark Anomaly fluctuates so sporadically. I've been working with ranges, not exact numbers, and even that is not guaranteed, of course. Look here."

She grabbed a data slate and slid it into her tablet frame.

"That's the visual of the energy field of the Dark Anomaly."

We lowered our heads over the screen with the 3D model of the Anomaly's disk slowly rotating on it.

"The main part of the Dark Anomaly is the field of energy that spins through space not unlike a whirlpool of water," Svetlana started. "It drags in objects as it travels, pulling them into the center of the field where the hard core of the crashed spaceships has formed over a long period of time. Just like a whirlpool, the energy spins around the edge of the disk, its pull growing stronger and faster the closer to the centre it gets. The power compresses the ships, with the pressure getting exponentially stronger the closer to the center they move."

She slid her finger along the radius of the disk toward the bulging center.

"All this energy needs to be released at some point. Similar to a whirlpool, it blasts out from the very center of the disk." She traced the thin dotted lines that came out from the bulging centre of the disk on her diagram. "Unlike a whirlpool, however, where the water is dragged down, forming a funnel, the centre of the Anomaly's disk is raised on both sides. Its disk actually has the shape of a flat, wide spinning top toy, with the rays of energy blasting out from both sides, the top and the bottom. The power of the blasts is strong enough to propel the energy out for long distances."

Vrateus scrubbed his chin.

"The same energy that dragged us all in here is blasting out into the space from the centre?"

Svetlana nodded. "Yes."

"So, all we have to do is make it to the centre of the Dark Anomaly then let the force field shoot us out?" Wyck asked, sceptically.

Svetlana swallowed hard, rubbing her throat.

"Technically, yes," she said. "In reality, there are some serious challenges."

"Like what?" Nadia shifted closer.

"The energy travels in a loop. The trajectory of the field is similar to that of an electromagnet. Most of what's released from the center curves, spreading like a fountain or a flower, then comes back to the edge of the disk."

Svetlana moved her finger in an arch from the center of the disk down to the outer edge of it.

"It sweeps through space in a curve, grabbing whatever objects happen to be in its path, then carries them back to the edge of the disk."

"That's how we all ended up here," Malahki concluded.

"That's how," Svetlana echoed. "I'm still not entirely clear on why it takes some objects and leaves the others, but I suspect it has something to do with energy waves. That's why the Dark Anomaly sucks in powered spaceships and probes, but doesn't touch asteroids and other celestial bodies."

"Fascinating." Vrateus shook his head, staring at her. It wasn't entirely clear what fascinated him the most, the discoveries Svetlana had shared or the woman herself.

Malahki kept his gaze on the tablet screen. "That means that even if we manage to catch a ride with the energy stream emitting from the center of the Dark Anomaly, we'll risk being dragged back where we started."

Svetlana heaved a long breath.

"Yes, but I believe a portion of the energy at the very center is blasted with enough power to separate from the field. The trick is for us to get to that precise location."

"Because if we're in any way off, we're dead," Malahki said what Svetlana wouldn't.

"And that is the biggest risk," she concluded, adding, "With a number of other risks too, like losing control and crashing into the center on the way to it or getting lost in space after we leave."

"How are we getting to the center?" Nadia asked. "Walking?" She touched her still perfectly flat belly.

"No, it's way too far to walk," Svetlana replied, adding with a small shrug, "and perilous. This ship is not designed to travel along a surface. We'd have to drive the escape capsule to the center."

Vrateus stared at his hands folded on the table in front of him. "If we succeed, what will happen next? After we're blasted into space?"

"The capsule is not designed for long-distance travel," I explained, thinking about all the perils we would have to face every step of the way. Would all of them think it was worth it? To risk everything for the slim chance of getting out of here?

"Our original plan was to send a distress signal once we'd left here," Nadia chimed in. "A ship was supposed to pick us up to take us back to Earth."

We all looked at Svetlana, since she was the one with the plan, now.

"That would still be our best…our *only* option. Except that no one will be waiting for us out there. Once we're clear of the Dark Anomaly's force field, we'd lay a course for the closest traffic route." She heaved a sigh. "Then, we'll turn our locator signals on and wait for someone to find us and pick us up. Otherwise…" Her voice trailed off.

It was clear what she meant without her voicing it.

"Otherwise, we'd be drifting through space in a craft the size of a bus until the oxygen ran out or one of the other life-support systems failed."

Silence hung over the table, as everyone was absorbing the words she had said and those she mercifully hadn't.

"It's been at least several decades since either one of us traveled through space." Nadia spoke first. "I hope traffic has increased since then, and someone will be out there to pick us up, eventually."

"Omphi is the closest planet. In my time, there was a human exploration station orbiting it," Svetlana said.

I searched my brain for the information on the water world Omphi among so many things I'd learned in preparation for our mission.

"There were several small floating settlements on Omphi, the year of our expedition," I said. "Most of them were from Earth, but in partnership with other species, too."

"They might've grown in the…how long has it been, now?" Nadia turned to me. "How much time would've passed on Earth since we've been gone? Sixty? Seventy years?"

I stared at her in silence. The enormity of the time warp rushed over me anew. I counted every day spent on the Dark Anomaly, yet the cruelty of it was to fully comprehend what it meant in terms of human lives. My brother and his wife would be dead by now. My baby nieces would be more than twice my age. They would've gone through a lifetime worth of experiences by now, all without me…

Malahki took my hand, squeezing it firmly.

"Yes, between sixty and seventy years," he replied to Nadia for me.

I swallowed around the tightness in my throat, composing myself. It'd been a millennium and a half since Malahki left his world. No one he ever knew would be alive anymore. If our escape worked, for him, it'd be like visiting a completely new world.

"I'll calculate the flight path that will take us to the closest most-traveled route," I offered. No one knew exactly how things would've changed out there while we'd been stuck in here. Like Svetlana, I hoped the space traffic had increased, but it could have very well gone the other way, too. Since our disappearance, the Federation might've imposed travel restrictions on this area. Omphi's exploration could have ended. So many things could've changed.

We all sat in silence again. None of us had ever had this possibility before—to leave here.

Finally, Svetlana cleared her throat.

"We need to consider the alternative," she said softly. "The risk of going through with this is great, every step of the way. Not all of us may make it, or none of us will…"

She swallowed hard, moving her gaze around the table, from one face to another.

"What is the alternative?" Nadia asked in a subdued voice.

"Staying here," Vrateus replied, raking his fingers through the wide stripe of long fur on his head.

"Staying? When we can leave?" Nadia narrowed her eyes at him. "The Dark Anomaly is worse than a prison. What do we have going for us here?"

"Well, the crew is less of a threat, now," Svetlana pointed out.

That was true. Most of the crew had died by now, either by exterminating each other or as a result of the chemical leak into the air-supply system. A few handfuls might be surviving on the different shipwrecks, but taking into account their propensity to self-destruction, they wouldn't last long. With the six of us coming together, we were stronger than ever as a group, capable of fighting and surviving.

Hers was the voice of reason, but getting even a sliver of hope for true freedom, my brain refused to listen. My mind clung to that one chance to be free.

I gazed at the faces of the others.

The reflection of my hope was clearly displayed on Malahki's face. Nadia bit her lip. Svetlana kept her expression neutral. But the expressions of both Vrateus and Wyck struck me the most.

Having lived on the Dark Anomaly all of their adult lives, I'd expected them to be most reluctant to leave. But there was so much light, hope, and excitement on their faces, it left no doubt they longed to break free from this place, too.

Svetlana must've seen it, too. She stroked Vrateus's hand on the table.

"You don't want me to risk my life," she said, "and I'd so much rather stay here with you than risk yours. I'm happy wherever you are, even here, as long as we're together. I don't mind staying."

Nadia glanced at Wyck, who remained silent, even as his face said it all.

"I do," she said quickly. "I do mind staying if there is even the slightest chance to leave. I'd risk it all, for the baby." She crossed her both arms over her belly as if trying to protect the tiny being inside.

"Wherever you go, I'll go." Wyck wrapped his arm around her shoulders, and she stroked the hard, dark ridges of his knuckles.

Even if her pregnancy progressed and ended well. I understood the added horror of their situation if we all stayed here. With all of us eventually aging and dying, Wyck and Nadia's son would be destined to live the rest of his days as the Dark Anomaly's sole survivor. He'd live and die completely alone—a future no parent would wish for their child.

The alternative of course carried the risk of all of us dying while trying to escape the clutches of the Dark Anomaly.

"Staying here carries challenges, too," Malahki commented. "The support systems are deteriorating. The six of us could never maintain them at the same level as before. We'd need to significantly reduce the habitable sector in size."

"We're running out of food," Wyck added.

Svetlana inclined her head, not meeting their eyes. "We can clean out and maintain a smaller section of the habitable sector. We can revive the gardens for food supply."

"Wyck needs meat to survive," Nadia argued. "His species require a large amount of it in their diets. He can't live on plants alone."

I suspected that would be an issue for Malahki as well. In his male form, he had developed a new craving for meat, when he'd abhorred even the smell of it before. With the *vasai* farm destroyed and the wild *vasai* possibly all exterminated due to the lack of oxygen, chemical leak, and overhunting, there was no source of meat on the Dark Anomaly at all.

Wyck gazed at Nadia warmly.

"With the baby coming," he said, "we'll need doctors. Even your machine here," he tipped his chin in the direction of the medical capsule, "is confused about what to do with the human-*errock* baby.

It doesn't have enough information even to monitor your pregnancy properly."

The system was definitely not programmed with detailed information on interspecies pregnancies. Something like that had not been planned as a possibility during this expedition.

Vrateus placed his hand on top of Svetlana's.

"You were ready to give up your life to leave here," he said softly, referring to Svetlana's failed escape attempt months ago when he stopped her from leaving, saving her life.

She lifted her eyes to his with a sad smile.

"Yes. I'll give up my life in a heartbeat if it leads to people learning something new. But I'm not ready to risk yours." She shook her head.

"Svetlana is right," Malahki said, unexpectedly. "We need to carefully consider the alternative, what we'd be giving up. Here, we have a relatively safe place, which we could possibly make habitable enough to survive for decades if not longer. That is something to think about before launching ourselves out there, to possibly face immediate death."

I stroked his hand with my fingers, making the multi-colored swirls come to life on his skin. The mesmerising colors easily rivaled the beauty of the Dark Anomaly's lights, in my opinion.

"Are you talking caution, my vicious *damirian* warrior?" I murmured, trying to lighten the heavy atmosphere hanging over the table. The choices we had to make weren't easy.

"I'm with Svetlana on this one," he said, the stern expression in his vivid eyes softening as he gazed at me. "If it were just me, I wouldn't think twice, but as far as you're concerned, I can't bring myself to endanger your life in any way."

"You'd rather I stayed here?"

He kept his gaze on me for a moment longer, then faced Svetlana.

"Are you sure it's not possible for one of us to go out there, take all the risks, then bring help to get the rest out of here, safely?"

I opened my mouth to protest, guessing Malahki wanted to be the one to do what he'd just said.

Svetlana beat me to it.

"How can anyone from the outside help us?" she asked. "If they come here, they'd end up stranded here with us. Then, we'd just have more people to worry about." She sighed deeply. "Like I said, it has to be all of us, together, or none at all."

On one hand, we had decades of survival on the Dark Anomaly, isolated from the rest of the world.

On the other, we faced the risk of immediate death in exchange for the chance at a better life.

Indeed, it was a difficult choice to make.

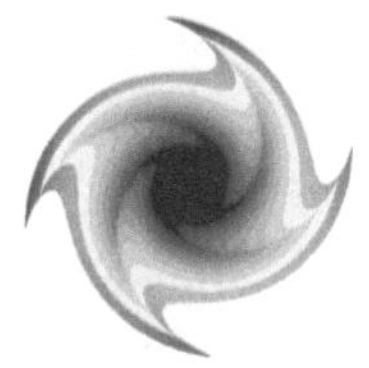

Chapter 18

Malahki

He adjusted his grip on his makeshift spear. Vrateus had offered him an entire arsenal of guns to choose from, but the solid weight of the metal bar in his hand felt most reassuring.

Wyck clicked on the camera that Nadia had clipped to the belt on his shoulder. He often wore it for her, recording the conditions of the Dark Anomaly outside of the ship. The *errock* then rolled open the massive door.

"I'll go first." Malahki stepped out into the corridor.

Outside of the clean environment of the ship, he placed the oxygen mask over his mouth and nose and opened the supply valve. According to the recent readings of the air analysis, the conditions in the habitable sector of the Dark Anomaly remained acceptable, but it had been decided between the six of them not to leave the ship without the oxygen masks anymore. None of them trusted the deteriorating air supply system. It hadn't been maintained at all lately, and could fail any time.

Vrateus joined him, his trusted guns firmly in his hands. Wyck rolled the door closed. The three of them waited until the clanking sounds came, confirming that the women engaged the locks from the inside.

Once satisfied that the women were now safe, the captain gestured for him to start on their way.

Malahki's heart gave a loud thud as the three of them passed by the white doors to the gardens. The lighting behind the doors appeared much dimmer than it should be this time of the day for the plants to thrive.

He was glad the purpose of today's trip did not require them to enter. Seeing the gardens in their current state would break his heart. The controlled destruction he'd done when Valya and he still lived there was hard enough—he had to let some plants die, making others grow out of control. Now, he suspected everything inside would be gone, dead, and rotten.

Coaxing plants to life in the challenging conditions of the Dark Anomaly had been one of the hardest tasks he'd accomplished in his life. It'd been one of the most rewarding, too. He loved watching the seedlings grow, transforming the dead world of metal and plastic into a green space. It had brought him peace and even an enjoyment among all the cruelties and devastation of this place.

He'd been proud of the hard work he'd done in the gardens. Seeing it all ruined now would be crushing.

Thankfully, they didn't need to enter the gardens today. Their destination was the spacesuit storage room on the opposite end of the main corridor of the habitable sector. Svetlana insisted all of them have functioning spacesuits for their journey to the center of the Dark Anomaly.

The day after she'd first informed them about the escape plan, the six of them had put it to a vote. Personally, he would've loved to take all the risk on himself, sparing the worst for Valya and the others, but there was no option like that. Like Svetlana had said, they had to be in it together.

"Watch out!" Wyck shouted behind him, yanking Malahki out of his thoughts.

A male he didn't recognize jumped at them from a side corridor, attacking from behind. Malahki swung his spear, whacking the male flat across his jaw with it. The blow didn't kill but stunned the attacker, tossing him against the wall.

A *raimoid*, Malahki finally recognized his species.

"I thought it was an animal." Wyck took a closer look at his former crew mate. The *errock's* mouth behind the clear material of the oxygen mask twitched in disgust.

Malahki was especially grateful for his own oxygen mask as he studied the male spread on the floor. The *raimoid* looked so filthy, he probably stunk unbearably.

"Leephron." Vrateus lowered himself to his knees next to the male.

Malahki knew the name the captain had said. It belonged to one of the very few *raimoids* on the Dark Anomaly. Leephron had come to the gardens with Urkril once. But the male was simply unrecognizable.

His normally purple skin had paled to light gray now, the typical for *raimoids'* bright blotches of color had completely disappeared. With not a shred of clothing covering his body, it was apparent how malnourished Leephron was—his skin stretched tightly over his skeleton with no fat and hardly any muscle tissue left. His two legs and four arms were almost as thin as the metal rod in Malahki's hands.

"He's starving," he said softly.

"Leephron." Vrateus touched the *raimoid's* face.

Snapping to awareness, the male jerked. His gray eyes bulged out of their sockets. Void of any emotion, they seemed muddy and unseeing.

With a feral growl, he launched on Vrateus, sinking his teeth into the captain's arm.

"Fuck!" Wyck punched the *raimoid* in the head the same moment as Malahki speared the male with the metal rod, pinning him to the floor.

Vrateus's chest rose and fell quickly as he ripped the bottom of his voluminous sleeve and tied it tightly over the fresh bite.

"We'll need to treat it when we get back," Malahki said. Even if the *raimoid* didn't carry any contagious diseases, his bite couldn't be clean.

The captain nodded silently, his gaze on the dead body at their feet.

"I didn't get a chance to talk to him," Vrateus said with regret.

Malahki lowered his hand on the captain's shoulder.

"I don't think he *could* talk," he said, remembering the unhinged expression on the *raimoid's* face. His bulging eyes appeared dead even before he died. No wonder Wyck had mistaken him for an animal, there was not a shred of intelligence or even self-awareness in the male.

"They can't be rescued anymore," he said, understanding the struggle Vrateus must be going through. "There is nothing we can do for them."

Frankly, most of the crew weren't redeemable even before the air supply malfunction or the chemical leak. But he understood the captain's desire to protect those he'd been responsible for. For more than seven years, Vrateus had protected the crew, often even against their wishes. Seeing them in this state must have felt in part like a personal failure to him.

Wyck frowned, heaving a long sigh.

Malahki yanked his spear from the dead body. If there was anyone still left alive around here, the body wouldn't be lying here for long. Overall, the corridor looked less disgusting than the last time he had walked here. The rotten remains were mostly gone now, only bones remained, cleaned of every shred of meat.

"They've made poor choices, captain, long before the air system malfunctioned. And even long before they got to the Dark Anomaly," he said to Vrateus.

Most of the crew came from questionable backgrounds. Smugglers, slave traders, and pirates, they travelled too close to the Dark Anomaly to avoid being caught and persecuted, ending up being sucked in here instead.

The bones crunched under his boots as he headed down the corridor, followed by Vrateus and Wyck.

The strings of lights had been torn in some sections. Wyck took out a flashlight from the tool belt across his chest and turned it on, allowing them to keep moving ahead.

In the bluish ray of the flashlight, the space looked even more wretched and desolate. The panelling had been stripped from most of the walls, baring scratched metal and torn cables. There was so much dirt and litter on the ground, the floors were impossible to see. Bones and pieces of chitin snapped and crunched under their feet, in every section of the corridor.

Worry racked him when he thought about all the challenges they would face when trying to escape this place. But watching the deterioration of life on the Dark Anomaly made staying here not just depressing but emotionally impossible. Even if he were never to see the sun of a planet again, any chance of getting out of here was worth taking.

"Here." Vrateus stopped shortly after they had passed the airlock.

The captain shoved the door to the storage room open, and Malahki braced himself for the sight of the dead *akuks* that Valya and he saw the last time they'd been here. However, the bodies were gone, now, and he decided not to dwell on what might've happened to them—eaten most likely, since the door didn't close properly.

"Well, this doesn't look as decimated as the rest," Wyck observed, taking in the storage room.

Someone had ransacked it after Malahki's last visit. It looked even messier than before, with most things that weren't attached to the walls now littering the floor. Wyck was right, however, the room's contents were misplaced but not taken. The crew, apparently, had little interest in what could not be eaten or used for a weapon.

Vrateus got to work.

"Check the spacesuits," he said, lifting one from the floor. "We need three functioning ones, with built-in locators. And be mindful of the size." He slid an assessing gaze down Malahki's large body, muttering, "You may want to try one on to make sure it fits."

The spacesuits that the humans had on their ship had proven too tight for either one of the three of them.

"We need *four* suits," Wyck corrected him. "Lesh is coming, too."

Vrateus turned to him.

"You're not planning to stuff the *mahdi* into a spacesuit, are you?"

"I'm not leaving him here." Wyck crossed his massive arms over his equally enormous chest, taking a wide stance.

Vrateus blew out a frustrated breath, shaking his head. "I don't want to leave him either, but it's not going to work."

"Why not?"

"Are you kidding me? For one, he has three heads and four legs."

"So?"

"We don't have the suit to accommodate that. How is he going to move?"

"I'll carry him," Wyck replied, unfazed. "I just need a suit wide enough to have him comfortable inside. It can be short, but it needs to be wide, with a large helmet."

Their arguing shifted Malahki's thoughts to their escape plan. Svetlana counted on the force of the Dark Anomaly's energy field to blast them into space. But what if they could aid the field in getting them out of here?

Stepping over the suits, he searched for power cells collected from the crashed spaceships over the years. The older ones had less energy stored in them than the newer ones. Their combined effect, however, would be substantial if set off at once.

"The spacesuits are just for a backup," Wyck stubbornly continued to argue with the captain. "We're taking the capsule, aren't we?"

"There is no seat in the capsule for him, either. It only has six." Vrateus clearly hated the argument. He had a soft spot for Lesh, all of them did. As the captain, he had to be the voice of reason, but Malahki already knew he was fighting a losing battle. Wyck wouldn't leave without Lesh.

"I'll put him in my lap," the *errock* kept going.

"How? He's almost the size of Nadia!" the captain exclaimed, whipping his long fluffy tail around his boots in irritation.

"And I have a big lap!" Wyck slapped his muscular thighs, the size of tree-trunks. "Nadia fits here perfectly."

Malahki headed for the exit, leaving the two of them to it.

"I'll get a cart from the waste processing room," he told them before exiting the room. "We'll need something to transport all of this back to the ship."

When he came back with the cart, Wyck had two suits set aside. Malahki guessed he'd won the argument and Lesh was coming with them. He knew Vrateus would concede eventually. Lesh had become a part of their small crew long before even Valya and Malahki had joined. Though, he still had no idea how Wyck would accomplish getting the suit on the *mahdi* if it came down to it.

After trying a few suits, Malahki finally found one that fit him more or less comfortably. It was an older model, but it seemed to function just fine. He'd need to test it more when he was back on the ship with Valya.

His thoughts drifted back to her. The desire to be near her itched deep under his skin. Being away gave him an anxious feeling he severely disliked.

"Are we all set?" Vrateus asked after they had loaded the suits into the cart. The captain obviously had no desire to linger here for too long, either.

"I want to take the power cells, too." Malahki lifted one shaped like a cylinder off the floor.

"What for?"

"I have an idea I'll have to run by Svetlana first, but we may as well take them now. It'd spare us another trip to get them later."

Vrateus regarded him carefully.

"How many do you need?"

"All of them."

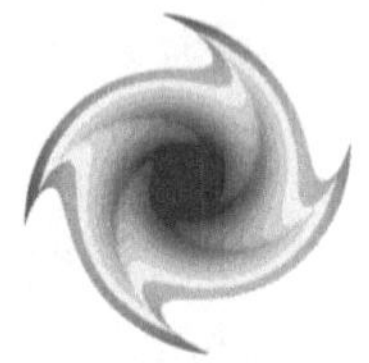

Chapter 19

Valentina

The night before our planned take-off, I turned to Malahki the moment we entered the capsule which had served as our bedroom for the past few weeks.

I needed to be close to him, as close as possible. Because tomorrow… So many things could go wrong tomorrow. If I thought about any of them for another minute, I'd lose my mind.

He understood perfectly. Without saying a word, he cupped my face, kissing me deeply.

My hands trembling, I fervently opened my suit then let him slide it off me. The glide of his large, rough palms along my skin felt invigorating, making each nerve in my body stand on end.

He got down to his knees, taking off my boots, and I raked my fingers through his long, dark-as-night hair. He'd been wearing it in one braid, lately. With all the preparations for our departure, there hadn't been much time for the elaborate braiding he'd done before.

Leaning over him, I took his braid and tugged at the end of the tie. The braid unravelled as he got up to his feet. When he kissed me again, the fragrant curtain of his hair draped around our faces, adding to the intimacy.

Suddenly, we were completely alone in the entire Universe. Just the two of us. And at that moment, I needed no one else in the world.

"I love you," I whispered against his lips. "I love you, Malahki, all of you. I love the person you've always been and the man you have become."

He inhaled sharply, breathing my words in.

"Spirits, I love you too, Valya." He pressed his forehead to mine, holding my face between his hands. "So, so much," he groaned.

I had to tell him how I felt because this might be the only chance I'd get, because tomorrow might be the last day of our lives or the last day of us being together or…

I grabbed his shoulders, finding his mouth with mine. I kissed him with the desperation of a drowning woman grasping for a life raft. He was my escape from the terror and despair that had been the past three months.

"I love you, I love you," I chanted like a mantra as I opened the closure of his pants and found his erection. "I love you," I repeated as he propped me against the back of one of the seats and gently slid inside me.

The feelers around his shaft caressed me tenderly, as if welcoming our connection. Their gentle rubbing grew more intense as his thrusts got stronger and more desperate.

"Valya…" he groaned my name, setting off the explosion of pleasure inside me.

Blinded by pure ecstasy, I gripped his shoulders. The orgasm was still rocking through my body as he pumped his release into me.

His hands wrapped around me tightly, he buried his nose in the dip between my neck and my shoulder.

"Hold me," I panted. "Don't ever let me go.

"Never," he said firmly, making the word sound like a vow. "You're my life, Valya. Whatever happens, we'll stay together."

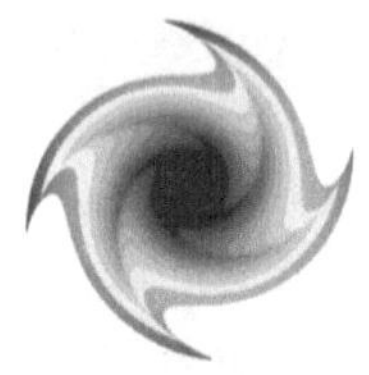

Chapter 20

Valentina

I flipped the front section of my transparent helmet back and clipped the gloves up, freeing my hands for a better grip on the controls. We'd decided to wear our spacesuits inside the capsule to be prepared for the unexpected.

Today was the day we were finally trying to say goodbye to the Dark Anomaly, and it felt surreal.

"Ready?" Svetlana asked from the co-pilot's seat of our escape capsule.

"No!" I wanted to scream.

I didn't feel ready. Not ready to die or potentially lose any one of our small team with whom I had connected so closely over the past weeks. Not ready to risk parting from Malahki.

But I nodded anyway, as calmly as I could manage.

Nadia was sitting behind Svetlana. Malahki was in the seat behind me, I couldn't see him unless I turned around, which I might not be able to do once we started moving. I turned to him now, while I still could.

"I'm ready," he said softly, giving me an encouraging smile. I smiled in return, grateful to hear his voice.

Vrateus was in the last seat behind Malahki. Wyck sat behind Nadia, with Lesh in his lap. He had managed to coax the *mahdi* into the spacesuit with only minimal protests from the animal. All three of Lesh's heads now were inside the wide, round glass bowl of the suit's helmet. Two appeared to have dozed off, while the middle one looked around, watching its surroundings intently.

At the very back, the power cells and batteries of all possible shapes and sizes were piled up. Tied together with cords, they were supposed to be set off when we reached the center of the disk.

Malahki's idea was to increase our speed by giving us a boost through an explosion. After a series of fervent calculations, Svetlana had agreed to it, saying that an explosion wouldn't hurt.

Svetlana joined me in surveying the cabin of the capsule.

"Well…" She straightened in her seat. "Let's go. Take us away, Val."

The air inside the capsule was charged with high energy from everyone present. I sensed their anxiety, their fear of what was to come, and their hope.

I chose to focus on the hope.

"Let's go," I echoed Svetlana, starting the engines.

We disconnected from the spaceship that had been our safe haven on the Dark Anomaly. Just like during our test drive with Svetlana, I took the capsule along the edge first. It ran rather smoothly despite the uneven surface of the dented hulls of the smashed ships.

"Going into the yellow zone now," I called out, shifting the controls to stir the craft from the edge onto the rim of the disk.

Far in the distance to my left, the black, bulging core of the Dark Anomaly glimmered under the colourful lights. That was our target, except that I had to approach it at an angle.

"Orange zone," I said, inching our craft more to the left and closer to the core, which looked even more menacing as it remained largely unknown.

Both Svetlana and Vrateus speculated that the core was soft, either gelatinous or completely liquid. Of course, no one had gone there to verify that. We were the first ones ever.

"Red zone." I kept getting closer, gripping the controls harder.

The pull of the core got stronger. To avoid being dragged to the centre too quickly and possibly crash or sink on impact, I had to move the capsule along an invisible spiral, like a needle moved along the surface of a music record in the old play-back devices. Starting from the edge, we circled the center in the tightening curve.

"Going in," I gritted through my teeth, holding on to the controls with all my strength.

We'd given no name and assigned no color to this zone. This close, it was all pure danger.

I bit my lip, forcing the capsule to proceed on the pre-planned course as Svetlana monitored the systems. Using the data from our test drive, I'd planned for the corrections to counterbalance the pull of the core. The brakes I had to engage and the reverse trust I had to apply on the engines were hard on the system, consuming a lot of power.

"Doing good, Val," Svetlana's strained voice reached me. She made an obvious effort to sound encouraging, but tension was evident in her tone.

"How far are we?" I asked, keeping my eyes on the trajectory line on the screen. Maintaining the course proved too difficult for me to even glance elsewhere.

Svetlana read the numbers to me out loud.

I nodded.

"Getting closer," she announced.

From the corner of my eye I saw the core rising to my left like a smooth, glossy mountain.

With another shift in its direction, something snapped. I still held the controls in my hands, but the capsule skidded and swerved, sharply turning toward the core.

"It's too fast!" Svetlana warned as the speed accelerated, propelling us forward.

The capsule completely abandoned our carefully planned route, heading straight into the core.

I reversed the engines, killing the forward trust completely and diverting all power into backward motion. Yet we kept speeding ahead, the dark mass of the core rapidly growing bigger.

"Turn it off!" Svetlana yelled over the sound of my thundering heart that echoed in my ears. "Kill all power completely."

Without the reverse trust, the core would only suck us in faster. I hesitated.

"Do it!" she shouted louder, more urgently. "The field reacts to energy waves."

My hands moved before my brain had fully comprehended her words. I shut the engines off, immediately turning off the back-up battery and the axillary power as well.

Everything went dark inside the cabin, illuminated only by the swirling lights of the Dark Anomaly outside. Every sound stopped too, except for our hard breathing.

The capsule skidded and rolled ahead, but without the pull of the Dark Anomaly's field, we no longer accelerated. In fact, the traction of the wheels on the bumpy surface slightly slowed us down.

"It worked…" Svetlana exhaled, slumping back against her seat.

"You weren't sure it would?" I asked, without taking my eyes off the approaching bulge of the core straight ahead.

"Well, you know, that was largely just a theory that the Dark Anomaly reacts to energy waves." I heard a smile in her voice.

Most of our plan was based on Svetlana's theories. Many were now being tested for the first time ever.

The capsule tilted, climbing the steep incline of the rising core toward the summit in the center. Our momentum slowed down significantly.

I clicked on the camera built into the underbelly of the capsule. The image of the wheels rolling along the smooth surface of the core came into view. Up close, the surface didn't look smooth at all, however. Wide ripples ran along it. As if someone poured thick caramel out of a bowl.

"The core *is* soft," Svetlana confirmed yet another theory of hers. And if so, the hard caramel would turn into syrup the closer we got.

"We'll sink." I placed my hands on the controls again, ready to restart the engines. "I have to take off!"

Svetlana frowned. "Val, we're on the core, now. That's where the energy stream starts lifting off. We need to stay on the surface or as close to it as possible. Instead of fighting moving forward, we'll be fighting to stay down. You understand?" She stared at me intently.

"I do." I nodded, gripping the controls harder.

"We'd better close the helmets, now," Svetlana said softly.

"Secure your suits!" Vrateus ordered, his voice booming through the capsule for everyone to hear.

I inhaled deeply, going over the sequence of the steps I had to take to start the engines then to prevent the energy field from sweeping us up and smashing us against the edge of the disk. I had to be quick.

From the back seat, Malahki placed his hand on my shoulder.

"I'll see you on the other side, my love," he said softly, before sliding the front of my helmet down for me and clipping it in place. The sound of his beloved voice and the tenderness in his words made my heart melt and brought tears to my eyes.

What could "the other side" mean in our case? Freedom? Or death?

I couldn't allow myself to dwell on that. So much depended on me keeping my head cool and my thinking straight.

I put my gloves on, sealing them with the cuffs of my suit and lifted my right thumb up, signaling everyone I was ready.

We had one chance at it.

The wheels of the capsule's landing gear had completely submerged into the thinning material of the core, effectively stopping any progress toward the summit, now.

I took a long breath, positioning my hands over the control panel.

"One…Two…Three…" I counted in my head then let my fingers do the rest. Quick and practiced, they flew through the sequence with lightning speed. The engines vibrated to life, and I shifted the

controls, forcing the capsule down against the stream of the Dark Anomaly's force field.

The capsule jerked up, out of my control. The wheels of the gear snapped off, stuck in the material of the core, the Dark Anomaly refusing to give up anything it had claimed.

Using whatever power the capsule had left, I set the engines full thrust forward. Our craft sprang ahead, jerking me back against my seat.

The next moment, a bright red dot flashed in the middle of the control panel. We were right above the center of the Dark Anomaly.

Svetlana grabbed my arm, urging me to act.

I yanked at the controls, sharply turning the capsule up. Instead of fighting the force field, I let it carry us up, now, away from the surface.

The vibrations of the engines reverberated through the capsule. I felt them with my hands, too, through the controls. The sensation halted suddenly. When it resumed, its rhythm was broken. The engines struggled.

The warning message on the control panel flashed red. Then the vibrations stopped completely, bringing our ascent to a sudden stop.

Svetlana glanced at me with a silent question in her deep-brown eyes. I met her gaze, but couldn't hold it. I couldn't give her anything good here—we were out of power. Completely.

The engines had been pushed to the limit to get us to the centre, exhausting the capsule's resources. Without the waves generated by the engines, the Dark Anomaly's force field wouldn't react to the capsule. For it, we were no different than an asteroid, now.

For a moment, we just hovered uselessly right over the gaping mouth of the crater of the Dark Anomaly's center. Then, the dreaded slide downwards began.

The Dark Anomaly's gravity was pulling us straight down into the gaping mouth of its crater, filled with the liquified bodies of the ships that crashed here millennia ago.

We needed some kind of energy waves for the force field to hold us. I turned off the engines then frantically tried to restart them. All in vain. Svetlana put her hand on mine, stopping me from trying again. Instead, she gestured at her back and at the built-in power pack of her suit.

Each of our suits was a mini-spacesuit, equipped with a power battery. We had the comm devices and locators there, too, to generate enough energy waves for the force field to carry us along. We just needed to get out of the capsule, first. The craft had become nothing but a dead weight. The speed of its descent was increasing exponentially, leaving us little time.

The black mouth of the center was closing in. I could already see the liquid inside it rising up in spikes and peaks with the release of the stream of energy in the center—the stream that could still take us to freedom if we just could make ourselves a part of it to hitch the ride.

I unclipped my seatbelt, and opened the front of the capsule, making the large glass portion of it slide back.

Svetlana had already gotten Nadia out of her seat. Together, they helped Wyck advance forward. Holding Lesh in a bulky suit, he moved awkwardly. Vrateus and Nadia held him from each side, as the three of them climbed over the control panel and out on the hull of the capsule.

Malahki grabbed my hand, tugging me to follow them and Svetlana.

The capsule now plummeted toward the bubbling crater at astonishing speed. Scrambling into a circle in the front, we turned on the power packs of our suits. The force field grabbed us immediately, helping the engines to propel us up as the capsule plunged down.

Svetlana frantically gestured for us to come closer, obviously worried someone might fly away from the center and into a weaker stream of energy that would end up curving under the gravity of the Dark Anomaly and drag them back to the edge of the disk.

Malahki yanked me closer, wrapping his arm around me. I grabbed on to Wyck, who held Lesh with one arm, having another one hooked with Nadia's. Vrateus had his arms around both Nadia's and Svetlana's shoulders on each side of him. And Svetlana closed our tight circle by linking her arm with Malahki's.

As we ascended higher and higher, away from the Dark Anomaly, we put our heads together, watching it move away from us.

The abandoned capsule plunged into the crater of the center, quickly absorbed by its black-as-night liquid. From what I knew about the Dark Anomaly, there was enough pressure to crush it into a pancake right away. The metal and plastic of the capsule would be liquified and assimilated into the body of the disk, eventually released in the form of energy with the bright, multi-colored light effects.

Suddenly, the liquid in the crater bubbled up higher, rising above the rim. A bright light tore through the bubble, ripping it into pieces that blasted up after us.

The core of the Dark Anomaly had crushed the power cells left on the capsule, setting off the explosion Malahki had set up.

The black pieces of the Dark Anomaly's matter rushed after us, catching up and passing by. Some were as small as a drop, others were huge like icebergs. Some seemed liquid like water. Others had the rounded shapes of blobs or ragged edges of solid material.

Our circle grew tighter as we flexed our arms, getting closer. No matter how hard I tried to hold on to them, however, I felt some invisible force trying to pry me away from them. The streams of energy shot out from the center of the disk. I remembered the 3D graphic on Svetlana's tablet, the rays then dispersed, opening up like a flower. Our tight circle in the middle was being forced to break up with the streams as well.

"No!" I yelled, even as no one would hear me.

I flexed my arms tighter, trying to hold on to both men on each side of me. My grip slipped off Wyck first. Thrown aside, Lesh was torn out of his arms, too. I saw Wyck try to go after the *mahdi*, but the energy field was now in charge, allowing no control over our own spacesuits.

Lesh didn't stop moving, however, and didn't go down like the capsule did, which told me that Wyck must've at least turned on the locator on the animal suit's before the *mahdi* had been ripped away from him.

The locator beacons on the rest of our suits went on the moment the power packs did. It reminded me of other systems we could use, too, now. I turned on the comm.

"Malahki?"

"Valya," his deep voice came through.

The sound of it resonated through my chest. Hope grew stronger.

"Stay with me," I begged, trying hard to hold on to him with both hands.

It was like fighting a centrifugal force, with no way to lessen the effect of it. My fingers kept sliding off his arm, no matter how hard I tried to cling to him.

"Wyck! No!" Nadia's panicky screams broke through the comm.

A large blob of the black material bumped into Wyck, sending him forward, far ahead of us. Nadia flailed her arms and legs, in a futile attempt to follow him. The energy stream kept her on course, making her slowly drift away from us, even as all of us flew further from the Dark Anomaly's disk.

"Hold me!" I screamed in panic, feeling Malahki being torn from me, too.

"Always," I remembered his reply from last night.

But he couldn't keep his promise this time. The invisible force ripped him out of my grip, our hands disconnected, the fingers pried open.

"No!" The agony of losing him lanced through me.

"I love you," he said as the comm crackled.

"No!" I cried. "Malahki, please. Stay with me…"

"Valya, I'll see you on the other side…" His voice broke off as he drifted out of range.

Through the fog of tears, I watched in horror as he floated farther and farther away from me. A large piece of matter from the core rushed between us, shielding Malahki from view.

I glared back at the disk of the Dark Anomaly as it steadily grew smaller and smaller. It was no longer perfectly round, however.

Deep cracks formed from the center all the way to the edge, crumpling its smooth, even form.

The explosion had disturbed the balanced flow of the energy the Dark Anomaly absorbed and released. The entire thing was imploding now.

The material bulged up along the cracks, thicker closer to the center. The edge crumbled up and broke, the distorted disk getting smaller as the Dark Anomaly consumed itself, shooting the pieces of its body out from its center, into the space after us.

Another piece rushed by me. The impact of yet another one sent me into a spin. I had to engage my stabilizers to get myself out of it. By the time the spinning stopped, and I got back on course, there was nothing but open space around me, with pieces of debris floating by.

"Malahki!" I screamed his name through the comm, but there was no answer.

There was no one around me, none of the five people who, like me, had risked it all for the tiniest chance of freedom.

Far in the distance, the remnants of the despicable place called the Dark Anomaly crumbled to pieces, leaving nothing left.

I turned my suit engine off. It had hardly any power left to keep it going, and it was useless now, anyway. The momentum would keep me moving through space, roughly in the direction of the travel routes that used to be in use over seventy years ago, back before I fell into the clutches of the Dark Anomaly.

Maybe, someone would stumble on the signal of my locator beacon. Maybe I'd run out of oxygen before then. Or maybe the suit's life-support system would fail first. There was nothing more I could do for my survival.

I'd done all I could.

Drifting through the dark open space, I felt more alone than ever. If this was my fate to die here alone, I just had one wish before I went. I wanted to see *his* face one last time.

I closed my eyes, recalling his beloved features in my mind. Every familiar line and curve of the face that had changed so much lately, yet always remained the face of the man I loved.

During all the dramatic physical changes that Malahki had gone through, the love and affection in his eyes always grew steadily. The warmth of it kept my heart and my soul alive in a place where everything wholesome and beautiful died.

"I'll see you on the other side, my love…"

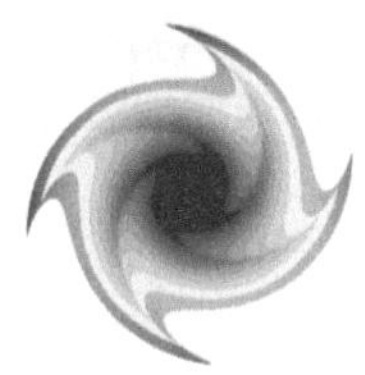

Chapter 21

Valentina

I'd thought our choice was either the life trapped on the Dark Anomaly or the risk of an immediate death while trying to escape it.

I'd been wrong.

An immediate death would've been too easy. Apparently, I was destined to die slowly while agonizing over every single choice I'd made in my life and mourning all the people I'd lost.

Breathing was growing harder. I panted in short, shallow breaths. As the oxygen level dropped, I inhaled slowly and deeply, trying to draw whatever was left into my air-starved lungs.

Eternal chill had set so deep into my bones, my body stopped shivering, giving up and growing numb instead.

I was no longer sure whether my eyes were open or closed—darkness was everywhere, with erratic light flashes slashing through it, either from space or from my vision shutting down.

It wouldn't be long before I crossed over to… Where? Would it be to "the other side" that Malahki had been talking about. Would he be there to greet me? Would I get to see him again?

A tear separated from my frosty eyelid, slowly crystalizing as it floated in front of my face.

A scraping vibration ran through my suit. I had no idea what it was. But my eyes must have been open because I saw a pattern across the glass of my helmet—black, thin lines that formed squares.

It took me another moment to place the image—a net. A net had been dragged around me, scraping against my suit. I couldn't move my arms or legs. It could be because I was trapped in the net. Or maybe because my body went numb. Somehow, it didn't really matter either way.

Nothing mattered anymore…

"Valentina, it's time to wake up."

Valentina…

No one I truly held dear used that name.

My friends called me Val. My family called me Valya.

Valentina was reserved solely for people who hardly knew me.

"Valentina," the female voice insisted. "Please, open your eyes."

He had called me Valya, too.

Malahki… The man who had become closer than family to me.

"You can wake up, now," the woman kept coaxing.

Wake up? Was I still alive then?

I tried to lift my eyelids. They felt so heavy as if laden with lead.

"Very good," the woman cooed approvingly at my efforts. "Can you see me?"

A middle-aged woman with dark skin and black hair that had been generously touched with silver gazed down at me. The expression in her golden-brown eyes was kind, and I managed a smile.

"Excellent." She gave me a wide, toothy grin in return. "Now, how are you feeling?"

A clear oblong shape hovered high above me—the cover of a medical capsule, I recognized. I lay on a padded surface with the woman leaning over at my side.

"I'm Doctor Kimathi," she said. "Can you move your legs for me, please?"

I glanced down my body. I was naked, save for two wide, glossy strips of material, one over my breasts, another one over my pelvis area. Pressing my elbows into the padded surface under me, I tried to get up. The white strips turned out to be not just to protect my modesty, they held me in place, gently but firmly.

"It's too early to get up yet." Doctor Kimathi stopped me by placing a hand on my shoulder. "Just try to move your limbs first."

The feeling returned to my body, though it felt not entirely my own, like a new suit that hadn't been broken in yet. I lifted a hand in the air, then the other one, followed by the right leg then the left. My limbs seemed to listen to me well enough.

"I'm good…" I croaked, my throat painfully dry. "Can I… Water, please?"

"Of course." The doctor nodded but didn't leave my side. Someone else handed me a glass of water. There were more people in the room.

I took a long drink of water. Not just my mouth and throat, all my insides felt like they had shriveled and dried from thirst.

"Where am I?" I asked the doctor. It'd just registered with me that she was human. A moment later, I remembered I was a human, too.

"On a passenger ship from Earth," she said. "We're currently orbiting the planet Omphi."

"Where is Malahki?" I asked. The sound of his name tugged at my heart with ache, pleasure, and longing—all at once.

"Who?" Doctor Kimathi blinked at me.

"Malahki. He is a *damirian*, from planet Ak'ae. He was with me…" My voice broke off, and my heart dropped into the hollow of my stomach. I already knew from her expression she had no idea who I was talking about.

"Valentina." Another woman came forward. She was younger, blonde, and dressed in a uniform I didn't immediately recognize. "My name is Sylvia Kraus. I'm with the Earth's Space Coalition, and I need to ask you a few questions—"

Doctor Kimathi stopped her by lifting a hand in the air. "She's still too weak for long conversations."

"It won't take long," Sylvia Kraus insisted.

I winced at a headache that started pounding inside my skull from their voices.

"Can I…sit up?"

"Sure." The doctor moved away, and two other women covered me with a sheet then removed the white bands, allowing me to sit upright.

I dropped my feet from the medical capsule bed, clutching the sheet to my chest.

"I'll answer any questions you have," I addressed both the doctor and the Coalition rep. "But only if you answer mine first. Who else has been found?"

They both just stared at me.

"Nadia? Vrateus? Wyck? Svetlana? How about Lesh, the *mahdi?* Anyone?" I felt like a piece of me died every time I said a name and found no recognition in their eyes.

"We only found you," Sylvia said slowly.

I pressed my hands so tight to my chest, it hurt, then realized the pain was actually inside me.

"Just me, then?" I said softly, dropping my head between my shoulders. Here, surrounded by people, my people, I felt more alone than ever.

"This ship was en route during its scheduled trip from Earth to Omphi when they caught the signal from the locator of your spacesuit," Sylvia hurriedly explained. "You were in poor condition when they brought you on board two weeks ago. They placed you in the medical capsule. Luckily, Doctor Kimathi also happened to be on board as one of the passengers. She kindly volunteered to oversee your recovery."

I nodded, blankly staring at one of the floor tiles in front of me.

Sylvia continued, "I represent the Earth's Space Coalition in Crystal Wave, the capital city of the planet Omphi. Once your identity was confirmed, it raised a lot of questions."

"I bet it did," I said flatly.

"Your expedition was thought lost without a trace. With your… um, re-appearance…" She drew in a long breath. "Well, we're wondering if you could provide an explanation on what happened to your ship and the crew as well as how did you suddenly re-appear seventy-three years after going missing, physically almost unchanged."

Physically? Maybe. Emotionally? It felt like much longer than seventy-three years had passed.

"Did you say it's been two weeks since you found me?" It finally registered with me.

"Yes." Silvia nodded. "It'll be exactly two weeks in Universal time tomorrow."

"The condition you were found in required some time to heal." Doctor Kimathi stepped in again. "We kept you under for the duration of the flight, letting your body recover. The damaged tissue needed to regenerate. But your muscle tone has been maintained artificially, so you can try to walk soon."

"And maybe answer some questions?" Sylvia clicked something on the wide bangle around her wrist.

I fought the overwhelming flood of darkness that threatened to suffocate me.

"I'll explain what I can," I said, staring imploringly at her. "I'll answer all your questions. But please, there were five more people with me. Please, please keep searching the area."

"The passenger ship is leaving for Earth in four weeks," Sylvia told me.

Our shuttle landed in Crystal Wave, the capital city on Omphi. There used to be several floating research facilities here the year Nadia and I joined our ill-fated expedition. By now, they'd built three real cities on this water world planet.

The huge buildings were constructed like icebergs, with their largest parts submerged under water for stability. They were connected by flexible bridges and underwater passages, creating a grid that floated in the endless ocean of the planet Omphi.

We walked through a passage from the office of the Omphi Government where my identity had once again been confirmed, this time for immigration purposes. The underground passage was a wide, clear, flexible tube with a rigid walkway inside it.

The light of the Omphi's sun pierced through the surface above, illuminating the horizontal platforms suspended under water outside of the tube. A variety of plants of different shapes and colors grew on the platforms, making the waterscape outside a true feast for the eye.

"These are the Crystal Wave's famous underwater gardens." Sylvia tipped her head at the gorgeous plant life outside. "The people here take a special pride in the aesthetic. Not to mention that the gardens provide close to ninety percent of the city's food supply."

"They are gorgeous," I said softly, admiring the clever way the plants had been arranged on the platform to showcase their colors and forms in the best light possible.

"Malahki would've loved to see this…"

The thought speared through my heart with so much pain, I staggered, nearly tripping over my feet. The long flowy dress I wore suddenly felt too tight in the chest area.

"Are you okay?" Sylvia grabbed my elbow.

Would I ever be okay?

I nodded quickly, closing my eyes for a moment and forcing the thick, heavy darkness out of my chest so I could breathe again.

Sylvia gave me a moment to compose myself then took me up an elevator to a room on one of the upper floors.

"Your request to contact your family had been sent," she said, using a wide armband on her left wrist to unlock the door.

My brother and his wife would be gone by now, but I hoped to locate my two nieces. They were so small the year I left, they'd be women in their seventies, now. They probably wouldn't even know me anymore, but they were the only family I had left.

"The Earth's Space Coalition will pay for your accommodation on Omphi for the next four weeks and for your ticket back to Earth with the passenger ship that brought you here."

"Why would they do that?" I stood awkwardly in the threshold of the spacious room. "I have little to do with the coalition. They weren't in charge of my expedition."

Sylvia turned around, waiting for me to follow her in.

"We know your expedition was organized privately, Valentina. But the company responsible for it is no longer in business. You will be needing some help with integration back into society, and we'll be happy to be there for you."

"In exchange for what?" I clasped my hands together so tightly my knuckles ached.

"We would like your cooperation in our investigation. We recovered some data from your spacesuit and would love for you to help with its analysis."

They needed Svetlana for that, not me. The amount of information that woman stored in her head was larger than any system could collect. She'd process, organize, and explain anything to them.

I thought about Nadia and the videos she'd made of our life on the Dark Anomaly. She'd taken all of them with her when we left. Her suit would've been much more valuable than mine. It had built-in cameras, too, as she'd wanted to film our escape as well.

My insides tightened again, twisting with pain and survivor's guilt. Why me? Why did I have to make it, and they didn't? Every single one of them was so much more worthy of life than me.

Sylvia came closer and placed her hand on my shoulder.

"Valentina, if you need anything, please let us know. I'll talk to you again tomorrow, and your therapy sessions will be starting tonight. Doctor Kimathi came to Omphi for work. She's staying in Crystal Wave and will be happy to talk with you as well, whenever you feel like you need it."

I just nodded again then struggled to keep it together as she showed me around the room, pointing out all its amenities and explaining how to use the latest models of the bathroom fixtures and the built-in food replicator.

After she left, I stood on the small balcony, looking out into the ocean beyond the floating buildings of the city, and watched the sunset.

The vivid colors of Omphi's sun sinking beyond the horizon brought to mind the shades of red, purple, and gold that lit up Malahki's skin when he made love to me. The color combination was different when he felt angry or ready to fight. When he took me, his skin came to life with a unique pallet of colors that only I got to see.

Memories flooded my mind, burning my eyes with tears, and I let them flow, unable to hold back the grief and sorrow I'd been struggling to contain all day.

My knees buckled, and I slid to the floor of the glass balcony as I cried.

It'd been two weeks since we escaped the Dark Anomaly and blew it the fuck up. I hoped against all odds the Anomaly hadn't managed to exact its revenge on us even while dying.

Logically, I understood that after two weeks, none of the space-suits would've made it. By now, all their life-support systems would've long failed. The suits were not meant for long-term travel.

In my heart, the stubborn hope refused to die. Many other ships traveled along the route where I'd been found. Other races and nations had regular transportation going through there. Even in today's age of instantaneous communication, the information could get lost for a little while. More of our group could've been rescued around the same time I was or even earlier. Those who'd found them just wouldn't think about searching for me to inform me.

Our team was a mismatched group of people of different races from different planets, separated by distance and time we'd come from. It would take a while for anyone to establish a connection between us.

The hope refused to leave me, giving me strength to go on.

But even if I lost everyone I held dear for the chance to come back to this life, I couldn't give up now. If I survived while they didn't, I couldn't throw it away.

I had to try to go on.

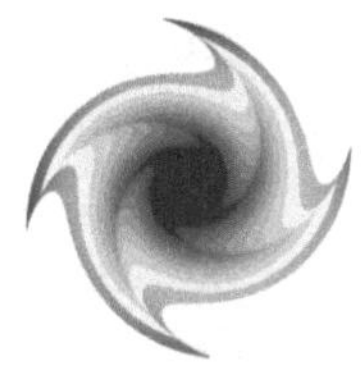

Chapter 22

Valentina

For four days I tried. I tried to go on as I'd vowed to myself I would. I'd started therapy. I'd met with Doctor Kimathi for lunch. I'd chatted with Sylvia about my employment opportunities. In the afternoon, I went for walks around the Crystal Wave, exploring all the amazing things this city had to offer.

But at night, I couldn't fight the darkness. I cried. Every time I closed my eyes, I saw *his* face and felt his touch on my skin. And every time I opened them, not finding him beside me, I died inside, over and over again.

Sylvia had given me a personal communication device. It wrapped around my left arm like a wide, flat bangle. Its surface on the top of my forearm was a curved screen.

The morning of my fifth day on Omphi, the device vibrated and the screen lit up with a call.

I was having breakfast—a cup of coffee and dry toast from the food replicator. I could've chosen anything from the long list of breakfast foods available from the replicator. I could've ordered anything fresh to be delivered, too. But day after day, I kept having the same breakfast I'd had on the Dark Anomaly—coffee and toast.

"Yes?" I picked up the call, but left the video off, not ready to face anyone yet.

"Valentina?" A male voice sounded.

"Yes."

"Another survivor of your group was delivered to the medical center earlier this morning." The male sounded irritated, as if complaining.

The toast fell out of my weakened fingers. I jumped to my feet, shoving back the chair I'd been sitting in.

Another survivor! I was not the only one.

My heart pounded so hard in my chest, the sound of blood rushing through my veins echoed in my ears.

"Where?" I asked, dashing for the door.

"He has violated the rules of quarantine, so he had to start over."

He.

"His name?" I croaked, fumbling with the door lock and the handle.

"Malahki."

I froze, my forehead pressed to the cool surface of the door.

"Thank you, thank you, thank you," pulsed through my brain as a prayer to every god of every planet out there.

I swallowed hard, trying to regain my ability to speak.

"Is he well?" I asked, finally opening the damn lock and hurrying down the corridor.

"Yes, but he's rather irritated," the man replied, the annoyance growing stronger in his voice. "Unruly and uncontrollable. Our tranquilizers have proven ineffective, so we can't even sedate him for long enough. He's been asking for you, and we were wondering if you could come down here to see him. Otherwise, we would need to take measures to physically restrain him."

"Don't." I ran into the elevator then found the location of the medical center on the electronic map on the wall and selected the floor it was on. "Please don't hurt him. I'm on my way. Tell him I'll be there."

"He's not cooperating," the man replied sulkily as the elevator, moving torturously slow, took me down to the floor with the passage to the medical center. "He is extremely *difficult* to communicate with, which is a major characteristic of all *damirian* males, really," he added with a frustrated sigh.

"I'm almost there," I panted into the communication device, running through the underwater passageway toward the building with the medical center. "Where exactly is he? What part of the building?"

He gave me the room number of the room, and I located it on the map on the screen of my device.

"I'm here." I stopped in front of a wide door with a narrow glass insert. Behind it was a small empty room with another door opposite of this one. "How do I open it?" I shook the handle of the locked door.

"You're at the emergency exit of the quarantine room, Valentina, with the decontamination chamber in front of it. But you'll have to go to the visitors' area just around the corner to your right," the male instructed. "There will be a glass wall with a microphone and a speaker on each side so you and the patient can see each other and talk. Since he is in quarantine, no physical contact will be allowed, of course."

Of course…

Disappointed, I was about to turn in the direction the man had told me to go to the visitor's area, when a large hand splayed on the glass of the door on the other side of the decontamination chamber. Then the face I'd only seen in my dreams for the past four days came into view.

"Malahki," I whispered, pressing my forehead to the glass.

His eyes met mine across the decontamination chamber and the two doors separating us. There was everything in his gaze—my hope, my dreams, and my entire life.

Shoving away from the door, he stepped back.

"Stay with me," I mouthed.

Not taking his eyes off me even for a moment, he charged the door, kicking it in. Alarms blared. A red light flashed over the last door that still separated us.

"Valentina!" the man's voice exclaimed in panic from my device. "You *must* go to the visitors' area. The patient is quarantined. You can only see him from the other side of the glass."

The other side?

"No." I said softly, as my man was breaking through doors and walls on his way to me. "We need to be together. He and I. On the *same* side. Always…"

From the decontamination chamber, Malahki gestured for me to step aside before crashing through the remaining door and into the corridor to me.

Air left my lungs as he crushed me to his chest. And with the air, a huge portion of the darkness left me. My next breath was filled with light, hope, and so many more wonderful things.

"Hold me," I begged as tears rushed down my face, happy tears, for once.

"Always," he murmured, holding me so tight, I couldn't move a muscle, and I loved it that way. "Valya, Valya, Valya…" he chanted, rocking side to side with me in his arms. "Don't ever leave me again, do you hear me? I won't survive watching you drift away from me ever again."

"Ma'am! Please step back into the patient's room immediately!" People in protective gear rushed down the corridor to us.

The alarms kept blaring, coloring the lifeless walls of the corridor with streaks of bright red light.

"Valentina!" the man on the call sounded outright furious, now. "I regret to inform you that due to the physical contact with the patient, you will have to be quarantined with him for the next two weeks."

I just smiled at that as Malahki showered my face with kisses.

"That's absolutely fine with me," I murmured, sunshine flooding my veins with each kiss Malahki placed on my skin. "I'm planning to spend much longer than two weeks with this man."

"The rest of my life," Malahki demanded between the nibbles

and kisses he peppered down my neck. "I'm not letting you go for the rest of my life."

We tried to stay at the medical center for quarantine, but it didn't go well. My presence soothed Malahki, but he took it upon himself to dote on me. If he believed I experienced the slightest discomfort at any time, he flew into a fit of rage against the staff.

His overreacting was deemed to be amplified by our forced confinement. After everything we'd gone through to regain our freedom, we ended up being locked up again. It was hard to take for him. I knew he tried to control his emotions, but it proved too much.

After some intense negotiations, the authorities granted us the permission to quarantine in my room, instead. I suspected they'd just gotten tired of dealing with Malahki's temper flare-ups.

Once they moved us to my room, things started improving. Technically, we were still locked up, unable to leave the room, but it was a much more comfortable environment than the medical center. We had more privacy here, less supervision, and a balcony—a window into the outside world, which made this feel less like a prison and more like a holiday.

When we first got to my room from the medical center, Malaki stopped in front of the closed glass doors to the balcony.

"I never thought I'd see a sunset ever again," he said in awe, staring at the setting sun.

"Did you get to breathe the ocean air yet?" I asked.

He shook his head, not taking his eyes from the horizon.

"Come." I gently took his hand in mine, leading him out to the balcony.

The neighboring buildings flanked ours, but our room was high enough to have an open view of the sunset.

Tall, massive spikes floated upright in the ocean in the distance. They were a part of the system that controlled the winds and broke up the ocean waves, preventing the massive turbulent storms that used to be a norm on Omphi. Thanks to the system, the storms never reached disastrous levels here anymore.

Today, the weather was lovely. A warm breeze gently blew from the open water, stroking my skin and playing with the long ends of Malaki's unbound hair.

Tilting his head back, he drew in a deep breath, his wide chest rising.

"I forgot how fragrant the air can be," he murmured, closing his eyes.

I had only been gone for seventy-three years, but the world had moved on so much in that time. I had to re-learn some things and learn anew so many others.

It would take time and work for me to hopefully stop jumping at every loud noise—one day. To stop working out an escape route the moment I walked into a room. To stop calculating the distance to the nearest exit in case there was a sudden attack and I had to run for my life.

It had been fifteen centuries since Malahki had left his world. I realized that everything I felt he must be feeling so much more profoundly. The issues I was dealing with must be multiplied by a thousand for him.

There were and still would be so many issues for both of us to overcome. But there were pleasures waiting for us, too.

The scent of the ocean mist. The view of the sunset. The caress of the wind. The simple things that people often took for granted held special meaning to us, now. Even more so for Malahki, because he had been deprived of it for so long.

"It's beautiful, isn't it?" I leaned my head against his arm.

He moved me in front of him, my back to his front. Wrapping his arms around my shoulders, he rested his chin on top of my head.

"I don't think I'll ever get used to seeing this every day," he said softly.

I thought the same about having his arms around me. Every hug, every kiss of his felt special. I didn't think I would ever get used to that or would ever take his attention for granted.

Having to stay in the room for two weeks, we finally had the time to enjoy each other in peace, without the fear of danger constantly looming over our heads.

We talked, learning more about each other. We made love whenever we felt like, which happened to be often.

One evening, as we sat on the balcony, watching the sunset again, Malahki told me about how he was rescued.

A small *dimo* ship had picked him up, apparently even before I'd been found.

"When I saw the *dimos* hauling me on board, I punched the first one before they even got me out of my suit. It was almost a reflex." He shrugged apologetically, and I understood what he meant. The only *dimos* he'd seen in the past five years were the ones who hurt and taunted him.

"That didn't leave a good first impression of course," he continued with a sad smile. "The four of them managed to maneuver me into a storage room where they locked me up until they arrived at their research station on the asteroid a few days away from here. They contacted the government of Ak'ae, asking them to come and get me. I stormed and raged all that time, knowing they had left you behind. I demanded they go back, but at that point no one really listened to me anymore, thinking me deranged."

I placed my hand on his, and he grabbed it like a lifeline.

"Ak'ae couldn't confirm my identity, because I'd been officially declared dead centuries ago. For a while, I was stuck in limbo. But the *dimos* really wanted to get rid of me. So, one of them finally requested information on the human expedition that disappeared seventy-three years ago, like I kept telling them. They contacted the Federation, and from them learned that someone from the expedition had been found and sent to Omphi." He stopped abruptly, swallowing hard.

Reaching over, he scooped me out of my chair and placed me in his lap. I leaned against his chest and wrapped my arms tightly around him. Even the smallest distance between us sometimes felt unbearable.

I understood the reasons for the *damirian* custom of self-isolation of all newly matched couples at the beginning of their sexual relationship. The explosion of emotions that came with the gender transformation needed some time for each person to sort through. The couple found comfort in each other's bodies, slowly processing their physical and emotional changes.

Malahki had barely had that time with me. Most of the time he knew me, we'd been fighting for survival. For the first time ever, we got a chance to slow down and connect while feeling absolutely safe.

During the days of our quarantine, Malahki was gaining more control over his body and his emotions. His behaviour was getting more stable, his confidence more solid.

"They brought me here, but wouldn't let me see you," he said softly. Taking apart my ponytail, he started spreading my hair strand by strand along my naked back. Neither of us wore any clothes. It made little sense to bother getting dressed with only the two of us being here. "They kept talking about another quarantine."

"Why did you have to do another one? Didn't the *dimos* keep you isolated already?"

"Not long enough. I tried to escape the research station on the asteroid, twice. I wanted to steal their ship and come back to search for you. Once they brought me here, they concluded that I had to be isolated again."

He slid his hand down my back to cup my backside.

"Little did they know," a smile filtered into his voice, "that I'd never agree to be isolated from you."

I thought about the damages sustained by the doors that had dared stand between us.

"My uncontainable." Smiling, I lifted my face to his, catching his kiss on my lips, and he shifted me in his lap, closer to his growing erection.

Straddling his hips, I rocked my pelvis against his hard length, the tantalising caress of the gentle feelers igniting my blood with desire. I lifted my hips, letting him slide inside me.

Growling, he covered my face and chest with hungry, biting kisses as I rode him hard, until both of us moaned with pleasure.

One part we still couldn't talk about was the moment we'd been ripped away from each other by the force field of the Dark Anomaly. That part would haunt both of us in our nightmares for some time still. Even while dying, the Dark Anomaly had found a way to exact its revenge on us by tossing all of us away from each other, to float in space completely alone.

Could anyone else have survived?

Malahki and I were researching the names and home planets of each transportation company that used the nearby routes. Through Sylvia, we sent out messages with the names and the detailed description of the four people still missing. Against Sylvia's advice not to divert the focus from people to the animal, I also insisted on finding Lesh. The *madhi* had become an important part of our team, too. He'd escaped with us, and he deserved every effort to be found.

Less than a week since our confinement began, another call with amazing news came.

"Nadia!" I rushed to Malahki as he exited the bathroom after taking a shower. "They found her!"

His eyes flew wide open with surprise and excitement.

"Where is she?"

"On a research ship from Earth, on her way to Omphi!" I pressed my hands to my chest, afraid it'd explode with relief and excitement filling me.

"How is she?" he asked, his brows moving into a concerned frown.

"They said she's well. The baby, too…" My voice shook and my lips trembled as tears of joy prickled behind my eyelids.

"Come here." Malahki took me in his arms, kissing my hair.

"Oh God…" I pressed my face into his chest, letting my tears mix with the shower water droplets on his skin. "I'm so, so happy," I sobbed. "I've never cried so much in my life."

He laughed, rocking with me in his arms.

"Let's hope this is just the beginning."

He was right. More happy news quickly followed. Wyck and Vrateus had been found together, by an *errock* cargo ship. Both had delayed the ship for over two weeks, making the crew search the area for more of us, but they'd only found Lesh. The ship was on its way to Hexol, the *errocks'* planet, when one of my messages reached them. The three of them then had to board another ship via a shuttle and were headed for Omphi.

Svetlana had actually been found before any of us. Her suit had been damaged from the collision with the debris of the Dark Anomaly. She was unconscious when the crew of a transport shuttle found her on their way to work at the station orbiting a small unpopulated planet nearby.

When she got better and was woken up from the medically induced coma they had put her under, it took them a while to confirm her identity and then find a transportation here, to all of us.

All of them were supposed to be on Omphi by the time Malahki and I had finished our quarantine. Everyone was alive.

The Dark Anomaly no longer had a hold on us. We'd escaped. So many possibilities awaited us now. We had our lives to leave any way we pleased.

We won.

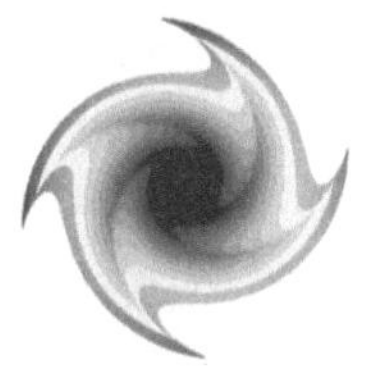

EPILOGUE

Valentina

"Ready?" Malahki leaned against the door frame of the bathroom, folding his arms across his chest.

The crisp white shirt stretched tightly over his shoulders. The short sleeves would've burst at the seams, struggling to contain his bulging biceps, if there were any seams at all. The latest human fashions weren't sewn, they were molded from one piece of material.

I'd never seen him wear a shirt before. Come to think of it, I barely remembered him in clothes at all. We'd spent the past two weeks not wearing anything.

Today, our quarantine was over.

I stood in front of the mirror.

"How do I look?" I smoothed my hands down my outfit—a loose, blush-pink blouse with a high collar and a long, ivory skirt. The light, flowing material felt like nothing against my skin.

"Gorgeous." He smiled, his intense gaze roving over my body. "Absolutely perfect."

My face heated, my cheeks taking the same shade as my blouse.

He tossed his long braid back over his shoulder, sauntering to me.

I twisted the end of one of my braids around my finger, taking a step back. It didn't take much more than that smoldering look in his gorgeous multi-colored eyes to make my heart race and my skin buzz with awareness.

"We'll have to go soon," I reminded him as he came closer, sliding his large hands up my bare arms. The same hands that so deftly braided my hair just a little while earlier. The weave of the five braids I wore reminded me of intricate macramé. This hairstyle must be severely outdated, even on Ak'ae, but I loved it so much. "We can't make them wait."

Wyck, Nadia, Vrateus, and Svetlana waited for us in the restaurant one building over. Today was the first day Malahki and I were free to leave our room after the quarantine, and we were about to finally meet everyone in person for the first time since our escape from the Dark Anomaly.

"Just one kiss," Malahki murmured, lifting my face to his with a finger under my chin.

"*Just one* doesn't happen with you," I smiled against his lips.

He placed a second kiss in the corner of my mouth, proving me right, then trailed more kisses down my neck.

"You're going to get hard," I warned with a giggle.

"Mm," he agreed, but kept kissing.

"And your feelers will start squirming," I added.

He leaned back a little, lifting an eyebrow.

"Squirming?"

"Like this." I wiggled the fingers of my both hands in the air.

He laughed. "I can't help it. Like me, they get excited. And like me, they love making you come."

Warm tingles trickled through my chest to my lower belly at the thought of having him between my legs again. We had no time for that, though.

"We can't do it, honey," I gently stroked his cheek. "We need to head out now, and you have to calm them down. Otherwise, they will be squirming in your pants, which are pretty tight by the way. So, everyone will see all that squirming."

He blew out a disappointed breath.

"I hate wearing pants."

I smiled, taking a step back and giving him a once-over.

"I do prefer you naked, but you look rather dashing in pants, my love."

He heaved another heavy breath, the pretty pink swirls on his skin fading away as he reined his desire under control.

"Fine. Me and my *squirmy* feelers will have to wait until tonight, then."

I laughed, heading for the door.

"Don't tell me you're not looking forward to seeing everyone again."

A huge smile spread on his face.

"I can't wait," he admitted.

I took his hand as we left our room for the first time in fourteen days. As we walked down the corridors then along the walkway, the space looked suspiciously deserted. The moment we stepped into the restaurant, I realized why.

The people at the tables turned our way the moment we entered. The patio was filled with photographers, a flock of reporter-drones hovering over their heads.

"What is all of this?" I muttered under my breath, stopping at the entrance and wondering if we should maybe do this some other time.

"We're celebrities, remember?" Malahki said softly. His voice sounded calm enough, but his hand tightened on mine.

Right. The news of our rescue had gone out. Sylvia had said something about a lot of interview demands. She knew about our plans for lunch and must've arranged for the hallways to be cleared. But this...

"Should we leave?" I fought the immediate desire to flee.

A person rushed to us. A *kreer*.

I sucked in a breath, gripping Malahki's hand tighter.

"Come with me, please." The *kreer* stretched his lipless mouth, displaying the sharp teeth. It took me a moment to realize he was smiling. The word *"Manager"* glowed on the lapel of his uniform.

I breathed slowly, trying to calm my racing heart. One day, I would be able to face a *kreer* or an *ognat* or the people of some other species without a jolt of panic or fear of an attack.

One day…

The manager took us upstairs, explaining over his shoulder, "We'll be serving you in our private room. Enjoy your lunch." He opened a door into a round space with a large table in the middle.

The four people I'd feared were dead just a few days ago were sitting around the table.

I forgot all about my apprehension or about the reporters outside. Pure happiness filled my heart, momentarily banishing every other feeling.

"Val!" Nadia shoved her chair back, jumping up, then rushed to me for a hug.

Svetlana and the two men got up too, coming closer.

The happiness inside me bubbled up to the surface. Tears of joy trickled down my cheeks. I opened my arms to them, and they all joined us in the hug.

Svetlana, Vrateus, Wyck, and Malahki put their arms around Nadia and me, making an even tighter circle than we'd formed when the stream of energy whisked us away from the Dark Anomaly and toward the unknown.

The six of us had been united forever by the place that now only existed in our nightmares.

When each of them first got to Omphi, I'd spoken to them over the communication device. I'd seen their faces on the screen. But having them all here in person, safe and sound, overwhelmed me with joy so much, I was crying and laughing at the same time.

"I can't believe this. I can't…" I wiped my tears with my shoulder, only for more of them to rush out.

"We're alive." Nadia laughed, gazing at me through her own tears. "It worked. We won!"

I caught Svetlana's eye.

"Thank you," I said to the woman who made it all possible. My heart filled with so much gratitude I thought it would burst in my chest.

Svetlana quickly brushed away a tear from her eye, too, shaking her head.

"We *all* did it," she said. "I couldn't have done anything without all of you."

We loosened the hug, eventually moving back to the table. I spotted Lesh hiding under Wyck's chair. I crouched next to him, gently petting his side.

"Hi buddy," I said to him softly.

Lesh's middle head flicked its long tongue out, tentatively giving my hand a sniff. He then pressed his nose to my palm, letting me know he recognized me.

"I'm so happy to see you here." I scratched the side of the middle head.

"He is a little overwhelmed by all of this," Nadia said, taking her seat next to Wyck's.

"Aren't we all?" Wyck laughed with a nervous edge in his voice.

Wyck was wearing dark sunglasses, even though we were inside. Both he and Vrateus avoided looking at the floor-to-ceiling windows surrounding us.

Neither of the two remembered the outside world. The Dark Anomaly, with its artificial lighting inside and the permanent darkness outside broken only by the lights of its energy field were all they had ever known, until now.

"How do you find it here?" I asked them both.

"Too much light," Wyck confessed with a wince.

"And space," Vrateus added with an uncharacteristically unsure smile. "I haven't been outside yet, but even what I can see through the windows is too much."

"We're working on it." Svetlana gave him an adoring look, taking his hand in hers. "There're amazing therapists here in Crystal Wave. They also managed to connect us with someone from Nofoi, Vrateus's home world."

Nadia gently rubbed Wyck's thigh. "It's getting better. The first day, Wyck refused to leave our room. But now, he likes going for walks in the underwater gardens."

"Oh, I need to take you there, too," I turned to Malahki. He'd seen the gardens on the screen of the entertainment unit in our room, but I couldn't wait for him to see them in person.

"Maybe we can go together after lunch?" Wyck suggested.

I smiled brightly. It felt amazing to be able to freely move around again.

A drone took our lunch orders then a robotized cart brought our food to the table. It was such a normal thing to do getting together for lunch with a group of friends. Yet I still couldn't wrap my mind around the simple fact we were now free and alive. We had reclaimed our lives to do with them as we pleased.

"What are you planning to do, now?" Svetlana asked, taking a sip of her sparkling water when we finished eating.

I glanced at Malahki. We'd spoken a little about the future while being locked in our room.

"We're considering staying here for a while," I said. "I could get a job as a space shuttle pilot. The Earth's Space Coalition has offered to help with my re-training."

Malahki took a long drink from his cup of the sweet tea imported from Ak'ae.

"I'm interested to see the underwater gardens," he said. "I've read a little about the technique they use to grow them here, and I wouldn't mind learning more about it. I may apply to work there."

"No joining the *damirian* army for you?" Vrateus smiled.

Malahki laughed, shaking his head.

"The army has never been my thing, either before or after my gender transformation. Though, I'll need to look into the local sports clubs," he added, rolling his massive shoulders back. "These muscles need to be worked out, and I'd rather punch a bag than people if I have a choice."

"Well…" Nadia cleared her throat, looking like she had something important to say. She took a brief pause, waiting until all attention was on her. "You certainly can have jobs if you want to, but it looks like neither of us may have to work for a living anymore."

"What do you mean?" I blinked at her.

All of us stared at her in question. Except for Wyck, who had a knowing smile playing on his full lips.

She clasped her hands on the table.

"I've been going through the videos I brought with me. There's some really good footage there, of all of us and our life on the Dark Anomaly. I want to put it all into a film, a documentary of sorts." She scanned our faces, tentatively, as if trying to gauge our reaction.

"You'll get to do your movie after all!" I felt my face stretch into a wide smile as excitement for her spread through my chest.

"I'm thinking about it." Nadia nodded. "But it would have a personal feel rather than scientific. Sort of a look at our entire adventure from the point of view of someone being there. Traveling to the Dark Anomaly, landing, surviving on it, and finally escaping it."

"It'd be neat to see it now that we're safely out of there," Svetlana mused.

"Well, a lot of people would like to see it, actually. The public interest is there." Nadia gestured downstairs, to the crowds of reporters we thankfully couldn't see from here. "So much interest, that I already have several huge companies wanting to buy the rights. They're offering a lot of money."

"Wow. This is amazing, Nadia." I gasped.

She shook her head.

"The most important thing for me is to have all of the people—those who passed and those still living—represented properly and with respect. I will be obtaining the permission of the families of our deceased crew. Also, if any one of you is uncomfortable with the idea of making this public, I'm not going to do it."

Nadia was not a stranger. As someone who'd lived through the experiences she wanted to depict in the movie, she was the one I trusted to tell the truth without sensationalizing it or exploiting her subjects.

"You have my permission," I said. "I trust you."

"Thank you," she replied. "We'll talk about all of it in more detail of course. I'll show the footage to all of you, too, whenever you think you may be ready to watch it."

"Are you planning to stay here on Omphi, too?" Malahki asked.

"Well..." She glanced at Wyck. "We may do a trip to Hexol, first. To see Wyck's home world."

"The crew of the *errock* ship that found Vrateus and me invited me to Hexol," Wyck explained. "I'd love to see the world I came from."

"We'll just have to decide whether we'll do it before or after the baby is born," Nadia added.

"How is the baby doing?" I asked.

"Oh, he's great!" She leaned over the table, showing me a 3D picture on her communication device. "Just look at his cute little face," she cooed.

"He is adorable," I agreed, admiring the tiny being, still shaped very much like a bean, with skinny legs and arms. The baby looked so defenceless and vulnerable, his survival appeared a true miracle after everything his mother had gone through.

"He is so big," Nadia gushed excitedly. "The doctor already told me to get ready for a C-section. There's no way I'd be able to deliver him any other way."

"It will be fine." Wyck kissed her face.

"I know." She beamed at him.

The dark worry I'd seen in her eyes before was gone. Now, there was just hope and pure happiness.

"How about you?" she asked Vrateus and Svetlana. "What are your plans?"

"In terms of babies, you mean?" Svetlana smiled, shooting a glance at Vrateus. "We've enquired about it, and apparently inter-species pregnancies are now much more common than ever before. There have been a number of children born to *themul*-human couples. I've heard *damirian*-human babies have happened, too." She winked at me.

Malahki squeezed my hand, and I smiled. We hadn't talked

about starting a family yet, but it was wonderful to have that possibility in the future—now, that we had a future.

"We want to do something else first, though," Svetlana continued. "We've been able to find the exact location that's marked here."

Lifting her hand, she gently traced the tattoos above Vrateus's pointy ear. Strings of numbers and symbols decorated the skin on his scalp below the wide stripe of long fur in the middle of his head.

"The captain's tattoos?" Wyck lifted both of his eyebrow ridges with the question.

Vrateus took Svetlana's hand and placed a kiss on it.

"My tattoos are the names of the home port and the ship of my family," he explained to us. "The location of the town I hail from."

"Do you want to find your relatives? The descendants of your family?" Malahki asked.

"No, that wouldn't be possible. Thousands of years ago, *themul* lived and travelled in clans. My entire family was on the ship when it crashed. They were merchants, but…" Vrateus frowned. "Like many others who ended up on the Dark Anomaly, they weren't always on the right side of the law. My family were smugglers."

"So," Svetlana blurted out excitedly. "We want to find some of what they smuggled."

"How?" Nadia asked.

"Ooh." I gasped. "You're going treasure hunting?"

Svetlana beamed, and Vrateus gazed at her adoringly.

With a glance over her shoulder, as if concerned about being overheard by anyone outside of our circle, she leaned over the table, bringing all of us closer, too.

"I did some research into this while being transported to Omphi," she said.

"Of course you did!" I laughed. "It wouldn't be like you to just relax and do nothing."

The busy brain of this woman wouldn't rest, even for a day.

She shrugged apologetically.

"I tend to always be thinking about something," she admitted. "Anyway. Vrateus's clan was fairly well known in their time.

However, not much information remained about them. Vrateus has read everything he managed to recover from their ship. We're going to follow some of their routes and revisit the stops they'd made, starting from their home port." She glanced at Vrateus's tattoos again.

"It sounds so exciting." Nadia gushed, her eyes lit up.

"A real adventure," Wyck agreed.

"What will you do if you find something?" Malahki asked.

"It depends on what it is," Vrateus replied. "By the law of the Federation, the finders are entitled to keep any treasure if it was lost or stolen longer than a thousand years ago."

"So, we'll keep it!" Svetlana announced. "Unless it happens to have some historical significance, then we'll donate it of course."

My device bracelet vibrated with an incoming message. While Vrateus and Svetlana continued to discuss their plans with the others and answer their questions, I quickly scrolled through the message.

"What is it, my love?" Malahki asked me, no doubt noticing that my expression had changed.

"My family…" I inhaled a shuddered breath, pressing my hand to my mouth as tears started to gather in my eyes again.

The conversation around us stopped, and I realized everyone's eyes were on me.

"Here," I said, pressing the audio button. I didn't trust my voice to read it out loud. "Just…listen."

"Dear Valya," the mechanical voice read in Universal. *"I've never met you, but I've heard a lot about you from my parents and my sisters. As children, we often watched videos of you playing with them, and I always wished I was born before you left, so I could be in those videos, too.*

"The hope of seeing you again one day always lived in our family. I wish our parents were still alive when we got the amazing news that you had been found, alive and well.

"Mom and Dad lived long and happy lives. They got to meet their eight grandchildren and six of their great grandchildren. We are a large but close-knit family, and you will always be a part of us, Valya, no matter where you are.

"My sisters agreed to let me write to you first because I never had the chance

to meet you in person. Well, now I have the real hope that I will get to meet you one day.

"Sincerely,

"Your niece Valentina."

"She has your name," Nadia whispered in the silence that followed.

I nodded, unable to speak through the tightness in my throat. My brother and I weren't close. Learning that he'd missed me, enough to name his third daughter after me, wracked me with regret. I wished I'd tried to be closer with my only sibling. I couldn't even remember if I'd told him I loved him the day I left Earth. I didn't recall when was the last time he'd told me he loved me, either.

At the same time, I was happy he lived the life he wanted. And I felt grateful he remembered me and kept the memory of me alive in his children. One day, I would share the memories of him with my children, too.

Malahki brushed away the tears from my face, bringing me out of my thoughts.

"I guess we're going to Earth for a visit, now?" He grinned.

"Really?" I blinked at him, smiling through tears. "You would do it? You would go to Earth to visit my family with me?"

He drew me closer for a quick kiss. "Of course, my love. Where you go, I go, remember? For the rest of my life."

Svetlana straightened in her seat with a deep breath.

"Wherever life will take us, please let's stay in touch," she said, her gaze sweeping over all of us at the table.

"We need to make it a regular thing," Nadia suggested, linking her hands with Wyck on one side and with Vrateus on the other. "Let's get together for lunch, every year. No matter where we are, let's make it happen."

Holding Malahki's hand in one of mine, I took Wyck's in the other. Svetlana gripped the hands of the men on either side of her —Vrateus's and Malahki's—closing the circle.

"No matter where we are," she said.

"No matter where we are," the rest of us echoed in unison, sealing the vow.

The Dark Anomaly might no longer be there, its disk gone, its field dying a slow death by dissipating into space, but the bond we'd formed by surviving it was stronger than ever.

Nothing was going to make us drift apart anymore. No matter where we were.

THE END

Thank you for staying with me through the darkness of the Dark Anomaly trilogy and for trusting me to lead you all the way to the happy ending.

I hope you enjoyed the journey. Your reviews are always deeply appreciated.

EXPERIMENT

CHAPTER 1

"Isabella Bruno." The man in a dark suit wasn't asking. Staring at me from the other side of the front entrance as I held the door open, he stated my name confidently, as if he already knew it was me.

"How can I help you?" I asked cautiously, glancing at the two others behind him. The large, black vehicles parked at the curb in front of our house did not put my mind at ease either.

"Michael Trevin." He offered me his hand. "May we come in?"

"Trevin?" I stared at him in shock, ignoring his hand. "The Michael Trevin?" I asked, dumbfounded, even as I had already recognized the face of one of the three North American representatives in the coalition of Earth Governments. "You're here? In Deer Rock?"

The fact that someone so high up in the government personally visited our small town—far up North on the territory that used to be Canada before the three countries of the continent had been merged into one—should be a huge event.

Had his visit been made public? How had I missed the news? And why was he at my house?

"Can we come in?" he asked more persistently, moving forward, which forced me to step back.

"Um, sure," I mumbled, as if my permission meant anything at that point—all three had entered our small hallway.

I smoothed my hair quickly and brushed my palms down my t-shirt, feeling painfully underdressed in my pajama pants. It was mid-morning on a weekday, but I had an evening shift at the store today and hadn't changed yet. Luckily, I had at least put a bra on.

"Who is it, Bella?" Mom came out of the kitchen, bouncing Lily, one of my sister's twins, on her hip. "Mister Trevin . . ." She stared at the representative, her eyes opened wide, her mouth agape. "In my house?"

"Mrs Bruno." He shook her hand energetically. "Where would be the best place for us to have a quick talk?" Without waiting for an answer, he shoved past her and into our kitchen. His escort followed.

"Um . . . About what?" Mom hurried after them. "Would you like anything? Tea? Water?"

"We don't have much time." Trevin pulled a chair from the table and sat down. "Secretary Carter. Agent Miller." He gestured at the two men accompanying him as they took seats at the table too.

"What is it all about?" Mom moved her gaze from one man to another. Both her and I remained standing.

"We are here to collect Isabella Bruno," Miller blurted out, earning a stern glare from Trevin.

"Me?" I stepped into the kitchen from the entrance where I had been standing.

Surely this was some kind of misunderstanding.

"What did she do?" Mom sent me a questioning stare.

"Before I explain," Trevin raised a hand in a calming gesture, "allow me to remind you that although our coalition is the main human governing body on the planet, it has been under the jurisdiction of the planet Keala for the past nine years. The extraterrestrials have left us to administer our population, but the Kealan laws take precedence over ours."

The aliens had come to Earth suddenly one day. Several giant flying saucers had hovered over a few major cities, and it didn't take long for them to make it clear they did not come in peace.

All military attempts by the coalition to attack the spaceships resulted in the immediate annihilation of our aircraft and missiles.

Then they attacked us. Entire populations of several towns and small cities around the world were eradicated within minutes when bright rays of light had descended from the ships. All structures, machines, and animals were left intact. However, the people in those places were turned to dust in seconds—white ash all that remained.

Human capitulation came right after the aliens threatened to annihilate the entire population of Earth in the same fashion if we didn't surrender.

As Trevin pointed out, the Kealans left the coalition in charge of Earth's administration, not getting involved much in our politics or our way of life. They built two facilities, one on each of Earth's poles, and implemented mandatory annual medical evaluations for all humans aged eighteen to sixty.

Other than that, it was easy to forget with time that Earth had been conquered at all.

"Please take a seat, Isabella." Trevin's stare carried a power I found myself unable to disobey. I sat at the table across from him, folding my hands over the large red strawberries printed on the plastic tablecloth. "About a week ago, the coalition received a request from the Kealans. They demanded you be handed over to them."

"Me?" I repeated, stunned, a fog of confusion and denial settled over my brain. "There must be some mistake . . ."

"No mistake. They want you," Miller bit off.

Trevin leaned in, resting his hands on the table. "We were able to negotiate some time to discuss the situation last week. However, this morning, their request was made urgent—" A sudden thought appeared to flash through his mind. "When was your last medical examination?"

"Yesterday," I replied, clutching my hands tight. "What do they want with me?"

The exams were done by the local doctor, for free and with no known health consequences observed. Alien robot-drones delivered the test kits and collected the data obtained. After nine years, the global medical exams had become the norm. By now, hardly anyone questioned it, begrudgingly accepting having to go see the doctor once a year as something that had to be done—kind of like renewing one's driver's licence, or filing taxes.

"You had one done yesterday?" Trevin exchanged a knowing look with the other men at the table. "That may explain the urgency."

"How?" Even more perplexed, I moved my gaze from one face to another. "What do they want?" I asked again, since no one had answered me the first time.

"Well." Trevin leaned against the back of his chair, stretching his neck and obviously stalling his answer.

"Your current physical state may be of some importance to them," Carter joined in.

"What do you mean? When will I be able to come home?"

Carter glanced at Trevin. Something in the expressions of the two sent a chill of trepidation down my spine.

"I will come back, won't I?" I insisted, louder.

"The extraterrestrials offered you Kealan citizenship. Through marriage." Trevin shifted in his chair, making it squeak. "To that extent, they also agreed to honour our traditions and have a proper wedding ceremony—"

"What wedding?" both Mom and I said at once.

Rolling his eyes to the ceiling, Miller leaned back in his chair and crossed his arms over his chest. "Yours," he explained, with a dramatic sigh of exasperation. "The aliens want one of them to marry you."

"Which is a good thing when you think about it," Carter rushed in. "It could be presented as a gesture of good will—"

"Presented to whom?" I jumped from my seat. All of it stopped making any sense whatsoever. "What are you all talking about? I'm not going anywhere. I'm perfectly fine where I am. Why would the aliens want me anyway? I've never met them and don't want to."

I'd watched the news broadcast of the few official visits of the

Kealans with the coalition. The images of their tall figures, draped in black cloaks, hoods drawn low over their faces, left an unpleasant impression on me, bringing the Grim Reaper to mind.

"And . . . a wedding? Really?" I wrung my hands, pacing in front of the table, as if moving could help me wrap my mind around all of this.

"Miss Bruno . . ." Carter jumped out of his seat, too.

"This is just stupid!" Skipping down the stairs, my sister, Mary, barged into the room, her son Luca under her arm. "His diaper is changed." She handed Luca to my mom, who put him on her other hip, opposite to his twin. "Honestly, guys." Hands propped on the tabletop, Mary stared down Trevin and his escort. Less than two years younger than me, she had always been the more assertive and outspoken one. "Just listen to you! An alien wedding? What the hell are you talking about? Is this some kind of a joke for reality TV or something?"

"It will be televised," Carter announced, brightly. "The preparations for the event have been in full swing since the initial demand was received."

"Even before I was notified?" I muttered, wishing I could just wake up and stop this nightmare.

"And who are you?" Mary threw at Carter sarcastically, one corner of her mouth lifting up. "The wedding planner?"

"Ma'am." Miller rose from the table and moved on to my sister. "It's imperative we deliver Isabella Bruno—"

"What do you mean by 'deliver?'" Mary scoffed. "Bella is a free woman, she has rights—"

"Exactly," Mom stepped in, balancing the twins on each hip. "You can't just come in here and take her—"

"You're forgetting that none of us are free, miss." Trevin got up, shoving the chair back with a screeching noise, his jaw muscles flexed. "Not since the capitulation to the Kealans nine years ago."

"We have orders to take your sister." Miller crossed his arms over his chest. "Your permission is not required."

"I don't want to go." Dread slithered up my spine, cold and sticky. "My home is here. My job. I have a life . . . I—"

“Isabella.” Trevin took a step my way.

“No.” I glared at him.

“She is not going anywhere,” Mary insisted stubbornly.

“This is all definitely way too fast.” Moving her gaze across the room, Mom appeared completely lost. “Why all this rush? Who is this man . . . um, this alien, who wants to marry her? Why? Does he like her? They’ve never met . . .”

“Like?” Miller grimaced. “What does that have to do with anything?”

The front door opened with a knock.

“Bell? Are you home?” I heard the familiar voice of Johnny, my boyfriend of four years.

Mom bounced on her heels to calm the twins who started fussing. “What I’m saying is that this is not a proper way to ask someone to marry you,” she argued with Miller.

Trevin pinched the bridge of his nose. “You’re missing the point, ma’am. We are not the ones who make demands here.”

“Who is getting married?” Johnny walked in, tossing back his shoulder-length blond hair, some of which perpetually hung over his face.

“The freaking aliens are planning a wedding with Bella!” Mary blurted out, gesturing at Miller and Trevin, as if they were the aliens in question.

“Mary . . .” I exhaled, feeling like my knees were about to give out, a pounding headache threatened to set in.

Johnny moved a confused glance from her to Miller then finally to me. “Is that true?”

“We don’t have much time.” Trevin ignored him. “The flight to Capital City will take at least two hours. With the ceremony scheduled for tonight, the team will have to start getting you ready soon.”

Ready . . .

Ready for what? The wedding?

Tonight?

My heart skipped at the realization that all of this was real after all. Fear settled heavily in my chest, threatening to turn into panic.

“How will you ever get anyone ready to marry some alien

dude?" Mary yelled at the three. "No matter how much time you have. Who the hell is he anyway?"

"We have not been given the groom's identity," Trevin replied coolly.

"Mary is right, though." Mom shook her head. "This is insane."

"Your family will be well compensated, of course," Carter started.

"This is not about money!" Mary snapped.

"Her dad is in the hospital," my mom muttered softly, shifting her pleading gaze from one of the men to another. "At the very least, you need to let her say goodbye . . . Why this rush?" she groaned.

"Johnny . . ." I grabbed my boyfriend by the arm and shoved him into the hallway, desperate to get away from it all, to shut the noise out, to get some time to do something . . . Anything.

"Is it true what they're saying, Bell?" Johnny asked as I dragged him around the corner and out of everyone's sight. "Are those SUV's outside theirs? And is that Michael Trevin, for real?"

"Miss Bruno!" Miller's voice thundered behind me.

"A minute, please. Give me one freaking minute!" I yelled back. "Johnny." I whispered quickly, panic vibrating through me. "This can't be happening . . ."

"Do they really want you to marry an alien?"

"Apparently, it's the aliens who want this. Johnny." Gripping his shoulders, I gave him a shake. "Please, help me. Let's run."

There was no way I was going to return to that kitchen where they all waited for me.

Until this morning, I'd been a regular small-town girl, working in a convenience store since I graduated high school eight years ago. With my oldest brother in and out of jail for the past several years and my father in and out of hospitals with his ailing heart and lungs, I had been helping my mom with my four younger brothers who were still in grade school and more recently, with Mary's ten-month-old twins.

My plans for the future had mostly included marrying Johnny—

whenever he saved up enough money to buy me a ring and asked me to be his wife—and eventually starting a family.

It was not a glorious life, but it was my life, and I was content, living right here in Deer Rock, where I knew everybody and everyone knew me from the day I was born.

This whole thing now felt surreal and terrifying.

"Get me out of here, please," I whispered, not sure myself how that could be accomplished or where I could run to. I just needed to be far away from here. "I'm not going with them. I need to hide."

"Bell." His hesitant expression broke my heart. "You know their drones can find you by your DNA?"

I knew—that was how the Kealans traced those who tried to evade the medical testing—but I couldn't think rationally at that point.

"We'll hide in a cave, somewhere, where the drones can't fly?" My voice dropped, however, as did the hope in my heart. "I can't do this, Johnny . . ."

"Maybe just for a little while?" he suggested.

"What?" I stared at him in disbelief. "You actually want me to go with them?"

"Tony should be out next month," he spoke quickly. "I'm sure your brother will think of something."

Tony—my oldest brother and Johnny's idol since we were little—always came up with something. I wished he were here. Unfortunately, Tony's ingenuity had been wasted on raiding gas stations and convenience stores, which had put him in jail for the second time in his twenty-nine years.

"Together, we will find a way to get you out later," Johnny promised.

"It means I'll have to go with them now," I whispered, every fibre of my being refusing to accept the idea of that.

"Listen," he said soothingly, stroking my arms, but his gaze flickered to the wall behind me as he refused to meet my eyes. "If they want you . . ."

"Then you don't?" I snapped.

"No, it's not that. Just, you know, they always get their way . . ."

"Johnny. Are you afraid of them, too?" I stepped back, not wanting to believe the obvious, but feeling completely alone already. "Are you breaking up with me?"

"There is going to be a wedding, Bell," he sounded apologetic. "I don't want you to end up feeling guilty over what may come afterwards."

"Are you kidding me?" My throat tightened painfully, and I brought my hand to it.

"I just want to make it easier for you," he continued in a rush. "No matter what, I won't see it as cheating on your part. Okay?"

"I can't believe it!" With a sob, I shrunk further away from him, feeling both ashamed and disgusted.

He reached for me. "You know we don't have a choice—"

"Isabella, it's time." Trevin walked out of the kitchen, his voice firm.

Breathing hard, I backed away from both of them, moving to the front door.

"Miss Bruno . . ." Miller came from around Trevin, but I was no longer listening to whatever either of them had to say.

Twisting around, I dashed for the exit.

"You go, sis!" Mary cheered from the kitchen just as one of the twins started crying.

Shoving at the front door with my shoulder, I ran outside, without having any idea where I was going. Panic overtook me, propelling me to sprint as far away from this place as possible, away from the men in suits.

"Miss Bruno!" The doors of one of the black vehicles in front of our house flew open, and two men in black uniforms leaped out. They cut me off and tackled me to the ground in our front yard.

"Quickly, in the van with her," Miller bit out the command, catching up with us.

"Let me go!" I screamed, fighting against the hands lifting me off the ground. "I don't want this! I'm not going!"

The last I saw before they shoved me in and shut the doors were the pale faces of my family standing in the doorway of the house where I grew up.

My sister, comforting Lily in her arms. My mom, her hand over her mouth, Luca crawling at her feet. The thought of Tony and my dad flashed through my brain. The images of my little brothers who would come home from school that afternoon and find me gone.

I never got a chance to say a proper goodbye to any of them.

AVAILABLE NOW

Also by Marina Simcoe

PARANORMAL ROMANCE

Serpent's Touch Duet *(World of River of Mists)*

Serpent's Touch

Serpent's Claim

Madame Tan's Freakshow (World of River of Mists)

Call of Water

Madness of the Moon

Power of Rage

Demons Series (Complete)

Demon Mine

The Forgotten

Grand Master

The Last Unforgiven - Cursed

The Last Unforgiven - Freed

Stand Alone Novels Set in Demons World

The Real Thing

To Love A Monster

Midnight Coven Author Group

Wicked Warlock (Cursed Coven)

Also by Marina Simcoe

SCIENCE-FICTION ROMANCE

Dark Anomaly Trilogy (Complete)

Gravity

Power

Explosion

My Holiday Tails

Married To Krampus

My Tiny Giant

My Birthday Getaway

New Year, New Planet

Mail Order Mom

Standalone Novels

Experiment

Enduring (Valos Of Sonhadra)

About the Author

Marina Simcoe likes to write love stories with characters, who may or may not be entirely human, because she firmly believes that our contemporary world could always use a little bit of the extraordinary.

She has lots of fun exploring how her out-of-this-world characters with their own beliefs, values, and aspirations fit into our everyday life.

She lives in Canada with her very own captain, their three little offspring, and a cat, who is definitely out of this world.

For more illustrations of all of her books please visit Marina Simcoe Author page on Facebook or www.marinasimcoe.com.

facebook.com/MarinaSimcoeAuthor

instagram.com/marinasimcoeauthor

Newsletter Signup QR Code

Facebook Readers' Group:
Marina's Reading Cave

Website:
www.marinasimcoe.com

www.ingramcontent.com/pod-product-compliance
Lightning Source LLC
Chambersburg PA
CBHW030346310726
48979CB00001B/209

* 9 7 8 1 9 8 9 9 6 7 1 6 4 *